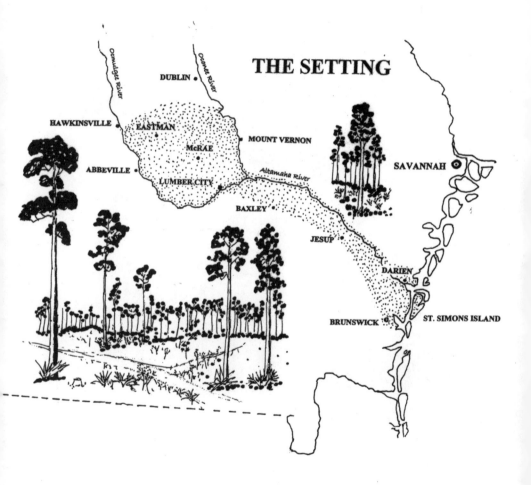

THE SETTING

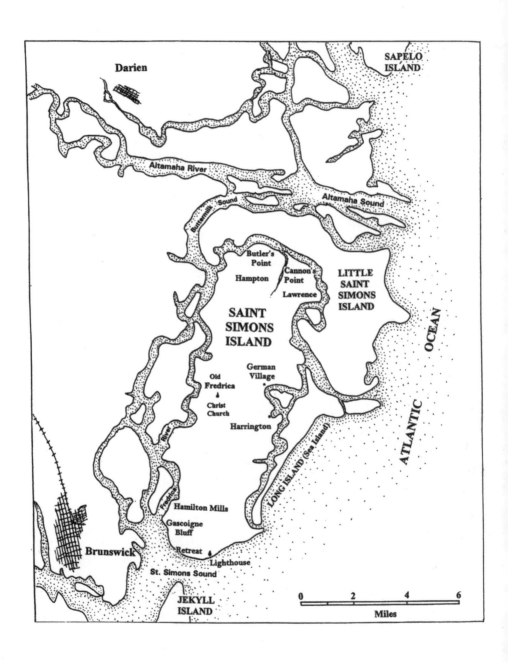

Widow of Sighing Pines

Jane Walker

Library of Congress Catalog Card Number
2002109827

ISBN: 0-9745650-0-8

Additional copies may be ordered for
$25.00
(Please add $5.00 for shipping & handling)
Jane Walker
P. O. Box 357
McRae, Georgia 31055
janehw@alltel.net

Wolfe Publishing
P.O. Box 8036
Fernandina Beach, FL 32035
1-800-475-6782

Dedication

For my husband, Bill, now deceased, who first introduced to me the intriguing history of this lovely piney woods/wiregrass area of Georgia

Scales of Justice Artwork by
Jo Ann Edge

In Appreciation

In writing first the novel, *Widow of Sighing Pines,* and then the history book, *The Dodge Land Troubles, 1868-1923,* which I co-authored with Chris Trowell, I was fortunate to have a number of people and sources, i.e., books, newspapers, masters, doctoral and other theses and dissertations, and maps which embraced the time periods of the south-central section of Georgia, the setting of both books. However, one person was my mainstay during the five years I have worked on the books. Chris T. Trowell, Emeritus Associate Professor from South Georgia College in Douglas, Georgia, who is a repository of historical and other information, was as near as a prompt email reply to my numerous email questions. To him, I am grateful for his willingness to help me - someone he had never known before - and for his steadiness and reliability during my years of putting the novel and the history book together.

One of Chris' first suggestions to me was to spend as much time on the rivers, where the rafting took place, as I possibly could. Not naturally being a "water person," I endured (with much enjoyment, to my surprise) many trips on the rivers. These forays onto the hitherto unknown waters of the Ocmulgee, the Altamaha, and the Altamaha Delta led me to many fascinating people who helped me in many ways.

The intelligent and colorful Carolyn Hodges of Darien, now deceased, conducted me in her motorboat on many trips on the Altamaha and the numerous rivers of the Altamaha Delta. Her special knowledge of the plant life and bird life, and the past rice culture of the area, were very instructive. Mattie Gladstone of Darien assisted me in many ways. Helping me comprehend the past history of Darien and Brunswick, especially pertaining to the rafthands' perception of the port towns, was Bruce Fendig, author of *Brunswick, the Ocean Port of Georgia.*

I traveled the Ocmulgee and Altamaha rivers by canoe, kayak, and motorboat. Here, again, I met interesting people who knew and respected our ancient rivers and waterways. Bob Strange was an authority on trees, pointing out different ones in the swamps on either side of the river. Lee Stallings, another knowledgeable river man, made kayaking seem safe and even pleasurable. Greg Varnadoe, Telfair County game warden with the Department of Natural Resources, was a pleasant and informative guide, carrying me to my first glimpse of the confluence of the Ocmulgee, the Oconee, and the Altamaha rivers. Special mention must also be made of Wanda Marchant, Executive Director of the Board of Tourism of Jeff Davis County, the sponsor of several canoe trips and a bird watching trip which were helpful in the writing of my novel.

Others who were especially helpful to us in the writing of the history book include my son, Billy Ware Walker, Jr., William Dopson, Judy Harris, Stephen Whigham, Steve Richards, Mark Wetherington, Frankie Snow, Del Presley, Buddy Sullivan, Janisse Ray, Milton Hopkins, Carlton Morrison, Ray Olivier, Jean and Olin Pound, James Angus, Phyllis Dodge, Jarrett Burch, Julian Williams, John Johnson of the Georgia Agrirama in Tifton, Georgia, Jeff Dukes, Sheila Willis, John Swiderski, Tad Evans, Paula Fraiser, Sue Sammons, Timme Feininger, Howard Snyder and the Remington Carriage Museum of Alberta, Canada, Edwin Gleaves, John Chapman, Jane Summey, Horace (Skeet) and Ruby Brown, Faye Jessup, Mary Ellen Wilson, Mercer University, Vanderbilt University, John H. Thurman and the Smyrna, Tennessee, Public Library, the Cleveland Dodge Foundation of New York, and the libraries and newspapers in the area. Jo Ann Edge rendered the watercolor of the Scales of Justice. Chris Trowell prepared the maps. Appreciation is extended to Roy Cowart, attorney, for his assistance with legal matters. I especially appreciate Janisse Ray's encouragement.

I am indebted to my sisters, Lydia Watson and Mary Ann Collins, the first "readers" of my novel, along with Chris Trowell, and to my attorney brother, Ashley Hawkins, for help with legal questions. Other family members, including my children, grandchildren, and the spouses of my siblings gave me encouragement and support.

Being an "outsider," myself, of the piney woods/wiregrass area of the state, having been born and having lived in Macon, Georgia, prior to my marriage, I had to dig for information even more intensely than I would have had to do, had I been a native of the area. I credit my deceased husband, Billy W. Walker, a native son, with instilling in me an avid interest in the history of this section of the state. Had he been alive, my writing of these works would have been easier, for he was an attorney, an outdoorsman, and an ardent history buff.

The latent lumber history of this piney woods area of the state is being scrutinized with a finer magnifying glass, as time marches on. May these works help all who study the history of this area during the latter part of the nineteenth century to a greater understanding of just what happened.

Chapter One

Fall, 1891

The stylish carriage swayed on the dusty road which led to the Yellow Pines Lumber Mill. Katharine Fremont shivered and looked out the window at the dense pine forest which towered on either side of the road. These tall, monstrous trees were the reason for her husband's death. The timber war had taken Frank, her husband, and now she was alone in an alien land. Though she had lived in the South nearly six years, she still felt like an outsider, an intruder.

She studied the stooped shoulders of Big Hill who sat hunched over the reins, quiet in his own thoughts. Loyal, colored Hill. He had stayed on after Frank's death in spite of her friends' predictions that he would be the first to leave. He helped her with the horses and with the few cattle which she still had not sold. In fact, it was Big Hill who had insisted that he drive her to the lumber mill this morning, maintaining in his gentle way that it was dangerous for her to make the trip alone.

Her heart beat hard against her bodice and her hand involuntarily moved to still it, feeling the tautness of her corset through the layers of her clothing. Had it actually been nine months ago? The memory was still fresh in her mind, as if it had occurred only the day before.

The posse of men on horses in her front yard had been real. And the Telfair sheriff, hat in hand at her door, his eyes first looking into her own, then lowering to study the wide planks of her front porch which extended as a veranda on three sides of her house...he, too, had been real.

Yes, there was a clarity about it all, which the passage of time had not eclipsed.

Her throat tightened and she found it difficult to swallow, as she retraced the events of that fateful day. She closed her eyes, remembering the halting, gruff voice of the sheriff.

"Mrs. Fremont," he had said, "something terrible has happened." With a shaking in his voice, he had continued. "Maybe you'd better sit down, for I bring the worst kind of news." She remembered touching the smooth white column nearest her, as if for support, for she had refused his suggestion that she sit down. She would remain standing. She would be strong.

"It's your husband, Mrs. Fremont," he had said. "He's..." The sheriff had looked toward his posse, and then she had seen the wagon hitched to a horse, with a deputy in the driver's seat. She remembered clutching the column then, desperately seeking in its stony hardness the reassurance that everything wasn't so terrible, after all, that she really wasn't experiencing the end of her life as she had known it in the piney woods of Georgia.

"Yes, Ma'm," the sheriff had said, "someone killed your..." Before he could complete his duty of informing the corpse's next of kin, she had felt her knees buckle, and only with iron resolve did she straighten them again. Something had warned her that these very men who faced her on their exhausted horses, with feigned expressions of horror and sympathy on their bearded faces, might well have been the murderers of her husband. She would not - and she did not - cower before them.

She remembered releasing the cold column and, holding up her long dress with one trembling hand, descending the porch steps. She had refused the outstretched arm of the sheriff. After all, the former Telfair County sheriff, before this one, had been convicted along with others of having John Forsyth, her husband's close associate in the timber business, murdered only a few months before. He was now serving time in the Ohio State Penitentiary.

Somehow, she had managed to walk without stumbling to the wagon, even as the sheriff beseeched her not to view her husband's remains. He was holding Frank's watch, with its gold fob and chain, and his initialed money clip, with the money intact, which ruled out robbery as a motive, he had said. These, he had assured her, would suffice for identification.

They had known Frank Fremont, anyway. Everyone knew who he was. He oversaw the smooth operations of the Dodge Company's turpentine still at Camp Six and its sawmill at Willcox

Lake on the Ocmulgee River, just as John Forsyth did at the Normandale sawmill.

Walking rapidly ahead of her, the sheriff had reached the wagon which had become a funeral bier, and he had held his arms wide across its side, as though wanting to shield her from the burden it bore. She had ignored his raised, uniformed arms which exposed weapons hanging from his gun belt, one over each hip, for she felt compelled to witness the wrong that had been perpetrated on her husband.

Nothing, however, could have prepared her for the brutalization of the body which rested on someone's quilts in the floor of the wagon, now soaked in her husband's blood. She had felt a retching in her throat, which she managed - she knew not how - to subdue. An unexplainable and invisible force had held her in its grip and had refused to let her faint...or weep.

She remembered the clothes that her husband had worn that day. Otherwise, she might not have recognized him, for his face had been blown away. No features were distinguishable. He had received bullets in the chest, also, for his fashionable brown coat still oozed blood onto the saturated quilts.

"Ma'm," the sheriff had pleaded with her, "let me help you back to the house. Do you have someone here...a maid perhaps? You need somebody, Mrs. Fremont."

"Yes," she had murmured coldly, trying to keep herself from falling to pieces, trying hard to repress the tears which wanted to gush forth. This time, she accepted his arm as he led her back to the house, for she knew she was too weak to walk alone.

"We found his body 'bout a mile from Camp Six," he had said. "His horse was nearby. We brought the horse back...we'll take him on to your stable when we leave."

"Oh," the sheriff had continued with relief in his voice, now that his duty had nearly been finalized, "let me give you these." He had held out Frank's pocket watch with its long chain and the money in its tight clip. Both were streaked with Frank's blood.

Katharine shuddered at the memory of it all. It had been rumored that angry "squatters" had waylaid her husband near Camp Six and had killed him. The murderer, or murderers, had never been found. She brushed at tears which stung her eyes. Her husband, like John Forsyth, had been a kind, gentle man. All that she knew about the tense situation in the Georgia piney woods was what he had told her, and Frank, not wanting to trouble her, had told her very little.

She remembered her initial grief and anger and solitude, enforced by her refusal to accept invitations from solicitous friends in the transplanted Northerners' timber circles. She had finally decided that she wanted to go home, back to New York. However, there were business matters to settle, especially the sale of her house and timber, the latter being the reason for her present trip to the lumber mill.

Suddenly, a heavy rumbling shook the ground, and Katharine was jostled from her reverie. The horses, wild-eyed and tossing their heads, slowed their gait, then began stepping backward, rocking the carriage from side to side.

"Whoa dar, Gen'l Lee an' Ha'ey!" Big Hill spoke soothingly to the matched gray geldings. "It dat lok'motif agin, and you's heard it befo'. Stop dat now, and git a move on!"

The horses lurched to a stop, their fidgety hooves swirling dust over the carriage. Only after more coaxing words did the frightened animals resume a slow trot, their sensitive ears twitching, as the train continued its whistling, steel-clanking journey along the railroad track which ran almost parallel with the eastern part of the dirt road.

Katharine straightened her hat, pulling the loosened wisps of her chestnut hair under the rounded brim. She still wore her widow's weeds, as she thought she should, since Frank had been dead now less than a year.

The groaning locomotive and the rumbling carriage arrived at the lumber mill almost simultaneously, the engine hissing to a stop at the depot, the carriage pulling up to the manager's office. The Negro driver slowly climbed down and opened the carriage door.

"Thank you, Hill," Katharine Fremont said, as she stepped to the ground. Drawing her long cloak about her, she moved toward the office door.

"I'll only be a short while, Hill, but you'll have time to go to the commissary."

"Ah sho' will, Miz Kat'rin. Ah be lookin' out fer you, w'en you's ready to go."

Katharine entered the office and was pleased to find the new manager there.

"Mr. Paul Owens, I believe?" As he nodded assent, Katharine held out her gloved hand.

"I am Katharine Fremont. My husband, Frank, was killed nearly nine months ago."

The portly Paul Owens studied Katharine intently. A pretty one, he thought, and a brave one to risk coming to the mill, even though there was a decided lull now in the land war.

"Oh, yes, I heard and read all about it, Mrs. Fremont. Your husband and Mr. Forsyth were killed about the same time. As you know, I have been trying to fill in here at the Normandale mill since their deaths. I'm so sorry about your husband, Mrs. Fremont. But I'm sure you know the local people have calmed down in their opposition to the timber company. Perhaps it took your husband's death to bring them to their senses. We haven't found any railroad spikes in the timber recently and we haven't lately heard of any squatter meetings." He paused, then adeptly changed the subject.

"Yes," he said, "I've been here at the mill about a year now. I'm originally from New York, as I believe you are, also, Mrs. Fremont, but I'd been working at the Dodges' sawmill on St. Simons Island for years. You know, they buried Mr. Forsyth there at Christ Church on the island. After Captain Forsyth's death, Mr. Norman Dodge asked me if I'd mind going upriver, into the piney woods, to manage the mill here at Normandale. You know, the mill here was named for Norman Dodge. Well, I had some qualms about it, at first, because of all the land troubles but he made the wages so good I couldn't turn it down."

Katharine found herself listening with interest to the talkative mill superintendent. Though she had been to the mill before, she had always waited in the carriage while her husband transacted business. She realized that this was the first time she had even been in the mill office and the first time she had talked with the mill superintendent.

"Yes," she said, "I knew the town was named for Norman, though I don't know him very well. My father, Mather Stuart, was a friend of William E. Dodge, Norman's father, who died around ten years ago."

"Yes, Ma'm, well...Norman and his brothers own over 300,000 acres of the finest longleaf yellow pine in the world. Of course, the squatters say they own the land, and some of them have deeds to prove it. Guess the Dodges' ejectment suits in this area have been going on for the past twenty years. I tell you, there's been a lot of blood shed over these land squabbles." The mill manager suddenly became contrite. "Oh, please forgive me, Mrs. Fremont," he said with sincere regret, "I didn't mean to bring up sad things and get you all upset."

"Oh, that's quite all right, Mr. Owens. I'm still trying to understand all that's going on with the Dodges and the squatters. I just don't understand how the squatters can possibly think the land belongs to them!"

"Well...some claim they bought it at the 1845 Tax Sale, and they've been living on the land and paying taxes on the land for the past forty-six years. Of course, a federal judge has said the tax sale was illegal but these Southerners just refuse to believe it. They have deeds and they've been paying taxes on the land...I tell you, it's a sad, mixed-up situation. We just don't know what's going to happen next. They're fighting over about 500 square miles of yellow pine that's over a hundred feet tall and big around as wagon wheels. It's virgin timber...been growing over a hundred years, some of it several hundred years." The mill manager smiled before continuing, "But you know the timber, Mrs. Fremont. You own some of it yourself."

"Yes," Katharine said, "my husband bought our lots from William Dodge before we even moved to Georgia, and that's what has brought me to the mill today, Mr. Owens. I need some help, some direction, actually. You see, I want to find someone to cruise my timber, get it to market, and sell it for me. As soon as I find an overseer to do this for me, I intend to move back to New York."

"You're not going to find anybody from the timber company to help you, Mrs. Fremont, since most of your timber, probably all of it, will have to be rafted. No, we Northerners came in and built the sawmills here and at Darien and St. Simons, but we don't have the rafting skills. We just don't know the rivers the way these local Crackers do."

Motioning for Katharine to join him at the office window and directing her to look across the mill yard, Paul Owens said, "There's your man, Mrs. Fremont...Micah MacRae...lives in Telfair County near Sugar Creek. Actually, you cross the old bridge over Bear Creek, and his place is on up the road to the right a mile or so."

Katharine's first look at Micah MacRae was forever welded like molten steel into her memory. He was a big man but he moved with the fluid grace of one accustomed to the rolling river under his feet. His clothes, befitting the backwoodsman he was, were of homespun and his coat and hat were of deerskin. As Katharine watched, other loggers joined him, and the raftsman, unaware of her gaze, withdrew some chewing tobacco from his pocket, cut off a plug, and implanted it firmly in his jaw. Katharine cringed slightly at this lack of civility, then turned to the mill manager who was still talking.

"He's the best you'll find, Mrs. Fremont," he said. "He knows the rivers and he knows timber. He'll take it down the river or he'll load it here at the railroad, just according to where the trees are located."

"I appreciate your help, Mr. Owens. I'll go and talk to Mr. MacRae now."

As Katharine moved to leave the office, the door opened, admitting a man with a jagged scar which joined his right ear with the corner of his mouth. Katharine presumed he was a mill hand, and it was on her mind to ask him to help with rafting her timber. However, the way he looked at her, leeringly, caused her to hurry on past him. It embarrassed her that he made intimate remarks, so that she could hear, as she walked across the front porch of the mill office, down the steps, and toward the group of loggers. Seeing her coming, the men hurriedly whispered among themselves, all except Micah MacRae who left the group and walked a few steps toward her.

"Hello, Mr. MacRae," Katharine said, extending her hand. "I'm Katharine...Mrs. Frank Fremont. Mr. Owens suggested that I talk to you."

"Nice to meet you, Ma'm" the backwoodsman said, removing his leather hat. "I'm sorry about your husband."

"Thank you, Mr. MacRae."

In spite of the cold day and the thin glove on her hand, Katharine felt the warmth of the raftsman as he took her hand. At that moment she had an irrepressible urge to be held by this man. An almost iron strength emanated from him, a strength that she desperately needed. A sense of shame flooded over her, that she should have such a feeling for this unschooled, uncivil man - or any man - with her husband not long cold in his grave. Gaining control of herself, she withdrew her hand and attempted to talk in a business-like manner.

"Mr. MacRae, I have some timber which I would like to get to market. I need someone to cruise and log it for me as soon as possible. Could you do this for me?"

Micah MacRae had known Frank Fremont. He just had not known Mrs. Frank Fremont. He looked at the lovely, upturned face, the slender figure not completely hidden by the loose cloak, the thick hair escaping the brimmed hat, and he marveled at her educated way of speaking.

Momentarily, he forgot his hatred of the Northerners who had come in with the timber company and the questionable deeds which had robbed so many local people of their land and timber. Of course, things had been carried too far with the murders of the timber company superintendent, John Forsyth, and his associate, Frank Fremont.

Hat in hand, his brown eyes inscrutable, he responded to her request. "Ma'm, I got more than I can handle right now, a-gettin' my own timber that's cut and on the ground to Darien. Let's see now...your trees are near the old River Road. That means they should be rafted, rather than haulin' 'em in to the railroad here." He paused, obviously considering the enormity of what she had asked him to do.

"Cuttin' the trees is only the beginnin', Miz Fremont. I'll need loggers and rafthands and oxen and carts. That'll take some time. You know, we raft in the cold months, and I'll be a-takin' my own logs to Darien in a few months."

Without thinking, Katharine said, "Since my timber is near the sawmill at Willcox Lake, perhaps you could use some of the Dodge facilities there at the sawmill." As soon as she had spoken, she regretted mentioning the Dodge name, for the backwoodsman's brown eyes narrowed and they took on a steel glint that made her gasp.

"Not likely, Ma'm," he said with a sneer in his voice, "though we might use some of their trams."

"Of course," Katharine said, trying not to notice the hatred now present in his demeanor. "How much will you charge, Mr. MacRae?" she asked.

"Well, I usually get a fixed rate for every thousand board feet cut, Miz Fremont. We can do it that way, or you can pay me by the job."

"I'll pay by the job," she said quickly, thinking it would be simpler and easier to pay in this way. "I'll go on halves with you, if you can help me... and if you think this is fair. And the sooner, the better. You see, I plan to move back to New York, as soon as the timber is cut and sold."

"Maybe in a month or two, I can see to it, Ma'm. I may just cut all along, once I've found some sawyers. Of course, a lot depends on the weather. Too much rain, and we can't get in to the trees. Too little rain, and we can't float the trees on the nearby creeks to the river. Let's see now...what we need is a freshet to drift the timber on your west tracts to the river. We can move the trams, as need be, to bring the other logs out. When I cut a lot, I always leave a few seed trees along the edges of the land lots, thinkin' this might help to reseed the pines."

"I know so little about rafting," Katharine said, not really grasping the significance of the seed trees, "but I do know the logs will have to be kept in a holding pond or boom before they are lashed together into a raft. My late husband oversaw the sawmill at Willcox Lake. I'm certain that the logs could be held there until you are ready to raft them."

"Yes, Ma'm, that's what I had in mind. We'll just leave the logs at the boom there until we're ready to peg them together."

Katharine felt relieved. "I'll have the necessary papers drawn up. Thank you, Mr. MacRae." She stilled the cordial impulse of offering her hand as a parting gesture. Instead, lowering her eyes, again she whispered, "Thank you," then turned to enter the carriage which Hill had waiting for her.

Her new business partner spat into the dust of the lumber yard, his eyes never leaving the departing carriage. Replacing his hat, he muttered to no one in particular, "Well, that's always a nice turnabout! A Yankee callin' on a white trash Southerner for some know-how!" He smiled as he relished the thought and the smile lingered over his memory of Katharine Fremont.

Chapter Two

Julia Winslow was insistent. "You must come, Katharine! After all, it's time for you to enjoy something. Nobody waits a year anymore. You need to get out of those dark, dreary clothes. The new timber inspector from Darien will be coming. He's not married, and you should be thinking about marriage again."

Unaware that the color in her face changed, Katharine replied that she wasn't thinking about marriage now. All she wanted was to sell her timber and to return home to New York. The two friends were seated in Katharine's parlor, sipping tea.

Tilda, her long white apron starched and ironed to stiff perfection, appeared in the arched doorway. Her welcoming smile softened the severity of the thin bun of gray hair on the back of her head.

"Will you be staying to eat with us this evening, Miss Julia? I'll lay another plate if you will."

"Oh, no, Tilda. I must be getting back home. Ben insisted that I not stay long, so I'll be leaving in a few minutes but I do thank you." Tilda bowed slightly and left as quietly as she had appeared.

"I know Tilda's a big help to you, Katharine."

"Oh, yes. You know, she helped Mother in New York for a number of years and when Mother didn't need her anymore, she agreed to come to Georgia with me. However, she's as ready as I am to make the move back to New York."

Katharine walked to the window and looked out, noting the camaraderie of Big Hill and Poke, her friend's colored coachman. "Julia, they're having a big time, catching up on all the latest happenings, as we are."

A troubled look came to Julia's plain face, as she joined her friend at the window, both of them observing the two colored servants outside.

"We hear they're having meetings again, just as they did right after the war. We're lucky, Katharine, to have Big Hill and Poke. They would never desert us." Julia's face in the sunlight, filtering through the lace curtains, had new lines which Katharine hadn't noticed before. It suddenly dawned on her that they were both getting older. Though they were both in their thirties, Julia was several years older than she. Time was going by too fast. But what had Julia said? Something about the coloreds having meetings again. Katharine looked at the jovial, graying drivers, standing by Julia's carriage in her circular front driveway. Their easygoing laughter and unhurried banter reassured her that Julia was right. These men who had been slaves, and whose fathers and grandfathers had been slaves, would never forsake them. After all, the Fremonts and the Winslows were on the right side of the war, weren't they? The winning side, which had freed the coloreds and their families from slavery.

"You're right, Julia. Remember when Frank died that everyone warned me that Big Hill would be the first to leave. Well, he's proven them wrong. We are lucky, as you said. They would never join with the insurrectionists!" She had heard of the uprisings, when the newly freed slaves would kill their former owners. These were, she was certain, cases where the owners had mistreated them. Katharine shuddered at her thoughts.

Julia was gathering her things, securing the ribbons of the riding hat under her chin. "Steve will be at our ball, and you know he's always adored you. Also, as I said, I want you to meet Sewell Siddon, the timber inspector I told you about from Darien. Will you come? It'll be the second Saturday in January."

Katharine smiled at Julia's mention of her younger brother, Steve. He was younger than Katharine, also, but he had never kept it a secret that he admired her. Steve with his fiery red hair! He was married to Victoria who loved him more than anything in the world and who had given him five children, but he persisted in his open flirting with Katharine, much to her embarrassment and his wife's chagrin. Katharine considered him the brother she had never had and kept their friendship on the same level, much to Victoria's relief.

"I promise I'll come, Julia. I'll be there." After a quick hug, the two friends parted ways.

Katharine watched from the front doorway as Julia waved from inside the graciously appointed landau. Pulled by two lively thoroughbreds with Poke in the driver's seat, the carriage hobbled along the brick driveway and through the open, black wrought-iron gates which revealed the name, Sighing Pines, hammered above in a majestic, towering arch. Katharine had long ago regretted this sobriquet of the Fremont estate, since with the escalation of the land war, it had taken on ominous tones in her mind.

***

Winslow Hall was aglow with lamps, candles, and blazing fireplaces. Its front courtyard was filled with horse-drawn coaches and carriages. The scrolled, white, Ionic columns, reaching upward to the second floor, gleamed in the gaslight of stately post lanterns and glowed a welcome to guests arriving from local and surrounding counties. Inside, toe-tapping music was bringing a few of the younger couples to the highly polished floor of the large ballroom. Servants in full livery carried silver trays of meats, fruits, and sweet pastries through the throngs of laughing guests.

This was the Northern timber company's social event of the bleak winter season in the wiregrass, and guests ate and drank in an attempt to forget their troubles. Though all were becoming increasingly wealthy from timber investments and sales, this was not without a price. The resulting land war attested to this. The deaths of two of their top men, John Forsyth and Frank Fremont, made them wonder and fear who might be next.

Katharine disengaged herself from the attentions of young Steve Winslow who in full view of his newly pregnant wife had given her a hug that was more than a brotherly one.

"Promise me your first dance, Katharine, please. Vickie can't dance - doctor's orders." Steve's red hair framed his boyish face and his lopsided grin made Katharine smile in spite of herself.

"Only if Victoria doesn't mind," Katharine said, smiling at his plump, attractive wife.

"Oh, Mrs. Katharine, it'll be fine," Victoria said. The "Mrs." attached to her name reminded Katharine of the age difference between herself and Steve's wife, although for the life of her, she couldn't remember Victoria's addressing her in such a way before.

Was Victoria a bit jealous, or was she just innocently acknowledging their age difference? Again, Katharine felt alone and she felt herself growing older.   Seeing Steve looking at her in a puzzled way, Katharine managed a smile and replied, "Of course, Steve, I'll save my first dance for you."

Suddenly, Julia Winslow was at her elbow with a man Katharine had never seen before. He was fairly tall and overweight with a thick moustache.

"Katharine, I want you to meet our new timber inspector from Darien, Sewell Siddon. Sewell, this is my friend, Katharine Fremont. I'm sure you remember the tragedy of her husband's death." With the introductions over and remembering that she had other guests to attend to, Julia excused herself and left the two alone.

"How do you do, Mrs. Fremont...uh Katharine? Yes, I heard about your husband. I'm so sorry." He edged closer to her until she could smell the sweetish cologne on his clothes and the liquor on his breath. His fumbling hand found her waist. Katharine felt angry at Julia for leaving her with this man who, from the outset, seemed too forward, too familiar with her, and yet she knew that knowing a timber inspector well might insure good money for one's timber. She was certain that was the reason her friends had invited him to their party. The Winslows were shrewd, she realized. They knew how to mix business with pleasure and their many social events were proof of this. Also, wouldn't she herself be in need of the services of a timber inspector before long, when her timber was rafted down the rivers to Darien? She made an effort to be nice to the man, continuing the conversation.

"How do you do, Mr. Siddon? I hope you're enjoying the party."

"I am, now that I've met you, Katharine, honey, and just call me Sewell."

A man Katharine did not know approached them and slapped the timber inspector on the back.

"Still grading the local Crackers' rafts, Sly?" The timber inspector reddened slightly and spoke a few words to the man who moved on through the crowd.

"Did he call you 'Sly', Mr. Siddon?" Katharine could not mistake the meaning of such a designation for a timber inspector. She prayed inwardly that he would not be the one inspecting her timber when it arrived in Darien. She wondered whether there would be a choice in the matter. She would find out from Micah MacRae, when she had a chance to talk with him further.

Sewell Siddon's face was almost livid now. "I think he mistook me for someone else," he said, his former assurance returning and his hand pulling her to him. "Come on. I want to dance with you." His manner was coarse and assuming too much, and Katharine longed to be free of him.

"Excuse me," she said, "I must go to the powder room." Not noticing his sullen disappointment, she swept away from the man and entered one of the bedchambers on the main floor, off from the drawing room, closing the door behind her. The music drifted in to her, and she heard people tapping their shoes to the beat. Slipping off her shoes, she stretched out on the chaise lounge and closed her eyes. She longed to be back home in New York, away from the fears of this part of the country, where she and her compatriots were hated and maligned.

Men's voices near the closed door filtered through her thoughts. They were talking timber again and she heard only snatches of their conversation. She caught the words, "Darien," "river," and "Micah MacRae." At that name, her heart pounded, and she felt lightheaded, giddy. What were they saying? She slipped on her shoes and moved toward the door, her ears straining for any tidbits of information.

"I heard he was invited to the party tonight."

"Oh, hell! He may have been invited, but I'll bet you a dollar he won't show. If he does, he'll be the only Rebel here. We could hold him for ransom." Laughter at this.

"Well, gentlemen, we all have to admit that his is the only voice of moderation here. He's the reason the land war hasn't escalated. Also, he's the damn best timber pilot on the three rivers, they say! A true river rat!"

Katharine slowly opened the door and listened attentively to the voices of the men who stood in a tight circle, only a few feet away. They were having their shot glasses refilled and they were feeling the effect of the whiskey. Slightly disheveled, their formal attire so impeccable when they had arrived now looked rumpled, and they had loosened their bow ties.

One of the men, his tongue set free with alcohol, inquired of the dead sober, somewhat pompous manservant whether the potables had been procured from the "blind tigers" around Eastman. The servant winced at the improper question, but assured the guest that the imported liquors were the best from the Winslow home, having been obtained from the finest establishments in Europe.

The Winslows' parties always celebrated the pleasures of libations, except for the rare occasions when William E. Dodge or his sons were present, for he had been a teetotaler and a Prohibitionist. Imbibing alcoholic beverages in any form was a sin, and he would not tolerate it among the members of his company. The Winslows, though loyal in every other way to company policy, refused to adhere to the strait-laced rule in regard to alcohol consumption. Rather, they kept the crystal glassware of their guests filled with the many fine wines from their own well-stocked wine cellar.

Suddenly, to Katharine's dismay, the house servant, Beulah, was opening the front door, and in stepped Micah MacRae. He was dressed in a Sunday version of his attire at the mill yard. His smooth deerskin vest had long strings at the top closure which tied at his throat, giving a semblance of a bow tie. His long-sleeve shirt of bleached homespun and his smooth, leg-hugging, deerskin pants, tucked into soft old leather boots, completed his coarse ensemble. Any other time, or at any other occasion, Katharine would have noted the difference in the way the raftsman was dressed and the manner in which the timber company associates were attired. However, for some reason, this difference was lost on her now.

As Ben and Julia Winslow hurried across the room to welcome him, Katharine gasped, her heart pounding. He must never know how he affects me, she told herself. Once again, she closed the bedchamber door. She looked at herself in the standing mirror. Her reflection revealed a woman whose hair was piled in an elegant coif atop her shapely head, with tendrils escaping around her lovely face. Her full gray gown with its becoming bustle emphasized her tiny waist which remained small, despite the fact that she had carried three children almost to full term, only to lose them in early childbirth.

Tears came to her eyes as she remembered her sorrow at being unable to have children. Oh, what a comfort a child would be to me now, she thought, dabbing at her eyes with a lace-edge handkerchief. The thought of Micah MacRae so nearby, in the next room, almost made her faint. She closed her eyes, leaning her head against the closed door. I must leave this room, she thought. I can't stay here all night. I don't know what's wrong with me. I need to brace up.

Again, she heard the men talking and she put her ear to the door, attempting to understand what was being said. Ben Winslow was introducing the Southern raftsman to the group of men.

"Now, Micah, here are some timber men who have been wanting to meet you. Stanley Agnew, Mr. Dodge's legal counsel, one of the foremost attorneys in the state of New York, Tillman Nash, esteemed attorney from Maine, William Hardison, timber official from Connecticut..." Ben's voice droned on, completing the introductions.

Katharine opened the door slightly. The timber men were all shaking hands with the raftsman who was cordial but aloof. A manservant offered him a choice of select wines and liquors which he refused with a slight shake of his head and a "No, thank you."

The men all talked at once, questioning Micah about the timber business in general and Darien in particular. Most of the men had been to Darien, the ocean port city where their timber was rafted for marketing, but they didn't go as often as Micah. They knew he would know the latest news from that fascinating place.

"Whoa, wait a minute," Ben said, laughing. "Let's give the man a chance to hear from all of you. Stanley, what were you asking?"

"Well, I'm just wondering about the ships putting into port there. Any new ones?"

Micah appeared to be choosing his words carefully. He was neither friendly nor hostile.

He answered the question tersely in the slow, Southern manner of speaking: "Oh, yes. Of course, some of these were making return visits, but I saw the *Josephine* from Boston, the *Mary Jenness* from New York, and others from England and South America. The loading facilities are even better now at Darien and also at St. Simons." As Micah continued, Katharine wondered why the Southerners persisted in pronouncing the town of Darien in such a way. They almost pronounced it "Dari-ann."

"Vessels drawin' twenty feet of water can load alongside now," he was saying. "There's a large European business, as well as South American, in addition to domestic shipments. No, there ain't a downward shift in the market yet. You'll make your money right on - as long as you have trees to raft down the river or load on the railway."

The thin Mr. Nash with the raspy voice asked about the quarantines at Darien.

"Yes, Darien escaped the yellow fever epidemics that hit Savannah and Brunswick, because of its quarantines. They're lifted now, though, and business is good again. Last week, I walked a mile from my raft to the derrick, walkin' on other rafts all the way. Rafts were backed up for two miles on Cathead Creek."

The timber man from Connecticut, William Hardison, pressed for information about the rafting trips to the coast. He was obviously impressed with the look of the lean, hard, wiregrass rafter, for he knew that life on the river either killed a man or molded him into a man of iron.

"What's it like - riding a raft of giant logs to Darien?"

"Well, sir," Micah paused, as though giving some thought to something he had never had an occasion to put into words. "Well, sir," he repeated, "it's like tryin' to break in a wild horse - guess that's the best picture I can give you - a wild horse that moves and shifts in different ways, all awhile you are a-tryin' to stay in control." He smiled and said, "You'll have to come along with us sometime, if you can take the cold. We have to raft in the cold months, 'cause plantin' time comes soon after and then gettin' in the crops we planted."

William Hardison shook his head, wryly smiling. "If I were younger, I'd take you up on it. Yes, I'm sure it's an experience to drift to Darien and see those large ships from faraway places, waiting for our timber from up the river."

"It's a way to make a livin'," Micah said quietly, looking around the large drawing room.

Stanley Agnew, the lawyer from New York, interjected at this point. "Mr. MacRae, I just want you to know that we all are aware that your level head has brought about a lessening of the tensions in regard to Mr. Dodge's rightful ownership of the land and timber here."

Micah MacRae's face and manner visibly changed from polite civility to stark hostility.

"Sir, I was against the killin' of the two timber company men, and I made myself clear on that. If that brought about a 'lessenin' of the tensions,' as you called it, so be it. But as for Mr. Dodge a-claimin' some 300,000 acres of land here...I say he's doin' it with some deeds that ain't what they should be."

As the stunned men pondered what to say next, a man on the sidelines who had been listening to the exchange and who was very drunk, sidled over to Micah and winked knowingly at the other men.

"We want to hear some more news from Darien," he said, slurring his words. "What can you tell us about 'May Belle's' place?"

Momentarily caught off guard, Micah nonetheless casually replied, "I couldn't tell you anything about it."

"Couldn't or wouldn't?" the man persisted, attempting a knowing smile with slack lips.

"Neither," Micah said curtly. Signaling that he'd had enough of their questions which were losing their cordiality, he excused himself and, with Ben by his side, was welcomed into another circle of timber men.

Katharine knew she had to leave the room which had become her haven during the party- the party which she had not wanted to attend, in the first place. She could hear Steve asking different ones whether they had seen her. She had forgotten that he had asked her to dance earlier. She hadn't danced in such a long time. Actually, Frank and she had never danced, but she had grown up with dancing lessons and dancing parties in New York. She and Steve had always managed to dance during parties such as this one. She used to love to dance but tonight she just wanted to be alone. She didn't want to get out on the dance floor. She wasn't ready.

Steve opened the door without knocking, and her startled look made him laugh. "Is this where you've been all night? Come on! It's dance time. Hear the music?" The music had picked up, and serious dancing was about to begin. The orchestra that the Winslows had hired from Macon was playing waltz music which Katharine loved and in a quick change of mood, she thought, "Why not?" Accepting his outstretched hand, she gave Steve a smile of anticipation, and they joined other couples on the dance floor.

With the waltz tempo filling her soul, for a few moments she closed her eyes and let the music soothe her inward turmoil. She dared not look toward the others, the spectators who lined the walls of the room, watching the dancers. No, she might meet the eyes of the "damn best timber pilot on the three rivers," as she had heard him described, and he might guess her strange feelings for him. He would probably find it amusing that a person of her background would even notice an uncultivated man such as he. He might even use her attraction to him as a way to extort more money from her in their timber partnership. She would be careful. She had to rid her mind of him!

The dance ended, and Steve was about to ask her for the next dance when the timber inspector, Sewell Siddon, walked unsteadily toward her. Never mind that he now reeked of whiskey, she thought. She would just try to get through this one last dance, and then she would say her goodbyes to Ben and Julia. It was another waltz, and the timber inspector pulled her to him. She strained to keep him at arms' length, as she had danced with Steve, but it was a losing battle. Embarrassed, she tried to maintain propriety, but it was difficult to follow the flow of the music while fending off a dance partner who pulled her ever closer to him.

His hair was waxed smooth with bandoline, the gummy hair dressing which she was certain he had used, also, to achieve his pointed mustache. Made from the boiled pips of the quince, the bandoline had, to her mind, a nauseous smell, and the timber inspector's barbed mustache stung her face with its close proximity. Remembering that he was a business acquaintance of the Winslows and not wanting to make a scene, Katharine endured the situation, but she vowed to herself that she would leave as soon as the dance was over.

Emboldened by the whiskey, the timber inspector whispered compliments in her ear, while his fleshy hand around her waist moved higher up the back of her gown and slid around to the beginning of her breast under the sleeve of her bodice. Katharine repeatedly moved his hands.

"Katharine, I must see you again. I'm leaving for Darien in the morning but I'll return in a few weeks. I want to see you then." As Katharine struggled for an answer that would deter him from ever seeing her again, her eyes inevitably found those of Micah MacRae. He nodded and smiled at her, and she thought how strange life was - that she was unhappily dancing with one man, when she would rather just be in the presence of another. She found herself smiling back at the raftsman. Finally, the music stopped and the dance ended. Not wanting to talk, yet feeling that she should say something to the timber inspector, Katharine murmured that she trusted that he would have a pleasant trip back to Darien.

"Goodbye, Katharine. I must tell you" he said, his voice thick with whiskey, "that Darien is filled with beautiful women but they can't compare with you. I didn't know that I'd find one even more lovely here in this Godforsaken wiregrass!"

Chapter Three

Rain was falling several mornings after the party at Winslow Hall. Katharine sat alone in her bedchamber, sipping hot tea from the breakfast tray which Tilda had brought her. Looking out at the rain-soaked yards and the surrounding woods of canopied pines, she thought about the evening at Winslow Hall, especially the moments filled with Micah MacRae's presence. Why hadn't Julia mentioned to her that he was invited to the party? But then, why would Julia have thought she would have been interested?

She never even spoke a word to him at the party, for fear that her attraction to him would show on her face, for him and for others to see. She had left shortly after the unpleasant dance with the timber inspector from Darien and had returned to her room. She left hurriedly, because she did not trust herself to be near Micah MacRae.

In the cold light of day, Katharine reasoned with herself, forcing herself to look at the raftsman with an objective eye. She asked herself why this Southern backwoodsman had taken possession of her. She was unaccustomed to the physical pull toward him, as she had honestly never experienced such before. Her marriage to Frank had been a good one. They had grown up together and their families were friends. It was expected that they would marry one day, after Frank graduated from university. Looking back, she realized that though she had loved Frank, it had been a quiet, passionless love. She had pleased her parents by marrying him and he had been a good, kind husband to her. She had loved Frank, she argued with herself, but she had never felt the passion for him that she felt for this stranger, whom she had seen only twice.

Groping for composure in her thinking, Katharine searched for something about him to criticize, because she knew that she did not want to be attracted to him. No, she did not want to be drawn to anything or anyone here in the South which she had lately grown to hate. He is uneducated, she thought. Her family had always valued education. She wondered whether he could even read, as many of the backwoodsmen could not. At this settling thought, something reminded her, however, that he knew timber and had the grudging respect of educated men. For probably the first time in her life, she acknowledged that one could be educated in ways other than books and traditional schools.

Noticing that the rain had stopped and the sun was peeking through the clouds, Katharine sipped the tepid tea and replaced the porcelain cup on the breakfast tray. Taking a chair by the slow-burning fire in the large fireplace, she closed her eyes and continued her musings. She'd overheard someone say that Micah MacRae had three children and that his wife had died in childbirth several years ago. His mother had moved in with him to look after the children, she had been told, and his father had died in the war during the battle at Gettysburg.

Opening her eyes, she mulled over the idea that she needed to talk to her new overseer. She had to recover from the feelings she had for him. She would go today to see him, and they would discuss her timber situation. After all, it had been months since their meeting at the lumber mill. She was determined that theirs would be a business relationship and nothing else. Besides, what would her family in New York and her friends think, if they knew she even entertained such thoughts about this wiregrass raftsman who showed open animosity toward her friends in the timber company? No, she would stifle her schoolgirl feelings for him. She would see to it that he got her timber to market. Then, she would go back home to New York and she would never see him again.

Pleased that she had decided on a definite course of action and that she was once again in control of herself, Katharine quickly put on riding clothes for the trip to the raftsman's house. The green wool riding skirt and fitted, basque jacket and vest made her dark blue eyes almost green. The matching green bowler tamed her thick hair after she secured the ribbons in a bow under her chin. She decided to dispense with the hat's veil for the ride.

She saddled the gray gelding General Lee herself, since Big Hill wasn't nearby. She remembered that her friends in the timber company had teased Julia and herself about their using thoroughbred horses in the piney woods of Georgia, both as carriage and saddle horses. However, she nor Julia regretted bringing their lovely thoroughbred geldings, for they fared well in the rural South. Actually, she thought to herself, they fared better than their carriages, for the rutty roads were rough on carriages. Also, the horses performed equally as well, whether pulling their carriages or doubling as saddle horses.

The lovely English saddle had been a birthday gift from her parents the past year. As she fastened it beneath the horse's slick belly, she longed for her parents and her home in New York. She had not seen her parents since Frank's funeral which they traveled by train to attend, but they did exchange letters.

The horseback ride over the rain-packed dirt road was pleasant, but she was glad she had dressed warmly for the day was cold. Warnings from her friends and family about the dangers of riding alone flashed through her mind, but she dismissed them quickly. Could she help it that she was alone? She couldn't travel by carriage everywhere. It was quicker by horseback. Anyway, a carriage was always breaking down and hers were constantly undergoing repairs. The backwoods roads with their deep ruts often snapped the spokes in the delicate wheels.

No, she had to fend for herself in this frightening world, without a husband or family to help her. Almost each new day, she had to summon courage or strength which heretofore she had not known she possessed.

The warnings about riding alone continued to haunt her and she peered into the dense woods on either side of the narrow road. Noises of animals, unseen, sent shivers up her spine and when a deer darted across the road ahead, her mount reared up, almost depositing her on the cold, wet ground.

"Whoa, steady...steady, fellow," she crooned into the horse's ear, patting his maned neck.

Throwing up his head, as if to sniff the air, the horse responded when she pressed her knees against his ribs by resuming a brisk gait. For several hours, Katharine rode the gray farther into the forested interior of Telfair County, along the dirt roads and paths which followed the Dodges' timber railroads and tram roads, known simply as Dodges' Roads.

The timber acreage of Micah MacRae finally came into view, just as the mill manager had described it to her. She had crossed the small, rickety wood bridge and, as she had been told, the MacRae property began a mile or two on the other side of the bridge over Bear Creek. She could now see the gray-boarded frame house through the trees. She was surprised to see a large, red bull in the pen near the house, for cattle usually roamed the open range of the wiregrass without restraint. However, she had heard that the backwoodsman was making money in the timber-rafting business, so he may have sold any other cattle, she reasoned. The bull was probably penned up, pending its sale to someone else.

She reined the horse to a stop and looked at the house where the raftsman lived with his mother and children. No one was in sight, so Katharine took her time observing the place the backwoodsman called home.

The large, cleared, and swept yard and house had towering trees surrounding it. Beyond the pen on the left, several cows ambled out of the woods and munched the winter's stubbles of grass. The large bull in the pen paced, snorting, around the confines of the wood rail fencing. Looking at the big, horned animal, Katharine thought that its hooves appeared to bounce from inward coiled springs, as it loped around the enclosure. She felt that she must be getting paranoid, for the bull summoned a sort of dread from deep within her.

Mesmerized, Katharine turned her eyes to the gray, weather-beaten house, enclosed by a picket fence and built in the double-pen style of the backwoods. It exuded a certain charm, with its chimneys rising against the big-barreled pine trees which nearly engulfed it. Smoke wisped from the front chimney, a sign that someone was home.

As Katharine prodded the horse up the dirt path to the house, she noticed the well on the far right side of the house, along with scuppernong arbors and a martin pole with gourds hanging from it. She could see the barnyard to the far left of the house which enclosed a shed with hay piled high at the top open window and a mule milling around the yard below. An old ox in a smaller pen nearby was drinking from a trough, hollowed out of one of the tremendous pine trees.

Upon reaching the gate, Katharine slid from the horse and looped the reins over the gatepost. Entering the gate, she walked toward the porch which ran the length of the front of the house. This awakened the hound dog sleeping under the front steps, which jumped from its lair, barking but simultaneously wagging its tail for her benefit. Katharine almost collapsed from the fright it gave her, but was calmed when the dog began licking her hand, in spite of the thick riding gloves she wore.

"Good dog...good dog," she murmured, thinking that she had always liked dogs but Frank hadn't, so she had never insisted that they own any. As she patted the dog's head, still talking to the animal, the front door opened and a woman in a coarse brown homespun dress, with a black shawl around her shoulders, stepped onto the porch. She couldn't have been much older than her own mother, Katharine surmised, but the woman's skin was parched and old from working long hours in the sun. Her hands clasping the shawl were gnarled and worn. Looking into her brown eyes, however, Katharine saw a strong semblance of the eyes of Micah MacRae, and she knew that many years past, his mother had been a strikingly beautiful woman. Katharine hurried up the steps to greet the older woman, when she noticed the children spilling out of the doorway behind their grandmother.

"I don't believe I know you, Miz...?" the woman said, hesitantly. "I'm Abigail MacRae, Micah's mother."

Fleetingly, Katharine wondered whether she would encounter here the bitterness and hatred which most Southerners foisted on outsiders, but was relieved when these were not apparent. However, she knew that by her speech and attire, she had identified herself as one of the Northerners in the area.

"No, we haven't met, Mrs. MacRae, but I have met your son who is going to oversee my timber cutting and marketing. Is he here? I need to speak to him. My name is Katharine Fremont."

"No, Ma'm, Miz Fremont. Micah ain't here now. He's a-workin' down at the river landin' a-gettin' his logs ready to raft 'em to Darien. Won't you come in and sit a spell? More'n apt he'll be a-comin' back shortly."

Katharine looked with delight at the smiling children who had remained silent during their grandmother's welcome.

"Yes, I would love to come in for a few minutes, if you think there is a chance your son might come home early."

"Well, come on in," Abigail MacRae said with a welcoming smile. She ushered the children and Katharine through the door and into the dark room on the right of the dogtrot, which ran through the middle of the old house. A burning fire in the smoke-blackened fireplace provided warmth and light, as the two women settled into small oak rocking chairs with thin cushions. The two girls stood nearby, smiling but quiet, as the little boy crawled into his grandmother's arms.

"These must be your grandchildren, Mrs. MacRae."

"Yes, this is Carrie. She's the oldest at ten year." Carrie clasped her hands behind her back, swinging them back and forth, as she eyed Katharine. Her somber dress of brown homespun set off the simple white pinafore. Her long, golden hair was braided in two thick braids which fell on either side of her neck. The color of her eyes could not be ascertained in the dim light of the room.

"This here's Mary Sue," Abby MacRae said, "She's eight year." Mary Sue, dressed almost the same as her older sister, appeared to be shy. She was but a smaller replica of Carrie, Katharine thought, as she spoke to the girls. The girls responded with soft hellos and full smiles.

"And this one?" The grandmother cuddled the brown-eyed, laughing boy on her lap. "This one is Little Roy, named for his grandpa. He's two year now."

"Well, you certainly have some fine grandchildren, Mrs. MacRae. Your son is fortunate to have you to look after them."

"Well, you know, his wife died when she had Little Roy. He ain't never knowed any ma but this old woman." Speaking deprecatingly of herself, Abigail MacRae smiled, pleased that her guest was interested in the children.

Katharine's eyes rested on a small, framed tintype of a woman in a dark dress, which stood on a table nearby. Seeing her looking at the picture, the grandmother answered the question which she knew the younger woman was about to ask.

"Yes, that's Jenny. She had a hard time with each baby, just couldn't seem to get well, and just didn't have the strength left for the last one. He had to have a wet nurse, and lucky we were to find one out here in the country." Katharine lowered her eyes, not wanting to appear too inquisitive but longing to know more about this woman's son, forgetting momentarily that she had vowed to herself not to think of Micah MacRae in any way other than her overseer.

As the burning logs in the fireplace cast moving shadows around the room, Katharine noticed an old upright piano near one of the windows in the room. Several of the stained ivory keys were missing, but they weren't crucial ones, she decided, as they were among the lower bass notes of the piano.

"Do you enjoy the piano, Mrs. MacRae?"

"Oh, I love to hear it, but Jenny was the one could play it. She never had no lessons, but she could play it some - by ear, she'd say. I wanted the girls to have lessons, but there ain't nobody to come out this far to give lessons in music." She looked at Katharine, especially noticing the Northern woman's white, soft hands.

"You most likely play the piano, Miz Fremont?" She made a statement and asked a question at the same time.

"I had six years of lessons and I know a little about music. I know just enough to know how very much I don't know," Katharine said with a soft laugh.

"Will you play somethin'? It's been two year, since anybody played the piano."

"I haven't played much myself, since my husband died, Mrs. MacRae, but I'll try to oblige." Katharine sat on the rickety piano stool and turned the pages of a ragged old Baptist hymnal which was propped open on the piano. The pages fell naturally to a song which must have been played often by the woman, now gone, in the picture on the table in the room.

Katharine played the song, *Amazing Grace*, stiffly at first, then with greater ease. After two verses, she realized it was getting late and she needed to be home before dark. She was embarrassed to have stayed so long. She rose quickly.

Her gaze turned to Micah's mother who was gently rocking back and forth, and she smiled at the little boy, now asleep. With a sureness born of much experience, the grandmother lifted the slumbering child, his little mouth open, to a small wooden crib which Katharine hadn't yet observed. It was to the right of the old piano, and Katharine could imagine the mother, Jenny, playing the piano with her child nearby. However, the child would not have been this one as she had died soon after his birth.

"It's late," Katharine said. "I must be going. I didn't intend to stay so long." She hastily gathered her riding coat and hat and smiled at the two girls sitting on either side of their grandmother. Abigail MacRae rose to show Katharine to the door.

"We enjoyed your visit, Miz Fremont, even though it weren't us you come to see. I'm sorry you missed Micah. He's due home most any time now. Sometimes he's in earlier and sometimes it's later."

The two women clasped hands, as Katharine turned to walk down the steps.

"I'll talk to him later, Mrs. MacRae," she said, and looking back over her shoulder, she was puzzled to see tears which had welled in the older woman's eyes.

Chapter Four

Since asking Micah MacRae to cut and market her timber, Katharine had considered going to the outlying logging settlements to find men willing to work with him. Today was as good a day as any to make the trip and Katharine had asked Big Hill to ready her carriage and horses. She planned to go after dinner.

Though Tilda had cut back in her cooking since Frank's death, she still managed to prepare excellent meals which were served in Katharine's china dishes and on Katharine's lovely damask and linen table coverings. Tilda had even cut and hemmed some of the cloths, after receiving Katharine's approval, so that they fit just the end of the large mahogany dining table.

After Frank's death, Katharine insisted that Tilda eat her meals with her, so the altered cloths covered the end of the table nicely, allowing room for the two of them to eat. Such a cloth graced the table today as Katharine took her chair across from Tilda.

"Mm..., what have you cooked today? Smells like vegetable soup. Vegetables from your last year's garden, right, Tillie?" The softened version of Tilda's name which Katharine used more often, of late, always pleased Tilda.

"Yes, Miss Katharine, and I baked some bread just like you and Mr. Frank used to like it."

"Oh, it's so good," said Katharine, sipping some of the hot soup. "Hot soup is perfect for a cold day. And your bread is just right, too. So good, Tillie." With a grateful sigh and smiling across the table at her aging housekeeper and cook, Katharine exclaimed, "Tillie, I know you are ready to go back home to New York. I want you to know that I have someone to cut my timber, and as soon as it's sold, you and I are going home. Won't that be wonderful?"

Tilda's passive face lit up with a smile. "Oh, Miss Katharine, I ain't wanted to bother you none. I know you've had a world of troubles on you, since Mr. Frank died, but I'm wanting to go back home just like you."

"Oh, Tilda, I miss everything about home - my parents, my friends...oh, Tillie, I miss civilization! The South is frightening to me. The war is supposed to be over but we're in the middle of another one here."

Sensing the fear in her mistress's words, Tilda responded with a rare lilt in her voice.

"How soon, Miss Katharine? How soon before we can go home?"

Katharine slowly finished her bite of the buttered, crusty bread and patted her lips before replying, choosing her words carefully.

"If all goes as planned, the timber will be cut this season. If not, we'll have to wait until next fall. I guess it depends on the weather and on the overseer I am going to hire to cut and market my timber. Big Hill is driving me to the colored settlement after dinner. I know the overseer will need extra help and I plan to get commitments from some of the men in the settlement to help him."

A worried look crept over Tillie's face. "Miss Katharine, it's dangerous for a lady like you to go to the settlements and Big Hill knows it, too. Ain't he told you it's too dangerous?"

"Yes, Tillie, but I have to go. I have to look after Frank's interests. I'm his widow. Surely, I can find some people to help me!"

"Miss Katharine, a lady that's a widow has to look out, because she's by herself and they all know it, and no telling what might happen to you." There! Tilda, who rarely spoke more than a soft greeting and who usually only quietly answered questions posed to her, had spoken her say. Katharine knew she should not act afraid, though her stomach was in knots with fear.

"I'll be fine, Tillie," she said lightly.

The two women rose from the table and Katharine again complimented the simple but tasty meal Tilda had prepared. Katharine had berated Tilda about the vegetable garden which she had insisted on planting shortly after Frank's death, for she only had Big Hill to help her. But how fresh tasting the vegetables were now in dead winter. Yes, she herself would help Tilda plant a vegetable garden this year! That is, if they had to wait until the fall for the timber to be cut. If not, why, they'd have a vegetable garden at home in New York! She, Katharine Fremont, who had never dug in the earth to plant anything, would have a garden!

Katharine had let go the servants who helped her when Frank was alive. She really thought she would be back in New York by now. Her parents had urged her to hire someone to see about the timber, so that she could go on home to New York. She had considered this in a weak moment, but she had sense enough to know that she needed to stay to learn as much as she could about the timber business and to try to make as big a profit from the timber sale as possible. After all, this would be the money which would be her livelihood for the rest of her life, unless she should marry again.

She had not told her parents that Frank had still owed money on their home. Since Frank never discussed business with her, she found out only after his death that money was still owed on the house. With his insurance money, she had managed to pay on the mortgage and to live, until her timber was sold. Then, she planned to sell the house.

The Brougham carriage was waiting for Katharine with the gray geldings hitched to it. Big Hill, holding the door for her, shook his head as he helped her into the carriage.

"Ah sho hates to see you go to the settle'mints, Miz Kat'rin. It sho dange'rus."

"But, Hill, you live there. How can it be dangerous, if you're with me?"

" 'Cause dey ain' satisfied, Miz Kat'rin. Dey allus wants mo'."

"I'm willing to pay them more, Hill. Tell them that for me, and I'll tell them, too."

"Mistuh Frank strap me to a tree, ef he knowed Ah wuz drivin' you to the settle'mint, Miz Kat'rin."

"Mr. Frank is dead, Hill, and I'm looking after myself. I'm not foolish, however. I did bring this along." Katharine reached into the folds of her skirt and produced a small handbag, which she opened, and took out a small gun.

"Frank bought this for me before he died. He said for me to carry it in my purse wherever I went. He was going to teach me how to use it, but he died before he could do it."

Big Hill's eyes widened. "Ef it doan' beat all Ah heered tell. A lady wid a gun, ridin' 'round, but dat jes' whut you needs, Miz Kat'rin. Mistuh Frank shoulda had a gun fer hisseff, too."

"He did, Hill, but he was shot from behind. They took his gun after they killed him, but I still have mine and I think I can use it, if I have to."

A new measure of respect gleamed in Hill's eyes and a smile crossed his weathered, black face. "Yas'm. Ah b'lieves you sho could, Miz Kat'rin," he said, as he closed the door and laboriously climbed into the driver's seat.

The drive to the settlement which was on the outskirts of the lumber mill, and not actually a part of the lumber mill, was a long one, and Katharine intermittently read and looked out the carriage window at the monotonous landscape of yellow pines which lined both sides of the road. Occasionally, cut-over timberland appeared and, more rarely, open pastures of grazing cows varied the interminable miles of longleaf pine.

Finding herself unable to concentrate on reading, she closed the book which she had borrowed from the new library in Eastman and let her thoughts wander. She intended to talk to as many loggers and raftsmen as she could to help her new overseer. Perhaps, if the weather cooperated, if she could find enough help, if everything fell into place, she'd be home within a few months.

A moaning murmur drifted through the swaying pine trees, interrupting her thoughts. "The sound is eerie," Katharine whispered softly to herself as she looked up the lengths of the tall pines. The needled tops of the trees, moving in the breeze, produced this sound which had always caused an uneasiness in her. She remembered telling Frank how the sound disturbed her but Frank had said that it didn't bother him. The trees meant money to him, he had said, and he could take the noise they made, because it just meant money in the bank.

And now Frank was dead. The insecurity which had assailed her at times since Frank's death now struck her anew. How she longed for a strong man to lean on, to help her! Katharine's cheeks flushed as the image of Micah MacRae was almost palpable in the carriage with her. Katharine scolded herself for thinking such personal thoughts about a rascal Southerner. He probably attended all of those squatter meetings, and he may even have been guilty of putting spikes in the timber company's sawlogs and wrecking the company's tram roads. She must look at him only as a means of getting her timber to market. At that moment she made a promise to herself that she would be strong and that she did not need a man to lean on. She would handle her business affairs herself, the sooner the better, and then she would go home, never to return to this angry land!

In spite of her vow, however, the truth that she had no business experience and no timber expertise kept clutching at her, and she felt almost ill because of it. She knew she would have to learn rapidly, and she would have to trust Micah MacRae as her overseer explicitly. How could she, a Northerner, trust a rebellious Southerner? Could the mill manager have led her astray in suggesting Micah MacRae as her timber overseer? "Oh, God," she prayed silently, "help me."

She cupped her face between her gloved hands and closed her eyes, moving with the carriage as it bumped and swayed, its wheels waggling along the rutted road. The movement of the sighing pines cast shadows through her closed eyelids, almost forcing her to look again at their crowning heads of long green needles.

The rhythmic staccato of the horses' hooves was slowing to a different beat, and Katharine realized they were nearing the colored timber settlement. She had been advised that they would be more likely to help her than the ones in the white settlement, as the latter still harbored hatred toward the Northern timber people. She would approach the colored loggers first.

The Negro settlement was a sad commentary on the lives of colored families in the area, Katharine thought, as her gaze took in the tiny shacks, the small church without a steeple or paned windows, the trash that no one bothered to pick up. Only half-naked children were in sight, playing with an almost deflated ball in the mud-streaked areas which served as streets.

"Whoa dar," Big Hill called to the horses, as Katharine surveyed the dismal scene.

Again, fear twisted in her stomach and she struggled to breathe calmly.

Hill was at the carriage door, opening it for her, as men appeared at the doors of the rundown shacks. Katharine walked ahead of Hill, her head up, emitting a confidence to the curious onlookers, which she did not actually feel. Stepping in the middle of the cluster of shanties, she found herself speaking clearly.

"Good day. My name is Mrs. Frank Fremont, and I need loggers and rafters to help in cutting my timber and getting it to market."

As she began talking, several of the men on their narrow porches ambled over to her. Hill introduced four of them as Shep, Luke, Bud, and Hoke. Trying hard not to notice the open hatred in their eyes, Katharine told them that an overseer would be cutting her timber and he would need men to help him.

Sullen and uncommunicative, the men responded in different ways, as she offered to increase the wages they usually earned for logging and rafting timber. Shep carved in the dirt with his torn boot, while Luke rolled a dirty cigarette. Bud whetted a knife blade on a worn strop, as Hoke emptied his 'shine bottle remains in the dirt near Katharine.

Not knowing how to end the one-sided conversation but determined not to show her fear, Katharine mentioned that some of them had likely helped her husband, Frank Fremont, at Camp Six or at Willcox Lake. Realizing she was getting nowhere, Katharine smiled bravely and said that she would talk with them again soon, when they'd had time to consider her proposals.

Big Hill was oddly quiet throughout her speaking. It was difficult to realize that this was his home, she thought, and he had a wife here, though she didn't know which of the dilapidated shacks was theirs. When she turned abruptly to head back to the carriage, her colored driver spoke for the first time since his introductions of the four loggers.

"You heerd Miz Fremont. She sho pay good wages, ef you he'p her." The loggers' icy refusal even to speak to Big Hill, or to her, made Katharine admit to herself the futility of her mission. She quickly turned to Big Hill and told him she was ready to go back home.

The distance from the mute loggers to her carriage appeared to lengthen as Katharine walked ahead of Big Hill. She had never been as frightened in her life, except when Frank was murdered, and she was thankful to reach the relative safety of the carriage. She wanted to fling the door open and throw herself inside, away from the hatred she had seen and felt. However, she forced herself to walk with measured steps and to wait for Hill to open the door for her. Nodding graciously at the group which was increasing as people spilled out of their hovels, Katharine settled in her seat and inwardly thanked the Lord for keeping her safe.

Hill, looking shaken, cracked his whip in the air, and the horses lunged forward. Glad that they were on their way home, Katharine looked at the small handbag on the seat and realized she had left her gun where it could not have been of any use to her. She vowed to keep it near her from now on. She would not likely forget about it again.

Chapter Five

Several weeks after the Winslows' party, Winslow Hall was revisited by officials of the Yellow Pines Lumber Company for their annual meeting. Since Katharine's husband had owned shares in the company, Katharine attended the meeting in his behalf.

Driving her phaeton carriage, Katharine guided the horse onto the wide brick driveway of the imposing mansion. Parked at the hitching rail at the side of the large home were gentlemen's fine carriages, some from a decade earlier and some of the latest types, such as Brewster Victorias, curtained five-glass landaus, coupe rockaways, and a wicker vis-a-vis. Yard grooms were leading some of the horse-driven carriages to the coach house where the horses would be unharnessed, and then they would be tended in the stables. Liveried Negro coachmen congregated together, sharing news and occurrences since their last encounters.

Men in top hats, cravats, and frock coats were moving across the vast grounds, calling out good-humored greetings to one another. Ben Winslow was at the front door, showing the men where to leave their hats and canes.

Katharine assumed she would be the only woman, other than Julia, at the meeting. Everyone would likely think it improper for her to have driven alone to the meeting from such a distance, but Katharine was learning, more and more, to depend on herself and not to expect Big Hill to drive her everywhere.

Yard servants, helping with the horses and carriages, came forward to assist her, and they guided her carriage to a mounting block near the front door. They knew her and called out courteous greetings which Katharine returned with a smile, asking about them and their families.

She was careful not to snag her blue wool dress and petticoats, as Poke helped her out of the carriage. As she walked up the front steps of Winslow Hall, holding up the front of her dress to avoid stepping on it, she wondered what was discussed at a lumber company annual meeting, as she had never attended one.

Julia was hastening out the door to greet her.

"Oh, Katharine, I'm so glad you could come. I do worry about your riding alone, though," she said, glancing at Katharine's carriage, with Big Hill nowhere in sight.

"I'll be all right, Julia," Katharine said, smiling, "I have to learn to be self-sufficient." She added, "I hope you'll sit in the meeting with me."

"As you probably know, I never do - attend the meetings, I mean - but I will, since you're here."

The two women walked to the large, walnut-paneled library where the lumber company men were waiting for the meeting to begin. Servants were entering the room with trays of hot beverages, non-alcoholic because of the presence of one of the Dodge sons, and cigars for the men to smoke.

Most of the men were seated in upholstered chairs around the carved mahogany table, but others stood near the burning lightwood fire in the cavernous, richly ornate fireplace. Some were lighting their finely chiseled pipes while others were enjoying the proffered cigars.

Those who were seated quickly stood when Katharine and Julia entered the library. Acknowledging the greetings with smiles and a few handclasps, the women seated themselves in the matching Hepplewhite chairs near one of the heavily curtained windows.

Ben Winslow remained standing after the men again seated themselves. He rapped on the lectern with the company gavel, making certain that he had the attention of everyone in the capacious room. Conversation ceased, as everyone waited for the meeting to begin.

Katharine had never seen several of the men, whom Ben hastened to introduce.

"Gentlemen," he said, "and ladies," nodding toward Katharine and Julia, "you know why we're here today. We're in a land war, and we've got to figure out how to win it. We've got six lawyers meeting with us, three from other states, representing the sons of the benefactor of this county, William E. Dodge, and three from Savannah, representing our Yellow Pines Lumber Company. And, of course, Norman Dodge is here today. We're honored with your presence today, Mr. Dodge!"

Everyone acknowledged Norman Dodge's presence with respectful words of greeting and handshakes. As Ben introduced the well-dressed lawyers, they stood up briefly, nodding and smiling.

Ben continued, "The battle is moving into the federal courts. These squatters sometimes win the land cases in the Georgia courts, but our company lawyers are moving the lawsuits to federal court where we'll get a fair trial."

"Hear! Hear!" This was interjected by one of the Savannah lawyers who pounded his clinched fist on the solid table, then raised it in a mock show of triumph into the air. Talking erupted among the timber officials, and Ben had to knock on the table to regain their attention.

"First things first! Mr. Paul Owens, we'd like to know about the latest shenanigans of the squatters. What are they up to now?"

The rotund mill manager stood before his chair and adjusted his eyeglasses.

"Ladies and gentlemen," he said, "there is still a definite lull in the land war. The mill is turning out more board feet than ever. The saws haven't been tampered with. No spikes have been driven into the timber. No tram roads have been blocked or damaged. Best of all, I don't believe the squatters are meeting anymore. Maybe they've learned their lesson." Everyone clapped at this, until Ben Winslow again rapped on the table.

Paul Owens continued, "Perhaps the battle is totally in the courts now. I'm thinking we can give Micah MacRae credit for stopping the day-to-day harassment of the squatters. They listen to what he says, and I believe we have him to thank for the respite we are experiencing now." The mill manager cast a sweeping look around the room before sitting down.

"Don't be fooled by Micah MacRae!" The voice was that of one of the Savannah lawyers.

"He's a dyed-in-the-wool Southerner, and don't ever forget it! I know some of you have hired him to raft your timber to Darien, and let me tell you, he knows timber. He can look at a log and tell you its board feet within a few inches. He won't be outdone by the timber inspectors, either. He already knows the value of his timber before the inspector can quote a price. Why, I've talked to a number of the inspectors there at Darien, and they say he's the best." The lawyer paused, then continued, "However, don't be fooled. He hates your guts and actually believes that all of your land deeds are invalid. Believe me, gentlemen...and ladies, I know!"

The room was silent, and Katharine felt her face grow hot following the lawyer's tirade. What had she expected? The lawyer was right, but she reminded herself that she was only hiring Micah MacRae to market her timber. After all, the lawyer did concede that he was the best, didn't he? When her timber was cut and sold, she would sever all ties with him.

In the short silence that followed, the Savannah lawyer who had been introduced as William Thornton, slowly stood up. Fingering the watch fob and chain across his ample vest, he cleared his throat, and his eyes moved around to each person in the room.

"I want each of you to know what we're up against. Yes, I am representing the Yellow Pines Lumber Company, along with my colleagues here. But I think it behooves each of us to understand just what is going on in regard to the squatters' claims."

Some of the men in the room uneasily shifted their weight in their chairs. Others riveted their attention on any words which might proceed out of the lawyer's mouth.

"Again," the lawyer reiterated, "remember I'm on your side, but it pays to know your enemy."

The men relaxed a bit as the lawyer walked to a corner of the room and brought what appeared to be a long scroll on wooden legs to the table. The scroll, unrolled, was a large map of land lots in the Georgia counties of Telfair, Dodge, Laurens, Montgomery and Pulaski. It was an area of about 500 square miles of land in the triangle formed by the convergence of the Ocmulgee and the Oconee rivers which together formed the Altamaha River. On many of the land lots was a ribbon with the letters, N.W.D., the initials of Norman W. Dodge.

Beneath the ribbons were names of the Southern squatters who were illegally claiming the lands. These were lands that William

E. Dodge's sons had agreed to sell to all in the Winslows' library, who were interested. Each land lot, the lawyer stated, represented 202½ acres.

Katharine stared at the land lots and at the squatters' names under the yellow ribbons. She swallowed hard when she saw four land lots in the northeastern part of Telfair County with the name of Micah MacRae on each lot. The ribbons attached to these lots claimed them for Norman W. Dodge! The Savannah lawyer resumed his seat, obviously awaiting a reaction to the beribboned scroll.

Katharine looked around the room, wanting to hear more, trying to understand what the land war was all about. Paul Owens was rising to speak again and she leaned forward to hear him.

"I'm not a lawyer," he said hesitantly, "but hardly a day goes by that I don't hear from the local people, or 'squatters' as you call them, about what the Georgia law says in regard to land ownership in the State of Georgia."

"Now, wait a minute, Paul. Whose side are you on anyway?" The voice belonged to one of the timber men, Silas Ewers, who had moved from Connecticut some twelve years prior.

"Silas," Paul Owens addressed him. "I don't know about you, but I agree with the lawyer from Savannah who said we should know our enemy. Of course, I'm on the lumber company's side. You all pay me my wages. All I'm saying is that we need to know what these Southerners are thinking. And, for starters, there's the law of 'adverse possession' in regard to land ownership. The squatters know that Georgia law says a land claim is good after twenty years' possession without a deed, and they also know that the Georgia law says their land claims are good after only seven years' possession with a deed!" Following his spiel, the mill manager resumed his seat and glanced at the scowling Silas Ewers who was vehemently shaking his head.

After a few moments of silence, Silas Ewers said, "To borrow a colloquialism from the local Crackers, Paul, 'your wits are always wool-gathering.'"

Following another brief silence, Norman Dodge, the only son of William E. Dodge in attendance at the meeting, stood up and walked over to the mantel where he rested his arm and looked down into the crackling flames. No one spoke, for this was the timber magnate's son, and everyone waited for him to speak.

"I'm sure you all knew my father, and I think you will all agree that my father was a good man. He had built at his own expense the Court House in this county. He was for national prohibition and he supported the Prohibition Party. He was for Christian temperance in all things. In fact, he served as president of the National Temperance Society. He also believed in keeping the Sabbath day holy. He was opposed to Sunday labor and refused to serve as director of any company which received a profit from such labor."

Ben Winslow interjected a word of encouragement. "Your father was a good man, Norman, and I don't think anyone here would deny it. I'm not a religious man myself, but I think we all know of the good that Dwight L. Moody has done, and your father, with the help of Cornelius Vanderbilt II and J. P. Morgan, once financed Moody's ministry. Yes, your father was a good man."

The mill manager was on his feet again, and everyone was shocked that he continued with his diatribe which obviously annoyed the son of William E. Dodge.

"With all due respect to you and to your father, Norman, and to you, Ben, I don't believe we're talking about the same thing. Being temperate and keeping Sunday holy and financing an evangelist's ministry are not the same as taking lands which the squatters feel are theirs. Again, with all due respect, we're talking about several different things here. The Georgians have won a number of the land title court cases against your claims."

Ben Winslow leapt to his feet. "That's because they've been tried in the Georgia court system, Paul. Let's see how they fare in the federal court which is where they'll all be tried in the near future." He sat back in his chair again and looked at the mill manager as if to say that the matter had ended, but the short, corpulent Paul Owens had no intention of sitting down, and he still commanded the attention of everyone in the room.

However, before he could continue, Norman Dodge commented that he had to catch the train back to New York, and that he regretted having to leave so abruptly but he was needed on a business matter back in New York. Everyone stood as he walked by, respectfully nodding their heads and some gripping his outstretched hand, as he left the room.

"I'm not trying to be a mule's behind, gentlemen," Paul Owens continued, as though there had been no interruption, "and as I said before, I'm on your side. I think most of you know my background insofar as the war was concerned, but I don't mind repeating it. I was in the Wilderness Battle in Virginia with General Grant. We suffered nearly 18,000 losses, and I can assure you that I am lucky and blessed to be standing before you now. No one need ever question my loyalty, but being loyal and being stupid don't necessarily mean the same thing." The mill manager looked around the room, letting his words sink in, before continuing on a different vein.

"How many of you know that this land in question, over 300,000 acres of land or, to put it another way, over 500 square miles of it, was once owned by the State of Indiana? Yes, I've been told that the State of Indiana came into possession of these lands, which in itself is illegal. Also, to further the illegitimacy of it all, the State of Indiana didn't pay taxes on the land during the year 1844, and, by the way, the squatters have paid taxes on this very land since they purchased it. Some of the local families have owned this land - or thought they owned it - for many generations."

"Paul, you're confusing everybody. As you stated earlier, you are not a lawyer, and what we need is to hear from our legal counsel, some of whom traveled for long distances to come today," Ben Winslow said.

Throwing up his hands, yet smiling good-naturedly, the mill manager concluded, "By the way, one of the ejectment suits will be tried this afternoon, if any of you would like to go to the Court House and hear it. It's probably one of the last ones to be tried in the local court, since you lawyers have had the ejectment cases moved to the federal courts."

The mill manager sat down, and the Savannah lawyer, William Thornton, again captured everyone's rapt attention as he stood up to address them. However, rather than offering an explanation as to why the deeds appeared questionable to both sides, the artful lawyer returned them to the pressing matter at hand.

"My friends, instead of arguing about something that has been bandied about for fifty years, without any more light being shed upon it, let's return to the reason for this most urgent meeting, and that is to inform you, as Paul just stated, that the battle will be fought in the federal court system now, and we have every reason to believe that ours will be the victory. You won the war, and this final land war here in Middle Georgia will be only a minor scuffle which our grandchildren will not even bother to know about or remember." William Thornton resumed his seat amid the low rumble of agreement around the room. However, he was seated for only a moment before rising again and addressing the group.

"Looking around at this assemblage, I can only count a handful of you who may have been present at the mass meeting here in Eastman, in 1874, when William E. Dodge formally presented the Court House to the people of Dodge County. Of course, he had the Court House built at his own expense, because this county was formed and named for him. I myself was at this meeting and I'll never forget, as long as I live, what happened during the presentation of the Court House. I believe you all would be interested in hearing about it, also." The lawyer paused as though gauging whether everyone would indeed want to hear. Satisfied that he held their attention, he continued with his recollection.

"In addition to being a financier and philanthropist, William Dodge was an eloquent speaker. He made a fine speech in presenting the Court House to the people at this mass meeting. Well, it was arranged that a Col. Dawson, a lawyer and resident of Eastman, would respond in behalf of the people with an acceptance speech. The lawyer, somewhat nervous and wanting to be equal to the occasion, took double his usual dose of morphine, and before he had proceeded more than three or four minutes into his speech, with his arm extended in Ciceronian style, he fell asleep.

"In the silence that followed, no one knew what to do, until a young man by the name of Ham stepped to the front and delivered a ten-minute address that completely captivated everyone, including William Dodge. In fact, Mr. Dodge asked for an introduction to the speaker, saying, 'That young man made one of the best short speeches I ever listened to.'"

After enjoying a laugh with the others about the in-depth preparation of the speaker in question, with his overdose of morphine, and insisting against their amused disbelief that the story was indeed true, the Savannah lawyer turned to another subject.

"I want to shed some light on what Paul just said about the State of Indiana owning a part of the State of Georgia. Indiana did own the land in question for nine years, I believe, from 1842 until 1851, and you're right, Paul, in saying that Indiana didn't pay the required taxes for the year 1844, but you're incorrect in saying that it's illegal for one state to own part of another one. In fact, I have committed to memory Judge Speer's ruling in the matter. He said, 'It must be understood that when the State of Indiana bought these lands, it came as a subject and not as a sovereign. If the State of Indiana is to be regarded as an alien, it is laid down in Washburne on Real Property that an alien may purchase and hold lands against all the world except the state; and Briggs, Hall and Sleeper may not say with Louis XIV: "I am the state."'" "For those of you who don't know, Briggs, Hall and Sleeper were the defendants in the case." Having stated his understanding of the law in the case, the eloquent jurist sat down.

Not intimidated at all by the learned lawyer, Paul Owens again stood up to add what he knew about the legalities of the case, which the Savannah lawyer had neglected to mention. Everyone now turned their attention to him, trying to comprehend the complexities of the serpentine links in the title which had been in question for so many years.

"I think everybody ought to know who Briggs, Hall and Sleeper were, other than just hearing that they were defendants in the case. Briggs was from Massachusetts and was a clerk in the office of Dodge's land agent. He knew that the deed to the lumber company had been lost, that it had not been properly executed, and that it was not entitled to record. Sleeper was a lawyer, also from Massachusetts, but living in Eastman. Hall, of course, was the lawyer in Eastman who's now in prison in Ohio. Hall found many defects in the Dodges' recorded title." The timber officials in the room appeared to be bored with the explanation of the mill manager, and their yawns prompted Ben Winslow to interrupt Paul Owens.

"Paul, we need to go ahead with other business. The title is so long and complicated, and we just don't have time to go into it today. Also, we probably need a lawyer to explain it again to us some other time."

The mill manager, looking somewhat defeated, nonetheless smiled and resumed his seat. Katharine was disappointed, for she wanted to hear about every link in the lengthy title chain.

The thin, quavering voice of Tillman Nash, one of Norman Dodge's lawyers, interjected an answer to what was on everyone's mind. The lawyer rose as he began talking.

"I'm sure you're all wondering why Mr. Dodge didn't attended the previous two meetings of the Yellow Pines Lumber Company. No, he doesn't have any fear for his own safety, though I think it would be wise for everyone here to be careful and not to take undue risks. But, no, Mr. Dodge could not attend the last two meetings because of urgent business to attend to in New York. We, of course, are representing him and will telegraph him about anything he needs to know."

As the aged lawyer took his seat, the thought crossed Katharine's mind that her husband and John C. Forsyth had paid the ultimate price here in the piney woods, while William E. Dodge had stayed a thousand miles away in the safety of his home in New York. Now, his sons rarely attended their meetings. As quickly as the thought came to her, she remonstrated with herself for thinking such a thing. However, the thought persisted that, with all of his immense wealth, William E. Dodge, who died in 1883, had never built a home here in the wiregrass, as others in the company had, though his son, Norman, did have a home at Normandale, the lumber town which bore his name. It seemed, however, that the sons spent most of their time at St. Simons or other places away from the piney woods area. Something akin to resentment settled around Katharine's heart and she could not make it go away.

Julia, who along with Katharine had remained silent during the meeting, now rose, suggesting to Katharine that they leave the meeting.

"How boring! I'm glad for the men to handle the business," Julia laughed, as they left the library. Looking at Katharine, she was surprised to see the morose look on her friend's face.

"Katharine, what is the matter? You look like you're worried about something."

"Oh, Julia, do you think Norman Dodge could possibly be wrong about some of the land he's claiming for his own? I mean, it's a lot of land, several hundred thousand acres of it!"

"Didn't you hear our lawyers? Of course, he has a rightful claim to the lands. Don't worry yourself about such. You're just not used to these business meetings, and it's upset you."

"But people are being thrown off their lands - some at gunpoint!"

"Well, that's not for us to worry about, is it? After all, that's what the courts are for. You know, Katharine, I think it would be interesting to watch one of these cases tried here at the Court House, as Paul suggested earlier. Let's go see how it's done. I've heard they're actually humorous parodies of what the court system should be. Do you want to go?"

"Yes, Julia, just so I can get back home before dark. Are they usually settled pretty quickly?"

"Well, that's what makes them so funny. See, the local juries usually favor the local people, so they're never out over a few minutes. They know what the verdict's going to be when they take their seats in the jury box." Julia hesitated before continuing, "Actually, they used to make me angry, but now that they're all going to be tried in the federal court where we'll get fair trials, I can see the hilarity of the local court. You'll see what I mean." Julia maintained, "I've attended several of the ejectment suits in Macon and Savannah, which were very professionally tried, but these local trials are but mockeries of our justice system. You'll see!"

Chapter Six

Poke guided the Winslows' Victoria through the dirt streets to the two-story, box-shaped, clapboarded Court House, a gift to the county which bore his name from William E. Dodge some eighteen years prior. Katharine studied the imposing building which reputedly cost its benefactor $25,000, with its green window-blinds, now in need of repairs, and green shingled roof.

She had read about the need for repairs in regard to the Court House and to the different gates to the entrances of the Court House yard, thereby preventing cows and hogs from being annoyances to persons in attendance at court. She also had read about the platform and wood foundation around the Court House well being in rotten condition and the need for repairs.

The Court House yard was dotted with horses, mules, and oxen, hitched to wagons, buckboards, buggies, and oxcarts, along with a few modest carriages. Obviously, Katharine thought, court was well attended, judging by the conveyances outside.

She thought of the many ways that Dodge money had helped the area. How paradoxical it was that a man who gave so much also took even more - and from innocent people!

With courteous aplomb, Poke had descended from the driver's seat and now proceeded to help the ladies from the carriage. Julia reminded him to wait for them, as they only planned to stay perhaps an hour.

Julia and Katharine quietly entered the Court House and ascended the stairway to the courtroom. They could hear mingled voices, drifting from the courtroom, and Katharine hurried up the last few steps, eagerly anticipating actually hearing one of the ejectment cases being tried.

They barely opened the squeaking courtroom door. A bailiff standing just inside held the door and motioned them to seats on the back bench. Settling back on the hard bench, they lifted their dresses from the dirty sawdust on the floor, acrid with the stench of stale tobacco juice. Though their row was empty, except for themselves, the rest of the courtroom was packed with local people and backwoodsmen who had come to witness the ejectment suit. The case involved Norman Dodge versus Norris Burch, a farmer well known in the county, whose large family and host of friends were seated in the courtroom behind him.

With surprise, Katharine saw Micah MacRae sitting on the second bench on the side of the counsel table. He sat among other backwoodsmen who, like himself, had ejectment suits pending against them. Some habitually spat streams of ambeer into nearby spittoons, oftentimes missing the mark and splattering the layer of sawdust on the floor. Though most were dressed similarly in brown jeans breeches with shirts of homespun and rawhide shoes, some boldly wore the frayed gray coats of the Confederacy.

While waiting for the trial to begin, Katharine looked around the courtroom, noticing that several lights of glass were broken and the walls were cracked in a few places. She remembered reading in the Eastman paper that the grand jury had recommended that thirty-six chairs be purchased by the ordinary and placed in the court and jury rooms for the use of the jurors. Also, a number of settees necessary for seats in the courtroom were to be purchased. She noted a number of settees which were filled with spectators. Judge Seymour McAfee sat behind a desk-like structure in the center of the raised platform at the center terminus of the courtroom. Lawyers and their clients sat at a table in front of the dais which also held a witness chair. Katharine recognized Stanley Agnew, attorney for the Dodge family, who had just left the meeting at Winslow Hall.

The rear courtroom door opened, admitting Paul Owens, puffing from the exertion of climbing the stairs, and William Thornton, the Savannah lawyer. Both nodded toward Katharine and Julia before hurrying down the aisle to the plaintiff's table, where they joined Stanley Agnew. Norman Dodge was absent, and Julia whispered to Katharine that he rarely was present for the local ejectment suits.

Norris Burch, the defendant, was dressed in clean overalls and a long-sleeve homespun shirt, his beard and hair trimmed and combed for the occasion. He sat quietly, at times glancing around at the array of supporters behind him. A gray Confederate jacket hung conspicuously from the back of his chair.

Julia whispered to Katharine that Burch's lawyer was Murray Hall, a relative of the lawyer, Luther Hall, who was one of the conspirators convicted of having John C. Forsyth murdered two years prior. Forsyth was superintendent of the Yellow Pines Lumber Company. Luther Hall, she reminded Katharine, was still in the Ohio State Penitentiary, serving his sentence of life imprisonment.

The clerk of court rose from his seat and announced the case which was coming before the court: "Norman W. Dodge versus Norris Burch." Following his pronouncement, Sheriff Buford Hargrove called out to twelve men, sitting on the front benches of the courtroom, to come forward and fill the jury box, facing the counsel table on the far side of the room.

Most of the jurors appeared to be backwoodsmen, dressed in homespun and brown jeans and overalls, their full beards and hair untamed by the razor. The only two local townsmen were recognizable by their neatly trimmed hair and beards, their plain wool jackets covering white shirts which were open at the neck.

Nearly all of the men, shuffling in an irregular file toward the jury box, made eye contact with the defendant who managed to control a smile at the corners of his mouth. Even from the back of the courtroom, Katharine noticed the tacit communication between the jurors and the defendant. She was beginning to understand what Julia meant when she said that the local ejectment suits were parodies of the judicial system, and the trial hadn't even begun.

The jurors somewhat noisily seated themselves in the jury box, then smugly surveyed the courtroom from its vantage point. Judge McAfee nodded toward the counsel table for approval of the jury selection and Murray Hall quickly rose to address the assembly.

"We accept the jury, Your Honor. We need twelve good and honest men and they're sitting right there in the box, waiting to hear our case."

Stanley Agnew just as quickly sprang to his feet, indicating that two of the jurors, Leon Mullis and Early Evans, would not be acceptable due to the fact that they had testified against the Dodges in previous ejectment suits. Within a relatively short period of time, two substitutes had replaced the dismissed jurors.

As the trial began, Stanley Agnew called William Thornton to the witness stand to explain the Dodge claim to the land lots in question. Katharine couldn't hear the lot numbers, but she inferred that the four land lots were in southern Dodge County near Sugar Creek.

William Thornton recited the title jugglery of the Dodge lands, which included the Burch lots in question, beginning with the purchase of all of the land lying between the Oconee and Ocmulgee River by the State of Georgia from the Indians in 1805. "It was the first land in Georgia to be disposed of by lottery," he said. "Under it every white man, widow and orphan was entitled to one draw, and every Revolutionary soldier was entitled to two draws.

"Since the big stretch of piney woods between the two rivers was never claimed, Peter J. Williams of Milledgeville, Georgia, amassed 300,000 acres of the land which he sold in 1834 to the Georgia Land Company. The imposing antebellum Williams home still exists at the corner of Liberty and Washington streets in Milledgeville," he added, as an interesting aside. "The Georgia Land Company owned 300,000 acres of the finest longleaf yellow pine in the world.

"Yellow gold, my friends," the Savannah attorney said dramatically, looking around the crowded courtroom. "Of course," he continued, "the local people did not know the worth of the yellow pines, but William E. Dodge knew. Mr. Dodge also knew that he wanted to help the people of this area...give them jobs and bring enlightenment to the people of this region. We are all sitting in this lovely Court House today because of the beneficence of William E. Dodge." William Thornton toyed with the fob on his gold watch chain which hung from his lower vest pocket.

"But I digress," he said, before continuing with his explanation of the Dodge claim to the land lots in dispute. "In no time, the Georgia Lumber Company was formed by Northern entrepreneurs who purchased this large tract of land lying in Laurens, Montgomery, Telfair and Pulaski counties. You remember, at that time Dodge County did not exist. It was formed from the four counties I just named in 1870 or thereabouts and named for its benefactor, Honorable William E. Dodge.

"Another purchase of land, 20,000 acres in Telfair County, was made by this group, which included the Old Flournoy Mill near Lumber City, said to be the largest sawmill in the South at that time. Though for several years, the mill appeared to enjoy great prosperity, it ultimately was forced to close.

"All of its property was conveyed in 1838 to the Fund Commissioner of the State of Indiana to cover debts that could not be met. For nine years, my friends, the State of Indiana owned 500 square miles of the State of Georgia.

"From the Governor of Indiana, the title passed through several links to William Chauncey and others of New York. There, caught by the outbreak of the war, it was for the duration of the war captive in the Northern enemy territory. After the war, it went to William Pitt Eastman of New Hampshire, who became owner in 1868.

"In that year, gentlemen of the jury, William E. Dodge, W.P. Eastman, William Chauncey and others organized the Georgia Land and Lumber Company, known locally as the Yellow Pines Lumber Company, under the laws of New York and established an office in Georgia at Eastman and later at Normandale. The president of the corporation was William E. Dodge, now deceased, father of Norman W. Dodge who is named in this suit today.

"I think we've brought the title up to date. It should be clear that Norman Dodge is the owner of these four lots in question and that the defendant, Norris Burch, should vacate the premises immediately."

Stanley Agnew formally thanked the Savannah lawyer for his astute mastery of the minute vagaries in the land titles and excused him from further witness in the suit.

Murray Hall, however, quickly stood up and announced his intention to cross-examine the witness. Stanley Agnew resumed his seat at the far end of the counsel table, clasping his hands together under his smoothly shaven chin as the cross-examination began.

"First of all," the Southern lawyer said, "I think most of us assembled here know that this is probably the last Dodge eviction case that will be tried in our state court, because the Dodges are having their ejection suits moved to the federal courts. You remember, last year the case involving the murder of John Forsyth was illegally moved from the state court, where all murder cases are tried, to the federal court by the Dodges and their big-city lawyers."

Stanley Agnew was on his feet. "I object, Your Honor! We are not here to review the Forsyth murder case."

"Objection overruled, Counsel," Judge McAfee said, nodding to Murray Hall to continue.

"Thank you, Your Honor. This is relevant to this case, because it will likely be tried again in federal court, not as a simple eviction case but as a case of conspiracy...conspiring to deprive the Dodges of their rights...or some such idiotic drivel."

Stanley Agnew silently fumed, looking at the ceiling and twiddling his thumbs as the upstart young lawyer faced the jurors, then turned to include the courtroom audience in his remarks.

"Your Honor," he said, "I'd like to quote from the defendants' counsel in the Forsyth murder case last year. He said:

> The real purpose of the indictment is to bring citizens of Georgia into a Federal court and try them on a charge of murder of which the State court alone has jurisdiction. Norman W. Dodge is nothing but a sham, a stalking horse, a decoy duck, to bring the case into the jurisdiction of this court. The slender excuse upon which it is brought here should not be allowed to wrest the case from the hands of the people of Georgia, whose rights are being eaten away as waves of mighty ocean wash the landmarks from the shore.

"I've been told," Murray Hall continued, "that the Dodges will use the same ruse to move their ejection suits into the federal courts: 'conspiracy.' Friends, our rights are still being taken from us, but here...today...we shall see justice done."

He addressed the plaintiff's lawyers.

"Your colleague in this case complimented your skill in relating the serpentine links in the titles in question, Mr. Thornton, but I must differ to the extent that I noticed several loopholes, sir, in the titles to most of the lands, in general, and to Mr. Burch's lots, in particular.

"We've gone through this in other suits such as this one, but I'll reiterate it again for those jurors who might not have heard about them." The lawyer paused for emphasis, then continued.

"It's on record that the State of Indiana never paid taxes for the year 1844, and a fi fa against the Georgia Lumber Company was issued by James Boyd, tax commissioner of Telfair County.

"During the Tax Sale of 1845, many local people bought these lands, including Norris Burch's father, Littleton Burch. Georgia law states that twenty years' possession gives a man absolute claim, Mr. Thornton, and under color of title, the claim becomes absolute after seven years. Being a member of the Georgia Bar Association, you know these to be Georgia laws.

"Gentlemen of the jury, Burches have been living on this land for nearly fifty years. To further solidify their claim, they've paid taxes on the lots in question each year - ain't missed a year," the lawyer said, reverting to the vernacular of the local backwoods people.

"Where are the deeds?" Stanley Agnew was on his feet, glaring at the opposing counsel.

Judge McAfee's gavel cracked on his wood desk.

"You're speaking out of turn, Mr. Agnew. You may reexamine the witness after Mr. Hall's cross-examination." The Northern lawyer sat down in exasperation, shaking his head at the absurdity of it all.

"Thank you, Your Honor," Murray Hall said, addressing the judge but looking at the opposing counsel. "However," the lawyer continued, "I was coming to the deeds in question. I have them here as evidence, Your Honor." The defense lawyer carefully extracted the deeds, discolored with age, presumably, from the papers in his attaché case. He handled them gingerly, attesting to the supposed brittleness of the papers.

Stanley Agnew leapt to his feet, pointing a long finger at the four deeds which Murray Hall held, two in each hand, before the hushed courtroom spectators.

"I say those are coffeepot deeds - every one of them!"

Again, Judge McAfee's gavel sounded on the rostrum.

"Mr. Agnew, one more outburst in my court and you will be held in contempt."

Murray Hall was magnanimous in his reaction to the invective of the opposing counsel.

He nodded, smiling, to the spectators in the courtroom and to the jurors in their box, holding up the four deeds as though the matter were settled.

"These are the deeds to the four lots in question. We have the tax receipts for every year since the land was purchased in 1845. The land belongs to Norris Burch!"

As the local lawyer resumed his seat, a smatter of applause issued from the spectators. Though Judge McAfee had a smile on his face, he held up his hand to bring silence to his courtroom.

"Now, Mr. Agnew, would you like to reexamine your witness?"

"No," the lawyer replied, succinctly. "Mr. Thornton, you may return to the counsel table." As the Savannah lawyer made his way back to the counsel table, Stanley Agnew remained standing, waiting for his associate in the case to resume his seat.

Katharine vaguely remembered a reference to coffeepot deeds, but she never really knew what they were. She leaned forward to hear the Northern lawyer, whose quick, clipped voice was in such contrast to the slow drawl of his opposing counsel. Adjusting his spectacles on the bridge of his aquiline nose, the lawyer walked over to a tin coffeepot which rested on the wood-burning, potbelly stove. Obviously having planned the procedure he was about to commence, he poured the coffee into a bowl on a nearby small table. Dramatically, he picked up the piece of paper by the bowl and held it up for the jurors to see.

"Gentlemen of the jury, note how new and fresh this paper appears. Now, I want you to observe how it can be aged." He placed the paper in the coffee in the bowl, swishing it back and forth, then holding it, dripping, over the bowl between his two hands for the jury to see. The paper looked mottled and yellow-brown, more like what a fifty-year-old deed might resemble.

Katharine noticed that the jurors and many of the spectators were uncomfortable with the theatrical presentation. Some looked away, others hung their heads, and a few smirked at the display. Obviously, this was a method some of the squatters were using to make their illegally executed deeds appear to be the proper age. It was absolutely incredible!

"Again, I say to you," Stanley Agnew continued, holding up the yellowed deeds, "having seen deeds aged in this spurious manner many times, I can say with some authority that these are worthless coffeepot deeds!" Shaking his head in disgust, the Northern lawyer threw the deeds on the opposing counsel's table and sat down beside William Thornton.

Judge McAfee cleared his throat and briefly charged the jury. The twelve men left the courtroom for their closeted deliberations. Within only a few minutes, to Katharine's utter amazement, the jury filed back to their seats in the jury box.

She looked at her locket watch in disbelief. Had they discussed the case at all? She doubted they had been sequestered even ten minutes!

The judge requested a copy of the verdict which the foreman of the jury gave to the bailiff, who in turn delivered it to the judge. Opening it, the judge asked the jury foreman to render the verdict.

"We, the jury, find Norris Burch innocent of any wrongdoing in regard to the four land lots in question. We believe the land rightfully belongs to Norris Burch."

The courtroom erupted in whistles and cheers and stomping feet. The defendant, Norris Burch, and his lawyer, Murray Hall, were immediately surrounded by well-wishers and sympathizers. Stanley Agnew and William Thornton hurriedly gathered their papers and made their way through the hostile crowd to the judge's bench, and Katharine heard them tell the judge that the case would be appealed.

Katharine whispered to Julia that she needed to leave in order to be back home before dark. She also didn't want to risk being seen by Micah MacRae, though she mentioned nothing of this to Julia. As they were about to leave the courtroom, she saw the defendant, Norris Burch, smiling broadly and shaking hands with Micah MacRae. Obviously, the squatters were having a meeting of sorts right there on the courtroom floor. The twelve jurors had joined the circle of men around Micah MacRae and Murray Hall.

As they walked down the stairway from the courtroom, holding up their long dresses, Julia could scarcely contain her laughter about the courtroom performance.

"Well, Katharine, what did you think about the circus we just saw? Can you believe that is the way our cases are being tried?" Before Katharine could answer, Julia continued, "I used to get furious when I watched our ejectment suits being tried, but knowing the case today was one of the last ones to be tried locally, I could laugh at the ignorance of the Southern courts. Most of them will be tried in federal court from now on, where we won't have to contend with these squatter juries!"

Katharine said nothing, as some of the backwoodsmen were coming down the stairway above them. They were jovially discussing the Burch case, praising Murray Hall and chuckling about the coffeepot episode.

"You reckon them deeds was aged in coffee?" one of them asked.

"If they was, they was jest like the ones that he lost," another one added.

"All he needed was his tax receipts, and he had all of 'em," a third one said.

A fourth one spoke up as though he had pondered the fine points of the case throughout the brief trial. He said, "Dadblame it, Dodge don't own none of this land! It was illegal in the first place for Indiana to own a part of Georgia, and when it didn't pay no taxes in 1844, why that stopped any claim they might of had. I ain't no lawyer, but that's as plain as hellfire to me!"

Chapter Seven

Since her unintentional but enjoyable visit with Micah MacRae's mother and children, Katharine found herself once more interested in her own piano. Almost daily now, she would sit at the lovely grand piano which she had brought from her home, in New York, and would play the music which had lain untouched since Frank's death. Without acknowledging it, her short, requested but unrehearsed, recital for Abby MacRae and the girls had brought about a revival of interest in the music she had always loved.

It had been several weeks since her trip to the MacRae home, and Katharine wondered whether her potential overseer had received her message in regard to finalizing plans for the cutting and rafting of her timber. She desperately needed to talk to him! She supposed she would need a surveyor to find her land lines, before the timber could be cruised and cut. Not having had any business experience, she would have to trust her overseer's honesty. Also, she was having doubts that the timber could be cut during this timber season. Why, spring was almost here, though the continued cold weather belied it.

Katharine stared at the sheet music open before her, as she sat at the piano. She used to love to play some of the war songs from both sides, but because of Frank's death, presumably at the hands of vengeful Southerners in the piney woods, she didn't believe she could bring herself to play Confederate songs ever again. She used to enjoy playing and singing the Southern song, *Dixie,* but the song with its snappy beat brought no pleasure to her now.

She walked over to the rosewood music cabinet and rummaged through the sheets and books of music which she had accumulated through the years. She hadn't attempted anything from Bach in some time. She found *Jesu, Joy of Man's Desiring,* one of her favorites, and opened it on the piano.

As she seated herself on the piano bench, she heard Tilda come quietly into the room and take a chair near the burning logs in the fireplace. Tilda had been pleased that Katharine was enjoying music again and, as her work allowed, she would sometimes come in to listen.

A sharp rap on the large front door, however, brought Tilda to her feet. "I'll see who it is, Miss Katharine," she said.

Katharine swung her slippered feet in their satin house shoes to the reverse side of the piano bench and awaited Tilda's return.

Tilda appeared in the door of the music room.

"It's Mr. MacRae, Miss Katharine, Mr. Micah MacRae." With this announcement, Tilda returned to the foyer and invited the visitor to take a seat in the parlor, assuring him that Mrs. Fremont would be in to see him shortly.

Katharine thought she would surely faint. Why was he here at her home? Then, she remembered that she needed to talk to him. Obviously, his mother had given him her message.

Katharine smoothed her hair which was braided into a chignon at the nape of her neck. She patted the full, lotus-blue dress with its small bustle and wondered how she would appear to the man waiting for her in the parlor. Chastening herself for such thoughts, she quickly brought to mind the vow that she would think of him only in a business way and nothing more.

Resolutely, she walked to the parlor, fuming with herself for becoming breathless in her anticipation of seeing him again.

If Katharine had known the effect she had on Micah MacRae when she stood in the doorway of the parlor, she would have, nonetheless, trembled with pleasure. However, she was not to know, because he steeled himself when he saw her and allowed nothing in his countenance to betray what he thought about the woman standing before him. He kept these thoughts hidden beneath the knowledge that she was the enemy, part and parcel of the Northern machine that was ravaging the piney woods. He intended to do her work and when he had sold her timber, to pocket the money she had promised him, and then to turn his back to her forever.

"Well, hello, Mr. MacRae." Katharine walked into the room and observed how the man's presence filled the large, formal parlor.

"Evenin', Ma'm. I got your message, and I came as soon as I could." His brown eyes were looking at her, and Katharine kept reminding herself that he was only the overseer and a Southern one, at that!

"Yes, I'm wanting to get my timber cut as soon as possible but it's already February, and I'm wondering whether it's too late in the season now."

"Yes, Ma'm. It'll have to wait until next fall, Miz Fremont. I'm still cuttin' on my land. I'd be glad to wait on mine but most of the logs are cut and on the ground. We're a-waitin' on a freshet to get 'em to the river." Katharine remembered her husband explaining that a freshet was a lot of rain at one time, which would float the cut logs in the swampy areas and make it possible to move them to the open river.

"Then," he continued, "it's goin' to be time to plant in another few weeks. Maybe by next fall, we'll get the freshets we need to float your timber out of the swamp. However, I got some help with my crops this year, and I'm a-goin' ahead and cuttin' your trees all along, as I can, and leavin' 'em at the boom at Willcox Lake. It'll take awhile for me and my logchoppers to cut your timber."

Strangely, Katharine was not as disappointed as she had feared she would be, though this meant that going home to New York would be delayed for probably eight or nine months. The thought inexplicably crossed her mind that she and Tilda would plant their vegetable garden here, after all. A small smile played on her lips and the new overseer looked away, not wanting to be drawn into whatever was bringing the smile to her lovely face. No, she was a distrusted Northerner, and he was only the overseer of her timber cutting. Also, he had qualms about broaching another subject which his mother had requested of him, but before he could mention it, Katharine politely remarked that she had enjoyed meeting his mother and children.

"Yes, well, that's somethin' else I had on my mind, to speak to you about. My wife, well, she always wanted the girls to have music lessons. My mother wanted me to ask you if you..." He paused, then haltingly resumed after noticing the surprise in

Katharine's eyes, "if you'd consider teachin' 'em how to play the piano."

Katharine was shocked but touched by this request which had obviously been difficult for the raftsman to deliver. She had never taught anyone music - not that she couldn't, she hastened silently to tell herself.

"I..I've never taught music, Mr. MacRae, but I'm willing to teach them what I know. Will...won't you sit down?" Where had her manners flown? She had forgotten to offer him a chair.

"Oh, no, Ma'm, I'd best be a-goin'. Won't be too long, it'll be dark."

"When do you want me to begin the girls' lessons?"

"They're a-wantin' to start whenever you can come, Miz Fremont."

"What about my coming once a week, maybe on Tuesday afternoons?"

"That'll be fine, Ma'm, but I'm sure you know how dangerous it is now, for a woman to ride alone. Don't you have a man that drives you?"

"Oh, yes, I can get Big Hill to drive my carriage, but actually, I'm not afraid to make the trip alone, Mr. MacRae. You see, my husband gave me a gun before he died and I never leave home now without it."

"Your husband was a wise and carin' man, Ma'm," he said softly. Fingering his deerskin hat, Micah MacRae moved toward the front door. He was again dressed in the plain clothes of the backwoodsman, and Katharine wondered whether he ever dressed like the local townspeople. He was at the door and as he stepped onto the large porch, he turned back to speak to Katharine, standing in the doorway.

"Ma'm, just know I'll see to raftin' your timber, 'long about next September or October, after we get all the crops in." He placed his hat on his head, then held out his large, strong hand, rough from the rafting of timber and the plowing of the earth, and grasped Katharine's small, smooth one.

"And we thank you for bein' the girls' music teacher. Let me know what's owed for the lessons."

Katharine feared he could feel her shaking. Why, in God's name, did he have such an effect on her? Had she detected a trembling in his handshake? She thought so, but realized that she was reading too much into a simple gesture of kindness. For a brief moment, as their eyes met, they were neither Northerner nor Southerner, only a man and a woman. Again, she sensed his strength, and she longed to hold on to it, just as he turned and bounded down the steps.

Chapter Eight

The morning sun streamed through the heavy lace curtains in Katharine's bedroom, striking her closed eyes and informing her that the day had already begun. Sleepily opening her eyes and stretching her full length in the large, warm feather bed, she realized it was Sunday morning. Sunday morning! She felt guilty. Though it had been many months since she had attended church services, the guilt had only lately surfaced, and today it was especially heavy on her soul.

She made up her mind, lying in the large, tall-postered bed, that she would go to church this morning. Words of her father came to mind, as she lay there thinking about her lapse in church attendance. Her father had always said that people didn't feel the need for the Lord until they reached a crisis in their lives. He further had said that the Lord wanted his people in church during the good times, too, not just when problems arose. She wondered what her parents would think if they knew how lax she had been about going to church.

Her grandfather Durham had been a Presbyterian minister and her parents both belonged to the Presbyterian Church, where they lived in New York. Katharine joined the church as a young girl and she remembered going regularly, until she and Frank made the move to Georgia. They attended only spasmodically then, and Katharine couldn't remember going since Frank's death. Though they had a church funeral service at Normandale, his body had been sent back to New York for burial.

Katharine tucked her left arm under her head and pulled the embroidered, feather-ticked comforter under her chin. Her thoughts wandered on about her negligence in not going to church. Part of her apathy stemmed from the fact that the Presbyterians did not yet have a church building to call their own, in Normandale nor in Eastman.

How she missed the lovely Presbyterian Church which she had attended in New York, with its richly hued, stained glass windows and its stately steeple which pierced the sky. She longed for a church here in the piney woods which at least had pews and an altar and a semblance of the church she had known near her home in New York.

She decided to visit the Methodist Church in Eastman. Maybe she would find there the rudiments of the church, as she had once known it. At least, the Methodist Church was housed in a nice building. As was her nature, once she had made a decision, she was ready to move forward with it. She would have to hurry.

Katharine breezed through preparations for the morning journey, pleased that she was doing something to assuage the guilt she had been feeling, for some time, on Sunday mornings. She prepared her small breakfast of fruit and toast and steeped her own tea, since Tilda was not yet stirring. Tilda, in fact, had kept to her bed for several days with a cold which she fell victim to each spring. She vowed it was the pine trees that caused her misery which she referred to as her catarrh, as she never suffered from such in New York, though the weather was much harsher there.

Though Katharine never disputed Tilda's assessment of her spring illnesses, she did know that many Northerners came to the piney woods area of Georgia with various health problems which they claimed the resinous air would heal. In fact, the Uplands Hotel in Eastman was filled with people from the North, seeking to be cured in the salubrious air of the piney woods.

She dressed hurriedly, holding her breath and lacing her corset herself and pulling the voluminous rose silk dress over her head and down over her full petticoats. She brushed her hair back on the sides, securing it with pearl-studded combs. Finding the matching silk hat, she placed it on her head and tied the wide ribbons in a bow next to her cheek.

Hoping to find Big Hill to make ready her carriage, Katharine hastened down the back steps and on down the brick path to the stables. She spied Big Hill, up and about, and was glad to see that he had stayed overnight. He had simple quarters in the stable and often would spend the night.

"Good morning, Hill."

"Good mo'nin', Miz Kat'rin. You sho is up and 'bout early dis mo'nin."

"I'm going to church, Hill. Please get the phaeton ready for me. Just hitch one of the geldings to it."

"Yes, Ma'm, Miz Kat'rin'."

Katharine stood by and watched Hill retrieve the gray from the stall, harness and hitch the horse to the carriage. She wondered whether the church she had seen in the colored settlement would be having services this day. As if reading her thoughts, Hill answered her silent question.

"Aer church doan meet 'til after dinner. Ah be goin' back to de settle'mint in time to go."

Big Hill led the horse and carriage to Katharine, then helped her up to the driver's seat. Katharine looked appreciatively down at the aging Negro who served her in so many ways.

"I just want you to know, Hill, that I am grateful for all that you do for me. Tilda and I want to plant a garden soon, and we're hoping we can count on you to help us."

"Oh, yes, Ma'm! Yes, Ma'm! Ah sho' he'p!" His voice which had risen in anticipation of the forthcoming garden became serious, when he cautioned her.

"Miz Kat'rin, Ah say it befo' and Ah say it agin - it sho be dange'rus fer a lady lak you to be drivin' and ridin' 'round by yo'seff."

"Hill, I'll be careful. I promise. Besides, I have my protection. Remember?" She held up the purse, opened it, and pulled out the gun which caught the bright glint of the morning sun.

Hill grinned. "Good 'nuf, Miz Kat'rin. But jes' be careful. Ah knows that's whut Mr. Frank would say."

"I will; I promise." Katharine clucked to the horse, lightly flicking the reins over his back. The horse started forward swiftly, pulling the drop-front carriage down the path leading from the house and through the large, wrought-iron gate at the end of the driveway.

Though it was a sunny day in late winter, it was cold. Katharine took the main road to Eastman, carefully guiding the carriage wheels into the established ruts of the dirt path. Deer and rabbits frequently crossed the road ahead of her. Once, a bobcat leapt across the pathway, chasing an elusive squirrel. Several cows ambled out of the thick woods, all bearing different brands seared into their hides. They eluded the oncoming carriage by entering the pine forest on the opposite side of the road, their cloven hooves trampling the thick carpet of wiregrass, now reddish-hued in the throes of continuing cold weather.

Katharine remembered a Northern journalist's description of the Southern wiregrass as being "famished grass, scattered thinly over the surface in tufts and patches like the hair on a mangy cur." Growing in over foot-high clumps which drooped from central shafts, the round-bladed, grayish-ivory perennial felt silky to the touch only in the spring but furnished food to the farmers' cattle and sheep throughout the year.

The trip was long, and Katharine was glad when the Methodist Church finally came into view. She realized she was late, as no one stood around outside, talking. Buggies, carriages and buckboards of every description, harnessed to horses, mules, and oxen, dotted the church yard.

As Katharine's carriage approached the church, she saw a mule and rider quickly enter the church grounds. The man dismounted and secured the mule. As he walked through the front door of the church, Katharine realized it was Micah MacRae.

She was unsettled. She didn't realize that the backwoodsman attended this church. She suddenly felt awkward and considered leaving. She reined in the horse, debating what to do. While sitting there, contemplating what to do, she overheard people talking. They were local townspeople, Southerners. She could tell by their voices, and they appeared to be two couples. They could not see her, because of the trees and the many buggies and carriages and other conveyances; and she could not see them, but she could hear them.

"I hear Micah MacRae's a-comin' today. He's found out his land lots are bein' claimed by the Dodges." This was one of the men talking, and Katharine strained to hear more. Another man spoke.

"We're meetin' again. Micah's slippin' ever'body word today after church, the time and place of our meetin'."

One of the wives began talking and Katharine could hear her clearly, as they were walking near her, on their way to the church door.

"I told Eulalie she ought to come this mornin'. What Micah needs is a good woman. Jenny's been gone now over two years and his little ones need a ma, too."

The second wife added her thoughts.

"I hear tell that the men that raft the logs to Darien...all of 'em end up at 'May Belle's.'"

One of the men, most likely her husband, reproved his wife.

"Now, Sugar, that don't mean that Micah's a-goin' there. You don't know that for a sure thing."

"No, but he's a man, ain't he? You all make out you can't do without, and he certainly ain't a-courtin' any of our girls here in the piney woods. Don't seem like he's interested in gettin' married again."

More talking ensued as the foursome moved on toward the church and out of Katharine's hearing. She could see them as they entered the church door.

Holding on to the carriage, Katharine lowered herself to the ground, lifting her silk dress to avoid tearing it. After securing the horse, she made her way to the church door.

She had always heard that the Northern timber company people sat on the right side of the church, while the local people sat on the left side. Opening the door, she found this to be true, and she hastened to a pew on the right side, which had an empty seat at the center aisle. She nodded and smiled at several people she knew, and they responded similarly, some reaching out to take her hand.

Music from the piano brought the congregation to their feet, and they began singing the hymn, *Amazing Grace*. Katharine's mind raced backward, remembering that she had played the song on the old piano at Micah's home. Then, she thought about the conversation she had just heard outside the church. Once again, she had heard a place called "May Belle's" mentioned. Where did she first hear it? She couldn't remember, at first, then clearly it came to her that she had heard of that place at the Winslows' party. She surmised it must be a bad house, a place where men went when they wanted to be with a woman. Katharine blushed, realizing that she was singing a hymn and thinking carnal thoughts at the same time.

She searched for Micah MacRae and saw him sitting near the front of the church, on the left with the other local people. She noticed an attractive young woman on the pew behind him, who leaned over and whispered into his ear. Katharine felt something akin to jealousy and she wondered who the woman was. She observed that the raftsman wore brown jeans breeches with a homespun shirt and jacket. Looking at the broad shoulders and his dark, neatly combed hair, she again felt the raw power that he possessed and she felt guilty about her thoughts.

Katharine didn't realize that the song had ended, but when she noticed everyone seating themselves, she hastened to do so, also. As the preacher began various church announcements, her thoughts again returned to the four people she had overheard outside the church. She was trying to assimilate everything that was said. Something was said about a meeting. Could this be another squatters' meeting, such as the ones which the mill manager, Paul Owens, had referred to? But he had said the squatters weren't meeting anymore. This must be a new development in the land war, if they were meeting again.

Attempting to concentrate on the church service, Katharine sensed the guilt that had brought her to church again, after such a long absence. Shouldn't she be worshiping the Lord, rather than mulling over the meaning of an imminent squatters' meeting? Still, bits of the conversation kept intruding on her thoughts, and she remembered what they had said about Micah MacRae's land lots being claimed by Norman W. Dodge. Didn't she herself see those lots on the large map at Winslow Hall?

They were rising for another hymn, and Katharine had to glance at the book of the person on the pew ahead of her, in order to know which page to turn to in the hymnal. As she sang, she forced herself to think of the words of the hymn and to try to find some peace to replace the turmoil of her thoughts.

Seating herself again, following the hymn, she listened intently as the preacher announced the text from the Bible. It was from the Old Testament book of *Micah*, but she missed the chapter and verses. Strange that she had never considered that the backwoodsman might have been named for the Biblical prophet, but this possibility tugged at her consciousness, as the preacher read from the text.

The sermon expounded on the deeds of the northern kingdom of Israel which was attempting to vanquish the southern kingdom, and the message rang a bell in Katharine's thoughts. Could the preacher be drawing a parallel with the tense situation in the piney woods? Was the congregation supposed to infer the similarity? Katharine resolved to read the short book of *Micah* before going to bed that night.

The stark contrast of the two sides of the church, separated by the center aisle, preyed on her mind. She couldn't help but note the difference, and she could not help but think how she had been blind for many years about the dissimilarities of the groups of people who were involved in the ongoing land war.

On the right side of the church, men were dressed fashionably in cutaway coats of serge and tweed, with high lapels and light trousers, and Prince Albert coats with long satin-lined lapels and light trousers, and loose sack coats with fuller trousers. Some wore single or double vests. Their shirts were pleated and slightly starched. Their overgarments included coats extending to the knee or shorter coats with velvet collars. With high, standing collars, they wore bow, four-in-hand and ascot ties, and they wore pointed-toe shoes which laced or buttoned.

The timber company wives wore dresses of silk, velvet, and faille. Some had furs of mink, sable, ermine, or Persian lamb draped around their shoulders. They were fashionable in their hats of flowers and ostrich plumes, some of which had sheer veils across their faces, covering their chins, or they wore bonnets matching their dresses, as Katharine did. Some carried lorgnettes, which they gracefully held before their eyes. Their chatelaine purses, muffs and gloves and elaborate long hat pins, along with high, laced, or buttoned shoes, completed their ensembles.

Katharine's eyes shifted to the left side of the church and she perceived that two groups comprised this section: the local townspeople and the backwoods people. The ones who lived in town wore similar, but simpler, clothes than the timber company people wore. The clothing of the men and the women was mainly of dark wool. The women's bonnets and hats did not have the flowers and feathers of those across the aisle.

However, the women of the backwoods provided the greatest contrast of all. Their dresses were of cotton or homespun and were ill-fitting. Their long sunbonnets were stiffened with tupelo strips. Some wore homemade hats of wattled shucks or palmetto with ribbons on them. The backwoodsmen were, for the most part, dressed like Micah MacRae - in brown jeans breeches, homespun shirts and jackets and rawhide shoes.

The preacher was asking everyone to stand for the last hymn. Katharine was ashamed that she had missed so much of his sermon, because of all that she was trying to absorb in regard to the obviously accelerating land war. She decided to leave before the song was over, so that she could get back to her carriage and perhaps find out more about the impending squatters' meeting, when the people she had overheard earlier would return to their carriages.

She slipped out the church door, braving the curious stares of those near her. Hurriedly, she returned to her carriage and freed the horse from his hitching constraint. She stepped up to the seat of the carriage, grateful that its drop-front allowed easy accessibility.

The church service was over and people were leaving from the front door. Katharine saw the local townspeople whose conversation she had overheard, making their way toward their buggies. They were talking animatedly among themselves, but she couldn't understand what they were saying. The men helped their wives into their respective buggies and then appeared to be waiting for someone.

As Katharine suspected, they were waiting for Micah MacRae. She saw him leave the church and walk over to a group of people who formed a circle around him. After a few minutes, he extricated himself from this group and walked toward the two men who were waiting near Katharine's carriage.

Katharine shrank back into her carriage, turning slightly, so as not to be noticed. She heard him speak to the two men in an audible whisper, and she caught some of the words.

"...the log boom at Gum Swamp...just as the light fades...around 7:30."

The men spoke quickly, at the same time, and their words were jumbled to Katharine's ears. Then, in the silence that followed, one spoke in a hushed but clear voice which she could hear.

"I hear he's got your land lots tagged on that big map of his. They're already a-cuttin' on our land. What're we gonna do, Micah?"

Micah spoke quietly, but hurriedly. "We can't win in court no more. They're tryin' the land cases in federal court now. We got plans - just gotta put 'em into action. Remember...tomorrow night at the log boom at Gum Swamp." He abruptly turned to leave, then called back in a low, urgent voice: "Pass it on!"

Katharine waited until the backwoodsman was well on his way back to another huddled group of local people, before clucking quietly to the horse. She kept her head turned in an attempt to avoid recognition on the part of the people who were leaving the church grounds.

She didn't notice much on the drive back to her Sighing Pines estate. Even the sparse raindrops which splashed on the carriage top did not raise her concern, though she did unroll the rainproof apron from the dashboard of the carriage and pull it over her dress.

Her thoughts hummed with all that she had witnessed and heard, and they were filled not with the words of the preacher, which she could not remember, but with the language of the squatters, which rang in her ears: "...boom at Gum Swamp...Micah's land lots...federal court...plans...pass it on." Katharine felt the excitement of one who newly discovers something. She realized how naive she had been during the years she had lived in the Georgia piney woods. She had turned a deaf ear to the squatters' cries, but now she was suddenly listening and even wanting to know more. Not wanting to admit it, she knew it was because of Micah MacRae.

The black wrought-iron gate beckoned to her as she rounded the last bend of the dirt path to her house. Again, the molded letters of "Sighing Pines" seemed to be portentous. The scattered raindrops had ceased, but now an ill wind was blowing.

Chapter Nine

The old clock on the mantel in her bedroom had just struck the early morning hour of 3:00 o'clock when Katharine was first aware of hoofbeats outside the house. She lay there, trying to awaken from what she first believed was a dream. The hooves were louder now and splotches of light danced on the shades which were pulled behind the lace curtains of her bedroom.

As she sat up in bed, reaching for her dressing gown, Tilda appeared at the door, her trembling hand cupping a small candle. Her frightened face, with the unrestrained gray hair framing it, brought cold fear into the room.

Katharine, fully awake now, quickly ordered Tilda to put out the candle. Pulling on her dressing gown, she crept swiftly to the window and barely lifted the side of the shade. Her heart jumped to her throat at the scene of horror outside. Horses, draped with white sheets, carried figures in white robes, with tall white hoods over their heads and slits for their eyes, as they galloped by the window. The riders carried lighted torches which shot yellow, spiraling flames into the moonless night.

Her whole body shaking with cold and fright, Katharine turned in the dark and bumped into Tilda who uttered a startled sob. Katharine quickly embraced the elderly housekeeper and tried to quiet the terror and mounting panic which were seizing both of them. She knew the riders must be the Ku Klux Klan, for she had heard that the Klan was functioning again in the area.

She wondered about Big Hill and prayed that he had not spent the night at the stables. Had they come for him? Katharine had heard of Negroes being tarred and feathered and hanged by the K.K.K. They were an outlaw group who feared nothing.

Katharine felt Tilda trembling, and she realized they were still holding on to each other in the still, dark room. Katharine eased the older woman over to the chaise lounge. She could feel her shaking sobs.

"Tillie, it's the Ku Klux Klan. Just sit here and try to be as quiet as you can. I'm going to get my gun."

"But, Miss Katharine, what are they doing here?"

"Shh...Sh...I don't know."

Katharine stole back to the window and looked through the small aperture she had created. She guessed that probably twenty-five horses and riders were in view, their torches lifted into the air. She could hear only fragments of what they were saying. She pressed her ear to the shade, trying not to cause it to move and to give away her whereabouts in the house. Not hearing anything, she again focused her eyes through the small crack between the window sash and the shade, and it was then that a low-hanging branch of a tree in the back yard ripped the hood from one of the riders, who appeared to be the leader.

Katharine's heart skipped a beat. It was the man she had seen at the mill several months before - the one with the long scar on his face! In the flickering light of the torches, the scar on his face seemed more snake-like, more sinister. He was saying something, and Katharine pressed closer to hear his words.

"Dammit...get that thing!"

"Can't...wind's got it!"

The wind whipped the robes of the riders into an eerie white display. It carried the torn hood to higher branches in the tree. The scarred man looked equally as fearsome without the hood, and the orders that he barked in a harsh nasal voice brought fresh terror to her heart.

"Burn the stables. Yeah, that Uncle Tom's prob'ly there, lessen he's up here in the big house." Coarse laughter followed this remark. Panic-stricken, Katharine folded her hands and prayed for Hill's safety and the safety of the animals in the stables.

Hearing Tilda's muffled crying, Katharine stole quietly to her. She wondered whether Tilda had heard the orders in regard to the stables and prayed she had not.

"Tillie, I'm going to get the pistol. Just wait here. I'll be back in a few minutes. Don't be afraid. Everything's going to be all right."

Tilda reached out in the dark, fumbling for Katharine's arm.

"Please, Miss Katharine, please be careful. Oh, I'm so afraid."

"I am, too, Tillie, but let's try not to be. I don't want them to know that we're afraid. Stay here. I'll be back in a few minutes."

Katharine groped her way out of the room, longing for a lamp or candle to light her steps but knowing she couldn't risk such. She silently scolded herself for not keeping the gun handy. Why hadn't she kept it near her in her room at night?

She could see the lurid patches of light cast on the shades of windows in other rooms of the house. Some of the rooms she crossed did not have the shades pulled, and her heart beat wildly in fear that she would be observed by the riders outside. In these rooms, she prostrated herself and crawled their carpeted length, feeling the cold, hard wood near the doors, where no floor covering reached.

She remembered leaving her purse on the marble-top table in the foyer, so she moved in that direction. The narrow hallway was void of carpet and Katharine felt its chilling hardness, as she pulled herself over it. The burning torches outside emitted enough light for her to see the form of the table, with her purse where she had left it. She grabbed it, feeling the unyielding steel of the revolver which she soon had in her hands.

Caution urged her to refrain from using the weapon, unless she had to. Her acute thoughts warned her not to leave the house, but to unload the pistol at anyone who dared to enter it. She quickly retraced her crawling passage back to the bedroom with the revolver in her shaky grip, back to Tilda who had recovered enough to peer out the window at the frightening apparitions.

"Oh, Miss Katharine, they're at the stables. Oh, Lord help us, they're setting fire to the stables!"

Katharine opened her mouth to scream, but no sound came forth. She couldn't stay here while Big Hill and the geldings were being threatened, if indeed Big Hill were at the stables. She felt loathing and anger rise in her breast and she knew what she had to do.

"Tilda, wait here for me. I'm going to the stables."

"Oh, Lord, no, Miss Katharine, they'll kill you, or worse! Oh, Lord, help us!"

Katharine crept to the back of the house and fully intended to fling open the rear door, when she realized that the hooded marauders had left the stables and were galloping down the front driveway of the house. She forced herself to refrain from running out of the house until the last masked rider had left the premises. She then lit a lantern and hurried to the stables.

Flames were licking at the outside stable walls when she arrived, and she was shocked but pleased to see Big Hill attempting to put them out. They found old blankets inside the stable and beat out the flames before they reached the stalls of the horses and Hill's living quarters. Hill hurried to the well and brought buckets of water to douse any remaining embers.

Tired, her arms aching, Katharine finally allowed tears to fill her eyes and to roll down her cheeks. She dabbed at them with the sooty sleeve of her dressing gown, not wanting Hill to see her in such a weak moment.

"Thank God you are all right, Hill, and the horses, too. I didn't know whether you had stayed overnight or not."

"Yas'm. Ah had some wuk to do on yo' cah'age, Miz Kat'rin. Ah sho glad Ah wuz heah to he'p. Ah jes wonder did dey go ober to de colored settle'mint."

The mention of the colored settlement rang a distant bell in her mind. Would she be the target of the K.K.K., rather than Big Hill, since she had recruited raftsmen from the colored settlement, rather than the white settlement? The jagged pieces of the puzzle began to fit, and Katharine longed for the morning to come, when she would bring the hooded varmints to justice.

***

The early morning after the Klan's ugly raid on her property, Katharine walked around the yards, bitterly regarding the mess that the legion of horses and masked riders had left behind. Droppings, still moist from the animals, assailed her senses as she lifted her skirts and proceeded toward the stables. The galloping hooves of the horses had left broken brick in her driveway and the several walkways around her home. The once-packed dirt in her yards was pockmarked with impressions of equine hooves.

Nearing the stables which were ringed with the soot of the fire, stamped and beaten out in the dark, early morning hours, Katharine thanked God that no physical harm had come to them or to the animals. She was also thankful to have been spared the burning cross which usually was left as a terrifying memento by the Klan.

Big Hill was feeding and watering the horses when Katharine entered the stable door. Harry and General Lee, the two geldings, watched her in anticipation as she walked toward them. She had remembered to bring apples with her, which they loved, and they greeted her with enthusiastic whinnies and gentle blowing, shaking their heads to and fro above the stall doors.

Katharine opened her hands with the apples displayed and held them under the horses' mouths. Their arched, nimble lips grasped them and their large eyes gave her a look of contented appreciation. She wondered what fear these fine animals had experienced only a short while before, and the thought brought hot tears to her eyes.

"Ha'ey and Gen'l Lee, dey sho laks dem apples you brings 'em, Miz Kat'rin."

"I have one for you, too, Hill."

A wide grin, showing missing teeth, spread across the Negro's face as he took the proffered apple.

"You knows Ah laks 'em, too, Miz Kat'rin."

Katharine laughed, and the thought of herself laughing, after all that had happened only a short time earlier, made her wonder at her sanity. She had heard of people laughing when under unusual strain, and she wondered if this were happening to her. Whatever, she shrugged, it felt good to be able to laugh and to forget, momentarily, anyway, the paralyzing terror she had experienced in the hours before dawn.

As she watched Hill and the grays devour the apples with relish, a measure of calm returned to her. She wondered what Hill had done during the raid.

"Hill, were you asleep when the Klan came? Where were you, and how did you keep from being seen?"

"Lawd, Miz Kat'rin, Ah heerd 'em and Ah wuz sleepin', and w'en Ah look mout and seed all ob dem, Ah say 'dat's de Klan,' and Ah knowed Ah had to mek tracks out ob de stables. Ah jump out de winduh an Ah lay low in de woods. It wuz cold, and Ah feared dey wuz comin' aftuh me, so Ah stay in de woods till dey wuz gone."

"I thought, too, that they had come for you, Hill, but now I'm thinking they were letting me know they were mad, because I went to the colored settlement to find rafthands, rather than the white settlement. Oh, me, things are so complicated here. I'd as soon have both colored and white to help me, but I had heard that the white people wouldn't help me, because I'm a Northerner. Anyway, I know who the ringleader is. I don't know his name but I'll find out, and I plan to press charges against all of them."

"Ah hopes dey all be put in de jail fer whut dey done to yo' propuhty, Miz Kat'rin. Ah'm jes wonderin' now ef dey made a trip to de settle'mint."

Katharine had wondered the same thing. "You go on home, Hill. I know you're worried about what they may have done at the settlement. Tilda and I'll be all right. We'll worry about getting everything cleaned up and repaired later."

"Ah be back soon, Miz Kat'rin'. Ah jes' wants to check on ma wife and mek sure she okay. Ah knows you wants to go to see the sheriff 'bout what happened, Miz Kat'rin. Won't take long to hitch Gen'l Lee to yo' cah'age." The old Negro led the horse out of the stable and expertly harnessed the animal, then fastened the traces of the harness to the carriage singletree.

Katharine rubbed the velvet nose of her favorite horse, laughing when this evoked a loud whicker.

"You're always ready to go, aren't you, big fellow? I'm as eager as you are to bring the nightriders to justice!"

Hill kept a mule in a section of the stables for his trips back and forth from his house in the settlement to the Fremonts' place. He now went to get the animal for the ride back to the Negro settlement. "Hattie," as he called the mule, came clopping out of the stall behind him.

He didn't use a saddle - never had, he said, and Katharine wondered how he could stay astride the sleek, fat animal. Katharine had kept hidden from the geldings' eyes one last apple which she fetched from the pocket of her apron. Hattie spied the fruit and plodded over for her customary treat. Since she was minus several teeth, like her master, Katharine thought it remarkable that both still could eat the hard fruit.

As Hattie clip-clopped down the driveway of broken brick, with Big Hill astride, Katharine thought of the man she intended to bring to justice about her ordeal. She remembered the hood that had been torn from his head and looked for it in the trees behind her house, but it was nowhere to be found.

Looking at the debris which the Klan had left in its wake, she was glad that the vegetable garden had not yet been planted, or it surely would have been trampled, also. The idea of a garden growing, putting out new buds and sprouts, brought hope, and she realized that it was time for the three of them to get some seeds and plant them.

However, first things first - she must see the sheriff right away! She quickly climbed to the carriage seat and clucked to the horse to begin the trip to Eastman.

Chapter Ten

The bight at Gum Swamp on the bank of the Little Ocmulgee River, the meeting place of the squatters, was aglow with a huge bonfire, set as much for its light as for its warmth. Conveyances of every description were interspersed among the tall timber which grew more sparsely near the water's edge. The cast-off, thick, brown pine needles provided a carpet for the oxcarts, buckboards, and wagons, pulled by oxen, mules, and horses. Mostly, however, the men rode horseback or muleback to the meeting, then hitched their animals to the lower branches of the lofty pine trees. Many who lived within a few miles walked.

Because the recessed area of the stream had been cleared to accommodate the making of log rafts during the daytime, it also afforded an open area for the nighttime meetings of the beleaguered squatters. Logs which were scattered on the riverbank, waiting to be transported on the high water of an anticipated freshet to the larger Ocmulgee River, were used as seats by those present.

Though the men greeted one another heartily, there was an air of angry expectancy about all who were arriving. Some warmed themselves at the fire, while others found more wood and added it, making the flames reach higher. With the narrow stream only a few feet away, the grunts and roars of alligators added an eeriness to the business at hand.

Because of the lingering winter cold, the usual insects and other flying pestilences of Gum Swamp did not harass the men, and what few did brave the cold were driven away by the intensity of the leaping flames. Swamp creatures such as deer, raccoons, panthers, and bears shied away from their usual habitat because of the sounds and the unmistakable smell of men. Many watched from the safety of the dark, impenetrable forest, knowing that the men would be gone before daylight and the riverbank would be theirs once more, that is, until the log cutters arrived soon after dawn to run them off again.

Some of the men who had ridden far distances led their animals to the water's edge and stood by as they imbibed steady draughts of the moving water. Others used old cloths and blankets to rub down the profuse sweat from their animals, accumulated during many miles of travel. Men were there from Telfair County and the surrounding counties of Dodge, Laurens, Montgomery and Pulaski, for the plunderage of the Dodge timber empire stretched like long, fat fingers into hundreds of miles of Georgia piney woods.

The bight on the Little Ocmulgee River was an area filled with water, which was recessed from the riverbank, so that logs could be held until such time they would be lashed together to form a raft. The logs had been square-cut at the site by some of the portable or pepperbox sawmills. Squared or scab timbers brought a better price at Darien. They also provided a flat area for the raftsmen to eat and sleep on their way down the rivers to Darien. According to the weather and to the problems encountered, the trip might take several days or, conceivably, a week or longer.

The men at the meeting alternately gathered around the fire for warmth, then returned to their log seats. The logs were so large in girth that their feet dangled over them, and the men engaged in guessing bouts as to the number of board feet in the timber. Some of the men began to question the whereabouts of their leader, Micah MacRae, and others took up the inquiry, peering down the dark path which wound through the swamp.

A splotch of light, bobbing up and down with the movements of the traveler, shone through the trees which stood between them. Several men who observed the light, waxing stronger, informed the crowd that their leader should arrive within a few minutes. The burning lightwood knot illuminated Micah MacRae until he reached the periphery of the bonfire's light, at which time he doused the flame in the dirt and brought the smoking pine knot into the enclave of the meeting.

Men crowded around Micah, grasping his hand and thumping him on the back. Others rolled a large pine stump, flattened by a broadax, to the front of the group and motioned for him to use it as a platform from which to address the assembly. As Micah moved toward the stump, several men came forward and told him that someone was going to introduce him, as people from some of the other counties would like to know more about him.

One of Micah's neighbors, Joe Little, a man in his late sixties, climbed on the stump and brandished a hammer and a metal bucket. He was wearing the gray coat of the Confederacy which he had served for two long years. Though his right leg had been amputated just below the knee, a testament of his sacrifice during the war, his wooden stump of a leg posed him no problems. Repeatedly, he beat the hammer on the bucket, until quietness settled over the group. Once he was certain he had everyone's attention, he put away the noisemakers and addressed the men.

"Evenin...my name's Joe Little. I'm a neighbor to Micah MacRae. I know all of you ain't been to the meetin's we had before, so you might want to know more about our leader. It's my job to innerduce 'im to you. He's worked up a name for himself on the rivers. He's been a-driftin' logs now for maybe fifteen years, and lak I said, he's made a name for himself. He can look at a tree and can tell you just how many board feet's in that tree. He's a-rafted many a log to Darien, and I reckon he's tougher'n a knot of lighterd. Many's the time, after raftin' 'is logs to Darien, he'd walk back home, a-killin' squirrels and rabbits to eat on the way back home. Ain't nobody like 'im. He's our leader. He's the one figured out how to mess up the tram roads of the timber company with spikes and poles and such and how to stop the big sawlog at the lumber mill, so just maybe that'd stop old man Dodge from takin' some more of our land." Joe Little surveyed the intense, attentive crowd of farmers and raftsmen, then continued.

"Well, Micah MacRae backed off from all this when Mr. Forsyth and Mr. Fremont was killed - and all of us here knows none of us ain't had nothin' to do with that! But now, we're a-findin' out that ol' man 'Dodge-a-mighty' is addin' more lots to that map of his, includin' some of yours, and just give 'im enough time and it'll be all of yours, and Micah MacRae's, too." Joe Little paused for a moment, then launched into some family history in regard to the neighboring families.

"Micah's father, Royston, was my best friend. We grew up together in these piney woods, swam in the same creeks, helped each other with log-rollin', cattle-brandin', sheep-shearin' - whatever's been needed - our families have always stuck together. In 1861, Royston and myself trained with some of you here tonight, with our militia at Concord Church, then marched away to the war. We stayed together, Royston and myself, two boys from Telfair County, Georgia, fightin' with Lee from the Seven Days Battles to Bull Run to Sharpsburg to Fredericksburg. At Fredericksburg, Virginia, I lost my leg."

The crusty Joe Little became silent, looking slowly around the group of Southern men, some of whom bore their own battle scars from the terrible war. Then, the one-legged man surprised everyone with a personal revelation about his war experience.

"I ain't never a-told to anyone what I'm about to tell you tonight. I haven't wanted to talk about it, didn't even want to think about it, but I especially want Micah to know this, and I want all of you to know about Micah's pa, Royston MacRae, just about the bravest man I ever knew, maybe so you'll know a little more about his son, Micah. I'm standin' here alive tonight because of Royston MacRae." The hush of the crowd was magnified by the hissing, spitting fire and the animal sounds which permeated the swamp, as the men leaned forward to hear. A woodland owl interposed its emphatic "whoohoo-whoohooaw" into the quiet, as Joe Little continued.

"I mentioned about losin' my leg at Fredericksburg. Well, if it hadn't been for Royston MacRae, I'd of died right there on the battlefield. My leg was shot and I was on the ground and a-losin' blood fast. Royston was right beside me and bullets were a-whizzin' and a-hittin' ever'body 'round us. Royston picked me up and threw me over his shoulder...like a bag of salt," he said, attempting to smile but failing. "He run with me, a-dodgin' bullets all the way, to the stone wall where some of our men were. I was a-losin' blood and really thought I was a-gonna die any minute. We were both barefoot - no shoes." The brave Joe Little stopped speaking, as if overcome by his memories of that life-threatening time in his life. He looked down at the ground, then up at the night sky, obviously attempting to regain control of himself. Finally, his voice breaking, he finished what he had to say.

"Royston MacRae saved my life that day in Virginia. He stayed by me when they finished hackin' off the rest of my leg. Then, after a time, he and the rest of the regiment moved on with General Lee to Gettysburg. I was left behind. That was the last time I saw my friend, Royston. But, friends, let me tell you, after my wound healed over and I made it back home, I saw Royston's little four-year-old boy, Micah, and I watched Micah grow into the man he is today." Joe Little's voice choked again, but he continued speaking. "Folks, when I see Micah here, it's like seein' my old friend Royston again, because he looks just like his pa, and he's brave like his pa, too. I love Micah like my own sons!

"Friends, we just can't stand idly by and see our homes destroyed and our land taken from us - not when we've lived on these lands for as long as we have and paid taxes these many years. No, it's time to fight agin', and that's what we're here for - we got a plan, a battle plan! Let's send the Dodges and their henchmen - the whole kit and caboodle of 'em - back to New York and wherever else they come from! Micah MacRae's a-gonna tell us how to do this. I innerduce to you Mr. Micah MacRae." He turned to Micah, saying his name again as he shook his hand, then pulled him up onto the big stump, alongside him. The two men embraced briefly, then Joe Little eased himself down from the stump, with Micah's help, and took a seat on one of the logs where others sat.

The throng of men let out whoops and hollers and pitched their caps into the air. Micah stood with clenched fists raised over his head as the men leapt to their feet, some wildly waving balled fists and others shooting weapons out over the river water. This frenzy lasted several minutes, as Micah repeatedly tried to restore calm with arms outstretched toward the crowd and palms flat, as though trying to stay the noise. Only his threatening to jump down from the stump platform was sufficient to lessen the outcry which finally dwindled to only a few soundings of the raftsman's name.

"Thank you. I appreciate your confidence in me." Micah turned to his neighbor and friend, Joe Little. "Joe, I never knew just what happened, and I didn't realize that Fredericksburg was the battle where you lost your leg, but it explains a lot of things about the war and about my pa's death. I appreciate you lettin' me know this. I think you know that I have always looked up to you as a father."

Micah turned and faced the crowd of men, some of whom had traveled for several days to attend the meeting. He boldly addressed them, holding out his arms in an inclusive gesture: "My friends, these invaders from the North are worse than all the carpetbaggers and scalawags and Sherman's army put together! Let's don't waste precious time. We got a war to fight, and we need a battle plan." At this, another hushed silence spread over the group, broken only by the croakings of frogs and the rumblings of alligators. The screech owl and the mockingbird could also be heard, intermittently, before Micah interrupted the relative quietness.

"I don't think you would be here tonight, leavin' your wives and young'uns, unless you had recently found out that Norman Dodge has now got your land lots marked, like they're his own, on that big map he's got." Angry protests started from the men, and Micah repeatedly shushed them.

"Men, we're all mad as hell, and that's why we're here. Let's keep it quiet as we can, so we can get through, and we'll all know what we're a-goin' to do. And by the way, don't tell nobody what we've talked about here tonight-nobody!"

"Not even our wives, right, Micah?"

"Especially our wives!" A man near the back of the crowd stood up and addressed everyone. "If our wives hear of this, they'll try to talk us out of it," he yelled.

Another man stated emphatically that women talked too blame much, so none should be told, if it was to be kept a secret. Micah stood with his arms folded across his chest, listening to the men talk.

A man from Montgomery County stood up and crossed to the stump, where he addressed the men. "I'm Wallace MacBryde from Montgomery County. I ask you what in the name o' lead-'n-powder can Dodge do with so much timber? That sawmill of his on the coast must be the master big! The henchmen from the Yellow Pines Lumber Company done run me off my land. They came with a posse of armed men, and they told me to pack a few household goods and some food and to get off my own land! I even had to leave my hay and fodder in the shed! My family's livin' with my brother and his family, and the Lord only knows how we're a-gonna get our own place again. It's another war, and we might as well get ready to fight it!"

The man from Montgomery County returned to his seat and, one by one, men left their log seats and addressed the assembly of men. Each had a similar frightening tale to tell, and each pledged his loyalty to the group and to their leader, Micah MacRae.

Knowing that it was getting toward the midnight hour and seeing the huge bonfire diminish to a few writhing flames, Micah once again addressed the gathering and related to them his plans for the war against Norman Dodge and his Yellow Pines Lumber Company.

"You remember what we were doin' a year ago, a-puttin' spikes on the tram roads and burnin' the bridges?" This brought on whistles and yells and stamping feet, which Micah again stopped by holding up his hand.

"Well, my friends, that's just the beginnin'. We start there, makin' it difficult for 'em to get the logs to the mills. Then, we work on the mill itself, a-plantin' spikes in the sawlog and doin' anything else you might think to do. We need to ask ourselves, 'who should rule, Dodge or the people?'" These final words were recognized as the battle cry of the passionate, one-eyed Eastman lawyer, Luther Hall, presently a prisoner, though considered by many to be an innocent man, in the faraway Ohio State Penitentiary.

"The people! The people!" chanted the men.

"We heard you had a new plan, too. We wanna hear that!" someone added.

"I got a new plan, all right." He paused for emphasis, looking around the large assembly.

"The new plan is that we're gonna burn the main mill down - burn it to the..." Before Micah could complete the sentence, the men leapt off the logs, again firing their weapons and throwing their caps into the air. General havoc reigned for some time, while Micah stood with his fists clenched over him in the night air. Again, however, he was forced to stop the display, as he knew the men had to return home soon, in order to plant crops when the first morning light came. Some had a day's or more travel before putting their crops in the ground. He opened his fists and waved them to an expectant silence.

"Men, I see we are of one mind here tonight. You have your guns...the nights are dark. You can do your own work. However, we got to time it right. We need to go ahead with plantin' our crops, then harvestin' the crops. At night, by the light of the moon, we'll fight the company. Those livin' near the Normandale timber railroad - you know what to do. Those livin' near the sawmills at Normandale and Willcox Lake - you know how to fight this war. You men from other counties...you know what to do." Men from these areas nodded vigorously, appearing ready to resume their nighttime tactics against the hated timber company. Micah asked all of the men to stand and raise their right hands.

Feeling the bonds of people of a kindred area, threatened by outsiders who not so very long ago had defeated them in a terrible war, the men again swore their fidelity to one another, to their cause, and to their leader.

***

During the weeks that followed the squatters' meeting, after waiting for the nights when the full moon cast its light, local men wreaked havoc with the Yellow Pines Lumber Company operations, burning company tools, blocking logging rail tracks with trees, and twisting rail iron.

On the thirty-mile Ocmulgee and Normandale timber railroad, the three Maloy brothers hacked and pounded the steel tracks with axes on a two-mile stretch between Normandale and Camp Six.

The next day, when the train made its usual morning run, it became derailed and almost turned over before the engineer could bring it to a halt, its steel wheels embedded in the soft dirt beside the beaten tracks. Hurling curses and snarling epithets, meant for the squatters who had long since fled the area, the engineer and the colored log choppers began the long, cold walk back to the Normandale sawmill.

Several days passed before the tracks were repaired, so that logs could once more be brought to the Yellow Pines sawmill from the interior of Telfair County. During this time, the timber company's logchoppers were, at gunpoint, run off lands which the Dodge family claimed as theirs. This happened repeatedly on lands where Lancasters, Burches, Grahams, Boneys, Maloys, and others refused to acknowledge the federal court's edict that their lands now belonged to the Dodge family from New York. Norris Burch, along with Littleton Graham and Hank Maloy, greeted the logchoppers with loaded shotguns, their hammers pulled back and ready to shoot at the first sign of encroachment. When the company choppers began their work, the backwoodsmen fired over their heads, sending them screaming for their lives, dropping their axes and saws in their hasty retreat into the dark safety of the surrounding woods.

Other backwoodsmen, working singly or in groups, burned the wood bridges which spanned the creeks in the timber railroad's path. These also had to be repaired before the timber trains could run, along with the wood crossties and beams of the tramroads which snaked through the vast interiors of the lands in the five counties, which the Dodges claimed as their own. Setting fire to these tracks diverted the lumber company, for a few days or weeks, from the perpetrators' lands and timber. While the lumber company was occupied with repairing the damage, the local people rushed to cut their timber and raft it to Darien without its deadly harassment.

On a moonlit night, two men rode their mules along the back road which followed the timber railroad to the Normandale sawmill. Tree stumps stood like silent sentinels over what once had been a towering forest of mammoth pine trees. The riders rode low in their saddles, silently urging their mounts toward the trees, yet a mile distant, whereby they and their beasts might find refuge from the moon's glare which cast their stark silhouettes against the barren landscape. Arriving at the shelter of pines, which hadn't yet succumbed to the company's choppers, the men paused in their saddles for a few whispered words.

"Joe, we oughta have the cover of the pines from here on to the sawmill. We should make it in another hour." Joe Little sat his mount as easily as any man in the piney woods, and nobody ever really noticed the stump that hung loosely down the right side of the saddle. He wanted no pity, and he received none.

"Micah, my friend, when is the real thing a-gonna happen? Tonight's jest a trial run, but when are you a-plannin' the big fire that'll burn down the durn sawmill?"

"Probably 'round the first week in September, Joe. Now, as I recall - and I ain't been to the mill in several months now - but, as I remember, there's a night watchman and there's some dogs."

"Don't worry, Micah. I ain't lost my leg for nuthin'. I been in the thick of battle before. This here stump is proof of it, and I ain't one to run." Joe Little brandished the stump as a badge of honor against his mule's flank, and Micah MacRae silently applauded the short, brave man - his father's age - who had survived the war, only to become embroiled in another one, closer to home.

"We better move on." Micah clucked softly to his mount and the mule pulled forward, followed by the one-legged Joe Little on his mule. The tall pines on both sides of the timber railway allowed only a ray or two of moonlight to glint on the cold steel tracks which led on through the dark backwoods to the main road. Reaching the open road, with the moon visible overhead, the men carefully looked both ways before venturing across it in the revealing moonlight. The sawmill was only minutes away now, and they stopped for a final quick review of their plans to inspect the sawmill before actually setting it on fire at a later time.

"I know what you said before, Micah. We ain't got room for mistakes, and I don't aim to make none. I'll do what you said for me to do. I'll get the dogs' attention and that'll bring out the night watchman. I got meat scraps for the dogs." Joe Little patted the large saddlebag which bulged with the necessities of their midnight mission. Both men carried loaded shotguns which hung down their backs from straps, running under their left arms and around the right side of their necks. Micah had soaked his boots in turpentine to confuse the mill dogs further, in the event any should attempt to track him.

"While I'm entertainin' the dogs and the watchman, like you said, you can be lookin' over ever'thin' and maybe even have time to drive a spike or two into the logs. Don't know whose logs they're a-workin' on now, but I saw their choppers on old man Thompson's place a week ago. It just might be his logs that you drive the spikes through. He'd be mighty pleased to know his trees helped in some way to plague the company."

"You got it right, Joe. Just remember, if the watchman shoots at you, don't wait on me. Run like hell, if you have to. I'll be all right, so don't worry about me, and don't come back a-lookin' for me. I'll be long gone. We might have to lay low in the swamp somewhere. Just remember to put your mule in the water, so the dogs can't track you. Oughta be more water now in Gum Swamp, because of it rainin' so much lately."

"I'm ready, Micah, whenever you are."

"Let's go." Micah's voice was low and urgent as he kneed his mount toward the sawmill, only a few hundred yards away. Through the lush overhang of tremendous pines, the two riders could see the openness of the compound. In the soft moonlight, each of the mill buildings was distinguishable, and on beyond them lay the steel tracks of the East Tennessee, Virginia and Georgia Railway which transported the heavy logs from the sawmill to Brunswick, where ships from around the world waited to receive them.

A guttural growl, not far from them, meant that one of the mill curs was aware of their presence. The dog started toward them, growling and barking. This alerted two other dogs which jumped from the porch of the mill office and ran, barking, toward the commotion. The noise brought the night watchman from around the corner of the mill office. He ran, shotgun in hand, toward the hidden riders at the edge of the woods. It was time for the men to carry out their plans.

"I'm gone, Micah. Good luck, man!"

"You, too, Joe. For God's sake, be careful!"

Joe Little flapped the reins on his mule's withers, and the animal lunged forward, moving yet unseen by the mill dogs, along a well-traveled path toward the dark recesses of Gum Swamp. With the dogs hot on his trail and the cursing watchman not far behind, he reached in his saddlebag and began dropping bits of deer meat to put a greater distance between himself and the animals. Since the plan was to lure them even farther into the swamp, he reserved the larger pieces of meat until the dogs were far enough away to allow Micah to complete his work.

He could faintly hear the watchman, still in pursuit though tiring from the chase, whose panting voice kept urging the dogs to find the "squatter," who he was certain had come to sabotage the mill. His continuous yelling to the dogs, Joe Little reasoned, should provide enough noise to drown out the sounds of spikes being driven through the sawmill logs.

After securing his horse, Micah MacRae ran, bent-over, an axe in one hand and several spikes in the other, from one building to the next, checking doors to see whether they were left unlocked and looking for kerosene which he planned to use in burning the sawmill at a later date. He found several barrels of kerosene in the commissary which was unlocked. He ran, zigzagging, to the office which was lit with a kerosene lamp. Peering through the front window, he looked at the huge map with the Dodges' land claims on the side wall. Swallowing with difficulty, he saw his own land lots on Bear Creek, now circled in red! His were next!

He felt emboldened for what he had to do. Running with new resolve to the planing mill, he drove the first spike into the log which was already on the carriage. He pounded the remainder of the spikes into other nearby logs, being careful to drive in the entire spike, not leaving any telltale metal heads sticking out from the rough bark of the logs.

He heard the dogs, though off in the distance, returning to the mill. Running another zigzag course back across the dirt compound, he reentered the woods and quickly untied his mule, as the dogs filed, growling and barking, back onto the mill grounds.

The sound of his mule's hooves on the hard dirt turned the dogs' attention his way, and he urged his mount to a fast trot as the dogs ran, yelping, after him. He never saw the watchman again that night, nor did he see Joe Little. He assumed his friend had gone on to Gum Swamp, then, once free of the dogs, had circled back toward the main road west of the sawmill. Their trial run had been a success. However, when they set the mill to the torch in early September, they would have to carry live decoys for the dogs. He was certain of that.

Chapter Eleven

Katharine had always thought that if something bad were going to happen, it would certainly happen at nighttime, when one was asleep and unaware of any forebodings. Ever since the move to Georgia and being caught up in the escalating land war, and especially since Frank's death, she almost dreaded each night's arrival. She fought this feeling and never let on to anyone that she feared the darkness and the feelings of loneliness, cut off from the life she once knew in New York and alienated by many in the desolate backwoods of the South.

Nighttime had once again arrived, and the fire was burning low in the fireplace in her bedchamber. Katharine sat at the dressing table which held a glowing kerosene lamp. Dressed for bed, she freed her hair of its pins and combs and braids and brushed it until the tight spirals, caused by the braiding, relaxed into thick waves. Sighing and laying down the brush, she rose from the dresser and picked up several pine knots from the wood basket by the fireplace. When she tossed them onto the slow-burning logs, the flames momentarily flared. She blew out the lamp and readjusted her eyes to the dim light of the glowing fireplace. Finding the steps to the bed, she climbed onto the linen sheets, fearing that she would once again toss and turn during a sleepless night. However, for some strange reason which she would later wonder about, she was asleep almost the moment her head touched the pillow.

Knock!! Knock!! Knock!! Knock!! Someone was at the front door, and Katharine struggled to wake up and to sort her thoughts. There it was again - rapid beating on the door, a girl's voice, crying! Cold reality set in, and sleep was banished for the night. Katharine felt for her dressing gown, then slid off the bed and into her slippers. She found the candle on the chamber stick and lit it, then tied the gown. Taking the burning candle with her, she padded down the hallway to the front door. The full moon provided enough light for her to determine the cause of such commotion. Looking through the vertical glass panes which ran the length of the door on both sides, she saw a colored girl, maybe eight or nine years old, who was alternately beating on the door and screaming for help.

Katharine unbolted the door and held the candle to the girl before her.

"O, Miz Fremont, pleez come! Ma mamma, oh, she dyin'! Dey sont me t'git you."

"Wait a minute. Who are you? Where do you live?"

"Ah libs in de settle'mint. Ah wuz dar w'en you come askin' fer he'p wid yo' logs. Ah's Ruthie Mae. Ah's Shep's girl."

Katharine remembered Hill's hurried introduction of the four surly men that day at the settlement and she remembered that one was named "Shep."

"What's the matter with your mother, Ruthie Mae?"

"Her got pneumonie agin', and de doctuh he say ef her git pneumonie agin', her die fer sho. Her got high feber. We kane find no doctuh." At this, the tears splashed down her dark face, glistening in the candlelight. Katharine found a handkerchief in the pocket of her dressing gown and gave it to the girl who proceeded to wipe her eyes and nose.

"Where is your father...where's Shep?"

"Mah papa and all de mens in de settle'mint, dey's raftin' logs on de ribber or workin' some'ers else. Dat de reason Ah had t'come - ain' nobody else could come."

"How did you get here? Surely, you didn't walk?"

"Yas'm, Ah stahted mout long time ago, away 'fo dahk, and Ah jes' kep walkin' e'en in the dahk, an' Ah 'fraid boogyman, he gonna git me or a big ba'ah comin' mout de woods, fer sho." The thin girl was crying and wringing her hands. Katharine found it difficult to believe that the girl had walked all the way, until she looked at her bare feet which were raw and bleeding on the cold front porch.

Katharine was afraid, and it was against her better judgment, to go back to a place where she had felt so hated and distrusted. However, the pathetic girl with the wrenching sobs made it difficult to know what was the best thing to do. Noting Ruthie Mae's bruised and bloody feet, Katharine told her to wait for her, that she would be back shortly. She had the child step into the foyer, out of the cold.

Holding the candle, Katharine returned to her room and found some shoes and a coat for the girl to wear for the horseback trip to the settlement. She hastened back to the foyer with a wet rag for the girl to clean her feet before putting on the shoes. Ruthie Mae's eyes, with the tears now stilled, were big with wonder and appreciation. Katharine was glad to see that she was calm now, and she told her to wait while she dressed.

The first thing Katharine did, upon returning to her bedroom, was to find her purse with the gun in it. She would put this in the saddlebag. She then quickly found an old riding habit that she had intended to add to the clothes which she gave to various charities every year. It would suit her needs, for it had pantaloons which would allow her to ride astride the horse, rather than sidesaddle. As she pulled on the brown wool riding habit, she involuntarily noticed her candle-lit reflection in the cheval mirror. The fear in her eyes made her cringe, and she purposely looked away, trying not to acknowledge the dread that was possessing her. She hurriedly scribbled a note to Tilda, leaving it on the desk in her bedchamber.

She knew she would have to saddle the horse herself, since she didn't want Big Hill to know she was going to the colored settlement in the middle of the night. She knew he had mentioned staying overnight in the stables and repairing the phaeton carriage in the morning.

Instructing Ruthie Mae to wait for her on the back porch, Katharine lit a kerosene lantern and followed the brick path to the stables. She retrieved her saddle from the saddle block in the tack room, then hung the lantern on the post by the first gelding's stall. Working hurriedly and quietly, she soon had the horse saddled and bridled. She also put the saddlebag, with her gun in it, across the horse.

She knew she would have to be back before daylight, so that Hill would not find the horse gone and be upset. She hated to leave without letting Tilda or Hill know where she was going, but she just couldn't risk letting them talk her out of her night journey. The note would have to suffice. Katharine knew that her fear was such that any remonstration on their parts would probably keep her safely at home. No, she couldn't afford to let them know what she was about to do, for though it was her conscience that was prodding her to go, every shred of her being silently screamed for her to go back to the house and wait for morning to come.

Her mind made up to make the trip, Katharine blew out the lantern and led the horse through the familiar stable walk. Thank God, it was a moonlit night, she thought. Otherwise, it would be impossible to make the trip on the dark paths to the settlement. She could see the girl huddled on the back porch waiting for her, and then she saw her running to meet her.

Katharine had realized that the child probably had no riding experience. Otherwise, she might have saddled the other horse for her. She was correct, for as she mounted the horse and instructed the girl to climb up behind her, Ruthie Mae almost became hysterical.

"Lawd, Miz Kat'rin, Ah ain' rode no hoss befo', an' Ah sceert." Her voice was quivering from fright, as well as the cold of the night.

"Come on, grab my hand." Katharine pulled the hesitant girl up behind her, and she clucked to the horse, pressing her knees simultaneously against his ribs. The gray leapt forward, following Katharine's guiding reins across the hard dirt of the yard, rather than the brick driveway, to avoid waking Tilda and Big Hill. Katharine had never ridden any distance alone at night, and she silently prayed that God would watch over them and keep them safe.

The night wind ripped through her clothes, and her cold hands reminded her that she had forgotten to wear gloves. She inwardly scolded herself for this omission for, besides the cold, she would probably sustain blisters from the reins. Trying not to think of all of her discomforts, she concentrated on taking the right roads and paths to the Negro settlement.

The horse settled into a strong trot, and it was a struggle for her to hold onto the reins and maintain her balance in the darkness, especially with another person in the saddle. Her young riding partner alternately laughed and cried during the frightening journey.

She saw only a few animals on the road ahead, as the horse's hooves announced their coming in time for the denizens of the woods which rose on both sides of the road to scurry into its black interior. Katharine knew that panthers and bears were often spotted in the vicinity, and she knew they would spook a horse, if they chose to venture out in his path.

In many parts of the lengthy back roads which led to the Negro settlement, the umbriferous tops of the pine trees admitted no light from the moon, and during these fearsome stretches, Katharine relied on the innate horse sense of the animal she rode. She felt that horses had good night sight and, perhaps by a combination of sight and instinct, could follow a path in the dark.

During these periods of sightlessness, when the darkness closed in like a black blanket, Katharine could feel the tenseness of the child behind her and could hear her whimpering. Then, coming into sections of the road, which were well lit by the moon, she could feel her relax and stop her crying.

"It shouldn't be long now, Ruthie Mae. I can smell the river swamp. We'll get more moonlight now that the trees are thinning out. See, it's better now." Katharine was grateful that the road now was bathed in dim light. She knew they were only minutes away from the colored settlement. Barking dogs let her know they had arrived, and she prayed they wouldn't frighten the horse.

She spoke calmly to the horse and slowed his trot to a walk. The first of many dogs which she did not recall encountering, when she was at the settlement before, ran barking to meet them. This alerted the sleeping occupants of the run-down shanties, who stuck their heads out of their doors as the horse and riders approached Ruthie Mae's house.

Before Katharine could help her, the child jumped to the ground and ran into the house. Katharine dismounted and secured the horse, then turned to speak to the people who were previously standing in their doorways. However, no one was there now, and the doors were closed. A shiver went up her backbone, and the knot of fear in her stomach began to grow as she entered the front door of Ruthie Mae's small house which, she observed, had only two tiny rooms.

The stench of sickness brought a wave of nausea which almost replaced the fear in Katharine's stomach. Ruthie Mae was kneeling by her mother's bed, with its tattered cornshuck mattress, and was holding her mother's limp hand. An old woman who introduced herself as Auntie Chloee rocked slowly in a squeaky chair near the small fireplace. The fire was but a few glowing embers and the room was cold.

Katharine walked over to the bed and looked at the sick woman who appeared to be too weak to move or speak. She touched her forehead and felt the hot, dry fever, though she knew the woman was probably having chills, along with the fever.

"Ma'm, you have a wonderful, loving child. Ruthie Mae brought me here to see about you." A hint of a smile curled briefly at the corners of the woman's mouth, but when she blinked her eyes, Katharine saw they were filled with tears which wet her cheeks.

"We've got to get some heat in here," Katharine said. "Ruthie Mae, where is some wood for the fire?"

"Ah fine some," the child said, as she hurried out the back door. Just as quickly, she returned with the wood which Katharine placed on the remaining embers. After several loads of wood and Katharine's stirring the embers, a blazing fire began to heat the room.

"Aunt Chloee, where are more blankets or quilts? We need more cover for Ruthie Mae's mother."

"Her ma name Rhody."

This was the first bit of conversation proffered by Aunt Chloee after her terse introduction of herself, and Katharine was glad to know the woman could communicate. Though she appeared to be very old, her mind was obviously intact.

"Well, can you tell me where I can find some quilts for Rhody. She needs to be kept warm."

"Ruthie Mae know." At this, the child left the house and shortly returned with some pieced quilts which Katharine doubled for warmth and tucked around the woman on the bed.

"We need to find a doctor for Rhody," Katharine said, looking from Aunt Chloee to Ruthie Mae.

Aunt Chloee was speaking and her voice was so low, Katharine moved over nearer to hear her.

"Dar nigger woman herb doctuh on de ribber. Ruthie Mae sceert ob her and wone go fetch her. She lib on de ribber on pas' de color grabeyard. Ruthie Mae, she sceert ob de haints in de grabeyard."

Katharine had heard of a mulatto herb doctor who lived on the riverbank. In fact, she remembered that one of the Northern timber men had a sick child with a rare kidney ailment, who had been treated by several medical doctors, some as far away as Atlanta and Savannah, only to be cured finally by the colored herb doctor. It was worth a try, to attempt to find her.

"I'm going to look for the herb doctor. I don't know that she can treat pneumonia, but maybe she can make Rhody comfortable until we can find a doctor tomorrow. Ruthie Mae, keep your mother warm. Add wood to the fire, if you need to, and keep her warm. Also, if you can find a pail for water, go to the well outside and draw some water. Then, wipe your mother's face. This should help to bring down the fever. I'll be back as soon as I can."

Aunt Chloee was murmuring something again, and Katharine leaned over to her, straining to hear.

"Deotha, her de nigger doctuh." The old colored woman repositioned the snuff in her cheek. "Her place on de ribber. Go on pas' de grabeyard, and de road lead to de ribber. De color grabeyard on de left. De white settle'mint on de right side ob de road. De white grabeyard on de right. Deotha house near de place whar dey puts de logs t'gedder at Gum Swamp. Go on pas' dat place, and her house on de right on de ribber."

Assuring them she'd be back shortly with the Negro herb doctor, Katharine hurried down the narrow wood steps and unhitched the horse. She quickly placed her foot in the stirrup and swung her leg over the horse. Clucking softly, she guided the animal onto the river path which continued on beyond the colored settlement. She was glad for the freedom of the separated riding habit and also for its warmth, for once again the wind tore at her.

Barking dogs followed her almost to the colored cemetery, and then she was alone with the swift-running horse. Once again, the path was difficult to follow, except in those places where the moonlight found its way through the tangled branches of the pine swampland.

Katharine noted the landmarks which Aunt Chloee had mentioned - the untended colored cemetery on the left, the white settlement on the right, and the equally unkempt white cemetery farther on the right. She looked for the bight on the river, which she could now see through the trees, and she shivered at the swamp sounds of bullfrogs and alligators. Her skin crawled with goose bumps as she neared the river dwelling of the mulatto herb doctor. Katharine had heard that the old woman was frightening to look at, and this probably explained Ruthie Mae's aversion to seeking her out for her mother.

She stared at the recessed area of the narrow river, and the realization hit her that this was the place where the squatters held their meetings. The difference in the meeting places of the two sides involved in the land war struck her anew. The lovely Winslow home in Eastman with its cherished antiques and its roaring fireplaces was far removed from the cold, windswept stream in the middle of Gum Swamp.

Katharine slowed the horse to a walk, looking intently through the trees for the herb doctor's place. She saw the small hut several hundred feet ahead on the right and guided the horse along the narrow trail which led off from the river path.

She called out to Deotha, hoping the woman would come to the door. As the horse came to a halt in front of the hut, its narrow wood door creaked open and the mulatto woman stepped onto the narrow porch. She was holding a small, burning lightwood knot in one hand and was bearing her weight on a crooked stick with her other hand. Her eyes appeared to be rolled back under her eyelids, except when she later spoke. Her appearance was both gruesome and ghastly, and Katharine's hands on the horn of the saddle were shaking uncontrollably. The colored woman's turbaned head made her appear taller than she was and her flowing robe of deerskin, with openings for her head and arms, hung from her shoulders to her ankles.

"Who are you...whaddayu want?" The apparition in animal skins squinted at Katharine as she spoke. Then, her eyes disappeared and only black sockets peered through the dark at her nighttime visitor.

Unnerved, Katharine spoke in a halting, low voice.

"Deotha, I'm Mrs. Frank Fremont. Shep's wife at the settlement is very ill, and she needs help. Can you come and see about her?"

"How is her sick? Is dar feber?" The mulatto's eyes appeared briefly as she spoke, only to vanish again.

"Fever? Yes, she is very hot. Her daughter thinks she has pneumonia again."

"Is her whoopin'?" The eyes were slits that receded swiftly.

"Oh, you mean coughing. No, I didn't hear her cough. She's very weak and appears to have ague."

"Ah be on...has t'git mah stew pots and medicines." Deotha returned to the darkness of her hovel, and Katharine turned the horse around and headed back to the colored settlement. Looking behind, she saw the shadowy figure of the herb doctor emerge from her door and untie the mule, which Katharine had not noticed, from a nearby tree. The mulatto slung her stew pots across the mule and climbed up without aid of saddle or stirrups. Thus lightly accommodated for her job of healing the sick, she followed close behind Katharine who was amazed that the woman could ride so well, at such speed, without a saddle.

The two women arrived at the colored settlement almost at the same time. They quickly entered the shanty of the sick woman, and Deotha went to work.

She first checked Rhody and pronounced that she didn't have pneumonia. Rather, she suspected a kidney ailment, and she had a remedy for that.

Deotha stoked the fire and hung two of her iron pots over the flames. She added more wood and soon the flames were reaching the pots, making their contents boil. Deotha extracted several burlap pouches from the pockets of her deerskin robe. From these, she lifted out several wilted herbs which she added to the pots. She made no attempts at conversation with anyone in the room, thereby keeping her eyes unseen under her eyelids. She turned toward Katharine and motioned for her to go on home. Katharine was grateful for someone else to be in charge of the situation.

"Ruthie Mae, I'm going on home now. I think Deotha will have your mother well soon. If not, the mill doctor should be at home tomorrow and he will know what to do."

"Goodbye, Miz Fremont," the girl said.

Rhody was stirring in her bed, and for the first time since Katharine had arrived, the ill woman attempted to speak.

"Ah thanks you, white lady, fer comin'. Deotha, she see 'bout me now."

"Yes, I've heard good things about Deotha's medicines. She'll have you up and about before long."

Ruthie Mae ran over to Katharine and threw her arms around her. This childlike gesture almost brought tears to Katharine's eyes. How she longed for a child of her own!

"Goodbye, Ruthie Mae. You take good care of your mother, all right? I'll be asking Big Hill about you and he'll let me know how you are. I must go now."

Katharine hurried outside into the early dawn of the day. She was thankful for light on the dark road back to her house. The ride was uneventful, except for the few animals which scurried across the path ahead. Sensing his rider's urgency, the horse broke into a long-stride gallop which soon brought them to the black, wrought-iron gates of home. Katharine sighed with relief that the Lord had indeed watched over her, and she prayed for Rhody's recovery.

Chapter Twelve

SPRING, 1892

Katharine retrieved from the barn the soft, old, burlap pouches of seeds, which Ben Winslow had gladly shared with her from his last year's gardens. She had never helped with planting a garden, and she was excited about doing something new and productive. She opened each of the pouches, attempting to guess what each vegetable would be, according to the appearance of the seed. Some were obvious, but others she only knew by looking at the strips of paper which Ben had thoughtfully pinned to the pouches, identifying each group of seeds. She had small tomato plants, also, which the Hardisons had gladly contributed, when they heard with some amusement that Katharine was actually helping to plant her own garden this year.

Hill and Tilda were waiting for her. Big Hill, dressed in overalls and large boots which once belonged to Frank Fremont, was making small holes for the seeds. He had already turned the earth with his mule pulling Frank's harrow. It was the same garden spot that he and Tilda had planted the year before. Tilda was dressed in an old brown work dress and she, too, had a spade and was working the black dirt.

Katharine herself had put on an old muslin dress with large pockets which she used to good advantage to hold the pouches of seeds. She had on cotton gloves to protect her hands and noticed that Tilda had on some old gloves, also. Both women wore large hats as protection from the sun.

Hill spoke with the gentle air of the professional speaking to the amateur.

"Now, Miz Kat'rin, Ah and Miz Tilda, us gwine make de holes and you puts de seeds in de holes. Dis heah hole, it fer de squashes."

Katharine was appalled at her own ignorance. She could only look into two pouches and recognize the vegetable from its seed. She pulled the small burlap bags from her pocket and laid them neatly in a row. Finding "squash" on the strip of paper, which Ben had pinned to one of the bags, Katharine reached in and grabbed a handful of the seeds, figuring that more would be better than less in the waiting hole.

"No'm, Miz Kat'rin," Hill said, stopping her, and Tilda suppressed a smile.

"No'm, jes' 'bout fo' ob dem seeds be 'nuff fer each hole...'one fer de cutworm, one fer de crow, one to rot, and one to grow.'"

Katharine laughed, "Well, I've never heard your rhyme, but it makes sense. You have to tell me, you know. I've never done this." She reached into the squash seed bag and began dropping seeds into each indenture, smiling over the planting verse and mentally adjuring all cutworms and crows to stay away from her garden.

The planting progressed, until the seeds of squash, cucumbers, butterbeans, peas, watermelons, eggplant, and okra were all embedded in their respective, straight rows which Hill had previously laid out with his mule pulling the turnplow. Hill and Tilda showed her how to cover each grouping of seeds with dirt, and Hill had buckets of water ready to pour over them. The tomato plants were next, and they were put into deeper holes. Hill had stakes to support the plants, once they became laden with their red fruit. Tilda had some practical markers which she'd made herself, and Hill had whittled some wood to points which he had attached to the stakes, designating the name of each row of seedlings and plants.

The earthy smell, the closeness of two dear friends, the spring sun on the damp earth, and the promise of ripe vegetables in the not too distant future, worked their charms on Katharine. Standing up from planting the last hole, she sighed with a sense of accomplishment. She wiped perspiration from her face with her sleeve, since her gloves were caked with dirt, and could not remember when she had felt such satisfaction. No, they might be delayed in moving back to New York, but that wouldn't stop them from having a vegetable garden again!

She had not even noticed the wet dirt stain which followed the hem of her dress, the dirt which leadened her shoes when she walked, nor the tiny rivulets of dirt on her face, neck and arms. She reckoned that her lovely claw-foot tub had never received such a soiled person to bathe, and she wondered what Frank would think if he saw her now. He certainly wouldn't approve; of that, she was certain. Nor would he approve of her going to the mill or the settlements near the mill, but Katharine knew she didn't have any choice in the latter matter.

As they gathered the tools and parted ways, with Katharine and Tilda heading toward the house and Big Hill the stables, the colored overseer stopped and called back to Katharine.

"Ah bin wondrin' whut's bes', and Ah doan know, but Ah thinks you ought to know, Miz Kat'rin'."

"Know what, Hill? What are you talking about?" Katharine stopped and turned back to talk to him, as Tilda proceeded on up the walkway.

"Ah thinks you should know. Dey done burnt a cross at de settle'mint - de same night dey come here. It wuz a big cross, and it burn fer a long time, till dey got 'nough buckets ob water to put it mout. Dey say dey is gonna kill a nigger, too, ef we doan do right, and Ah reckons doin' right is doin' whut dey say."

"Oh, Hill!" Katharine was horrified. "At first, I thought they were after you. But now, I really think they were showing me just what they thought of my going to the colored settlement and asking for help with my timber, rather than the white settlement. As I told you earlier, I went to the sheriff's office that very morning after the Klan was here, and I told Sheriff Burch about the man with the scar. He knew him - said his name was Harold Diggs, but people call him 'Crow.'" Katharine did not tell her colored servant that she suspected this was because of the man's Jim-Crow ways and, also, because of his frightening, scarecrow look.

"Anyway," she continued, "the sheriff said Diggs had been in trouble with the law before, and he didn't seem surprised that the man was involved with the Klan. However, they can't find him to arrest him. And since the other men had on hoods, and I don't have a clue as to who they were, there's no way to make any arrests."

"All dem Klan - dey bad news, Miz Kat'rin. Dey be back." The colored man sighed, "Us jes' doan know w'en."

Chapter Thirteen

Katharine could not pinpoint the time when the idea formed in her mind that she would accompany her logs on their rafting trip to the port city of Darien, but the idea persisted and she mulled it over on an almost daily basis. She wondered what Micah MacRae would think, if he knew her plan, but something told her he would think it too dangerous for a woman to make the trip. She was undecided whether to tell him that she planned to ride the raft with him and the other raftsmen or whether just to show up at the riverbank on the day they set out for Darien on the raft which was to be built from her trees.

Katharine pondered these matters of adventure and daring, as she rode the gelding, General Lee, on the sandy path which led to Bear Creek. Thinking back, she remembered telling Micah's mother, during the girls' music lessons the past week, that she had never seen trees harvested and would like to know how her own would be cut in the fall. At the next music lesson, Abby MacRae remarked that Micah said to tell Mrs. Fremont that she was welcome to come to the logging site near Bear Creek, where he was cutting his own timber for rafting within the next few weeks, so that she might see how the trees were cut.

The April day was pleasant, though the smell of the past two months' burning of the piney woods still lingered in the air. The singed wiregrass now sprouted new, tender, green growth, as did the bushy elderberry with its early spring blossoms of creamy white and the tall, graceful ty-ty, whose racemes of early greenery would change to white within a few weeks. The rod-straight canebrakes around Sugar Creek had glossy stands of moist fever bush, its burgeoning pink display emerging among the green foliage.

The sighing of the lofty pines which swayed on both sides of the narrow path reminded Katharine of a conversation which she and Abby MacRae had had several weeks past, when Katharine remarked on the eerie sighing of the pines. Mrs. MacRae had smiled her gentle smile and had said, "Here in the South, we call it 'soughin'. The pines 'sough.'" Katharine had stored away this bit of information along with other sayings and words of wisdom which Abby MacRae always appeared to have at her fingertips.

Once, when Katharine had arrived for the girls' music lessons, Abby had stayed unusually busy with the chores of a farm household. A mattress of corn shucks was partially completed in a corner of the room. Cotton thread was assembled on the spinning wheel in another corner. One of the girls' dresses was nearing completion on a table in the room, hand-sewn from the thread Abby had separated on the spinning wheel. Its buttons were made from acorns, hand-covered with the material from Abby's loom. She had also sewn "water wings" for Little Roy, which consisted of gourds sewn at both ends of a flour sack. She had explained that the sack would be placed under his arms, and the stitched-in gourds would hold him up in the water, until he was old enough to learn how to swim. Micah, she said, had learned to swim that way, as had Carrie and Mary Sue, in the creeks which ran through their homeplace.

Abby had attended to yet another chore, the churning of butter on the back porch, while Katharine taught her granddaughters music. When Katharine had later told her how remarkable she was to find a use for almost everything, the older woman had smiled and said, simply, "A willful waste makes a woeful want." She then had continued, "That's what we all learned durin' the war, to make do with what we had and to be careful not to waste it."

Katharine pressed her knees against the horse and urged the animal on. Getting to know more about Micah MacRae, through his mother and children, had only whetted her desire to know him even better, and her heart almost leapt within her at the prospect of seeing him again!

She had dressed carefully, as a woman dresses for a man, all the while not admitting to herself that she wanted to see appreciation, and yes, desire, for her in his coldly inscrutable, brown eyes. She did not chide herself for these longings, though they represented a part of herself with which she was only recently becoming acquainted. The other part of her being, which had been her true self for over thirty years, rebelled at life in the backwoods of the South and yearned to be away from the ignorance and the lawlessness and the fears. How then could she be so mesmerized with a man who was a Southerner, and a backwoods Southerner, at that? She, as yet, had no explanation.

The muffled sounds and acrid smells of logging assailed her senses, and when the horse rounded a bend in the narrow path, Katharine could see a large, sunny area ahead, where several tremendous trees lay on the forest floor. She slowed the horse to a halt and studied the scene before her. Not seeing Micah MacRae, at first, she did see other loggers, some of them shirtless, their white and black backs gleaming with sweat and creased with dirt.

Twelve yokes of oxen, chewing their cud, were hitched to a timber cart with two large wheels. The action of the moment appeared to be the lifting of the nearest felled tree beneath the cart for transporting to Bear Creek, probably a half-mile away.

Micah MacRae suddenly stood up on the other side of the cart, and Katharine's heart skipped a beat. He obviously had been checking or repairing the cart, and he brushed the back of his large hand across his brow which was beaded with sweat.

Katharine nudged the horse forward and they entered the clearing, the horse walking between two of the huge, felled trees which had their branches removed. She slid from the saddle as Micah walked over to her. As usual, his eyes were smiling, but unreadable. Any pleasure, which she had striven to evoke, was not present in his eyes. Though disappointment raged in her heart, Katharine had the diabolical feeling of gladness that she didn't have to choose her reaction. He made it easy for her, so she greeted him with a nice smile.

"So this is the way the trees are harvested? It's all very interesting."

"Yes, well...this is it. We're about to load one of these on the cart there and..." The raftsman hesitated, then talked hurriedly.

"Miz Fremont, I realize it's none of my business, but it's dangerous for a woman to ride alone. I never, for a minute, thought you'd come here..."

Before he could say, "alone" again, Katharine plucked her pistol out of the bag on her saddle, where she always kept it.

"Mr. MacRae, I keep this near me always."

"Yes, but can you shoot it?"

"Actually, I've never had to, but I know I could, if I had to." Katharine was feeling somewhat intimidated with the line of questioning. He probably thought her just another incapable woman, riding around with a loaded gun which she had just inanely admitted she had never fired. She could feel the redness creeping up her neck and face, but he mercifully did not appear to notice her discomfort. Rather, his eyes were on the gun, and he gently took it from her.

"It's a derringer, I see. And, I'm sure you realize it has two chambers for shells. You can fire twice. Then, you must reload. Are you carryin' other shells with you?" His tone was courteous and instructive, not at all patronizing, and Katharine warmed to it.

"No, I guess I never really thought, deep down, that I'd actually have to shoot it."

"Miz Fremont, have you heard of the problem we're a-havin' now with wild dogs?"

"Wild dogs? No, I don't know what you're talking about."

"I've lost at least half of my herd of sheep, and my neighbors for miles around are havin' the same problem. Sometimes, the dogs don't even bother to eat the meat. They just kill because they're wild and mean. Also, a number of 'em are rabid."

Katharine felt a chill go up her spine as she listened to him. He handed the derringer back to her and said nonchalantly, "You know, of course, to pull the hammer back each time, before you shoot, like so." He took the gun again and pulled the hammer back, then eased it back into place.

"Here, you try it," he said. Katharine awkwardly held the gun and attempted to pull back the hammer. The cold steel resisted and she pulled the hammer with a stronger grip.

"There! That's it! Now, if for some reason you don't fire it, you must ease the hammer slow... ver...y slow..., back into position." Again, he replaced the hammer and handed the gun back to her.

"Thank you for the lesson in weaponry. I suppose I need to practice shooting it," she said with a little laugh.

"You do, at that," he said, as she replaced the pistol in her saddlebag. Katharine nodded toward the cart.

"Is that a timber cart?" She guessed its huge wheels were around nine feet in diameter.

"Yes, it's a type of oxcart, called a balance cart. Now, that one..." He pointed to a two-wheeled cart among the standing trees. "That's a rule cart. It's for usin' when we need more than one cart to carry a tree. As soon as we can get these trees loaded and sent on to the creek, we'll be a-cuttin' some more, and I'll show you how it's done."

"Mistuh Micah, dis cart - it still ain' fixed." One of the Negro hands required his attention.

"Excuse me, Miz Fremont."

"Oh, please, don't let me interrupt you. I realize you're paying these men, and you don't need anything to slow you down. I've heard of how the trees are harvested, but..."

"But now, you can see for yourself, right?" His eyes were gentle and kind, belying the hardness of his appearance, and Katharine once again basked in the strength of his presence.

As he walked over to the oxcart, she found a fairly smooth tree stump which was free of pine sap, and used it as a seat, while she watched the drama unfold before her. Micah was working on the axle of the cart, and he yelled to the Negro driver to straddle the log with the cart. The cart appeared to be in working order, and Micah jumped out of the way as the oxen pulled the cart over the log.

The cart tongue was hoisted, letting down a set of hooks, or "dogs," that bit into the middle of the tree. When the cart tongue was pulled down again, the log was lifted from the ground. It was then dragged on the worn path to the creek. As the oxen left the clearing, dragging the tremendous tree trunk and following the grunted commands and cracking rawhide whip of the Negro driver, Micah instructed three of the loggers to prepare to cut down another one of the large trees.

The colored logger with the ax approached the tree which Micah had selected to cut. His bare back rippling with the hard muscles of heavy labor, the Negro woodchopper struck the base of the mighty pine repeatedly, each time slowly widening the grooved cut.

Two men followed him with a cross-cut saw which they pulled forward and backward through the freshly-hewn tree trunk. Sap oozed from the teeth of the saw, and its pungent odor filled the air. When resin built up on the saw blade, impeding its progress, one of the logchoppers remedied the problem with kerosene from a nearby barrel.

After many minutes of hard sawing, the harsh cracking of the nearly severed tree trunk heralded the disembodiment of the tree from its centuries-old roots. Katharine was unprepared for the raw power of the tree, swaying in a deathly slow motion, momentarily suspended against the blue of the sky, before crashing to the ground with a thunderous impact that made her tremble on her nearby perch.

As the loggers rushed to cut the limbs from the tree's torso, four men boldly rode their horses into the clearing, invoking everyone's attention and causing the colored loggers to drop their axes and saws in their rapid retreat into the nearby woods.

The man in the lead was Paul Owens, who nodded and tipped his hat at Katharine, all the while looking embarrassed and uneasy. Behind him rode a United States Marshal, attired in uniform replete with the gleaming badge of his profession. The other two men appeared to be Yellow Pines Lumber Company people, though Katharine didn't recognize either of them.

The mill manager, breathing hard from the unaccustomed exertion of the lengthy ride, dismounted and stepped gingerly across the clearing floor to Micah MacRae. He cleared his throat and glanced at Katharine.

"Mr. MacRae," he began.

"Yes, how are you today, Paul?" Micah met the mill manager halfway but refused his outstretched hand.

Dropping his pudgy hand, Paul Owens again cleared his throat and spoke almost inaudibly.

"Micah, I hate doing this, man, but the law's the law. This land has been claimed by Norman W. Dodge, and you are trespassing."

The U.S. Marshal nudged his mount over to the nearest large tree, where he hammered a notice of criminal trespassing, signed by the federal judge in Macon, on its huge trunk. Without directly looking at Micah, he intoned, "By the law invested in me as United States Marshal for the Western Division of the Southern District of Georgia, I find you, Micah J. MacRae, guilty of trespassing on the property of Norman W. Dodge. Unless you vacate the premises immediately, we shall have no alternative but to take you into custody."

Katharine never saw Micah reach for his gun. Actually, she hadn't even seen his gun, until the marshal finished his spiel and turned to face the accused trespasser.

Micah stood immobile, the loaded pump shotgun cocked and aimed at the posse who all now held their hands over their heads, their foreheads beading with the perspiration of fear. They knew the weapon which the raftsman aimed at them, and they knew that several quick blasts from such a firearm could kill or seriously injure all four of them. The men began shaking, almost uncontrollably, as the armed backwoodsman spoke to them in the low, measured tones of one who was ready for battle.

"The war ain't over, is it? It took my Pa, but it won't take 'is land, this land that was his pa's before him. We've lived on this land for goin' on seventy years, and we've paid taxes on it -never missed a year! It's ours, and I'll fight to keep it! I reckon this'll be the last battle of the war, and we'll see who wins this one! Now, I'm countin' to three, and whoever lags behind is a dead man."

The frightened men lashed their mounts during their fevered retreat. The loggers who had stood in the nearby woods with mouths open and hands raised, when the marshal had hammered the trespassing notice on the tree, now burst into guffaws and raised balled fists at the vanishing backs of the enemy, as they returned from their forest refuge.

During the jocular talking which followed the posse's hasty exit, Katharine didn't quite know what to do or say. Several times, she opened her mouth to speak, but then realized that Micah was ignoring her, on purpose. It suddenly dawned on her that he must think that she had something to do with the events of the past few minutes. Hadn't they nodded and spoken to her, as if she were one of them? And wasn't she?

Katharine yearned to know more about the escalating land war. Why were women kept in the dark about so many things? Why had Frank kept so much from her? As she stood there in the middle of the pine forest, undecided about what to do, the realization that women could not even vote came back to haunt her. Sighing, she climbed into the saddle and ran her gloved hand over the thick mane of the gray gelding.

"General Lee," she said, in a dejected whisper, "it's time for us to go home." Not looking back, she turned into the woods trail and retraced their path back to the wider dirt road which she followed for several miles. She kept reliving in her mind the events of the afternoon.

Suddenly, the horse whinnied and broke stride, then pawed the air before landing on all four hooves with a jolt that threw Katharine forward, almost out of the saddle. With alarm, she finally heard what the gelding's more sensitive ears had already picked up. It was the high-pitched, frantic bleating of sheep, mingled with the bone-chilling snarls of pursuing animals. The woods to the right, probably ten yards ahead, yielded the cause of the blood-curdling ruckus, as two sheep, an ewe and her lamb, crashed through the thicket and onto the dirt road, followed by a pack of six wild dogs.

Katharine froze, along with her mount, at the death duel before her and watched, terrified, as the lead dog seized the lamb and savagely tore out its throat, leaving it bleeding and dying only a few yards away. The mother sheep was surrounded by the other dogs which circled her, apparently biding their time before lunging in for the kill.

Katharine reached in the saddlebag for the derringer, trying to remember everything that Micah had taught her only a short while past. She realized she only had two bullets, but maybe they would scare the dogs away.

She quickly retrieved the pistol and pulled the hammer back, then fired to the side of the dogs, as she didn't want to risk killing the ewe. The dogs momentarily stopped their attack, allowing the sheep to bound into the woods. Though several of the dogs pursued the sheep, three of them turned toward the gun blast and spied Katharine.

Though the dogs were of different breeds, they all had the same wild ferocity of feral beasts, and Katharine noted with terror the bloodlust that smoldered in their eyes, as they slunk toward her, snarling, with fangs bared. Frantically, she engaged the other bullet, knowing that this one must count, as it was her last. Pulling the hammer back with more practiced fingers, she fired point-blank at the dog in the middle and felt a mixture of relief and pain as it fell bleeding and dead before her. The other two animals fled into the woods, and Katharine seized the moment to speed her mount down the road, her shaking hands repeatedly lashing the reins against the frightened animal's neck.

Her heart beating wildly with fear that the dogs might follow, she kept the horse at a rapid pace, feeling his long neck as it curved sideways, his large, expressive eyes rolling backward. After several minutes of steady galloping, Katharine gently pulled the trembling animal to a brisk trot, attempting to calm her own shaking self, as she talked softly into his twitching ears. Taking a deep breath, she settled back in the comfortable saddle for the remaining miles, and home had never seemed so welcoming as when she saw the iron gate, with its climbing roses rambling over the gate posts, and Tillie standing on the porch, looking for her return.

Chapter Fourteen

Several days passed, following the tragically eventful day with Micah MacRae, but notwithstanding all that had happened, Katharine was looking forward to the music lesson which she taught to his daughters on Tuesdays of every week. It was Saturday morning, and she strolled around her capacious yards, observing the flowers which were beginning to bloom again.

Yellow daffodils had sprung up overnight, followed by gold and rust-colored daylilies. Climbing pink roses twined around the wrought-iron fence which encircled the yard, and dewy roses in her rose garden were ablaze in vibrant reds, yellows, whites, pinks, and corals. The scent of roses had always meant springtime to her.

The vegetable garden had green shoots, and Katharine thrilled at the idea of eating their own fresh vegetables within several weeks. Tiny green tomatoes, hard with unripeness, clustered on the staked tomato plants.

Hoofbeats on the front carriage driveway drew her attention away from the garden, and she saw a young colored boy, on an old mule, approaching her.

"Miz Fremont?" he called to her.

"Yes, I'm Mrs. Fremont."

"Mistuh MacRae, he sont me wif a message fer Miz Fremont."

"Yes, well, I'm Katharine Fremont."

"Well, he say he daughtuhs, dey doan need no mo' music lessens. He done sont me to tell you dat. He say to gib you dis."

The boy leaned down from the mule's back and handed her an envelope.

"Mistuh MacRae, he say dis be payment fer all de music lessens." Without waiting for a reply, the boy trotted the mule back to the front driveway and on through the iron gates. Tears sprang to Katharine's eyes as she fingered the envelope. She would have sent any payment back with the colored boy, but he left too fast for her to realize what he had given her. She had always refused money for the lessons, though Micah's mother always offered it to her.

Slowly, she broke the wax seal of the envelope and took out the money which she didn't want. This was proof that Micah did indeed consider her one of the hated lumber mill people, one of the enemy. She wondered whether he would even refuse to raft her timber in the fall!

They are filled with pride, these Southerners, Katharine thought, too proud to accept her free music lessons, especially now that the land war was accelerating. No, he didn't want to be beholden to anyone, much less a Northerner who had connections with the hated Yellow Pines Lumber Company.

What Micah MacRae didn't know, and what Katharine had never admitted to herself, was that his mother and children had unknowingly filled a void in her life. Katharine rarely saw her friends, including the Winslows, anymore. In fact, since Sewell Siddon was a frequent guest now at Winslow Hall, Katharine made excuses about not going there.

Also, Katharine dared not admit to herself, nor to any of her family and friends, that she was becoming increasingly undecided about the heightening land war. She was consumed with wanting to know everything about the land problems, and she felt compelled to do almost anything to find out.

Her thoughts raced on, and her steps quickened as she walked toward the back door. She had decided what to do. She would go to see Micah MacRae early Monday morning. After all, she had to know whether he still planned to raft her timber in the fall. Also, she wanted to see Abby MacRae and the children. They had become an important part of her life, and she could not bear the thought of being denied their friendship.

***

Several months passed, however, before Katharine could make the trip to the MacRae homeplace, for Tilda had become bedridden with her illness, and Katharine was afraid to leave her. In fact, before Tillie's hip gout had worsened, Katharine had planned to put her housekeeper on the train for a short visit to her home in

New York, thinking the trip would cheer her and perhaps help her to recover, but she was too ill to make the lengthy trip.

Finally, Tilda revived to the extent that she was up and about and insisting that she felt like making the trip to New York. Katharine suggested that she should leave the following day, for this would give her an extra day to gather her strength and would give Katharine time to ride to Bear Creek, and if she were lucky, to talk to Micah MacRae about rafting her timber. She wondered what his mother and children thought about her absence during the past months.

The morning had dawned clear with only a hint of the late-August heat which would follow as the day progressed. Katharine had dressed carefully, choosing a riding outfit which brought out the gold in her chestnut hair and the natural glow of her skin. The green-gold poplin hugged her small waist but flared from her hips, then followed closely the curves of her legs to her ankles. Straps from the leggings slid under the insteps of her feet which were encased in riding boots. She tied the matching hat with ribbons under her chin, and she was set for the somewhat lengthy ride to the MacRae place.

She checked the derringer, making certain the two bullets were in place. Something told her that she needed a gun capable of shooting more bullets, but she didn't know what kind it would be or where to get one. She resolved to ask Ben Winslow about it...or her father. Katharine felt guilty about her parents. They kept writing her lengthy letters, urging her to come back to New York. They even suggested that perhaps Ben Winslow, whom they personally knew, would handle the harvesting and sale of her timber for her.

As Katharine walked to the stables, her thoughts kept dwelling on her parents. They knew only smatterings of what was happening in regard to the land problems in the Georgia piney woods. Of course, Frank's death had told them that the situation had evolved from land troubles to outright war, with killings on both sides. However, things had quieted down following the murders of her husband and John Forsyth.

Beyond this, Katharine didn't know what her parents knew, and she wrote or wired them little about the escalating war. She did not want them to worry about her and she assured them that she would be home for good, following the sale of her timber in the fall.

She had told them nothing about Micah MacRae or his family or her questions in regard to the practices of the Dodges and the Yellow Pines Lumber Company. She knew they would never understand the changes which had come over her, following Frank's death. They would be upset with her for doubting for an instant the veracity of the Dodge sons, whose father had crusaded against the evils of alcoholic beverages and who never allowed anyone in his business to work on the Sabbath. No, her parents who had been staunch friends of the powerful and wealthy William E. Dodge would be heartsick if they knew what their only child had been up to during the past few months.

As she neared the stables, Big Hill led General Lee out, saddled and bridled and ready for the ride. The horse's sleek, thoroughbred body was fairly bursting with pent-up energy for the anticipated jaunt, and he lifted his hooves in quick jerks, as Katharine gracefully stepped up and into the saddle.

"Hill, I'll be back later this afternoon. By the way, I looked at the garden yesterday, and it's coming up nicely. We should have tomatoes before long. You're doing a good job, watering and looking after it."

Big Hill beamed, for he took seriously his role of gardener.

"Yes, Ma'm, ever'thin' comin' up jes' fine. Ah waters it jes' about ever' day. Ah be heah to he'p you and Miz Tilda, w'en you is ready to put up de vegta'bules fer de winter. An' speakin' ob Miz Tilda, she ain' herseff lately."

"No, Tillie isn't well. She says it's the dampness here in the South. She says her hip gout is getting worse. Anyway, she may have told you...I'm sending her home to New York for a week or so. She has a sister still living there, and some cousins she hasn't seen for awhile, so she'll be leaving by train tomorrow."

"Dat do her good."

"Yes, we'll both be going back home, once my timber is harvested, but until that time, just short trips home every few months should help us."

"You sho ain' been home in a long time, Miz Kat'rin."

"No, I have to tie up loose ends here, Hill, especially looking after my timber harvesting. Well, I'd better go. As I said, I'll be back probably late this afternoon."

Katharine flicked the reins lightly over the gray's neck and the horse eagerly lunged forward, trotting down the front carriage way and through the iron gates. The dirt road beckoned, and the horse broke into an enthusiastic gallop which brought color to Katharine's cheeks and sparkle to her eyes. The brisk ride was pleasant and Katharine let the gelding run wide open for miles on the narrow dirt road. The redolence of honeysuckle hung heavy in the air, and Katharine was aware of the beauty of the tangled plant that, each summer, crept through the piney woods and wound its yellow blooms around trees and shrubs on both sides of the shadowed pathway.

She wondered what Micah would be doing today. In spite of all that had happened, she still looked forward to seeing him. In fact, if she could recognize the truth of the matter, she yearned to see him, to talk to him, to feel his eyes on her.

"Oh, God," she prayed out loud, "let him be home."

***

It was mid-morning when Katharine arrived at the MacRae place, and she quickly dismounted and secured the horse. Abby MacRae was coming out of the door as Katharine ran up the steps. Her welcoming smile told Katharine that she either knew nothing of Micah's land troubles or, if she did know something, she refused to let it hurt her friendship with Katharine. Abby opened her arms, and Katharine went into them.

"Well, dear, it's good to see you. Micah said you wouldn't be teachin' the girls music no more, and I didn't know what to think."

So, she does know, Katharine thought.

"I'll teach them as long as you'll let me, Mrs. Abby, but I've come today to talk to Micah about my timber. Is he here?"

"He's up in the cotton fields. Just walk behind the house. You'll see a footpath that leads to the east field where he's planted an acre or two of sugar cane. The first cotton field is just beyond the cane field. You might rather ride up there. He's got ol' Jack up there today, a-plowin'. He's supposed to raft his logs to the coast. I think he said they was leavin' tomorrow."

Katharine was surprised to hear this news. Obviously, Micah had gone ahead and finished harvesting enough trees to complete a raft which he was to drift down the rivers to Darien. He would probably be gone a week or longer, depending on the weather and whether he stayed in Darien for any length of time.

"Well, I need to talk to him about my trees. You know, he's supposed to raft them for me within the next few weeks. Goodbye, Mrs. Abby. I'll come back tomorrow for the girls' lessons." She almost added not to say anything to Micah about the resumption of the music lessons, but something told her that Abby MacRae knew what to tell and what not to tell her son.

"Goodbye, Katharine. We'll look forward to seein' you tomorrow."

Katharine mounted her horse and headed for the pathway through the woods behind the house. She tried to quiet her heart which she felt would burst through her bodice, so full it was of anticipation of being with Micah MacRae, if only for a few minutes. She passed the cane field of about an acre, noticing that the rows between its tall sugarcane had already been recently plowed. The cane stood ten to twelve feet high and was green with a reddish cast, ready for harvesting. She prodded the horse on along the cool path to the cotton fields ahead.

She saw him through the trees, holding the middle-buster plow steady as the ox pulled it through the black soil. She dismounted in the woods and tied the horse to the nearest tree before walking on toward the clearing. Looking through the trees and across the acreage of square-bolled cotton plants, planted in their neat rows, she noted the creamy white flowers which presaged the stark white tufts of cotton. It would soon be ready for picking. She knew he would plow the last furrow near her, so she waited until the ox pulled directly before her to step out of the woods and into the open field.

"Whoa, there, Jack!" Micah pulled the animal to a halt before regarding her with a questioning look in his brown eyes. Katharine never realized exactly what happened next, but she must have tripped on a root which the plow had unearthed. Micah quickly released the plow and caught her as she fell directly into his arms.

Embarrassed, she struggled to stand up, but he lifted her and held her, squirming, against him. His arms were like steel bars across her back, and she had difficulty breathing. What was he doing? She had longed to be in his arms. Of that, she was guilty. But not like this. She wanted tenderness, not this roughness. What in the world was he thinking, to treat her like this? He released his grip somewhat, allowing her to breathe large gulps of air, but still holding her against him.

"What are you doing? You have no right to treat me like this! Let me go!"

Without any explanation, his arms slackened and his hands moved over her body. He pulled her again to him gently, and his mouth was hot against hers, his tongue tasting her lips.

Katharine realized she had never really known, until now, what being with a man meant. She had heard women complain about their wifely duties, and she had always been taught that only loose women enjoyed the physical side of marriage. Rather, she had inferred an active disdain for such from the women she had known in her family, and she had unknowingly modeled her own thinking on the subject from these inhibitions which had been passed down from generations. What would these members of her family think of her, if they knew that she longed for this man's touch, for the sensations which coursed through her body in such a pleasant way?

Yet, something was wrong. Something was terribly wrong. He was holding her again in that strange way, lifting her up, pinioning her against him. Then, just as suddenly, he dropped her and turned his back to her, his hands on his hips, his elbows jutting outward. Katharine heard herself whimper and she involuntarily raised the back of her hand to her mouth. When he turned back to face her, arms at his side, his face was a contortion of murderous rage. Katharine stifled a scream.

"What is it? Why do you look at me like that?" Her voice broke.

"Because you're a part of 'em, the thievin' Yellow Pines Lumber Mill!"

"Micah, I'm trying to understand what's going on. I'm confused. Frank never told me anything."

"You're tryin' to understand what's goin' on, huh?" His brown eyes with flecks of gold were unbelieving. "While ago, I took advantage of you. I could have easily stripped off your clothes and taken you there on the ground. But, you see, Ma'm, we Southerners have some honor, or decency, or whatever you want to call it, that you Northerners just don't have. Otherwise, you folks wouldn't be here, a-tryin' to take somethin' by force that don't belong to you!"

"I tell you, I'm trying to understand. Mr. Dodge was a friend of my father's. He was a Prohibitionist and a Christian man."

"That long word just means he was against whiskey, and if he was a Christian man, then he knew for a fact that Jesus' first miracle was turnin' the water into wine. And if he was serious about 'is religion, then he knew what the Lord said about those who steal from others."

"Believe me, Micah, when I say that I've never had any of this explained to me. Frank never told me anything, and only since his death have I realized that I have got to find out for myself what's going on. No one else seems to be able to explain it to me."

"You want an explanation? You really want to know what's goin' on? I want to show you somethin' that just might help to explain things." His voice was sarcastic, and Katharine yearned for the tenderness he had shown toward her earlier.

"I'm through a-plowin' for the day. Get on your horse and follow me back to the barn. I'll bring ol' Jack and pen 'im up, then hitch the mule to the wagon, and I want to show you somethin'! You want an explanation? I've got one for you!"

Katharine dutifully followed him back to the barn where she tethered the gelding and watched Micah hitch his docile mule to the old wagon. She had never ridden on a wagon, but knew from the looks of it that it would be an open, bumpy ride.

What was he about to show her? Her skin fairly prickled with anticipation and a certain dread. She was finally about to learn some great truth about the land war.

The ride was even more bumpy and jostling than she had guessed it would be, and often she was unseated and thrown against Micah, as he guided the mule over sandy trails which led deeper into his forested homestead. If she had been alone, she would have been afraid, as she had left the derringer in her saddlebag.

She saw that Micah had a gun strapped around his waist, and even if he were without a weapon, she had to acknowledge that she felt safe with him. However, the pistol definitely made her feel even more secure. She wondered what kind of weapon it was and how many bullets it would shoot.

Strange, she thought. A year ago, she would never have even thought about a gun, and now she not only carried one with her wherever she went, but also she was interested in finding a more useful one than the two-bullet derringer she had. She sighed. Such was life here in the piney woods of Georgia!

The trail led them ever farther into the thick woods, and Katharine realized they were nearing the clearing floor, where she had witnessed logchopping and attempted land confiscation only a few days prior. She noticed the several seed trees which Micah had left along the borders of his land lots. They were perfect specimens of longleaf yellow pine, reaching over a hundred feet into the open blue sky. She remembered his explaining to her during their first meeting at the lumber company that such seed trees would be left to replenish the stump-laden wiregrass with future pine seedlings. This was the only method known to restore the depleted forests. She was gradually beginning to understand the meaning of a few good seed trees.

Micah turned off onto another woods path, and before long, she could see a small clearing through the large trees. A small, one-room shack, of sorts, appeared to be built up on stilts.

"What is that?" she innocently inquired.

"That, my dear Miz Fremont, is a pole shanty, and you'll find 'em scattered throughout the piney woods. It's what your friends, William E. Dodge and sons, have brought about. You see, when they take someone's land, where do the people go, and how do they live? Well, they go where someone will let them go, and they live the best way they can!"

Micah pulled the mule to a halt, and Katharine uneasily surveyed the tragic scene beyond the edge of the woods. She had never seen a pole shanty, had never even heard of one.

Children's playful cries drew her attention, and she counted five children, all appearing to be under the age of nine or ten years, taking turns swinging on a large rope, knotted at the end, which hung from a tree. Beyond the children, she could see a vegetable patch which a thin, haggard-looking woman was hoeing.

Micah was speaking, "That's Maude Ivey. She and Pete were thrown off their land by your friend, Mr. Dodge, last year. They asked me if they could use a little corner of my land to put up a pole house. There's a spring nearby, so they don't need a well. My mama takes clothes and food to them. Pete stays sick all the time. Maude has a hard time, but you never hear her complain. Come on. I want you two ladies to meet. Giddyup there, Doll!"

Maude heard them coming and stopped hoeing, looking toward them with her hand over her forehead like a salute, shielding her eyes from the bright sun. The children crowded around the halted wagon.

"Maude, I want you to meet someone."

"All right. I'll just put down my hoe and rest a minute. How are you a-doin', Micah?" Maude, her coarse and ragged brown dress covered with dirt from the pea patch, made her way over to the wagon, looking from Micah to Katharine. Her thinness was such that her skin barely covered her bones. Micah was again speaking, while Katharine attempted to recover from the terrible shock which she had felt when she first saw the spindly pole shanty and realized that it was home to seven people.

"Oh, I'm fair to tolerable, I guess. Maude, I want you to meet Miz Fremont, Miz Katharine Fremont."

Maude raised her head in greeting, showing a toothless smile.

"It's nice to meet you, Miz Fremont."

"A pleasure to meet you, Maude. You have some precious children."

Maude positively glowed at this and picked up the youngest one, a little girl around the age of two.

"Thank you, Miz Fremont. They're my whole life - them and Pete."

As if hearing his name mentioned, Pete appeared at the door of the shanty, his body stooped from the waist.

"Howdy, Micah."

"How is ever'thin', Pete?"

"Could be better, but I won't complain. I got a good wife and good young'uns."

"Pete, this is Miz Fremont. I'm a-goin' to do some log raftin' for her."

"Hidy-do, Miz Fremont. Well...you picked the best man to raft your trees, Ma'm."

"So I've heard," Katharine said with a smile.

Turning to the business at hand and ignoring Katharine's presence, Micah looked from Maude to Pete and said, "I guess you heard that Dodge is claimin' my land as his, too."

The reality of their own situation had not yet registered with the displaced family.

"No, Micah," Pete said, slowly. "We ain't heard that. What you gonna do?"

"Well, it looks like I gotta answer to a court summons, sometime in September. All the land cases are bein' a-tried now in federal court, and we don't stand a chance. When they were tried in state court, Dodge and his group would sometimes lose, because Georgia judges and jurors would just about always rule in our favor, but now that they're a-bein' tried in federal court, we don't have a chance. When that fella Dodge gets through with cuttin' down all the trees here in the piney woods, all we're gonna have left is a lotta big stumps and wiregrass!" Micah paused, looking around at his surrounding, virginal forest which hadn't yet felt the invasive blows of the Northern timber company's large broadaxes and newfangled skidder.

"Maude and Pete," he continued, "I just want you to be thinkin' of where you might go, because whatever happens to me and my land will also affect you."

"What will you do, Micah?" Maude's face, old with worry and the day-to-day struggle for survival, was heartbreaking to see, and Katharine looked away.

"Well, I don't rightly know yet just what I'll do. I'm leavin' tomorrow, takin' some of my logs to Darien. After I get back, I'll finish with my crops. I planted more this year, since I'll need the money."

"What you got planted? I seen the cotton over here near us. What else you got planted?"

"I planted cotton, corn, sweet potatoes, peanuts, melons, sugar cane, oats, vegetables, and cowpeas. Joe Little and his boys are goin' on halves with me, so I can take my logs to Darien and finish cutting Miz Fremont's trees, too, when I can find the time."

"We'll help you, when you get back from Darien. Our older ones can help, too," Maude said, nodding toward the larger children. "They usually help me with my hoein', but I told 'em they could play today. You ain't a child but oncet."

"Well, we'll be gettin' back. I'll probably be gone a week with the raft. I'll depend on you folks, then, to help us with the crops when I get back."

"We'll be there, Micah. You all be careful on that raft." Maude put down the youngest child she had been holding throughout the conversation. She and Pete and the five children all waved farewell, as Micah turned the mule around, and they entered the woods trail for the trip back to his barn. Katharine was silent, and Micah finally turned to look at her.

"Well," he said, "do you understand the situation about the land problems a little better, Miz Fremont?" Katharine wondered why he was now formally calling her "Mrs. Fremont," as though he hadn't kissed her sometime earlier. She turned to look at him, and her deep blue eyes met his impenetrable brown ones. In the shadows of the forest, his eyes had lost their gold flecks, and they seemed to be opaque, she thought. He put his large hand on her hands which she held in her lap, and his fingers were like a metal vise.

He has such anger, she thought, and she really didn't know how to respond to his question or to his grip which was so tight, it hurt. She made an attempt to answer him.

"Micah, of course, it's terrible, but I know if I talked to Ben Winslow or any of the timber mill people, they would explain it all in a different way. The truth has to be somewhere in the middle."

At this, Micah pulled the wagon to a halt and jumped to the ground. Ignoring her startled look, he reached over and pulled her to the ground beside him. A mutual anger welled inside her at his ragdoll treatment of her.

His hands held her shoulders, and his breathing was deep and ragged.

"You can't tell me, Miz Fremont, that you could look at Maude and Pete and their young'uns, and the pole shanty they call home, and not realize what a monster your friend Dodge is!"

"Micah, please calm down." She pulled both of his hands from her shoulders, then stepped back several feet.

"I intend to help Maude and her family. I'm glad you brought me there today."

"How old are you, Katharine?" The direct question, with its change of subject, confused and somewhat embarrassed her.

"Why do you ask?"

"How old are you? Tell me."

"I'm thirty-two, but why do you want to know?"

"Because Maude is your age, but she looks thirty years older. Women here in the wiregrass ain't young for many years. And, women whose land and homes have been taken from them age overnight."

He drew near to her and she smelled the leather of his clothes and the slight tobacco odor on his breath. She trembled as his rough hands cupped her face and turned it up to him.

His mouth was on hers again, but this time, she resisted and pulled away. His fingers followed the lines of her face, and their eyes met, as he pulled her to him again.

"Miz Fremont, you're a beautiful woman!"

Katharine's heart melted within her at these words, but not for long. His anger which she had experienced before returned, and he ordered her back to the wagon, roughly assisting her as she climbed up. He jumped up himself and briskly flicked the reins over the mule's broad back. Both were silent for some time. Finally, Katharine spoke.

"I intend to help them, too, Micah."

"What?"

"I have clothes for Maude, and I still have Frank's clothes in an armoire. Of course, they're mostly suits, but maybe Pete can wear them."

It was Micah's turn to be silent. He didn't speak until they could see the barn and the gelding waiting for her. Then, he surprised her by answering the question which she hadn't yet had the opportunity to ask.

"I been a-cuttin' your trees all along, and I plan to start a-raftin' 'em sometime in September. I'm gonna need more men to help though, with the cuttin' and the raftin'."

"I've talked to some of the woodchoppers in the colored settlement near Gum Swamp, and I think you'll find some there who will help you." Katharine did not tell him how she had inadvertently won over the four loggers, after they found out she had helped in saving the life of Rhody. Big Hill had told her all about how the colored hands had been astonished that a white lady - and a Northern one, at that - had come in the dark of night to help one of their own.

Micah's face registered surprise that she would have actually gone to the colored district with such a request. Perhaps, he thought, she did not realize just how dangerous the times were.

"Miz Fremont, let me give you some advice. A good many of those colored people near the mill settlements came from North Carolina. In the first place, they ain't local colored people. In the second place, a white lady don't need to be a-ridin' alone, period! You're gonna get yourself killed or worse!"

"I have no choice, Mr. MacRae. I'm a widow. I'm strong. I can look after myself. Besides, I have my gun, remember?"

A flicker of admiration for her courage, mingled with exasperation at the risks she had taken in going to the colored settlement, appeared briefly in his brown eyes.

"That 'gun' you keep tellin' me about ain't much protection. Two bullets won't help much."

Katharine's memory was instantly jolted back to the episode with the wild dogs, and she didn't realize that her face reflected the terror she had felt. His hands were again at her shoulders, shaking her.

"What were you a-thinkin'? What made you look that way?"

"You remember telling me about the wild dogs? Well, I saw a pack of them near your land and I killed one of them. They were after some sheep and they killed a little lamb right in front of me. I think the bullets scared them away."

"That passel of dogs stays close to Camp Six. Every camp has trouble with dogs. They roam through the woods and kill sheep and hogs and anything else they come across. They'll track a man walkin' a back road. You were lucky they didn't follow you. I'm not goin' to say, 'I told you so,' but now you see what I mean about it bein' dangerous for you to ride alone. Here, I want to give you somethin'."

Before she could wonder what he was about to give her, he had unbuckled the weapon from the leather strap around his waist.

"Here, I want you to use this. I'll a-take it back when you head back to New York, after your trees are sold. Didn't you say you were leavin' these parts, after your trees are sold?"

"Yes, but, I really can't accept this. I..."

"I'm not givin' it to you - just lettin' you use it."

Katharine was momentarily touched, though she knew that, to him, she was just another helpless female, another Maude, for whom he felt compassion, as the strong occasionally felt for the weak. After all, he had mentioned her returning to New York in the fall. Certainly, neither of them had thoughts about any relationship, other than a business one. However, the memory of his mouth on hers made her wonder about his intentions. She was as guilty as he, for she had not resisted.

She reached out to accept the gun which was heavy and unwieldy in her hands. In fact, she could barely lift it, much less cock and fire it. What had seemed not very large, around his waist and in his large hands, was impossible for her to hold and use.

"I appreciate your concern, but as you see, it's just too large for me."

"So it is, I guess," Micah said as he smiled and strapped the pistol around his waist again.

"It's a Colt six-shooter. It'd give you four more bullets before reloadin'. I just can't stress enough how careful you - or any woman - should be. You need to carry extra bullets with you and you need to practice reloadin' 'em."

"I know. I have extra ones in the saddlebag, and I have practiced, a little, reloading them." She reached in the saddlebag and brought out some money which she held toward Micah.

"Please give this to Maude. I'll be bringing some clothes later. Well, I must go." Micah stashed the money in his saddlebag, then untied the horse and helped her into the saddle.

"I'm sure Maude will be grateful for any help you give her. She and Pete can sure use the money."

"I hope you have a safe trip to Darien."

"Thanks, Katharine. You be careful, hear?"

"I will." Katharine turned General Lee toward the dirt road, and the horse quickly broke into a trot. She looked back before rounding the corner of the yard and saw Micah standing there, looking at her. She waved and he waved back, still looking, as she left the yard and entered the hard-packed dirt road. When she looked back the second time, she could see nothing but the huge pines between them. The strength that she had felt in his presence began slipping away from her with every thud of the horse's hooves, and she checked the thick part of the saddlebag for the derringer, feeling reassured that it was there.

The trip home, however, was uneventful, and she relaxed somewhat in the saddle. The events of the day crowded her thoughts, and a smile tugged at the corners of her mouth, parting her lips and shining in her eyes, when she remembered that Micah MacRae had told her that she was beautiful.

Chapter Fifteen

The following day brought the heavy smell of rain in the air, as Katharine made preparations for the trip to the MacRae house. However, her first concern was to drive Tilda to the train depot at Helena and to see her board the afternoon train for the first leg of her lengthy rail journey to New York. Katharine had decided that Tilda should take the new S.A.M. train to Savannah. It stopped for passengers in Helena. She would avoid a six-hour delay in Jesup by doing this. However, this meant a two-hour, or better, carriage trip to Helena. Katharine knew this would make her own arrival at the MacRae homeplace close to nightfall.

Tilda had recurringly suffered from bouts of homesickness and other ailments, especially since Frank's death and the acceleration of the land war, and Katharine hoped that the trip home would help her aging housekeeper and friend to recuperate. They prepared to leave following the midday meal. Both of them carried rainproof coats because of the likelihood of rain.

Tilda had a small array of boxes and bags which Katharine helped her carry to the front porch. Big Hill had hitched General Lee to the phaeton carriage, and he led the prancing horse onto the circular driveway in front of the house, stopping in front of the wide front steps. He placed all of the boxes and bags in the break, hitched to two draft horses, as he was to follow Katharine and Tilda to the train depot with Tilda's baggage. He assisted Katharine and Tilda as they stepped up to the carriage seat.

Katharine remembered that Abby MacRae had suggested that she stay with her and the children while Micah was away on the raft, but she had not definitely decided what to do. However, she felt she should let Hill know that she might be gone for several days, though she hadn't packed any clothes for such a possibility.

"Hill, I may be gone for several days, or maybe longer. If I do decide to stay with the MacRae family, I'll probably come back and pack some clothes. However, you might be gone, so I thought it best to let you know, just in the event you're not here when I return."

"You jes' be careful, Miz Kat'rin. Yas'm. Ah be comin' and goin', an' Ah look aftuh de place. And Miz Tilda, Ah sho hopes you feels better. Mebbe dis trip do you good."

"Thank you, Hill," Tilda whispered with a sigh. "Yes, I'm looking forward to going home."

Katharine flicked the reins over the gray's long neck, and the horse began a slow trot down the brick driveway. She reached back and checked her purse for the loaded derringer. It was there, along with extra bullets, and she felt safer, just knowing it was nearby. Also, she felt better, having someone with her for the ride but dreaded being alone again, once Tilda boarded the train at Helena.

When the horse reached the hard-packed dirt road, Katharine noticed that Tilda winced every time the carriage bounced over the wheel ruts, and she did her best to guide the carriage, so that the wheels followed the established grooves.

"I'm sorry you aren't feeling well, Tillie, and I know the bumps in the road don't help any. Is it your hip gout again?"

"O-o-oh, yes, Miss Katharine, and every time the carriage shifts, I feel worse and worse."

"I'm trying to stay in the wheel paths, so maybe we won't bump around so much. I think it'll be good for you to go home and see your sister and your cousins. I almost wish I were going with you."

"You ain't been home in a long time, Miss Katharine. I wish you would go with me."

"Don't think I haven't thought about it, Tillie. I keep getting letters from Mother and Father, begging me to come home, but it won't be too long before we'll both be going home for good - just a few more months. I believe we should be home before Christmas. I've just got to see about my timber. I'm trying to find out everything I can about it, so I'll know what's going on. You know, I don't know anything about business, and I'm having a time, just trying to find someone I can trust to help me."

"I know you've had a time, Miss Katharine. I've been a widder all these years, and it ain't been easy." Tilda flinched with pain, as the carriage wheels jumped the ruts and then fell back into the deep furrows.

Lightning streaked across the sky, visible above the tops of the waving pine forests on both sides of the road. Thunder followed, and soon raindrops began pelting the carriage top. Katharine and Tilda hurriedly pulled on their rainproof coats. Katharine quickly tugged the weather-proof lap robe from the inside of the dashboard and spread it across their legs, so as to keep their dresses from being soaked. She wondered how far behind them Big Hill was and whether he had remembered to wear the weatherproof coat she had bought for him.

The wind grew stronger, and the pine branches reached across the three-path road, almost touching the carriage. The rapid lightning and ensuing thunder made the rain-drenched horse uneasy, as he pulled the phaeton down the road which had turned to mud.

Katharine and Tilda huddled under the carriage apron, attempting to deflect the rain from themselves. Finding the well-traveled ruts in the road was increasingly difficult, and Katharine allowed the horse to pull the carriage without her guidance, thinking that horse sense was better under such circumstances. The rain poured for many miles, and the women attempted to console each other with light conversation.

"I reckon our garden'll be coming up for sure by the time I get back. This rain ought to help it along." This was the second planting of vegetables, the first garden having already been harvested and put up under Tilda's and Big Hill's experienced supervision.

"Yes, you and Hill are doing a great job."

Katharine's thoughts kept returning to her parents.

"Tillie, I hope you see my parents while you're there."

"Yes, you know my sister helps your mum now, Miss Katharine, and the days she works, I can go with her. It'll be like old times, helping your parents again, and I'll give them any news you want me to."

"Just tell them, Tillie, that I have an overseer to help with my trees, and I should be coming home before Christmas."

"I'll sure tell them, Miss Katharine, and I know they'll be happy when all this is over and you're back home for good."

"Tillie?" Katharine had debated whether to request something of her housekeeper.

"Yes, Miss Katharine?"

"Please do something for me, Tillie. Please don't tell my parents about all the frightening things that have happened to us here. I will tell them myself, some day, but now they would only worry."

"I've thought about the same thing, Miss Katharine. No, I won't say a word about the Ku Klux Klan or anything. It would just upset them, and they're a thousand miles away."

"Thanks. I knew I could count on you," Katharine said.

Each of them became immersed in her own thoughts, as the rain slackened to only a few large drops for the next several miles, then returned as a light shower which continued all the way to Helena.

The train station was just ahead, and from the sparse assortment of conveyances which were parked or leaving the vicinity, only a small number of people were waiting inside for the train. The rain had stopped, and Katharine was thankful for that, as she guided the horse to a mounting block at the depot. She and Tilda had removed their rainproof coats, and Katharine spread them and the lap robe to dry while they waited on the train.

As they stepped from the carriage, they spotted Big Hill arriving in the break with Tillie's luggage. After securing the horse, Katharine turned to speak to the old driver who had pulled up to them and inquired whether he should carry Tilda's baggage into the depot.

"Yes, Hill," Katharine said, "that will be fine. We'll probably have to wait awhile for the train. It won't be necessary for you to wait, Hill. You can take the break on back home. The porter will help us with Tilda's luggage."

"Yas'm. Ah sho do dat, Miz Kat'rin," Hill said, as he reached into the break and grabbed all but several small packages of Tilda's assortment of baggage. He headed on into the depot, followed by Tilda and Katharine who carried the remaining pieces. Katharine was pleased to see that he wore the weatherproof coat she had purchased for him. He obviously was so proud of it, he still wore it, in spite of the fact that the rain had ceased, and it was a warm day. Once his mission was accomplished, he muttered his goodbyes again to the two ladies and walked slowly back to the break. Climbing up to the driver's seat, he popped his whip and turned around the horses for the trip home.

Inside the depot, they walked into the "White Only" waiting room, and Katharine thought how those two words still denied the Negro true freedom, one of the central issues over which men lost their lives during four long years of war, some thirty years before. With Tillie and her baggage deposited on one of the wood benches, Katharine walked to the office window to purchase her housekeeper a ticket.

The depot was hot and humid, and Katharine found herself feeling sad about the whole situation. Micah was gone, Tillie was going, and though she felt like weeping, she knew she had to cheer up, or else she would upset Tillie.

"One ticket to New York City, please," she requested of the ticket agent. As the agent handed her the ticket and she gave him the money for it, she inquired how long it would be before the train arrived.

"Well, Ma'm, they just telegraphed us that they're runnin' a little behind schedule."

"Thank you, sir."

Katharine noticed that the telegraph operator appeared to be receiving a wire, so she walked over to him.

"Sir, is the train still running late?" she asked.

"Well, they just now wired me, and they're makin' better time now than they first thought. They say it'll be maybe an hour late now." As if offering an explanation for the few people waiting to board the train, he added, "Guess the rain has kept a lot of people away today. They're stayin' home, tryin' to keep dry!"

"I suppose so. Well, if you hear anything different, will you let me know?"

"Yes, Ma'm. I sure will."

"Thank you," Katharine sighed, as she turned and made her way back to the waiting room, where Tillie was seated.

"It'll be a short wait, Tillie - maybe an hour," she said."

"Well, no need grumbling. Guess they're doing the best they can." Tillie managed a half smile, and Katharine knew she was trying not to complain and not to worry her.

The day wore on, and the heat and dampness became even more oppressive in the depot. Finally, they heard the whistle before they actually saw the locomotive, but it was soon followed by the train itself, and Katharine and Tillie made their way outside, each holding various boxes and bags.

The porter jumped from the train and immediately began gathering Tilda's baggage, while the two women said their last goodbyes. As they embraced, each saw tears in the other's eyes.

"Now, you take care, Miss Katharine. It's dangerous for you to ride alone so much. You know, I've been telling you that."

"I know, Tillie, but it's something I have to do sometimes. I will be careful, though. Remember to give everyone my love, and tell them that I'll be home before Christmas, for sure."

"I will. Goodbye, Miss Katharine."

"Goodbye, Tillie." Katharine waited while the porter showed Tillie her baggage which he had placed above her seat. Tillie was seated and she proceeded to wave to Katharine, as the train chugged from the station. Katharine couldn't remember when she had felt so alone, and when the tears began spilling from her eyes, she turned her head, so that Tillie would not see. Dabbing quickly at them, she made herself smile as she turned back to the departing train. Tillie was looking back and waving, and Katharine threw up her hand in a final wave, as the passenger car rounded the bend out of sight.

Drops of rain were falling again, and Katharine opened the parasol and walked back to the hitching post, where the horse and carriage were waiting. She freed the horse, then gathered the reins and climbed onto the carriage seat.

"Let's go, General Lee. We surely don't want to be on the road after dark."

Chapter Sixteen

Katharine arrived at the MacRae homeplace at dusk. She was weary from the trip and from the melancholy of bidding farewell to Tilda, her only link to the life she had known in New York. The thick pine woods which rose before her in every direction were especially oppressive, as she drove the carriage on to the barn where she intended to leave it during her short visit of a day or so.

She eased down from the driver's seat and set about the unfamiliar task of unhitching the horse from the carriage. How she missed Big Hill and the way he looked after such things for her! Hearing footsteps, she turned to see Abby MacRae, lantern in hand, coming toward her, smiling and calling out to her.

"Katharine, dear, I'd just about given you out, thinkin' you decided not to come, after all."

"I think the rain slowed down everything, Mrs. Abby. You know, I had to drive Tilda, my housekeeper, to the train depot at Helena. She hasn't been well lately, so I made arrangements for her to go back home to New York."

"Well, I know that's a long ways to New York. I ain't never been there, but I heard tell of it. Well, the girls are waitin' up to see you. It's too late for a music lesson. I done told the girls that. That'll wait till tomorrow."

Abby hung the lantern on the barn gate and helped Katharine finish the process of unhitching the horse from the carriage. Katharine then pulled a blanket from the carriage and began rubbing down the gelding, which seemed to bring some relief to the exhausted animal.

"There's oats inside the barn, and I don't know of a horse that don't like oats. 'Course, there's water, too." Abby MacRae smiled and lifted the crossbar of the barn gate, and the horse languidly clopped inside the barnyard.

"Come on, dear, it's almost dark. I saved supper for you." Abby retrieved the lantern and held it before her, then put her right arm across Katharine's shoulders in a motherly gesture, drawing her to her.

"I know you're dead tired. You made a long trip today."

"Yes, it was exhausting, and it was also sad for me to see Tillie go. She's my housekeeper, but she's more than that. She just helps me in so many ways and I know I shall miss her." Tears filled her eyes as she spoke and she was glad for the mantle of darkness which shielded them from Abby's gentle eyes. "I want you and the children to meet her when she comes back."

"Well, dear, the chill'un and me, we want you to stay with us while Micah's on the river. Sometimes, he's gone a week and longer."

"Did you know, Mrs. Abby, that I neglected to pack clothes for myself? I was so involved with helping Tillie pack, and I just didn't pack anything for myself. But I'll only stay a night or two, and I can sleep in my chemise."

"Never you worry about not packin' for yourself. Why, the chifforobe in Micah's room is still full of Jenny's clothes, and I reckon you are about the size she was when she died."

Katharine stiffened at the thought of wearing the dead woman's clothes. They had reached the back porch, and Abby shooed Katharine on up the steps ahead of her.

The dogtrot which ran through the middle of the double-pen house was dark, except for the lantern light which shifted with Abby's every movement.

"Come on. Little Roy's asleep in the crib in my bedroom, but the girls are a-waitin' for you in the front room."

Giggles and whispers issued from the front room. When Abby opened the door, Carrie and Mary Sue MacRae rushed across the wood floor to give Katharine a hug.

"We thought you wasn't comin'," Mary Sue said, holding on to Katharine's skirts and looking up at her."

"Papa said no more piano lessons 'cause he ain't got no money for such." Carrie's face was crestfallen.

"Well, as I've heard your grandmother say many times,

'Where there's a will, there's a way.' If you girls want to learn music, then I'll teach you."

The girls hugged Katharine again and with an arm around each of them, she heeded Abby's invitation to sit on the old settee, across from the piano.

Abby set the lantern on a nearby table and then sat in the wooden rocking chair near the settee. Rocking slowly, she spoke quietly to the girls.

"You two can stay up just a few more minutes. Then, it's bedtime. Miz Katharine is tired from her long trip today and I know she's ready to get some rest, too."

The girls were full of conversation.

"What did you see on your trip, Miz Katharine? Any bears?" Mary Sue leaned forward to hear.

Katharine smiled, "No, I've never seen a bear around here, though I know they're in the woods. I did see some deer and rabbits and racoons and opossums. Also, a number of squirrels. Near Longview, a bobcat dashed across the road ahead of me. He was gone in a flash!"

Carrie continued the line of conversation.

"What about a catamount? Did you hear any?"

"No, I'm not sure just what a catamount sounds like, but I think I heard a wolf howl a few miles from here."

Abby stopped her rocking.

"Micah says there's a wolf that's taken up here. He's found some of his hogs and sheep killed, and he says they kill different from the wild dogs. I been hearin' a wolf howl at night for the last few nights, and I think he's a-stayin' on our land."

Icy shivers crept up Katharine's spine, for she realized that other women, such as Abby MacRae, had to fight the lonely battles of fear without men to help and protect, just as she did. However, she hadn't had to worry about wolves and she wondered how people in the backwoods coped with them. Before she could ask, Abby stood up, slightly yawning, and ordered the girls to bed.

"Tomorrow is my spinnin' day. Miz Katharine can teach you two about piano music in the mornin'. Then, maybe you girls can help me finish up the spinnin' in the afternoon."

"I'll help, too, Mrs. Abby." Katharine had never spun wool, but she would willingly help Micah's mother with anything. She and her family always bought wool clothing, ready-made, and she couldn't imagine actually having to spin the wool, then having to make the clothes.

Abby smiled. "We'll see how everythin' goes tomorrow. I may be able to finish, myself. Carrie is comin' along. She's a pretty good spinner to be as young as she is, and Mary Sue has tried, but she needs a little more practice." She turned to her granddaughters. "Now, off to bed."

The girls walked over and kissed their grandmother goodnight. Carrie asked one final question. "How long before Papa's home from the river? We don't never see him no more."

"It might be a week - could be longer," Abby replied.

"Will he bring back a lot of money?" This was asked laughingly by Mary Sue, and the question brought smiles to the others' faces.

"Hope so," Abby said, and again she admonished the girls to go to bed.

"Goodnight, Miz Katharine."

"We're glad you're stayin' with us, Miz Katharine."

"I'm looking forward to it. Goodnight. I'll see you in the morning."

"'Night." The two girls reluctantly left the room, and Abby stirred herself to get Katharine's supper.

"I know you're hungry, dear." Abby picked up the lantern. "Let's go on out to the kitchen. I left somethin' on the table for you." Katharine knew this meant a walk across the yard to the kitchen which was separate from the house, and she couldn't help but wonder whether the wolf was nearby. However, noting that Abby didn't see any danger, she followed her out to the kitchen. She was hungry, and the food, though cold, was inviting. The plate had ham, peas, corn, and cornbread on it, which she ate with relish. She looked around the kitchen with its clay floor, in the dim light of the kerosene lantern, thinking that this was where Micah MacRae ate his meals when he was home.

"Mrs. Abby, this is refreshing. I didn't realize I was so hungry!"

"Yes, and I know you're tired, too, Katharine. I've changed the bedclothes in Micah's room, and you can sleep there for the time you're here. We got an important church meetin' comin' up this Sunday, and we'd like for you to go with us."

"Where do you go to church, Mrs. Abby?"

"Oh, we go to the Primitive Baptist Church in Helena, dear - have ever since I can remember. I'm worried about Micah, though. He ain't been to church much since all these land squabbles began, and I'm wonderin' when he'll ever come back. He shouldn't raft logs on Sunday. We got a sayin' in the piney woods that says, 'A Sabbath well spent brings a week of content...And strength for the toil of the morrow...But a Sabbath profaned, whatsoever gained...Is a certain forerunner of sorrow.' I know it takes a week or longer to raft all those logs, though, and I'm sure the Lord knows when the old ox is in the ditch and it's a case of havin' to raft on the Lord's day, sometimes."

Katharine wondered whether Micah's mother knew about his meetings with local people at other churches, but she wasn't about to mention this to Abby. Katharine was unfamiliar with the Primitive Baptist denomination, and she looked forward to going with Abby and the children on Sunday. She finished the meal and rose to wipe out the plate. Abby took it from her and placed it in a pan of water where she washed and dried it, along with the fork, knife, spoon, and glass, which Katharine had used. Then, drying her hands, she picked up the lantern and the two of them walked back across the yard to the house.

Inside the house once more, they walked down the dog run until they came to a closed door near the large front room. Abby opened the door and motioned for Katharine to enter. Katharine wondered what Micah would think if he knew she were going to sleep in his room, in his bed. She observed the simplicity of the room, as Abby set about pulling the covers back, and noted that water was in the washbowl on the dresser with clean, though threadbare, towels and washrags.

"Goodnight, dear, hope you rest good. We'll see you in the mornin', and you just sleep as long as you want to. You're tired and you need to rest."

"Thank you, Mrs. Abby. I'm looking forward to a good night's sleep." Abby found a candlestick and lit the candle for Katharine before leaving with the lantern.

"If you need anythin'," she said, " I'm right down the hall, and the girls' room is across from this one."

"Oh, I'll be fine. Goodnight."

"Goodnight, dear."

Abby left, and the room was in semi-darkness as Katharine undressed. She sat on the bed which had a cornshuck mattress. Probably one which Abby had made herself, she thought. She had never slept on a cornshuck mattress, and she wondered what her friends in the timber company and her friends and family in New York would think, if they knew where she was at this particular moment. The thought made her almost laugh out loud, as she crawled between the rough and frayed homespun sheets. Faint scents of tanned leather and tobacco wafted from the bed, and they reminded her of Micah as she drifted off to sleep.

***

She was dreaming surely, she thought, but then the bloodcurdling howl came again, mingled with the pitiful baaing of a young lamb. Katharine sat up straight in the bed. The room was pitch black, the candle having burned to the bottom of the wick. There it was again, a howling, a bleating, and now the frantic barking of the hound which always greeted her from under the MacRae's front porch. The howl was unmistakable, though Katharine had never had experience with such, other than hearing it the day before, but she knew it had to be the wolf. Did it have one of the MacRae sheep? Was it nearby, under the window?

She knew there were open places in the wood floor of the room, and she wondered whether the wolf might be able to chew through the wood to one of them in the house. Oh, for a man to help them! Why did Micah go off and leave his family to fend for themselves in his absence? She knew the answer, of course. He did it to make money for them, but they were surely left defenseless. She felt herself quivering, as the enraged howling continued, blending with the anguished cries of the sheep. She felt her way over to the unused candlestick which Abby had left her, in the event she needed some light before daybreak. She felt on the dresser for a match and lit the candle, glad to have light to dispel the darkness.

Hearing a knock at the door, she said, "Come in," and Abby MacRae entered the room with a candle on a stick.

"It looks like Micah's done caught the wolf. He's got a wolf pit out near the sugar field. He tied a lamb there on the middle part, before he left yesterday, so the wolf is most likely in the pit. Brownie's out there at the pit, too. I can hear 'im barkin'. Just try to go back to sleep. I'll see about it in the mornin'."

"But, what will you do about a live wolf, Mrs. Abby?"

"Why, I'll have to kill it. I got a shotgun. It was my husband's, and I shoot it when I have to. That wolf's not goin' anywhere. It's a eight-foot pit, so he'll be there in the mornin'. I just wanted to let you know what it was, so you wouldn't be upset." Katharine marveled at the calmness of the older woman, standing there in her coarse night clothes, with her gray hair freed from the harsh bun and spilling about one side of her neck.

"Yes, I had guessed it was the wolf, but I didn't know anything about the pit. I feel better, knowing it's not likely to get into the house."

"No, it might make a racket all night, but it won't bother nothin'. Just try to go back to sleep, and I am, too. Goodnight. I'll see you at breakfast in the mornin'."

Katharine sighed and yawned, "Goodnight. Mrs. Abby, will you blow out my candle, please?" Abby obliged, then carried her own candle back through the door which she closed behind her. The black silence of the night was again and again shattered by the doleful howls of the trapped wolf and the quieter bleating of the sheep. The dog appeared to have gone to sleep, as his barking became more infrequent as the night wore on.

Katharine rose early and noticed that Abby had laid out a dress for her to wear - one of Jenny's, she guessed. It was a plain cotton dress without even pockets to alter its severity, and the scant fabric without pantaloons or petticoats made the dress almost straight as it draped over a chair.

A long, mournful howl broke the stillness of the morning and Katharine felt shaky, envisioning the wolf in the nearby pit.

Obviously, Abby hadn't disposed of it and Katharine wondered whether this would be the first order of the day. She dressed hastily, trying not to notice the lackluster dress or the fact that it was too short and too large for her.

Abby knocked, then opened the door.

"Breakfast time, seein' as how you're awake."

"What about the wolf? I just heard it again."

"Yes, well, we'll have some breakfast first. The girls are already at the table."

They crossed the backyard to the kitchen, and the wolf was strangely quiet. Katharine half expected it to show itself before they reached the safety of the kitchen, but then it howled again - a long, bewailing cry that brought gooseflesh to her arms - and she knew it was still in the deep pit, awaiting its fate.

The two girls were unusually quiet, but spoke warmly to Katharine as she sat down at the table with them. She inquired about Little Roy, and Abby said he was still sleeping.

Katharine attempted to eat the simple breakfast, but the cries of the trapped wolf made the food stick in her throat. The girls, with their heads bowed over their plates, ate little, also.

Only Abby appeared unperturbed by the situation. Though never a hearty eater, she nonetheless ate calmly, as if this day were no different from any other.

The sharp, plaintive howls intensified as they washed the few breakfast dishes. The girls were unusually quiet, but Abby talked more than usual, again reminding Katharine about the Singing School at their church on Sunday.

"Gramma, that wolf might hurt you. You best wait for Papa to come back." Carrie's voice shook with fear. Then, Mary Sue added her thoughts.

"I don't want you to go out there, Gramma. That wolf might be just walkin' 'round. It might not even be in the pit that Papa dug."

"It's in the pit, all right, baby. It's in the pit, and the lamb's all right, just scared to death. I'm gonna get the shotgun and I want you and Carrie and Miz Katharine to go to the house and wait for me."

Katharine spoke quickly, "I'm going with you, Mrs. Abby. I'll bring my gun."

Abby smiled. "That's not necessary, dear, but come on, if you want to."

The girls hastily left the kitchen and ran to the back door of the house. Katharine started out the kitchen door.

"I'm going to get my derringer. I'll only be a minute."

"All right, dear." Abby smiled, though Katharine sensed that she was making a brave attempt to be strong for all of them. She was loading the shotgun, as Katharine raced across the dirt yard of the house.

Finding the loaded derringer, she hurriedly grabbed it, along with several additional bullets, then headed out the back door again. She saw Abby walking the trail behind the house, which led to the sugarcane field, the same path Katharine had guided General Lee over, only a few days prior. She had not known, that day, that a deep wolf pit was only a stone's throw through the woods.

Katharine quickened her steps and followed closely behind Abby. For the first time, she noticed the painful stiffness of the older woman's walk, a sign that she suffered from the miseries of rheumatism, common among the backwoods people who had overused their bodies in the rigors of daily existence.

The lamb, tied to a stake on the middle post which rose out of the pit, saw them coming and emitted pitiful bleatings without ceasing.

The wolf alternately snarled and leapt toward the top of the pit. Katharine could hear its claws as they gripped the dirt walls, then pulled loose, thrusting the wolf back to the bottom of the abyss.

They had reached the pit and Abby pulled the hammer back on the shotgun. Katharine made herself look over into the pit. The sheer size of the wolf startled her. The black animal's eyes, looking up at them, reflected fear and savagery. It snarled, wrinkling its dark lips over long, pointed teeth.

Abby was talking. "Another thing you have to think about is the animal bein' mad. See how this one's a-foamin' at the mouth. Could be mad."

The wolf lunged upward toward them, its guttural grunts only a few feet away. Katharine stepped back involuntarily, but Abby took several quick steps to the edge of the pit and, with the gun raised to eye level, fired several times into the wolf which dropped to the floor of the pit. The recoil of the shotgun nearly cost Abby her footing, and as she groped backward, Katharine helped her away from the yawning precipice which was filled with smoke from the shotgun blasts. Abby rubbed her shoulder, sore from the powerful kick of the gun.

The wolf appeared to be dead, but Abby threw several pine cones over its body to observe whether any life-like tremor might yet remain. Satisfied that there was no movement, she audibly sighed with relief.

"That was somethin' I'd been dreadin', but I knew it had to be done."

The two girls were on their way to the pit, giggling and talking now that the wolf was no longer a threat. They ran to their grandmother and hugged her.

"Gramma, that was good shootin'," Carrie complimented her grandmother.

"Is the wolf dead?" asked Mary Sue.

"It's dead, chill'un. Now, let's see 'bout little lamb." The lamb's baas were only intermittent, now that the worst danger was over. All it lacked now was being delivered from its perch on the central dirt pillar of the pit.

Abby found a sturdy log nearby, and she had brought along an ax to score it on one side. With the help of Katharine and the girls, the log was extended to the central post and Abby walked across it, refusing Katharine's attempt to do it for her. She untied the lamb, then carried it back across and set it free. It took off, running and kicking, looking for the herd of sheep which foraged on the thick wiregrass on the forest floor.

"Gramma, was the wolf a mad wolf?" Mary Sue wanted to know.

"Sugar baby, I don't know. He did have white foam 'round 'is mouth, and he was off to himself, but I don't know for sure, honey."

"Gramma?" Carrie now was full of conversation. "Why don't you tell Miz Katharine 'bout the little girl who got bit by the mad fox?"

"Oh, honey baby, Miz Katharine don't wanna hear 'bout such bad things."

"Oh, please, Gramma!" "Yes, please!" Both of the girls were in good spirits again, wanting their grandmother to recount for them, once again, one of the stories of her childhood, which they loved to hear, though it made the usual chills go up their spines.

Katharine had no idea what the sisters wanted their grandmother to tell to her, but she went along with them and urged Abby to tell the story.

"Well, this is true," Abby began, as they walked slowly back to the house.

"A little colored girl was playin' not too far from here in the woods with her sister, and a mad fox come along and bit the little girl. Well, the two of them decided they wouldn't tell their mama and papa, because they had been warned to stay away from all wild animals, and they had not obeyed their mama and papa by goin' in the woods, in the first place, to play. Well...," Abby paused for emphasis, "Well, a few weeks went by, and the girl that was bit got to actin' sort of strange."

"How did she act, Gramma?" the girls asked almost in unison.

"Well, she kept sayin' she wanted to bite somebody, and she weren't eatin' the way she should."

"So, what happened, Gramma?"

Katharine almost dreaded to hear the rest of the story, but she found herself listening to every word.

"Well," Abby continued, "the mama and papa kept wonderin' what was wrong with the little girl, and finally the sister told them that a mad fox had bit her. Well, the mama and papa knew what they had to do, and it was terrible, 'cause there ain't nothin' can be done if a mad animal bites you. It's a slow and awful way to die. Well, they had to tie the poor li'l thing to the bed, and they got a spoon with a long handle to feed her." Abby held out her hands, one holding the gun and the other the ax, to demonstrate

153

the size of the spoon which must have measured about three feet in length. Katharine's face was a grimace of horror, as the girls urged their grandmother to finish the story.

"Tell Miz Katharine what the poor girl said, Gramma," Mary Sue interjected.

"Well, the poor li'l thing kept sayin', 'Come over closer. I wanna bite you.' But, of course, the family had to stay away from her or they, too, woulda caught the mad dog disease. But the hardest part was when the child said, 'Come closer. I wanna kiss you.' Of course, they couldn't risk her possibly bitin' 'em and givin' 'em the sickness."

"That was sad, wasn't it, Miz Katharine?" Mary Sue said, with tears in her voice.

"Yes, it's one of the saddest things I've ever heard. And you said it was a true story?"

"Yes," Abby said. "It happened to a colored family that lived not too far from us when I was growin' up. And, of course, the poor li'l thing finally died."

Abby continued, "'Course, ever' dog and some of the cats we had through the years have gone mad. That's why I tell you chir'run not to be too friendly with 'em. There was a man just in the last month I heard tell of was bit by a mad cat. I ain't a-tellin' you such to scare you, but to let you know to stay away from 'em.

"Well, as I was a-tellin' you, a man was bit by a mad cat 'bout a month ago. Said he was a-walkin' along a road, and a cat draggin' a long string crossed the road in front of 'im. He grabbed the string and pulled the cat to 'im, when the cat bit 'is thumb, and wouldn't let go. He and 'is friend with 'im tried to open the cat's mouth, but the cat bit down on another thumb, so then it had 'is two thumbs in its mouth.

"Well, they finally got 'is fingers outa the cat's mouth, and they healed up, and he thought he was all right. But he weren't. A few weeks later, he went to the well to draw up a bucket of water, and it choked 'im. He started havin' a fit and a-fell to the ground. They say he suffered somethin' terrible...had to be chained to 'is bed, and couldn't drink no water. They put a madstone on the bites, but it didn't help none. A lotta doctors come from all around to visit 'im and study 'is case. Said he frothed at the mouth like the wolf was a-doin'."

"What's a madstone, Gramma?" Carrie and Mary Sue asked in unison.

"It's somethin' like hard salt, comes from a deer's stomach. Sometimes, it'll draw the poison out. Some folks say that chewin' the leaves of the alyssum plant'll keep a person from goin' mad, but I don't put much store by that."

Katharine remembered reading about President Lincoln's son, Robert, who had been bitten by a dog, and the president had carried him to Terre Haute to have a madstone applied to the wound. She refrained from mentioning the incident, as she didn't know how Abby MacRae regarded the former president whose armed forces had taken her husband away from her.

They had reached the house where Little Roy was on the back porch, crying and raising his arms to be held. Carrie ran up the steps and picked him up, and his crying ceased abruptly.

Abby headed to the kitchen. "Bring Little Roy on to the kitchen so he can have some breakfast, sugar baby." The girls followed Abby back to the kitchen while Katharine walked on to the house. Katharine called back over her shoulder.

"Carrie and Mary Sue, how about a piano lesson in maybe an hour?"

"Whenever you can teach us, we're ready, Miz Katharine," Carrie said, smiling, and Mary Sue echoed, "Yes, we're ready whenever you are, Miz Katharine."

"Well, give me an hour to freshen up and we'll learn something else by Beethoven today. I brought two of his songs for you to learn."

"What are they?" Mary Sue wanted to know.

"It's a secret. I'll tell you when we have our lesson. Meet me in one hour at the piano."

"All right, Miz Katharine." The girls disappeared into the kitchen, as Katharine entered the house and walked down the dogtrot, back to her room - Micah's room, she reminded herself, as she slipped off her shoes, wet with the morning dew - and lay down across the bed. The frightening excitement of the morning and the pitiful stories she had just heard had taken their toll on her spirits.

The melancholy of the day before assailed her anew, and she fought against the tears which tugged at her heart.

Directly in front of her was a small book shelf with several bound, though worn, books. The titles interested her, and as she softly repeated them, her doldrums went away.

"*Pilgrim's Progress,*" she whispered. Then, "John Milton's *Paradise Lost* and Shakespeare's *Julius Caesar.*" She had wondered about Micah's education, but had he read these works? Her eyes drifted to other titles and other authors, then suddenly she was on the floor in front of the bookshelf, fingering the books, opening them, pondering whether Micah had ever read them. If not, then perhaps Jenny had read them. Otherwise, why were they in the room?

In the social circles of her family in New York, education was everything, but here in the piney woods, where survival was on a day-to-day basis, education had taken a back seat. She wondered where and when the books had been obtained. She resolved to ask Abby MacRae about them. There were not many of them - nothing to compare with her home library or the larger one of her parents.

Katharine straightened her clothes and brushed her hair into a chignon which she secured with combs at the nape of her neck. The day was warm and humid and it was cooler with her hair up. She searched for the music which she had brought for the girls to learn and, finding it, proceeded down the dogtrot to the front room. The girls were waiting for her and smiled expectantly as she opened the door. Little Roy was happily occupied with large wood blocks which he alternately stacked and knocked over. Abby was seated at the spinning wheel in the far corner of the room in preparation for spinning the bats of wool which she had carded the day before into separate rolls.

Katharine watched the procedure with interest, never having witnessed such a thing. Abby smiled at her, realizing that the method she was using was probably unknown to Katharine.

"Mrs. Abby, before we begin our music lesson, I just have to see what you're doing. Isn't this a corn shuck?" She felt of it, almost unbelievingly.

"Yes, Katharine, dear, it's the inside leaf of the shuck that's soft. You just cut off the ragged ends, then roll up the leaf. You leave just a little openin' at the bottom, like this, then you a-sew it in place and slip it over the spindle." Abby quickly stitched the rolled leaf in place and put it on the spindle. Then, she picked up some breaking cards and a bat of wool which she began carding.

"I'm not gonna spin anymore today, bein' as how it makes such noise and you-all 'bout to have your piano lesson. I got plenty to card here and I'll just card and listen." The girls were enthusiastic about beginning their lesson and playing for their grandmother.

"What did you bring from Mr. Beethoven, Miz Katharine? You said you was bringin' some more of 'is songs," Mary Sue inquired.

"I hope they ain't too hard for us," Carrie interjected.

"No, but you will have to practice them. I brought two more of his works. You remember the last several lessons, you practiced a song from Beethoven's *Ninth Symphony*, his *Ode to Joy*, remember? Today, I want you to practice these two." Katharine held up two pieces of sheet music, one in each hand.

" One is his *Moonlight Sonata*," she said, "and the other one is *Für Elise*."

"Carrie, let your grandmother hear you play, first. Mary Sue, I want you to do some written music work." Katharine had wondered whether the children were going to school, and this should provide an opportunity for her to find out about the girls' education, or lack of it. Mary Sue took the practice work sheet and pencil from Katharine and waited for instructions.

"Just follow the directions, Mary Sue. Can you read them?"

"I can make out most of the words," the child said, as she eagerly began working on the practice sheets.

"Play the *Ode to Joy* for your grandmother, Carrie, and then we'll look at the other music."

With the sheet music already open and in place on the old piano, Carrie played it childishly, but with stilted correctness, and Abby's wrinkled face glowed with pride in her grandchild's accomplishment.

"Very good!" Katharine said. "Now," she continued, opening one of the new pieces on the piano, "now, let's practice *Moonlight Sonata*. By the way, has your father heard you two play?"

"Only two times," Carrie said with a small sigh. "Papa just ain't home no more."

"Well, I want him to hear you and Mary Sue when he comes back from the rafting trip," Katharine said firmly. "Remember to sit up straight, Carrie, dear, and remember your timing."

"Yes, Miz Katharine." Carrie began slowly playing the strange notes, at times looking discouraged.

"It's going to take a lot of practice, just as the other song did. You and Mary Sue both have talent, but practice is so very necessary. All right, let's try the other one now and then you and Mary Sue can change places. You can do the pencil work while she practices on the piano." Katharine opened the sheet music, *Für Elise*, and placed it before Carrie who began picking out the notes on the piano.

The morning progressed to midday and the sisters took turns playing for their grandmother and practicing the new music. Abby put down her carding cards and patted the neat rolls of wool which were ready to be spun into thread for the clothing of the household. Taking Little Roy by the hand, she told her granddaughters that she had to go to the kitchen and prepare the noonday meal for everyone. Also, she had to prepare the food to take to the church the following day. Then, she kissed both of them and told them how very proud she was that they were learning to play so well. The young girls beamed at their grandmother's approval.

Katharine, also, was pleased with the girls' performances. Of course, they both faltered over the new music, but Katharine was delighted with their progress and she told them so. She was always surprised that Mary Sue could almost keep up with her older sister. She let them practice awhile longer, then ended the day's lesson.

"Well, girls. I'll bet your grandmother is waiting for us. Let's go help her."

"I'm hungry!" Mary Sue exclaimed.

"Me, too!" Carrie chimed in.

The frightening hours of the past night and early morning had given way to serenity and a degree of contentment. Katharine and the girls walked across the swept-clean dirt yard to the kitchen, its shuttered windows propped open to mingle the heat from its old wood stove with the cooler air outside.

The meal of fresh peas, cornbread, and fried fatback was good, and Katharine was surprised at herself for liking the greasy fatback. Afterwards, the girls and Little Roy went outside to play, and Katharine and Abby watched them draw the squares of hopscotch on the dirt of the yard. Even Little Roy participated in the game, his little legs attempting the hops of his older sisters.

Abby stirred from the table and Katharine followed, helping her with the few dishes.

"I reckon I best get busy and fix my dinner for the church tomorrow."

"Let me help you."

"No, dear, you ain't used to workin' and cookin', 'specially in this heat. I'm gonna take one of the hams what Micah smoked, out in the smokehouse, and I'm gonna a-cook some fresh corn and butterbeans. I'm gonna look for some berries, when it's a little cooler, for a pie. The chir'run like to help with that."

"I'll go with you - when you look for the berries, I mean, but I want to help you with the cooking, also."

"Don't Tilda do your cookin', Katharine?"

"Yes, but it won't hurt me to try my hand at it. In fact, I really do want to."

"All right, dear. We first got to get some water from the well."

"I'll get it," Katharine offered.

"It's heavy, chile. We'll both go."

They brought back two buckets of water, and Katharine agreed that they were heavy. She was used to having Tilda and Big Hill do such for her and she had never realized how heavy a full bucket of water was, especially when it was carried all the way from the well to the inside of the kitchen.

The cooking made the large wood kitchen hot, though the open shutters did allow a breeze to stir through it. Abby went ahead and rolled out her biscuits, using the thick, curdled milk which she called "clabber," and Katharine could not help but admire her industry, though she could see the toll it had wrought, over the years, in her lined face and gnarled hands. Katharine was embarrassed that she had to ask directions about cooking the corn and peas.

Abby instructed her in pulling off the husks and silks and scrubbing the ears in some of the water which they had just brought from the well.

"I cut my corn three times, and then I scrape it," Abby said meaningfully, though Katharine did not grasp the importance of cutting the tiny kernels of corn so many times before scraping it. Nor did she know how to do it. She attempted it with one ear, but couldn't cut it the third time and gave up, laughing.

Abby smiled at the younger woman's trouble with the corn.

"I reckon you never had to do it, so it's new to you. Just you never mind. When I finish with this cornbread, I'll do it myself. I do appreciate you a-shuckin' the ears and pullin' out the silks."

Katharine put the peas on the stove to boil, and Abby produced a smoked ham hock to boil with them. Abby then quickly cut the corn, and Katharine was amazed at her skill in easily cutting each ear three times.

Time passed by and toward the afternoon a stronger breeze drifted through the open shutters of the kitchen. The children continued to play outside, alternately fussing and laughing, and Katharine wondered what it would be like to have a child of her own.

"Time to pick berries. You sure you're up to it, Katharine, honey? I think you need to rest."

"No, I'm going with you. I can rest tonight."

"All right, dear, but some of the huckleberry bushes are back in the woods, so it's a good walk from the house."

"Oh, I'll be fine. I think I'll bring my gun, though."

"No need to. I'm bringin' the shotgun." Abby went out on the back porch of the kitchen and found several baskets which she brought back with her. Katharine had never seen baskets quite like them and she inquired where Abby had gotten them.

"Oh, I made these...out of grapevines."

"Is there anything you can't do, Mrs. Abby?"

"Yes, there's a lot I wish I could do - like readin'. I wish I could read better. I can make out most of the words in the Bible, but I'd like to know all of the words."

"Do the girls go to school?"

"Yes, they go to the school not far from here - just a little one-room school - what we call a old field school, but both the girls are a-doin' just fine. They go four months out of the year. Carrie and Mary Sue, too, can read good."

Katharine wanted to know about Micah, but hesitated to ask. After a few moments, however, her curiosity overcame any hesitancy on her part.

"What about your son, Mrs. Abby?"

"Micah finished the ninth grade. He wanted to go on and graduate, but he had to work. Of course, the schoolmaster gave 'im all the work that the eleventh graders were doin', because he said Micah was smart and could keep up with the older ones. The school only had eleven grades. I hated for him to have to quit school, but I was doin' the plowin' myself, waitin' for 'im to be big enough to help me, since his pa died in the war. I was where I couldn't hold out to do it no more."

"Mrs. Abby, don't tell me you plowed! How in the world could you do that?"

"I don't know, but I did it. It's man's work, but when you don't have no man to do it, why, you just do it yourself. You know, my husband was killed in the war, and Micah was only two years old when he marched away with his regiment. That was in 1861. Well, he died in the little town of Gettysburg, Pennsylvania, in 1863. Our men were lookin' for shoes to wear, when they ran into the Union soldiers on horses. Roy, my husband, was in the group of Confederates what attacked a hill called 'Little Round Top,' right near Gettysburg, and that's where he was shot and killed on July 2, 1863. There was a lot of us widder women left - the war took all our husbands. But thank the Lord, He gave me Micah!"

"You never wanted to marry again?" The question was asked before Katharine could question its propriety, but Abby didn't appear to be offended.

"Sugar pie, if I had wanted to marry again," she emphasized 'wanted,' "it would've been too bad, because there weren't no men left. They was drafted up to the age of sixty year, so there weren't no men left. All 'round these parts, widder women were left to fend for themselves, and it weren't easy. But, when I'd start to feelin' sorry for myself, I'd look 'round and see Widder Burch down the road a few miles with eight chir'run and no husband, 'cause he was killed in the war, or Widder Willcox, ailin' with the rheumatism, and can't hardly walk, with six chir'run to feed, and no husband, 'cause the war took 'im." Katharine's eyes were brimming with tears and, seeing them, Abby was filled with remorse that she had upset her.

"Let's stop thinkin' 'bout sad things that's over and done with and start thinkin' about those huckleberries, plump and juicy, just waitin' for us to pick 'em," Abby said with a gentle smile. "Here's you a basket, dear, and I got one for each of the chir'run."

Katharine wiped her eyes with the tattered handkerchief which Abby found in her pocket, and accepted the woven grapevine basket which she handed her. Meeting Micah and his family had put names and faces on the Confederacy, which in her mind had always been just the other side in the war. The two started out the kitchen door and the children abruptly ended their play, running to get their baskets.

"Time to pick berries...the huckleberries are ripe in the woods, long about this time, and we might find some blueberries, what we always called rabbit berries, but they're prob'ly all gone by now. Y'all be careful 'bout snakes, 'cause they like to stay 'round berry bushes."

"We will. We'll be careful," the children promised, as they ran toward the berry bushes in the woods on the side of the house and immediately began filling their baskets.

Katharine had never gathered berries, though her parents' acreage in New York contained many blackberry bushes. Tilda, or one of the servants, had always gathered the berries for tarts or pies.

The wild berries hung like smooth, blue-black jewels, unlike the multifaceted drupelets of the blackberries of early summer. The children popped as many into their mouths as they gathered and Katharine found herself doing the same. Everyone had stained lips and hands, and all laughed at one another, as they pulled the plump berries from the bushes. Abby finally said they had enough, and everyone was glad, as mosquitoes were whining around them, eluding their slapping hands.

"Guess you can say summer is here in the piney woods when the mosquitoes start to buzzin' 'round you," Abby said with a smile, "but here it is the end of August, and they're still a-buzzin'."

All followed Abby back to the kitchen where they combined the berries into one bowl. Little Roy had picked exactly nine berries, but his baby hands holding tightly to them had extracted juice which dripped through his fingers to the floor. This didn't matter to Abby one whit, for she opened his little hands and scraped the crushed berries into the bowl, noting with a smile the happy expression on his face. Katharine wet a dishrag and washed the stickiness from his hands, though the stain remained, as Abby wiped the juice from the floor.

The children were out the door again, mosquitoes or not, and Katharine knew they would be brown as little berries themselves, before the summer was over. No thought of shielding their skin from the sun to maintain a delicate whiteness, the way the ladies in town did. Soon, she could hear their infectious laughter and their funny bickering, as they played the games of childhood.

Katharine washed the berries while Abby made the crust for the pie. She thought again of the books, some of them classics, which she had found in Micah's room, and she decided to ask Abby about them.

"Mrs. Abby, the books in your son's room. Has he read all of them?"

"Oh, I should think so...when he was in school, I'm sure he did. But he don't never have time now - to read or to do nothin'- but work. It worries me that he don't spend more time with the chir'run or go to church."

"Mrs. Abby, you never finished your spinning today, did you?"

"No, but it won't hurt nothin' to do it later, maybe next week sometime. Ain't been too long since Micah sheared his sheep, and I like to do my spinnin' pretty soon afterwards, but it can wait awhile. I wouldn't take anythin' for hearin' my girls play the piano so pretty today. The spinnin' can wait!"

"Mrs. Abby, I've been thinking...I need to go back home, probably Monday. Maybe you and the children could come and spend some time with me while Micah's gone."

"Katharine, dear, I got my hands full here, what with spinnin' and lookin' after ever'thin' here. Have to feed and water ever'thin'. I would love to go, but just don't see how I can."

"What about the girls? Do you think they could come home with me for a few days?"

"Yes, I know they would enjoy it. They ain't much used to a-spendin' the night away from home, but they love you, Katharine, and I'm sure they'll be a-wantin' to go."

Katharine had, for some time, wanted the girls to come for a visit and to play the songs they had learned on her grand piano. She knew that they would hear and appreciate the difference in the sound of the music.

Abby had finished putting the pie together and she slipped the deep dish, filled with unbaked crust and berries and water and sugar into the oven of the hot wood stove to bake. Yellow flies made their stinging way into the open kitchen windows, and Katharine thought that insects were so much more worrisome in the South than at her home in New York.

"Seems like flies and mosquitoes were earlier this year and there's more of 'em. I'm gonna burn some herbs and pine straw tonight, and maybe they won't give us such a fit. I got three washpots and I'll put one in each room." Katharine didn't know exactly what Abby was talking about, but she looked forward to anything that would help in deterring the mosquitoes and flies.

After an hour or longer, when the aroma of Abby's baking filled the kitchen and wafted out into the yard, informing the frolicking children that the berry pie might be done, three dirty, hot, tired, and bedraggled children took their places at the table. Abby wet several rags and had the children wash their faces and hands. She washed Little Roy's herself before checking on the pies in the oven. First, she removed a small pie which Katharine had not even seen her place inside the stove.

"This is for now, and I'm gonna let the bigger one cook some more. We'll take it to the Association meetin' tomorrow."

Abby put the berry pie in small bowls for everyone, then skimmed the cream off of the milk which she had in a large covered bowl on an old serving table in the kitchen. As she worked, she informed everyone that Betsy, the cow, had enough milk for them and for her little calf, also. In fact, the cow had arrived early at her kitchen door, almost begging for her swollen bag to be relieved of its rich milk.

Katharine realized that Abby had milked the cow before breakfast, while the wolf snarled only a short distance away. Obviously, Micah's mother had nerves of steel. The farm work never ceased. Abby MacRae could certainly vouch for that!

Abby proceeded to beat the cream with a fork, adding sugar as she beat it. They all took turns beating the sweet cream which gradually thickened. Abby then spooned the whipped cream on top of the individual bowls of pie, and they all ate the rich dessert, oohing and aahing at its rich, full taste. Abby's face glowed from the compliments on her cooking, but she reminded all of them, even Little Roy, that each one had a hand in making the pie.

The sun was setting low in the sky when the MacRae family and Katharine finished cleaning the dishes from the table. Abby gathered some herbs from a cupboard in the kitchen and put them in one of the larger baskets. Katharine and the girls helped her carry the three washpots into the house, and they gathered pine straw to mix with the herbs which they would burn to ward off bugs.

Abby lit the herb mixture in the pots which were placed in each of their rooms and reminded Katharine of the big day at her church the next day. They would leave in the morning, because the trip would take several hours and they wanted to be back before dark, surely. Everyone said goodnight and the children, including Little Roy, each gave a hug and kiss to their grandmother and to Katharine. These childish, loving gestures were almost too much for Katharine, whose tears seemed ever ready to come forth.

Upon closing the door to Micah's room, she sat on the simple bed, head in hands, and the flowing tears brought her some relief. She opened the wood shutters of the pane-less windows and watched the smoke from the concoction in the washpot, as it drove away the bugs of the night.

Chapter Seventeen

The rooster crowing from his perch on the barnyard gate signaled the arrival of Sunday morning, and Katharine lay in the bed, listening to his masterful crows which set off a cacophony of other daybreak sounds. Abby's brood of guineas, perched high in a chinaberry tree near the kitchen, emitted their harsh, potracking cries which were muted somewhat by the soothing cluck-clucks of her dominecker hens, pecking and scratching beneath the window of Micah's room. Off in the woods, cows lowed softly and sheep occasionally joined in with their muffled bleating.

The herbs in the washpot had long ago stopped burning and smoking, but the smoke had left its residue on her skin and even a faint taste in her mouth. She must wash herself. She would go to the well and bring back water for a bath of sorts.

She slipped on the dress she had worn the day before and her shoes, not bothering to lace them. How she longed to put her feet in a pan of clean water.

Katharine could hear Abby stirring in the kitchen and she momentarily felt guilty for not going in to help her. The need for washing herself, however, overrode any feelings of guilt, and she hurried to the well, bucket in hand.

Drawing the water and lifting it were more difficult without Abby to help her, and she struggled with the nearly-full bucket all the way back to Micah's room. Abby had left a cake of her soap which she had made, and Katharine stepped out of her clothes and proceeded to wash the grime and smoke from her skin.

She brushed her hair, dipping the brush in the water in an attempt to remove the soot from it. The quick bowl bath did wonders for her spirits and she looked forward to what the day might bring, especially going to Abby's church. She hurriedly put on an old, worn dressing gown which she had found, folded, on the sole chair in the room.

She heard Abby at the kitchen door, calling her. Obviously, she was late, and she was ashamed of herself for not being on time for breakfast. She hurried to the kitchen and found everyone waiting for her.

"I'm so sorry to be late. I should have helped you with breakfast, Mrs. Abby."

"Katharine, dear, I don't expect you to do any such thing. You ain't used to cookin', but I been a-cookin' all my life, just about."

"Well, you don't need another one to care for. By the way, when will we leave for church?"

"It's a right smart piece away - take several hours to get there, so we'll be leavin' soon. We're havin' the Singin' School today and we all like to sing. Hope you do, too, Katharine."

"Well, I sang a little in school and some in my church choir when I was growing up, but that's been a long time ago."

"We ain't havin' foot washin' today. That'll probably be sometime in September."

"Foot washing?" Katharine inquired. "What do you mean?"

"The old school Baptists believe in washin' feet, just like Jesus did."

"Well, how is it done in your church?"

"Ever'body sits on the front bench, and those that's a-gonna do the washin's got their bowls of water and their towels, and the men wash the men's feet and the women wash the women's feet."

Katharine had never witnessed a church foot washing and she was somewhat disappointed that it would not be today.

The meager but tasty breakfast was over, and after washing and putting away the dishes, Abby and Katharine began setting out the food which they were going to carry with them to the church.

"Katharine, dear, just look in the chifforobe there in Micah's room and find you somethin' to wear today."

"Thank you, Mrs. Abby, I may do that," Katharine said, hesitating before broaching another subject. She took a deep breath, then said, "Mrs. Abby, I've been wanting to ask something of you, but I really don't know how to say it."

"Now, Katharine, honey, you can say anythin' to me and you know it. What's on your mind?"

"Mrs. Abby," Katharine blurted out, "I'm looking forward to going to your church, but please don't tell them who I am."

"Katharine, honey, I thought about that, too. Somebody killed your husband and nobody knows who it was. I pray to the good Lord it weren't nobody in our little church, but we just don't know who did it, and I guess you're scared."

"No, really, I'm not scared. It's not that. It's just that I would rather that no one know that I am associated with the Yellow Pines Lumber Company. There are so many ill feelings left from the war, and I would rather you just introduce me as a friend and let it go, at that."

"I'll do that, Katharine. You'll be fine."

Katharine went over to Abby and put her arms around her.

"Mrs. Abby, you're just about like a mother to me. I just want you to know that." Abby smiled, and though several of her teeth were gone, Katharine had always thought she had the smile of an angel.

"Well, you're the daughter I never had, Katharine, dear. Now, let's us get busy and put on our Sunday clothes. I gotta get the mule and buggy ready first, so's I won't get all messed up a-tryin' to hitch ol' Doll to the buggy."

"We could use my carriage, Mrs. Abby."

"Well, if you don't want nobody to know who you are, better not use your nice carriage. It'd have folks talkin' and wonderin', for sure. No, our old wagon'll be fine - get us there and back, anyways."

The women walked to the barnyard and General Lee clopped over to the wood fence, leaning his large head over the fence toward Katharine.

"Hey there, fellow. You ready to go home?" Katharine patted the velvet muzzle of the gelding and he playfully pulled at her fingers with his large gray lips.

Abby opened the gate for the large mule which followed her obediently, just by the touch of her hand, to the lean-to where the wagon was. Abby had no trouble at all getting the sleek animal to back into the shafts of the wagon. Katharine helped her hitch the mule to the wagon and then led her to the front yard, where they tethered her under a shady live oak.

"Now, Katharine, honey, you find the prettiest dress in that chifforobe and put it on."

"Thank you, Mrs. Abby. I won't be long."

Katharine hurried to Micah's room and closed the door. The small chifforobe in the corner seemed to beckon to her, after Abby's words of encouragement, and Katharine walked across the plain wood floor and opened it. As she looked at the clothes, she thought of the dead woman, Jenny, whose small framed picture rested on the little table in the front room. As Katharine had noticed the first night she had spent in Micah's room, there were no pictures of Jenny in his room, and she wondered why.

Life goes on, she thought. That's why. You pick up the pieces and you keep on living. She thought of Micah intensely at that moment and, closing her eyes, she imagined him on the raft - strong, capable, his brown eyes with flecks of gold mirroring the similar brown of the river water with the golden sun playing on it.

Her thoughts went back to the day he had held her and kissed her, the magic of the few moments before he pushed her away in anger. Katharine opened her eyes and tried to banish her yearning for this man. She had never felt this utter longing for anyone before and she seriously questioned herself, as she fumbled through Jenny's few dresses. Katharine wondered what had come over herself to the extent that she was wearing clothes which neither fit her nor were attractive on her. Why, a year past, even six months ago, her life as she was living it now would have been preposterous.

Her hands stopped on an undyed muslin dress, and she decided to try it. Though it was a better fit than the one she had worn the day before, it was still too short and too large, and she laughed at the way she would look if her family and friends were to see her. However, it appeared to be the best choice of the clothes in the chifforobe, so she decided to wear it. Because of the warmth of the day, she braided her hair across the back of her head - something Tilda often did for her.

Abby and the children were waiting on the porch. Abby had driven the mule and wagon around to the kitchen and had put the food, including the smoked ham, into the wagon. The children scrambled into the back of the wagon, and Katharine climbed onto the front seat next to Abby.

Ol' Doll appeared eager for an outing, and under Abby's gentle guiding rein, the mule stepped from the established road in front of the MacRae homeplace into the woods across from it. This confused Katharine, for she didn't know the shortcuts through the woods that the local people knew. The woods were burned often in the piney woods and this allowed one to see far in the distance through the tremendous longleaf yellow pine trees. The path the mule followed was hardly wide enough to accommodate the wagon, but obviously Abby MacRae had traveled it often, for she handled the driving with ease.

Cows and sheep foraged on the wiregrass that newly carpeted the forest floor every spring and provided year-round food. The razorback hogs of the piney woods upturned the palmettoes which grew beneath the pines and feasted on their roots. Cattle roamed freely during the year, but were rounded up every spring and accounted for by their owners, according to the brands which were seared into the animals' flesh.

The ride was pleasant, and the dim light filtering through the huge pines, whose tops provided a needled canopy far above them, refuted the fact that it was actually a sunny and warm day. The animals, which they could see through the trees, regarded them with non-curious eyes, as they pulled on the rough wiregrass with their large, blunt teeth and chewed on their cud. Katharine noticed different brands on the cattle and realized that it didn't take long, after the spring roundup, for the animals to commingle again until the next roundup the following spring.

Abby MacRae informed them that the trip would take several hours, so everyone should just sleep or sing to pass the time away. They were all in for some good preaching and singing, she said, when they reached the church.

Katharine, however, was unprepared for the intensity of the church meeting and the duration of the service. She had never heard the Sacred Harp music which the church people performed, sitting on benches arranged in a square at the front of the church. Since their faith forbade the use of musical instruments in the church, their voices alone created the euphony.

She was intrigued by the shaped musical notes in their hymnals, some in the shapes of squares, triangles, diamonds, and other geometric shapes. One song which they sang, *Leander*, was especially beautiful. Another old hymn, *Amazing Grace*, had words in the chorus which were unfamiliar to her. She would always remember them, for they were sung with clear enunciation and zeal:

> *Shout, shout for glory, Shout, shout aloud for glory,*
> *Brother, sister, mourner, All shout glory hallelujah.*
> *Shout, shout for glory, Shout, shout aloud for glory,*
> *Brother, sister, mourner, All shout glory hallelujah.*

***

The religious fervor of the Primitive Baptist Church meeting the day before brought about a night of tossing and turning and wakefulness before Katharine realized that it was morning, late morning. She had overslept, but it was a wonder that sleep had come at all, she thought, after hearing the church elders speak on the perils of sin and the fires of damnation at the church meeting the day before. Lying in bed, she felt guilty. Was what she felt for Micah lust? Did women lust, as men did? Women in her family had never openly discussed such and Katharine felt guilty even thinking about sins of the flesh. The chanting elders of the little church had unknowingly probed her mind and pointed invisible fingers at her.

Oh, well, she thought. We have kissed and that's all. What's wrong with that? The invisible fingers kept pointing at her. Ah, yes, it was more. She admitted it. She remembered that day in the freshly plowed field, when he held her and she clung to him, and his mouth was on hers and his hands were moving over her. Did he think less of her because she had enjoyed kissing him back that day? Only now, after hearing the church elders, did she question how she had behaved that day in the field.

Her face flamed when she remembered what he had said about not taking advantage of her that day. In fact, he had compared his behavior with that of the Northerners with the Yellow Pines Lumber Company and how they had raped the piney woods while he refrained from treating her in such a way.

Katharine sat up in bed. She needed to go home, away from this room which brought Micah so close, yet didn't allow her to touch him, to lie with him and to be held by him. She had to get over her grade-school infatuation for the man and it was never too late to begin.

Fresh water was in the large bowl on the dresser, and Katharine knew that Abby had brought it to the room for her. Dear Mrs. Abby! Could she possibly have guessed Katharine's feelings for her son? No, she reasoned, she had not yet guessed, and she must never know, because she, Katharine, did not intend for the relationship to go any further. As soon as she had the money in hand from her trees, she intended to go home, away forever from the desolate stretches of monotonous pines which lined the roads for hundreds of miles, and away from the man who called this forbidding part of the world his home.

It was quite obvious at the church meeting the previous day that several women, younger than she, were more than interested in Micah MacRae, and they were disappointed that he had not come with his family. Also, they gave Katharine looks which made her uncomfortable, as though they questioned who she really was and whether there was anything between Micah and herself.

Katharine eased out of bed and peeled off the shimmy of Jenny's, which she had slept in. Abby had also left a clean, though ragged, washcloth which Katharine dipped into the cool water and commenced her morning bath. How refreshing just wiping one's skin with a wet cloth could make one feel!

She opened the chifforobe and found her dress which she had hung up the past Friday evening. Stepping into it, she almost felt back to normal again, wearing a dress which fit her and was the proper length. She brushed her long, thick hair and plaited it in one large braid which hung down the middle of her shoulders.

Though she felt the need to go home, she almost dreaded going, as Tillie would not be there. Also, the girls were only going to stay one full day and then she was to bring them back home the following day. It would be really lonesome then, all by herself, and Katharine wondered whether she could stay alone for several weeks until Tillie returned. She might decide to visit the Winslows, after all.

She admonished herself to brace up. After all, other widows faced the world alone, and she could, too. She spread up the bed and straightened the room, pouring out the bath water through the opening in the room, which was the unshuttered window. She checked the derringer in her purse and made sure the extra bullets were also there. Gathering the few things she had brought with her, including the sheets of music for the girls, she looked around the simple room once more, mouthed the word, "Goodbye," then hurried out the door. She could hear giggling and talking from the girls' room and she knew they were getting ready for the trip home with her.

Seeing activity in the kitchen, through the open windows, she dropped her things on the floor of the dogtrot and proceeded across the yard. Abby saw her coming and spoke to her from the nearest open window.

"Katharine, dear, breakfast ain't ready yet, but don't you worry none 'bout helpin'. You can be a-hitchin' your horse to your carriage. The girls are gettin' ready. They're sure lookin' forward to goin' home with you."

"All right, Mrs. Abby. I won't be long."

Katharine headed toward the barn, where General Lee was waiting for her, his large head bobbing up and down as he watched her approaching the gate.

"Hello, fellow, have you missed Harry and Big Hill? Are you ready to go home?"

The horse's intelligent eyes rolled in their sockets, acknowledging her voice, as he clopped along the fence to the gate. As Katharine crooned words to the big gelding and lifted the crossbar of the gate, the horse playfully nibbled at her fingers. She slipped the bridle over his angular head, then led him, his long tail swishing back and forth, to the carriage where he obediently backed into its sidebars to be hitched for the trip home. Katharine walked the horse, pulling the carriage, to the front of the house, where it was cooler under the large live oak. She tossed the reins over the bottom, low-lying limb and loosely tied them.

Abby was calling her and the girls to breakfast and she hurried back to the old kitchen. The smells of a Southern backwoods breakfast drifted toward her and she could detect the distinct aroma of fatback which Abby fried on the old wood stove each morning for breakfast. Though Katharine had never eaten it before her visit, she had to admit that it was tasty and filling.

The smiling girls, Little Roy, and Abby were standing before their plates at the simple pine table when Katharine entered the kitchen and she quickly took her place at the table. Abby led them in a blessing of thanksgiving for the food which they were about to receive, then all sat in the hewn pine chairs, worn smooth with years of living.

After the meal, Abby urged them on their way, noting the rather lengthy trip and always the risk that the carriage might fall into disrepair and the danger of nightfall and its attending perils descending upon them. Katharine went with the girls and helped them put their few bags and her own belongings into the boot and rear of the carriage. Abby and Little Roy came around the house to tell them goodbye and Katharine experienced the choked feeling she always had when she left Micah MacRae's home. The girls hugged their little brother and grandmother and climbed up to the carriage seat. Katharine scooped up Little Roy, and he planted a child's wet kiss on her cheek, bringing tears to her eyes. Putting him down, she and Abby embraced, and Katharine quickly climbed up beside the girls. It would be a close ride home in the small carriage.

"I'll bring them back day after tomorrow, Mrs. Abby. Don't worry about them. We'll be fine. I enjoyed everything."

"And we enjoyed havin' you so much, Katharine, dear. Bye, now. Carrie, you and Mary Sue, be sweet now."

"We will, Gramma. I love you, Gramma," Mary Sue said.

"I love you, too, Gramma," Carrie chimed in. "Bye, Little Roy. We love you, too."

Katharine lightly flicked the reins over General Lee's back and the horse moved forward, quickly breaking into a trot, as he pulled the carriage down the path and onto the narrow dirt road. Before long, they were following the Chauncey timber railroad line which led to the wider main road at Normandale.

Immersed in her own thoughts, Katharine finally realized that her young charges were unusually quiet, so she thought of ways to make the trip not so long and warm.

"Why don't you two sing a song?"

Smiling, shyly, they looked at her, and their smiles broadened for they loved to sing.

"All right, Mary Sue," Carrie said, with older sister authority, "let's sing *Red River Valley*." Katharine didn't know what inspired Carrie to suggest such a song, but the words were rather fitting, as the two girls lifted their yet childish voices in song. Katharine sang parts of it with them. The warmth of the day and the dust from the horse's hooves were not as oppressive because of the sweet melodies which issued from their throats.

After singing several songs, including church hymns, Mary Sue wanted to sing *The Homespun Dress*. Katharine knew the girls were innocent of the implications of this Southern Civil War song, and she listened to their rendition of it with a strange sense of detachment. She had heard it sung several times, but never as well nor as meaningfully as the girls now sang it. Katharine smiled at the words, "Three cheers for the homespun dress that Southern ladies wear." The girls in their home-dyed, homespun dresses gave the song an appealing aura of simple authenticity.

One war song brought on another, and Carrie began the Southern battle song, *Dixie*, with a joyful rush of the catchy words, "I wish I was in the land of cotton..." Katharine laughed and joined in the song which she had always enjoyed until Frank's death, but now she seemed to be over any reticence in singing it, and she knew that she would once again be able to play it on the piano.

The girls soon tired of singing, and they began to look for animals in the thick, pine-laden woods on either side of the road. Cows foraged quietly on the wiregrass on the forest floor, flicking flies with their tails and looking up briefly as the carriage passed by.

They reached Normandale about noon, and the horse pulled the carriage over the timber railroad tracks which intersected the road. The railroad began at the sawmill which was located a quarter of a mile away at the Yellow Pines Lumber Mill and continued on across Telfair County, going through Camp Six and on to Willcox Lake on the Ocmulgee River, some thirty miles away. Willcox Lake was the center of the Yellow Pines timber operation on the Ocmulgee River. Katharine knew that the lake would be the embarkation point for her own timber, once it was cut and made into rafts, probably within the next few weeks.

Hearing a clanking and a whistling through the woods on the left side of the road, she urged the horse forward, fearing that the noise of the oncoming locomotive would cause the animal to panic. The horse, however, did not shy, but slowed to a halt when Katharine pulled gently on the reins after crossing the tracks, allowing the girls and herself to look back at the iron horse on wheels.

Puffing steam from its boiler and clacking on the forest tracks, the train, laden with huge trees from the interior of the county, whistled on its journey to the sawmill which Katharine knew to be one of the largest in the Southeast. The girls had never seen the train, though they lived only a few miles away, but they had often heard the whistle and bell from their house on Bear Creek. Their eyes were round with wonder and a little fear, as they gazed at the iron monster bearing down upon them. The noise was deafening and the girls held their ears, though they could not tear their eyes away from the strange conveyance which moved on iron wheels. The engineer and fireman waved and smiled at them from their seats inside the locomotive.

The girls sighed, almost with relief, when the last, tree-laden car of the loud, clanging train left their sight, vanishing into the dense forest on the right side of the road and shortly arriving at the Normandale sawmill where, abruptly, the locomotive noises ceased. Katharine clucked to the horse, and the carriage was once again pulled along the three-path dirt road.

Passing in front of John C. Forsyth's two-story executive house, Katharine asked the girls whether they knew whose house it was. No, they said. They had never seen it. Katharine told them that a good man named John C. Forsyth used to live there. She did not mention his murder at the hands of Southern squatters and the children did not ask anything about him. They did comment, however, on the enormity of the house and the fact that it had two levels. They had never seen such a fine house, they said. Katharine smiled at their childish candor which was refreshing to her.

The horse realized he was nearing home and Katharine let him have almost a free rein, watching him with some amusement as he pulled the carriage with renewed vigor and ever faster strides. She and the girls were holding on to their bonnets with one of their hands and the carriage crossrail with the other, laughing at the horse's antics on the dusty road.

Though Katharine had dreaded returning home to an empty house, she nevertheless had missed the comforts which the large house afforded, and she looked forward to its many amenities, including running water. She hoped that Big Hill would be there to tend to the horse and carriage. How she had missed his and Tilda's assistance with the myriad chores which sprang from one's everyday existence!

Katharine realized that the horse was tiring when he abruptly slackened his frenetic pace and slowed to a trot, his mouth frothing from the heat and exertion. She would have Big Hill give him a good rubdown. He also needed water to drink, as did she and the girls.

The last few miles went by swiftly, and soon Katharine could see the wrought-iron fence through the trees and then the large house itself, situated a distance back from the road. Without her prodding, the big gray turned left onto the brick half-circle driveway and the carriage passed under the Sighing Pines archway.

The horse eagerly continued toward the stables and Katharine was happy to see Big Hill as he shuffled out to meet them. Behind him was a plump colored woman who flashed white teeth inside a face as brown-black as tree bark. Though she appeared to be somewhat younger than Big Hill, Katharine felt almost certain that this woman must be Ollie, his wife. She followed in the footsteps of Big Hill who reached up to grasp the horse's bridle.

"Whoa, dar, Gen'l Lee...whar you think you is goin'? Good day, Miz Kat'rin, glad to see you back home." Big Hill extended a long arm and helped Katharine from the carriage.

"And I'm glad to see you, Hill. Who is this with you?" Katharine looked at the smiling colored woman who wore a colorful turban on her head.

"Ah's Ollie, Big Hill's wife, Miz Kat'rin. Ah's come to he'p you anyways Ah can. Big Hill done tole me yo' he'p done gone back to NooYawk, so," she repeated, "Ah's here to he'p anyways Ah can."

Bless her, thought Katharine, for she knew that meals would have to be prepared and more housework done with the girls visiting her.

"Ollie, I'm so glad to meet you. Big Hill has worked for us for six years, and he's always spoken of you, but until now I hadn't met you." Katharine turned to Big Hill, "Well, how has everything been here - quiet, I guess - since I've been gone?"

"Not hardly, it ain'," Hill said, first looking at her, then looking away. A sense of alarm gripped Katharine, and she stepped closer to the elderly Negro, clutching his upper shirt sleeve.

"What do you mean? What has happened?" She walked around him a few steps, until he looked at her and she saw rekindled fear in his black eyes which gazed at her from almond-shaped, white orbs.

"Dey come back, Miz Kat'rin."

"Who? What? What do you mean?" Katharine almost felt like shaking him to make an explanation come forth.

"De Klan. Dey come back."

The Ku Klux Klan! Katharine bit her lip, visualizing the horror of their first visit some months prior. She wondered what evil mischief they had wrought during this return visit and she noted that Big Hill hung his head.

"What? Tell me! What did they do? Did they set fire to the stables again?"

"No'm. We wuz blessed dat dey left de stables alone. No'm, but dey did tear up yo' garden, Miz Kat'rin."

"What?"

"Yas'm. Dey all rode wid dar hosses all up and dahn de garden, and Ah wuz inside de stable, peepin' out, and Ah couldn' do nuthin' to stop 'em. Den, jes' to make sure we knowed who been heah, dey burnt a big cross on de front ob de house. Dey had on dem white sheets and had 'em on dar hosses, jes' lak de last time, and dey had burnin' tawches in dey hands."

Katharine felt sick. Why wouldn't they leave her alone?

"How did you put out the fire, Hill?"

"Ollie wuz wif me, and we bof carried buckets ob water from de well and jes' kep' pourin' water on it. De fire finally went mout, and de wood too hot to touch but it rain a little de next day, and we carry it mout in de woods."

Katharine thought of the late garden which she had lovingly planted with the knowledgeable help of Tilda and Big Hill, and she tried not to be visibly upset, for she suddenly remembered the two young girls who were sitting perfectly still on the carriage seat, their eyes large with fear. They had never heard of the Ku Klux Klan, and they were holding hands, as if to ward off such an enemy.

With great effort, Katharine regained a measure of composure and she introduced the girls to Big Hill and his wife. Big Hill moved slowly to the carriage seat and helped them down. They both uttered quiet but mannerly thank-you's.

"I don't think I can bear to look at the garden yet, Hill. I guess it just wasn't meant to be, but we still have plenty of vegetables which Tilda put up last year."

Katharine didn't share her final thoughts, for they dealt with her longing to go far away from this angry, unfriendly land, back to her home and her people. However, she stifled her thoughts about the unpleasantness of her life in the piney woods and, with concentrated intent, turned her attention to Micah's daughters who stood watching her, as if to determine where they were to go and what they were to do, now that they had come to visit her.

"Girls, I'll show you to your room. Ollie, bless you! I'll meet you in the kitchen and show you where everything is, just as soon as I show the girls their room. As you may know, there is still meat in the smokehouse, and Tilda has some chicken coops behind a fence on down the road there." Katharine nodded toward a narrow path which led from the back gate to the chicken yard.

As Ollie headed for the kitchen, Katharine led the girls into the large, comfortable house, thankful that Big Hill had had the foresight to bring his cheerful wife to help her, now that Tilda was gone. The house, though a little musty from being shut up for several days, was nonetheless inviting with its luxurious rugs, its furniture of fine-grained woods, its gleaming hardwood floors, and its ornate tapestries and oil paintings.

Both girls were wide-eyed at the elegant refinement and beauty of the place and they hesitantly asked Katharine what some of the different furnishings were, such as the gleaming claw-foot tub in the bathroom near their room, which had running water. They had never seen an indoor bathroom and they most certainly had never seen water which emerged from a gold spigot at the twist of a porcelain knob. Katharine turned on the water for them and suggested that each one have a bath before going to bed. Both girls were readily agreeable to this, though an all-over bath was something they rarely experienced and the gleaming tub with water which flowed into it was something unheard of.

Katharine left them, giggling and talking in their room, and proceeded to the kitchen to familiarize Ollie with everything. The butter and milk, she told her, were in glass jars in the well on the back porch, though she was certain that Ollie would have known such.

The colored woman was quick to learn and immediately began preparations for their midday meal. Katharine took this time to go to the garden and see what damage had been done by the Klan.

As she walked to the area, her tears fell unchecked down her cheeks. Again, she questioned why? Why was she a target of the Klan's hatred?

On reaching the garden, she was shocked at the brutality of the raid. Horses' hoofprints pockmarked every inch of the garden plot. The vegetables, heretofore almost ripe for picking, were pulled up and trampled on, and nothing was left. The tomato stakes and vegetable markers, which Tilda and Big Hill had painstakingly made, were broken and strewn in bits across the entire garden site.

Katharine wondered whether the man with the scar on his face had led this raid, also, and she felt certain that he had. She would put in another request to the sheriff for his arrest, but she knew they had no way of finding him and no evidence that he was even involved in this trespass on her property. What would they do, if the Klan returned again? She shuddered at the thought. She really didn't feel safe anymore. She might consider going back home to New York for awhile. She would give it some thought.

She heard a shuffling walk on the hard-packed dirt behind her and turned her tear-stained face to Big Hill who stopped near her. He threw up his big hands, palms upward, and sighed.

"It wuz a lotta wuk to come to nuthin'."

"I know, Big Hill. You worked so hard to keep it thriving and I really thought I'd be putting up vegetables again with Tillie's and your help. I'm thankful they didn't tear up the brick walkways again though, the way they did before."

"Dat's de strange thing. Seems lak dey pickin' out sumpin' diffrunt ever' time to mess up and tear up. Miz Kat'rin, Ah hates to say it, but Ah think it be dange'rus fer you to stay heah now."

"I've been thinking the same thing, but I've got to stay on to see about my timber." Katharine waited a few moments before asking, "Was Ollie here when the Klan came?"

"Oh, yes Ma'm! She wuz wantin' to run mout in de woods, but w'en I seen dey waren't comin' to de stables, I tole her we jes' needed to lay low and jes' mebbe dey'd go on, and dey did. Dey kep' shootin' up in de air and Ah thot dat Harry and mah mule, Ol' Hattie, wuz gonna bust outa dar stalls. Dey made a racket, but de Klan dey made a heap bigger racket, so dey never heerd dem."

Katharine began moving toward the house, and as Big Hill began his slow walk back to the stables, Katharine spoke to his retreating back.

"What's done is done and we can't bring it back. Let's be thankful that no one was hurt."

"Yes, Ma'm, dat all we can do - dat and pray."

Katharine reached in her pocket for a handkerchief and wiped her eyes. She must present a calm demeanor for the sake of the young girls in her care and she made up her mind to do just that.

As she walked past the kitchen, Ollie stepped outside and asked her where she wanted to have dinner - in the kitchen or the dining room. Katharine answered that the kitchen would be fine, but they would have their evening meal in the spacious dining room.

"I done got yo' dinner ready, Miz Kat'rin," the colored woman said.

"All right. I'll get the girls and we'll be over in a few minutes. I'm sure they're hungry after the long trip this morning."

Katharine hurried into the house and found the girls sitting quietly in the bedroom where she had left them. With worried expressions on their young faces, they walked over and put their arms around her.

"We're sorry about what that awful Klan did, Miz Katharine. We don't know all that they did, but it must be bad," Carrie said.

"Yes," echoed Mary Sue, "they must be bad to mess up your garden."

Katharine realized at that moment how much she loved these simple, unaffected children. She gave each a hug and their childish embrace and sweet words brought a measure of comfort to her. She then feigned a happy, carefree manner, so that they would quit thinking about the Klan.

"Come on, dear ones, and let's go to the kitchen and eat dinner. Ollie says it's ready."

Smiles appeared on their faces as the girls followed Katharine to the kitchen, each embellishing her account of just how hungry she was. When Katharine motioned for them to be seated, however, they stood before their plates, as was their custom at their home, and Katharine said a table blessing before they sat down to the meal.

Though Katharine was grateful for Ollie's help, she couldn't help but notice the difference in the table and the food in comparison with that which Tilda prepared. She acutely missed her housekeeper and cook, but she reminded herself how fortunate she was to have Ollie to fill in during her absence. She resolved to show her appreciation to Big Hill's smiling, turbaned wife whose cheerful outlook on life was contagious.

Tasting the food prepared by the Negro woman, Katharine was pleased to discover that Ollie was an excellent cook and the food, to their hungry mouths, was delicious and reviving. The lace cornbread which she fried on the stove was similar to that which Abby MacRae cooked. Katharine noticed that the girls consumed it with relish. This obviously was a Southern way of preparing cornbread, for Tilda usually baked their breads. Katharine had to admit, however, that she had grown to like the fried cornbread.

After the meal was over, Katharine and the girls praised Ollie's cooking, then walked across the yard to the main house. Katharine was eager to have her pupils try their new songs on her grand piano.

"Would you two like to have a music lesson now - maybe play your new songs on the piano here?" she asked.

"Is it a very big piano, Miz Katharine?" Carrie asked.

"Yes, it's one of the largest ones made, and I think you'll see a difference - or hear a difference - in your music played on an upright piano and a grand piano."

They had reached the back steps of the main house, and Katharine was surprised at her own enthusiasm in wanting to hear the girls play the large concert piano.

"Come with me to the music room. I already have your sheet music just waiting for you on the piano."

They entered the large music room off the long hallway which led to the front parlor and the girls stood, looking shyly but expectantly, at the large piano.

"Carrie, why don't you begin? Mary Sue, we'll let her play first. Then, we'll listen to you."

Carrie slid onto the piano seat, and Katharine showed her sister to a chaise lounge in the room, a comfortable piece of furniture with which Mary Sue was not familiar, but which she appeared to enjoy, as she stretched out on its long expanse.

Carrie leaned over to decipher the unfamiliar word which was etched in gold letters above the middle keys of the piano.

"S-t-e-i-n-w-a-y," she spelled, haltingly. "Is it 'steenway' or 'stineway,' Miz Katharine?"

"It's pronounced 'stineway,' Carrie. A concert piano produces a rich vibrancy of sound when it's played, that cannot be matched by an upright piano. Let's see whether you and Mary Sue can detect the difference."

Carrie began with the familiar music from Beethoven's *Ninth Symphony* which she had practiced more, then progressed to *Moonlight Sonata* and *Für Elise* which she had only recently learned. The music, played wistfully and unerringly, with a talented beginner's attempt at finesse, was a balm for her soul, Katharine thought, as she leaned back in the large, old, brocaded chair which once had belonged to her mother.

Katharine closed her eyes, thinking how proud she was of her young music pupils and how quickly they were learning. The music stopped, and Katharine waited, as Carrie and Mary Sue wordlessly changed places. Mary Sue played the three pieces almost identically in the manner her sister had played them, and again

Katharine felt a surge of pride in their competence, which she had been instrumental in bringing about.

The girls tilted their heads as they played, listening for the richness of sound which their teacher had promised them. Katharine beamed with delight when each revealed she could hear the difference in the way the music sounded on her grand piano.

After their short recital, Katharine found a hymn book and other pieces of music which the girls enjoyed practicing, and again she was pleasantly surprised at their emerging skills. She wanted to introduce them to other great classical musicians, such as Mozart and Bach and Vivaldi, but she wanted to nourish their buoyant pleasure in the music, as well as their learning more difficult pieces and the preciseness of timing, which sometimes took away from the joy of the music.

Time passed quickly, and Katharine knew that it would be suppertime, then nighttime, shortly thereafter. If the girls were going to have baths in the "beautiful bathtub," as she had heard them refer to it, then they needed to go ahead before dark and accomplish this.

"Girls, you have played so well and I am very proud of you. However, it's not long before suppertime and then it'll be dark. Unless you want to bathe by candlelight, you'd better go ahead and get your baths now. I'll have Ollie bring in some hot water from the reservoir on the stove."

The girls were excited about their upcoming baths and they hastily repaired to their room. Katharine went to find Big Hill and Ollie to bring hot water to the tub. She glanced at the cypress vat, suspended high in the air beneath the windmill which pumped its contents into the lavatories and tubs in the house. The water, however, was necessarily cold, but this was rectified by hot water from the reservoir on the kitchen wood stove.

Ollie and Big Hill saw her coming, and she called out to them to help her bring hot water into the house. The two colored people were inside the kitchen before Katharine arrived, finding large, clean buckets in which to pour the hot water. They carried the hot water to the back porch; then Katharine showed them where to carry it to the guest bathroom.

Katharine turned on the water in the tub and Ollie added the hot water, until it was warm to the touch. She left towels and bathcloths and a cake of scented soap, then called the girls to their baths.

She could hear them laughing and talking excitedly, and she guessed they must be in the tub together. Obviously, the bath in the lovely, brass-footed tub was a new experience for them, and they were gleefully enjoying the novelty of it all.

While the girls finished bathing, Katharine put away the few things she had carried to the MacRae home, then decided to take a tub bath herself. She found a bucket of the scalding water from the reservoir, which Ollie had left on the back porch, and carried it to her bathroom. Oh, for a nice tub bath, something she had not had in quite some time.

She prepared the water, then took off her dusty, travel-soiled clothes. Stepping into the slipper-shaped porcelain tub, she silently thanked the Lord for the many comforts of her home. She luxuriated in the clean, warm water and washed away the dust from the trip. She washed her hair, also, then reached for a soft, linen towel to rub away the water from her skin and hair.

Dressing quickly, she brushed her damp hair back over her ears and secured it with simple combs. Darkness was approaching and she wondered whether Ollie had brought their supper to the dining room.

She hurried to the dining room and found the meal on the table and candles lit. Ollie had found an appropriate cloth for the table, and everything appeared to be in order. She had made biscuits and though they were not of a dainty size, they looked tempting and tasty.

"Ollie, you learn quickly. I see you found the cloth all right."

"Ah hopes it all right, Miz Kat'rin. Yas'm, Ah look in de drawer dar." She motioned to the large sideboard. "And Ah fine de cloth, and Ah say dis mus' be whut Miz Kat'rin want to put on de table."

"You're right, Ollie. Now, if you'll call the girls, we'll go ahead and eat, before it gets dark."

Ollie left to call the girls and soon they were at their places at the table, waiting for the blessing.

Darkness set in before the meal was over. Katharine was grateful that Ollie had lit a sufficient number of candles on their sticks in the room. Their shadows played on the walls with every movement. Katharine listened with amusement as her young visitors described their baths in the "beautiful bathtub."

Ollie came in to gather the dishes for washing and she was helped by Katharine and the girls. Then, with a lighted lantern in one hand, she led the way to the kitchen where Big Hill was finishing his meal. He and Ollie had eaten together in the kitchen. Katharine thought that Ollie had easily fit into her household. She would be worth the extra pay it would take to keep her.

"We're going on back to the house, Ollie. We're all tired. We'll see you in the morning," Katharine said, as she lit a lantern for the walk back to the house.

"Yas'm, Ah'll have yo' breakfast ready soon after first light, Miz Kat'rin."

"Goodnight," Katharine said.

"Goodnight," the girls called out, as they and Katharine returned to the house.

Katharine couldn't remember being so tired. She looked forward to her large, goose-down bed. She bade the girls goodnight. They gratefully returned to their room, each holding lighted candles, for they were exhausted, also, from the long trip and the events of the day.

***

Katharine sat up in bed, feeling rested and looking forward to a new day. She wondered whether the girls were up and about.

She made her preparations for the day, putting on a cool crushed-linen dress with short sleeves and a scooped neckline. She braided her hair in two braids, then crossed them at the back, bringing up the ends and fastening them under the thick part of the braids on the opposite sides.

She went to the girls' room and knocked on the door.

"Come in," they said in unison.

"Are you two ready to get up?"

"Yes, Ma'm. We're dressed, too, Miz Katharine," Carrie said.

"Well, it's time for breakfast."

Something told Katharine that breakfast would be waiting in the dining room, rather than the kitchen, and she was right. Ollie had everything ready for them, including biscuits and sausage which she had found in the smokehouse. Katharine felt there was more than likely enough meat to last until she moved back to New York, following the sale of her timber. Frank had always kept it full and she was glad to have it so readily available.

The morning was consumed with the girls exploring everything within the Sighing Pines compound. Katharine accompanied them to the stables to see the horses, and she gave them each a carrot to give to the geldings and to Hattie, the mule. They spied the two Percheron draft horses and fed them carrots, also.

They wanted to see the chickens which they had overheard her talking about the day before, so she led them down the woods path to Tilda's chicken coops. They wondered why their grandmother's chickens clucked and pecked all over their yard, while Mrs. Fremont's were kept hidden from view. Mrs. Fremont's chickens had an aura of secretiveness which attracted the young girls to their coops. They brought back fresh eggs for their breakfast the following morning.

Then, they wanted to pick some of her roses and she went to the kitchen and got a knife to cut the stems. These they arranged in a large crystal vase which they placed on the dining room table. When she mentioned that "Queen Anne's Lace" would look pretty with the roses, they followed her into the woods surrounding her yards and watched while she cut some of the flat, lacey blooms. She commented to them that the flower was actually a wild carrot, though it was inedible. They were surprised by this revelation and pulled up one of the lovely, wild-growing plants to look at its roots, which did resemble carrots.

After the midday meal, they sat at the table, talking. Since the dining room was on the front of the house, Katharine could easily see out the lace-curtained window and she was surprised to see Julia Winslow's carriage, with Poke in the driver's seat, pull into her driveway. As she rose from the table, she observed the Negro driver helping Julia to the ground. Next, he reached up and helped

Julia's sister, Blanche, and Blanche's two young daughters from the carriage.

Though Katharine looked forward to seeing Julia, she did not relish the idea of a visit from Blanche. She had never met Blanche's two girls and she wondered whether they were as haughty and snobbish as their mother. Blanche Hughes looked down her sizeable nose at everyone who didn't conform to her exalted paradigm of education, old money, and family background.

Katharine led Carrie and Mary Sue to the parlor, where she suggested that they sit and wait for her to answer the door. Then, with some apprehension, she walked to the door and opened it.

"Katharine," Julia said, rushing inside and hugging her friend. "We were returning from the sawmill at Normandale and thought we'd stop for a visit. You remember Blanche."

Katharine smiled gamely and greeted them all, asking everyone to come inside. She waved to Poke who removed his cap and, with a big grin on his weathered face, nodded toward her. Big Hill was rounding the corner of the house and Katharine knew they would have a fine time, catching up on all of their happenings.

"Katharine, these are Blanche's girls. This is Andrea, the eleven-year-old, and Marsha, the nine-year-old." Same age as Micah's daughters, Katharine thought.

"Well, no, I haven't met your daughters. I'm glad to know you, Andrea and Marsha. And," Katharine said, turning to their mother, "how are you, Blanche?"

"Oh, I've never been better, Katharine. I see you're answering the door yourself. Where's your help these days?" Blanche's thinly arched, raised brows silently repeated the question.

"You mean Tilda, of course. She's in New York now. She won't be back for several weeks."

Katharine blushed in consternation. They would have had to come when Tilda was gone! She wondered whether she could put up with Blanche's sharp tongue without being ugly herself. Katharine feared for Micah's daughters, for she knew that Blanche could be cutting and mean. She was prepared, however, to go on the attack herself, if Blanche should use her poisonous prattle against the two young girls who waited with anticipation in the parlor.

As the visitors moved into the parlor, Katharine could not help but notice the difference in the lovely clothes of Blanche's daughters and those of Micah's children. Blanche's girls were dressed in the latest fashion which included matching hats for their travel ensembles. Though they were not pretty girls, they were already aware of their social status and Katharine could see that they were well on their way to being like their arrogant mother.

She looked at Carrie and Mary Sue, sitting together on the love seat in the parlor, their plain homespun dresses showing not only their sunbrowned skin but also their complete lack of style. The girls stood up when the visitors entered the room and their too-short dresses hung without much fullness from their sash-less waists. Katharine had not even noticed the way they were dressed until now.

She saw them as they must appear to Blanche and the others, and she thought instantly that she should have helped the girls with their hair or maybe looked for sashes for their dresses. Julia was speaking to the girls and Katharine realized that Blanche was staring at the girls, as though she wondered who they were and what in the world they were doing in Katharine's home. Katharine was annoyed with herself for being vulnerable to their thinly-veiled contempt, though she knew that she would leap to Micah's children's defense, if need be.

"Julia and Blanche, I want you to meet Carrie and Mary Sue MacRae. And, Carrie and Mary Sue, these are Mrs. Hughes' daughters, Marsha and Andrea, I believe." She wasn't sure she had remembered their names correctly. The four girls stared at one another, each of the two sets of sisters adroitly sizing up the other.

"Whose girls are these, Katharine?" It was Julia speaking, and she was smiling in a kind but still somewhat condescending way.

"They are Micah MacRae's children." Before Katharine could further explain, Julia's eyes registered recognition at the name.

"Oh, of course, the backwoodsman from Telfair County. He has been in our home several times, and to some of our parties, and he's always welcome."

Blanche looked surprised that Julia had invited any of the backwoods people to her parties which were the most important social events of the year, in her mind. Though Blanche lived in New York, she visited her sister in Eastman several times during the year and sometimes attended her parties, but she said she didn't remember meeting anyone named Micah MacRae. In fact, she said, she hadn't met any of the backwoods people.

"No," Julia said, "you weren't here for those parties, Blanche, but Micah MacRae is probably the best timber raftsman on the Ocmulgee and Altamaha rivers. He has rafted some of our timber and got the best prices for it at Darien, and he's going to harvest and raft Katharine's timber in the fall." She looked at Katharine, stating, "You're fortunate, Katharine, to get him. We've been unable to hire him to raft any more of our timber. He's just too busy now."

Blanche raised her finely penciled eyebrows, still gazing at the MacRae children, who looked sweetly from her to her daughters, obviously not picking up on the pinching curiosity of the haughty woman in regard to themselves.

The Hughes children stared at the MacRae girls as if they were watching a circus act, waiting to see whether the girls might stumble and fall right before their very eyes. Katharine was nervous, though she was determined not to show it.

"Won't you sit down? Carrie and Mary Sue are my music pupils. I wanted them to come home with me and try their pieces on my large piano." Why did she feel the need to explain the girls' presence? She inwardly reproved herself, waiting to see how the conversation would turn.

"Oh," said Blanche, her eyebrows still aloft, "and how are you girls progressing?" Before Carrie or her younger sister could answer, Blanche put her arm around her daughters and bragged to everyone that Andrea and Marsha had been taking piano lessons for three years and they would like to play something for everyone on Katharine's piano.

"Of course," Katharine said, for wont of something better to say. "Let's go into the music room."

Julia spoke up, apparently attempting to give the MacRae girls the same opportunity to show their musical talents, but Katharine knew that this would only allow another sharp contrast between the MacRae and Hughes children. She wasn't sure how to handle the situation and only wished that Blanche and her brood had never even come to her home.

On reaching the music room, the older girl, Andrea, sat at the piano and looked at the music which Carrie and Mary Sue had left open on the instrument.

"Mmm, *Für Elise*," Andrea said. Yes, she said, she and her sister had the very same music and they had both learned to play it. She began playing it, missing almost every other note, and Katharine found it hard to believe that the child had had three years of music instruction. She played the other pieces which were, also, on the piano, in the same broken manner, followed by her younger sister who played even worse than she.

"Thank you, girls. That was nice," Katharine said, literally stretching the truth so as not to hurt their feelings, and almost in the same breath, she said, "Carrie, let's hear you play, dear." Carrie's lovely smile lit up her face as she slipped onto the polished piano bench. Her small brown hands quickly played the eighth notes which comprised every measure, and after playing one song, she quickly played through the other Beethoven selections. Gracefully, she rose, and Mary Sue swiftly took her place, playing as well as her older sister the lovely songs, albeit simple renditions, of Beethoven's classical music.

Katharine felt she would surely burst with pride, as both girls stood up and performed a quaint curtsy of sorts before everyone assembled in the music room.

Julia Winslow and her sister, Blanche Hughes, looked stunned at the girls' performances. Though Blanche quickly regained her composure, Julia was the first to speak.

"Katharine, I'm amazed. I knew you had studied music and could play well yourself, but I've known you all these years and I didn't know you taught music."

"Oh, I don't, Julia. I mean, I never have, until now. These two are my only students," she said with a laugh, gesturing toward Carrie and Mary Sue who were returning to their places on the large chaise lounge.

"They also played well," Blanche said, in perhaps the only way she knew how to give a compliment, as an extension of one which she gave to her own children.

"Thank you," Carrie and Mary Sue said, smiling. The two Hughes girls looked at them with grudging new respect.

Almost abruptly, Blanche said that they really should be going, but that it was good seeing Katharine and knowing that she was faring so well, since Frank's death. And, she said, she thought it nice that Katharine was teaching the backwoods children music. Why, she, Blanche, would not dare to venture off the well-traveled, main road into the obscurity of the backwoods. Also, she had heard that these backwoods people, or squatters, as she'd heard them called, couldn't be reasoned with and were the cause of the murder of John Forsyth. Aside, she whispered to Katharine, "They are dangerous people!"

The two MacRae girls did not understand everything that Blanche was saying and they weren't sure what the term, "backwoods," meant, but they intuitively understood that she must mean that they lived in the woods area of the county, which they couldn't deny. However, when the name, John C. Forsyth, was mentioned, they quickly remembered the house where he once lived, on the McRae-Eastman Road which they had traveled the day before. They were startled to hear that he had been murdered and this lady visitor was saying that the backwoods people had done it. Also, though Blanche's last words were whispered, they were loud enough to reach the MacRae girls' ears, and they heard that the people in the backwoods were dangerous! Carrie and Mary Sue looked at each other in puzzlement, their innocence gradually giving way to spurious knowledge.

Katharine was filled with loathing for this woman who was using her home and hospitality to heap invectives on the young children in her care, and she was about to retaliate when Julia spoke to her sister.

"Blanche, I'm sure that many of the backwoods families are charming people, such as the MacRae family and, as I remember, the sheriff of Telfair County, Hugh Cole, was found guilty, along with a well-known lawyer from Eastman, Luther Hall, of the murder of John Forsyth. They are still serving time in the Ohio State Penitentiary. They were townspeople, not backwoodsmen."

"Julia," Blanche said with vehemence, "surely you remember reading all about it. A man named Rich Lowery killed Mr. Forsyth.

I believe the papers referred to him as a Scuffletonian, a man of mixed race - part white, part colored and part Indian - from Roanoke Island, North Carolina. The newspapers were full of it."

"Of course, I remember reading about it, but the main ones involved, besides the gunman you just mentioned who was not from this area, were the sheriff of Telfair County and the lawyer of Dodge County, not exactly your average backwoodsmen," Julia said with some sarcasm.

"Well," Blanche continued, unruffled, "they were called 'squatters,' as I recollect, but that's the same as backwoods people. Also, Katharine, wasn't it generally believed that they killed Frank, too?"

Katharine could remain silent no longer. She stood in front of the MacRae girls, trying to shield them as she faced Blanche Hughes.

"It was never decided who killed Frank, Blanche, but let's get something straight. Squatters are people who settle on other people's land with no right to do so. It is not synonymous with backwoodsmen," she said.

"But this war you all are engaged in, off and on, is called the 'Squatters' War.'"

Katharine did not want to argue. She just wanted Blanche Hughes out of her house and well on her way back to Eastman or, preferably, back to her home in New York. Katharine turned and glanced at Carrie and Mary Sue who were still sitting quietly on the chaise lounge behind her. Their faces reflected both apprehension and the dawning of realization of how their people in the backwoods were regarded by this wealthy woman from the North. They were somewhat embarrassed and looked at themselves as with new eyes, studying their plain dresses and sturdy shoes that had seen much wear. They noticed the fair skin of the Northern women, then looked at their own young skin, brown from the sun. They looked at each other as if to decipher that they both were experiencing and thinking the same things, and the recognition in the other's eyes said that they were.

Katharine was speaking, and the girls sensed that she was fighting a verbal battle with the woman, Blanche Hughes, who was pleased that she had evoked such spirit from a Northern compatriot.

Why, Katharine really should be more careful about mingling with the outlaw squatters and having their children as her houseguests. Blanche was aghast. Why, these people were what some people called "white trash," though she as a Christian woman had never used the term herself. Why, they would be stealing from Katharine, and worse!

Julia knew that Katharine was upset and she gave her sister a look that would have wilted a less confident woman, but Blanche's nostrils only flared briefly under the scrutiny. Julia put her arm around Katharine, hoping to ease the tension in the room.

"Katharine, I have been missing you. You haven't been to any of our parties during the last several months. We're having a ball Wednesday night and that's the main reason I stopped by to see you - to invite you to the ball on Wednesday." As if reading her friend's mind, Julia interjected that Blanche would be returning home on tomorrow's early train which would free the guest house for Katharine.

Julia continued, "I want you to stay for at least a week's visit, as you used to. We'll also be having another company meeting which you should attend. And..." Julia paused, looking undecided about revealing a final reason for Katharine's timely visit. "And," Julia said again, "Sewell Siddon is coming to the ball, Katharine, and he wants to see you. You're going to be sending your timber to Darien before long and, believe me, it helps to have a friend who also happens to be a timber inspector. He has never inspected our timber, but we have had some who did not give us the best prices when we knew our timber was the best money could buy. We are hoping that Sewell will be our inspector and will give us a better inspection report, when we send more of our trees down to Darien."

Katharine wondered about Julia's inability to see Sewell Siddon as she, Katharine, had seen him at the Winslows' home some months ago. It seemed like such a long time ago, now. His nickname, "Sly," said it all to Katharine, though she didn't doubt that what Julia said was true about having a timber inspector friend. Katharine realized that while the Winslows embraced him as an ally in the timber business, she preferred to avoid him for personal and business reasons. However, the thought of being alone for several weeks gave Katharine a change of heart, and she welcomed the thought of a change of pace at the Winslow home, with people to talk to and events to share. She smiled at Julia.

"I would love to come up for a few days, Julia," she said. "It'll be lonely here for me, without Tillie, and I'm taking the girls back home tomorrow."

Julia looked pleased that Katharine had accepted her invitation and she moved toward the front door. Blanche motioned to her daughters who followed after their mother, emulating the way she thrust her head back with her lips pursed. Blanche's figure had grown rounder with the passing years and Katharine thought she resembled a proud, plump hen, strutting along with her brood of equally proud and plump chicks. Katharine was glad for them to go. She hardly felt like being civil to the woman. Goodbyes were said at the door, with Julia reminding Katharine that she was expected for a week's visit.

"I'm coming, Julia. I'm looking forward to it."

Julia looked at the MacRae children, standing near Katharine.

"I suppose you know that your father is the top raftsman and timber dealer on the Ocmulgee and Altamaha rivers," she said to them.

"No, we didn't know that," Carrie said modestly, shaking her head.

"Well, he is. He's in great demand now. We all want Micah MacRae to raft our timber." Julia held out her hand to the girls and each shook her hand.

"You girls are quite talented. I hope to hear you play the piano again sometime." The girls smiled at her kind remarks and thanked her.

As Blanche and her daughters were helped into the waiting carriage by Poke, Julia seized the opportunity for a few private words with Katharine.

"Please look over Blanche's behavior, Katharine. She's my sister, but sometimes I can't stand her high-minded ways. I hope she didn't upset you."

Katharine stepped away from the MacRae girls and walked down the front steps with Julia.

"If I seemed upset, Julia, it was because of Carrie and Mary Sue. I didn't want them to be hurt or embarrassed," she said.

"Actually, if I'd known you had guests, I wouldn't have stopped by, because of Blanche. You know, I think she's always been jealous of you, Katharine. You are beautiful, and she's not. Also, I think she resents our friendship. She's my sister, but I have never felt close to her because of her arrogant ways. However, I did want to invite you up for a visit and I did accomplish that. We have missed you, Katharine. Oh, and Steve will be there! He and Vickie recently had their sixth child, another little girl."

"My, Julia, how time flies! At your last party I attended, Vickie was expecting the baby and now it's here! I can hardly believe it! Talk about being jealous! Here, Vickie has six children and I'm a widow with no children! I'm afraid I'm just a little jealous," Katharine laughed.

"Well, it's certainly not too late, Katharine. You'll meet someone before long. I know you don't seem to be interested in Inspector Siddon, but he certainly wants to know everything about you. He kept asking where you lived, as he wanted to come to see you, but I avoided telling him, because you asked me not to." Julia paused. "Well," she said, "they're waiting for me. We'll see you soon. 'Bye, Katharine. 'Bye, girls." She turned around and waved to the girls who smiled and waved back.

"Goodbye, Julia," Katharine said.

Katharine walked back to the MacRae children, and the three of them stood in the large doorway, watching the thoroughbreds clop briskly down the driveway and out of sight. Katharine sighed, wondering what the girls were thinking about the bizarre visit with Blanche and her daughters. She didn't really know how much they had heard nor how much they had understood, so she waited for them to talk to her about it.

However, the MacRae children didn't even mention Blanche or the Hughes girls. Rather, though they were quieter than usual, they engaged in their usual girlish chatter, devoid of anything vengeful or mean, and Katharine attributed this to their innate good manners, for she knew with a certainty that they had comprehended some of the boorish Blanche's comments. She attributed their sweetness and kindness to Abigail MacRae whose gentle upbringing had cradled them from the harsh realities of life, which included the rudeness and meanness of people like Blanche Hughes.

Katharine devoted the afternoon to activities which her young visitors would enjoy, attempting to help them forget the unpleasantness of the strangers' visit. She found interesting puzzles for the girls to put together, then surprised them with samplers which she had purchased for them in Eastman several weeks before, replete with fine threads of varying hues. She taught them the intricacies of fine embroidery and marveled at their quick minds and the deftness of their young, brown fingers in manipulating the embroidery needles.

As evening neared, Ollie had supper ready in the dining room and Katharine and the two girls took their places at the table. Candles had been lit to ward off the approaching darkness which appeared before they had finished the meal. Katharine reminded the girls that they would leave early the following morning for their return trip home. They promised to be ready by daybreak.

***

The dawn of a late summer morning is a beautiful sight, Katharine thought, as the horse pulled the carriage in an eastward direction along the main dirt road. Sunlight trickled through the apertures where the pine boughs intertwined over a hundred feet above the sandy road. Cattle sounds drifted through the thick trees on both sides of the road, mingled with the caws of crows and the distinct "keeer-r-r" call of a red-tailed hawk, circling high above them.

Carrie and Mary Sue had talked between themselves for several miles, leaving Katharine to her own thoughts, but when she heard them mention their father, she was drawn to their conversation. It occurred to her that she had never seen Micah MacRae with his children. He was always away, though she knew that he was home with them at nights when he wasn't rafting on the river. And now, he was faced with the fact that the Dodges were claiming his land! Katharine knew that he was in something akin to a death struggle, but she didn't think his children knew anything about his problems. She listened to their innocent words.

"I wonder when he's a-comin' back," Mary Sue said.

"He said he was a-comin back this weekend, lessen somethin' kep' him from it," Carrie said.

"He ain't never home much no more," Mary Sue said, and Katharine was glad that Blanche Hughes didn't hear Mary Sue's incorrect usage of the English language.

"Well, he has to make money for us," Carrie replied.

This seemed sufficient for Mary Sue. The girls lapsed into silence, broken soon by the whistle of the train leaving the sawmill at Normandale and crossing the road on the railroad tracks ahead of them. They were excited about seeing the clanging locomotive again, but this time its flatcars were empty, as it followed the long railroad track into the forested, shared border of Dodge and Telfair Counties.

Crossing the railroad track after the last rail car had jangled and clanged out of sight, Katharine turned the horse onto the road which followed the track for several miles into the pine forest. Presently, they came upon the train, halted in a clearing, being loaded with the huge trees which lay strewn on the stump-scarred ground between the railroad tracks and the peripheral forest. Katharine reined in the horse and she and the children watched the logging procedure, now accomplished on a much larger scale than that of Micah MacRae's, which she had seen several weeks prior. This was the Yellow Pines Lumber Company, and the very latest in tools and equipment were at its disposal.

The place teemed with activity as the colored and white loggers, some with shirts removed and sweat glistening on their torsos, readied the felled trees for their transport back to the East Tennessee, Virginia, and Georgia Railroad which ran by the huge Yellow Pines Lumber Mill. Two men were about to cut down a tree, a forest giant which towered a hundred feet above them. Its lowest branches were around seventy-five feet from the ground, and its huge trunk was at least three feet in diameter at its base. One logger held a double ax with a cutting edge on both ends of the ax head.

Before chopping the tree the axman cut a notch into one side of it to determine which direction he wanted it to fall. He then began chopping on the side of the tree opposite the notch. Two men used a ten-foot crosscut saw to complete the cutting of the tree. After a long period of tedious sawing, the loggers cut close to the last remaining wood fibers, allowing the staggering tree to crash to the ground, midst the scurrying away of nearby loggers.

Katharine glanced at the girls who looked frightened, holding their hands over their ears to lessen the deafening noise of the plunging yellow pine. They appeared less fearful, however, once the tree was on the ground.

Loggers hastened like ants to strip the tree of its top and limbs. One of the loggers used the broadax to square the sides of the tree. Katharine was surprised at herself for remembering the procedures and terms which Micah had explained to her. This timber was to be sold as hewn or squared timber, according to Micah's explanation, as hers would be when it was cut in the fall.

She couldn't help but notice the difference in the landscape where the big trees had been cut, several years past. Large stumps stood as monuments to all the trees that were logged. Patches of wiregrass, dog fennel, ragweed, goldenrod, and broom sedge competed in hiding the jagged scars of merciless logging. She thought about the cattle and wildlife that lived in the forest. What would happen to them when all the trees were gone? She also thought about the fact that the lumber company was edging closer to Micah MacRae's land lots. She marveled at his daring in ignoring the claims of the Dodges to his land and timber and going ahead and rafting his timber to Darien. She knew that other Southern landowners were doing the same thing, attempting to squeeze any profit from the timber before the Dodges' logchoppers invaded what, they thought, were rightfully their own land and trees. She also knew that they risked jail or prison terms in doing this and she feared for Micah MacRae!

The company woodchoppers were getting ready to transport the logs to the waiting rail cars, and Katharine observed that the girls were as interested as she in watching this take place. Actually, she knew that they had never witnessed any of the timber harvesting which was quickly encroaching on their family's property; nor, of course, could they know that a vastly wealthy man by the name of Dodge had recently claimed the land, where their house and surrounding timber stood, as his very own. Katharine knew with a certainty that it was just a matter of time before the land war turned even more violent and ugly.

Several drivers, or teamsters, worked together to connect the twenty-four-yokes of oxen with the massive balance cart which was to be used to move the largest logs to the waiting flatcars. The balance cart had nine-foot wheels, held together with an inverted u-shape axle which allowed an opening for the log to go through. The axle was covered by a frame of hickory wood, held together by huge u-bolts. A pair of log tongs was suspended from the top of the frame at the rear by a large metal ring. At the front of the cart a tongue projected at the top of the frame. The oxen were harnessed to this tongue, which was made from a strong wooden pole about ten feet in length.

The drivers pulled the timber cart lengthwise over the log until the rear of the cart reached the center of the log. A teamster then uncoupled the oxen from the tongue and pushed it upward, dropping the cart on its backside. This lowered the tongs at the rear of the cart where the logger could sink them into the log. The tongs had hooks which caught hold of the log and held it in place.

Next, the oxen were hitched to the tongue and as they pulled, the cart was lifted into an upright position and the weight of the log forced the hooks of the tongs into the log more deeply, securing it more firmly. Once the cart rotated past the center of gravity, the weight on the tongue pressed downward. Then, the drivers tied a chain around the log and tongue, and the cart was ready to move.

Katharine could hear only fragments of the workers' conversation, but she did hear one say that they might need a rule cart with this tree, because of its vast size; however, the logging overseer ruled this out, stipulating that only one cart should suffice. Again, Katharine was surprised and somewhat proud of herself for remembering that a rule cart was a second cart which was sometimes used to move especially large trees.

The strong, patient oxen slowly moved the first of the large logs to the nearest flatcar, heeding the ever-cracking rawhide whips which sang near their ears. Katharine remembered hearing that the "Cracker" designation for the local people derived from the cracking sounds of the rawhide whips which could be heard before the arrival of the men and their animals into outlying towns, such as Savannah, where the local farmers formerly made yearly ox-and-wagon trips, sometimes lasting weeks and months.

Workmen placed skids diagonally against the railcar over which the log was to be rolled. They then pulled a chain under the log and fastened it at two points on the railcar side, which was opposite to the log. This formed a loop of the chain with the tip of the loop protruding from under the log.

Then, a second chain lying across the top of the log was fastened to the tip of the loop. Lastly, the teamster linked this second chain to the oxen. As the team pulled forward, the chain dragged the log sidewise up the skids and onto the flatcar. The loud thud as it dropped into the flatcar shook the forest floor. Midst all of the sounds of logging came the monotonic chant of the teamsters: "Rain or shine, money is mine, Work or play, a dollar a day."

In addition to the oxen and mules, Katharine saw a skidder in operation several hundred yards farther down the timber railway. She urged the horse forward so that they might see the unusual machine in operation, stopping as the noise became deafening. The children covered their ears. She had heard Ben Winslow describe the new machine which greatly facilitated the removal of felled trees to the waiting railroad cars.

The noisy skidder was firmly staked to the ground beside the timber railroad track. It looked like a heavy wooden sled, around twenty feet long and eight feet wide. A small, upright steam engine boiler was on one end, with the hissing, puffing steam engine in the middle. Two big winches, the size of fifty-five gallon drums, were on the other end. Steel wire cables, unwound from the winches, ran to pulleys attached to the top of one of the tall trees across the railroad track. From this tree, the cables ran across the woods to another tree about five hundred feet away. With one of the cables guyed taut, the other ran beneath it through a trolley. Several sticks of timber were attached to the alternately creaking, grinding, pounding trolley cable and were being pulled toward the railroad cars.

When the logs were cut from the area that could be reached by the cable on the trolley, the tight line would be moved a hundred feet or so, and the process repeated. The acreage where the skidder had been used was already resembling a large asterisk.

Katharine turned the horse around to proceed toward Bear Creek. Again, she thought about the differences in the way the

Dodges harvested their timber and the methods of the local farmers who had few tools and animals to help with their home logging operations. Regardless, the tree cutters led hard and dangerous lives. She knew that accidents happened on a regular basis and loggers were often killed or maimed for life.

"Well, girls," Katharine said, clucking to the horse and urging him down the Bear Creek path, "you have seen how trees are cut and placed on the rail cars. It's been a new experience for you, I suspect, as it has been for me."

"Yes, Ma'm," Carrie answered. "It's really hard work."

"Oh, I'm sure it is. These are such old trees, such tremendous trees. They're probably hundreds of years old. Someone said they were around two hundred, or maybe even three hundred years old," Katharine said.

The girls appeared to be deep in thought and Katharine was surprised at Carrie's foresight when she next expressed her feelings.

"I'm just a-wonderin' how it's all a-gonna look here in a few years. There's just a-gonna be big tree stumps all around."

Mary Sue added her not so childish thoughts which brought chills to Katharine's spine.

"Prob'ly for miles and miles and miles - nuthin' but big ole tree stumps!"

They were entering the forest domain of Bear Creek now, where the distant lumbermen's shouts and the muffled sounds of logging gave way to the gurgle of water, the chirping of birds, and the snapping of twigs in the creek underbrush by animals, both domesticated and wild. The coolness of the pathway provided a welcome relief from the heat they had experienced in the timber railway clearing floor earlier. Only a few of the sun's rays filtered through to the ground below, providing the usual dim light which marked the backwoods even during the sunniest of days.

The horse clopped on for a number of miles farther on the woods path which followed the nearby creek. The creek broadened as it flowed southward into Horse Creek, but it still would have accommodated only one, or at the most two of the large logs which Micah had floated on down to the mouth of Horse Creek, where he had assembled them into a raft. Horse Creek emptied into the

Ocmulgee River. It would have taken some time to have floated enough logs to make a sizable raft to drift on to market at Darien. Katharine was only beginning to comprehend the plight of the independent raftsman who probably had to beg and borrow tools and draft animals to accomplish the harvesting of his trees.

The old wood bridge spanning Bear Creek came into view through the trees, and Katharine guided the horse over it. They were now on the larger dirt road which ran in front of Micah's house. If she followed it to the left, it would lead back to Longview which was several miles north of McRae. She might return home that way, once she carried the girls home.

She reined the horse to the right and followed the road for several miles, until the MacRae farmstead came into view. Katharine was surprised to see a large black bull inside the wood rail fence, which was several hundred yards from the old double pen house. She remembered seeing another bull, a red one, months ago, the first time she ever visited the MacRae home, and she idly wondered why these had been pent up, while other cattle grazed freely in the open woods.

They pulled up to the picket fence which surrounded the house and Katharine climbed quickly from the carriage. The girls clambered down and she helped them gather their few belongings from the boot of the carriage.

Abby was on the porch, speaking to the girls and inviting Katharine in. The girls unlatched the gate and raced up the steps to their grandmother's arms. Little Roy, she told them, was asleep.

Katharine hurried on inside the gate and was startled by the dog, Brownie, barking at her from his refuge under the front doorsteps. He pulled himself out from the snug enclosure and proceeded to wag his tail in greeting. Katharine had never understood why the dog usually preceded his welcome with barking; nor could she understand why the barking always alarmed her, if only momentarily. She patted the large dog's thick neck, reminding him that they were friends. Then, she joined Abby and the girls on the wide-timbered front porch.

"Katharine, dear, come on inside and stay awhile."

"I can't, Mrs. Abby. I must be getting back, but I want you

to know how very much I enjoyed having Carrie and Mary Sue for a visit."

Before Abby could reply, the girls were talking at the same time, eager to tell their grandmother of their new experiences at "Miz Katharine's" house. Abby and Katharine couldn't help but laugh at their descriptive accounts.

"Gramma, we had a tub bath in Miz Katharine's big, claw-foot tub," Carrie said.

"Yes," Mary Sue added, "it had feet on it, and they were like claws."

"And it had water a-runnin' in it. I ain't never seen nuthin' like it," Carrie continued.

"And then, awhile ago," Mary Sue said, changing the subject, "we saw big trees a-bein' cut down and put on a train. We saw the train, too."

The expression on Abby's face changed. Katharine could see worry in her aged but still expressive brown eyes.

"Where are they a-cuttin' now?" she asked.

Katharine answered, quietly, "They're cutting along the timber railroad, Mrs. Abby."

"Well, I ain't been that way in a long time. I keep hearin' that Mr. Dodge is a-sayin' that a lot of our neighbors' land lots are his. I don't know what to make of it. All I know is that the people who live around here have been a-payin' taxes on this land for years. The same fam'lies have a-been a-livin' here in the piney woods since they bought the land at the tax sale in 1845."

Vaguely, Katharine remembered someone saying that the State of Indiana had owned over 500 square miles of this area of Georgia, but the state didn't pay the Georgia property taxes, so the Telfair tax collector had issued a fi fa upon the entire acreage. Now, she remembered it was the Savannah lawyer at the last Company meeting who explained everything. He had said that hundreds of lots, at 202½ acres per lot, were sold at a private sale, the usual price being six cents a lot. She was beginning to understand a little better why the "squatters," as they were inappropriately called, were outraged. Katharine wondered whether Abby MacRae knew much about her own involvement with the timber company. All

Katharine realized, at the moment, was that she hurt for the MacRae family and for all of the families who were being dispossessed.

Suddenly, they all jumped at a loud bellow from the caged bull inside the rail fence near the house. The animal was trotting round and round the enclosure, stopping now and then to butt at the fence with his long horns. Katharine was afraid the fence would give way, but Abby assured her that Micah had firmly secured the rails and there was no danger that the animal would escape.

"I'm curious, I suppose, Mrs. Abby, but why is the bull in the pen? The other cows are all grazing in the open woods."

"Micah's a-gonna sell this one to breed. The man's supposed to come and get 'im before long," Abby said. "He sure don't like bein' pent up," she said, with a smile, as the bull continued to rake the fence with his sharp horns.

Katharine turned from watching the animal, repeatedly smashing its head into the stacked rail fence, for it frightened her with its brute strength. A sense of foreboding gripped her, for the bull's savagery seemed symbolic of the increasingly violent land war which was inching ever nearer to the MacRae homeplace on Bear Creek, and she longed for a peace which appeared to be ever more elusive.

"Mrs. Abby, I must go," Katharine said, abruptly. She gave Abby and her granddaughters a quick hug, then hurried down the steps and out the narrow front gate.

"You be careful, Katharine, dear. Goodbye," Abby called, as Katharine quickly climbed up onto the carriage seat and clucked the horse down the yard path and on to the road in front of the house. She could hear the girls bidding her goodbye, and she turned to wave with a lump in her throat, as the horse pulled the carriage onto the white sandy road.

Heretofore, she had only been concerned with the plight of Micah and his family, insofar as losing their land and home was concerned, but it struck her now that Micah could be involved in actual warfare. She had seen enough of him to know that he was a fighter and that he was unafraid. Abby MacRae had lost her husband in a war. Would she lose a son, also, in another war?

And what was she, Katharine, to do? Micah resented her association with the Yellow Pines Lumber Company, but this was her livelihood, just as his was his farm and his timber. She really didn't know what to believe and she certainly didn't have anyone to turn to.

Already, the war had claimed too many lives, in addition to her husband's and John C. Forsyth's. Also, five local men were yet in the Ohio State Penitentiary for conspiring to kill John Forsyth. The actual perpetrator, Rich Lowery, was also killed, supposedly by some of the conspirators. The men involved, naively or perhaps desperately, believed that their murder of the Dodge Company superintendent would alarm the Dodges to the extent that they would abandon their claims to over 300,000 acres of the finest yellow pines in the world. Obviously, the men who planned Forsyth's and her husband's murders conjectured that the land would revert back to the local people who were forcibly being evicted from their lands and homes.

Katharine knew that Luther Hall, the prominent lawyer in Eastman presently serving time in the Ohio Penitentiary for conspiring to murder John Forsyth, had found several important discrepancies and outright breaks in the labyrinthian titles to the lands in question. In fact, Hall had exposed the weakness of Dodge's "short chain of title," so that the timber baron was forced to exercise his "long chain of title," which though also fraught with weak links was upheld by several successive federal judges during the years of ongoing court battles, involving the tremendous tract of land.

She mused on, as the horse followed the dirt road into Longview. Pulling the reins to the left, she guided the horse onto the main road which connected Eastman to the north with McRae to the south. Her Sighing Pines homeplace was on this road, nestled far back against the tall pines, but it was still an hour's drive away. Her thoughts shifted from the escalation of the local land war to her upcoming visit with the Winslows, and her spirits lifted somewhat. She would try to forget for a few days the heightening land war and the latest Klan raid on her property. Since she longed for a safe place to go, perhaps a visit to Winslow Hall would be both timely and enjoyable.

Nearing the Yellow Pines Lumber Mill, Katharine heard the indisputable sounds of logging. Looking through the trees on the right side of the sandy dirt road, she saw a twenty-four-yoke ox team pulling a timber cart, loaded with a huge felled tree, in the direction of the sawmill. Other loggers were busy with crosscut saws, cutting down more of the trees, their trembling bushy crowns silhouetted like thin emerald splinters against the open blue sky. This had taken place since she and the girls had passed by earlier in the morning.

Already, a dead landscape of bare tree stumps was taking shape, rivaling the one which she and the children had seen earlier in the day near Bear Creek. She remembered the remarks of the MacRae girls about all of the tree stumps being left behind. "For miles and miles...," one of them had said.

Though Katharine knew nothing of proper logging procedures, she felt that the Yellow Pines Lumber Company was somehow being careless and wasteful. It was strange that she never thought of such when Frank was alive, or she would have questioned him about many of the practices of the lumber company.

In the distance ahead on the dirt road, Katharine saw a covered-wagon train approaching her, loaded with people who were going to settle on some of the cut-over land in the area. She had heard of this happening repeatedly. Often, after the Dodges confiscated someone's land and harvested its timber, they would sell the land back to its original inhabitants. Then, again, the Dodges might sell the land to someone else.

Katharine studied the faces of the people who passed by in the wagons. For the most part, they looked tired and apprehensive, fearful of what awaited them on their lands, pockmarked in every direction with hundreds and thousands of large tree stumps, limbs, and treetops. Katharine shuddered at the thought of eking out a living on the desolate lands which bore the scars of the logging saws.

The sight of small children, riding in all of the six wagons, tugged at her heart. What future awaited them on the cut-over land which would be their homesteads? These new settlers would, necessarily, have to live in the wagons until they could erect their double-pen houses. Just thinking of the hardships and deprivations which, of a surety, lay in store for them caused her to offer up a silent prayer for their well-being. As the wagons passed within a few feet of her, some of the people nodded and smiled, some called out greetings, but others only looked straight ahead, oblivious of her in her fine carriage.

Home wasn't far away now and the gelding knew it. Katharine could hardly restrain the horse, as he raced headlong toward home and his manger of oats. She pulled on the reins, fearful that the carriage would lose a wheel on the bumpy road, and the horse was subdued, somewhat. However, the last few miles were covered quickly, and she was relieved to see the Sighing Pines nomenclature arched over the iron gates of her homeplace.

She was also glad to see Big Hill and Ollie who were in the process of grooming the other gelding, Harry. Big Hill was cleaning the horse's front, left hoof with a hoof pick, while Ollie brushed his large sleek body with a currycomb. They grinned broadly when they looked up and saw Katharine returning home.

The horses greeted each other with snorts and head bobbing, each rubbing his large head against the other. Katharine and the two colored people laughed at their display of recognition toward each other. Big Hill gave Katharine a helping hand from the carriage.

"General Lee could surely use some grooming, too, Big Hill. He's also quite thirsty. He rushed the last few miles, thinking about his oats, I guess," Katharine said with a laugh.

"Sho thing, Miz Kat'rin. Ah's gonna see 'bout Gen'l Lee now. Ah's been cleanin' Harry's hoofs, but Ah's thu now, and Ollie's 'bout thu combin' 'im." Ollie nodded and smiled, as Big Hill began unhitching the horse from the carriage.

"Ah feed and water Gen'l Lee, den we give 'im a good rubdown."

"He'll like that," Katharine said, as she turned to walk toward the house. Then, looking back, she said, "I can't remember whether I told you or not, but I'm planning to visit the Winslows in Eastman for a week. I'm leaving early Saturday morning and should return the following weekend. Will you two be staying here?"

"Yas'm. Ollie might not stay here all de time, but Ah plans to. Ah'll see 'bout de hosses, and Ah's still wukkin' on yo' other cah'age, Miz Kat'rin. It still ain' fixed so's you can use it."

"Well, I'm glad you'll be staying, Hill. I'm always grateful that I can count on you and Ollie."

"Yas'm, Miz Kat'rin," Ollie said. "Ah be here most ob de time, 'cep when Ah has to go back to the settle'mint to see 'bout ma daughtuh. She gonna have a baby, and she ain' feelin' too good." Ollie reached for the bridle of the gelding, Harry, and led him inside the stable to his stall, followed by Big Hill, leading General Lee.

Katharine continued on toward the back porch steps. She needed to pack some things for her visit at Winslow Hall during the upcoming week. She looked forward to seeing everyone. She needed to rid her mind of worrying about the local land war. After all, she didn't understand it and no one seemed to be able to explain it fully to her. She had made up her mind that the truth was somewhere in the middle and there was nothing she could do to rectify the situation. She had also done some serious thinking about Micah MacRae. She had decided that she was infatuated with him only because she had let herself be cut off from her family and friends.

Well, she thought, as she slowly ascended the back steps of the house, she would rectify the situation by enjoying herself at the Winslows' and by trying to forget how she had become too involved with Micah MacRae and his family. She would keep her relationship with the backwoodsman on a business level only. She would not let him kiss her again. He probably took her for a fool, she thought, but not anymore. She would keep him at arms' length until he had sold her timber for her. Then she would return home to New York, never to see him again.

Chapter Eighteen

The rain pattered outside against the paned windows of her bedchamber as Katharine sat at her desk, alternately composing a letter to her parents and gazing at the quickening rain. In contemplating the trip to the Winslows', she didn't mind the rain so much, but the muddy roads it engendered made travel by carriage uncomfortable and even risky. She would wait several hours and maybe it would let up, though the roads often remained mucky for several days following a hard downpour. She knew the farmers would welcome the rain, however, for the area had experienced drought conditions for some time.

She stared at the daguerreotype of her parents on her desk. The hand-colored photograph in its oval cut-out of the leather case was a decade old, but her parents had changed very little, she thought. The photographer had rather singularly captured the thrust of her father's chin and the upswept hair of her mother. Both pairs of blue eyes, though frozen in time, met her own.

The letter to her parents drew her attention again, and she replenished the pen with ink from the desk inkwell. The words would not come easily. Several times, she wadded the linen writing paper and began anew. Finally, after completing several sentences, the letter began to take shape and the words spilled forth onto the page. She loved her parents, but how could they understand all she had endured, a thousand miles away, since Frank's death?

What would they think of her feelings (and she, herself, didn't know exactly what they were!) for an illiterate farmer-raftsman whose land was being confiscated by the sons of their now deceased, good and honorable friend, William E. Dodge? Her parents must never know of her association with this backwoodsman who, some said, was the leader of the infamous "Squatters." "Squatter" was a misnomer, she knew, but she would never be able to explain this to her parents.

Would her parents really think that their late, wealthy friend, William E. Dodge, was the upstanding Christian he had held himself out to be, if they could see the ravaged, cut-over lands which so altered the towering piney woods landscape? He, and now his sons, had filled their pockets with lucre from piney woods land and timber, using questionable deeds and strong-arm tactics.

What would they think if they knew of the Ku Klux Klan raids on her property and the fact that the perpetrators had not even been caught and brought to justice, free to strike again? She had felt the urge for some time to go to New York for a visit with her parents, and now that the latest Klan raid had made it dangerous for her to stay at her home in the piney woods of Georgia, she felt she should go ahead, following her visit with the Winslows in Eastman, and make the trip to New York. She and Tillie could then make the return trip, back to Georgia, together.

She penned all of this in her letter, telling her parents that her timber was to be cut soon, probably sometime in September, but that she would be coming for a visit with them within the next few weeks. She was fine, she said, dipping the pen into the inkwell again, but she missed them and didn't want to wait until her timber was cut to make the trip to New York, though she would be home in New York for good, probably in October or November, once her timber was cut and sold.

She wrote of her love for them, with tears filling her eyes, then folded the several pages and placed them in a matching envelope, sealing the flap with hot wax. She would carry the letter with her to Eastman and leave it at the post office there.

Glancing out the window, she saw sunshine glistening on drops of rain, falling intermittently from the window sashes, the house eaves, and the countless green pine needles, shimmering in the late summer breeze. The road to Eastman might be muddy, but she would have a sunny day to travel it, now that the morning rain was gone.

She rose from her desk, glad finally to have written to her parents and to have decided to go home to New York for a short visit, right away, rather than waiting for her timber to be sold. She also felt better about her resolve to distance herself from the troubles in the piney woods of Georgia and to reunite with her family and friends who were, after all, her kind of people. Once this frightening chapter of her life was over, she would never look back.

She went to the back porch and rang the bell to summon Big Hill to hitch her horse to the carriage and to bring it on around to the front drive. Having done this, she went back to her bedchamber and gathered her bags for the trip to Eastman, making several trips to the front porch where she deposited them for Big Hill to place in the break. Later, he would make the trip to Eastman with her baggage.

She had included several new dresses in the latest fashions which her mother had sent her from New York. They had arrived only a few weeks ago. She had tried them on before her bedchamber mirror, but she had had no occasion to wear them, until now. Knowing Julia and Ben, she could probably count on several parties at Winslow Hall during her week's stay, and it would be nice wearing such lovely dresses again, as she used to. Each dress was secure in its own original large box in the break.

Big Hill appeared around the corner of the house, driving the phaeton to the front door. He slowly stepped down from the low carriage.

"Miz Kat'rin, you be careful, now."

"Oh, I will, Hill. It's only an hour's trip to Eastman, and I have my derringer with me. I carry it with me wherever I go."

"Yas'm, well, dat's de best thin' to do, seein' as how dar's so many mean peoples now."

"Goodbye, Hill. You and Ollie, please look after everything for me."

"Miz Kat'rin, don' you worry none. We see 'bout ever'thin'." He extended his arm for her to hold on to, as she climbed to the carriage seat.

***

The road was muddy, as Katharine had predicted, but halfway to Eastman, it became dry and sandy, indicating that the rain had not fallen there. The carriage which Hill had cleaned was dirty again, splattered with mud.

On reaching Eastman, Katharine guided the carriage to the post office on the main street which was bisected by the railroad tracks, the same rail line which ran by the Yellow Pines Lumber Mill at Normandale. Several cows, munching on tall grass near the railroad track, refused to budge, even as a proprietor of one of the nearby businesses ran at them, yelling and waving his arms. For only an instant, the cows observed him before returning to their feeding, slowly ambling along as the grass supply diminished.

Katharine was reminded of the ditty she had read in the local newspaper about the town of Eastman which the writer referred to as "Hogville": "Piggies, piggies on the street, All around you nice and sweet, When we go our friends to meet, Piggies, piggies we will greet." Katharine smiled ruefully at the truth in the words, for hogs, cows, and sheep wandered freely throughout the towns of the wiregrass, frequently sauntering through yards and into homes and businesses.

She had also read about a recent Dublin law calling for the sale of all loose cattle not claimed within three days. It proved to be so unpopular that it was repealed within three months. As a result, their streets also were cut up by cow paths and hog wallows and blocked by droves of hogs, sheep, and cows. It was said that Hawkinsville's rat population, which grew uncontrollably when the town was used to store Confederate corn during the war, had increased by 1880 to such an extent that merchants had imported ferrets to attack the rats. It was no wonder that the wiregrass area of the state continued to have sanitation problems!

Holding her parents' letter, she stepped down from the carriage seat and was about to enter the grocery store which housed the post office, when a two-story, brick building, newly erected next to the store, caught her eye. She wondered what it was and resolved to ask the postmaster.

As she entered the nearly empty store, the proprietor who also was the postmaster greeted her warmly, silently observing to himself that she was one of the rich Northerners who were affiliated with the timber company at Normandale.

"Good day, Mrs. Fremont. May I help you?"

"Yes, I have a letter to mail," Katharine answered. "By the way, sir, what is the new building next door?"

"All I know about it, Mrs. Fremont, is that it's gonna be a place where the new electric lights are gonna be sold."

"Who owns it?" she inquired, thinking to herself that an electrical company would certainly be timely and should prove to be very profitable to the enterpriser who was starting the business.

"Don't know for sure. I've heard it's a man who lives in Telfair County."

"I'm sure it's just a matter of time before all the businesses and homes in town have electric lights. Won't that be wonderful?" Katharine smiled at the idea, and the storekeeper smiled in return, agreeing that it would indeed be very nice.

Katharine remembered the letter to her parents, which she was still holding, and gave it to the postmaster.

"Please mail this for me, sir."

"Be glad to, Ma'm. Train'll pick up the mails here."

Katharine thanked the proprietor and hurried out the door. She was eager to go to Winslow Hall. After settling herself on the carriage seat, she flicked the reins and guided the horse toward the Winslows' home.

The dirt road carried her by the three-story Uplands Hotel with its mansard roof, widow's walk and tall brick chimneys. Built in 1876 by the Northern capitalists whose presence the local people now deplored, the hotel was magnificent, nestled as it was among the sheltering pines. It had quickly become a place where Northerners, desperate for a cure for their respiratory diseases, could come for an extended stay in the salubrious South. Katharine remembered reading about the New Jersey man with damaged bronchial tubes and a severe cough, staying at the Uplands, who left several weeks later, eleven pounds heavier with his health much improved.

There was also the man from Boston who was looking for "a winter home in a sunnier land" for his sickly son, who remarkably recovered in the piney woods. A man from Brooklyn declared that his daily walks among the pines had restored him to the "bloom" of good health. Katharine had even heard of old-timers in the area who wore lightwood knots around their necks, purportedly to alleviate heart palpitations.

She remembered asking Big Hill once to explain to her just what a lightwood knot was. She kept a basket full of the knots of wood by each of the fireplaces in her home, but she wasn't sure what part of the longleaf yellow pine they were. Some were a foot long. Others were smaller or larger. Her colored servant had looked amazed that she didn't know such a thing.

"Law, Miz Kat'rin," he had said with a smile, "a lighterd knot comes from the ji'nin' ob a limb ob de tree with de trunk ob de tree. It swell up wid resin, den it be hard. It burn fer a long time. It be only on a ol' tree. It drap off de tree, den we come along an' pick it up and use it."

She had never forgotten this explanation of a lightwood knot and every time she started a fire with one, she remembered what Hill had said. A lightwood knot was somewhat metaphoric of the people of the piney woods section of the state, she guessed, for she had often heard Southerners say that one of their own was "tough as a lightwood knot."

However, she had to disagree with those who felt the piney woods were so very healthful. After all, hadn't her Tillie felt that her hip gout had worsened? And what about the colds which Tillie suffered each spring?

Nevertheless, she always enjoyed looking at the Uplands with its lawn planted in trees and shrubs and surrounded by a quaint white picket fence. Its one hundred rooms, elegant parlors, and lovely dining rooms were comfortably furnished, and its spacious veranda was lined with Boston rockers. It was necessarily staffed by managers, chefs, and other personnel from Adirondack resort hotels and New York restaurants and was a favorite stopping place for Northerners on their trips through the Deep South.

Katharine thought how ungrateful the Southerners were because of all the money which the Northerners had invested in the area. The causes for the land war began to recede in importance. She felt almost desperate to see things through the eyes of the timber company people again, as she had in the beginning, before she had let the MacRae family become too important in her life.

She could see Winslow Hall through the tall pines. It was a breathtakingly beautiful place, she thought, as she neared the grounds of the in-town estate. Its scrolled columns, embodying Greek classicism at its finest, were imposing yet welcoming. Though

Widow of Sighing Pines

designed and built by Northerners, it reflected the architecture of the South, so evident in the antebellum homes of Atlanta and other Southern towns. Its graceful paned windows glowed at night with the light of many candles, illuminating the myriad faces of the Yellow Pines Timber Company's shareholders and administrators who were often guests at Winslow Hall.

Katharine turned into the long front driveway which formed a half-circle in front of the mansion. The yard servant, Poke, appeared near the mounting block and assisted her from the carriage.

"Welcome, welcome, Miz Kat'rin. Did you have a nice drive, Miz Kat'rin?"

"Oh, yes, thank you, Poke."

"Miz Julia done tol' me you be stayin' for a visit, Miz Kat'rin. She comin' now." Katharine looked up to see Julia descending the curved brick steps, and she hurried to meet her, holding her dress up to avoid tripping on it.

"Katharine, you're late. I've looked for you all morning," Julia said, laughing.

"I waited until the rain was over, Julia. We surely needed the rain, but as you can see, my carriage is muddy from it."

"Well, Poke will clean it for you, Katharine. I wish it had rained here. We need a week's deluge or a freshet to help in floating our logs out to the river."

The friends walked arm in arm to the double front doors which had above them a large, arched transom, inlaid with beveled lead glass. A uniformed house servant held the door for them. She courteously greeted Katharine. As always, Katharine thought, Julia had trained her help well, though this was one she had never seen. She was surprised when the woman called her by name, but then, Julia knew how to train her servants!

"We glad to see you, Miz Kat'rin."

Julia quickly informed Katharine. "This is Beulah, Katharine. I told her you were coming."

"Hello, Beulah. You are helping some good friends of mine."

"Yas'm, and Ah enjoys it, too." She nodded and beamed as Katharine and Julia walked through the massive double doors, then left the two friends alone.

"Katharine, I'm having Cook bring us some mint juleps. That's something Southern that I like, as you well know, that along with the big pine trees here." She said this with a laugh, and Katharine couldn't help but laugh, too, as they entered the beautifully appointed drawing room.

The Winslows had brought "Cook" with them when they made the move to Georgia some ten years prior. Since her name was actually Su-Ling Cook, in light of her avocation, the appellation had stayed with her through the years. Her husband having died in the war at the tender age of twenty years, following their marriage of only eleven months, the broken-hearted Su-Ling had devoted herself to the Winslow family for nearly thirty years. A matronly woman of middle age now, she was the autocrat of the kitchen at Winslow Hall. Though she had help from several other would-be cooks in the capacious kitchen, hers were the hands that shaped the breads and cookies and mints that issued forth on the silver, porcelain and china dishes, bearing the Winslow monogram and family crest. Hers were, also, the hands which selected the hand-embroidered linen and damask table covers with matching cloth napery for the four long mahogany tables in the company dining room, which would seat one-hundred guests at the time.

Cook appeared in the drawing room with the mint juleps in their delicate silver and crystal highball glasses, perched on a silver serving tray. Her oblique Asian eyes smiled at Katharine, and her lips turned upward at the corners, revealing straight small teeth.

Katharine, smiling, rose to greet her and the two embraced as dear friends.

"Cook, I've missed seeing you the last times I've visited Julia and Ben."

"Yes, Mrs. Katharine. I've missed seeing you, too," she said in her birdlike, singsong voice. "I don't know. Guess I'm always in Mrs. Julia's kitchen, cooking something good for you to eat." Her mouth curved again in a broad smile which also twinkled in her slanted eyes. She picked up one of the frosted glasses and handed it to Katharine.

"For you, Mrs. Katharine."

Warm and thirsty from the trip, Kathrine welcomed the cold drink which had crushed mint leaves floating near the rim of the glass. It had been quite a while since she had drunk anything alcoholic, other than the usual table wines which she had always enjoyed with her evening meals.

"Thank you, Cook. It looks most inviting." She sipped the julep, smiling in appreciation as Cook delivered the other drink to Julia, then quietly left the room.

Katharine joined her friend on the lovely old settee which had quite a grand history, as she recalled, dating back to an ancestor who was a close friend of Thomas Jefferson. When Jefferson made his trips to France to furnish his home, Monticello, he so inspired Ben Winslow's great-great-grandfather with his selections, that James Winslow had replicas of several pieces made for his own home in New York. Katharine had visited Monticello and the likenesses of several of the furnishings were indeed evident. The family legend contended that Jefferson was good-humored and even pleased that his taste in furnishings was shared by his old friend.

The two friends sipped their drinks and caught up on the latest events in their lives.

"Will Steve and Vickie bring their new baby while I'm here, Julia?"

"Vickie and the children won't be coming, but Steve should be here for the ball on Wednesday night. He'll be stopping by on his way to Savannah. He has business in Savannah, so he'll leave early the next day. By the way, Katharine, he told me to tell you...he wants to teach you the *Terpsichore*."

"The what?" Katharine laughed, just thinking of Julia's younger, irrepressible brother.

"The *Terpsichore*. It's one of the latest dances. I've heard that the town people in Savannah and Atlanta are dancing it up a storm."

"Guess I've been in the backwoods so long, I haven't kept up with the new dances. I'm afraid I'm getting a little old to dance them, anyway," Katharine said, ruefully.

"Nonsense, Katharine. Steve has tried to teach me, but I've never caught on to dance steps as quickly as you two. I've heard so much about the dance and I want to see someone dance it," Julia said.

"Well, I'm looking forward to seeing Steve and I'm also wanting to learn the new dance. Steve always makes me laugh and I need to laugh."

Julia looked quickly at Katharine. She had felt for some time that Katharine was not herself. Julia gazed steadily at her friend, until Katharine met her eyes with a slight shrug.

"Katharine, is everything all right with you? We haven't really talked in so long..."

"Everything's all right, Julia." Katharine had weighed in her mind the need to confide in Julia about her ambivalence in regard to the escalating land war and the risk that she might shock and alienate her friend. She knew that Julia never questioned the Dodge family about anything. In fact, if any of the Dodges declared that black was actually white, Katharine felt sure that Julia and Ben Winslow would find a way to agree.

Katharine wondered whether she herself might have been as unquestioning as Julia, if she had not allowed herself to become too involved in the lives of Micah MacRae and his family. She was not aware that just thinking, momentarily, of Micah MacRae had brought a glow to her face and a softness to her dark blue eyes that Julia had never before seen. Julia was taken aback and looked more keenly than before at her friend.

"Have you met someone, Katharine?" Julia asked quietly.

Startled, Katharine looked quickly at Julia and said, "What?"

"I mean," Julia continued, "have you met a man you might be interested in?"

Katharine struggled not to look at all aware of what Julia was asking, for she never intended to tell Julia that she had ever been even remotely interested in Micah MacRae. The stakes were just too high, for though the Winslows feigned a business sort of friendship with the raftsman, Katharine knew that they still looked upon him as the enemy. Also, even though they touted him as a shrewd raftsman and timber dealer, he was still a semiliterate backwoodsman to them. Katharine studied the mint leaves in the drink which she sipped only infrequently. She realized, more and more, just how far apart their worlds were - hers and Micah MacRae's. With a start, she realized that Julia was looking at her oddly.

"You didn't answer my question, Katharine. I asked whether you had met a man you might be interested in."

"Oh, I'm sorry, Julia. No, actually there isn't anyone. No, I plan to sell my timber and move back to New York, probably around October or November of this year."

"You know, Katharine, Ben and I have talked about doing the same thing. We're ready to make the move back...to New York, I mean."

"Well, what would happen to Winslow Hall?"

"I've wondered, too, what would happen. I suppose we would sell it."

"Nobody down here has that kind of money, Julia, to buy it and keep it up."

"Well, we just might have to lease it. I don't know. What I do know, though, is that I'm frightened by the escalating war, and I don't want to wait around and see who gets killed next." Julia paused and looked mortified that she had spoken so candidly about someone getting killed, when Katharine's husband had been murdered and she was dredging up painful memories for her.

"Katharine, how dreadful of me. Why am I talking about such sad things, when I asked you here to have an enjoyable time? Let's talk about the ball on Wednesday night. We've hired a chamber music group from Atlanta. We heard them in Atlanta a few weeks ago, at the Masquerade Ball, and Ben hired them on the spot. They're charging a fortune to come, but believe me, they're worth it. I think you'll agree when you hear them."

"I haven't danced since your last party I attended, Julia."

"Oh, and Sewell Siddon will be here also. He'll be staying at the Uplands Hotel and will be returning to Darien the morning after the ball. We are hoping he'll be the inspector when our rafts reach Darien a few weeks from now. They're still cutting our timber near the railroad right-of-way. Some of it borders the River Road. They'll use mules probably to drag those logs to the sawmill there at Willcox Lake. It's drier land there, they say. They use oxen in the swampy areas. Though they are slower than mules, their cloven hooves are more adapted to boggy ground."

Katharine, looking surprised, laughed.

"Well, you are quite the timber businesswoman, Julia. I didn't know why they used mules sometimes, rather than oxen."

"Actually, I guess it really depends on what are available, but Ben did tell me that about the oxen's hooves." Julia paused a few moments, looking at the massive old grandfather clock, visible in the large entry hall adjoining the parlor.

"Katharine, Cook says supper will be served promptly at 8:00 o'clock. Let me show you to your room. I've had Beulah prepare one of the upstairs rooms for you."

"That's fine, Julia. Anything's fine with me."

Katharine followed Julia out into the spacious entry hall where wide, beautifully carved stairs ascended to the balconied second floor. A house servant whispered something to Julia and Katharine heard her name mentioned. The servant bowed and disappeared into another room.

"Poke had your things put in your room," Julia said, as she and Katharine climbed the stairs, holding up their long dresses and petticoats. Obviously, the faithful Hill had already delivered her gowns and luggage.

The parquet hardwood on the balcony floor gleamed in the afternoon light as Julia opened the guest room door. An oriental rug of muted pastels covered most of the hardwood floor, extending almost to the wide baseboards that followed the rose silk-hung walls of the room. A Federal bed with ivory silk coverlet and matching dust ruffle was centered on the back wall of the domed room, which featured raised panels, also in pastel hues, on the circular dome. Other lovely pieces of Federal-era furnishings graced the room, each piece complementing the others - a lady's writing desk, a chaise lounge, several lovely chairs in rich velvets and brocades, a stately armoire with the ornate carvings of the central bed. Katharine had always loved this room, but until now, had never slept in it. Its beauty was rarely seen by the many guests of Winslow Hall, for most of the visitors usually stayed in the guest house, removed from the main house, or in one of the lower level rooms which were almost as lovely.

"The room's as beautiful as ever, Julia, but I thought I'd be staying in your guest house."

"Well, we want you to be comfortable, Katharine, and to enjoy your visit. I'll put Steve in the cottage. As you know, Ben and I are right next door. If you need us, we'll be near. Remember, supper is at 8:00 o'clock. That'll give you time to relax and maybe even take a little nap. Of course, we'll dine in the private dining room."

"See you at 8:00."

Smiling, Julia closed the door, and Katharine began undoing her dress and tight corset. Free of the steel-like restraint of the corset, she pulled on a rose combing sacque and lay down on the chaise lounge, plumping a large feather pillow under her head. She was quickly asleep and dreaming that she and Micah MacRae were drifting down the Ocmulgee River on a tremendous log raft which rolled and pitched in the strong river current.

**

She sat straight up, breathing hard, and realized that she had only been dreaming. She opened the locket watch, hanging around her neck, and knew she had slept longer than she meant to. She had to dress for supper.

Beulah had hung her dresses in the large armoire, and Katharine decided hurriedly to wear the ecru linen one. She pulled the bell cord for help with lacing her corset, and a housemaid promptly appeared at the door.

Katharine held her breath while her corset was laced and tied. Next, she was assisted with the voluminous petticoats and dress. The housemaid offered to help her with her hair, but when Katharine declined, she bowed slightly and quietly left the room.

Sitting at the large Regency dressing table, Katharine brushed her hair, then braided it into a chignon at the nape of her neck. Using the large gilded hand mirror, she had a rear view of herself, which included the swags of the linen dress, caught up into a small bustle which fell over her hips. She knew that the Winslows dressed beautifully for the evening meal, and she wanted to be attired accordingly. Oftentimes, they entertained other guests at supper and she did not want to be lacking in her appearance.

For the first time since she had entered the room, she heard the methodical ticking of the mantel clock above the ivory marble fireplace. Noting that its chiseled hour and minute hands registered almost the time for supper, she quickly completed her toilette. Stepping out of the room onto the balcony floor, she walked to the wide stairway which offered a panoramic view of the lower floor.

Graceful, candle-burning chandeliers hovered below her. Although Winslow Hall was one of the first homes to employ electricity from a home generator, it still relied on candles and lamps for its extensive lighting needs.

Descending the finely carved stairway, Katharine heard mingled talk and laughter, emanating from the drawing room which opened away from the pentagonal entry hall. She recognized the Winslows' voices, and though another male voice sounded strangely familiar, she momentarily could not recognize it. As she paused at the open doorway, the occupants of the room stood, as if of one accord, and Katharine realized with a sinking heart that the oddly familiar voice belonged to Sewell Siddon who obviously was to be her supper partner for the evening. Masking her disappointment, she braved a nice smile and entered the room, as Julia moved toward her.

"Katharine, you remember Sewell Siddon...oh, I'm sure you do."

"Yes, of course. How are you, Mr. Siddon?"

Sewell Siddon moved toward her, taking her hand.

"It's Sewell, remember," he said, taking her hand and bringing it to his lips.

Ben also crossed over to her, giving her a light embrace and welcoming her to Winslow Hall again. "Glad you could come, Katharine, honey," he said in his somewhat gruff voice. "We've been kind of worried about you - haven't seen you in several months."

"Oh, you musn't worry about me, Ben. I've had business affairs to see to, and Tillie hasn't been well. I really hated to leave her to go anywhere."

"Well, I certainly hope she's feeling better. We're just glad you're here. We're having a timber company meeting Tuesday. It's good you'll be here for that."

Before Katharine could answer, Beulah appeared in the doorway and announced that other guests had arrived. When Julia instructed her to bring them on to the parlor, she ushered in the lawyers, whom Katharine had met at the timber company meeting some months ago. This time, Katharine put the names with the faces, as they were reintroduced: William Thornton, Ashley Hall, and Charles Mitchell from Savannah, representing the Yellow Pines Lumber Company, and Stanley Agnew and Silas Carey from New York, along with Tillman Nash from Maine, representing Norman Dodge and his brothers.

Julia was speaking. "I believe everyone's here. Cook has prepared us a quail supper. Ben goes quail hunting often and this time he brought home fifty birds."

The talkative Savannah lawyer, William Thornton, interjected, "Are they fried?"

"No," Julia said, laughing. "I know you Southerners believe in frying everything, but she baked them in white wine and they are even better than fried."

Arriving at the private dining room, Katharine and the other guests found their names on the place cards which were erect in their sterling silver holders. As she had suspected, she and Sewell Siddon were seated together, facing four of the lawyers, with the other two lawyers to Katharine's right. Julia and Ben sat at the ends of the table, facing each other as host and hostess.

Fresh roses from the Winslows' rose gardens, placed decoratively in a graceful cut-glass epergne, were the centerpiece for the table. The gleaming silver candelabra each held twelve burning candles which beamed their pulsing light over the fashionably attired assembly and the beautifully appointed table. Fine china gleamed, crystal wine glasses sparkled, and sterling silver serving pieces and flatware glowed on the massive mahogany table, covered with a richly embroidered, antique white satin cloth.

With the first course of the sumptuous meal in place before each guest, lively conversation erupted around the table. As usual, national political affairs took priority, and the opening discussion centered around the policies of the current occupant of the White House. The Savannah lawyer, William Thornton, was speaking.

"I don't see how President Harrison can be elected again. He may be the Republican nominee, but Grover Cleveland will be the next president." He said this with conviction.

"I agree with you," Stanley Agnew said, sipping his wine. He continued, "You recall, of course, that Harrison was barely elected at all in '88. He carried the Electoral College, but Cleveland had 100,000 more popular votes than he did. You're right. Cleveland is going to serve a staggered second term. I'm afraid."

As political and other comments swirled around her, Katharine sat with her left hand in her lap, which from time to time Sewell Siddon covered with his own. This annoyed her, but she forebore making a scene and strove to hear the various conversations during the course of the meal. Invariably, as she expected, someone mentioned the land war and all other talking ceased.

"How is everything now?" William Thornton inquired. "Are the squatters still behaving themselves?"

Katharine cringed at the term, "squatters," for she knew this was a blanket designation for all of the people whose land Norman Dodge was confiscating. She wanted to cry out that all of the Southerners in the piney woods were not squatters and that Dodge's son, Norman, was wrong in taking some of the lands, but she knew better than to allow herself such an outburst. She was glad when the meal was finally over and Julia and Ben were rising from the table.

"Let's all go to the parlor. We have some chamber music for you and we'll have after-dinner drinks, if you like."

Everyone rose from the table, murmuring to Julia and Ben how very much they enjoyed the meal. William Thornton even allowed that the quail were equally as good cooked in wine as fried with gravy. Julia smiled and thanked him in an indulgent sort of way and, taking Ben's arm, led them to the parlor.

Katharine accepted Sewell Siddon's arm, and they followed the Winslows. The lawyers, engaging in conversation inaudible to the other guests, trailed behind them. Music from the five-piece chamber group drifted from the parlor, and again Katharine silently applauded the way her friends entertained their guests, always thoughtfully and flawlessly.

After seating guests in the parlor, white-uniformed servants brought in silver trays with tiny porcelain demitasses, filled with hot coffee. Some had dollops of cream for those who preferred Irish coffee.

Stemmed, crystal, after-dinner goblets sparkled on a silver tray with wines and liqueurs. Delectable cheeses and fresh fruits in season were also available. The guests helped themselves to the beverages and foods. Some of the men, led by Ben Winslow, excused themselves to go to the library to smoke their cigars. Katharine rather hoped that her supper partner would go with them, but no, he had no intention of leaving her.

Remembering, however, that she was trying to distance herself from the MacRae family and the attending land war and also reminding herself that she would be rafting her own timber to Darien within a few weeks, Katharine decided to make an effort to be friendly with Sewell Siddon. After all, she thought, his background was more like her own. Though he was a Southerner, Katharine had heard Julia say that he had attended university in the North. He was affiliated with the newly established Darien Bank and was active in the social affairs of Darien and the surrounding islands, including St. Simons Island. Julia had continued in her self-chosen role of matchmaker, and Katharine smiled at her friend's determination to find a husband for her.

"I don't know what brought that smile to your face, Katharine, but if possible, you're even more beautiful when you smile." Sewell Siddon reached for her hand and she wanted to withdraw it quickly, but she allowed him to take her hand in his, while the others in the room were at the serving table, with their backs to them.

Before Katharine could reply, one of the New York lawyers, Silas Carey, moved their way, imbibing the coastal rice wine which, Katharine knew, would quickly make one tipsy. However, he appeared to be quite dignified still, as he addressed Sewell Siddon who mercifully had released her hand.

"Well, Mr. Siddon, how is the yellow pine business in Darien?"

"I don't believe it could be much better, Mr. Carey. We've had several fires in Darien this year. Lost almost an entire block of businesses in February and then another fire, which we think was intentionally set, destroyed the McIntosh Academy in March."

"Yes, we keep hearing about the fires at Darien. Too bad."

The lawyer shook his head, sipped his rice wine again, and continued his questions about Darien.

"How many board feet of timber have left Darien this past year?"

"It's been around ninety-five million board feet, so far. By the end of the year it could be even more."

Two other lawyers stood near them, holding their brandies and listening attentively to the conversation about Darien. William Thornton interjected comments from time to time, since he regularly visited the port city, which was only around fifty miles south of his hometown of Savannah. The New York lawyer, Silas Carey, had never been to Darien, and he was as curious as Katharine about the ocean port, known worldwide for its timber enterprises.

Katharine was determined to go to Darien with her raft of logs when they were rafted in the fall. She listened with mounting interest to everything that was said, trying to visualize the booming little coastal city that lured rafthands and timber magnates alike to its shores.

Stanley Agnew from New York spoke up: "I've always called trees lumber. Who started calling them 'timber'?"

William Thornton answered, "My understanding is that the English use the term, 'timber,' rather than lumber, and it's caught on in Darien."

Katharine looked around the room for Julia, then realized she was probably attending to her hostess duties elsewhere. Though she usually enjoyed her friend's company, she was glad for the opportunity to learn about life outside the piney woods from the men who brought news from the large cities of Savannah and New York, and she especially wanted to hear more about Darien.

"How many foreign consulates are in Darien now?" Stanley Agnew asked the question. Katharine observed that Sewell Siddon was literally basking in the attention he was receiving. He began naming them, and Katharine was surprised at the number of consulates and at the international atmosphere that must prevail in the port city, because of them. Stanley Agnew, cupping and rolling the bottom of his brandy glass with bowl-shaped fingers, continued questioning the timber inspector.

"You see many steamships?"

"Some of them are calling at Darien now. They can carry much larger cargoes than the sailing ships."

"Do you deal with the backwoodsmen from this area, who raft their own logs to Darien?"

"I've dealt with some. Knot-plugging is a common practice among them."

Katharine wondered what he meant. The New York lawyer urged him to explain what he meant by knot-plugging and the fleshy inspector sat back in his chair, clasping his entwined fingers over his chest. He glanced at Katharine out of the corner of his eye, enjoying being the center of attention and the fountainhead of knowledge concerning Darien and the timber business.

"Well, as you may know, knotholes detract from the value of timber, so these local Crackers plug the knots with wooden pegs. They plane the pegs smooth and try to hide them with mud."

Katharine didn't like the trend of the conversation and was considering leaving the room, when Ben Winslow, Julia, and the other lawyers returned to the room. Julia chose a chair near Katharine. Several of the lawyers seated themselves as others stood nearby. William Thornton addressed Ben Winslow about the now latent land war.

"Are the squatters still calm or have there been some flare-ups?"

"No," Ben Winslow answered, "I really think things have calmed down for good, though Paul Owens may tell us differently tomorrow at our meeting. They're busy with their crops now, for the most part. The coming months will tell how things are going. I don't trust them but I certainly think the killings have stopped. We are all careful to carry our weapons with us, but it's just a matter of time before Dodge's sons have cut all of this timber, and then we can all go back to New York and New Hampshire and wherever."

"What? The timber business is supposed to go on and on. Don't talk about it ending," one of the lawyers interjected.

"Well," Ben persisted, "it won't end within the next few years, but at the rate Dodge is cutting, it can't go on much longer than that."

Katharine thought of the stumps left behind from the logging operations she had recently witnessed, and she opened her mouth to mention this to the others. However, she thought better of it and instead thanked the colored servant, Beulah, for replenishing her demitasse with hot coffee.

The evening wore on and eventually several of the lawyers excused themselves from the group, saying that they needed to prepare for the upcoming lumber company meeting the following day. The rest of the lawyers followed them, saying their goodbyes and thanking the Winslows for another "brilliant evening," as they expressed it, filled with the "best of foods, potables and repartee." The musicians had also long ago departed.

Katharine herself was ready to be alone and she chafed at sitting near Sewell Siddon and enduring his attentions which increased in direct proportion to the cognac he drank. He held her hand now and as he spoke, his words were slurred.

"How 'bout a game of croquet in the morning, honey?"

Katharine did not like being called such a term of endearment by the man, but she did enjoy croquet once in awhile, and the manicured lawns of Winslow Hall included a charming croquet court, replete with the necessary accouterments of the game.

"Oh, I want to play, too," Julia said, tugging at Ben's arm. "We'll play them a game, won't we, Ben?"

Ben, holding a stemmed glass of rice wine, also appeared somewhat inebriated. Solemnly, he lifted his glass and offered a toast to the proposed game the following morning. Katharine raised her cup and the others touched it with their goblets.

"To the strongly competitive game on the morrow. And may the best couple win!" Ben laughed and reeled somewhat, and Julia announced that they all needed to get their rest for the big game the next day.

Sewell Siddon stood, somewhat unsteadily, and as Katharine rose also, before she realized what was happening, he kissed her on the mouth. The revulsion she felt from the alcohol on his loose lips and the fact that he dared to take such liberties, and in front of the Winslows, made her long to slap him. How she yearned to be free of the man! She wondered what Julia could possibly think of such behavior on his part, and she quickly looked directly at her.

Julia, to Katharine's dismay, looked all approving as if her role of matchmaker were bearing fruit. Katharine attributed her friend's smiling reaction to the boorishness of the timber inspector to be either Julia's over-consumption of brandy or the fact that he would be judging her lumber at Darien within the near future. People tended to overlook faux pas where money was concerned. This, Katharine was realizing more and more. Without caring whether the timber inspector or the Winslows noticed, Katharine withdrew a tiny handkerchief from her hidden dress pocket and wiped her mouth. Everyone appeared oblivious of the gesture and she restored the handkerchief to her pocket.

Sewell Siddon's arm remained around Katharine's waist, as he informed the Winslows that he needed to get back to the hotel himself. Holding his liqueur goblet toward the house servant who was in the process of clearing the room of soiled dishes and left-over foods, he silently demanded by a shake of his glass that she refill it immediately. Katharine was appalled at his conduct and she noted a similar feeling on the part of the servant. It was obvious that she and the servant viewed the situation the same, since they had not drunk the alcoholic beverages which had wrought such coarse and callous behavior on the part of the others, especially Sewell Siddon. She watched with disgust as he loudly swallowed the drink in several quick gulps.

Julia herself had had far too much to drink. In fact, Katharine could not remember having ever seen Julia over-indulge in drinking. Her mouth was drooping and her eyes were red and not steady in their orbs. Her fashionably lovely gown which, however, could not hide her increasingly plump figure, had several soiled places where she had unmindfully dropped food and drink during the course of the evening.

The paradoxical thought came to Katharine's mind that with the near reverence of the Winslows for William E. Dodge who had been a strict Prohibitionist, they let the alcoholic beverages flow freely at Winslow Hall. Of course, the parties which the timber financier attended before his death in 1883 were quiet, stiffly elegant affairs, Katharine had been told. These occurred during the years before she and Frank had moved to the Georgia wiregrass.

Katharine slipped nimbly out of the half-circle of Sewell Siddon's arm as he moved unsteadily toward the side courtyard of Winslow Hall. Julia had rung for his carriage to be brought to the *porte cochere*, and it was waiting for him. Once again, he bade them farewell, then climbed shakily into the curtained rockaway laudaulet, its door held open for him by the liveried coachman.

"Where to, Mr. Siddon?" the driver queried.

"Back to the Uplands...where else?" he grunted. The coachman closed the carriage door and resumed his seat, clucking to the horse which jumped forward at his command.

Katharine couldn't remember when she had been more ready for an evening to end. It had been a long one and she was tired of putting up with Sly Siddon's tasteless behavior.

They were at the spiral stairway in the foyer, and Katharine related to the Winslows again that the meal was excellent and that she enjoyed hearing the talk about Darien and other places.

"Honey, you've been down there in the backwoods for so long, I guess you were ready for some intelligent conversation and some refined people." Ben Winslow said, his grinning, slack mouth belying his own words.

"That may be true," Katharine said, somewhat reluctantly. "Well," she continued, "I'm ready for some sleep." Pausing, she then inquired how long Sewell Siddon would be visiting in Eastman.

"Oh, he'll be here at least until after the ball on Wednesday night. He wouldn't miss that for anything, especially since you will be here," Julia said.

As Katharine started up the graceful stairway, Julia added, "You go ahead, Katharine." She nodded toward the guest room on the second floor where Katharine was staying during her visit. "Ben and I have got to make sure everything is in order in the rooms we used tonight."

"All right. I'll see you two in the morning."

***

Katharine was awakened the next morning by a knock on the bedroom door, followed by, "It's me, Miz Katharine, it's Beulah. Ah done brought you some breakfast."

Rubbing her eyes and reaching for her dressing gown, Katharine told Beulah to come in. Another house servant opened the door, as Beulah entered with a large silver service holding Katharine's breakfast. A dainty vase of freshly cut rosebuds of varied colors, still moist with morning dew, was surrounded by silver tea and coffee pots, steaming from their spouts, and various porcelain dishes of breakfast foods, including fresh fruit, poached eggs, tiny sausages, and buttered toast. An assortment of individual jellies and jams and conserves complemented the savory tray.

"Good morning, Beulah. What a feast you have brought. I see you have coffee and tea. I would love some hot tea."

"Yes, Ma'm. Let me pour you some." Beulah expertly poured the steaming tea into the translucent china cup.

"Lemon, Miz Katharine?"

"Yes, please, Beulah. Oh, what a nice breakfast. I'm not used to this anymore, especially since Tillie, my housekeeper, has been ill. I'll be spoiled for sure!"

"It doan hurt nothin' to be spoil' once in awhile, Miz Katharine." Beulah smiled when she said this, and Katharine smiled back, thinking that Julia was lucky to have Beulah to help her.

Turning to leave, Beulah instructed Katharine to ring when she was ready for her to come for the breakfast tray. On leaving the room, she quietly closed the door.

Katharine enjoyed the luxury of eating the delectable breakfast alone, before dressing for the day. She had always enjoyed her visits at Winslow Hall, and she looked forward to not only its gracious amenities but also the exciting conversations which, she knew, would be forthcoming from the big city lawyers and the Yellow Pines Lumber Company affiliates.

After finishing her breakfast, she rang for the tray to be removed and for help with her corset. She opened the large armoire to decide on something to wear for lawn croquet. She had brought different sports outfits, as the grounds of Winslow Hall were demarcated with several tennis courts in addition to the croquet court and lawn layouts for other outdoor games.

A different maid arrived and pulled the corset strings until her natural hourglass figure was even more accentuated. Over the almost inflexible corset, she stepped into several layers of petticoats, followed by the white pique sailor blouse with its wide collars, stitched with navy blue thread and undergirded by a white broadcloth scarf which she tied in a large knot at the joining of the collars. A long, flowing pique skirt, white kid slippers, and a straw hat completed her fetching attire, though she left the hat on the bed until she decided how she would wear her hair for the croquet game.

Before the house servant left, she left a message with Katharine that Mrs. Winslow had asked whether Mrs. Fremont was ready for the croquet match. She and Mr. Winslow were waiting at the croquet court, and she said that Mr. Siddon's carriage should arrive soon.

"Yes, please tell her I'll be there within five minutes." Katharine quickly brushed her hair and fastened it with a large ribbon, letting its thick tresses fall down the middle of her back. Then, she placed the straw hat on her head, and she was ready for the game. Though she dreaded spending the morning with Sly Siddon, she was looking forward to a delightful game of croquet. Also, she doubted there would be alcoholic drinks available so early in the day, so maybe the timber inspector would be on better behavior.

She hurried down the stairs and out the courtyard side entrance. Ben and Julia were seated in one of the several charming and airy gazebos which graced the lawns of Winslow Hall, tiny complements of the mansion itself. Sewell Siddon had already arrived and was in the process of selecting mallets for himself and Katharine. At least he's sober, Katharine thought, as he handed her a mallet. His small eyes examined her figure in quick detail and his large mouth emitted a combined sigh and grunt.

"If I'm not the luckiest man in Eastman and Darien, just tell me now but I won't believe you. This woman's the prettiest one I've seen in a long, long time." Katharine blushed as his eyes lingered on her bodice and moved on to her hips. The man has no shame, she thought, and again she felt the urge to slap him and put him in his place. Julia and Ben were smiling their good-mornings and laughing at Sewell Siddon's cold sober assessment of Katharine.

"She's beautiful all right, Sewell. My brother, Steve, has always said that if she hadn't been married the first time he met her, he would have married her himself." Julia laughed and concluded, "and Steve is nearly five years younger than Katharine."

Sewell Siddon looked slightly intimidated. "Is your brother, Steve, married?"

"Oh, yes," Julia answered, "and he and Vickie just recently had their sixth child. They come to some of our balls, but you may not remember him. He loves to dance with Katharine."

"I do remember a red-headed young fellow who danced with you, Katharine, at the Winslows' ball several months ago."

"That's Steve," Julia recalled. "Yes, you can't miss his red hair. He'll be here for our ball tomorrow night." Sewell Siddon did not look pleased at this revelation. However, he was secretly glad the young man was married and therefore no competition for him.

Katharine had remained silent during the conversation. She felt like an inanimate object being discussed and slavered over. She couldn't understand why Julia did not sense her humiliation by Sewell Siddon. The possibility that Julia was aware of it, but allowed it because of business considerations, made Katharine's blood almost boil.

Ben had returned from checking the wickets and pegs and was carrying the colorful balls for the game. Everyone held a long-handled mallet. With a coin toss deciding which team would lead, the Winslows won the toss and Julia putted the blue ball through the first wicket. The game quickly became competitive, with it being obvious early on that Ben and Katharine were the better players of their respective teams.

Julia good-naturedly fussed and chided her wayward balls which strayed more often than not from the narrow wickets, but Sewell Siddon cursed his erratic ones which not only avoided the wickets, but more often than not landed in some distant shrubbery or flower bed, refusing to be found by the huffing and puffing timber inspector.

Nevertheless, Katharine was the first to garner the necessary points to win the game, and this somewhat mollified Sewell Siddon, as if he had helped in any way to acquire the twenty-six points. Two more games were played, with Ben winning one for himself and Julia, and Katharine winning the last one again, virtually without any assistance from her inept partner.

Since it was nearing time for dinner, Julia suggested that they all freshen up before the meal which would be followed shortly thereafter by the lumber company meeting. She invited Sewell

Siddon for dinner and he quickly accepted, pulling a silk handkerchief from his breast pocket and patting the beads of sweat on his balding head. His and Ben's Norfolk jackets, though quite the fashion, were a bit warm for a summer's day in South Georgia. Ben also was dabbing at his upper lip with his handkerchief.

"No offense to you folks here in the piney woods but this heat here is almost too much. Guess I'm just used to the coast and those ocean breezes," the timber inspector said.

Ben offered his sincere apologies about the overly warm weather, as Julia gestured toward a guest room near the stairwell where the timber inspector might freshen up for the noonday meal. Then she and Ben hastened up the stairs, with Julia calling back over her shoulder that dinner would be served in the private dining room at 12:00 noon. As Katharine turned to go up the stairway to the guest room she was using, Sewell Siddon seized the opportunity to speak with her alone.

"Katharine, honey, I want you to come to Darien and return to civilization. You've been buried in this wild backwoods of the state too long."

"Darien?" Katharine inquired somewhat incredulously. "Darien is a 'return to civilization'?"

"Darien itself is only a starting point. We've got the steamer, *Hessie*, now that runs from Brunswick to Darien, stopping at St. Simons and Frederica. My home on the Ridge has a number of bedchambers." He looked meaningfully at Katharine, and she averted her eyes.

"Also," he continued, "I have a summer cottage on the south end of St. Simons. We could go surf bathing in the ocean."

He caught Katharine's interest, not realizing that her interest was in hearing about life in places where she longed to go. But not with him. Why would he even entertain the idea that she would stay in his home or even go there at all? The man assumed too much, Katharine thought, instinctively pulling away and turning her head as he attempted to kiss her.

"I really must get ready for dinner, Sewell," she said, beginning the long stairway climb. A wicked grin met her backward glance for he would not be dissuaded.

"I like a hard-to-get woman, Katharine, and believe me, I won't give up. I intend to put a big diamond on your finger before the year's end. It may take some doing on my part, but I'm not one to give up. I think I've found the woman I want."

Katharine stopped midway up the staircase, then turned and stared at the man who had once again pulled out the rumpled handkerchief to wipe his damp face.

"I'm afraid you assume too much, Mr. Siddon. I'm not interested in marrying again, at least not any time soon."

"You may change your mind, Katharine. It's difficult for a woman to live alone. Oh, I know you've got your timber to fall back on, but sometimes timber prices are not what you think they should be."

A chill edged its way up Katharine's spine. What was the man insinuating? How did he know about her timber? He was saying she might not receive top prices for her trees. Oh, Lord in Heaven, what if he were the inspector of her logs and purposely gave her a reduced price? What should she say to him now?

She chose not to say anything. Lifting her skirts, she looked directly at him, then turned and headed back up the stairs. She heard him emit a coarse laugh as he moved toward the guest room which Julia had offered to him on the lower floor.

Katharine entered her room and locked the door behind her, then began peeling off her clothes which were somewhat damp from the warm morning's croquet match. She pulled back the covers of the freshly-made bed and lay down, feeling the coolness of the bedclothes against her bare skin. How she would like to remain here, she thought, and never have to put up with Sly Siddon again!

She even considered the possibility of going back home early, in order to escape his unwanted advances, but she would just upset Julia and Ben who had been too good to her during her six years in Georgia, though their acceptance of Sewell Siddon deeply annoyed her. Lying there, her mind drifted to the places he had talked about - Darien, St. Simons, and other places. She would be going to Darien within just a few weeks.

What would Sewell Siddon think, if he knew that she would be on her raft of logs when it arrived in Darien? For that matter, what would Micah MacRae think? She had talked to no one of her plans to ride the raft to Darien. After all, there was no one she could tell.

Her mind in a dither, she realized with a start that she had to dress for dinner and the lumber company meeting which would follow soon afterward. The company meeting would be held without Sly Siddon's presence. Of that she was certain. He would be on his way back to the Uplands Hotel by then.

She found fresh water in the bowl on the dresser and proceeded to wash her face and hands, patting herself dry with the hand-embroidered linen cloth which was folded nearby. She pulled on her silky batiste chemise and drawers and corset, then rang for the house servant who soon appeared at the door.

"I need help with my corset, please."

"Oh, yes, Ma'm. You jes' hol' on to sumpin' an' suck in yo' breaf, and Ah tie it fer you, Miz Kat'rin." The colored servant flashed white teeth in a full smile, confiding, "Ah he'ps some ob de white ladies and dey wears de pads, 'cause dey ain' got 'nuff paddin' ob dey own. But you, Miz Kat'rin, you done blest wid 'nuff paddin' in all ob de right places." Katharine had never heard from a servant such an appraisal of herself and she joined in the housemaid's sustained laughter.

"No'm," the talkative servant continued, "you done got dat hourglass shape dat all de white ladies wants." Katharine smiled and thanked the housemaid for her compliments. In fact, the servant had, without realizing it, lifted her spirits and she looked about for something to give her in return. Her eyes settled on some pearl hair combs, and without any hesitation, she picked them up from the dresser and gave them to the unbelieving house servant.

"Take these. I want you to have them," Katharine said.

"Oh, Miz Kat'rin, Ah kane take yo' jew'l combs." Katharine smiled at this description of the combs as she put them into the servant's hands and closed her fingers around them.

"Oh, thank you, thank you, Miz Kat'rin."

"Thank you...I'm sorry, but I don't know your name, but I was going to say, 'thank you' for making my day a happier one."

"My name Mattie, Miz Kat'rin. Now, let's pull dis cawset tight." With the corset duly tied, the servant helped Katharine with petticoats, then held the tailored dress which slipped over her head. After helping with buttons, hooks, and eyes, the housemaid left, reminding Katharine of the dinner time within only a few minutes.

"I'll be there, Mattie. Thanks for your help."

"You sho is welcome, Miz Kat'rin." As the servant quietly closed the door, Katharine quickly twisted her hair into a chignon at the nape of her neck. Then, finding the dress's matching sailor, trimmed with ribbons, tulle, and plumes, she placed it on her head.

Standing before the full-length mirror in the center of the large, double armoire, Katharine surveyed herself. The bulging, leg-of-mutton sleeves on the gray linen dress tapered to her wrists. The white lace cascade enclosed her neck, then dropped - jabot style - almost to her narrow waist. Lifting her long, smooth skirt, she revealed gray pointed-toe shoes with buttoned high tops. Feeling appropriately dressed as the wife, albeit widow, of a timber company executive, Katharine pulled on short gray gloves and carried a white lace fan as she left the room and descended the precipitous stairway.

The lawyers had returned for the midday meal and were standing in the foyer, conversing with the Winslows and Sewell Siddon. Katharine felt her face grow warm as all heads turned to watch her entrance to the foyer from the balcony above. Several of the lawyers moved toward her, in gentlemanly fashion, to offer an arm in assistance as she neared the bottom stair. William Thornton of Savannah, reaching the newel of the stairway ahead of the others, offered his arm which Katharine gladly accepted. He was probably old enough to be her grandfather, but he was courteous and kind and intelligent, and she looked forward to sitting by him at the dining room table. Why hadn't she thought of such before?

She made herself look at Sewell Siddon and she didn't like the look on his porcine face. His nostrils were flared and his face flushed. She couldn't decide whether he was angry with her or the unsuspecting, elderly William Thornton. She felt like a rabbit escaping a fox. But what if the place cards at the table paired her with the timber inspector again? She would cross that bridge when she came to it.

Julia was commenting on her dress, and the lawyers all nodded and slightly bowed.

Easygoing Ben Winslow related to everyone that Katharine had won two out of three croquet games that morning and Sewell Siddon reminded him that he was Katharine's partner. Katharine almost rolled her eyes at this, being unable to remember more than two or three points credited to the timber inspector.

Cook appeared in the dining room doorway.

"Dinner is served, Mrs. Julia," she said with great dignity.

"Thank you, Cook. We are coming."

Still holding the crook of William Thornton's arm, Katharine and the Savannah lawyer followed Julia and Ben to the private dining room. Quickly, Katharine glanced at the lovely table, set with different china, and was relieved to see no place cards designating where each one should sit. Though a butler stood nearby to assist the ladies with their chairs, William Thornton courteously seated Katharine by him, leaving a silently fuming Sewell Siddon to seat himself at the opposite end of the table across from Katharine.

The conversation quickly grew interesting as one of the Savannah lawyers began asking general questions about New York City, which each of the New York lawyers took turns answering. Katharine listened eagerly to news from the outside world.

"What's happened about the World's Fair? Will New York have it?" Ashley Hall was the inquirer.

Stanley Agnew answered him. "Looks like Chicago will get it. You know, 'Anything to beat Tammany.'"

Katharine realized he was talking about the political machine which had been in power for so many years, Tammany Hall. The piney woods of Georgia did not have a monopoly on greed and corruption. She had often heard her father speak of the red light districts which flourished under the protection of the police and the patronage of Tammany Hall politicians, creating a town more wicked than any metropolis on earth, he had said.

Stanley Agnew continued, "I'm a Methodist myself, but we've got a Presbyterian man of the cloth who's trying to clean up the city." Katharine was intrigued. Since she was Presbyterian, she listened with acute interest.

"He's the Rev. Dr. Charles H. Parkhurst of the Madison Square Presbyterian Church. I have committed to my memory his denouncement of the 'polluted harpies that, under the pretense of governing this city, are feeding day and night on its quivering vitals...a lying, perjured, rum-soaked and libidinous lot.'" Stanley Agnew's voice had deepened to its most lawyerly tones. Silence greeted the conclusion of his quotation.

Silas Carey spoke quietly into the silence. "Given the debauched history of New York City, what a diamond came through the fire in the person of William E. Dodge." Another silence followed this statement but Ben didn't allow it to linger.

"He may have been looked upon as a diamond in New York, but here in the piney woods of Georgia, he's been hated and reviled. And they hate his sons about as much, also. I tell you, as soon as our timber is cut and rafted or shipped to the coast, we're moving on back to New York. We were talking to Katharine about it today. And Katharine's going back, too, as soon as she sells her timber. Right, Katharine?"

"Er...yes, er...right, Ben." Katharine wished Ben would hush. Was the table wine loosening his tongue? She didn't want her business made known to Sewell Siddon. She covertly glanced at the Darien timber inspector who was staring open-mouthed at Ben, as if by gazing hard enough and long enough, he might elicit more information from him. Finally, he turned and looked directly at Katharine.

"Katharine, where is your timber that you're wanting to sell?"

Katharine felt as though her breath had been knocked out of her. She didn't want to tell him or anyone where her timber was located. Before she could give a deflective reply, Ben was telling all he knew, and more, about her land and timber and she squirmed in her seat, longing to flee the room and the presence of Sewell Siddon. Ben, innocent of any wrongdoing, explained in careful detail just where Katharine's timber was located.

"It's there, facing the River Road, Sewell. It's fine timber, all right. Most of it'll probably be rafted. It's near Willcox Lake."

Again, Katharine glanced at the timber inspector and noted a decided gleam in his eyes.

"I know that timber, Ben. You're right. It's large timber, but..." He lowered his voice to a whisper which Katharine, nonetheless, easily overheard. "It's got large knotholes, as I recall."

Katharine breathed deeply. She couldn't recall Frank's ever saying it had knotholes or any other imperfections. She had the distinct impression that Sly Siddon was bribing her, using her timber, or his possible inspection of her timber, as his bribe. Julia, noting that everyone was through eating, had risen from the table.

"Let's all move to the library. Other timber company members may be arriving at any time now."

Everyone rose from the table, and again the courtly old lawyer, William Thornton, offered his arm to Katharine who was grateful to anyone who, though unaware of the situation, nevertheless, removed her from the confinement of Sewell Siddon's smothering and unwanted attentions. She avoided looking at the timber inspector who was talking with Julia and Ben. Obviously, he had brashly inquired whether he might attend the lumber company meeting. Katharine was appalled at his brazenness. Julia was apologetic.

"If it were allowed, we would love for you to attend the lumber company meeting, but I'm afraid it's against the rules, Sewell."

"Oh, I don't need another meeting to go to. You all go ahead and have your meeting."

"Your carriage is waiting for you at the *porte cochere*. Don't forget the ball tomorrow night, Sewell."

"Wild horses couldn't drag me away," the inspector said, his mouth slack as he looked steadily at Katharine who was entering the library on the arm of the elderly Savannah lawyer.

"You folks, excuse me. I need to see Katharine before I go."

Katharine was annoyed by the appearance of Sly Siddon, standing in front of her. At his words, "Katharine, honey, I need to talk to you before I leave," the distinguished old lawyer, William Thornton, excused himself and entered the library alone. Katharine resented the timber inspector's behavior, but felt that she should make an effort not to incur his wrath. However, no words were forthcoming and she waited with trepidation for him to speak.

"Honey, you'd better hope that I inspect that timber of yours, when it reaches Darien."

Katharine still could not bring herself to speak. Her worst fears were being expressed and she did not know what to say to mitigate the situation. For some strange reason, she suddenly longed for Micah MacRae. If only he were here, he would know what to say about her timber. Micah MacRae knew just about everyone's land and timber in Telfair County, and he would tell this impertinent timber inspector that her timber was sound and worthy of the highest prices. Dear God in Heaven, she silently prayed, Micah MacRae will either make or break my fortune, though this insolent timber inspector fully believes that he himself holds me in the palm of his hand.

Without being fully aware of Micah MacRae's incorporeal impact, Katharine found herself becoming calmer and more at ease. Unconsciously, she felt his strength pervade her and she was able to speak.

"Sewell, my trees are virgin timber, possibly several hundred years old, and I have been told that they should command the market's best prices. If you should be the one who inspects them, then I would hope that you would give me a fair inspection."

"Fair? What is fair? Believe me, when your timber arrives in Darien, I'll make it my business to inspect it myself. If you want the best for your timber, then you should give your best..." He paused, his eyes ravishing her, then reiterated, "...your best. You understand what I'm saying?" He leaned over to kiss her on the lips, but a quick turn of her head planted his mouth on her cheek instead.

"You're not giving your best, honey."

"I have a meeting to go to, Mr. Siddon. Excuse me," Katharine said, as she walked around the spurned, angry timber inspector and through the library door. Something told her she would have a difficult time, trying to get her timber's worth at Darien. Again, Micah MacRae loomed in her thoughts and again his strength undergirded her and made her feel that, somehow, everything was going to be all right. Heretofore, she had skirted around the realization that her lifelong livelihood directly depended on the profits made from her timber. Now, she knew with a certainty that her timber would largely determine her lifestyle for the rest of her life.

As Katharine entered the library, Julia nodded to her and gestured toward a chair near her. At the last meeting, they had sat in the same two Hepplewhite chairs while the men took seats around the long mahogany table. Other timber company shareholders were coming into the library and finding chairs at the table. Some sat in other chairs in the spacious room.

Paul Owens, the Normandale mill manager, was one of the last to arrive and someone pulled up another chair to the table for him. Katharine noted that he was even more corpulent than when she last had seen him with the eviction posse on Micah MacRae's land. He nodded his head toward her and Julia, but did not appear as talkative and demonstrative as he usually did.

Ben Winslow cleared his throat and banged the company gavel to gain everyone's attention. The meeting moved forward, as servants brought in fresh fruits and petits fours, along with other delicate pastries. Lemonade was served in tall slim glassware.

Paul Owens was asked to report on the status of the Yellow Pines Lumber Mill, and he gave a cursory report, citing the continuing success of the large lumber mill. When he sat down, everyone stood and applauded, though Katharine only went through the motions to avoid bringing unwanted attention to herself.

Someone spoke from the center of the room. Katharine never knew who it was.

"What happens when all the timber is cut?" A deafening quiet did not answer the question. Paul Owens stood up again and everyone strained to hear what he had to say.

"That's a question we're all going to have to answer," he said, his voice registering a tone of finality.

"Now, Paul, let's not be melodramatic. The end of timber cutting here in the piney woods is nowhere in sight...yet. However, when the end does come, everybody will do as I plan to...pack up and leave." The words were Ben Winslow's.

The vision of stumps, as far as the eye could see, reappeared to Katharine. She wondered whether the other company officials had ridden much over the territory and observed the desolate landscape of the once tree-canopied piney woods.

She found herself standing alone, as everyone except Ben Winslow was now seated again. She had remained quiet at the only other company meeting she had ever attended, so everyone looked at her with surprise and interest as she stood before them.

Feeling their curiosity in regard to what she was about to say, she once again had the oft-recurring thought that since she could not even vote, why would men listen to her? She had something to say but would it carry any weight? She squared her slender shoulders and looked at each man as she talked, her eyes moving steadily from one to another.

"I don't profess to be a businesswoman, nor do I claim to know anything about the protection of forests and the animals which live in the forests. I only know what I have seen and it hasn't been pretty. Have you ridden across Telfair and this county lately, and have you noticed the lands where the trees have already been cut, especially the areas near the river and Horse Creek in Telfair County? I tell you, when we all go back to our homes in the North, we'll be leaving towns of stumps! How long does it take for a yellow pine to grow? Some of these we are cutting are several hundred years old! I don't have an answer. I'll be cutting my own within a few weeks. I suppose what I am asking is: Are we doing this in the right way?"

Katharine sat down, mid comments that she shouldn't worry her pretty head about such things. Julia leaned over and sympathetically offered her friend advice.

"You worry too much, Katharine. I just let the men worry about such things. Actually, I guess we all came to the piney woods of Georgia because of William E. Dodge and we have just trusted that he knew what he was doing. Since he's been gone for the last ten years, we've looked to his sons to carry on the timber operations."

Katharine barely heard what Julia was saying, because she had just realized that she had not even once glanced Julia's way while she was addressing the men about the stumps on the cut-over lands. We women perpetuate our own indifference and ignorance, Katharine thought, by not including one another in our deliberations and thereby attempting to solve some of life's problems. The pudgy Paul Owens stood up, his face more heavily lined than Katharine remembered and his jowls shaking, as he addressed the group.

"Mrs. Fremont is correct about the cut-over lands being unsightly. It's also not easy to farm with the large stumps left behind, and wagonloads of people are beginning to come to settle on these cut-over lands. All I can say is that it's going to be tough to eke out a living on this treeless land. You may remember, as early as 1881, the *Macon Telegraph* warned about the 'wanton destruction' of South Georgia forests, stating that present rates of cutting would turn the piney woods into a 'barren waste' within twenty years. Though that was before my time as manager of the mill, I remember reading that sawmillers and turpentiners had abandoned the Old South practice of cutting only mature trees in favor of the despoiling policy of harvesting almost any tree of size, including 'half grown' saplings. Thereby, the young stands that had through the ages replenished the forest for succeeding generations were now 'blasted and cut off.' In fact, it can be said that this unrestricted cutting is destroying 'the goose which lays the golden egg.'"

"Sounds like you're on the side of the squatters, Paul." This was bluntly stated by the Savannah lawyer, Ashley Hall.

"No," the mill manager replied. "I've been accused of that before, however, Mr. Hall, but as I recall, we decided at our last meeting that we should know our enemy. I think this means trying to understand what he's thinking, so we can always be a step or two ahead." He continued, "Someone mentioned the 'latent land war.' I would take exception to those words. Why, almost every week or so, our woods riders are shot at, and we've had several killed. In fact, I heard someone say recently that close to thirty people have been killed, already." Everyone in the capacious library leaned forward to hear what the mill manager had to say.

"Why, this past week, an unusual thing happened. Several months ago, one of our woods riders was riding his horse through the woods near Gum Swamp in the northern part of Telfair County, when he had an overpowering feeling that he was being watched and that his life was in danger. He told me this himself. He said he reached in his saddlebag for his gun but couldn't find it, so he slipped off his horse and fell to his knees and started praying. He thought he was about to be killed. He heard someone walking in the woods not far from him but he didn't look up, just kept praying out loud. He soon had the feeling that whoever it was had gone, so he got back on his horse.

"Well, the really unusual part of the story is that this same woods rider was just this past weekend called to the death bed of a certain man in Telfair County. The man's last words were directed to our woods rider. He asked his forgiveness for the time, several months prior, when he was about to kill him. He said that when the woods rider dropped to his knees to pray, it took away his desire to kill him, but he still wanted his forgiveness before he died. Of course, the woods rider willingly forgave him. You can call this land war 'latent,' if you want to, but in my book it's out in the open and getting worse every day."

"You're sounding more and more like a backwoods Baptist preacher, Paul," Ashley Hall said in a half-teasing, half-scathing tone of voice. He continued, "It might be that you've been in the piney woods too long. You might need a replacement, so you can go back home to St. Simons or New York and rest awhile." Paul Owens sighed heavily and, wearily shaking his head, resumed his seat. Ben Winslow banged the gavel, reminding everyone to return to the lumber company business.

"Paul, we want you to give us some facts and figures about our sawmill at Normandale and also the one at Willcox Lake. We're relying on you to keep things running smoothly. We want a detailed report on the lumber mill's operations."

Paul Owens raised his glass for a quick sip of lemonade before rising to his feet again. He shifted some papers on the table before him and looked around the room.

"Gentlemen, our mill at Normandale is the largest in the Southeast, as some of you may know. We still miss Mr. Forsyth and Mr. Fremont but the groundwork they laid for the mill continues to contribute to its success. We have a sawmill with a capacity of 50,000 feet per day, a planing mill with a capacity of 800,000 feet per month, and a dry kiln with a capacity of 50,000 feet per day.

"Our loggers are paid according to the number of trees they can fell in a day. We expect our axmen to cut down ten trees in a day's time. However, we do have a few exceptional workers who can cut as many as twenty trees per day, and we gladly pay these loggers double wages.

"Our machine shop can do all kinds of machinery repairing, from the turning of a shaft or cutting of a bolt to the remodeling of a locomotive. As an example of what we can do, we changed our locomotive from narrow gauge to standard gauge ourselves. We have also overhauled and remodeled several locomotives, steam pumps, and stationary engines. We have the latest and most improved lath and stave machines. We also have a Lidgerwood skidder which is much quicker in moving the felled trees, though we continue to rely also on oxen and mules. We have around 225 mules in our employ which bring the logs from the forests to the railway and, of course, a number of oxen which fare better than the mules in the swampy areas.

"Our sawmill on the Ocmulgee River, at Willcox Lake, has a capacity of 40,000 feet per day, and our turpentine distillery has been turning out 275 barrels of spirits and several hundred barrels of rosin per month. We have nearly thirty miles of track, built with thirty-pound iron rail and forty-three inch gauge, from Normandale to Willcox Lake with four steam locomotives and forty-two cars that operate there.

"Of course, in comparison, the Amoskeag Lumber Company, situated near Eastman and controlled by Savannah businessmen, has a ten-mile long railroad with forty-pound iron rail and a sixty-nine inch gauge. It has nine locomotives and sixteen cars.

"Also, the Empire Lumber Company has a logging railroad that stretches from Dublin on the Oconee River to Hawkinsville on the Ocmulgee River. It crosses the East Tennessee, Virginia, and Georgia line at Empire which is around thirteen miles north of Eastman. Some of you may know that they built a one-hundred-thousand dollar, nickel-plate lumber mill there in 1887. Indeed, what I'm saying, gentlemen, is that Empire's investment in both the railroads and the mill is so enormous that the company cannot operate profitably, and they're beginning to realize just that.

"I think we all appreciate the business acumen of William E. Dodge, and now his sons, for they have known how and where to invest their money, making all of our profits greater than those of the lumber companies around us. William E. Dodge was a 'Connecticut Yankee' in the finest sense of the words! I'm sure you all realize that the Legislature named this county after William E. Dodge because in his capacity as Chairman of the New York Chamber of Commerce, he induced, and I quote, 'Congress to remove the burden of taxation from the great staple of our State and of the South....' The 'great staple,' of course, was cotton and, my friends, no one benefitted more from this inducement than William E. Dodge himself, for the taxation was removed from his own vast cotton interests. My friends, the Dodges know what they're doing and we are all the beneficiaries of their expertise!

"I'm sure most of you know about the Dodges' lucrative 'cotton triangle,' which has been operative for most of this century, exporting their cotton from Charleston, New Orleans, and other ports in the South to England in return for tin plate. Of course, the Dodges have had the largest business in metals probably of any mercantile house in the world...and cotton has made this possible. The tin plate is shipped from Liverpool to New York, thus completing the 'triangle.' I might add here, also, that when increased duties on wool, woolen goods, flax, and iron were proposed by the thirty-ninth Congress in 1866, W. E. Dodge made sure that tin plate, in which he had a vested interest, was in no way affected."

Hearty applause followed this assessment of the Dodges' shrewdness in knowing how to protect their own interests and how to use their considerable resources to the greatest advantage, both in their capital outlay and also in their knowledge of even the minutiae of the logging, sawmilling, rafting, and railing facets of the gigantic and complex timber industry. The mill manager continued with his praise of the Dodges.

"Yes, the Dodges are quick-witted and competent, all right. As I recall, in 1877, the Georgia Legislature passed an act requiring all foreign corporations holding more than five thousand acres of land in Georgia to incorporate under its laws within one year. Well, as you know, the Georgia Land and Lumber Company was incorporated under the laws of New York. Did this deter the Dodges? No, my friends, not one iota! No, two days before the law became effective...two days, my friends,...the Georgia Land and Lumber Company conveyed all of its lands to George E. Dodge, a citizen of New York, but a natural person. The title remained in George E. Dodge and his successor and brother, Norman W. Dodge, also a citizen of New York, but the development here in Georgia continued to be carried on by foreign corporations. I must say, this was a remarkable way to...shall we say,...circumvent the law?"

Or an "unscrupulous" way, Katharine thought to herself. She had never heard this before, and she wondered how the Dodges were able to evade the law. She didn't really understand the "natural person" conveyance to the sons of William E. Dodge, if the timber harvesting continued to be carried on by "foreign" corporations, which the law was meant to preclude.

Apparently enjoying the endorsement of what he was saying, evidenced by the hand-clapping of those around him, the company superintendent launched into a human-interest story in regard to one of the competing sawmills. The timber officials listened attentively.

"I mentioned the Amoskeag Lumber Company a few minutes ago. I was talking to one of their officials the other day, and he was telling me an unusual but true story about a mule that hauls dust from the mill. After the driver dumps the load of sawdust, the mule returns to the mill without his driver and will go to the places where the sawdust is usually deposited. If there is none there, he'll go to another place where there is a pile and will back up and wait for his load. The timber official says it's amusing to watch him, as he'll do it every time. The mule is blind in one eye and deaf, too."

"If Norman Dodge hears about the mule, he'll be wanting to buy the animal for our Normandale mill. He's always interested in a good bargain," someone said, with a laugh.

Paul Owens chuckled. "I don't think the Amoskeag people will part with the mule. He's been a part of the mill now for a number of years and he gives everybody a good laugh every day."

The mill manager paused, observing the smiles and amusement of others in the room. Katharine also enjoyed the lightheartedness of the mule raillery for it eased, momentarily anyway, the conflict which raged within her about the Dodge family. She had never really thought about the fact that William E. Dodge's having the taxation removed from the cotton in the South had been more profitable for him than for anyone else, though this was obvious since he had owned major cotton-exporting businesses in New Orleans and other Southern ports. He probably benefitted more than anyone else from having the tax on exported cotton removed, yet the impoverished Southerners thought he did this to help the vanquished South. A new county had been created in his honor in the State of Georgia, because he had been instrumental in having the "burden of taxation from the great staple of our State and of the South" removed. What duplicity, she thought!

Paul Owens continued with his report on the Yellow Pines Lumber Mill at Normandale and she tried to concentrate on what he was saying.

"At Normandale, we now have seventy-five houses, two churches - one for whites and one for coloreds - a community hall, school, and commissary. Our company employs over 500 men with a payroll of $8,000. All of our buildings are either painted or whitewashed, with attractive green shutters, and fenced. Of course, we also have the two beautiful executive mansions that belonged to Mr. Forsyth and to Mr. J. B. Knox who was assistant to 'Captain Jack,' as we all called Mr. Forsyth.

"I'm sure most of you know that we've ceased using the Horse Creek Railroad. Actually, most of our timber has been cut from that area of Telfair County and rafted on to Darien and St. Simons. Of course, we still have some acreage around Bear Creek, so we may be using the upper half of the Horse Creek railway to move that timber out. It'll be a simple matter of replacing the portable tracks and maybe clearing the weeds around the tracks."

When he said this, Katharine stiffened and noted that Paul Owens momentarily flickered his eyes her way. Did he know? Could he possibly know the extent of her involvement with Micah MacRae and his family? He was, of course, aware of the location of the MacRae land, as he and the posse had been driven off the land at gunpoint. He probably had wondered until this day why she, Katharine Fremont, was sitting on a tree stump, watching the logging procedure that day in the woods when he and the posse had arrived. His brief glance her way told her that he remembered.

At that moment, Katharine realized that the mill manager was purposely dropping information about Bear Creek for her benefit, because no one else in the room likely knew or cared that the MacRae land was situated there. She knew with a sudden clarity that he would never be openly ambivalent about the escalating land war, but for some reason, he was trying to get a message to Micah MacRae that his land lots on Bear Creek had been circled in red by the plumed pen of Norman Dodge. Blood red, Katharine thought - a pen dipped in the blood of the local landowners.

She looked at the wealthy men in the room with new eyes. Some, like Paul Owens, were corpulent from too much food and too little physical labor. Their hands were smooth and manicured, their clothes fashionable and well-made, tailored to their fleshy, inactive bodies.

The images of the MacRae family came to her mind. Abby's gnarled hands, along with Micah's large, rough ones. The land which both had tilled for so many years had belonged to Micah's father and grandfather and to his father before him. How in heaven's name could Norman Dodge honestly believe it was his? The sound of the gavel adjourning the meeting caused Katharine to jerk forward in her chair, much to Julia's amusement.

"Katharine, you nearly jumped out of your chair. Whatever has kept you so preoccupied?" Katharine searched for a ready answer.

"I guess I've just been thinking of all the timber that Norman Dodge has cut, and I can't help but think of the local people who have lost their land and timber."

"There you go again - worrying about something that can't be helped. I think these meetings always upset you and me. By the way, I thought we'd visit the Hardisons and Woodruffs tomorrow. They were telling me recently that they haven't seen you much since Frank died and they have missed you. Then, the ball is tomorrow night."

"Julia, that sounds great - I mean, all of your plans to visit Eleanor Hardison and Joan Woodruff and their families. I'm looking forward to it. However, I feel that I must go on back home the following day."

"But, Katharine, I thought you were planning on staying through the weekend. You don't need to go back home without Tilda there."

"I know. I really don't look forward to it, but for some reason I feel compelled to go back Thursday."

"Well, at least you'll be here for the dancing tomorrow night. I think Steve would be terribly upset if he didn't have a talented dance partner."

"Vickie won't be coming, I believe you said?"

"No, it'll be awhile. She doesn't enjoy dancing much, anyway, as you know. I think she's glad for Steve to have you as his partner, since you and Steve have known each other for such a long time, and she doesn't feel threatened by your friendship."

"As you already know, Julia, Steve is the brother I never had. I'm looking forward to seeing him."

As Katharine and Julia talked, the timber men quietly left the room, discussing company business and nodding toward the two ladies as they passed by them. Servants entered the room and busied themselves in collecting the glassware and trays and carrying them from the room. Julia whispered confidentially, "If you're like me, you're ready to get out of your corset and relax for awhile before supper. However, you haven't put on any extra pounds like myself, so you may not be as uncomfortable as I am."

"Oh, I agree with you, Julia. It would be wonderful to put on something loose and comfortable and maybe lie down for a few minutes."

The two friends walked from the room to the spacious foyer and, lifting their long dresses, ascended the tall stairway. Reaching the balcony, Julia reminded Katharine about the evening meal and the friends parted ways.

Closing the guest room door behind her, Katharine quickly undressed and untied the tight corset. She pulled the rose silk combing sacque around her and climbed onto the inviting chaise lounge. Stretching her arms and legs, unhampered by anything tight and binding, was like a bit of heaven, she thought, and with the passing of only a few minutes, she was asleep.

The steady ticking of the mantel clock which had lulled her to sleep now awakened her with its persistent ticktocking.

Chapter Nineteen

The ballroom of Winslow Hall was gleaming with the gaslight of crystal chandeliers and the flickering flames of many candles. Guests were arriving by carriages and other horse-drawn conveyances at the *porte cochere*, and servants were directing them to the large ballroom where dancing was already underway. The large chamber orchestra from Atlanta was playing the lilting strains of Strauss' *On the Beautiful, Blue Danube*, and the ladies' full dresses looked like butterflies cavorting on the highly polished dance floor. Their courtly husbands and suitors gave the appearance of large black moths in their formal tuxedos, twisting and turning their partners in the sweeping waltz steps.

Katharine stood at the wide arched doorway of the large ballroom, observing the rhythmical cadences of the dancing couples whose shadows replicated their movements on the walls of the room. She was unaware of the stir she caused among those in the room, even when they whispered among themselves and looked her way. Her thoughts were crowded with the social calls she and Julia had made during the morning, visits which Julia had painstakingly planned in advance, leaving her calling cards at the homes of the Hardisons and Woodruffs. Though Katharine had tried to enjoy the visits, she had felt a detachment from the wives whose husbands had been present at the lumber company meeting only the day before. Their prejudiced conversations about the illiterate, mean squatters were difficult for Katharine to hear, and she had to restrain herself not to enlighten them about the situation, as she now saw it, in the piney woods. She knew that she could not visit any of them, even Julia, on a regular basis anymore without letting her true feelings surface. She felt trapped and longed to be free of her ambivalence in regard to the situation in the Georgia piney woods.

With a start, Katharine wondered how long she had been standing in the doorway of the crowded ballroom. Her white silk dress with its voluminous leg-of-mutton sleeves of pale turquoise blue shimmered on her slim figure. Her soft pompadour hair, tilted plume, long gloves, and folded fan were but subtle composites of the fashionable appearance she made in a still, almost portrait-like, pause at the entrance of the domed ballroom.

A guest on the far side of the ballroom was having his liqueur glass refilled. Upon seeing Katharine, he quickly set the glass on the nearest table and moved purposefully toward her. The sleek lines of his black dinner jacket failed to camouflage the man's pudginess. With a certain dread, Katharine realized the man was Sewell Siddon. However, before she could enter the room, someone crept behind her and covered her eyes with two large hands.

"What? Who...?" Katharine pulled vainly at the hands, attempting to dislodge them from her eyes.

"It's me! No, before you correct my grammar, it's 'I.' Guess who, lovely Mrs. Fremont?"

"Steve! It's you! I'd know that voice anywhere." Katharine tugged at his hands.

Steve dropped his hands as Katharine quickly turned around to face her youthful admirer, his eyes dancing with mischief under a thatch of neatly combed, red hair.

"My, but you do look quite the young gentleman in your resplendent tuxedo, Mr. Winslow," Katharine laughed, genuinely pleased to see the irrepressible Steve. How especially wonderful that he had arrived just in time to foil the timber inspector's clumsy pursuit of her. She felt almost like an animal's prey. She was glad to see that Steve's presence had stopped, for awhile at least, the man's advance toward her. He was glaring at the oblivious Steve with bloodshot eyes and Katharine knew he would be even more inebriated as the evening wore on. She did, however, manage a smile and nod toward him, though he made no attempt to hide his displeasure that she had somehow managed to elude him again.

"As you may know," Katharine continued her banter with Steve, "you are the brother I always wished I had."

Steve scowled, then warmed to a bright thought.

"Glad to know I have a place somewhere in your affections," he mocked, then laughed somewhat derisively.

Katharine said, "I heard about your new baby daughter. In fact, I was looking forward to seeing her."

"She's still a little young to make the long ride here. Actually, I'm just passing through town on my way to Savannah."

"Yes, Julia told me you had business in Savannah. My, but you're young to have such important business so far away from your home in Macon."

"Well, the business is growing. Maybe Julia mentioned that, too. When she told me about the ball, I told her I wouldn't miss it, so she's put me out in the guest house, which suits me just fine. By the way," Steve continued, "did Julia mention the new dance to you?"

"Yes, but I hadn't heard of it. She says they're dancing it in Savannah and Atlanta."

"They're dancing the *Terpsichore* just about everywhere. I can't believe you've never heard of it. Mrs. Fremont, you've been in the backwoods too long. Now that you've returned to civilization, if only for a few days, I will be your *Terpsichore* dance instructor."

"I'm looking forward to learning it, Steve," Katharine said. Steve began describing the whirling *Terpsichore* to her, then stopped talking as the music from the last dance ended.

"Come on...what are we doing, standing here talking, when we could be dancing?" Steve took Katharine's gloved hand and the two stepped inside the ballroom where a liveried manservant, stationed just inside the room, made the expected announcement:

"Mrs. Frank Fremont with escort, Mr. Steve Winslow."

A patter of applause followed the announcement. As Katharine curtseyed and Steve slightly bowed, the orchestra, screened in the musician's gallery, burst forth with *Tales from the Vienna Woods*, another waltz which brought Steve and Katharine into the whirling midst of the dance floor. Katharine closed her eyes and surrendered herself to the tempestuous, pulsating waltz music. Opening them a few moments later, she thought that the room appeared to spin with the synchronous movements of the dancing couples.

How beautiful everything is, she thought, but beneath her appreciation of it all was an emptiness which she could not fathom. In fact, she was somewhat surprised at herself for longing to be away, to leave as soon as possible.

Silently, she berated herself. What was wrong? Didn't she usually enjoy dancing and especially her visits at Winslow Hall? She looked around the lovely ballroom, then abruptly met Steve's quizzical eyes.

"You're a thousand miles away from here, Mrs. Fremont. Whatever can you be thinking?"

Katharine smiled, attempting to deflect any curiosity on his part.

"I don't know really, Steve. Guess I'm just getting older and more contemplative."

"Contemplative...hmm, let's see. I think I learned that word in spelling - or maybe it was English Literature."

Katharine laughed. "Same Steve. Trying not to let the world know that you're a Harvard graduate."

"My dear Mrs. Fremont, you know me quite well. However, I'm unable to keep such a secret, especially in view of the fact that everyone knew that I was out of circulation for four long years, due to my heavy studying schedules."

"What heavy studying are you talking about?" Katharine said teasingly. "As I recall, your father threatened to cut off your matriculation money if you didn't start studying."

"You're right," Steve grinned, "about the studying, I mean, but you're wrong about my being a Harvard graduate. No, I went four years, all right, but had to repeat some courses. Then, I got into the timber export business and I decided I didn't want to go back to the halls of ivy. I'm doing all right without that degree, Ma'm," Steve said, grinning.

The waltz ended and a lively polka issued from the musicians. A man Katharine did not know tapped Steve on the shoulder, informing him that he would like a dance with the beautiful lady. Steve faked a good-natured smile as Katharine and her new partner joined the other couples on the dance floor in managing the quick steps and graceful hops of the buoyant Bohemian dance.

As the polka ended, leaving everyone breathless, Steve and Sewell Siddon simultaneously appeared as Katharine's partner for the quadrille-type dance known as the lancers. As her last partner courteously thanked her for a wonderful dance, Sewell Siddon elbowed a provoked Steve Winslow away from Katharine and took her hand.

"Come on, honey. You're dancing this one with me," he said, and Katharine forced a smile to her lips, because he was a Darien timber inspector and he might soon be inspecting her own timber. The smile became genuine, however, when she heard Steve's assessment of her latest dance partner as they passed before him. "The big lummox!" he said, and Katharine's eyes meeting his told him that she agreed.

As the couples positioned themselves on the dance floor, a manservant quietly appeared at Katharine's side. Bowing slightly, he said that a gentleman wished to speak with her. He, the servant, had informed the gentleman that Mrs. Fremont was occupied in the ballroom, but then the gentleman insisted that it was a matter of some urgency.

Katharine looked quickly at the arched doorway of the ballroom and was startled to see Micah MacRae, dressed in his usual homespun and leather attire. Her heart leapt to her throat. His large presence appeared to fill the entire ballroom. His steady gaze was undaunted by the formally garbed guests who were now openly staring at him.

Whispers of "That's Micah MacRae!" and "That's the best timber pilot on the three rivers!" and, finally, "What's he doing here?" assailed Katharine's ears.

"Thank you, Sylvester," Katharine said to the servant, then spoke to Sewell Siddon.

"Excuse me, Sewell, I must speak with Mr. MacRae."

"Who? What the…" The timber inspector looked annoyed and irritated. He followed her part of the way across the dance floor, until she turned and said again, "Please excuse me." The inspector stopped trailing behind her, but waited as she lifted one side of her long dress and moved rapidly toward the raftsman whose presence suddenly made the ballroom an unimportant place to be, an insignificant place which he appeared to dismiss with one brief glance around the room. What was this matter of great urgency which brought him here? How did he know she was here? Her jumbled thoughts raced on.

Katharine stood breathlessly in front of the large raftsman, feeling the strength which always flowed from his body to hers. Her gloved hand reached out almost instinctively, and he covered it with his large one. Looking up into his opaque brown eyes, she as usual could not fathom his thoughts.

"Good evening, Mr. MacRae." Some charade, Katharine thought, calling him 'Mr. MacRae,' when she had been held and kissed by the man. Yet, she knew that she must keep up appearances before her Northern friends who must never know of her feelings for this man, recognized by his clothes, speech, and demeanor as a Southern backwoodsman and squatter. She removed her hand from his strong grasp.

"Evenin', Ma'm." Micah MacRae knew how to play the game, also. Though the music had begun again and some couples were dancing, others were openly curious about the stark contrast of the couple standing in the arched doorway of the ballroom - the beautiful Katharine Fremont and the ruggedly handsome backwoodsman. Though Micah MacRae had rafted some of the guests' timber down the rivers, and though he was recognized as the foremost raftsman on the rivers, he was also suspected of being the leader of the squatters in their assaults on the timber company's property. There was a mystery about the man.

"Ma'm, I need to talk to you."

"I see. Let's walk into the foyer where we can hear better. I didn't realize the music was so loud, until now." They were soon alone in the large foyer and Katharine was eager to know what had brought Micah MacRae to Winslow Hall.

"Miz Fremont, we finished cuttin' all of your trees now and I'm ready to take your first raft to Darien. You said to let you know when I was ready, so that's why I came on here." The fact that he was at a formal ball without benefit of an invitation did not deter him in the least, and Katharine had to hide a smile at his innocence regarding the intricacies of the social conventions which had always governed her life. It was amusing to her that an invitation to Winslow Hall, so coveted by everyone who received one and by many who did not, was of no importance to Micah MacRae. Rather, he appeared to view these formal affairs as wastes of time.

"How did you know I was here?" Katharine inquired.

"I went to your house first and old Hill told me you were here."

Katharine decided the time had come to tell him her plan. She paused and took a deep breath, feeling a sense of relief at finally being able to divulge her secret. Looking steadily at the raftsman, she said, "I'm going to Darien, also."

"What?" The raftsman thought he had not heard correctly.

"I plan to go with you on my raft to Darien."

The backwoodsman's breathing was labored.

"I won't allow it," he said, flatly.

"You can't stop me, Mr. MacRae," Katharine said cooly. "After all, it's my raft. It's something I have planned to do for the last several months."

"It's too dangerous, and I can't let you. It's just too dangerous for a woman - and especially a woman like you..." His voice trailed off, unbelievingly.

"What do you mean by 'a woman like me'?"

Micah looked her up and down and Katharine's face grew pink under his glare.

"I mean you ain't worked a day in your life and you don't know how hard and dangerous it is, even for a man, out on the river."

"I plan to go, Micah," she said quietly. "I promise I won't be any trouble and I can take care of myself."

"Ma'm, sometimes men get killed on trips down the rivers and we're a-gonna have only one other man, besides myself, who's made the trip before. That means two of 'em will be dead weight for half the trip, not knowin' what to do. I tell you it's too dangerous for a woman." Micah paused, then continued, "Why do you want to go, anyway, Ma'm? I'll see about your timber and get you the best prices. Besides, I'll be a-takin' many more of your rafts down, unless you want to send your logs to Brunswick by rail. You might rather wait and go on one of the later ones. However," Micah paused again, "guess if you wait 'til later, it'll be a-gettin' colder."

"That's true, also," Katharine said, "but, no, I want to go on the first raft, because I believe it'll pretty much determine the prices of the later ones, and I want to be assured of the best prices possible. Anyway, I've been wanting to go to Darien and this will be my chance."

"Ma'm, you'd be a lot more comfortable a-goin' by train to Brunswick, then catchin' the *Hessie* steamboat over to Darien."

"I've pretty much made up my mind to go," Katharine insisted.

"Suit yourself, Ma'm. As you said, it's your timber but I want you to remember how I tried to talk you out of it, and you can be sure that you will regret ever even thinkin' about livin' on the raft for seven or more days. It ain't no place for a fragile woman."

Katharine smiled at his assessment of her. She supposed that in comparison with his mother and wife who had tended crops in the fields and plowed behind oxen and birthed children in their beds at home, she must portray a weak, fragile woman, but she would show him! Yes, she would show him so that he would know that she was strong and capable. Just how she was going to accomplish this, she wasn't at all sure, but she resolved as she stood looking at him that she would prove to him that she wasn't the Southerners' notion of the stereotypical rich but weak woman from the North.

"I appreciate your concern, Mr. MacRae, but I promise I won't be any trouble to you."

"I'm ready to leave in the mornin', at sunup," the raftsman said.

"What?" Katharine was incredulous.

"Yes, Ma'm, that's the reason I came on here tonight, to let you know I was a-leavin' in the mornin'. I ain't had no idea you were a-plannin' to go, too, but if you're set on goin', why you need to go on home tonight and catch the early timber train to Willcox Lake. That's where we push off, first light. I can't make no changes here at the last minute, 'cause the blacks are a-goin' to be at Willcox Lake at sunup, and they'll be a-walkin' thirty miles in the dark to get there. Ain't no way to change ever'thin' here at the last minute. Also, the freshet should give us enough water in the Ocmulgee for your raft. It's prob'ly ten feet or more wider and it's longer than I'm used to driftin'. It'll be all right, once we reach the Altamaha, and if we go on now after the rain we had, the raft should make it down the Ocmulgee."

Things were moving too fast for Katharine to make a hurried decision as to what to do. The only thing she knew to do was to pack her things and leave Winslow Hall immediately, but it was nighttime and she didn't relish the hour's trip home in the dark. Micah MacRae seemed to read her thoughts.

"The moon's out tonight and I'll follow you home, if you're a-wantin' to leave now."

"I need to see first whether a timber train will leave early enough for me to get to Willcox Lake by daybreak." Katharine turned abruptly and almost bumped into Sewell Siddon. It was obvious that he had come looking for her when she didn't return to the ballroom. She wondered what he had heard of her conversation with Micah MacRae. He did not seem aware of anything that had been said, and for that Katharine was grateful. She knew that the two men knew each other, but when neither spoke to the other, she felt compelled to introduce them.

"Mr. Siddon - Mr. MacRae," she said.

"We've met, Ma'm," Micah MacRae said evenly, nodding to the timber inspector.

Though Sewell Siddon made no attempt to speak to the raftsman, he turned back to Katharine with a craftiness that made her realize that she had underestimated his meanness.

"So...," he said, slowly, emphasizing each word, "the great river runner is going to raft your timber to Darien, is he, Katharine, honey?"

"He may at some point, Mr. Siddon." Katharine noted the puzzlement in Micah's expression, but only briefly. He obviously knew that she was keeping any knowledge of the imminent rafting trip from the timber inspector for a reason, and Micah was quick to understand. He had never had dealings in Darien with this particular timber inspector but he knew raftsmen who had, and they all said what a dishonest fellow he was.

Just as Katharine was wondering how to elude Sewell Siddon, Ben Winslow appeared at the doorway of the ballroom, looking for the timber inspector.

"Sewell," Ben called over to him, "one of our timber men has a question for you. I know you hate to leave our beautiful Katharine, but it won't be for long." Ben paused, spying the backwoodsman.

"Well, Micah MacRae!" Ben Winslow strode over to the raftsman, his hand extended. "I didn't realize you were here. Welcome back to Winslow Hall!"

"How are you, Ben?" The two men shook hands as the timber inspector looked on, obviously annoyed by Ben Winslow's warm greeting to the backwoodsman.

"Come on in to the ballroom. You know you're always welcome here. I've got some men here who would love to talk to the top river runner. You're already a living legend, you know."

"Thanks, Ben, but I gotta go - just had to say a few words to Miz Fremont."

"Well, excuse us, then. We've got a timber discussion going on and we could use a timber inspector's opinion." Sewell Siddon strutted alongside Ben, feeling his importance as the two men entered the ballroom.

Katharine seized the moment to complete her plans before his return.

"As I was saying," she said, turning to the raftsman, "I need to talk to Paul Owens about the timber train schedule, then pack my things and speak to Julia and Ben."

"I'll see about gettin' your carriage ready, Miz Fremont."

"Just talk to Poke and he'll bring it around to the *porte cochere*." Thinking he might not understand the French terminology, she gestured toward the side entrance.

"I know, Ma'm," he said quietly, making Katharine feel somewhat embarrassed by her assumption that he wouldn't know what the word meant.

Micah was heading for the front door.

"I'll see about your carriage," he repeated.

"I'll be out in a few minutes," Katharine replied as the raftsman stepped outside, pulling the door behind him.

Katharine heard her name called, then saw Julia hurrying toward her.

"Katharine, I've been missing you. I wondered where you were." Julia's voice was that of the continuing matchmaker. "The gentleman who danced the polka with you has been asking me all sorts of questions about you. Katharine, he is a wealthy timber official from Maine. He's looking for you right now. He is very eligible, Katharine. His wife died just last year, and..." Julia paused, noting the faraway look on her friend's face.

"Yes, well, Julia, I was on my way to find you. You see, I'm going to have to leave early, in fact, right now. I have some business to tend to tomorrow and I really must be going."

"Business? What on earth can be so important that you must leave at nighttime?"

"Well, you see, Micah MacRae is going to raft my first timber to Darien tomorrow and I really want to see it - the raft, I mean."

"Did I just see Mr. MacRae leaving?" Julia inquired.

"Yes, he says he'll follow me home so I won't be alone. He's gone to talk to Poke about getting my carriage ready."

Julia laughed, "Well, we've had many rafts run to Darien and I never saw one of them. Actually, I never even thought of going to see one. Guess I just wanted to see the money after the rafts were sold."

Katharine smiled, determined not to reveal her plan to go to Darien herself on the raft. What would Julia think? She would be unbelieving. Of that, Katharine was certain.

"Julia," Katharine said, "thank you for a wonderful visit. You and Ben are the perfect hosts, and Winslow Hall has never been more beautiful. Please tell Ben I had to leave hurriedly, and please tell Steve that we'll dance the *Terpsichore* another time. I was looking forward to learning the steps from him." The friends hugged each other and Katharine longed to tell Julia what she was about to do, but she knew with a certainty that she couldn't risk it.

"Oh, and Julia, I'll send Hill and Ollie in the break for my things. Ollie can pack the dresses in the boxes again."

"Katharine, we'll get everything back to you. Poke can carry them to you, for that matter."

"No, you need Poke here, with so many guests, Julia. Hill will come tomorrow. Now, I need to find Paul Owens to ask about the timber train."

"I'll get him for you. Wait here."

Julia returned with the mill manager who assured Katharine that the train would be leaving early in the morning, as it would be loading logs near Camp Six for rail transport.

"However," he said, "regardless of picking up the sticks, as we call them, I'll send the train out any time that you say you will need it."

Though Paul Owens may have been curious about Katharine Fremont's abrupt departure from Winslow Hall and her boarding of the timber train in the early morning hours, he was nevertheless uninquisitive, realizing that it was her business and hers alone, and he wasn't about to question her.

"I'll be at the Normandale sawmill at 4:00 in the morning," she said.

"The train'll be ready to go, Mrs. Fremont."

Chapter Twenty

The hurried carriage trip back home in the darkness would have been a frightening one, except for the fact that Micah MacRae rode along beside her. Because of his presence, Katharine found herself actually enjoying the night sounds and the full moon which shone down on the winding dirt road.

Katharine had wondered whether the backwoodsman might tie his mule to her carriage, then sit with her on the driver's seat, maybe even take the reins and guide General Lee home, but he chose to ride along beside the carriage and there were few words between them. She guessed that he was purposely putting a distance between them, because things had gotten out of hand the day she had stepped out into the furrows of his cotton field and had fallen into his arms. The memory made pleasant shivers course through her body.

However, she was determined that such intimacy would not be repeated and she was glad to see that he felt the same way. She cast a side glance at the raftsman and again felt his great strength. He was looking straight ahead, apparently lost in his own thoughts. He would have a lot of riding to do before the night was over. She had suggested that he board the timber train, as it would cross over Sugar Creek near his homeplace, but he disdained the suggestion. She knew it was because the train was timber company property and he wanted nothing to do with the hated timber company, even if it saved him hours of torturous muleback riding. Stubborn these Southerners are, Katharine thought!

Ahead on the moonlit road, a bear and her two cubs lumbered toward them. Katharine felt her horse balk just as Micah leaned out of his saddle and took the reins from her, bringing his own mount and General Lee to a complete halt.

The bear stood on her hind legs, facing them only a few feet away, but when the backwoodsman gave a bloodcurdling yell, she reverted to all fours and moved quickly into the woods on the left side of the road, her cubs bawling after her. Katharine felt her breath coming in short gasps. Her hand slid to her purse where the gun's small bulk let her know it was there. She realized that Micah hadn't even touched his gun. Obviously, he was used to warding off bears just by yelling at them. Katharine knew that the horse had been frightened, for though the gentle animal pulled the carriage again, his large hulk was trembling from the bear encounter. It was most likely the first bear he had ever seen, she thought, and she hadn't seen but a few herself.

The remainder of the trip home was uneventful with only the usual deer and raccoons and opossums crossing the road ahead of them. They soon entered the wrought-iron gates of her home and Micah jumped from his mount and helped her from the carriage. He then reached into the boot of the carriage and grabbed her bags, easily carrying all of them, with a single bound, up the front steps. After Katharine opened the large front door, he placed them inside and waited while she lit a nearby candle to light her way through the house.

"I'll see to your carriage, Miz Fremont."

"Thank you, Mr. MacRae," Katharine said, deciding that she could be just as formal with him as he was taking great pains to be with her.

"Oh, please tell Hill I will need him to go with me to Normandale in only a few hours. We'll need to leave here around 3:00 in the morning, so I can board the timber train around 4:00 o'clock."

"I'll be sure to tell him, Miz Fremont. And, by the way, I ain't a-tryin' to tell you what to do, but you need to wear some old clothes on the river. It ain't no place for fancy dressin'."

"I will certainly heed your advice, Mr. MacRae." Holding the burning candle, she watched him negotiate the several front steps with one jump, while another upward leap landed him in the seat of her carriage. His own mount clopped behind, as he guided her carriage on around to the stables where Big Hill had been roused from his sleep and was waiting to tend to the horse and carriage.

Katharine spent some time emptying her bags of the assortment of accessories which she had carried to Winslow Hall.

Then, she quickly made decisions about what to take and wear on the rafting trip. For some weeks, she had been washing and boiling some of her dead husband's clothes in an attempt to shrink them and to make them look older. She wanted to blend in with the rafthands as much as possible, and she was pleased at her anonymity when she put on the clothes and looked at herself in the long, stand-up mirror in her bedroom.

She coiled her hair in a neat ball on top of her head and pulled on Frank's floppy leather hat which she had pounded with a rolling pin and, also, washed in the washtub outside several times over the past few weeks. It should certainly conceal her identity, especially from Sewell Siddon, if he should be the inspector of her raft, once they reached Darien.

She decided to pack one travel suit for the return train trip home. She chose one which her parents had sent her. It was the latest style, a tan, short-jacketed walking suit with a large sailor collar. The collar, cuffs, and skirt were trimmed with brown braid. The white blouse was tucked, with a high collar which encircled the neck. She also included a flat sailor trimmed with feathers, ribbon, and plumes, and a pair of high top, lace-up shoes.

Katharine wrapped the clothes in a clean muslin sheet and placed them in a large leather hunting bag which was her late husband's. She decided not to pack a petticoat or pantaloons because of the lack of space, but she included several silk drawers and, of course, her corset. She tucked in a small cake of soap, several washcloths, and a towel.

She found another leather bag of her husband's and stuffed a pillow, two sheets, and a warm blanket in it. The nights were becoming cool now. In this bag she also placed her gun and bullets and several books. Then, she set out a kerosene lantern and stuffed some matches in the bag with her bedclothes.

Afraid to go to sleep, lest she might not awaken in time, Katharine lay down on the settee in the front parlor and waited for the early hour when an adventure, unlike any she had ever known, would begin. Though she had some fear of the unknown in regard to the rafting trip, she couldn't deny that she was looking forward to a week or more in the close proximity of Micah MacRae. Also, she wanted to get the backwoodsman out of her mind, and the rafting trip with all of its perils might be the way to do it. She would have her fill of him and then she would go home to New York and would never see him again.

She knew that her family and friends would think she had lost her sanity, if they knew what she was about to do, and that was precisely why she told no one of her plans. For some reason that even she did not know, she felt compelled to ride on her raft to Darien. With these thoughts swirling in her head, and without meaning to, she drifted off to sleep.

"Miz. Kat'rin! Miz. Kat'rin! Time to go! Miz. Kat'rin!" It was Big Hill, banging on the front door!

Katharine rubbed the sleep from her eyes and stumbled across the parlor floor, on into the foyer. Yawning, she opened the heavy door and waited while the faithful old Negro picked up the leather bags and placed them in the carriage. The Brougham's burning lamps and the moon overhead would light their path to the lumber mill.

"Miz. Kat'rin, it ain' none ob my business, an' Ah knows it, but it sho be dange'rus fer you to be goin' places in de middle ob de night." Again, Katharine felt the urge to reveal her plans to someone, but again she thought better of it. She was surprised that he didn't notice that she was wearing Frank's clothes. She attributed this to the enveloping darkness which the moon could not dispel and especially to the aging Negro's failing eyesight.

"I'll be fine, Hill. I'm going on the timber train to Willcox Lake. It'll take probably several hours, so I should arrive around sunup. I have some timber to check on over there. I plan to be gone around a week. I'd like for you to meet me at the train depot at Godwinsville with the carriage next Thursday. I should be arriving by train at that time."

The old Negro was trained not to inquire into white folks' business, and he knew better than to ask questions. However, Katharine knew that he was wondering where she would be during the week's time. She had friends living on the River Road and she had often visited with them, so he probably assumed she would visit with them, then return by the timber railway. However, the timber railway terminated at Normandale, and she had asked him to meet the passenger train at Godwinsville. Katharine didn't offer further explanation and the faithful Hill didn't appear to expect any.

Hill clucked to the horses and they were on their way to the lumber mill. Though Katharine had had only a few hours of sleep, she felt wide awake with a sort of dreaded anticipation of the rafting trip. Micah MacRae's words in trying to dissuade her from going made her wonder just what dangers loomed ahead in the murky waters of the Ocmulgee and Altamaha rivers.

It was then that the thought came to her that she should have brought food and spring water with her. What would Micah think? She had promised him she would be no trouble, and she had forgotten the fact that she would have to eat and drink! Oh, he would really think she was spoiled and dependent! Well, she was bringing some money with her. Surely, she could buy some food somewhere. Big Hill looked at Katharine through the carriage window.

"Miz Katharine, is you all right?"

"I'm fine, Hill. I'm just not used to looking after things and being on my own, and I'm having to learn everything in a hurry." She paused, then turned to him with such profound words that he scratched his white head at the perplexity of it all.

"Hill, do you realize how fortunate you are?" Hill was looking dubiously at her.

"Do you realize that a terrible war was fought to give you the right to vote, but it did not give me that same right?"

"No'm, I din' know it, leastways not de way you is sayin' it, Miz Kat'rin." The old Negro was staring at her, suddenly mystified by her assertion that he was more fortunate than she in having the right to vote. He did not think to tell her, though she probably already knew, that he hadn't even once exercised this hard-won right, mainly because he couldn't read and really had no idea how to utilize that right.

They arrived at the sawmill and passed by the kerosene-lit train depot with its "White Only" waiting room. Katharine knew Hill couldn't read but she was willing to bet that he knew what the two words on the door were.

"Hill, what are the words on that waiting room door?"

"Miz Kat'rin, you knows as well as Ah do dat it say 'White Only' on dat do'."

"Well, that proves another point I want to make, Hill...that the black woman is the most repressed in our country. She can neither vote nor use any waiting room she wants to. She is the most restricted of all."

Katharine fell quiet, leaving Hill to his own mute interpretation of what she said, and of why she said it, during the early morning hours to a poor old, illiterate Negro. Katharine wasn't sure herself why she uttered, at this time, thoughts she had pondered through the years. But then it all became clear to her. She was in her own way rationalizing the unusual trip she was about to take. Few women ever made the trip and probably no women of her background. She had always felt keenly the deprivation of voting rights and this spilled over into other areas of her life. In a way, this wild trip on the raft was an assertion on her part that she would not be restricted in her life, that she would control her own destiny, and that she did not need a man to do this for her or to restrain her from going.

The timber train engineer was in the locomotive of the train when Katharine boarded the passenger car. Big Hill set her leather bags and kerosene lantern by her seat, and she reminded him to be at the Godwinsville station on the following Thursday with her carriage.

"Ah sho will, Miz Kat'rin. Me and de hosses be dar, sho as de worl'. Now, you jes' take cahr ob yo'seff, Miz Kat'rin."

"Goodbye, Hill. I know you'll look after everything for me. I'll see you in one week."

The timber train engineer nodded toward her, and Katharine smiled and wished him a good morning. Several colored loggers sat on the empty log cars, their legs dangling over the sides. In such fashion, they would ride into the dark interior of the county where the longleaf yellow pines grew to be over a hundred feet tall.

The engineer blew the whistle and clanged the loud bell to alert anyone who traveled on the nearby road in the dark, early morning hours, that a locomotive was coming through. After crossing the Eastman dirt road, the train began its thirty-mile journey to Willcox Lake on the west side of Telfair County. This was the hub of the Dodges' vast Ocmulgee River timber enterprise and was the embarkation point of its rafts, now that the Horse Creek timber supply had been depleted and that railway was no longer in use.

The inky darkness pervaded the timber train whose tracks ran through the middle of the pine forest. The top overhanging limbs of the large trees almost met over the railway, thereby hiding the full moon and myriad shimmering stars. Only intermittently, when the train clacked through acres of cut-over land, could Katharine see the jagged tree stumps, bathed in moonlight.

As the train chugged on and on, its metal wheels clickety-clacking on the metal tracks, Katharine rested her head on one of her leather bags and fell asleep. Dreams of rafts and alligators and river water and Micah MacRae were only fleetingly interrupted by the whistle of the train as it neared dusty crossroads. At Camp Six, the former lumber camp and turpentine still in the middle of the arboreal forest, the train stopped for additional loggers who swung their legs over the logging cars and held on, as the train gathered some speed for the rest of the journey to Willcox Lake.

Katharine awoke, feeling somewhat refreshed, and felt the train slowing to a crawl. In the clearing ahead, in the rosy light of the coming dawn, she saw huge trees lying on the forest floor. Two Negro loggers were in the process of hitching twenty-four yokes of oxen to one of the enormous trees. The engineer brought the train to a halt, as its loggers jumped from the log cars and, picking up broadaxes and crosscut saws, proceeded to their early-morning tasks. Katharine had heard timber men talk about the hard work involved in logging and about the great endurance of the loggers whose day's work was from "kin to kant," from the first light of day until dark.

The train started again, with a jolt, and was soon clacking along the tracks toward its final Willcox Lake destination. Before long, the River Road came into view, and Katharine knew with an almost sinking feeling that the rafting trip would soon begin. For the first time, she felt real qualms about the lengthy trip by water to Darien, but there was no turning back now. The time had arrived.

The train crossed the River Road which ran a close parallel with the winding Ocmulgee River. This was one of the busiest areas of Telfair County, a place called Temperance which boasted a large, two-story commissary, a hotel, and over 300 houses built across the River Road from the commissary. To Katharine, just emerging from the nearly three-hour trip through nearly thirty miles of tall trees, and little else, the early-morning activity of the bustling river town was a reminder that this was the headquarters of the Dodges' vast river timber-rafting operation.

The timber train slowed down as it approached the Ocmulgee River, now only a short distance through more pine woods. In only a few minutes more, the locomotive came to a clanging, whistle-blasting stop at Willcox Lake.

Katharine stepped down from the passenger car, unused to being by herself and not having someone to meet her and to handle her bags. She gathered the leather bags and kerosene lantern and proceeded toward the river, where she assumed the raft lay waiting.

The engineer was starting the train again, but he hollered back to Katharine, asking her if she needed his help. When she assured him she didn't, he waved farewell and guided the locomotive around the wye for the return trip to pick up the large trees on the ground near Camp Six and to transport them back to the East Tennessee, Virginia, and Georgia Railroad at Normandale.

Noticing a flurry of activity near the water, Katharine walked in that direction. She knew she had to look as strange as she felt in her husband's clothes, but she received only cursory glances as she neared the riverbank. She saw the raft before she saw any of the rafthands. It was tied to a stout sapling at the river's edge. The muddy Ocmulgee River flowed slowly beyond the raft, its placid surface belying its treachery in the forms of sunken logs, whirlpools, sandbars, shoals, and alligators.

She paused and studied the raft which bumped gently against the riverbank. It was in six long sections, or cribs, with squared logs measuring thirty feet in length in each section. It appeared to be around 200 feet in length and perhaps thirty feet wide. She counted 150 logs or sticks, as the rafthands called them, in its assembly which was v-bowed or sharp-chute, rather than square-bowed. She had picked up some knowledge of raft construction from hearing Ben Winslow and the timber men talk.

Iron spikes called "dogs," inserted in the rear of each log, held the next log back.

Micah MacRae saw her before she saw him, through the trees on the riverbank, and he strode up the bank to help her with her belongings.

"Oh, no, thank you, Mr. MacRae," Katharine said. "I don't want to be any trouble. I can carry my own things." The backwoodsman, ignoring her protests, took her bags and lantern with one hand and deposited them on a squared log on the bank of the river.

The three colored rafthands, whom she had met during her ill-fated trip to the colored settlement some six months before, were busy at work on her raft. They all looked up with broad, respectful grins when they saw her and quit their occupations to speak to her.

"Which one of you is Ruthie Mae's father?" she asked.

"Ah is, Ah's Shep," one of the rafthands said, his ragged old shuck hat in his hand.

"I thought you were. I can see Ruthie Mae's resemblance to you." She also remembered how he had drawn in the dirt with his torn boot that frightening day. "Now, let's see..." Katharine turned to the other raftsmen. "I don't remember your names, but..."

"Ah's Luke."

"Oh, yes." Katharine didn't tell him that she vaguely remembered his rolling a cigarette while she talked to him that day.

"Ah's Hoke," the third, short rafthand said, and Katharine recalled with clarity his emptying the dregs of his 'shine bottle near her feet, but she put these negative thoughts from her mind, for she was thankful to have their help with her raft.

Micah MacRae stood by, listening to the reintroductions. He appeared somewhat amused by Katharine's attire and said he was surprised that anyone would recognize "Miz Fremont" in her husband's clothes.

"Us knows her dressed fer de ribber. Kane dress up in no fancy clothes on de ribber," Shep said.

"All right, men, I want you all to get back to work. We oughta be a-leavin' now, but the raft has to be right before I'll run 'er. You, Luke and Shep, find me some white oak. I see you found the black elm for the binders." He paused, then said to no one in particular, "Build a raft right and it'll make it to Darien. Build it wrong and we could all end up in the water." Shivers went up Katharine's spine at the thought.

Micah looked at Katharine.

"Miz Fremont, might as well make yourself comfortable. That log there..." He motioned to the log which held her leather baggage and kerosene lamp. "That log'll do for a seat while we wait on the raft. It'll be another few minutes before we shove off, Ma'm."

Katharine took his suggestion and sat on the log with her belongings while watching the finishing work on the raft. Shep had found some white oak and had cut off several thick branches for the pins which he gave to Micah. Micah called his three rafthands together to demonstrate the shaping of the pins from the hard wood. Using an axe, he rounded each one a little larger at the top and bottom than in the middle. He then scored each pin with well-placed hacks from the ax. He told each of the men to get to work and make the pins needed to bind the outer logs to the hard, heavy binders. The rivers could tear the raft apart, he told them, with the soft wood pins which the unknowing rafthands had already hammered into the binders. Even Shep, a skilled raftsman in other respects, had never fashioned binder pins like Micah's, but he quickly learned, along with the others. The pins were soon constructed, holes bored, and the pins driven into the black elm binders.

Micah MacRae leapt up the riverbank again, gathering Katharine's bags and lantern with one hand, but Katharine shrugged away from his outstretched hand to help her down the bank and onto the raft. She decided to set the boundaries of the trip at the outset, insofar as what help she expected from Micah MacRae was concerned. She knew he would have his hands full and she didn't want to be an added burden. Grabbing on to saplings near the river's edge, she half-stepped, half-slid down the embankment.

Stepping onto the shifting logs of the raft, which were half-submerged in the brown water, she struggled to keep her balance and felt relieved, however, when Micah MacRae supported her with a large hand under her arm. He suggested that she sit down near one of the lean-tos, fashioned out of pine boughs, that were midway the first section of the long raft near the bow oar. Katharine did as he suggested and he set her bags and lantern down beside her.

She observed the two oars, or sweeps, with Micah at the bow and Shep at the stern. The other rafthands walked the length of the raft, examining it for missing pins, as Micah had instructed them to do. The oars, made of hickory saplings, were around fifty feet long and had gator tail blades at the lower ends. They were mounted on wooden blocks at the point of the bow and the middle of the stern.

Micah jumped off the raft and unhitched it from the sapling on the bank, then bounded back onto it. Grasping the bowsweep and pulling in synchrony with Shep at the stern oar, he yelled, "Bow Injun!," guiding the raft toward the opposite side and into the mainstream of the Ocmulgee River. Katharine remembered that the "White" and "Indian" sides of the Ocmulgee River dated back to the time when Indians lived on the opposite side of the river from the newly-settled white people, often frightening them with their raids.

As the raft approached the "Indian" side of the Ocmulgee, Micah commanded, "Bo-o-ow White!" The raftsmen plunged their oars toward the left or "White" side of the Ocmulgee. The raft was drifting down the middle of the Ocmulgee River now, and the other two rafthands dropped down to the floor of the raft on its last section where Shep still manned the stern oar. Micah relinquished the bow oar and stepped over to speak to Katharine.

"I had the blacks build two lean-tos, thinkin' you oughta have one just for yourself, Miz Fremont. They built it this mornin', when they first got here. I had 'em make yours with some boards pegged together to keep out the rain and sun."

"I appreciate your thoughtfulness, Mr. MacRae," Katharine said.

Chapter Twenty-one

The morning passed rather peacefully. Katharine inspected the raft, walking across the binders to each section and examining each log in the raft's assembly. She could see her own timber brand, registered in the Dodge County Court House, on the logs. Forged by the local blacksmith, the hot brand had been hammered into each log. She had heard Micah refer to this as "water-logging." Each huge log was straight and free from wind-shakes and knotholes, and she suspected that the other sides of the logs, half-submerged in the water, were the same. She had near-perfect timber which should bring top prices in Darien, that is, if they had an honest timber inspector.

The raft floated on for several hours, and as the noon hour neared, Katharine began to feel uncomfortable. Though she was beginning to feel the need of a water closet, she reasoned that the raft would be pulling over for the noon meal shortly. Then, she would escape into the sheltering woods for a few moments of privacy.

However, noontime came and Luke approached the clay hearth near the lean-tos to start a fire. He lit a lightwood knot and placed it on two logs which soon started a fire fit for cooking. He then looked in the lean-to, covered with pine boughs, and brought out an old iron spider, corn meal and fatback. As he proceeded to fry the meat, Katharine realized that the raft would not be pulling over to the bank, after all. Rather, they would cook and eat as the raft drifted on down the Ocmulgee River.

Surely, the men had to visit the water closet, too, she thought, but no one seemed to feel the urgency that she did. She was embarrassed to ask Micah to stop the raft, yet what alternative did she have? The lean-to provided no privacy for such, nor any means to use it in such a way. She knew that the men had to be suffering as much as she, but no one made any complaints and the raft drifted on. Finally, Katharine could stand it no longer. She felt she would surely faint, or worse, if she didn't have some relief soon. She approached Micah MacRae.

"Mr. MacRae, aren't we going to stop and have our midday meal on the riverbank?"

The backwoodsman looked steadily at her. Something...was it amusement?...flickered in his eyes.

"No, Ma'm, we can make better time if we drift on durin' the day."

"Do you mean we'll continue on until nightfall?" Katharine was almost hurting with the urgency of the situation and again she saw his eyes momentarily flicker...with what?

She became bold in her distress. "Don't the men have to go...er...to the woods for privacy? We've been gone since early morning and I would think the men would need..."

Before she could continue with her indelicate concern for the men on the raft, Micah MacRae said swiftly, "The men have been a-goin' all mornin', Ma'm, off the side of the raft, but if it's you that needs us to pull over, why, we'll tie up and wait for you."

Katharine's face flamed red. She hadn't seen any of the men "goin'" off the sides of the raft, but then they often had their backs to her and it would be easy for a man to do such. She was embarrassed and again she was silently reminded that a woman could feel most unwelcome on a raft, even her own. However, she had no alternative but to insist that they pull over. Before she could do so, however, Micah spared her having to make her needs known to the others by yelling to the rafthands that they were going to stop and eat on the riverbank, after all. The rafthands looked surprised but didn't question their bossman. His word was what they lived by on the raft.

To Katharine's utter relief, Micah and Shep pulled the bowsweep toward the bank in an attempt to check the raft, as Hoke paddled the bateau to the riverbank. Hopping from the bateau, he caught the thick rope which Micah tossed to him. Pulling the raft with all of his might, the diminutive Hoke circled a tree near the bank with the rope, finally tying the raft for their midday meal.

Katharine was surprised at her agility in stepping on the walk board to the side of the raft, then jumping unaided to the riverbank. Mindless of their respectful avoidance of looking at her, she headed for the privacy of thick trees and undergrowth, heeding only negligibly Micah's called-out warning to avoid poisonous plants and snakes.

The briars and nettles and thorns which pierced her clothing were only minor annoyances, so great was her need. The ground with its cover of leaves and moss and pine cones was as good as any chamber pot, and Katharine pulled down her husband's pants and relieved herself on the ground. Not exactly a lady's boudoir, she thought ruefully, but she had brought this trip on herself and she was determined to overlook its inconveniences and humiliations.

She remembered the amusement at her predicament in Micah's eyes, and she couldn't help but laugh at herself, also. He had just bided time, waiting for her to ask him to pull over the raft and tacitly letting her realize that she was delaying the raft's arrival in Darien with her trips to the dirt chamber pot! Oh, well, he had warned her, hadn't he?

Katharine walked with as much dignity as she could muster, considering the circumstances, back to the raft. The cornbread, cooked in the grease from the fried fatback, was ready. This, along with the fatback and the spring water which everyone else had brought, was their noonday meal. Katharine ate on the raft, away from the others, accepting a tin cup of water from Micah MacRae who still looked at her with something akin to amusement but, also, perhaps a touch of sympathy in his dark brown eyes.

"Mr. MacRae," she said, "I left in such a hurry this morning, I foolishly forgot to bring food and water with me. However, I did bring some money and will gladly buy food along the river, if any is available."

"Yes, well, don't worry about it, Miz Fremont. I brought enough for two and I brought plenty of spring water."

Katharine appreciated his kindness but she felt like a helpless woman, a burden to him, having to stop the raft for her and now sharing his food with her. She wanted to be of help to him, but how? She would look for ways.

She had heard that fresh fish were sold along the river. It would be a good change from the fatback which she knew was a staple in their meals. She would buy some fish along the way.

With dinner over, Luke washed the iron spider in the river and wiped it clean, but was surprised and sufficiently contrite when Shep informed him that cleaning the spider in the river would bring bad luck. He said he thought, for sure, that Luke knew that. The repentant Luke promised never to clean the pot in the river again, as he returned the meal and salt and fatback to the croker sack in the lean-to and joined the other Negro rafthands on the end section of the raft. Katharine supposed this was some river superstition which the seasoned rafthands sprang on the unsuspecting newcomers, and she was amused by the drollery of grown men being bound by the river's rituals.

The quiet drifting of the long raft rendered a certain tranquillity, broken only now and then by Micah's commands of "Pull to the White" or "Bow Injun." Several times, the raft became grounded on sandbars, but the raftsmen pushed away with their pike-poles, then oared back into deeper water.

A great blue heron with at least a six-foot wing span flew before them for several miles, occasionally dipping toward one side of the river, then flying to the other side, before resuming its flight over the middle of the Ocmulgee River. Katharine noted how strange it appeared in flight, for it soared with its long legs straight out behind and its head curled between its shoulders. Its odd beauty was its color, a downy blue-gray.

Great egrets, standing on thin, black, jointed legs, in silhouette against the tree-and-vine-covered riverbank, bore rich snowy plumage which flattened to their tail feathers. Usually motionless in the shallow edge water, at times one would quickly dart its head toward the water to grasp a minnow or a bug in its long, yellow, pointed bill.

Though hardwoods dominated the landscape on both sides of the river, including varieties of moss-laden oak trees, tupelo, sweet gum, sycamore, yellow poplar, ash, willow, and ironwood, the tall, longleaf yellow pines stood majestically atop the bluffs. Wild magnolias, now laden with cones and red seeds, were bereft of their velvety white blossoms of late spring. Ty-ty bushes which also bloomed white in the summer, along with black-fruited gallberry and scrubby palmettos, vied for space on the riverbank.

Bald cypress, its wide knobbed knees growing out of the water at the river's edge, gave the effect of large, twisted roots which guarded the dim, tangled recesses of the swamp beyond. Willow trees leaned gracefully over the river's edge, their leaves touching the moving water and casting intricate shadows in the afternoon sun.

The raft passed the old town of Jacksonville which had built the first courthouse in Telfair County, before the seat of county government was moved to the railroad town of McRae in 1871. The railroads had changed everything, establishing the towns of Eastman, Chauncey, Helena, and McRae, places which were formerly known as the backwoods. Now, these towns represented the dawning of civilization for the piney woods.

Katharine could see cattle roaming freely through the areas of more sparse vegetation. Often, they passed by cows standing with their forefeet in the flowing current, their heads lowered to draft water.

The raft floated on past the river hamlet of Clayville, then negotiated a bend in the circuitous river. Around the bend on the right, or "Indian" side of the river, Katharine noticed more cows, five in all, taking great draughts of the moving water. A movement on the bank caught her attention, and to her horror, a large alligator slid rapidly into the water and was under the nearest cow before the struggling animal could flee, catching hold of its smooth, bovine nose and pulling the large beast under the water. Katharine stifled a scream as the rapid flailing of hooves, thrusting upward in the air, became slower, then ceased, altogether. The animal was drowned.

"Just nature, Ma'm," Micah said, looking at her, "but sometimes it ain't a pretty sight to see."

Katharine felt nauseated. She hadn't seen many alligators, but she knew the rivers in Georgia were full of them. She had seen one of the rafthands sitting on the edge of the raft with his feet trailing in the water. Surely, he would realize now what a chance he was taking!

The rafthands were shaking their heads over the alligator episode, recapitulating the cow's ordeal. Katharine could hear parts of their conversation. She heard one say that the alligator was twelve feet long. She had no idea herself how long it was, but it had easily pulled a large cow under the water and held it there until it died within a matter of only a few seconds.

The whole event which occurred so quickly seemed ominous in her mind, especially happening at the beginning of their long journey. Also, she had not even seen the alligator, until it moved. They could be just about anywhere, camouflaged by their dark coloration which blended with the dark hues of the swamp on both sides of the river.

Micah motioned to Shep, yelling, "Bo-o-ow White! We'll pull in for the night at Horse Creek!"

So soon after the alligator incident, Katharine was fearful of leaving the relative safety of the raft. Also, she promised herself she would be more watchful during her excursions into the nearby woods. The languid, peaceful outset of the rafting trip was but a dull memory now, replaced with the vivid picture of the large reptile which so quickly pulled an animal as large as itself into the water and drowned it. Micah was right. A rafting trip was not for the fainthearted.

The raft was heading toward the "White" side of the river, just beyond the estuary of Horse Creek. Katharine realized that this was where Micah had drifted his own logs from Bear Creek, then held them in a boom at the mouth of Horse Creek. There, he had built his rafts.

The Ocmulgee River was a brown, watery cradle for Telfair County, being its western and southern borders. The "Indian" side of the river, across from the Telfair or "White" side of the river, included the counties of Wilcox, Irwin, and Coffee. Their night encampment would be at the bottom of the Telfair County line, with Coffee County directly across the river from them.

Micah and Shep, still pulling the oars to the north or "White" side of the river, let the raft drift into the still waters of an eddy away from the main channel. As the raft floated parallel to the riverbank, Hoke jumped into the shallow water, rope in hand. Running to a large tree, he looped the rope around it twice, then double-looped the end around the part stretching between the tree and the raft. Holding to the end, he leaned backward with his full weight, tightening the loops and checking the movement of the large raft.

From their lean-to, two of the Negroes picked up guns and headed off into the river swamp. Hoke and Micah began building a fire on the riverbank, as a deterrent to night bugs and animals. Holding a small lightwood knot to the flickering fire, Hoke carried the lighted torch to the clay hearth on the raft, where Luke's cooking would soon begin.

Katharine watched the proceedings from her place on an uprooted tree, shorn of its limbs, which lay perpendicular to the riverbank. Looking into the now roaring fire, as night approached, she pondered her strange situation. She was in the river swamp, away from even the remotest civilization with four men, three of whom were Negroes with guns. The only white man in the group was the suspected leader of the fanatical squatters, some of whom had killed John C. Forsyth and possibly even her own husband. He also had a gun which he kept near him at all times.

A chill went up her spine. She felt like a child, wanting to be held, wanting to know that everything was going to be all right. She heard a rustling noise behind her, and the indelible picture of the large alligator with its mouth open loomed before her. She screamed as she fell off the log, tearing her clothes on the tree's rough bark.

Like a pouncing cat, Micah MacRae was before her, lifting her, asking if she were all right. Katharine was embarrassed and confused. She looked back over the log, half expecting to see a large alligator. Instead, the two Negroes, each carrying several dead squirrels, were coming through the woods. She vaguely remembered hearing their shots fired, which had killed the squirrels.

"Oh, I'm sorry, Mr. MacRae. I don't know what came over me. I heard something and all I could think about was the large alligator we saw."

"Well, we'll see plenty of 'em before we get to Darien, Ma'm, but they won't likely come around a fire. You're safe, Ma'm. We got guns to take care of any that does come around."

Katharine backed away from his helping hands which had lifted her up, and from his very presence which had allayed her fears. She longed to throw herself into his arms because she was afraid and the night was rapidly descending, but instead, trembling, she walked back to her log seat and tried to sort out her conflicting feelings.

During this trip, at least, she told herself, she had to forget that Micah MacRae was on the other side in the land war. Hadn't the manager of the timber company suggested to her that Micah MacRae was the man to raft her timber? He had certainly been kind to her, she thought, and she felt safe with him. However, she knew he was capable of great anger, for she had experienced it first-hand that day at the sugar field, when he held her against his hard chest, apparently as proof of what he could do to her, if he so much as had the slightest inclination.

Katharine swallowed hard. She had to be strong. She also wanted to be helpful but didn't know how to be. She decided she would watch Luke and try to learn how to cook on the clay hearth on the raft.

The Negroes were still in the process of skinning the squirrels and Katharine looked away, afraid of being sick at the messy, bloody procedure. She had never eaten squirrel. The thought of eating the rodent which so resembled a rat made her feel queasy. She gradually became aware that Micah MacRae was beside her, talking to her.

"You ever eat squirrel, Miz Fremont?"

"No," she said, trying to sound nonchalant.

"You think you can eat it?" He had one boot-encased foot on the log by her, his folded arms resting across his raised knee. Katharine was determined not to let the thought of a squirrel supper daunt her. She would not let him or the colored raftsmen know just how repugnant was even the idea of putting the rat-like meat in her mouth. She put on a brave front.

"Oh, I'll be fine. Don't worry about me, Mr. MacRae."

"If it's cooked right, it's good," the raftsman said, "but if it ain't, we won't want it, for sure. The blacks got fishin' lines on the end of the raft. We oughta have enough fish for a fish supper tomorrow night." Katharine was surprised. She didn't realize that fishing lines were trailing behind the raft.

"You eat bacon, Ma'm?" Katharine didn't know what to think of his referring to her as "Ma'm" and "Mrs. Fremont," but then, what should she expect him to call her, especially in the presence of the rafthands?

"Er...yes, of course," she said, "I like bacon."

"Well, I'll have the cook fry you some. I don't think you're a-gonna want any squirrel, seein' as how you turned a mite green awhile ago, just lookin' at 'em." Again, Katharine thought she saw a brief flash of amusement in his eyes, and when he smiled broadly, she knew she did.

"Really, I don't expect nor want any special consideration, Mr. MacRae."

"You gotta eat, Ma'm, or you'll be a-gettin' sick. The cook'll fry some bacon."

The squirrel meat was washed in the river, then put in the iron pot of boiling water, which Luke was tending on the raft hearth. Rice was added to the pot, and while this was cooking, he mixed meal and water for the cornbread. He fried some strips of bacon for Katharine, as Micah told him to do, then fried hoecakes of cornbread in the bacon grease.

Though the other Negroes ate on the raft, Luke stayed near Micah and Katharine, serving Katharine's plate and bringing it to her. He also replenished the fire, for the evening air was turning cooler.

Katharine was surprised that the food was as good as it was. She wouldn't touch the squirrel and, mercifully, Luke refrained from spooning any onto her plate. However, the rice was tasty and filling, as was the cornbread and bacon.

Nighttime had arrived and with it all of the nocturnal swamp sounds...the croaking of frogs, the hooting of owls, the howls and cries of strange animals, and the earth-trembling roars of alligators. Katharine thought it was as if the river swamp came alive at night, just as they were making preparations for sleeping.

The colored raftsmen made their own fire a hundred yards down the riverbank, away from them, though Shep settled down to talk to Micah, and Katharine found herself listening with fascination to their somewhat one-sided conversation.

"Mistuh Micah, mos' lakly you heard 'bout de lynchin' las' week?"

"Heard somethin' about it, Shep. It was some colored fella near your settlement, I heard."

"Yassuh, it wuz Bud, Bud McLeod. You seed 'im, Miz Kat'rin, dat time you come to de settle'mint."

Katharine gasped, unbelievingly, "You mean Bud was hanged?"

"Yas'm. Not only dat, dey shot at 'im fer twenty minutes whilst he wuz hangin' on de tree. Put thousands ob bullets in 'is body. 'Fore dat, whilst he wuz still 'live, dey cut off 'is finguhs and toes, and pulled out 'is teef wid pliahs."

"What?" Katharine's lip was quivering. She was so aghast at the description of torture that she was ready to burst into tears or faint.

Micah MacRae spoke up quickly. "Let's leave off talkin' about the lynchin'. Miz Fremont's about to be sick."

"No," Katharine said, "I want to hear what happened. What did Bud do that brought about the lynching?"

"Ah doan think he done nuthin', Miz Kat'rin. No'm, Ah doan think he wuz guilty, but dey claim he try to rape a white woman. Bud say dey had de wrong man, but de mens got 'im outa de jail and hang 'im. Dey say he one uppity nigger."

"You mean, he didn't even have a trial to determine his guilt or innocence?" Katharine asked, her voice shaking.

"No'm, de possee ob 'bout one thousand mens come to de jail and took de law in dar own hands. Dey got ol' Bud and carry 'im near de white settle'mint whar de lady say she wuz attacked, and dar dey kilt 'im." Shep's face in the firelight reflected the terror of his friend's agony.

Katharine herself was horrified at the brutality of the punishments of the alleged perpetrators, usually black, who were rarely allowed to prove their innocence in a court of law. She remembered reading only the past week about another lynching in the nearby small town of Mt. Vernon where 5,000 people congregated to witness it. She knew that women and children attended these events, along with their menfolk. However, she knew that she could never witness such herself. Just hearing about it made her sick and she regretted having listened to Shep's description. She looked over at Micah who was shaking his head at the colored raftsman. Shep quickly construed the hint and launched into a different colloquy.

"Ah sho is glad, Mr. Micah, dat we ain' raftin' in de winter, tho' dat's mos' use'ly de time to take a raf' to Dari'n."

"Yes, well, I had to take this one durin' the off season."

"Yassuh. It sho' bettah dan w'en it be so cold. Last Jan'airy, Ah wuz he'pin' some niggers wid dey raf' an' it wuz cold! It be so cold, aer clothes dey froze on aer back. De weathuh now, it nice, jes' cool a li'l at night." The talkative raftsman cut off a plug of tobacco and settled back against a tree, not far from the crackling fire. Micah had made himself comfortable, also, leaning back against the same overturned log that Katharine was using as a chair back. The three of them sat on the ground, looking at each other through the flickering light of the fire.

"Mistuh Micah, you heah 'bout de raf' dat broke up and de rafthand kane swim?"

"Just tell your story, Shep," Micah said, with an encouraging grin.

"Well, dis happen not too long 'go. De rafhand, he nebber go to church, and he nebber pray. Well, w'en he raf' break up, he grab ahole ob a tree limb and he kane swim, so he start to prayin'. He kane hold on no longer to the tree limb, so he drap into the watuh, only to fine de watuh ain' but knee-deep. He say, 'What a fool Ah is, prayin' in shalluh water.'" The Negro's full lips spread over his few remaining teeth in a big grin, followed by a contagious chuckle.

Micah smiled, as did Katharine, and she had the feeling that Micah had heard the story many times before, but was allowing the Negro to talk, perhaps to ward off feelings of loneliness and isolation which they were all experiencing on the dark, swampy bank of the Ocmulgee River. Shep was beginning another tale, encouraged by his audience's amused attention.

"Now, Mistuh Micah, Ah hear tell dis one jes' t'othuh day. Dis raf'hand he kill a turkey, and he take it to a boardin' house in Dari'n, and he mek a bargain wid de boardin' house lady. She say she cook de turkey and let 'im eat whut he wants ob it, den she pay 'im a dollah fer de res' ob de turkey. Well, suh, he ate all dat turkey 'cep' one wing and de feets, so he put de lady's dollah in he pocket, and he go 'way still hongry." This elicited a laugh from Katharine, and she was surprised at her own merriment. Somehow, the frightening swamp sounds did not seem as threatening while the Negro was talking. She was certain that Micah had heard all of the yarns being told, though he chuckled, also, and she really felt that he was trying to make her feel more at ease. Other stories issued forth from the loquacious Negro as the full moon cast its light on them.

Loud snores from the Negro rafters' camp downriver reminded them that they, also, were sleepy and tired. Rising from their now-cramped positions around the fire, they were ready to make their own makeshift beds and to go to sleep. As Shep moved toward the colored camp, he remarked with a grin, "Dem niggers is still sawin' lawgs in dey sleep."

"Sounds like it, all right," Micah said. "It's time we all got some sleep. Mornin's gonna come soon. We push off at first light."

"Yassuh! Ah knows it," Shep said, as he disappeared through the trees along the riverbank.

Micah said, "Miz Fremont, will you be a-sleepin' on the raft or here on the bank?"

Katharine didn't know what to say. What if the raft came loose from its mooring?

"Where will you be sleeping?" she asked.

"Oh, I usually sleep on the riverbank. I keep my gun handy."

"Well, I'll get my things, and I'll sleep nearby," she said, quickly.

"Suit yourself," Micah said, and seemingly from nowhere he found an old quilt and pillow which he spread on the ground. Before Katharine could move to retrieve her leather bag, he boarded the raft and brought the bag to her.

"Oh, please, I don't expect you to wait on me. Thank you," she said as he handed her the bag.

Katharine spread the doubled blanket on the ground, then put sheets on the blanket and the pillow at the head. Crawling between the sheets, she lay on the hard ground, thinking that she certainly could not rest on such a bed. However, within only a few minutes, as she gazed into the cracking, popping fire, her eyelids drooped and finally closed in deep sleep.

**

Midst the sounds of morning on the Ocmulgee riverbank was the unmistakable patter of raindrops. Struggling to open her eyes, Katharine felt the wetness on her cheeks. She also felt someone nudging her gently at her shoulder.

"Miz Fremont, it's rainin'. We're about to push off. You better stay in the lean-to on the raft."

Katharine sat up, trying to awaken and to get her thoughts together.

"Did you sleep all right? Looks like you did." Micah smiled, and Katharine could only think how nice it was when he smiled.

"Actually, I think I slept all night, and I'm amazed because I really didn't think I'd sleep at all." The rain was pelting them a little harder now, and Micah helped her gather her things and put them back into the large leather bag.

The fire had been out a long time. Though the rain was sprinkling the few remaining embers, Micah kicked dirt on them as a safety measure.

As they boarded the raft in the early dawn, an eerily distinct call sounded from downriver, and Katharine jumped as Micah cupped his hands about his mouth and yelled back.

"Nothin' to scare you, Ma'm. It's just somebody a-hollerin' to see if anybody else is on the river. We call it the river holler."

"Well, what's it for?" Katharine asked, somewhat shaken.

"It might be for nothin', just somebody feelin' good, or it might be somebody needs help. We'll see when we pull on out to the river and drift 'round the bend."

It had almost stopped raining, but Katharine sat in the lean-to as Micah and Shep eased the raft out of the eddy and parallel to the main riverbank.

"Bo-o-o-ow Injun!" Micah commanded at the bow oar, while Shep followed his exact sweep with the stern oar. Walking with the oars from one side of the raft to the other, the two raftsmen quickly steered the large, cumbersome raft into the main channel where the current, quickened a little by the light rain, carried it on down the river. The rain, however, had now ceased.

Micah's prediction about a raft in trouble proved true, for soon they came upon a raft grounded on a sandbar. Push as they might with their pike-poles, the two stranded Negro raftsmen could not dislodge the huge logs from the treacherous shoals. The pilot oarsman hollered to Micah, who told them they would either have to wait on a freshet to raise the logs off of the sandbar, or they could disassemble the raft and start over. If they were lucky, a passing steamboat might pull their raft to deeper water.

Noting that they were without fire, Micah lit a lightwood knot and tossed it to them. The pilot waved his thanks to him, as he and the other rafthand watched the larger raft drift on by. Then, they set to the immediate task of preparing something to eat, using the burning lightwood knot to start a cooking fire. This would precede the tedious and dangerous work of disassembling their raft, so that they could free it from the perilous shallows, before reassembling it in deeper water.

Luke had a fire going on the clay hearth and coffee perked in the tin coffeepot. Before long, fatback was sizzling in the iron spider, followed by battercakes. Though Katharine longed for cream for her coffee, the hot black liquid was, nonetheless, welcome and reviving in the cool morning air.

As the ponderous raft made its tortuous journey down the twisting, turning river during the early morning hours, raftsmen hollered back and forth to one another, more out of sheer exuberance at being alive for one more day than for an other apparent reason. The sound was like none other that Katharine had ever heard. It brought to her mind the infamous Rebel yell which Northern soldiers had tried with some success to imitate, though it had a different lonesome poignancy about it. Within her soul, she knew that the lonely hollers, up and down the river, were unique to the extent that she would remember them for the rest of her life, and just the memory of them would never fail to raise gooseflesh on her arms.

Luke was cleaning up after his breakfast cooking, washing the iron spider and returning the food staples to the croker sack in the lean-to.

"Dey's mo' raf's dan Ah wuz 'spectin' fer dis time ob year," he said.

"I don't know for sure," Micah said, "but sounds like it's the same ones doin' all the hollerin', leastways they're on the same raft. We oughta see it in a minute or two."

Katharine had heard of the Ocmulgee River's winding convolutions, often turning back so sharply that rafters could see and talk to one another across the narrow isthmuses of swamp which separated them. They could see the other raft now, a small one, through the tangled undergrowth. Two rafthands, one colored and one white, walked its length, taking turns venting the haunting river holler.

Spying the large raft behind them, across the projecting swamp, the vocal colored raftsman engaged in conversation.

"Whar you comin' from?"

"Left Willcox Lake yesterday."

"We's from Dodge County. We been on de ribber three days now. We done rafted fer Mistuh Dodge many times, but we ain' nebber carry aer own raf' to Dar'in. So far, ain' had no trouble."

Though the rafthand was still talking, the winding river took his raft and his words away. Katharine noted the difficulty which her own raft presented when the river turned back almost upon itself. However, with adeptness, Micah and Shep worked these hairpin curves, pulling their oars together as Micah yelled the commands of "Pull t'the Injun!" or, simply, "Bo-o-o-ow White!" The raft shuddered around the sharp bends, at times touching sandbars, where the rafthands used long pike poles to push back into the main channel.

The morning passed swiftly and Katharine whiled away the peaceful hours reading and walking the long sections of her raft. She heard the Negro rafthands commenting on the fish which they had caught on their hooks, and she anticipated a fish supper that evening.

Luke was readying the cooking apparatus for dinner. She expected more of the same fatback and cornbread. She was correct in her thinking, though he did cook potatoes, too, which was some variation. They ate on the raft, then pulled over to the bank for a short while, allowing Katharine to attend to personal duties in the seclusion of the shadowy swamp. These private forays into the inner recesses of the swamp were always terrifying for her, as she could never erase from her mind the picture of the large cow being brought down so easily by the monstrous alligator. It was during these times that she thought about her porcelain tub and about how nice a leisurely bath would be. She had been in the same clothes for two long days and nights.

Once again on the unmoored raft, they drifted farther down the Ocmulgee River. Micah mentioned that they were passing McRae's Landing and were nearing Lumber City, the last Telfair County town before the Ocmulgee joined with the Oconee River, around ten miles downstream, to form the mighty Altamaha River. Katharine knew that the Altamaha was much larger than its main tributaries, the Ocmulgee and the Oconee rivers, and she almost dreaded leaving the more familiar Ocmulgee River. However, she thought that the greater width of the Altamaha should allow her large raft easier passage, unless of course it had as many sandbars as the Ocmulgee River.

As the raft drifted under the railroad trestle at Lumber City, Katharine noticed the ferryboat which was loading passengers on the Coffee County, or "Indian" side, of the Ocmulgee River, obviously intending to cross to the Lumber City side. It appeared that several members of a family were aboard the ferry and were attempting to lure their recalcitrant horse onto the floating platform with them. Everyone on the raft heard the shrill whinnies of the frightened animal and its front hooves kicking away from the ferryboat for a long time, as the raft continued toward the forks of the three rivers.

Floating a few miles downriver from Lumber City, the raft passed by several steamboats, laden with guano from South America and phosphates from the new mines in Florida, which were anchored at wood pilings near the docks on both sides of the river. Workers were busy unloading the fertilizer. Katharine had heard Ben Winslow and others talking about the increased use of fertilizer which was relatively new in the piney woods. Ben had said that many of the wiregrass farmers would borrow money to buy the fertilizer, then when their crops failed during years of drought, they would have to mortgage their farms or sell their trees to pay for it. It seemed that fertilizer was a mixed blessing in the piney woods!

"Ocmulgee...," "Oconee...," "Altamaha...," The Indian names were strange but sonorous, almost rolling off the tongue. She wondered about their meanings. The ancient names were so fitting that the alien white man had written them on his maps and claimed them as his own.

Sitting in front of her lean-to, hugging her drawn-up knees, Katharine looked at the rippling brown water just beyond the edges of the raft, and she wondered how long she had been staring at the water without actually seeing it. It was unlike her to sit and daydream in the presence of other people. Perhaps the raft trip was getting to her. Her eyes momentarily shifted from the water near the raft's edge to the "Indian" side of the river. Her heart leapt to her throat at the sight of three human skulls, with crossbones under each skull, hanging from a tree limb which projected over the river. Her hand flew to her mouth to stifle a scream.

Micah looked from her horrified face back to the skulls which he had already noticed, before anyone else. The superstitious Negro rafthands now saw them, and their fear in regard to the bleached skulls and crossbones only added to Katharine's unease. Shep had abandoned the stern oar and was running across the raft sections toward Micah.

"Ah ain' nebbuh seen no man's bones on de ribber, Mistuh Micah," he said, stopping on the binders of the first two cribs of logs. "Dey's jes' been put mout on dat tree, 'cause dey wuzzen dere last week. Ah wuz on Mistuh Burch's raf' las' week, and dere wuzzen no bones dar den."

"You're right, Shep. I don't recall ever seein' any skulls on the river. I've seen cow and other animal skulls, left by the gators, more'n apt, but I ain't never seen no man's skull strung up like that."

The whites of Shep's eyes grew larger and rounder as his fear increased.

"It de Klan done dat, sho as de wuhl," he said, his bottom lip quivering.

Micah sought to put the distraught Negro at ease.

"I don't think so, Shep," he drawled. "I just think whoever hung those skulls was tryin' to warn the rest of us that we're about to reach the Altamaha River and it's a bigger and more per'lous river than our Ocmulgee is. It's sorta tellin' the one who ain't never been on the Altamaha to be careful, 'cause it's a mighty river."

Shep was calmer now, and as if the other Negroes took their cues from their brother oarsman, all quieted down about the hollow-eyed skulls.

"Better get back to your oar, man," Micah told Shep, who jumped over the raft sections and scurried back to his stern oar position, satisfied with his boss's answer.

Katharine didn't know what to think of Micah's explanation about the skulls. It certainly didn't address whose they were nor how they had met their demise. Obviously, Micah was only trying to calm the Negro rafthands, and it worked, for none seemed concerned about how anyone could have come into the possession of three human skulls. The thought of them left a chill in her bones.

Shadows along the river were lengthening as the sun rode into the western sky, almost hidden by the tall trees and vine-tangled swamp. Katharine knew they must be nearing the juncture of the Ocmulgee and Oconee Rivers which formed the larger Altamaha.

"Bo-o-ow White!" Micah yelled back to Shep at the stern oar.

"We gone pull in, Mistuh Micah?"

"We're close by a good place to stop for the night. In the mornin', we'll be on the Altamaha. We'll spend the night here at The Forks."

The two oarsmen guided the unwieldy raft into a slough near the landing site, thereby removing it from the main river channel, as they were wont to do each evening. Hoke rowed to the bank in the bateau, then secured the raft with the rope to a black gum at the river's edge.

Luke was checking the fishing lines, removing the fish hooks and throwing the flapping fish onto the raft. After nearly losing some of the smaller ones through the cracks which separated the squared logs of the raft, the Negro hollered for the iron pot to put them in, and Hoke came running the length of the long raft, swinging the heavy pot by its metal handle. After filling the pot to its brim with fish, the Negroes all worked together to clean them.

Katharine couldn't resist walking the sections of her long raft to see the fish which had been caught. She was hungry for something other than the usual fare of fatback.

She could hear the Negroes talking among themselves as they cleaned the fish and she heard them mention catfish, bream, and shad. She had eaten catfish and liked it, but had not eaten the other fish. She noticed that they scaled the fish, except for the catfish which had no scales. These they skinned. She had never really thought about such, as she had never watched fish being cleaned, until now.

She walked back to the bow of the raft where Micah had made a fire on the clay hearth. She sat nearby and watched the proceedings, as Luke arrived with the cleaned fish. She could sense that everyone was hungry, as she was, for something different from the usual monotonous fare.

Micah and the other Negroes began building a fire on the riverbank, as Luke found another iron pot in the lean-to, into which he poured grease for the fish frying. Placing this on the clay hearth fire, he busied himself with mealing the fish while waiting for the grease to boil.

Even the fish would taste like fatback, Katharine thought, as it would be fried in its grease. No escaping it. Why, oh why, had she forgotten to bring food with her? She could only attribute her omission to the surprise nature of the trip and the fact that she was unused to preparing for such an undertaking. Again, she was reminded of how protected and, yes, spoiled she had been all of her life - always expecting someone else to look after her. What would have happened if Micah hadn't brought enough food for her? Even if it were fatback!

The time had long passed for her to be of some use on the trip. But how? She watched as Luke dusted the fish with cornmeal before dropping them in the bubbling grease. She took a deep breath, then raised herself from her comfortable vantage point near her lean-to. She would help with the cooking! Walking toward the fiery clay hearth, she startled the Negro cook with her offer to help.

"Oh, no, Ma'm, Miz Fremont! Ah's done got ever'thin' a'cookin'. Ah doan need no he'p. Ah's gwine mek up some co'n dodjuhs. Dey be good wid dese fish."

"Tell me how you do it, Luke. I want to learn."

Luke looked surprised and somewhat embarrassed. His facial expression conveyed that she was a rich white lady and she shouldn't worry herself with helping with the cooking.

"Mistuh Micah, he get ontuh me ef he see you worryin' wid de cookin'. You is a rich Nawthen lady and you doan s'posed to fret yo'seff wid sech. Ah's de cook, and Ah see 'bout dese fish."

Katharine decided it was useless to insist, so she turned abruptly to go back to the lean-to and fell against the hard, unyielding body of Micah MacRae who was standing directly behind her.

"Oh, I'm sorry, Mr. MacRae. I didn't realize you were behind me." Katharine almost fell again as she tried to step backward, but Micah's hand steadied her as she regained her balance.

"I was just telling Luke," Katharine said, "that I'd like to help with the cooking. I would like to feel that I am helpful in some way." To her dismay, Katharine saw that Micah's brown eyes were dancing with laughter, though his straight face belied them. He actually thought she was incapable of cooking. How she would love to show him how wrong he was! If the puzzled Negroes weren't looking on, how she would love to give him a piece of her mind. She was about to retreat to the lean-to when Micah unexpectedly spoke up on her behalf.

"Let her help, Luke. Better yet...I'll take over for you, Luke, and you can help the others get the fire on the bank goin'. We need more lighterd."

"Yassuh, Ah sho he'p wid dat, Mistuh Micah." Luke was pleased with a reprieve from cooking for at least the one meal. He hurried across the raft and jumped onto the bank and joined the other Negroes in their search for fat lighterd.

Katharine didn't quite know what to think of her new cooking instructor, other than it was obvious that he was willing to let her learn something about cooking, whereas the former one adamantly opposed it. She couldn't see Micah's eyes, as he was busy turning the fish, but his manner still suggested that he was enjoying something at her expense. The muscles around his mouth twitched, as if it were an effort for him to keep a poker face.

Oh, well, she thought, let him be that way. She was sincere in wanting to be helpful, and if he found it amusing, well, he would just have to be amused. She meekly asked how to make the corn dodgers and she noticed how the corners of his mouth wanted to smile, but he willed them not to. He said in a dead serious voice that she needed to mix meal and salt and water. Salt would make it taste better but the salt from the fatback grease would lend it some saltiness. He continued to lower his eyes, as he took up the browned fish and put newly-mealed ones into the hot grease.

Katharine found the bag of meal and poured some into a tin pot. To this, she added some of the spring water which Micah had brought. She didn't know what consistency to make the things. Actually, she had never heard of such. She assumed they were something like cornbread, but she wasn't certain.

She brought the mixture over to Micah and asked him if it were the right consistency for corn dodgers. He told her to add a little meal, as the dodgers should be thicker to be dropped into the hot grease.

As she added the meal and practiced molding the dodgers, she looked up to find Micah looking intently at her, only to look away quickly from her gaze.

"Is this the right size?" Katharine held up the rounded cornmeal paste which she had attempted to shape.

"Too large," he said, solemnly. "Middle won't get done."

"Well, how large should they be?"

"Oh, maybe two inches long and one inch wide, or somethin' close to that," Micah said, and he turned away, so she could not see the smile which he could no longer suppress.

Katharine worked with the wet cornmeal, forming oval balls of the smooth damp paste of the proportions which Micah had told her. She momentarily forgot her cooking ineptness and became absorbed in making the dodgers as exactly alike as possible. Before she realized what was happening, Micah scooped them into the hot grease, alongside the last fish which were nearly done.

"I'll be glad to turn them," Katharine said.

"You might get burnt," he said.

"Please, I want to learn how. I'd like to know I'm of some help on the raft."

"Well, now's not the time to learn. You ain't used to cookin', and you could get burnt to where you'd need a doctor, and there ain't one nowheres around. No, Ma'm, raft cookin' ain't for one learnin' how to cook. You might get hurt."

At least, he wasn't laughing at her anymore. Rather, he appeared to be tersely sober when he spoke.

He gave her a tin plate and told her to get the fish she wanted and some corn dodgers. She took two catfish and he put two of the corn dodgers on her plate.

The laughter, gentle though it was, had returned to his eyes. "Guess I have to admit, they're the dadgum prettiest dodgers I ever did see. Looks like you used a measurin' stick to get 'em all the same size."

Katharine decided to take his words as a compliment and she smiled as she watched him take up the rest of the fish and the browned corn dodgers.

She looked toward the bank where the fire was now blazing. The Negroes, except Shep, had gone on farther down the riverbank, as was their custom, to make their own fire which Katharine could see faintly through the trees. Their fire reminded her of the fictional "wil-o'-the-wisp," the blazing wisp of hay which misled unwary foot-travelers into treacherous bogs. Oh, but her imagination was running away with her!

Micah carried the hot grease to the bank where he emptied it on the ground. He set the pot aside to let it cool before washing it out, then called the Negroes to come and get their supper. Katharine could barely make out their forms in the gathering darkness, as they moved along the edge of the bank toward the raft. Luke and Hoke sat on the raft near the hearth fire and filled their tin plates with the fish and corn dodgers.

Katharine and Micah joined Shep near the leaping fire on the riverbank. The talkative Negro immediately launched into his river stories which Katharine enjoyed hearing, partly because they banished the feelings of loneliness and fear, as darkness descended upon them.

The fish were especially satisfying to her taste. She also enjoyed the corn dodgers. She couldn't imagine why in the world they were called such, unless perhaps it was because they "dodged" the fish in the hot grease. No, she was certain that wasn't the reason, but then maybe there was no reason. Southerners just wanted to call them that. All right. It was fine with her. She did have some satisfaction in having helped with the cooking, especially when she heard the complimentary murmurs from the Negroes and from Micah, as they ate the fish supper. Micah especially bragged on the corn dodgers, saying they were just about the best he had ever eaten. She didn't know whether he was teasing or whether he really meant it, but it pleased her, nonetheless.

When supper was over, all the Negroes, including Shep, left hurriedly for their camp down the river. They departed with few words and oddly with a united purpose which appeared to have more to it than just getting a good night's sleep. Micah stared after them with the hint of a frown on his face.

Then, he turned to Katharine and she was tremblingly aware that they were alone and that it would be so comforting to her to go into his arms. However, looking away, she remembered that she had vowed to herself never to let him kiss her or in any way be intimate with her again. She knew that nothing must ever develop between them, because after this raft trip, she planned to go home to New York. She would get Ben Winslow to oversee the sale of the remainder of her timber. She would not be humiliated by any man and certainly not by an uneducated backwoodsman!

She looked up at him as he threw more fat lighterd on the lowering flames. His strength, which was not only physical, reached out to her and enveloped her and when he turned his eyes to her, she gasped, for it seemed he would come toward her, and could she deny him? Dear God in heaven, she prayed silently, please give me the strength I need to refuse this man, for I am weak....

A piercing shriek from the Negroes' camp was an answer to her prayer, for Micah grabbed the glowing lantern from the tree limb and headed toward their camp. Katharine hurriedly followed after him, though he turned to her several times and told her she should have stayed where she was, that he would be back shortly. However, she told him she had no intention of staying by herself, that she was going with him, whether he liked it or not.

Another shattering outburst and angry words from the Negroes' camp elicited further advice from him.

"Miz Fremont, you don't need to see what I suspect is a-goin' on. I don't allow no alcohol on my rafts, but that don't always mean that there ain't none. Thought I smelled liquor while ago, so they musta been a-drinkin' it on the raft. From the sound of things, they all been a-passin' the crock, and now they're mad about somethin'. I'm worried about you, Ma'm. You don't need to see 'em in such a state."

"I'm fine, Mr. MacRae," Katharine said, her teeth chattering. "I'm fine, really. I just don't want to be left alone."

Realizing she was upset, Micah reached for her hand and pulled her to him. As they neared the Negroes' camp, he handed her the lantern and ordered her to wait for him.

Loud bickering erupted among the Negroes. Katharine shivered from the night air and from her fear of what might happen when Micah accosted them. The smell of whiskey assailed her senses.

"All right, what's a-goin' on here?" Micah asked, as he stepped into the circle of light from their campfire.

"He stole mah knife," Hoke said, pointing an unsteady finger at Luke.

"Ah ain' stole nuthin', honest t'Gawd," Luke said, holding on to a low-lying tree limb, as he turned to face Micah.

Shep, his voice thick with whiskey, interposed for the other two.

"We doin' all right, Mistuh Micah. We jes' playin' 'Skin' and 'Seven-up.' Luke here, he done won de knife and Ah done won mos' ob 'is pay w'en us gits to Dar'in."

"Who brought this stuff?" Micah picked up an empty jar and held it to his nose, noting others thrown randomly on the ground.

"Ah knowed not to bring none, Mistuh Micah," Shep said, though his drunken condition reflected that he was not averse to imbibing what the others had brought.

"What did I tell you about a-bringin' this stuff on board?" Micah said, with rising anger in his voice.

Shep appeared to be the only one able or willing to communicate.

"Ah done tol' dese two. Ah say, 'Mistuh Micah, he gonna be mad wid you fer bringin' dis likker,' but dey say, 'Mistuh Micah, he ain' gwine know nuthin' 'bout it.' All us aimin' to do wuz jes' have us a good time wid playin' 'Skin' and 'Seven-up.' We ain' mean nuthin' by it, Mistuh Micah."

Through the trees, Katharine could see Micah's face in the flickering light of the campfire, and it was a study in restrained fury. She had seen the same expression on his face when they were returning in the wagon from Maude Ivey's pole shanty. She was reminded again that Micah MacRae was capable of great anger, and Lord help the one on whom it was unleashed.

With great effort, however, the large raftsman checked his rage. After all, these men had to live together and work together for at least several more days and they had a large raft to deliver intact to Darien. With these realities in mind, he visibly quieted his temper and spoke in a tight but calm voice.

"Where's Hoke's knife?"

"Ah done won it, fayuh and squayuh," Luke whined, retrieving the knife with shaking hands from his pocket.

"Ain't no 'fair and square' in 'Skin' or 'Seven-up,' neither," Micah said. "Give Hoke 'is knife."

The errant Negro slowly handed the knife to Hoke who almost fell as he walked unsteadily to receive it. His thick lips managing a weak smile, he opened and closed the knife several times, as if verifying that it was still as he remembered it, before shoving it into his pants pocket.

"All right, what else did you say was won tonight?" Micah's face betrayed his pent-up anger.

"Ah say Ah won 'is pay we'n we reach Dar'in, Mistuh Micah," Shep said, adding with rising respect, "but ef you doan woan me to collect, why you's de boss man, and Ah does whut you wants, Mistuh Micah."

"Well, I don't want you to collect and I don't want you a-playin' no more of these games that'll get you in trouble. Understand?"

"Yassuh." The three chastened Negroes all answered as if with one voice.

"All right," Micah said, his jaw tightening. "I want you all to bury these empty bottles right now. No use in leavin' trash like this. Now..." Micah paused, "any more whiskey?"

The men looked at one another and at first were silent. Then, Shep spoke.

"You, Luke and Hoke, you got any mo' moonshine?"

"Get it and pour it on the ground now," Micah said, staring hard at the tipsy Negro raftsmen.

"De ghosts dey sho' be glad," Shep said in a shaking voice. "Dey laks 'shine. Only way to git away from de ghosts be to pour it on de ground, den run to a safe place." The other two Negroes both produced full crocks from their hiding place behind a tupelo tree. Walking unsteadily away from the group and farther into the woods, they took Shep's advice and poured the whiskey on the ground, then shuffled back as quickly as they could, in their intoxicated state, to the supposed safety of the campfire.

"All right, men," Micah said, still in a tight voice of suppressed anger, "we got a job to do and that's what I'm a-payin' you to do. When we get to Darien, you're on your own, and you can do what you want to do but while you're a-workin' for me, you do as I say. Does everybody understand?"

"Yassuh." Again, the three spoke as one.

"No more games and no more whiskey, you hear?"

"Yassuh." As the men were busy burying the bottles of mischief, Micah turned back to Katharine who waited in the woods just beyond the light of the campfire and out of sight of the drunken Negroes.

Micah took the lantern which she had gripped tightly throughout the frightening episode and guided her back to their camp. Before she could think to help him, he had readied their makeshift beds before the campfire, and she crept into her enfolding blankets as a frightened animal would retreat into its lair.

Holding the lantern, Micah foraged for more lightwood to add to the now-dwindling fire, and her shaking finally ceased in the warmth of the crackling flames. She must have fallen asleep, she later thought, before Micah even lay down on his old quilt.

***

The rain set in heavily sometime after midnight. Katharine awoke to a doused fire and a cold, wet chill. The lantern, its feeble glow rocking on the tree limb in the blowing rain, provided the only light, now that the fire and the moon ceased to shed theirs.

Micah was immediately over her, lifting her out of the blankets and, at the same time, grabbing the bedding.

"Make a run for it," he told her. "Get in the goat-shed. It's the only dry place."

Katharine didn't have to be told twice. She climbed onto the raft and ran, half-asleep, to the lean-to, where she sat shivering in the dark. She had never heard it referred to as a "goat-shed." At that moment, the full impact of rafting caused her to question her sanity when she had first decided to make the trip to Darien.

Her warm feather bed at home kept inching into her consciousness and she remembered Micah MacRae's words in the foyer of Winslow Hall, when she had told him that she intended to go to Darien on her raft. He had said that she would regret even thinking about living on the raft for a week, that it was no place for a fragile woman.

Well, she didn't consider herself a fragile woman, as he had said, but she supposed that every woman liked to be comfortable and clean. She was neither, she thought, as she huddled shivering in Frank's dirty old clothes in the cold lean-to.

Also, she was frightened. She struck a match and lit her lantern which cast a soft glow inside the lean-to. However, she could see nothing outside in the wet, moonless darkness except the shifting lantern which Micah was carrying to the Negroes' camp. Obviously, their lantern was out, and they were unable to light it, for no light shone from their camp through the woods. She was cold and damp and miserable, and the pangs of homesickness set in.

Micah returned with the jabbering Negroes who stumbled after him along the riverbank. He urged them to get in their lean-to and try to get some sleep. The river would probably be too swift for them to push off at daybreak.

Katharine was glad for Micah's return, but was somewhat surprised when he dropped to the open door of her lean-to and walked in, sideways, on his knees.

"Hope you don't mind me a-sharin' your lean-to, Ma'm."

"No, I mean, it's fine with me. I had wondered how four of you were going to fare in the other one, and I confess I was feeling rather selfish, having this one all to myself."

Katharine wondered what the Negroes must think about her and Micah together in the cramped lean-to, but it was too late to worry about such. She should have realized the total lack of civilities on a rafting trip, but she would just have to survive the rest of the harsh trip as best she could. She was determined not to complain to Micah, as she had heard the Negroes doing.

Also, her damp clothes reminded her that she needed some clean, dry ones. In her hurried attempt to pack only stark necessities, she had only included the sole outfit which she planned to wear on the return train ride home. It was several days away. Actually, the trip was not even halfway over. She cringed at this thought and closed her eyes, resting her forehead on her bent knees and hugging her ankles to herself for warmth.

"You all right?" Micah's brown eyes were filled with concern as he studied her in the lantern's light.

"Oh, I'm fine," Katharine said with a nonchalant smile. She would die before she would let him know just how miserable she was. She noted that he hadn't changed clothes during the trip, either, but he looked the same as he did when they pushed off from Willcox Lake, which now seemed a long time ago, though it had actually been only three days since then. His face, however, usually clean-shaven, now had a rough beard.

The rain had let up but the wind continued to blow, pushing the groaning raft repeatedly into the riverbank. The night was still inky black. Katharine wondered what time it was. She fished the locket watch which she wore around her neck from under Frank's shirt. Its delicate hands pointed to the hour of 3:03. Daylight was several hours away. She closed the locket and dropped it back under the shirt.

Micah was looking at his watch, too, which he had pulled from his shirt pocket.

"Yours have somethin' after 3:00 o'clock?" he asked.

"Yes."

"Well, we might as well all go back to sleep." Muffled snores from the Negroes' lean-to told them that they had already unknowingly taken his advice.

Sudden loud yelling and desperate rantings issued from the main river channel. Katharine didn't need anyone to tell her that a raft was out there in the dark oblivion, and its men were in a frantic struggle to survive. They obviously had seen the light from Micah's lantern, off in the slough, and they were calling for help.

Micah was out of the lean-to in a flash, holding the lantern and picking up several dry lightwood knots from the Negroes' lean-to, moving with such deftness that none awoke. He ran the long lengths of the raft sections, rummaging in his pockets for a dry match. He seemed oblivious of Katharine who had trailed closely behind him, once she realized what he was going to do. The lantern which he held out toward the river dimly illuminated the huddled, frightened Negroes on the wayward raft out in the main river channel. They were yelling for help.

"Tie a rope somewhere and throw me the other end," Micah yelled to them.

The Negroes, wild-eyed, looked for a rope but couldn't find one in the darkness on the raft.

"All right. I'm sendin' over some fire." Micah lit a lightwood knot and threw it to the raft, but it landed in the flowing water, several feet away from its destination.

"Here's another one!" Micah handed the lantern to Katharine, as though he knew she were standing there all along, and heaved the second burning lightwood knot all the way to the other raft where it landed still afire. One of the men picked it up, his terror-stricken face revealed in its flare. He and the other Negroes shouted something but their voices were muffled by the swamp sounds and the swirling, gurgling water, which pulled them on downstream.

At least, they won't be in the dark, Katharine thought, but she wondered how they could manage the raft in such swift water. They must have given up trying to steer the raft toward the bank with the bow and stern oars, as they couldn't fight the surging water. Also, they didn't appear to have pike-poles onboard, as none held any.

If the raft should be torn apart, it would mean almost certain death for those on board. It was a life-and-death situation for which she had no answers. She knew now why Micah had said they couldn't push off at daylight, for the water was moving too fast, following the early morning shower.

They trudged back over the sections of the raft, and Micah found his old quilt and spread it near the clay hearth. Since it had stopped raining, he said, he would sleep outside.

Katharine knelt and crawled back into the lean-to and spread her blanket over the floor of squared logs. The inside of the blanket was relatively dry, as was the underside of her pillow. Covering herself with the blanket, she made her bed and prayed for the safety of the rafters who were yet adrift on the swift and swollen river. God help them, she thought, as she remembered the terror in the face of the one who had picked up the burning lightwood knot. She wondered how long they had been without light or fire. At least, they would know where the edges of the raft were and wouldn't inadvertently step off into the black water, for it was a moonless night. The sloshing of her raft against the riverbank soon rocked her to sleep.

***

She awoke to sunshine beaming into the lean-to. Micah and the other raftsmen were talking among themselves on the riverbank, as though nothing had happened the night before. How wonderful light was, she thought, as she sat up in her hard bed, for it dispelled the fears of the night. She remembered something from the Bible that she'd heard Micah's mother often repeat. The words eluded her but it was something about the morning time. She reached back into her memory and Abby MacRae's voice could almost be heard. Oh yes, she would say, "Weeping may endure for the night, but joy comes in the morning." Katharine could imagine the raftsmen, if they survived the night, rejoicing now in the morning light. She wondered whether Micah's burning lightwood knot which he had tossed to them had lasted throughout the night. Again, she offered a prayer for their safety.

Coffee perked in the old tin coffeepot as Luke prepared breakfast. Katharine idly watched his mixing the flour and water for the usual battercakes. The fatback had been fried and its smell vied with the coffee in pungency. She had no desire to try to help with any more meals. This was Luke's domain. She would not attempt to enter it again.

The day was a long one, with little to do but wait for the river's rapid flowing to subside. The sunshine, however, did wonders for everyone's spirits. The colored rafthands congregated on the end section of the raft which was closest to the main river channel. After reattaching their fishing lines, they passed the time talking and squabbling among themselves.

When one of them produced playing cards, they cajoled Micah into being a fourth participant. Katharine guessed that he was keeping them occupied at something less threatening than their prior diversions of "Skin" and "Seven-up," which she had vaguely heard referred to as games which Negroes played. In fact, he warned them ahead of time that there would be no betting and no money or anything else changing hands.

Katharine wondered what Micah's mother would think of his cardplaying. She was certain that the strict Primitive Baptist Church, which she had attended, would not condone playing cards. The men's laughter and open enjoyment, however, registered their disregard for any such restriction.

Left to herself, Katharine rummaged around in the large leather bag for a book to read. She had brought Coleridge's strange poem, *Lewti*, which had a reference to the Altamaha River, though he spelled the river, "Tamaha," and he referred to it as a stream. She reread the poem which she had never especially liked, thinking that maybe she had overlooked another reference to the Altamaha River. She, however, found no more mention of the river by name.

Having enjoyed the literary works of Oliver Goldsmith, she had brought along his *The Deserted Village*, a fairly long poem which she hadn't read. She had attended the performance of his play, *She Stoops to Conquer*, in London where she had visited with her parents during one of her father's several European business trips, before she and Frank married.

She reread parts of William Bartram's *Travels Through North and South Carolina, Georgia, East and West Florida*, dated 1791. She was especially interested in the "Lost Gordonia," the rare and beautiful flowering tree found only around the lower Altamaha River, near Barrington's Bluff. Actually, Bartram wrote that it was not the "Gordonia," though it was very much like it. He called the new tree, "Franklinia alatamaha," named for Benjamin Franklin and the nearby river. Bartram had collected specimens and sent them to

Philadelphia, where they were the source of present-day plants by that name in botanical gardens.

According to Bartram, the tree grew to be fifteen to twenty feet in height. The large, lovely flowers were of "snow white colour, and ornamented with a crown or tassel of gold coloured refulgent staminae in their centre, the inferior petal or segment of the corolla is hollow, formed like a cap or helmet, and entirely includes the other four, until the moment of expansion; its exterior surface is covered with a short silky hair; the borders of the petals are crisped or plicated; these large white flowers stand single and sessile in the bosom of the leaves, and being near together towards the extremities of the twigs, and usually many expanded at the same time, make a gay appearance: the fruit is a large, round, dry, woody apple or pericarp, opening at each end oppositely by five alternate fissures, containing ten cells, each replete with dry woody cuneiform seed...We never saw it grow in any other place, nor have I ever since seen it growing wild, in all my travels, from Pennsylvania to Point Coupe, on the banks of the Mississippi, which must be allowed a very singular and unaccountable circumstance; at this place there are two or three acres of ground where it grows plentifully."

Katharine made a mental note to look for the beautiful tree, though she didn't know whether it would be in bloom during early September.

Several years past, she had belonged to Eleanor Hardison's book club in Eastman where they met in her home once a month. Someone had given a review of *The Deserted Village* for the book club, and everyone present was surprised to learn of Goldsmith's reference to the Altamaha River in Georgia, some one hundred years prior. It seemed that the botanist, William Bartram, traveling in North America in the 1790's, had written enough about the river to influence the works of not only Goldsmith but also other writers as well, including Samuel Taylor Coleridge.

Katharine turned quickly to the first lines of *The Deserted Village*, eagerly looking for any reference to the Altamaha River. However, as she became engrossed in the meaning of the poem, her heart beat faster, because it was obvious that there was a parallel between it and the situation in the piney woods of Georgia. She read on, bemused by the fact that something written over a hundred years before, in England, was occurring again in the region referred to by Goldsmith as "Altama," across the wide ocean. Goldsmith had written that the yeoman farmers of "Sweet Auburn! Loveliest village of the plain," had been forced out of their village where they had lived for generations, by "the tyrant's hand," and some had fled to America to the "Altama" area.

Now, a century later, was it possible that some of the progeny of these families were being threatened, though by a different tyrant, who was again taking their land? Katharine looked up, staring straight ahead at the dense swamp.

Hearing a noise in the water, just beyond the raft's edge, she saw a blue dragonfly alight on a large oak leaf which floated on the water. She had once heard someone refer to a dragonfly as a "devil's-darning-needle," and she stared at the one on the oak leaf, envisioning it as part devil and part needle. She supposed the bugged eyes might be satanic, and the slim body like a needle. Other than that, she saw no resemblance, for its diaphanous wings were lovely in the sunlight.

A shadow fell across her shoulder and she looked up into the smiling face of Micah MacRae.

"We call the small ones 'skeeter hawks.'" He nodded toward the dragonfly.

"Oh, is that what you call them? I've heard them called dragonflies and, also..." Before she could repeat the other name, he said it at the same time... "Devil's Darning Needles." They laughed together at this.

He dropped down by her and gestured toward her book.

"What are you readin', Miz Fremont?"

"I'm reading a poem by Oliver Goldsmith. Did you ever study any of his works in school?" The question was asked before Katharine could think better of it, for she didn't want to embarrass him with his lack of education. Before he could answer, however, she quickly changed the subject.

"I'm just curious about the Indian names of the rivers here. They are beautiful names but I wonder what they mean."

"I might can help you there. I was curious myself 'bout 'em. 'Ocmulgee' means 'boilin'' or 'bubblin'' water. Why, I don't rightly know. As for 'Oconee,' Micah nodded toward the river on the left which fed directly into the Ocmulgee River. "A man..., an Injun agent by the name of Benjamin Hawkins said that 'Oconee' was the name of a Creek Injun village. Mary Musgrove, called Queen of the Creeks, once had a tradin' post here. And, as for the big 'Altamaha,' well, I've heard lots of dif'frent meanin's of its name."

"What meanings have you heard?" Katharine was breathlessly hanging on his every word. She was surprised that he himself had been curious about the Indian names.

"An ole Injun village was here at The Forks, where we're camped now, called the 'Tama.' One meanin' is that the river name means 'the road to Tama.' Some say it was an Injun word for their chief. It's spelt dif'frent ways, too."

"I see that it is. I'm reading *The Deserted Village* by Oliver Goldsmith, which he wrote over a hundred years ago, and he spells it 'Altama.' I'm afraid he doesn't brag on it...the river, I mean."

"Oh?" Micah smiled broadly, "what does he say?"

Katharine read the poem, hardly able to concentrate, for his brown eyes looked steadily at her and it was difficult for her to think of anything else. She made an effort to keep her voice calm and passionless, as she read the poet's references to the Altamaha River.

Through torrid tracts with fainting steps they go,
Where wild Altama murmurs to their woe.
Far different there from all that charmed before,
The various terrors of that horrid shore;

She looked up. "Shall I go on? It's not very flattering to your river here."

"I like it. It can't be all bad."

Katharine read the rest of the lines, pertaining specifically to the Altamaha River, mischievously emphasizing the negative adjectives and glancing up frequently to view their impact on Micah's face.

Those blazing suns that dart a downward ray,
And fiercely shed intolerable day;
Those matted woods where birds forget to sing,

But silent bats in drowsy clusters cling,
Those poisonous fields with rank luxuriance crowned,
Where the dark scorpion gathers death around;
Where at each step the stranger fears to wake
The rattling terrors of the vengeful snake;
Where crouching tigers wait their hapless prey,
And savage men, more murderous still than they;
While oft in whirls the mad tornado flies,
Mingling the ravaged landscape with the skies.

"That's it," Katharine said, closing the book. "Well, what do you think of it?"

"One man's opinion," Micah said briefly. "Guess he's entitled to it." He paused, looking toward the wider Altamaha River where they would be rafting the following day. His eyes were brooding, meditative.

"Guess it ain't much changed in a hunerd years, maybe in a thousand years. Prob'ly pretty much the same fish and animals. Reckon the 'tiger' he's talkin' 'bout is the catamount. I heard one close by last night."

"You heard one near the raft?" Katharine's heart was beating rapidly.

"Weren't very far off." Micah stood up, hands on hips, looking toward the Negroes still occupied in their cardplaying.

"How 'bout steppin' to it, Luke, and get some dinner a-cookin'."

The rest of the day passed uneventfully and as nighttime set in, the Negroes decided to sleep on the end section of the raft. They kept their kerosene lamp burning and Katharine could see its glow down the length of the raft. Micah made his bed near the hearth fire which he had replenished with dry lightwood from the lean-to. He spread his old quilt on the squared logs and threw his old, cornshuck-stuffed, flour-sack pillow on the quilt.

Katharine had heard him tell the Negroes that they would push off at first light. She was somewhat apprehensive about the Altamaha River which they would enter during the early morning, but her worst fears now centered around the catamount which Micah had nonchalantly mentioned only a few minutes earlier. Some of the old-timers called them painters, or panthers.

In moments, Katharine heard the raftman's heavy breathing and she knew he was asleep, his arm bent under his head and his large body turned slightly toward the leaping flames on the clay hearth.

Katharine stared at him, longing to creep over and fit her body into the nook of his own, bringing his protective arm around her. Instead, she put the two leather bags at the door of her lean-to as a sheltering shield, of sorts, and crawled between the folds of her blanket, plumping the pillow under her head. She lay there, listening to the night sounds of the swamp.

Midst the constant croaking of frogs, alligators bellowed, sending chills up her backbone. She had heard of alligators actually climbing onto rafts and the thought made her hands clammy and her heart faint. She closed her eyes, trying to calm herself and get some sleep. She could hear the hearth fire spit, as bits of lightwood became embers. She opened her eyes and watched the shadows inside the lean-to, reflecting the dancing of the fire outside. She closed her eyes, sighing as she snuggled under the blanket.

A soft whistle sounded close by. Katharine's body stiffened. Everyone was asleep. Who could it be? She was afraid even to open her eyes. Another whistle was nearer the raft. Was someone testing them, to find out whether anyone might be awake? Katharine opened her eyes in terror. She had heard of escaped convicts eluding the law by hiding out in the river swamp. She must wake up Micah!

She sat up, peering over the leather bags which she had positioned at the lean-to door. At that moment an unearthly scream shattered the night, and a large animal crept silently onto the second section of the raft. Katharine could see its large, cat-like form silhouetted by the faint moonlight, its long tail moving back and forth as it padded slowly, deliberately, toward her.

As she felt frantically for her gun in the leather bag, she saw Micah quickly reach for his weapon and fire upward into the air. The animal half-crouched, its cat eyes shining in the firelight. It began backing away, its ears flat against its feline head and its lips curled over sharp, flashing teeth. A guttural snarl noised its displeasure with the gunfire, which Micah, now on his feet, repeated.

The animal crept backward as Micah reloaded his gun. The Negroes, now all fully awake, were terrified. They had lit lightwood knots from the burning kerosene lantern which they brandished before them in an apparent attempt to stave off the catamount's movement in their direction.

Micah again shot upward into the air and ran at the animal which ripped and clawed its way off the raft and bounded into the safety of the dark swamp. Micah laughingly told the Negroes they could put out their burning knots and get back to sleep.

Katharine didn't see anything to laugh about. They could have all been killed.

"You should have killed it!" she exclaimed, when he turned to ask if she were all right.

"I don't kill nuthin' I don't have to, Ma'm. It was just a hungry catamount. He could smell where Luke had cooked supper and he thought he'd get a easy meal."

Katharine glared at his back as he continued to laugh with the now jovial Negroes about the close encounter with the catamount. She was angry and upset. He should have killed the animal. Now, she would worry the rest of the night that the "tiger" of the Altamaha would return.

As she had predicted, she slept fitfully, expecting to hear the chilling whistle or the nerve-shattering cry throughout the night. Only when she reminded herself that this was the last rafting trip of her life, and it would be over in only a few more days, could she gain a better perspective of her frighteningly dire situation. She yearned for her safe home in New York, but she was surprised that the prospect of returning to New York, soon after the rafting trip, seemed distant and, for some reason, unreal.

Her heart was heavy but she couldn't pinpoint why. Perhaps her nerves were just shaky from the catamount episode. She sat up in her lean-to and waited for the first welcome streaks of dawn, when coffee perked and battercakes sizzled, side by side, on the cooking hearth.

After their early breakfast, Katharine stood near her lean-to and watched the customary procedure of casting off from the riverbank. Micah and Shep took their places at the bow and stern ends of the raft, with Luke walking along the middle sections. Hoke jumped to the bank and unhitched the raft, then hurriedly hopped aboard again and joined the other rafthands in pushing against the river bottom with their pike-poles and easing the raft out of the eddy and into the main river channel.

"Bo-o-ow Injun!" Micah yelled to Shep who pulled the stern oar simultaneously and in the same direction as Micah directed the bow oar. They guided the raft into the wide expanse of the Altamaha River.

To Katharine's surprise and amusement, Shep dropped the stern oar and cut loose with quick, rhythmic dancing, while at the same time singing at the top of his lungs.

> Look-a-yonder! Look-a-yonder! Yonder!
> I see Sunday, I see Sunday -
> Sunday, oh Sunday!

His caper was infectious, for the other two Negro rafthands quickly imitated him on the middle section of the raft, all three now quick-stepping, clapping their hands, and repeating the chantey.

Micah, too, joined in singing, and Katharine not to be outdone sang along with him, trying to remember the unusual words.

Shep soon returned to the business of guiding the raft at the stern oar, and the other Negroes gradually ceased their exuberant dancing. Micah hummed the chantey and Katharine stood by him as they drifted down the Altamaha River. His eyes shifted to hers. Katharine wondered what he must think of her in her husband's too-big clothes, now dirty, which she had been wearing since the rafting trip began. Also, her hair which she kept penned up under Frank's old hat was dirty and unkempt. She must look a fright, she thought, under his gaze. To her complete surprise, in one fluid motion, he removed the wide-brimmed hat from her head, then quickly removed the large pins which held her hair, allowing it to tumble around her face and shoulders.

Before she could react, he leaned over and brushed his lips over hers. His strong presence could be felt in the cool morning breeze and she longed to go into his arms, but caution prevailed.

She quickly looked at the colored raftsmen whose backs were turned to them. Katharine knew that this could not go on, though every fiber of her being wanted it to. What they felt was not love, she reasoned. It couldn't be. And she had no intention of any further relationship with him. This must stop!

His hand was on the curve of her face, now on her chin which he tilted up to him. His lips were on hers again, parting them. She felt her iron resolve weakening, then thought again of the colored raftsmen. This was neither the time nor the place, but then, there would never be a time or place for them. He must think her a trollop, like...like those women at...at...she tried to remember the name of the place in Darien. She had heard it mentioned several times at the company parties but the name would not come to her.

She stepped back from Micah, saying, tersely, "You had no right to do that, Mr. MacRae."

"Will you forgive me?" He appeared to be teasing.

She reached for the hairpins and coiled her hair on top of her head, securing it again with the pins, then replaced Frank's droopy hat on her head. Tears stung her eyes and she didn't know why. She only knew that this trip must end soon, and she must separate herself forever from this man who stirred such conflicting feelings within her very soul.

She turned away, so that the tears on her cheeks could not be seen. Under the pretext of looking at something away from him, she dabbed her face with her shirt sleeves. Why, in God's name, was she crying? She was glad for the floppy brim of Frank's old hat, for it hid from Micah not only her tears but also her strange feelings about so many things which crowded her head during the rough rafting trip.

Having left behind the twisting, turning sinuosities of the Ocmulgee River, the raftsmen welcomed the relatively straight course of the mighty Altamaha. Katharine sat, knees bent to one side, listening to the odd river names, exchanged with loud yells among the raftsmen, and observing the strangeness of the Altamaha swamp on both sides of the wide river.

"We gotta stay away from Jack's Suck," Micah yelled, "but Hell's Shoals oughta be covered since the rain."

"Yassuh," Shep yelled back.

The raft continued its snake-like drift down the river. The swamp on either side varied from low land with thickly growing trees and underbrush to pine-laden, high bluffs overlooking the river. Sturgeons, harvested for their roe during the spring months, leapt from the water, revealing their slender bodies covered with rows of bony plates, their long snouts projecting over their toothless mouths and their thick, sucking lips. Katharine had heard that sturgeons were also fished for their oil and for their flesh which was smoked. Though the ones leaping from the water were not so large, she had heard of some measuring fourteen feet in length. She had also heard of men spearing the fish with their iron harpoons or "gigs."

A soaring flock of swallow-tailed kites circled and crossed high above them. Their breast and belly feathers so immaculately white upon their arrival in the spring were now stained an ineradicable tobacco-juice brown, due to the spurting of the body fluids of their prey which they crushed in their talons. The birds took turns swooping down to the river, gradually lowering themselves, then stooping to drink while on the wing. The largest ones had wingspans of likely four feet.

"Comin' up on Hell's Shoals," Micah hollered to the other raftsmen. "Looks like a raft in trouble!"

Katharine could see jagged, reddish-brown rocks which jutted out from the banks on both sides of the river and a small, stalled raft which appeared to be grounded in some way by the protruding rocks. Two men, one Negro and one white, walked back and forth on the several sections of the raft, talking and gesturing to each other. Neither appeared to know what to do. They looked up, seeing another raft approaching, and yelled for help. Micah shouted to them that they would have to regroup their logs, but they would have a hard time with the rocks in the way.

"We seen you back on the Ocmulgee," the white man said, snapping the galluses of his overalls. "We was makin' good time 'til we got stuck here. The river was a-runnin' pretty good."

"It was a-runnin' pretty good, as you said, but it's hard to control a raft in a freshet. We waited a whole day yesterday, a-waitin' for the water to slow down."

Without warning, a loud cracking noise signaled that the binders on the grounded raft had snapped. The white man was killed instantly as he lost his footing and fell between two of the huge, shifting logs. Katharine would remember his startled face for the rest of her life, for it became one of fear and pain as the logs, pushed by the river current, crushed him to death. His body sank immediately into the swirling water.

The Negro, panic-stricken, teetered precariously on the outside log and hollered that he couldn't swim, before disappearing into the water between the two rafts. Horrified and unable to speak, Katharine and the Negro raftsmen watched incredulously as Micah quickly removed his boots and dived into the water. The Negroes then tried to stop the movement of their own raft by feeling along with their pike-poles along the river bottom which wasn't so deep at the shoals.

Micah finally surfaced with the Negro's body, but decided it was too dangerous and futile to attempt to recover the other man's body under the binderless raft. He heaved the drowned man's body over the raft, then climbed aboard himself, gasping for air, his wet clothes clinging to his body. After catching his breath and pulling on his socks and boots, he leapt up and grabbed the bow oar.

"Bo-o-o-ow White!" he commanded, and the two raftsmen walked with their respective oars toward the "White" side of the river. The raft became embedded in a sandbar, but Micah was confident that they could easily free it, once they had buried the Negro from the doomed raft.

Katharine, still unable to speak, stumbled after Micah. He turned back silently and helped her from the raft to the sandbar. The Negroes had an ax and were cutting down small saplings to fashion a crude coffin. They made pegs to hold the boxlike receptacle together. Katharine stood on the open sandbar, watching their efforts which ultimately culminated in a rough casket. Micah retrieved the body from the raft and placed it in the long wooden box. They fastened the lid with the remaining wooden pegs.

Carrying the coffin beyond the edge of the swamp to higher ground, they dug a shallow grave with an old shovel from the lean-to on the raft and placed the oaken box in it. After covering it with dirt, they cut down tree limbs and placed over it, to keep the "'gators" and other animals away from the body, they said. Katharine could see them standing with their heads bowed, and she bowed her own, assuming they were saying words of Scripture over the body.

The fate of the corpse of the other man remained unspoken but the meaning was terribly clear. Katharine looked across the river's expanse to the opposite bank and saw several large alligators basking on the flat sandbar. Micah had said that sometimes nature was not pretty. To her, it was often terrifying!

The somber group boarded the raft again and the two oarsmen assumed their positions at the opposite ends of the raft. Katharine sat near her lean-to, grateful to be alive, thankful that her raft was still intact and that it was in the capable hands of Micah MacRae. She closed her eyes and prayed that they would arrive safely in Darien. As Micah had predicted, they easily pushed off from the sandbar. Katharine knew that Micah's wet clothes had to be uncomfortable, but she also knew they would dry quickly in the warm sun.

For the first several miles of drifting, no one talked. Only the occasional bird call and the water gurgling around the raft's half-submerged logs disturbed the quietness. They drifted on, the funereal silence onboard almost deafening.

"Comin' into Iron Mine Reach! Half-a-lick to Injun, Shep!" Micah hollered back to his stern oarsman, finally breaking the dead quiet. Shep matched his oar with Micah's, with "half" a pull toward the "Indian" side of the river.

"This is where they say the river boils, Ma'm," Micah said, turning to Katharine.

"Boils?" Katharine questioned apprehensively.

Micah explained, and Katharine thought he was teasing.

"They say that anybody who falls overboard at Iron Mine Reach will drown, for sure."

Katharine contemplated this latest frightening legend of the Altamaha, growing even more anxious for the perilous trip to end.

"Yassuh, de ribbuh sho' straight. Ain' lak de Ocmulgee," Luke yelled to him, as he began walking the long sections to the clay hearth. Shep had dropped the stern oar, since the raft was now drifting on a straight reach or unwinding path down the large river. He was following Luke, with Hoke trailing behind.

"Mr. Micah," Shep shouted, "dey all gotta treat Rag Point."

"Yes, well, we'll just have to see that they all do," Micah

said, looking at Katharine. "They treat the point, treat the crowd, or take a duckin' in the river."

"How does one 'treat the point'?" Katharine asked in a suspicious voice.

"Ever'body leaves some of their clothes there, just a piece or a rag," Micah said. "You'll see. We should get there tomorrow."

"Luke and Hoke gotta throw dey knifes up Bugg's Bluff, too," Shep asserted, glad that he was a veteran raftsman and didn't have to risk losing his own knife in the rites of initiation for first-time raftsmen. Luke and Hoke were skeptical about participating in such a ritual, but Shep assured them that they would never become the seasoned rafthand that he, Shep, was, unless they took part in the inviolable rituals of the river. In fact, Shep continued in a tone of confession, he himself had lost his knife on the bluff years ago, and for all he knew, it was still up there on the high cliff.

The two neophyte Negro raftsmen looked at each other in consternation, beginning to worry over the almost certain prospect of losing one of their very few possessions. Luke set about making preparations for the noonday meal, as Shep hurried back to the stern oar and Hoke sprawled out on the middle section of the raft.

Four moving objects in the river ahead caught their attention and Micah hollered back that deer were crossing ahead. Katharine could make out a buck with large antlers and three does. Hoke and Luke both started running toward the lean-to for their guns but Micah stopped them, saying there wasn't time to bother with deer meat. Looking disappointed, the two rafthands returned to their positions on the raft. The deer swam hard, trying to elude the oncoming raft, finally climbing up the bank on the "Indian" side of the river. They were quickly enveloped by their surroundings, their brownish-grey coats blending into the early autumn hues of the Altamaha swamp.

Katharine listened to the strange, wild names of the Altamaha, which the men muttered and bandied among themselves. She heard them mention Eason's Bluff, the Mouth of Old River, the Mouth of Ten Mile Creek, and Carter's Bight on the "Indian" side of the river. On the "White" side of the river, they pointed out the mouth of the Ohoopee River and Cypress Nursery.

At times they saw bears feeding on the dwarf chinquapin trees which grew on the riverbanks on both sides of the river. To make their food more accessible, the animals crawled through the several sprawling trunks of the small trees, straddled them, then rode them to the ground. Though the bears were aware of their presence on the slowly gliding raft, they continued their meal of the thorny-husked chestnuts, cracking them with their powerful jaws and teeth and extracting the savory nutmeat.

The oarsmen tied up at a place called Carter's Bight for the noonday meal, though no one was very hungry. This was Katharine's opportunity to retreat to the woods for a few moments of privacy, which though necessary were always frightening. Bears could be just about anywhere around. Also, she had seen a water moccasin slither into the water while Luke was hitching the raft and had heard Micah call it a "cottonmouth." He said when the snake opened its mouth, it looked like white cotton.

The water moccasin was poisonous. That she knew. But the snake she most feared was a rattlesnake because its bite was often fatal. She had always been careful to look before venturing into the underbrush. So far, she had been lucky in only seeing the moccasins and copperheads near the riverbank. However, she had heard Micah say that snakes were on the move now during the early fall of the year.

She stepped gingerly into the underbrush of leaves and twigs, seeking privacy within the tangled vines and palmettos. Finding her own nature's chamber pot, she made hurried use of it. Pulling up the too-large pants which she had tightened with elastic in the waist, she turned to head back to the waiting raft.

A whirring rattle caught her attention, and she found herself face to face with a large rattlesnake, its body in a thick coil with the vibrating, horny rattles on the end of its segmented tail perpendicular to the ground. It was poised to strike!

Involuntarily, she screamed, her hands clutching her throat. She dared not move again, not even breathe!

Like an apparition, Micah MacRae stood in front of her, the snake between them. She was surprised at the clarity of her thinking that the man moved so quietly, she hadn't even heard a twig snap.

"Don't move, Katharine!" he whispered, hoarsely.

She choked down a scream, afraid to look at the snake, but even more fearful of looking away. She slowly looked into its reptilian eyes, noticing the hideous forked tongue which licked the air and the quickened, whirring rattles, which often presaged a deadly attack.

Before she realized what was happening, Micah struck the snake with his gun barrel, holding it writhing on the ground.

"Run to the raft!" he shouted, and as she quickly ran past him, she looked back and saw him shoot the snake. She quit running, waiting for him to catch up with her. He had probably saved her life. She wanted to throw herself into his arms but she thought better of it. Instead, she held out her hand, trying to calm herself, and he took it.

"Thank you," she said.

"You're shakin', Miz Fremont," he said, smiling at her.

"It's because I was scared to death," she said, and she realized her teeth were chattering.

"I wish I could make it easier for you, Ma'm. Raftin's hard on a woman. Not many women ever gone all the way to Darien on a raft. As I said, if I could make it easier for you, I would."

"You have, Mr. MacRae," she said meekly, and she accepted his help in boarding the raft.

"You kill somethin', Mr. Micah?" Shep asked.

"A rattlesnake, big 'round as my arm," Micah replied to the round-eyed stares of the Negroes. "Let's push off. We got a raft to get to Darien." After unhitching the raft, the men used their pike-poles to push it away from the riverbank. Then the oarsmen walked their oars toward the middle of the river upon the command from Micah to "Bo-o-o-ow White!" Katharine settled down near her lean-to and watched the raftsmen maneuver the cumbersome raft around the sandbars which lined both sides of the river and extended out beneath the raft.

Farther on down the river, she heard the unusual names of Sister's Bluff and Sister's Bluff Reach on the "Indian" side of the river, along with Owl Head, Fort James Reach, Beard's Bluff, Marrow Bone Round, and Yankee Reach. The "White" side had fewer names, but they were equally interesting, she thought. Some she mulled over in her mind were Medlock Water Road, Stooping Gum, Beard's Creek, Tom's Creek, and Hughes Landing.

"See that bluff yonder," Micah said, looking at Katharine and pointing to the high yellow bluff.

When she nodded, he said, "That's Oglethorpe Bluff. Seems that General Oglethorpe jumped 'is horse from it, runnin' from the Injuns."

It was a long way for horse and rider to jump, Katharine thought, looking at the high bluff. In her mind, she had always associated Oglethorpe with the seaside towns of Savannah and Brunswick. She never had considered that he traveled this far inland along the Altamaha River. Also, she was surprised that Micah even knew anything about Oglethorpe. She guessed she always underestimated the man.

"It's a long jump," Katharine said, picturing in her mind the uniformed general on his horse and his red-skinned pursuers.

Drifting on downstream, Micah remarked to Katharine that they were approaching Doctortown, so named because a celebrated "medicine man" once lived there in his Indian village. The present bustling, industrial town had sawmills, stave mills, and shingle mills. On the riverbank was a tremendous wharf, grain elevator, and warehouse. Several steamboats, loading and unloading goods and passengers, along with a number of rafts from upriver, were anchored at the docks. The recently built steamboat, *Altamaha*, was also moored at the long wharf. Doctortown once had been known as the industrial hub of the county, following the war. The nearby town of Jesup was now the primary trade town and county seat of Wayne County, because the railroads ran through it.

Katharine thought that this was the most activity she had seen on any of the rivers, since their rafting trip began. She had never even heard of Doctortown and was surprised when the backwoodsman related that General Sherman had attempted to capture the railroad trestle there during his march to the sea in 1864, but was unsuccessful.

Next was a place on the Altamaha called Pullaway and Be Damned, an odd name that brought a chill into the air.

The raft drifted on toward an island on the "White" side of the river, and Katharine asked Micah whether it had a name.

"Oh, yes," he said, his expression serious and his eyes betraying that he knew something about the island.

"Well, what is its name?"

"That's Hannahs Island, Ma'm. Wouldn't ever wanna tie up there." She thought he was half-teasing, but she wasn't sure.

"Why? Who was Hannah?"

"Well, durin' the war, she was brought over to this island by a band of soldiers. She was used and mistreated by all of 'em. They all went back to their camp 'cross the river over there." He motioned to the other side of the river. "I've heard some say they left her a-cryin' there on the island, but others say she died." Micah paused, looking steadily at Katharine. "They say if you tie up on that island, Hannah's still there and she'll reach out to you with her milk-white arms and tears on 'er cheeks."

Katharine looked into Micah's brown eyes, trying to decide whether he really believed the superstition. She thought of all he had encountered and endured since their rafting trip began. She realized then that with all of the hardships of rafting that were real, one didn't need any additional perils, regardless of how superstitious they might be.

"I agree with you," she said. "I certainly wouldn't want to tie up on Hannahs Island."

Micah smiled, and this time she definitely saw an amused gleam in his eyes. She was smiling, too, though she meant every word she had said. The island gave her the shivers as they drifted by. A moaning sound emanated from the bank and Katharine turned toward it, almost expecting to see a tearful young girl, pleading with outstretched arms. She quickly turned back to Micah and realized that he had heard it, too. She smiled nervously, feeling ridiculous that a silly local legend could seem so real. The place would be doubly eerie at nighttime. She was glad when the raft drifted on past the island and its haunting myth.

Without any warning, Katharine sensed a visible change in the river. It appeared to narrow, rather dramatically, and she wasn't surprised when Micah said they were at the Upper End of the Narrows.

"Gotta find a place to tie up for the night," he shouted back to Shep.

"We passin' Mad Dog now."

"Comin' up on First Water Oak Round. It's good as any. Bo-o-o-ow White!" The oarsmen walked their oars in unison to the left, or "White," side of the river. Using their pike-poles, they guided the huge raft into a slough out of the main river passage. As if by rote, Hoke tested the water depth with his pole, then jumped into the waist-deep water. He snubbed the motion of the raft by twice looping the rope, tied at one end to both a boom log and a binder pole, to a good-sized tree. He double-looped the end and leaned backward with his full weight. The raft's momentum was duly checked.

Katharine dreaded another night on the river. No one else appeared troubled about what the darkness might bring but she was almost sick with anxiety. She heard one of the Negroes whistling as they headed for the woods to kill some squirrels for supper.

The next thing she knew, two of the Negroes were dragging the whistling Hoke toward the water. Hoke was protesting loudly, trying to free himself from their grip.

"Hey, hey! What's a-goin' on?" Micah looked up from making the fire, a large piece of lightwood in his hands.

"Hoke, he get a duckin'," Shep said. "Ain' no whistlin' allowed. It be bad luck."

"It ain't 12:00 o'clock yet. Reckon he can whistle 'til then," Micah said, with a patience that Katharine didn't realize he possessed. Obviously, superstitions abounded along the rivers, but as she had decided earlier at Hannahs Island, raftsmen pretty much respected them, even if they were only Negro lore, because the perils of rafting elevated them to the realm of belief. If she had to hazard a guess, Shep knew good and well that, "whistlin'" didn't bring bad luck until 12:00 o'clock, when he also knew they would all be asleep. He just wanted to give poor old Hoke another initiation. Katharine shook her head at their pranks.

The Negroes accepted Micah's reasonable assessment of the taboos about whistling only after midnight, but Hoke didn't appear to be eager to claim his right, for no whistling ensued as the colored rafthands charged through the swamp, looking for squirrels for supper.

As usual, Luke cooked bacon for Katharine, as she still could not make herself eat the bushy-tailed animals. She noticed that all of the raftsmen, including Micah, apparently relished the taste of squirrel, perhaps because they were just hungry, she thought, and it was something to eat. She also noted that no one but herself ate bacon, and she surmised that Micah had brought it especially for her. Again, she remonstrated with herself for neglecting to bring food for the trip. She especially missed fruits and vegetables.

With the evening meal over, the Negroes, except Shep, repaired to their camp down the river. Katharine sat on her blanket near the fire, listening with mounting dread to the chirping crickets and other, more ominous swamp sounds. She curled her arms around her drawn-up knees and tried to focus on the stories which, she knew, would be forthcoming from Shep. After cutting a plug of tobacco and stashing it in his jaw, Shep related one of the few tragic stories he was ever known to tell.

"Mr. Micah, Ah doan know whethuh you heard tell 'bout de young fellah, jes' ober a case ob de measles. He wuz on de raf fer de fus' time, and dey wuz runnin' day an' night, tryin' to meet de deadline. Dey wuz runnin' at night an' de young fellah, he fell into de ribber, an drownded. You hear tell ob it, Mr. Micah?" At Micah's nod, Shep further told how they found his body a few days later, many miles downstream. Yes, Micah said, he had known the boy and his family.

Micah was sitting on the ground with his back resting on a tree stump. His clothes, Katharine noticed, appeared to be completely dry. Usually letting Shep do the talking at night, he now appeared to have a yarn of his own to tell, and Katharine had the distinct impression that he was attempting to lighten their lonely situation on the morassy bank of the Altamaha River with something humorous, especially for her benefit, and she was grateful.

"There was a man lived in Tattnall County," Micah began, looking idly at his audience of two. "Didn't matter whether it wuz hot or cold, or whatever, he always wore a vest and a hat." He continued, "Well, one year, he wuz a'raftin' 'bout four hunerd logs down the river when a wind storm blew the goat-shed on the raft down and ever'body got their clothes wet.

"They decided to tie up and get their clothes dry and cook supper. They all took off their wet clothes and hung 'em before the fire to dry. Well, two hog bears came a-runnin' and began a-tearin' up ever'thin' and turnin' over ever'thin', so the man hollered for ever'body to jump on the raft. Ever'body jumped on the raft, and the man grabbed the fryin' pan but forgot 'is clothes a-dryin' on a tree. After driftin' a long ways down the river, ever'body began to see that the man only had on 'is shoes and 'is hat and 'is vest. They talked it over, what to do, and decided not to go back. Instead, they pulled a lot o'moss a-hangin' on trees along the banks of the river and made 'im a grass skirt to wear 'til they made it to Darien."

Encouraged by the amusement of his small but laughing audience, he launched into another yarn, even more bizarre than his first one.

"You might of heard this one, Shep. Seems that two men rode their raft wearin' homemade britches. It rained and their britches got wet and began to stretch. As they got too long, they whacked off an inch or so. When they got to Darien, they made a big fire to dry their clothes. Then, their britches began to shrink. They had to go home in freezin' weather with bare legs."

As the night wore on, the tales became even more preposterous, and Katharine found herself doubting the veracity of some of them. However, Shep assured her that the one he was about to tell was the "Godawful truth."

"So he'p me, Gawd," Shep said, as he began his tale, "dis is de trufe."

"A man wuz runnin' de ribber and 'is bow oar broke. Well, 'is raf' wuz driftin' mout ob control and he seed a light up ahead on 'nothuh raft dat stopped fer de night. Well, he seen two niggers sleepin' by de fire and he holluh to 'em to he'p him, but dey woan wake up, even w'en 'is raf' bump dey raf'. He knowed what he had to do, so he jump from 'is raf' to dere's and run past 'em sleepin' and tied 'is rope to dere bow oar, den he jump back on 'is raft, befo' it drif' on pas'. When 'is rope get tight, it pull dere oar into de water, and it wake up one ob de mens sleepin'. De man he look out but doan see nuthin', 'cause it be so dark. De man, he say, 'What de hell wuz dat?' S'cuse me, Miz Kat'rin, but dat what he say. Well, dey doan fine' out 'til de next mo'nin' whut it wuz. Den dey spend 'bout three hours mekin' a new bow oar." Again, Shep begged "Miz Kat'rin" to please forgive him for using such a word in her presence, but, he said, he was just repeating what one of the niggers said. Katharine told him, with a smile, that she forgave him.

Micah was now rising to his feet, stretching and yawning, a signal that the river yarns and odysseys, interesting though they might be, were over for yet another night. Again, Katharine thought how true it was that such yarn-spinning helped in warding off the demons of isolation and darkness and the almost impenetrable swamp which rose around them on both banks of the river. As Shep picked up his lantern and hurried toward the fire at the Negroes' camp, Micah jumped onto the raft and brought back his old quilt and pillow and Katharine's leather bag.

Katharine thanked him, adding that she did not expect him to get her things for her, that she was perfectly capable of doing such. However, deep down, it pleased her that he was so courteous and so manly. In fact, she thought, looking at him - something she rarely allowed herself to do - if their worlds were not poles apart and if they were not on irreconcilably opposite sides in the land dispute, if...if...if...!

She sighed. Micah looked up from throwing his old quilt and pillow on the ground.

"You all right, Ma'm?" She detected added respect in the way he addressed her. She was instantly glad that she had reproved him for taking liberties with her that morning. Remembering how he had uncoiled her hair, she took the hairpins out herself and shook it about her shoulders. She didn't look Micah's way but she could feel his eyes on her and she ached to go to him. Respect? Yes, it was something a woman wanted but it could not take the place of a man's warm bed. She longed to lie down beside him and feel his arms about her.

As she crawled into her cold, hard bed, she knew that her strict Calvinist upbringing had rescued her from something that she would surely regret later. She must cease thinking of Micah MacRae as a man, though God help her, such would be difficult. He was only an employee of hers. He was considered the best pilot oarsman on the rivers and that was the reason she had hired him. With a peace in her soul which comes to one who has wrestled with sin and prevailed, she closed her eyes and was soon asleep.

***

The river hollers awakened her just as the rosy streaks of dawn in the eastern sky were banishing the night. Realizing that the others were up and about, she quickly and quietly sought the shelter of the woods for some moments of privacy. How she would love a lingering bath, she thought, or a short bath, or any kind of bath. She felt the need for an all-over bath before they reached Darien, for she knew there would be no time nor place for such, once they drifted into the port city. She wasn't sure just how she was going to manage changing into the outfit which she had brought along for the return train trip home. However, she would worry about that after they had sold her logs. Right now, the uppermost thing in her mind was washing herself.

Maybe there was a place on the river where she could bathe. She almost laughed out loud when she compared herself with the Pharoah's daughter in the Bible, who bathed in the river Nile. Yes, she thought, there just might be a place on the river where she might go, away from everyone, and wash away a week's accumulation of grime. Just thinking about it made her feel better. She would look forward to it. There had to be such a place.

She hurried back to the dead campfire to roll up her blanket, but found Micah stuffing her bedclothes into her leather bag.

"Please, I'll do that," she said.

"Good mornin', Miz Fremont," he said, resisting her attempt to take her bag. "I got it. Watch your step, Ma'm," he said as he helped her onto the raft.

"Thank you," she said. As always, she appreciated his courtesy, and just his touch under her arm conveyed his strength and assurance. She knew she had never known anyone like him.

Everyone else had eaten breakfast, but Luke had saved hers, complete with hot coffee. She thanked him and ate it, sitting in front of her lean-to. She then disappeared into the lean-to, placing the bags on top of each other at the front door for some semblance of privacy. Finding her hair brush, she brushed her long tresses, finally twisting them into a knot on top of her head.

Extricating a washcloth from one of the bags, she wet it with some of the spring water which Micah had insisted on leaving in her lean-to. She dared not undress but she washed her face and hands, then pushed up the sleeves of Frank's old shirt and washed her arms. Next, she rolled up the pants legs, as high as they would roll, and washed her legs. Her mind was now fixated on the river bath that she had planned. She wondered if there might be a place where she could just sit in the water. She would take her cake of perfumed soap with her and maybe even wash her hair.

Only today, she thought, then tomorrow they would drift on down to Darien. Oh, how she was ready for the trip to end!

She removed the bags from the front of her lean-to and crawled out. What would her family and friends think, if they could see her now? What would Sewell Siddon think? He must not see her, at least not until her logs were sold. She hoped to avoid seeing him at all, ever again!

Shep was reminding Micah that they were coming to Bugg's Bluff. Since the raft was now drifting down a reach, Shep had momentarily abandoned his position at the stern oar and demanded that Luke and Hoke throw their knives to the top of the bluff. When both men hesitated, Micah promised the one who could do it a brand new Barlow. This provided the necessary incentive, and both men willingly attempted to throw their cherished blades, old and homemade though they were, to the pinnacle of the bluff. One knife dug into the face of the bluff near the top, for a few moments, only to fall with the other thrown knife, straight down into the water.

Katharine couldn't help but feel sorry for the newly initiated raftsmen, for they looked distraught over the loss of their knives. Their faces brightened, however, when Micah produced two simple pocket knives from the lean-to and tossed one to each raftsman.

Their wide grins showed their appreciation as they stuffed them in the pockets of their ragged pants. A knife was a knife, but now they had passed the first ritual of initiation into the world of experienced rafthands. They returned to their posts on the raft with self-perceived respectability, only to be alerted by Shep that Rag Point was just ahead. Somebody might get a "duckin," he said, if they didn't "treat de point."

"All right, all you first-timers," Micah said, looking specifically at Katharine. "Gotta treat the point." Katharine looked ahead at the point of land which jutted out into the water on the "White" side of the river. Hanging haphazardly on the trees and bushes was every imaginable article of clothing ever worn by male or female. Shirt tails, old breeches, socks, drawers, handkerchiefs, caps, shirts, all adorned the limbs and branches of Rag Point.

Katharine didn't really have anything to leave on the peninsular land jutting out into the river with its thick growth of willow and bushes, but she thought of an extra ribbon which she had brought and quickly retrieved it from the bag in the lean-to. This delicate bit of blue ribbon she looped around a drooping willow bough. Hoke and Luke had no choice but to cut a piece each from their ragged pants and stick them down in some bushes at the edge of Rag Point as the raft drifted by. Katharine looked back at her ribbon fluttering in the river breeze. For some strange reason, she felt a pang of sadness and she turned her eyes away from it.

They were coming to the end of the Narrows, Micah said, noting that they were at Phenholloway Creek on the "Indian" side and Hell Bight on the "White" side. Within a few minutes, they were at Upper Sister's Point on the "White" side, then Lower Sister's Point on the "Indian" side.

"Comin' up on Old Box Point," Micah hollered back to Shep. Katharine observed that the river made a ninety-degree turn here, and the oarsmen had to take care to avoid the sandbars on both sides of the river, once they had completed the turn and traveled a short distance.

Beyond the mouth of Ellis Creek on the "Indian" side of the river, jetties protruded outward from the bank, not far upriver from Alligator Lake and Red Breast Lake on the "White" side of the Altamaha.

"Ain't far to Barrington Bar," Micah called to Shep. "That's where we'll tie up."

"It still be daylight den, Mistuh Micah," Shep replied.

"Yes, but the tide'll be a-comin' in. We'll tie up, then drift on down tomorrow when the tide goes out."

"Yassuh, dat sho right," the Negro agreed.

"We're a-driftin' down Sans Savilla Reach now."

"Yassuh, and dat's Old Cypress ober dere and Knee Buckle."

"Just a little ways ahead and we'll be at Barrington Bar!" Micah yelled.

Barrington Bar! Why hadn't she thought of it? A sandbar with shallow water should be an ideal place for a bath of sorts, Katharine thought. She needed to talk quickly to Micah, before the raft was tied up, so they would be near such a place. She was shy about broaching the subject, but she gathered her courage and approached Micah at the bow oar.

"Mr. MacRae, when we arrive at Barrington Bar, is there a place where I might..." She found herself stammering, "where I might be able to...to...to...bathe a little, I mean, before we go on in to Darien?"

She was surprised that he didn't seem taken aback at all by her request. Rather, he seemed to think it reasonable.

"Yes, Ma'm, we can tie up on the main channel, and there's an eddy or slough with the prettiest sorta white-yellow sand and clear water where you might like to wash off. We all will be busy a-cleanin' the fish and you can go back into one of them sloughs. You'll have it all to yourself. Just be careful, Ma'm," he said, "to watch out for snakes!"

"Oh, I will!" Katharine almost sang the words as she hurried into the goat-shed to get her brown leather bag. She made sure her cake of soap, wash cloth, and towel were in the satchel, along with the derringer. It also contained her clothes which she planned to wear on the train when she returned home.

"Bo-o-ow to the White!" Micah yelled to Shep, and the two oarsmen rhythmically walked their oars toward the "White" side of the river. As the raft drifted toward the bank, Hoke paddled the bateau to the bank and performed his usual duty of tying the thick raft rope to a sturdy tree on the riverbank. Luke was taking the fish off the lines and putting them in the iron pot which he had brought to the stern section of the raft. Hoke hurried on down to help with the cleaning of the fish, as Micah turned to Katharine.

"Miz Fremont, as I said awhile ago...we all will be a-cleanin' the fish, so you'll have some time to yourself. I know it's been hard on you this week. We'll all a-stay on the raft, 'til you're done with your bathin'. You'll be safe from us. I'll see to that, Ma'm."

"Thank you, Mr. MacRae," Katharine said. "Now, where do I go?"

"Just walk on around that bluff there and you'll see a place where there's a lot of sandbars. This is the off season for raftin', so there ain't many rafts out here on the river. In the wintertime, you can just about step from one raft to another, there's so many on the river, but now as you can see, ain't no rafts in sight."

"I shouldn't be long," Katharine said, as she walked away from the raft, carrying the large leather bag with her. She walked along the exposed sand ridge, scattered with tufts of greenish-gray deer moss, and on around the bluff. She paused at the scene before her. Micah was right, she thought. It was a slough unlike any she had seen on the Altamaha or the Ocmulgee. It was a hidden nook with yellow-white sand surrounding a small, shallow pool of water. It was completely separated from the river which flowed a few yards away by a large sandbar. My own outdoor tub, she thought, testing the water, which was cool but not cold. It was early afternoon and the sun's rays were warm.

She lost no time taking off her shoes and stockings which she wore under Frank's old pants. She dug her toes into the warm sand, then sat down near the water, letting it cover her feet.

She rummaged in the leather bag for her soap and washcloth, laying them, along with her towel, on the satchel. She dipped the cloth in the water and rubbed the soap into it, making a lather. She washed her face and hands, then proceeded to her arms and legs, rinsing herself as the bathing progressed.

How strange that she trusted Micah MacRae utterly, that she didn't fear any unwanted attention from the raftsmen. Her parents and friends would never believe that here she sat on a sandbar in a slough off the Altamaha River, washing herself. She found it difficult to believe herself, but here she was, letting the water lave over her feet and legs.

She removed Frank's pants, so they wouldn't get wet and sat in her drawers in the small pool of clear water, as if she were sitting in her claw-foot tub at home. She also removed Frank's shirt, laying it and his pants, folded, on the leather bag, so as not to get them wet. She looked around her. No one, of course, was in sight. She pulled out her derringer and placed it on top of the bag, also, just in case some wild animal came out of the swamp, but everything was peaceful and idyllic, and she basked in the solace of the secluded, sunny area. She felt totally alone, though oddly secure.

She looked at her chemise. She would put on the clean one, along with the clean drawers in the bag. She took off the chemise and stored it in a corner of the large bag.

Rinsing the cloth, she applied more soap and washed her breasts and back. She rinsed the cloth again, then squeezed water over her body, until the suds dripped off into the shallow pool. She washed her lower body also, reaching under the wet drawers. She honestly could not recall when she had ever needed or appreciated a bath more than this one!

Her hair! She dreaded washing it, but knew that it needed it after a week of exposure to smoke from the campfires and the cooking hearth. She unpinned her hair and brushed it, freeing it of tangles. She then washed her brush and comb and shook them in the balmy air to dry them.

Leaning forward, she dipped her hair in the pool, using the soap cake to work up a lather. This she did several times, rinsing the suds in the pool until her hair felt clean. She poured some of the spring water, which she had brought along, over her hair and body.

Now chilled in the September air, she towel-dried her hair, feeling some warmth return from the sun's rays. A certain peace enveloped her as she began brushing her damp, snarled tresses.

She stood up and looked around her, enjoying the solitude and the privacy. She slipped out of the clinging, wet drawers and dried off her lower body. She put on the clean white drawers in the leather bag and reached for the clean chemise.

A soft whistle came from the woods to her left. Another catamount! She froze momentarily, looking toward the tangled swamp. Cautiously, she reached for the derringer, but couldn't find it under the wet clothing which she had inadvertently dropped over the gun. Now frantically trying to put her hands on the weapon, she heard a guttural laugh as a man stepped from the thick swamp to the open sandbar.

"Looks like Miz Fremont is gettin' all prettied up today." The man's coarse twang was terrifying and familiar. As he rapidly approached her, mouthing vulgarities, his jagged facial scar which linked his right ear with the corner of his mouth was red and pulsating.

Horror-struck, she screamed as she crossed her arms in front of her naked bosom, trying in vain to cover herself. The memory of the Klan raid on her property came to her sickeningly, as the man drew nearer. She screamed again, attempting to dislodge the gun from the entangled clothes with her bare foot, still trying to hide her nakedness with her bare hands.

As the Klansman lunged forward to grab her, a gunshot sounded and he was knocked off his feet. Flailing on the ground, he stumbled to his feet and ran haltingly, holding his side, toward the swamp, as another bullet tore through his shoulder. Grunting and howling with pain, he fled into the sanctum of the swamp.

Turning as if in slow motion, Katharine saw Micah MacRae standing, his rifle raised to eye level, at the mouth of the slough.

Embarrassed and still terrified, she groveled for the wet towel and wrapped it around her upper body. When she looked back at the entrance of the slough, the raftsman was gone. She called to him but he didn't answer.

Shaking, she hurriedly pulled on the old pants and shirt. Quickly, tremblingly, she pinned up her damp hair and replaced the floppy brown hat on her head. Seeing the nose of the derringer sticking out from under the wet clothes, she grabbed the gun and pointed it toward the swamp where the scar-faced man had fled.

"You all right, Ma'm?" She jumped at the sound of the raftsman's voice, then turned about quickly to thank him.

Instead, wordlessly, she threw her arms about his neck and they stood there on the yellow sand, locked in each others' embrace. Katharine fought back the tears as she nestled against his hard, unyielding body. Being weak with fright, she felt his great strength and it steadied her. She looked up into his brown eyes and her lips found his. His lips were hot on her mouth and her neck and her throat.

Then, as if a distant bell rang, they both stiffened and pulled away. The backwoodsman was the first to speak.

"I'm sorry, Ma'm. I didn't set out to do that."

Katharine reached up and kissed him again, this time on the cheek.

"I wanted to thank you. That's three times you've saved my life. The man with the scar - he's the one who led the Klan raid on my property. The sheriff said his name is Harold, or 'Crow" Diggs, but what is he doing here in the swamp?"

"Lots of criminals and convicts hide out in the swamp, Ma'm. Either that, or he's been a-followin' our raft, tryin' to get to you." She shivered at the thought.

Micah MacRae continued, "He'll be a-lookin' for a doctor now. He's hurt pretty bad. He's probably got a dugout somewhere nearby, and he's probably wantin' to row himself to a doctor in Darien, but it'll be hard rowin' against the tide. He just might not make it into Darien." He gently took the derringer from her.

"I'm afraid you're a-gonna get hurt with this, Ma'm, you're a-shakin' so." He paused for a moment, then changed the subject.

"You hungry? I guess Luke oughta have dinner near about ready." Though Katharine wasn't especially hungry after the frightening experience, she was glad for some return to normalcy.

"I think I smell fish cooking," she said.

"They are mostly catfish, but that's what you like best."

They walked back to the raft and the Negroes plied Micah with questions about the two gunshots.

"You kill 'nother rattlesnake, Mistuh Micah?" Shep asked as soon as they were within hearing distance.

"He was a snake, all right, but a different kind of snake. He walked on two feet," Micah said, then added, "must be a convict on the loose, a-hidin out in the swamp." The explanation appeased the Negro rafthands, for they asked no further questions.

The late midday meal of fish was appreciated by everyone, though Katharine found she was unable to eat much. Her throat felt constricted when she tried to eat and she knew that the terror which she had felt on the sandbar had not completely subsided. She wondered whether the Klansman had left in his boat, as Micah suggested, or whether he might still be in the area.

The rafthands spent the rest of the day making new pegs for the binders to replace those which had loosened or broken during the trip. The raft must be in good shape for the final drift into the port of Darien on the following day, Micah said.

Katharine sat huddled near the lean-to, dreading what the night might bring. Not much more could happen, she thought. She was ready for the trip to end but now she kept thinking about her timber and the price it would bring. Would "Sly" Siddon be at the Darien wharves when they arrived on the morrow? She determined to maintain her disguise in Frank's old clothes until her timber had been sold.

Micah had made a quick trip to the other lean-to and now sat, sprawled, near the door, looking at something. She moved over near him and realized he was looking at a newspaper. Was he reading it? Strangely, she had never even considered that backwoodsmen read newspapers or kept up with news of the outside world in any way. He noticed her nearness and looked up from the paper.

"Just checkin' timber prices in the *Gazette*."

Well now, that's a smart thing to do, she thought. He was thrusting the paper toward her.

"Look for yourself. This is the *Darien Timber Gazette*. Your timber oughta bring top prices."

Katharine took the paper and looked at the listings of board feet and prices.

"How many board feet are in my raft?" she asked.

"I'd say close to 73,000, Ma'm. This is one of the biggest rafts I ever drifted to Darien. And, of course, you're a-gonna have others like it, so whatever you make today can be multiplied by that many more."

Before Katharine could recover from her surprise that the backwoodsman kept up with the fluctuations of the timber market, she was further astonished when he muttered, almost as an afterthought, that he wanted to look at the timber prices in New York, also, as that was her home town. Of course, the timber prices in New York were, necessarily, much higher, as there was no local timber source for longleaf yellow pine. She felt ashamed that she had constantly underrated the man. He was a budding businessman.

Yes, she thought, she would like to compare the timber prices at Darien with those in New York. She really hadn't even thought about it.

Also, she had just assumed that the timber inspector's word was final. Could it be debated? She would find out. One thing was for sure. He would probably be surprised that a backwoods rafthand kept up with the mercurial timber market. This would be interesting to watch, though she planned to remain as invisible as possible during the inspection.

Katharine had no way of knowing that everyone in the timber business knew that Micah MacRae followed the timber market on a regular basis and that he could haggle and bargain and hold his own with the best of them. He also knew lumber and could usually name his price for the rafts he brought to Darien.

"I didn't realize that you kept up with timber prices, Mr. MacRae," she said.

"I look at 'em pretty regular. I asked Shep to bring me back this paper when he took a raft down last week. I got my issue of *The Southern Lumberman* here, too. Let's see what they're a-payin' for longleaf pine in New York." Katharine watched as he found the New York prices. He seemed satisfied that they were comparable in a relative sort of way with the timber prices at Darien, though he explained that there was really no way the two markets could be strictly compared.

"By the way, Ma'm, I'm plannin' to tie up at the public boom at Darien, if it's all the same to you."

"Well," Katharine said, "where else might we go? I know nothing about the procedure."

"The Dodge family has their own sawmill and booms at Lower Bluff, on down the river."

"No, I think I'd risk being recognized there, rather than the public boom. I'd rather tie up at the public boom, also."

Micah was pleased that they were of one accord in regard to where they were going to tie up. Katharine knew he wanted nothing to do with the Dodge lumber business.

"It's suppertime but we ate the fish so late, I'm thinkin' we can put off eatin' again 'til breakfast in the mornin'."

"That's fine with me," Katharine said. She still felt shaky after her terrible ordeal on the sandbar. She wasn't hungry in spite of the fact that she had eaten very little of the fish Luke had cooked.

The Negroes had a card game going at the end section of the raft. Their lantern vaguely illuminated their silhouettes as night fell.

Micah gathered wood for a fire on the clay hearth. The raft groaned as it bumped repeatedly into the bank.

"Tide's a-comin' in," he said. He jumped to the bank and unknotted the rope, repositioning it higher up the tree.

Katharine sat, unmoving, at the door of her lean-to. She felt stunned and listless, almost lifeless from the events of the afternoon. Her limbs felt heavy and she felt no desire to move or even to talk. She sat staring at the now-crackling flames on the clay hearth, feeling their warmth as the evening coolness set in.

As she sat looking into the fire, listening to the gathering symphony of nighttime swamp sounds and fearing the night, she heard the dulcet, plaintive notes of a harmonica and she knew without even glancing up that it was the big, strong backwoodsman evoking some of the sweetest music she had ever heard. Slowly, as the notes swelled on the night air, her taut body and soul relaxed and she leaned back against her lean-to and closed her eyes. Oh, God, she thought, would any music in heaven be as sweet?

From under her long wet lashes, she stole a look at him. He was only a few feet away from her and she restrained herself from reaching out and touching him.

His large capable hands gently but purposely found the holes of the harmonica to cover, as his pursed mouth alternately blew and sucked in air to create the different tones. She had never heard even a flute played more beautifully. He played a tender old love song and a hymn.

Katharine couldn't remember ever experiencing the tranquillity which she now felt and when he paused between selections, she waited with bated breath for the next one to begin. His ensuing songs, however, brought tears of joyful disbelief, for he played on the mouth instrument the lilting music of Beethoven, which she had taught to his young daughters. So, he had heard the girls play the music which she had taught them!

Lingering over the final notes of *Moonlight Sonata*, the large raftsman looked sideways at Katharine with a half-smile on his face.

"Teacher, how did I do?" he asked teasingly.

"I believe it's the most beautiful solo rendition I've ever heard," she said softly. "I didn't know you played a musical instrument."

"I don't play it much, just when the notion strikes me. I'd hear Carrie and Mary Sue play the music you taught 'em on the piano, then on my raftin' trips, I'd pick it out on the harmonica."

He paused, looking steadily at her. "I saw where you were uptight and I thought some mouth harp playin' might ease you a little."

"You're right," Katharine said, adding, "and it did. I...I feel better, just still a little unnerved, I guess."

She could feel the tide surging under the raft, pulling taut the rope which held it to the water oak on the bank.

"I see what you mean about the tide coming in. It seems to be pushing the raft back upstream," she said.

"Yes, well, the rope oughta hold it secure, but it'd be nigh impossible to drift against the tide. It'll raise the water level here, so ever'thin'll look different in the mornin'. The river'll look wider. We're at Fort Barrington now, or close to it, and it's the first place on the river, goin' down, where the tide is noticed. You'll see the difference in the mornin', Ma'm."

Picking up the lantern, he jumped off the raft to look for lightwood for the lowering fire. Katharine shivered in the near-darkness, longing for his return. She followed his whereabouts by the lamp's glow, watching as he picked up large chunks of wood for the fire. He also found several lightwood knots which he piled on top.

He made a quick return to the raft, where he threw several of the pieces of fat lightwood onto the fire, making it snap and crackle as the flames engulfed them.

Shep had returned for the nightly yarn-swapping, and Katharine was surprised at herself for the eager anticipation with which she awaited the stories. Though some bordered on the absurd, she knew with a certainty that a strong thread of truth ran through all of them. Some of them, however, she knew, were seasoned with the humor, exaggeration, and imagination of whoever might be relating them. She leaned back against the lean-to, wondering what tales would be forthcoming, as Micah sat near her with his back against the other side of the lean-to. Their hands almost touched on the squared log floor of the raft.

Lights flickered through the tangled swamp on the opposite side of the river, producing a ghostly bluish haze which shone sporadically through the blackness of the night. These were the foxfires of the Altamaha Swamp which had brought an uneasiness to many a traveler.

Sprawled near the fire on the clay hearth, the colored rafthand bit off a plug of tobacco, then thought to offer a chew of it to Micah who refused with a shake of his head and a "No, thanks." Katharine remembered the first time she had ever seen Micah MacRae. He was chewing tobacco then, but she hadn't seen him indulge in the messy habit since that day. She wondered why.

Micah cleared his throat, then nodded Shep's way.

"When we tie up at Darien tomorrow, you and the other two are a-gonna be on your own. You know that, don't you?"

"Yassuh."

"I'll pay all three of you. Then, you'll be free to go and do as you like."

"Yassuh. We's prob'ly gonna spend a day or two in Dar'in, Mistuh Micah."

"Well, as I said, that's your business, but I'll give you a word of advice, though you ain't asked for it."

Micah looked intently at the Negro rafthand.

"Just don't go and spend all your money, so you ain't got none to get home on."

"Nawsuh, Ah done learn ma lesson 'bout dat, Mistuh Micah. Ah did dat one time befo' and dat learn me not to do it agin. Ah had to walk all de way back home and lak to died."

Micah showed instant admiration for the Negro.

"I walked back home many a time myself, when I didn't have money for a train ride. A lot of the old-time rafthands walked that distance - must be 200 miles or more - but that was in the 1870s, I guess. Ain't heard tell of nobody lately a-walkin' back home since the railroad came through. 'Course, those that didn't have the money for train fare had to walk. You take the old River Road?"

"Yassuh. Ah jes' folluh it all de way back to Lumbuh City, den jes' folluh de road to Longview. Took me three days to walk back, and it wuz rainin' part ob de time and freezin'. Ah lak to died. Ef a man make it home, dey say he tougher'n a ol' lighterd knot. Guess Ah is dat tough, but Ah doan wanna walk dat road agin. Nawsuh, Ah sho woan be spendin' all mah wages agin dat way. Naw-w-w-suh!"

"Good. Now, another thing...," Micah said to the colored rafthand as he gestured toward the cardplaying raftsmen on the tail section of the raft, "tell your friends not to get too friendly with the crewmen on the big ships. I heard tell of men bein' taken to other countries, away from their homes and families for months at the time."

"Nawsuh, you ain't," Shep said, his mouth hanging open in baffled disbelief.

"It happened to a colored fella I knew. He kept a-hangin' around the big ships loadin' there at Darien and watchin' everthin' goin' on, and a sailor asked 'im if he'd like to go to Holland. Well, the colored fella asked 'im how far away was Holland, and the sailor said, 'a little farther than from Lumber City to Darien.' 'All right,' the colored fella said, 'but when Dock Burch comes down on his raft in the mornin', ask him to tell my wife, Mabel, that I'm goin' to Holland and won't be back for two or three days.' Well, of course, he was gone more like three months," Micah said to the wide-eyed Negro.

"All I'm sayin' is to be careful and look out for the other two. They ain't never been to Darien and you need to look out for 'em."

"Yassuh, ah sho do dat," Shep said, still awe-struck over the possibility of being unknowingly conscripted for ship service for long months away from home. The horrible idea had never occurred to him. He shook his head slowly back and forth, scowling at the very thought of it.

Having dispensed his advice to the naive rafthand, Micah MacRae settled back against the sidepost of the lean-to and asked Shep whether he knew the steamboat captain named Hank Durham.

"Yassuh, Ever'body call 'im 'Hoot, Mistuh Hoot.'" Shep's black eyes glistened in the firelight. "He one mean man. He come up in 'is steamboat awhile back and de waves from de steamboat so strong, dey break up aer raft. He jes' laugh at us and made 'is steamboat go real fas' by us, wid him a-turnin' round and laughin' on down de ribber. Den we had to put our raf' back t'gedduh agin. It took us a whole day to git our raf' back t'gedduh."

"Well, I ain't had nothin' happen between him and me, but I know of a lot of rafthands who've had trouble with 'im just like what you just told. I guess he's about the most hated man on the river."

"Yassuh," the colored rafthand agreed softly. He looked expectantly toward his bossman, waiting to hear the latest news about the despised steamboat captain.

Katharine, too, was listening, intrigued by the river people and occurrences which so greatly impacted the rafthands' lives.

"There was a rafthand from Montgomery County," Micah began. "He rounded a bend in the Oconee River and saw a rope strung cross the river, a-runnin' from the captain's boat on one side of the river to the other side of the river. The rafthand saw that the rope was just high enough to rake the shack off 'is raft, so he yelled to the captain to lower the rope so the raft could drift over. The captain yelled out, 'Lower it yourself.' The cap'n knew that weren't possible and the rafthand told him so. Well, the rafthand told his bowhand to play his oar under the rope, and when he did, the rafthand took his ax and chopped the rope in two.

"Well, the cap'n started a-cussin' and a-threatenin' to kill the rafthands, and he jumped into his bateau that was 'longside his steamboat and had his deckhands paddle over to the raft. The rafthand watched 'em for a little while, then he walked over to the goat-shack and just stood there with his back to the captain and his paddlers. When he turned to face 'em again, he was a-holdin' a twelve-gauge shotgun. When the cap'n saw the gun, he looked like he was struck dumb, and the deckhands just about turned over the bateau a-paddlin' in the other direction."

"Good 'nuff, dat sho good 'nuff," Shep exclaimed, grinning and chuckling out loud. Katharine, too, was smiling at the antics of the Montgomery County raftsmen. Obviously, the overbearing Hoot Durham had finally met his match on the river.

"Speakin' of steamboats," Micah continued, "sometimes the inspectors at Darien will come up the Altamaha in steamboats to meet the rafts. Seems they get a fee for every thousand feet of timber they measure and grade. They don't do it much now, this time of the year, because there ain't many rafts on the river, it bein' the off season."

Katharine was upset when she heard this. What if Sly Siddon met her raft? It would make him jealous and furious to see her on her own raft. Then, if he should be the one to inspect her timber, he might not give it the grade it deserved. She would have to tell Micah MacRae about Sly Siddon and his intentions toward her. She must not even wait until the morning to tell him, as the inspector could possibly arrive by steamboat at her raft. If such occurred, she thought, devising a plan of action, she would have to hide in the lean-to. She wondered whether the inspectors ever boarded the incoming rafts. It would be a ticklish situation. She did not look forward to seeing the overbearing Sly Siddon. She could only hope and pray that he would not inspect her trees. Yes, she had to talk with Micah about everything, and the sooner, the better!

Shep had spit his mouthful of tobacco juice unerringly over the side of the raft and he was now in the process of cutting another plug of tobacco. Placing it in his jaw, he sensed that another evening of tall tales had come to an end, for his bossman was rising to put more wood on the fire.

"Better get some sleep," Micah said, throwing some fat lightwood on the fire and watching its flames leap skyward. Shep ambled toward his fellow raftsmen on the stern section of the raft, shaking his legs in their ragged pants to free them from what he termed his "charley hawses."

Katharine seized the opportunity to relate to Micah the harassment she had endured from Sly Siddon and her fears about his inspection of her timber.

"Mr. MacRae, could we talk for a few minutes?"

"Sure thing, Ma'm. What's there to talk about?" The backwoodsman stoked the fire on the clay hearth, then dropped down beside her.

Katharine hesitated, looking at the handsome face so near hers, the week's growth of beard not at all detracting from it. Again, she felt the iron strength that emanated from him. His eyes caressed her and she yearned to reach out and touch him. They were both alone and they were lonely but each knew the boundaries which existed between them and each knew the penalties for violating those boundaries. After this trip was over, she fully intended to go back home to New York. Likely, she would never even see him again. She certainly would not act on her feelings of the moment. She would feel quite differently, once she was back home. Then, this frightening raft trip and its bow oarsman would be but fading memories.

"Mr. MacRae," she said, "if by any chance the inspector of my timber is Mr. Siddon, well...I think I need to tell you a few things."

"I'm listenin'," the backwoodsman said, often sparing with words.

"I'm afraid my timber won't get a very high rating if Mr. Siddon inspects it," Katharine said.

"You have to watch all the inspectors, Ma'm. Sometimes, I think the sawmills give 'em somethin' on the side to make the prices low."

"I don't know anything about that," she said, mentally adding this bit of information to her list of worries about her timber. "No," she said, "I'm talking about something personal. You see, Mr. Siddon has asked me to marry him and even threatened to lower the price of my timber, if I refused him." Katharine was somewhat embarrassed to be relating her personal ordeal, and she kept her eyes lowered as she talked.

Hesitating, she waited with her eyes averted for the backwoodsman to say something. Noticing his silence, she quickly glanced at him and found him gazing at her with a look that she could not fathom.

"You didn't tell me much I didn't already know, Ma'm," he said quietly. "There won't be more'n a few inspectors at the booms in Darien this time of the year, because it's the off season for raftin'. More'n apt, if he's workin', then he'll inspect your trees but I don't think we'll have a problem."

"Another thing I want to talk to you about..." Katharine hesitated as the raftsman's level gaze caused her some distraction.

"I...one of the reasons I wore these old clothes of my

husband's..." Katharine paused again, as the raftsman's dark eyes traveled over her figure.

"I didn't want anyone, especially Mr. Siddon, to recognize me. I want to leave the raft without his seeing me when we reach Darien. However, a few minutes ago, I heard you say that sometimes the inspectors will come up the river to meet the rafts. I don't know what I'll do if Mr. Siddon should happen to meet my raft. He'd be furious if he saw me on the raft, making the trip with four men. Actually, my friends and family would be shocked at this imprudence on my part, also, Mr. MacRae." Katharine returned the raftsman's steady gaze. Then, she noted a smile tugging at the corners of his mouth.

"It was surprisin' to me, too, that you'd make the trip, Ma'm. A woman like you a-puttin' up with all you had to put up with. I know it ain't a-been easy. But don't worry about your timber. It's some of the finest I've seen. Old man Dodge and his sons sure knew how to pick the best timber for them and their friends."

Something about the confident air of the raftsman eased her worries and she purposely overlooked his reference to the Dodges. Once again, the thought of Sly Siddon coming to meet her raft worried her.

"Do you think Mr. Siddon might actually come in a steamboat to meet my raft?"

"If it was the raftin' season in the wintertime, he might, Ma'm, but he ain't gonna come, bein' it's the off season." Again, she observed the man's quiet confidence and her worries ceased.

"Better get some sleep, Ma'm. Mornin' comes early." The backwoodsman picked up a lantern and lit it with a burning stick from the hearth fire. Jumping off the raft, he called back to her that he was going to look for some lightwood for the hearth fire. He also said something about the tide coming in and that they'd all better sleep on the raft.

Sighing, Katharine lit her lantern and crawled into her lean-to. As she reached for the leather bag which held her blanket and pillow, she for the first time realized that the other satchel was gone!

She had left it on the sandbar! She panicked, realizing that it held her money as well as her traveling clothes for the train trip back home. How could she have forgotten it? She was undecided about what to do.

Micah MacRae had returned with a large armload of fat lightwood which he dropped near the hearth fire. He added several pieces of wood to the fire, making the flames leap higher against the black night sky.

Katharine decided not to worry the raftsman further with her problems. He had rescued her several times already from disastrous situations and she did not want to trouble him anymore with her difficulties. She would get the bag in the morning and unless the tide had covered it, everything should be as she left it. She was embarrassed even to mention it to the backwoodsman.

"Goodnight, Ma'm," the subject of her thoughts said. He had spread his old quilt and lumpy pillow near the fire. He lay down with his arms under his head and one knee raised, looking upward at the stars.

"Goodnight," Katharine answered back with a sigh that he heard.

"You all right, Ma'm?" he asked, looking toward her as she unfolded her blanket in the lean-to.

"I'm fine," she said and involuntarily sighed again as she crawled between the folds of her blanket. The log raft was especially hard and unyielding as she pulled the edges of the blanket around her.

Remembering that she hadn't placed anything in the doorway of her lean-to, which had been her practice since the episode with the catamount, she reached for the satchel and stashed it in the opening of the lean-to. In doing so, she met the eyes of the backwoodsman who now lay on his side, facing her, his elbow raising the upper half of his body. Their eyes locked and Katharine felt a warmth coursing through her body. How easy and momentarily gratifying it would be to invite him into the lean-to. In her situation, what woman wouldn't?

Realizing that he wouldn't be the one to look away, Katharine knew it was up to her. She lowered her eyes and lay back on her pillow. She sighed again, praying that he did not hear her, because she knew that her resistance to him was becoming more difficult to maintain. Lord help me, she prayed, for this man-woman thing was too strong for her to handle!

Again, as she lay on the hard raft, she wondered what he had done since his wife's death, when such needs became more and more insistent. She knew there were brothels and women to be had in Darien. Also, she remembered the women at his church who were plain-spoken about their interest in him.

Katharine knew that the Negroes' presence on the raft had been a major deterrent to any intimacy between the backwoodsman and herself and for that she was thankful. She had never experienced such a strong attraction toward any man in her life. Only God knew how she had had to struggle against it.

Not realizing the degree of her weariness, she closed her eyes, listening to the cracking and popping of the fire, mingled with the whoo-whooing of owls and the croaking of frogs. Now added to these swamp sounds of the night was the regular, heavy breathing of the backwoodsman who lay asleep in the moonlight. She finally closed her eyes and she, too, slept.

Chapter Twenty-two

With the first rosy streaks of dawn came the ebullient river hollers. Katharine first heard them from a mile or more up the river, then again as the men aboard the upstream raft neared her own. Micah and Shep let loose with responding hollers that effectively jarred her awake. She sat up and looked over the top of her satchel in the doorway of her lean-to and spotted the small raft descending upon them. They were close enough now that the men could talk back and forth.

"It's rainin' north of here," one of them said. "Freshet'll be down here by tomorrow mornin'. We done talked to the steamboat captain. He prob'ly passed by here durin' the night."

"We gonna be outa here in a little while," Micah said. "The tide'll pull us on in to Darien."

"It's a-pullin' now. Hope there's enough water so we don't get stuck on Couper's Bar."

Micah MacRae spoke up. "You can take that tadpole through Rifle Cut. Mine's too big, but yours oughta drift through just fine, and you'll miss Couper's Bar."

"How ya get to Rifle Cut from here?" yelled the colored raftsman as the strong tide pulled his raft on down the river.

"Turn left to Stud Horse," Micah hollered, "and go around Lewis Island. You'll see Rifle Cut to the left, this side of Vivians Island. It'll take you on in to Darien."

The raftsmen took off their shuck caps and acknowledged the directions by waving them over their heads. They were soon out of sight.

Katharine crawled out of the lean-to and spoke to Luke who was flipping battercakes over the hearth fire. Micah, hands on hips, turned around to face her.

"Well, Ma'm, hope your sleepin' was good."

"Yes, I slept well," Katharine said as she walked toward the side of the raft. She could tell that the tide coming in the night before had raised the water level over the sandbar where she had walked the day before. She knew it was too late to worry about the satchel with her money and travel clothes in it. It was probably at the bottom of the river somewhere. Oh well, she could wear her dirty clothes one more day, and she would be getting paid for her timber sometime during the day, so she just refused to worry about the leather bag.

She also thought about the fact that she hadn't seen anything resembling the flowering tree called the "Franklinia alatamaha." It had ebbed in importance since the terrifying encounter with the Klansman. She had no desire to go traipsing off into the swamp beyond the boggy bank to look for it!

For some reason, she remembered the words of *The Deserted Village* which spoke of the dangers of the Altamaha. She remembered reading them out loud to Micah and laughing about Goldsmith's descriptive language, but hadn't she met with all three of the major ones, including the "vengeful snake," the "crouching tiger," and the "savage man"? She turned around to find Micah MacRae looking at her curiously.

"You all right, Ma'm?"

"Yes, I'm fine. I'm just going to leave the raft for a few minutes. I won't be gone long." As she stepped off the raft, with the backwoodsman lending a helping hand, she wondered why her private journeys into the woods were always well documented by the others on the raft, whereas they managed to keep their own trips unnoticed by her.

"Watch out for snakes!" Micah called to her as she walked into the woods and stood behind a large oak tree which shielded her from those on the raft. It had sprinkled rain during the night and the leaves and bushes were still laden with moisture. A large spider web in the vicinity of her outdoor water closet caught her eye and she walked over closer to examine its intricacies. Its dew-pearled web glistened in the faint, early-morning sun. A slight breeze puffed it toward her, so that its fine gossamer threads were shown in their exquisite patterns. The breeze gently blew its dewdrops until some fell, one by one. The thought came to her that she alone had seen its beauty and she felt strangely uplifted that she had been chosen to witness it.

Straightening her dirty, wrinkled clothes as best she could, she trudged back to the raft. She knew that they were waiting for her, but she was past being embarrassed by having the four raftsmen know about her private moments. Such was life and she had no apologies for it.

Hoke began unhitching the raft rope as Micah helped her back on the raft. As Hoke jumped back onboard, the two oarsmen assumed their positions at both ends of the long raft.

"Bo-o-o-ow to the Injun!" Micah called out, and both oarsmen walked their oars toward the "Indian" side of the river, until the raft was in the main channel of the river and the tide was pulling it toward the sea.

Luke handed Katharine a tin plate of battercakes and a cup of steaming coffee before moving toward the other Negro raftsmen at the stern section of the raft. She sank to the floor of the raft and ate her breakfast, relishing the idea that the raft trip would be over in only a few hours. She felt like shrieking her happiness to the world!

"What the...? What is that?" Micah's voice was quizzical, unbelieving.

Katharine stood and looked where the backwoodsman was pointing and saw her corset floating along beside the raft. The bosom of it was standing above the water as if it were already filled. Its unbreakable French wire and steel supports were visible, now that the satin material was water-soaked.

Katharine wanted to laugh and cry at the same time. Now, she knew what had happened to the contents of the leather satchel! She looked farther across the river and saw her tan jacket with its large sailor collar drifting along with the tide, followed by her tucked white blouse and tan skirt. Her flat sailor hat with its feathers, ribbon, and plumes looked bird-like as it floated on farther down the river.

Blushing a deep pink, she looked at the bow oarsman. He was looking from the clothes back to her as if expecting an explanation.

"I'm afraid they're mine, Mr. MacRae. You see, I left my satchel on the sandbar yesterday after I was so frightened, and I forgot about it until last night, when I realized my other bag wasn't in the lean-to. It was dark and I was afraid to go back to get it. Actually, I thought it might possibly still be there this morning, until I saw how the water had risen during the night."

"Ma'm, I'd been glad to get it for you, if you'd just told me."

"I've been enough trouble already. I didn't want to worry you anymore."

Micah picked up a pike-pole. "I can lift 'em off the water with this pole, if you want me to."

"No," she said, "thanks, but I don't want them now. However, I had some money in that bag, also. If it comes floating by, I'd surely like to have it back."

Micah scoured the river with his eyes but confessed he didn't see anything resembling greenbacks. His mouth kept twitching, and Katharine knew he was struggling to keep from laughing.

A large black crow alit on her sailor hat. Cocking its shiny black head, it eyed the feathers and other adornments as if trying to determine the specie of the odd-looking creature. Pecking and pulling at the white ribbon, it dislodged it and held it trailing in its beak, as it flew away.

Micah laughed out loud at the antics of the crow and Katharine found herself laughing, too. She threw out her hands toward her ruined clothes and smiled ruefully.

"It's better to laugh, I guess, than cry," she said in a soft voice. "I'll just have to wear these same clothes when we ride the train back home." She looked toward the Negroes at the far end of her raft. They were all in a huddle, talking about something else, and none appeared to notice her garments floating on the river surface. She was spared further embarrassment!

The early fall foliage of the lower Altamaha River was a study in changing colors and textures. The supple green willow trees of the summer were now drooping thin limbs of red and orange. The sourwood bushes had clusters of brown sweet gum balls which hung down over the riverbanks along with the brown beans of catalpa trees. Pinnacled goldenrod with its clusters of wand-like flowers fluttered among the river leafery. The hemp-like sisal plant, used to make rope and twine, grew near the water's edge, while wild persimmon trees laden with fruit flourished in the forest's dim recesses.

Fiddler crabs clawed up the sides of the deep mud banks in squirming masses around the greyish-green cypress knees. Some of the more inland cypress trees appeared to be over a hundred feet tall, as tall as some longleaf pine trees. Dragonflies and migrating swallowtail butterflies, also known as sulfur butterflies, added their beauty to the unfolding panorama.

Blue kingfishers, with their white collars and blue crests, made whirring noises as they dived toward the water to snare their fish meals. Wood ducks alternately flew to their nests in the nearby woods and paddled near the shore. White egrets stood on thin stilted legs in the shallow tidal pools.

Deciduous oak and pecan trees, draped with filamentous Spanish moss, had evergreen clusters of mistletoe in the crooks of their topmost branches. Large aeries of the bald eagle, the red-tailed hawk, and the golden eagle filled the top notches of the dead cypresses, crafted by their feathered denizens with the skilled use of twigs and leaves.

Pulled seaward by the strong, outgoing tide, the raft drifted past Clark's Bluff and a place called, simply, Clay Hole on the "Indian" side of the river. Entering the maze of islands which formed the delta of the Altamaha River, the raft glided alongside the delta rice islands of Cambers and Butlers, its vigilant oarsmen steering it on the usual watery path to Darien. The complex labyrinths of land and water had often brought delay and even peril to those raftsmen who did not know the islands and creeks, and sucks and cuts, that comprised the Altamaha Delta.

Looking toward the East as the sun began its daily journey just above the marshy horizon, Katharine's eyes momentarily dropped to the undulant river water beyond the bow of the raft. What appeared to be little sprites jumping together just above the surface of the water caused her to look again. Micah's low voice explained the apparition.

"You see the water fairies? Must be a million of 'em today a-dancin' on the water."

Katharine shook her head in disbelief and smiled.

"Yes, I see something," she said, but when she looked again, the sprites were gone, having ended their delta dance. This, she assumed, was another legend of the "Jolly God Altamaha," as she had heard the mighty river referred to, mainly because its antics of careening freshets and sluggish droughts simulated the erratic behavior of a reeling drunk. The river certainly had a celebrated life of its own!

Katharine was excited about the close proximity of Darien. She looked up and saw a lone seagull swooping high above the raft, reminding her that the ocean was not far away. The landscape had dramatically changed from tall pine and liana-entwined swamp to rice-cultivated islands. Raucous crows swooped down to the raft, pecking at crumbs of food and noisily defending their turf from others which hovered over the raft, their harsh caws an early, brash welcome to the Altamaha Delta.

The almost treeless rice islands were in stark contrast to the upriver swamps of the Altamaha. Here, the land was boggy and flat. The islands under rice cultivation were laid out in great squares, separated by ditches for irrigating. Orange and pomegranate trees flourished on the banks, their limbs sagging from the weight of the succulent fruit.

Yellow and black bobolinks, called rice birds, now joined the crows which scavenged the rice islands, constantly circling the grain as it was being harvested and often gliding downward for their share of the rice pickings. These small marauders could strip a field of sprouted rice and destroy it completely, as they headed north in May, or do the same in August and September as they returned to South America. Bird-minders, former slaves, armed with guns and clappers, shot into the air, clapped boards together, and built fires on the banks to repel the birds from destroying the rice crop.

Micah explained to Katharine that the rice birds were good to eat and were hunted by the local people during the rice season. He himself had enjoyed some at eating establishments in Darien and could vouch for their tastiness.

"Bo-o-o-ow White!" Micah called back to Shep, and the men pulled their oars to the left, guiding the long raft over the treacherous Couper's Bar which separated Vivians and Butlers islands. Another raft ahead appeared to be broken up, its two rafthands busy reassembling it. They wearily acknowledged Katharine's raft as it approached them.

"Had to take our raft apart - got stuck on the sandbar yesterday. Then, we got up this mornin' and the water's up three feet at least, and it ain't rained none," one of the raftsmen groaned.

"This your first trip?" Micah inquired.

"Yassuh."

"Tide comes in about every twelve hours. It'll raise the water level eight or nine feet up to Fort Barrington, but only around three feet here on the sandbar. That's the three feet of water you're talkin' about. If you ever get stuck again, just wait it out and the next day, when the tide comes in, you can go again. No need to take your raft apart."

The raftsmen looked exasperated at their own ignorance and thanked Micah for telling them about the tide. They didn't know to ask and no one had bothered to tell them, before, that the sandbar would be flooded with water on the following day, enough to lift up their raft so they could float on over the bar. They had wasted a whole day, breaking the raft apart, so as to drift each log separately to deeper water.

After Katharine's raft drifted out of the beleaguered raftsmen's hearing range, the two first-time Negro rafthands burst into laughter at the plight of the stranded raftsmen. It never dawned on Luke and Hoke that they would probably have been in the same predicament if they had taken a raft down to Darien alone, without the experienced rafthands onboard who knew the hazards and caprices of the chameleonic Altamaha River. With more than a degree of self-satisfaction, the fledgling raftsmen found much mirth in the green, country rafthands who didn't know about the changing tides in the river delta.

Colored freedmen, women, and children were harvesting the golden rice on Butlers Island which had first been banked and cleared for rice cultivation early in the century. For then slave labor, working with hand tools, it had been an awesome undertaking.

Standing in knee-deep water and singing to the rhythmic cadence of the rice hooks which they swung to cut the rice, the men wore old brown jean britches which were rolled to their knees. The women had cords around their waists which, to some degree, held their dingy dresses above the water. Some wore drab kerchiefs on their heads. Small children held to their mother's knees or clung to their backs.

During the times of slavery, before the War, drivers with whips kept the slaves constantly working. Though the lot of the Negro had improved somewhat with his status as freedman, he still contended with the same pestilences of disease, mosquitoes, sandgnats, alligators, and poisonous snakes during the laborious rice culture.

In fact, Micah informed Katharine, the rice business was slowly dying because it was more and more difficult to get Negroes to work in the disease-filled rice fields. Standing ankle deep in mud, ditching, drawing, weeding, or turning over wet ground, the workers were susceptible to constant exposure to dampness from working in wet fields. Though some of the Negroes were immune to malaria, the bane of the white man, because the Negroes' blood contained the sickle cell, they, however, readily succumbed to the disease-inducing, boggy rice fields, being especially vulnerable to pulmonary sicknesses. White plantation owners fled the rice fields during the summer months because of the fear of contracting malaria.

Visible on Butlers Island were the rice mills consisting of three threshing mills, an overseer's house, slave cabins now occupied by freedmen and their families, blacksmith's and cooper's shops. The tall, obelisk-shaped rice chimney on the far end of the island was a reminder of the days of plentiful rice harvests which produced the coastal aristocracy of the Old South. Katharine was horribly fascinated by the island and the idea that slaves were imported from Africa to work and die in the unhealthy rice bogs. Micah further told her that sometimes Negroes wouldn't last a week in the rice bogs before becoming deathly sick.

Floodgates affixed to wood culverts, called trunks, were strategically placed in the high banks, allowing water to flood or drain the areas as needed. Rice cultivation required four irrigations during the growing period, each followed by drainages of the squared fields, bordered by ditches and canals. Dikes surrounded the fields to protect them from the usual rising of the tide.

"About twenty-five years ago," Micah said softly, "a man named Pierce Butler owned this island and he had slaves workin' it 'til the war freed 'em. Then, most of 'em came back to work as freed men. One of 'em was a colored man named Liverpool Hazzard. When Mr. Butler was a-dyin' of the country sickness, what we call malaria now, this young Liverpool Hazzard, about sixteen years old, rowed 'im from Butlers Island to Darien to see Dr. Holmes. Nothin' could save 'im, though. He died, and I believe Dr. Holmes died in the early 1880s. Anyway, Liverpool rides around Darien now in his oxcart with 'is ox a-pullin' 'im. He's usually there around the log ponds. You'll prob'ly see 'im."

"Liverpool...that's an English name. It will be interesting to see him."

"Another thing about 'im...durin' the war, he was a cook for a company of Confederate soldiers. One of the things he tells about the war was the time he and some of the Rebs hid the horses in the swamp, so the Federal troops wouldn't find 'em. They held their hands over the horses' mouths, so the Yankees wouldn't hear 'em."

Katharine had heard of the Butlers and the coastal rice plantations. The older Pierce Butler had been one of the signers from South Carolina of the United States Constitution. He also had authored the Fugitive Slave Law which was incorporated into that document with little change from his original resolution.

The war had devastated the rice culture, freeing the slaves on whose shoulders rested the backbreaking toil which the crop demanded. Now, these slaves' descendants labored as freed men, still planting and harvesting the golden rice for the younger daughter, Frances Butler Leigh, presently a woman of middle age, who divided her time between homes in England and the Georgia coast.

Frances, or Fanny Kemble Butler, divorced wife of the younger Pierce Butler and mother of Frances B. Leigh, was a brilliant English actress who gave up her career to settle on Butlers Island with her husband. However, her condemnation of slavery, upon which the rice industry was forced to rely, and her husband's infidelities were such that they broke up her marriage, and she returned to England, being estranged also from her two children. Katharine remembered reading about Fanny Kemble in her old age.

She had dropped the Butler surname following the bitter divorce. She, Fannie Kemble, was trying to persuade a visiting friend not to leave her, saying, "No, do not go yet. I am old and lonely and never again will you have these chances to talk with a woman who has sat at dinner alongside of Byron, who has heard Tom Moore sing, and who calls Tennyson, Alfred."

Mother and younger daughter had written journals about life on a Georgia rice plantation, especially expressing their opinions on slavery, the mother adamantly opposing it, the daughter almost as adamantly upholding it. Katharine had read both of the works during one of her trips to London before her marriage, and she found it beguiling that she was actually viewing the island where the storms of marital troubles and civil war and even the rice culture itself had been weathered. Now, only the rice culture remained and it was slowly dying. Within only a few years it, too, would probably be a thing of the past, a few pages in the cloistered books of history.

On Vivians Island, directly across the Butler River from Butlers Island, a Negro baptism was taking place. Robed in white, the families and friends of those being baptized stood on the boggy shore, witnessing the baptisms of their loved ones. As the Negro preacher, dressed in his dark, Sunday-best suit, laid a parishioner back in the gray-brown river water in the Christian rite of baptism, those onshore rhythmically swayed and sang, "Swing low, sweet chariot, comin' for to carry me home...." After the first church member came up out of the water, others followed, until the five candidates for the day's baptism were duly submerged and their sins swept out to sea by the outgoing tide.

As their raft drifted on by, the large backwoodsman in a low whisper explained this lore to Katharine. An ebb tide, they believed, would wash their sins out to sea, never to return, whereas a flood tide would carry their sins back up the river, only to come back to them when the tide ebbed again.

The Hilton cypress booms were visible ahead on the Butler River. The huge cypress trees were a thousand years old. Katharine learned these facts from the knowledgeable backwoodsman who never ceased to amaze her.

The raft floated on past Generals Island which had already been harvested of its rice. Katharine remembered reading in the

Gazette that a Darien rice planter by the name of John Legare had shipped 500 bushels of new rice only a few days prior to Savannah. It was the first rice shipment of the season and was the first in the Savannah market. Shiny black crows and rice birds were still feasting on the chaff that was left after completion of the harvest, pulling at the cast-aside hulls in an attempt to dislodge any remaining grains of rice.

As the raft approached the convergence of the Darien River, the realization of the importance of the little town of Darien to the world market was suddenly obvious to Katharine when she saw the tall timber schooners with pointed sails, the square-rigged barks, and the steamships at anchor along the various wharves and booms of Cathead Creek, to the left, which fed into the Darien River. These were the public booms which ran from Cathead Creek, on the west of the town, to the Darien River and on beyond the town of Darien. Several rafts were already tied to the pilings.

Micah commented to Katharine that during the regular rafting season, usually from late October through the early spring months, one could walk from raft to raft for several miles along the wharves of Cathead Creek and the Darien River. In fact, he added, during the winter months, rafts would be lined up and touching one another all the way from Cathead Creek to Rifle Cut, a distance of several miles.

As Micah and Shep guided the large raft into the Darien River, Micah suggested to Katharine that she should sit inside the lean-to, as they were entering some rough water. There was always a strong crosscurrent where Cathead Creek entered the Darien River, and sometimes rafts were difficult to manage because of it.

Katharine did as he suggested and crawled into the lean-to. The raft began to shudder and shake as its oarsmen attempted to guide it into Cathead Creek. Micah and Shep burst forth with lusty river hollers, trying to get the attention of someone at the public boom.

Only a few men were working the booms since it was the off season. As they saw the large raft approaching the booms, they hollered back to the raftsmen, motioning to the pilings where they should tie up for inspection.

Sitting in the lean-to and watching the oarsmen's expert handling of her raft, Katharine could hardly believe that she had made the torturous trip and that she was about to receive money for her first raft of timber. Also, the city of Darien was now only a few steps away!

However, she had to elude Sly Siddon some way. She wondered whether Micah could recognize him, if he were at the wharf. She whispered loudly to her bow oarsman.

"Mr. MacRae, do you see Mr. Siddon, the timber inspector?"

"No, Ma'm, he ain't come down from 'is office yet," the raftsman said in a bemused tone of conspiracy.

He continued, "I been thinkin', Ma'm, if you're a-wantin' to stay hid, best way is just to stay in the lean-to. Put your leather bag in the front of it, and I'll give you a croker sack to put on top of it." He momentarily turned loose the bow oar and grabbed the croker sack from the other lean-to, then handed it to Katharine. Katharine placed it on top of her leather bag as he had suggested, then huddled inside the small shed, wondering with some trepidation what was about to occur.

"There he is, Ma'm. Your timber inspector. He's a-comin' to the log pond to meet us." The backwoodsman whispered this to Katharine before yelling back to Shep to bow to the "Injun" side. The oarsmen skillfully played their oars against the side of the bank, as the raft groaned to its final berth.

Katharine heard Micah tell Luke to "step to it" and bring the other raftsmen to him. As they huddled together, she knew he was apprising them of her whereabouts and not to let the inspector suspect anything. Though the Negroes did not understand the necessity of Mrs. Fremont's secreting herself in the small lean-to, they had enough loyalty for her and the bow oarsman and sufficient distaste for the arrogant timber inspector to act as accomplices in the matter.

Katharine found a hole in the lean-to and peered through it. Sly Siddon was, as usual, dressed in the height of fashion as he gingerly moved his corpulent bulk toward the wharf and the docking raft. His long-sleeved white shirt with the Prince Albert wing collar was held in check by the double-breasted, gray cloth waistcoat and Ascot puff tie at his throat. His below-knee pants met high socks that issued from black shoes with gaiters of white linen. On his head was a gray straw boater with white silk band, which he failingly attempted to place at a jaunty angle on his glabrous head. A burly Negro log-turner followed him.

Unbeknownst to him in his self-perceived grandeur was the object of his affections on the incoming raft, suppressing laughter at her own preposterous situation in the cramped lean-to, now abetted by the comical appearance of the foppish, bandy-legged, timber inspector who withdrew a white handkerchief from his hip pocket and mopped his face and hands, all the while jabbing with a thick forefinger toward the piling where the raftsmen were to tie up for his inspection.

As Hoke jumped off at the piling to secure the raft, the inspector jammed his handkerchief back in his pocket and, holding on to the piling, managed to work his way down the high bluff, huffing and puffing and finally boarding the raft. He gave Micah a brief nod and ignored the Negroes. The colored log-turner jumped easily from the bluff to the raft below.

"Well, now, you've got a big one today, especially for it to be the off season. I know whose it is and I've been expecting it. I've seen these trees growing, walked all over the acreage. It's got knotholes, and 'shakes, if I remember correctly. That'll certainly decrease the value of it."

"Don't think you remember correctly, Inspector," the backwoodsman drawled.

"What?" The florid face of the timber inspector deepened in color. His loose mouth hanging and anger building in his narrow eyes, he stared at the uppish raftsman and, for the first time, acknowledged with a squinted glance the colored raftsmen's presence.

"What?" He repeated. "What did I hear you say?"

In a slow, even voice, Micah repeated, "I said I don't think you remember correctly, because these trees are among the finest in Telfair County, selected by Mr. William E. Dodge as bein' the best his money could buy. Surely, Inspector, you would agree that Mr. Dodge would have only the best."

Sewell Siddon hadn't considered the far-reaching impact of his inspection of Katharine's timber. In his hurry to make her capitulate to his open, sexual advances, he hadn't thought of the close relationship between Katharine and the Dodge family and the fact that he would, in essence, be devaluing what the Dodges deemed the ultimate in timber.

However, he thought quickly, her timber would probably be bought by the Dodge company there at Darien and he would be doing them a favor by giving it a low rating. But then, his mind hurried on, the Dodge business couldn't hope to sell it for much without a better rating. He stalled for time, mopping his brow in the warm September sunshine. His attitude toward Micah MacRae was patronizing.

"I'm going to walk over the raft and look at the logs," he said, as Micah walked along with him and the log-turner rolled the inside logs for his inspection. Katharine listened and looked through the slit provided over the top of the croker sack.

"That's a plugged knothole," the flustered inspector said, pointing toward a knothole on one of the logs. Micah whetted the hole gently with the tip of his knife, cutting into the rich yellow pine.

"Your eyes are foolin' you, Inspector," he said, not letting on that he knew who was trying to fool whom. "Ain't nuthin' but pine wood. No line of a peg."

The inspector moved on to the second and third sections of the raft.

"Looks like a catface over there," he said, gesturing to a dark spot in the grain of the timber.

"They mighta burned the wiregrass every year, Inspector - we all do that for better grass for the cattle - but you know as well as I do, these trees ain't been hurt. That ain't no catface - just a darker brown in the wood."

The timber inspector looked scathingly at the rugged raftsman. He was uncomfortable with a rafthand who could hold his own against his intimidation.

"As I recall, some of Mrs. Fremont's trees had wind shakes. Might not be any on this raft, but those on her east tracts had some."

"Inspector, I've cruised all of her trees, and I ain't seen even one with 'shakes. As I said before, Mr. Dodge claimed these trees for his own, before sellin' to the Fremonts, and we both know that he knew 'is lumber."

Again, the inspector paled at mention of the powerful Dodge name. To save face, he ignored the raftsman and began placing his tape to measure the raft. The backwoodsman watched carefully as the inspector recorded the sizes in his notebook.

"That ain't what the tape measured, Inspector," Micah said, hands on hips, looking over the inspector's shoulder at the notebook.

"Oh, and how's that?" Sewell Siddon said, belligerently, his eyes narrowing to thin slits as he glared at Micah.

"I saw the readin', myself, on the tape. It was 180 feet. Looks like you put a zero where the eight oughta be. You're eighty feet off. I'd like to see you a-measure it again."

"What's it to you, what it measures? You're getting paid the same, aren't you, whether it's 100 feet or 180 feet?"

"Eighty feet times the width of the raft is a lotta wood, aside from the depth of the logs, but even if it ain't but a foot difference, I want the right measurement, Inspector."

The portly inspector glowered at the raftsman but entered the correct measurements in his notebook. He then called to one of the workmen on the bank to hand him a dip rod. After securing this, he proceeded to dip the rod into the water to measure the size of the logs. With the Telfair County oarsman watching his every move, the hostile inspector duly recorded the correct measurements of the logs.

Katharine sat breathlessly awaiting the outcome of the timber inspection. She was thankful for Micah MacRae's insistence on true measurements of her timber, and she was pleased to the point of admiration with the way he comported himself in dealing with the overbearing and corrupt timber inspector.

Though somewhat cramped in the small lean-to, she was thankful to be hidden from the vengeful eyes of Sly Siddon. He would never cease telling everyone of her making the raft trip alone with four men, and three of them coloreds, at that. No, because she had refused his advances, he would besmirch her character to anyone who would listen. He wasn't a much better man than the Klansman who had brought her such terror, she thought.

The inspector, appearing to be in a hurry now that his dishonest attempts to reduce the rating of Katharine's timber had come to naught, gave the inspection sheet to Micah MacRae, then without any further comment, grasped the nearest piling and heaved himself back over to the bank. He was mopping his face again as he and his log-turner proceeded to another raft which was drifting on the Darien River near the public booms.

Micah reached into his jeans pocket and pulled out a wad of bills to pay the waiting raftsmen. He counted out each man's wages and gave them their money.

"Shep, you remember what I told you, 'bout lookin' out for these two," Micah said, his hand on Luke's shoulder.

"Yassuh, Ah remembuhs," Shep said. He was busy in their lean-to, pulling out the rope and cooking utensils, the ax, and the auger. He gave the rope and skillet and coffee pot to Luke to carry, showing him how to suspend the cooking utensils from his belt, then handed the heavy maul, used to drive pegs in raft construction, to Hoke to carry. Shep himself carried the lighter ax and auger. The pint-sized Hoke looked miserable as he stepped off the raft, lugging the thirty-pound maul.

As the Negroes made their way to the streets and saloons of Darien, Katharine thought how unfair it was for the smallest one to carry the heavy maul. Seeing her questioning look, Micah told her of yet another rafthand custom.

"He won't carry it all the way home, Ma'm."

"What?"

"The maul. No, Ma'm, Luke's in on the joke with Shep. We throw away the mauls when we get to Darien, but Hoke don't know that. They'll make 'im carry it for awhile up the bluff and down the streets of Darien, 'til he's just about wore out, because it's heavy. Then, they'll tell 'im he ain't got to carry it no more and they'll get rid of it. It's easier for us to make a new one, the next time we take a raft down, than to bring one all the way back when it's so heavy. The old-timers get a chuckle out of seein' a new rafthand a-luggin' it around town."

Katharine smiled weakly. This last ritual was too much. They never gave up, these raftsmen. Poor Hoke. He was in for some sporting humiliation.

Micah reached in to retrieve her leather satchel from the lean-to.

"No," she said, "I don't want it. Just leave it. Maybe someone here will find a use for it. I have my books."

"All right, Ma'm, I'd be glad to carry it for you, but whatever you say. I got your derringer in my pocket."

He paused, then asked, "You a-gettin' hungry?" He had his hand under her elbow.

"Somewhat," Katharine said, "I guess I've been so fearful that 'Slyboots' Siddon was going to recognize me, I haven't thought much about food." Her fitting name for the nefarious timber inspector brought a quick grin to Micah's face.

"We'll get somethin' to eat shortly," he said, still smiling, "but we need to make the rounds of the timber offices and get your money. I got the bill of measurement. Think you can climb the bluff?"

Katharine had wondered herself whether she could climb the almost vertical bluff. Before she could attempt it, however, the backwoodsman lifted her and told her to hold onto the piling and pull herself up the bank. As she held on to the piling, she felt his strong arm holding her around the waist and lifting her up to the bank. With consummate ease, he was on the bank beside her.

She looked at the raft below them, which had been their home for a week. She had mixed feelings, now that the difficult trip was over. She knew without doubt that she probably could not have survived without Micah MacRae's protection. She remembered how naive she had been when she first mentioned to the backwoodsman that she planned to make the trip to Darien on her raft. She could now vouch with him that it was a dangerous trip! However, she was aware that she had survived a trip which few women ever even attempted. Again, she reminded herself that this was only because Micah MacRae had rescued her on three different occasions.

Standing there, looking at her tremendous raft below, she silently thanked the Lord for bringing them all safely to the end of their watery travail and for keeping the raft intact. Now, she was anxious to get her money's worth for it! They began walking in the direction of the timber company offices.

Though the rafting season was not yet upon the tiny port city of Darien, its streets were filled with sailors from coastwise vessels and foreign ports. The town's twelve saloons were doing a thriving business and the atmosphere on Broad Street, the sandy road which ran parallel with the river, was carnival-like.

Sailors from foreign countries, attired in their native dress, lounged on the streets, guzzling down the liquors and ales and brandies which were so readily available in the swinging-door saloons. They talked and sang in strange tongues to the accompaniment of harmonicas and accordions.

Early-season rafthands, jangling as they walked the streets with cooking utensils suspended from their belts, were also recognizable by the coils of manila rope which hung over their shoulders and the axes and two-inch augurs which they carried. Grimy and sweaty from a week or more on the rivers, their unwashed bodies made others move away from them as they passed by. Katharine marveled that Micah did not smell. Undoubtedly, he must have washed himself during the raft trip, though she was never aware of it.

They made the rounds of the timber companies on Market Street, comparing prices and finally selling to the Hilton and Dodge Lumber Company because it offered the best price for her raft. Katharine considered the irony of the chain of events involving her timber. Frank had first purchased it from W. E. Dodge in 1882, before they moved to Georgia. Now, even though they had avoided the Dodge booms, upon arriving at Darien, they had ended up selling it back to the Hilton and Dodge Lumber Company, ten years later.

Katharine let Micah do all of the talking with the timber officials. She kept her head lowered and the slouchy hat pulled down, so as to make herself unrecognizable. In a town with such strange people parading through the streets, no one noticed the slender figure in a man's old, dirty clothes and floppy hat. For this, Katharine was thankful, because she feared, at any moment, that the maliciously cunning Sly Siddon might arrive at one of the timber offices while they were there.

After receiving her money in cash, Katharine immediately paid the raftsman his half, as she had initially agreed to do. Then, they started walking toward the eating establishments on Broad Street.

Bustling activity along the riverfront was the wealth of the Altamaha delta town. Huge cotton bales from upriver were arriving on wide flatboats as well as atop the few upstream rafts of yellow pine and cypress and other woods. Flatboats containing large sheaves of rice were poled from the surrounding rice islands to the riverfront wharves. A new wharf, said to be 180 feet in length, was being built on the riverfront by one of the large timber companies. The pile-driver, the *Gazette* newspaper said, had been working day and night.

Docked at her usual mooring on the waterfront was the small steamship, *Hessie*, which plied her course from Brunswick to Darien, and back, six days of the week. Micah remarked that they would board the *Hessie* at 3:00 o'clock, after they had eaten and looked around the town, though he alerted her that sometimes the trips were rough, not so much from the water as from the rowdy rafthands on their way back home.

Women in suggestive clothing and heavy makeup sashayed along the waterfront, openly accosting sailors and rafthands who had just been paid their wages and who were likely candidates for the local brothels. Negro paramours stood in the doorways of bawdyhouses or leaned out of the windows, half-dressed, willingly subjecting themselves to the lewd remarks and rapacious scrutiny of men who had been without women for weeks and months.

Men drifted shamelessly in and out of the brothels, straightening their clothes after giving up their hard-earned money for the quick, pleasurable sins of the flesh. Katharine was appalled at the easy existence of these houses. Also, for the most part, she thought, the women looked old and hard-faced, working their trade where the pay was steady and lucrative. Katharine was glad that Micah appeared oblivious of them, even the ones who flaunted themselves before him.

A fine carriage passed by them, pulled by a prancing thoroughbred with a Negro coachman in full livery. Seated within the carriage was an attractive, buxom woman. Though overly dressed and too heavily rouged, the woman appeared to be striving for the perception, by others, of a respectable, well-to-do woman about town.

The carriage pulled up to one of the two-story houses on the waterfront, not far from where Micah and Katharine were walking. The colored driver jumped down and opened the door for his passenger. As the woman stepped from the carriage, two sailors approached her, calling out greetings.

"We're coming to see your girls tonight, Miss May Belle," one of the men said.

"Well, come on. We have two new ladies now, and I think you will like them."

"We'll just have to come and look them over, Miss May Belle," the other sailor said.

As the woman proceeded up the walkway to the house, the Negro coachman drove the horse and carriage to a stable behind the house. The men left, laughing and talking and looking back at the inconspicuous house which promised them such hidden delights. Every sailor and rafthand alike knew that May Belle had the prettiest girls to be had in Darien. And she had just let them know that two new ones were there, waiting for them. Darien was the port of gratification for sailors who had been on the seas and away from home too long. The two men could hardly contain their anticipation of what the evening would bring.

So that was "May Belle"! Katharine wondered just how many raftsmen had succumbed to the charms of "May Belle's girls." Obviously quite a few, she thought, for the woman appeared to be doing well financially, and she had heard the name mentioned several times at the Winslow parties and also at the church in Eastman. Darien seemed to be a veritable den of iniquity in so many ways!

Micah took Katharine's arm and guided her into an eating house which, he said, had recently been repainted and refurnished. The establishment included not only tables for eating but also billiard and pool tables. It was also a fine saloon, featuring excellent brandies, imported and domestic wines, gins, beer, whiskeys and imported ales.

Sailors, speaking in foreign languages, and rafthands, talking in the blended syllables of the wiregrass backwoods, ate at the same tables, each acutely aware of the geographical and cultural chasms which set them apart. Each stared at the others, trying to fathom what they were saying and from where they had come.

Micah seated Katharine at one of the long common tables, away from the crowd, before taking a chair by her at the end of the table. Hardly had the backwoodsman sat down before he was up again, speaking to someone. As Katharine looked up, she saw a woman hurrying toward them. She scarcely glanced Katharine's way but threw herself into Micah's arms.

"Micah MacRae, you handsome devil! Why didn't you let us know you were coming down the river? My boarding house is full. Otherwise, if I had known, I'd have kept a bed for you."

"Hello, Flo, I didn't know myself, 'til the last minute, that the raft would be ready. But, no, I ain't plannin' to stay the night. We're leavin' on the *Hessie* in a little while." Micah turned to Katharine.

"Flo..., I'd like you to meet a friend of mine, Miz... uh, Miz Fremont. Miz Fremont hired me to raft her timber."

"Oh?...I mean, I didn't realize. Forgive me, but I didn't know this was a lady friend. I mean..." Flo looked at the slender figure in the man's clothing.

"How do you do, Ma'm?" she said, bending slightly to get a better look at Katharine under the soft-brimmed hat.

"Miz Fremont," Micah said, "this is Flo Palmer. She and her husband, John, own this place, along with other businesses in Darien."

"A pleasure to meet you, Mrs. Palmer," Katharine said, quietly.

The woman turned back to Micah and began moving toward the counter, her arm around the backwoodsman's waist. He walked a few steps with her as she was still talking to him. Katharine heard every word of their conversation.

"I didn't know you had a lady friend, Micah, though I shouldn't be surprised, because of the way the ladies in town are always wanting to know when you're coming back to Darien. Why, I've had young ladies from some of the leading families in town asking about you. You know, you're already a legend, Micah. They also say you're about to start your own business there in McRae or Eastman and that you've made a killing from rafting timber."

Micah laughed warmly but evasively and asked, "Flo, where in the world have you heard such?"

"Oh, everybody talks about it! They say you know the rivers better than anyone else, and you are the only raftsman who can hold your own with the timber inspectors. In fact," Flo said, speculatively, "John is on the Darien City Council now and the city's wanting to hire you as Inspector General. John told them you'd make a good one but no one could get you to leave Telfair County. Of course, you'd have to live in Darien."

Micah, looking mildly surprised, answered, "John's right. I bring the rafts down, but I'm always ready to go back home."

Flo continued, as though she thought she might talk the backwoodsman into considering the lucrative offer.

"The raftsmen claim the timber inspectors aren't fair, and they have no recourse, once they've brought their rafts down."

"That's right," Micah quickly replied. "We can't take our rafts back up the river and the inspectors know that. We're at the mercy of the timber inspectors, and believe me, Flo, you've got a number of dishonest ones here!"

"I know you're right, Micah. The Darien newspaper has run several articles lately about the bad blood between the rafthands and some of the timber inspectors. That's the reason the council is wanting to hire you as Inspector General. You would know both sides of the problem, and you're honest. You also know how to measure and grade timber. The other Council members know of our friendship with you, so they asked John and me to approach you about their offer."

Flo hesitated, then said, "Well, Micah, will you just consider it? We need you here."

"Several years ago, Flo, I probably would've agreed to it, but now that I'm starting some new businesses upriver, I wouldn't be able to leave." Noticing her disappointment, he added, "As for the job of Inspector General, I'm afraid it won't last much longer, anyway, and that goes for the inspectors' jobs, too, because the timber won't last much longer."

"Oh?" Flo was wanting to question him about this when she paused, looking toward the doorway.

"Speaking of timber scalers, look who just walked in."

As Micah looked toward the door, Katharine knew without turning around that Sly Siddon had just entered the building. She shrank down in her chair, turning her head so he might not recognize her.

Micah disengaged himself from the lady proprietor's attentions and returned to the table where Katharine sat.

"I'm coming over to see you again before you leave, Micah," she called back to him as she walked over to greet the timber inspector.

Katharine cautiously peeked at the timber scaler as he made his way to a bar stool. Flo asked if he were having his usual, but he laughed and said, no, he was on the job, so he couldn't drink anything. However, when Flo left to greet other customers, he promptly ordered whiskey to drink, downing several shots in rapid succession.

Flo returned to a bar stool by the timber inspector and the two appeared to be in deep conversation. From time to time, Katharine observed the proprietor looking her way, then turning her attention back to the slurred, idle talk of the timber inspector. Once, Katharine thought she heard her name mentioned but she then considered it unlikely.

Katharine picked at her food, finding it difficult to eat because of the presence of the timber scaler at the counter bar. After the sameness of the food on the raft, she had looked forward to the sea food, in fresh abundance from the nearby Atlantic Ocean. However, it stuck in her throat, her nervousness making it difficult to swallow.

Micah ate his shrimp and oysters with obvious enjoyment, looking at Katharine frequently during the meal, his dark brown eyes dancing with unconcealed merriment at her predicament. Katharine wondered whether the day would come when she could look back at these events in her life and laugh. At the moment, she only wanted to flee and board the *Hessie*, where she knew Sly Siddon would not follow.

A noise from the counter caught her attention. The timber inspector was paying his bill, telling the proprietor that he had to get back to work. More rafts were coming in than usual, he said, for this time of the year. Flo walked with him to the door, then returned to Micah's and Katharine's table as she had earlier promised to do. She sat down, staring at Katharine.

Whispering, she asked, "Are you Katharine Fremont...Mrs. Frank Fremont?"

Katharine didn't know what to say or how to react. However, with the departure of Sly Siddon, she felt more at ease about revealing her identity.

"Yes, Mrs. Palmer, I am Katharine Fremont."

Flo's eyes widened with disbelief as she stared at Katharine.

"You didn't...you couldn't possibly have been on a raft for a week...not you...not the widow of Frank Fremont...why, you were both close associates of the Dodge family!" she exclaimed, trying to keep her voice down.

Micah, worried that Katharine might be upset with Flo, was about to intervene on her behalf, when Katharine quickly spoke for herself.

"How did you find out who I am?"

"Well, Micah introduced you to me as Mrs. Fremont, but he didn't say your first name and since he hesitated when he introduced you, I was a little uncertain just what was going on. Then, when Sly came in and the whiskey loosened his tongue, he started telling me about the beautiful Katharine Fremont from Dodge County."

Flo Palmer stared at the woman before her as if attempting to discover the hidden beauty under Katharine's floppy brown hat. All three of them laughed at Katharine's effective disguise, but quickly hushed when they drew the attention of others in the room.

Again whispering, Flo said, "You are beautiful, Katharine, but why in the world are you avoiding Sly Siddon? Didn't he scale your timber?"

Katharine weighed in her mind whether to confide in the inquisitive yet likeable proprietor.

"Yes," she said, "he measured and graded my timber but he didn't know I was onboard the raft. You didn't tell him that I was here?"

"No, I figured if Micah wanted him to know, he'd tell him himself." Flo looked from one to the other. "As I said, I couldn't decide what was going on, but felt that there was some reason you didn't want Sly to know you were here. Otherwise, you'd have made your presence known," Flo continued, placing her hand on Micah's shoulder and turning to Katharine.

"Micah is the best friend we have, Katharine." she said. "John and I have a lumber company here in Darien and Micah has helped us in so many ways. He knows more about lumber than anybody I know and the timber scalers realize that. They can't measure low with any raft that Micah brings down and get away with it." She patted Micah on the arm and resumed her praise of the backwoodsman who was shaking his head but obviously enjoying the flattering words thrown his way.

"What I'm wanting you to know, Mrs. Fremont...Katharine..., is that your secret is safe with me. I never let on to Sly Siddon that you were sitting over here. Actually, I wasn't sure myself that you were the same Mrs. Fremont he was talking about." Flo caught her breath, again considering the fact that Katharine had made the perilous trip down the rivers.

Then she observed, "Why, even seasoned rafthands sometimes get killed on the raft trips. I just find it hard to believe that a fine lady like you would even want to make the trip."

Flo looked, wide-eyed, at Katharine, hoping to evoke a response that would clarify in her mind the ambiguities of the whole situation. Before Katharine could reply, however, Micah MacRae leaned forward and startled Katharine with his own assessment of why she made the hazardous trip. If he hadn't smiled at her as he talked, Katharine might have taken offense.

"I can tell you why Mrs. Fremont made the trip. She didn't want to trust a Southern Cracker to get the best price for her raft." This made Katharine squirm, for she had to admit that she had some doubts at the beginning of the raft trip about Micah's loyalty to a Northern woman, given his heavy involvement in the land war. She set about trying to explain why she made the trip.

"Actually, Flo, I've wanted to visit Darien for some time. I've heard so much about it. Also, since my husband died, I've desperately tried to learn something about business. You have been in a position to learn about business matters, but I have literally been thrown into everything since my husband died, and I'm still trying to learn. First of all, though, I'd really like to know more about Darien. I know it's an important international port."

"Oh, yes," Flo said, "we have a number of foreign consulates here now. We have a Customs House. Our new bank was chartered just several years ago. We had an artesian well dug a year ago and many of our houses now have indoor plumbing and running water. Our lumber industries here expect to have exported 100 million board feet by the end of the year, and as you know, the lumber is loaded on ships from many different parts of the world."

Flo glanced outside, through the front windows of the building, then continued, "Of course, I'm sure you noticed our terrible streets. Editor Grubb in our *Timber Gazette* keeps reminding the city officials to repair our streets. The large holes and bumps of every description and mud, when it rains, make Broad Street almost impassable. Also, the weeds that have sprung up make an unpleasant stench."

Flo paused, smiling, then said, "But if you all will keep on rafting your beautiful yellow pine with hearts of gold," she laughed, then repeated, "and I do mean literally hearts of pure gold, then Darien will continue to grow and thrive."

"I give it maybe another ten years, not much longer than that," Micah said slowly.

"Oh, Micah, you can't mean that. Why, you can ride for hundreds of miles and see nothing but tall longleaf pines. It'll be forever before all those trees are cut," Flo said.

"Dodge and his logchoppers are cuttin' trees every day in Telfair, Dodge, Laurens, Pulaski, and Montgomery Counties, and they can't be replaced. In fact, they're clear-cuttin', harvestin' even the young saplin's that should be left to replenish the forests. There oughta be a law against clear-cuttin', like they're doin'. Sometimes, you can ride for miles and miles and see nuthin' but stumps. The big trees they're a-cuttin' are maybe two to three hundred years old, and big around as bulls' bellies. They won't ever be replaced." Flo was momentarily distracted about the possibility of the lumber from upriver declining in the not so distant future. Then, she remembered that Katharine was about to explain the problems relating to the timber inspector and she quickly returned the conversation to that subject.

"Mrs. Fremont, you were going to tell me about Sly Siddon, I believe. What has he done now?"

"Well," Katharine said, looking embarrassed, "he told me that if I refused to marry him, he would give my timber a low rating, and I wouldn't receive much money for it. No, if he knew I rode my raft with Micah and three colored men, why, he would tell the world about it. I plan to move back to my home in New York very soon, likely within the next few weeks. Frankly, I hope I never have to see the man again."

"Oh, he can be very obnoxious," Flo said. "We put up with him because he's a paying customer, but I can certainly understand why you feel the way you do. He probably felt that he could take advantage of you, because you're a widow."

"Exactly. I have run into this so much since my husband's death. My mother and father are still living in New York and they keep wanting me to find someone to see about my timber for me, so that I can move on back to New York. This, as I said, I plan to do within the next few weeks."

Unintentionally, Katharine glanced at Micah, and a fleeting expression in his eyes, as he looked at her, made her catch her breath. However, he quickly looked away and she was left wondering what he was thinking. She did not realize that her face softened and glowed when she looked at the large backwoodsman and that Flo could read yet another secret of hers, which she had never divulged to anyone.

In the silence that followed, the backwoodsman told Katharine that they really needed to board the *Hessie*, for it always left promptly at 3:00 o'clock for the four-hour trip to Brunswick. Flo spoke up quickly. "You two have plenty of time, Micah. I was hoping Katharine could see some of the beautiful homes here and maybe hear about our parties during the year. Darien does offer more than what first meets the eye when you step off a raft at the riverfront." Flo laughed when she said this, eliciting smiles from her guests.

"Katharine, we have three balls a year. The Hiltons always have a masked ball and the Fosters have a dance of some kind each year. Both of these families have lovely homes at the Ridge. Sometimes, we floor over a big lighter which is towed by a tugboat and we dance on this. We'll go to St. Simons, Fernandina, and Brunswick. Of course, we always get stuck in the mud but we don't mind. It just makes the trip longer. Baseball is big here, too. Darien is our team and the Ridge the rival team. We deck our horses and whips and buggies and yell for our teams. We have a glorious time!"

After stopping to catch her breath, Flo Palmer mentioned to the intrigued Katharine that Darien was put to the torch and nearly completely destroyed during the war, in 1863, by Negro troops acting under orders of white Northern officers. The fire, she said, burned almost all of the homes and public buildings of Darien, including the school and churches. Within less than thirty years, Darien had managed to rebuild and to become one of the busiest ports on the East Coast, a testament to the courage and ingenuity of its people. It had the largest pitch pine concern on the eastern seaboard, she said.

Micah stood up. "We're enjoyin' this, Flo, but it's time for us to go." Katharine and Flo rose from the table at the same time.

"I'm so interested in your history. I've enjoyed hearing about your town," Katharine said.

"You must come back soon, Katharine. You could stay with us at our boarding house. Micah's stayed with us many times, though it's been awhile since you've stayed overnight in Darien," she said, turning to address Micah.

Before Micah could answer, the talkative Flo broached a different subject, looking hesitant about treading on uncharted territory. Glancing quickly from Katharine to Micah, she asked Micah what was happening up his way in regard to the disputed Dodge land titles.

"We keep hearing that people are getting killed," she said, again looking quickly at Katharine, as if she were trying to determine Katharine's feelings about the land war. Katharine said nothing but waited to see how Micah would reply. The backwoodsman's face was a study in anger and hostility.

"You're a-hearin' right, Flo. We had a number of people killed. Dodge is a-claimin' my land now. When I get back home, I just might see his logchoppers on my land. They came once but I ran 'em off with my shotgun."

"Oh, Micah, what will you do?" Flo asked with genuine concern in her voice.

"There ain't much any of us can do. All the cases are now bein' tried in the federal courts, rather than the state courts, and we don't stand a chance in the federal courts. The judges there always rule for the Dodge family."

"Well, you be careful, Micah. They are powerful people, as you well know. They have sawmills here and on St. Simons. One of the younger ones has rebuilt Christ Church which was nearly destroyed during the war. It's really difficult to realize that these wealthy, educated, seemingly good people are involved in a bloody land war."

"Some folks'll do anythin' for the almighty dollar. You know yourself, Flo, that the Georgia law says a man can claim land without a deed after twenty years' possession and, with a deed, after seven years possession. I believe this is called adverse possession. Our Georgia law is no longer upheld. People are bein' thrown off their lands that have been in their families for fifty years and more. And they been a-payin' taxes all along. The Dodges have woods riders with guns that ride the woods and scare people and, at gunpoint, take their land. The Dodges have friends in high places, such as the federal judges who ruled in their favor, in spite of the fact that their deeds ain't what they should be. There's no other way to explain it. Cases that should be tried in the state courts are now bein' tried in the federal courts. It's a continuation of the war, and our hands are tied when the federal judges rule for the outsiders with their questionable titles. They haven't payed the taxes, either, every year, as we have. They don't have a right to our land." Katharine still remained silent, remembering the day Micah had driven her in the wagon to witness for herself the dire situation of Maude and Pete Ivey. Flo was talking again, her hand on Micah's arm.

"You be careful, Micah. John will be sorry he missed seeing you." She turned to Katharine.

"Goodbye, Katharine. I just enjoyed meeting you so much. Don't stay up there in New York too long. Come back to see us."

"I would love to, Flo."

When Micah began counting out money for their meal, Flo castigated him in no uncertain terms, telling him to put away his money.

"You know you never pay when you eat with us, Micah!" she said reprovingly, refusing the money which he held out to her.

"I'll pay for mine," Katharine said.

"No, you won't. You're my guest today, since you're with Micah. Let me tell you, Micah has helped us so much, in so any ways, that we never charge him for his meals or his room, either, if he comes to our boarding house. We consider it's small return for all he's done for us!"

The demonstrative Flo gave Micah another hug, but this time she included Katharine, too. Micah mentioned that he'd be returning before long as he'd be bringing many more rafts of Katharine's timber for the next several months. Flo extracted a promise from him that he would stay at her boarding house, if he should spend the night in Darien.

Micah and Katharine stepped out into the September sunshine. A black police officer was patrolling the street. Micah explained to Katharine that the man had the several titles of constable, deputy sheriff, and city marshall, and with all the saloons in Darien, he was constantly being shot. However, the sheet-iron underclothing, which the officer wore, had always deflected the bullets. The officer's name was Alonzo Guyton and he was highly respected and appreciated by the law-abiding community in McIntosh County. Micah further explained that he needed to report the shooting of the Klansman at Barrington Bar.

Micah approached the colored officer whose face wreathed in a smile of recognition. As Katharine looked on nearby, the men shook hands with each other, while Micah began relating the incident involving the man at Barrington Bar. He told the officer that the man who was shot was named Harold Diggs and that he was wanted in Dodge County for Klan raids on Mrs. Frank Fremont's home. He also was attempting to harm someone on his raft when he was wounded, and he fled into the swamp. Katharine was relieved that he didn't mention her being on the raft.

Alonzo Guyton meticulously wrote down the information about the Klansman and told Micah that he would pass it on to other law enforcement officials. They would check the local hospital, also, to see whether anyone had checked in with bullet wounds. However, he said, he agreed with Micah that the man could not possibly have rowed against the tide. He more than likely had died of his wounds there in the swamp, or if he started out in his bateau, he could likely have drowned. The officer thanked the backwoodsman for reporting the incident and promised him that everything possible would be done to apprehend the man who had brought such fear to Mrs. Fremont and such destruction to her property and who had attempted to harm someone on his raft.

After reporting the incident, Micah and Katharine began walking in the direction of the *Hessie* steamboat which was waiting at its usual docking place on the Darien riverfront. Rafthands and other passengers, some well-dressed, were boarding the vessel.

Looking down the sandy riverfront pathway, Katharine saw a large pied ox pulling an old oxcart which held an upright, thin-lipped colored man with a head and goatee of white wool. The ox, obviously many years old, walked slowly as its dark-skinned driver puffed on his pipe.

"From your description, the man in the oxcart must be Liverpool Hazzard," Katharine said.

"That's Liverpool. Thought he'd be out with his oxcart. He's the last of the Butler slaves. He was a house servant and, also, an oarsman for the Butlers."

The dignity of the aging Negro, garbed in a dusty old suit and buttoned-up shirt, was a reflection of his life. He was known to hold the interest of anyone who questioned him about the war, the Butlers, the rice culture, or the boat races on the river. He was a relict of the past, a bridge between Pre-War Darien and Post-Reconstruction Darien.

As the ox plodded past, Liverpool Hazzard smiled and nodded. When Micah called out greetings, the black freedman laughed with delight at being recognized and responded, "And how might you be, Mistuh Micah?"

"Doin' good, Liverpool. We're 'bout to board the *Hessie* to go to Brunswick."

"Watch out fer de 'gators!"

"We'll do that," Micah said, as the ox pulled the cart on past them.

Micah and Katharine hurried on to the *Hessie* which was still loading passengers. The unwashed, rowdy, and smelly rafthands congregated on the lower deck. The stench of sour liquor hung over them. In addition to the coils of manila rope which hung from their shoulders, some of them had suspended from their belts the usual skillets and coffeepots, axes, and augurs. All of them carried their loaded, dark-barreled rifles.

Micah quickly led Katharine past the rough crowd who appeared ready to fight anyone who lingered near them. Some of the noisy group recognized the backwoodsman, as one of them, and called out to him. He acknowledged these with a nod and a few words as he hurriedly guided Katharine into the lower deck of the steamer. Several other passengers, fashionably dressed, eyed the new arrivals as they took seats near them. Katharine wondered what they thought of her in the floppy brown hat and soiled clothes. They probably thought that she and her companion should be out on the deck with the other rafthands. The thought made her smile and she caught the eye of one of the ladies, who nodded unsmilingly back at her.

With a shrill blow from its steam whistle, the *Hessie* promptly began its journey down the Darien River between the log booms which extended for several miles on both sides of the river. Some of the ships at the sawmills were taking on timber, and Katharine found it fascinating to watch the procedure, for she knew that her own raft would be broken apart and the logs, or sticks of timber, would likely become the cargo of one of the vessels waiting to be loaded.

As the timber was moved in place alongside one of the wooden sailing ships, ports in the bows were removed to receive the heavy logs, muddy from the river. The logs were then placed on rollers, rolled to their positions in the ship, then turned by cant hooks into place. Other smaller timbers were loaded over the side as deck cargo or through the hatches.

The boss stevedore, a large man of indubitable skill and brawn, directed the colored stevedore hands whose large torso muscles rippled under their taut black skin in the afternoon sun. The stevedore hands sang chanteys as they worked, their leader singing a line, followed by the others singing in rhythm, ending with a loud "Ho!," as all heaved together on the big stick, dropping it into the ship's hold. Their nonsensical but rhythmical words drifted over to those on the *Hessie* steamboat:

> Ragged Leevy! Oh - Ho!
> Do ragged Leevy
> Ragged Leevy! O boy!
> You ragged like a jay bird!
> Mr. Sipplin! Ha-n-nh
> Goin' to buil' me a sto'e fence
> In the mornin' Oh - Ho!
> Soon in the mornin'!
> Hos' an' buggy - O - Ho!
> Hos' an' buggy
> Hos' an' buggy - O boy!
> Dey's no one to drive 'um.
> Mr. Sipplin! Ha-n-nh
> In de mornin'
> When I rise
> I goin' to sit by de fire.

As the *Hessie* passed by other ships, loading timber, their stevedores sang different chanteys. Katharine listened closely to the one about a "Mr. Foster" who, Micah explained to her, was the "big boss" of the Dodge Company's St. Simons mill. The stevedores often sang the chantey when they saw him coming. Katharine wondered whether the man might presently be in the vicinity of the company's sawmills on the Darien River, for the stevedores were now singing the chantey:

> Wish't I was Mr. Foster's son
> Pay me my money down

I'd set on the bank an' see the work done
Pay me my money down.

Micah explained to Katharine that the chanteys helped the stevedores to load the ships faster. If a ship was loaded in less time than expected, the shipper received "dispatch" money from the ship's owner; however, if it was loaded in more time than expected, the shipper paid "demurrage," a cash penalty for unduly detaining the vessel. Fast loading was an economic necessity and the rhythmic, pull-together chantey was definitely a factor in accomplishing this.

The *Hessie* steamed on behind a long raft of logs which stretched out behind a towboat. When the tug turned into a creek to the right of the Darien River, the backwoodsman related to Katharine that the stream was called Three Mile Cut. As Katharine listened with interest, he commented that when the water was high, the *Hessie* could make it through and it would save forty-five minutes on the trip from Darien to Brunswick. However, he said, the water was now too low for the steamboat, so the Captain would have to take the longer route to Brunswick.

"Oh, how I wish we could have taken Three Mile Cut!" Katharine exclaimed as they passed the narrow creek.

"I don't think you would like it, Ma'm," he said, "It's got mud banks with high marsh grass and big 'gators come down when a raft goes by. I've heard tell they try to get on the rafts."

Micah continued, warming to the frightened look on Katharine's face, and Katharine sensed that he was teasing her with rafting experiences, but she knew that it was probably just as frightening as he was making it out to be. She had heard enough to be grateful that she didn't have to travel on a raft, or even a steamboat, through Three Mile Cut, even if it did shorten the trip by almost an hour!

The rowdy rafthands on the outside deck, with their jangling utensils and tools, became noisier as the *Hessie* headed toward the sea. Several times, the Captain sent his mate, formally attired in white cap and coat, to calm the disturbances. After the mate's latest departure, the rafthands crooked their fingers around their jugs, resting them on their shoulders as they swilled the fiery contents.

Their curses on the Captain and his mate were delivered with more frequency and acrimony as they became more inebriated.

As the *Hessie* steamed on past the tall ships in the Darien River and approached the Rockdedundy River, Katharine noticed that some of the ships had rails around them, where stevedores pushed wheelbarrows filled with large smooth rocks. Noting her questioning look, the backwoodsman explained that the ships carried ballast in the place of cargo to stabilize them. Before they could load timber, they had to dump the ballast. Sometimes the deposits formed islands, called ballast islands. The ballast was unloaded in the marsh grass or sometimes in deep water. Doboy Island, which they were approaching, had ballast deposits in abundance.

Looking across the brown salt marshes, Katharine could see the mast tops and riggings of the huge ships at the loading docks of Doboy Sound. In contrast with the brown marsh grass, the many islands in the seaward delta of the Altamaha were lushly green. The awesome pristine beauty of the triangular delta, where the blue of the ocean and sky met over fingers of marsh grass and verdant islands, was invaded by the tall ships with their noisy crews.

One of the passengers in the steamboat remarked that it was still quarantine season in the delta. Another replied that, yes, the quarantine season began the first of May and would end the first of November. They looked at Micah as if attempting to verify that they were correct.

When Micah acknowledged that they were right about the quarantine months, the passengers launched into a serious conversation about quarantine procedures, asking many questions which the backwoodsman patiently answered. Katharine assumed that the other passengers had overheard him talking to her about the stevedores and ballast and other sights during the trip, and they had inferred that he was something of an authority on the area. She was amused and also interested in their queries and his replies.

"Didn't the quarantine station used to be on Queens Island?" another passenger asked, as the *Hessie* steamed past a black nun buoy into the Little Mud River which was a part of the intracoastal waterway, with Queens Island and Wolf Island on the left and Rockdedundy Island on the right.

"Yes, Ma'm, but it closed in 1891. The main quarantine station has always been on Blackbeard Island, since it was opened in 1880. They got a wharf with disinfectin' tanks and a rail track for unloadin' ballast, built out about 300 feet into the water on the north end of the island. All the ships arrivin' at Doboy or Sapelo Bar from tropical waters durin' the quarantine season are required to report to the National Quarantine Station at Blackbeard Island. The ones with disease onboard fly the yellow flags."

"Is that because of the yellow fever epidemic in those countries?"

"That's right, Ma'm. A Cuban doctor says that yellow fever is caused by a kind of mosquito, and he just may be right. Just like malaria. They're a-sayin' now that it's caused by another kind of mosquito."

As some of the passengers offered their own opinions about the different tropical fevers, the rafthands on the outer deck became more boisterous, openly guzzling the liquor from their jugs and crocks which they had refilled from the saloons in Darien. The passengers looked at them through the cabin windows, their faces betraying their feelings of disgust and apprehension.

The *Hessie* was now steaming into Buttermilk Sound, a continuation of the intracoastal waterway. One of the passengers, an elderly man sitting near the cabin door, remarked that Buttermilk Sound was named for the white-capped, churning surf which formed when "nor'easters" blew across the sound. Buoys, placed in the water as navigational aids by the U. S. Lighthouse Board, marked the ever-changing, perilous shoals, while seven-day, oil-lit post lanterns mounted on pilings indicated the entrances and exits of different river channels. At nighttime, now only a short time away, these would be indispensable to light the ships' passages through the intricate maze of islands which comprised the Altamaha Delta.

To Katharine's horrified surprise, one of the raftsmen in full view of the passengers in the cabin aimed his rifle at the nearest buoy and shot at it, making it bob erratically before sinking. Loud, raucous laughter erupted from the other rafthands who praised the accuracy of the buoy marksman. Suddenly, all fifteen of the raftsmen hoisted their rifles to the rail, using it as a fulcrum as they shot at other buoys, several hundred yards away, and at the oil-burning post lanterns, howling with success as each one succumbed to a simultaneous spray of bullets and sank in the water.

Just as suddenly, the shooting stopped and the drunken rafthands turned to face the white-uniformed Captain, striding toward them.

"I'll not have any more shooting on my boat. This is a public conveyance. I'll have you locked up when we reach Brunswick."

"You talkin' mighty big, lak you gonna mek it to Brunswick, Mister Cap'n," said a tall, thin raftsman with a black wool cap on his head.

"Yassuh," a short Negro raftsman spoke up, taking his shuck hat off and holding it to his chest in mock deference, "Yassuh, it sho sound to me lak he plannin' on steamin' on inta Brunswick."

The other raftsmen on the deck and the passengers inside the cabin watched the confrontation in silence, the former with grinning amusement, the latter with mounting anxiety. As the angry, red-faced Captain continued his tirade and threats, pointing his finger at the stinking river men, a large Negro raftsman moved like a black panther from the foredeck where he had been sitting on the capstan. Without saying a word, he shoved the startled Captain over the rail, so that his head and torso were parallel to the churning water only a few feet below.

The sick fright on the Captain's face, along with the helpless flailing of his arms and legs, reminded the passengers in the cabin of their own vulnerability. Some of the women were shaking with fear. Others were crying, holding on to their husbands who were undecided about what to do.

Katharine never knew when Micah left the seat beside her, for she sat mesmerized at the cabin window, watching with dread the Captain's ordeal. However, like the calm in the midst of a storm, she heard the sure, strong voice of the backwoodsman as he moved through the crowd of raftsmen to the large Negro who was still dangling the terrified Captain over the water.

"Set the Cap'n back down on 'is ship, Blue," he said.

The Negro immediately pulled the Captain, now more angry than scared, back over the rail. Sputtering, the Captain straightened his clothes, looking at his hat which had fallen from his head during the ruckus and now drifted out of reach near the *Hessie's* prow.

Before anyone said anything, Micah MacRae had a pole from the boat's foredeck in his hands, which he thrust over the rail and under the stiff hat. Within seconds, the hat was rescued and in the hands of the Captain who held it, dripping, in one hand while he vigorously shook the backwoodsman's hand with the other.

Having recovered his dignity somewhat, the Captain now turned to the mob of rafthands who appeared subdued, following the appearance of Micah MacRae. However, before he could continue with his threats of punishment, the backwoodsman intervened.

"Mr. Cap'n, I know almost all of these men, and they are good men. They just had too much to drink and this time tomorrow, they won't even remember this boat trip. It weren't right how they treated you, and I ain't excusin' 'em. I'm just askin' you, Mr. Cap'n, not to put 'em in jail when we get to Brunswick. Ever' one of 'em has families a-waitin' on 'em - wives and young'uns."

As Micah paused, the Captain wiped his brow and glared at the wild-eyed group who appeared to be struggling to return to the proper state of sobriety. Some removed their tattered caps as gestures of belated respect. All were silent, looking from the Captain to the backwoodsman. The possibility that they might be thrown into jail was imminent as the *Hessie* steamed on to the Frederica River.

"I don't know that they should go unpunished, sir. I'm a-thinkin' they ought to tell you they're sorry for actin' like a bunch of liquor-heads, and I'm a-thinkin' they might give up some of their hard-earned money to pay for the markers they shot at."

The Captain had regained his complete shipboard authority. He scowled at the rafthands who all now removed their scruffy hats and muttered in low voices their apologies, broken by the hiccups and the belches of the intoxicated.

Raising his eyebrows and again dusting off his uniform, the Captain sighed and held out his hand to Micah MacRae.

"Thank you, sir, for coming to my assistance. If I'd known you were onboard, I wouldn't have been as worried. You've helped us out many times when the rafthands gave us trouble. As for paying for the buoys they destroyed, I have no idea what they would owe. I'll let them go this time, but if they ever give us more trouble, they will go to jail. I'll see to that," the Captain concluded, again shaking hands with the backwoodsman and eyeing the rafthands with contempt.

"I'm going back to piloting this ship," the Captain said with great dignity. "I'm counting on you, Mr. MacRae, to help me keep order until we reach Brunswick."

"I'll see to it, Cap'n," the backwoodsman said as the Captain returned to his post.

Micah turned to the rafthands and told them to line up their whiskey jugs and crocks against the outside wall of the cabin and not to touch them until they reached Brunswick. The raftsmen obliged, grudgingly placing their libatory vessels in the suggested area, as the backwoodsman reentered the passenger cabin.

Katharine could hardly believe the ease with which Micah MacRae had handled a potentially dangerous situation. She had heard a collective sigh of relief from the other passengers when he had restored order on the outside deck and had induced the Negro to release the Captain from his precarious dangle over the side railing. Katharine herself had silently thanked the Lord.

The backwoodsman returned to his seat amid murmurs of appreciation from the other passengers. Katharine, too, complimented his handling of the drunk rafthands, and he replied that all of them had homes and families up the river and only drank to excess when they sold their rafts in Darien and had a little extra money. He said most of them wouldn't even remember their escapades after they sobered up.

As he settled back in his seat, he muttered that all of the rafthands, at one time or another, had been mistreated by the Darien timber inspectors who consistently low-graded their rafts, knowing that they couldn't be rafted back upriver. His voice trailed off, but Katharine inferred that this was the reason he had intervened and had successfully kept the rafthands from being arrested. In other words, the rafthands were only avenging, whether rightfully or wrongfully, their mistreatment at the hands of the authorities in Darien in not receiving honest payment for their rafts. Because they had no way of dealing with the malfeasance of the timber officials who often appeared to be in league with the lumber companies, the beleaguered raftsmen vented their frustrations in other ways, lashing out at innocent people.

As calmness returned to the steamboat passengers, Katharine looked through the windows of the cabin, noticing the rookeries of snowy egrets, roosting in the trees near the water. Several flew past the boat, their yellow feet curved backward.

The somber gray ruins of Fort Frederica were visible on St. Simons Island. Before Katharine could inquire about the meaning of the fort, Micah informed her that General Oglethorpe had the fort built in the early 1700s as a protection against Spanish invaders. Only the one tabby building remained, though the fort at one time had several buildings of tabby and brick, which were used as storehouses, along with others, long gone.

"You've heard the legend of the Ibos?" Micah asked

"The what?" Katharine replied.

"The 'who,'" Micah said, gently.

"Oh, no, I don't know what you're talking about," Katharine said, waiting expectantly for him to explain.

"Some Ibos were brought over as slaves from Africa. There's a landin' on the back of St. Simons Island where, it's said, the Ibos chose to walk off into the water and drown, rather than live as slaves." At Katharine's horrified look, Micah softened the impact of his words by concluding that some said it was just a legend, that the Ibos chose to swim away from their captors and drowned. Either version of the story intensified the plight of the Negroes who were uprooted from their ancestral homes, separated from their families, shackled below decks of slave ships, and transported to foreign shores. Those who survived the inhuman deprivations of the ocean voyages faced existence as slaves, working the rice fields and the cotton plantations, often under the cowhide-thonged lash of drivers who strove to exact the expected quota for the day.

The newly-restored serenity of the slow-moving steamboat caused the passengers to comment on the tranquillity and beauty of the waterways. Mullet fish leapt from the river, their glistening, writhing forms making splashing sounds as they reentered the water.

Behind the white-blooming sea myrtle on the riverbank were cypress trees with Spanish moss trailing in the breeze. Some of these trees had large osprey nests high in their branches, and even higher near their treetops were distinct bald eagles' nests. Here, too, as on the Altamaha River, the stark, thick limbs of the dead cypress held these lofty aeries.

The *Hessie* now entered the deep and wide expanse of water called St. Simons Sound. Cries of seagulls, soaring overhead, mingled with the flapping of pelican wings. Pelicans were perched on buoys and on tree limbs. Some skimmed along the top of the water in a line, driving fish ahead of them to more shallow water, before scooping up the catch in their pouches on the undersides of their long, straight bills.

Lengthening shadows on the water were reminders that dusk had arrived and as the steamer passed the end of St. Simons Island, its red and white lighthouse, built in 1872, was visible. Its kerosene-burning lamps' rays were diffused through a third order Fresnel lens, according to the backwoodsman who apprised Katharine of these interesting tidbits of information, and she wondered where he had learned such details and how he could remember them. He was obviously, she thought, quite intelligent though uneducated.

"Old-timers used to tell me to look for the 'whiskers' on the lighthouse. Just as it's gettin' dark, it looks like whiskers comin' out from the lighthouse. I can see 'em now," he said.

"What?" Katharine asked, straining her eyes at the far-off structure. "Oh," she said, laughing, "I do see whiskers!"

"It's the light rays, of course, but they look like whiskers this time of day."

Katharine looked at the range lines down the middle of the channel which was marked with burning lighter knots, mounted on pilings suspended above the water. She was glad the steamer trip was nearing its end, especially when she considered that something could possibly extinguish the lighter knots and thrust them into darkness.

They were in Glynn County now, made famous by the immortal words of the Georgia poet, Sidney Lanier, in his *The Marshes of Glynn* which she had brought with her to read while they were surrounded by the very marshes he had written about. She opened the thin book and read the musical cadences which so beautifully and accurately described what she was seeing:

Look how the grace of the sea doth go
About and about through the intricate channels that flow
    Here and there,
    Everywhere,
Till his waters have flooded the uttermost creeks and the low-lying lanes,
And the marsh is meshed with a million veins,
That like as with rosy and silvery essences flow
    In the rose-and-silver evening glow.

She finished the poem, then gave it to Micah's outstretched hand. She was surprised that he was interested in reading it. He read it quickly, then gave it back to her.

"He can paint a picture with words," he said with a smile, and Katharine agreed.

The *Hessie* steamed into the Brunswick River and finally into the East river, slowing down and inching into its berth at the foot of Mansfield Street. The subdued rafthands now resumed their rough speech and rowdiness as the steamboat docked, grabbing their jars and crocks and leaping onto the pier. The passengers, cramped from four hours of inactivity in the cabin of the *Hessie*, now walked with unsteady legs, reaching out for a helping hand to step up to the pier.

Having sat for so long, Katharine and Micah welcomed the opportunity to walk around and see the sights of Brunswick. They had three hours time to pass before the next train left for Longview and Godwinsville. They strolled along the road called Bay Street which ran parallel with the Brunswick Harbor.

Tall ships lined the busy harbor, along with small work craft and pile-driving equipment on the waterfront. A voluminous, six-masted schooner, flying the American flag, lay at anchor in its tremendous berth. The backwoodsman, noting that Katharine was observing it, commented that only two or three of them had been built, and Brunswick was one of the few ports it could enter.

Large freight wagons filled with cotton, lumber, and naval stores rumbled over the brick roads, pulled by strong draft horses. Horse-drawn carriages for hire were available for those who could afford them. To the south was Cook Brothers sawmill, whose steam whistle periodically proclaimed the time for the port city of Brunswick. To the north were the Mallory/Clyde Lines steamship terminals. To the east, the spire of City Hall was prominent in the background of saloons and brothels. Micah remarked that the rafthands aboard the *Hessie* had lost no time in seeking out the pleasures of "Hell's Half Acre" in the eastern, downtown sector of Bay Street.

"You don't mean they'll start drinking again?" Katharine asked, worriedly.

"More'n apt they will, Ma'm," Micah said, evenly, refusing to be judgmental.

"Where were they from? You seemed to know them," Katharine said.

"They were Oconee rafthands, but I've known 'em for a number of years. The big fella named Blue...he's meaner'n a snake, gets in fights...he'll kill a man over nothin', but I helped 'im once, and he ain't never forgot it. He'd spent all his money in Darien, and it was wintertime and freezin', and he didn't have money to catch the train back home. I let 'im have money for a train ticket and food, and he still talks about it. He appreciated somebody helpin' 'im."

"Well, he should have. Not everyone would have been as kind," Katharine said.

"We help each other, Ma'm. I'm sure Blue would help me, if ever I need it."

"I would certainly hope so," Katharine said, remembering the large, sullen, and arrogant Negro.

Looking ahead, Micah nodded toward a multistory brick building near the river.

"That's the new Oglethorpe Hotel," he said, "built in 1888, I believe."

"Very impressive," Katharine said, noting the tall chimneys and large pointed turrets, silhouetted against the darkening sky. Each of the many elongated windows, some singular and others alternating in pairs, had fans of brickwork above them. Tall, white spindles, reaching to the second floor, carved with simple elegance and joined with narrow, decorative arches, denoted the several entrances to the fine hotel.

Katharine sighed, looking down at her unkempt self. Visions of the tan walking suit which she had packed for the train trip home, but which was likely still floating down one of the rivers, came to her mind, causing her to laugh out loud. Noticing Micah's puzzled expression, she explained her amusement.

"I was looking at the beautiful hotel, thinking how nice it would be to go inside and look around but I'm afraid we're not dressed for it. Then, I thought about the tan suit I had packed, which is somewhere in one of the rivers, or maybe even the ocean by now, and it just made me laugh."

Micah chuckled at the remembrance, and then Katharine started laughing again, until both were laughing hard and tears were trickling down Katharine's cheeks. Embarrassed, she wiped them away with her hands. She didn't know whether they were tears from the laughter or from the anguish she felt over her predicament, knowing she would soon board a train, wearing the too-big, soiled clothing which had been her attire for a whole week. She thought of the huge armoire in her bedchamber at home which bulged with beautiful clothes, some unworn, and the absurdity of it all almost made her laugh again.

They walked through the town of Brunswick, carefully avoiding the part of Bay Street known as "Hell's Half Acre." The name of such a place had piqued Katharine's curiosity. She was reminded of the place in New York City, called "Hell's Kitchen," thinking it likely that every town had its sleazy quarter which catered to the low instincts of man. She wondered whether the backwoodsman, striding beside her, had ever visited the area which seemed to be the place where rafthands celebrated, once they had brought their rafts to Darien and had been paid. Darien and Brunswick both offered places for merrymaking and mischief.

However, though they shunned the tawdry section of Bay Street, they could not escape the sensuous music which issued from the brothels and dives or the slatternly women whose mincing presence attracted lustful men with money to spend on them. Katharine had heard of these saloons where cards were played on the first floor, often provoking customers to draw their weapons on one another or to engage in fist fights, and where ladies of the night entertained their paid clientele on the second floor. She couldn't help but wonder what the backwoodsman would be doing now, if he didn't have her to look after.

The rafthands were a wild lot. She had seen enough to know this was true, but Micah MacRae seemed to be cut from a different cloth, though he was accepted as one of them. He obviously had the high regard of not only the raftsmen but also the officials in Darien. She thought it most unusual that the City Council wanted to hire him as Inspector General. Why, he would have had authority over all of the timber inspectors, including the ostentatious Sly Siddon, if he had accepted the offer.

Katharine knew that Sly Siddon had always looked down on the backwoods people from upriver, belittling their lack of education, their rustic manners, and their perceived poverty. Without doubt, the Darien City Council was comprised of men who could grasp the worth of a man by looking beyond the shallow differences of speech and dress, and by recognizing his quick mind, his acumen in regard to the timber business, and his ability to deal with all types of people.

She thought it was so typical of Micah not to be impressed by the job offer. Having been reared among people who treasured education, culture, and family lineage, she was constantly baffled by the backwoods people who instead seemed to eschew these same values. Rather, she mused, the backwoods people placed more worth in ability, land ownership, and industry than in the acquisition of material possessions, other than land or stock, or intellectual achievements.

She supposed that was why she had always sensed a contentment among the isolated backwoods people that she had never found anywhere else. Yet she did feel that Micah's family respected education, though they had never had the opportunities to acquire it.

She supposed that their lack of interest in material things could be traced to their Primitive Baptist faith, a stern and disciplined religion, well-suited to their isolated, backwoods existence.

"Gettin' tired?" Micah asked, and his voice made her jump.

"Didn't mean to scare you, Ma'm," he said.

"Oh, you didn't. I mean, I guess I just had my mind on other things."

Micah suddenly stopped walking and became very still, listening.

Katharine heard it, too, the long, wailing whistle of their train just north of Brunswick. It was a little ahead of schedule.

"You feel like walkin'? The depot's maybe a half mile away. We'll be ridin' about five hours on the train so you might want to walk now. If you'd rather ride, I can hire a carriage."

"No, I'd just as soon walk, if you think the train won't leave us."

"It's scheduled to leave at 9:45, so we've got a good fifteen minutes until that time," Micah said, looking at his watch which he quickly dropped back into his chest pocket.

Something about the watch caught Katharine's eye, and the way that Micah hastily looked at it and as quickly disposed of it made her wonder about it. She really did want to see it but she wasn't sure just why.

"Your watch," she said, nodding toward his pocket where his fingers were securing the leather strap, attached to the watch, around the button on the pocket. "May I see it?" she added, momentarily forgetting that they had a train to meet.

The backwoodsman hesitated, as if undecided about something, before loosening the strap and holding the watch for her perusal.

"Why, it's a railroad watch," she said, looking closely, "a 23- jewel Hamilton - one of the best." Katharine hesitated, looking at the backwoodsman intently. "Where did you get such a watch?" she blurted, without thinking.

"Won it in a card game, Ma'm, from a railroad conductor," he said easily, dropping the watch back into its pocket repository and twining the thin leather strap around the safeguarding button.

He said no more and she asked no more, but the interchange revealed to her that Micah MacRae had undoubtedly played his share of cards when the stakes were high. It made her wonder again what vices he would be indulging, if he didn't have her tagging along. However, when he spoke again, he clarified what she had been pondering.

"Just in case you're a-wonderin'," he said, his eyes dancing with mischief, "I don't play cards for money anymore. In fact, I took the watch back to the conductor who lost it to me in the card game and tried to give it back to him. I didn't feel right about keepin' it but he wouldn't take it back – said I won it fair and square."

Another louder train whistle resounded through the night, informing them that the train had now arrived at the depot in Brunswick. As they hurried toward the depot, they passed by the building which housed the foreign consulates of Norway, Portugal, Spain, Great Britain, and the Argentine Republic. Micah explained that one man, Rosendo Torras, served as Consul for the five countries. The presence of foreign consulates amplified the importance of the port city of Brunswick.

The route to the passenger depot of the East Tennessee, Virginia, & Georgia railroad led through the infamous row of brothels and saloons on Bay Street, known as "Hell's Half Acre". For once, Katharine was glad to be dressed in loose-fitting men's clothing, her hair in a ball, tucked up inside the slouch hat. She kept her head lowered as they walked quickly through the red-light district.

Some of the saloon doors hung open, exposing cigar-puffing men sitting at tables, playing cards, their whiskey jugs and crocks within easy reach. Curses and other vile language issued forth from the dimly-lit rooms. The smell of rum and tobacco and overflowing privies saturated the air.

A rafthand in front of them staggered into one of the barrooms. He asked the bartender for a drink of "Old Squirrel." Having none of that brand, the bartender offered him "Old Crow," instead, which the raftsman refused with an oath, saying he only wanted to "hop, not fly." Though she made an effort not to be amused by the drunken rafthand's reply, Katharine had to laugh, and when she caught the backwoodsman's eye, he was laughing, too.

A vaguely familiar Negro's voice carried from one of the ground-floor rooms, as they hurried by, and when Katharine surreptitiously glanced inside, she recognized the large, surly Negro named Blue, from the *Hessie* trip. He was collaring two of the card-playing rafthands, jerking them away from the table.

"That's our train!" he rasped. "Just heard the whistle!"

Katharine walked faster, unconsciously putting some distance between herself and the wayward Negro.

"Whoa, where are you a-goin' in such a hurry?" Micah laughed.

"I just saw those Oconee rafthands back there and I heard one of them say something about hearing the train whistle and boarding the train. I had no idea they would be riding the same train." Katharine's voice revealed her fear.

Micah was smiling. "Now, wait a minute. We don't have to sit in the same coach with 'em. They won't bother you, anyway."

"I'm not so sure," Katharine said, her voice unsteady. "You said the one named Blue would kill people."

"Ma'm, you don't have to worry when you're with me," he said, looking down at her. "Now," he continued, quietly, "we better get to the train."

The brick streets of in-town Brunswick had given way to a shell road which they followed to the depot. The train station was a hub of activity with the steam locomotive, *Number 14,* spouting dense black coal smoke from its smokestack and periodically blasting steam onto its front wheels. Small coal cinders stung the eyes of everyone in the vicinity.

Having purchased their tickets at the ticket office, Katharine and the backwoodsman boarded the train, taking seats in one of the white-only passenger coaches, which was darkly lit with hanging kerosene lanterns. Micah opened the window by Katharine, as the air in the coach was warm and stagnant, reeking with unemptied cuspidors of tobacco spit.

Looking out the window, Katharine saw the Oconee rafthands boarding the train. They were loud and boisterous, and the conductor appeared to be having heated words with them. The large one, Blue, asserted his control over the five rowdy rafthands, clapping several of them on their heads and propelling them up the steps and into the coach which was designated for colored passengers.

Katharine rested her head on the back of her seat, realizing for the first time that she was tired and sleepy. After all, it was nearly 10:00 o'clock at night, and home was five hours away. She knew she'd be asleep before long and she felt safe and secure with Micah MacRae beside her. With her eyes closed, she thought how nice it would be to stretch out on a soft, clean bed and to lie her full length against the lean, hard body of the backwoodsman.

Hardly had the thought come to her mind before she reproved herself. She remembered reading about a "reprobate mind" in the Bible, and she was certain that she was guilty of having one. However, dear Lord, she prayed, still with her eyes closed, you have made him so attractive to me that I long to touch him and to hold him and, yes, to lie with him. She further prayed that God would forgive her for thinking such troubling thoughts about the man who would be only a memory to her, once she returned home to New York.

She opened her eyes as the shrill train whistle preempted the locomotive's chugging journey into the interior, piney woods area of the state. Passengers began closing their windows as the smoke from the coal-burning engine poured into the coach. Micah closed the window by Katharine, because the coal cinders in the rushing air were burning their eyes.

Katharine settled back in her seat, feeling lulled by the rocking of the train. Other passengers also prepared for the lengthy trip, resting their heads on the backs of their seats. Several children, all in one family, talked and fussed among themselves.

Her glance fell on the potbelly stove. In a month's time, the weather would be cool enough for a roaring fire in it. However, the air in the coach now needed cooling, rather than heating, and soon the passengers were raising their windows again, trying not to notice the black residue that clung to their skin and clothes, or the coal cinders that burned their eyes, for the cool night air gave them some relief.

A foul odor pervaded the coach, vying with the stench of the full cuspidors, and Katharine traced it to three bedraggled rafthands who sat away from the other passengers at one end of the coach. She asked Micah in a whisper whether he knew them and he replied that he didn't, but he thought they were Ohoopee River rafthands. Several times, she heard the raftsmen allude to the Ohoopee River, so she assumed Micah was correct. Micah remarked that the Ohoopee River emptied into the Altamaha, probably forty miles below the Forks, and Katharine remembered that they had spent one night near the mouth of the river. Obviously, all of the creeks and rivers in the area, which had any depth at all, were used to raft logs to the Altamaha and on to Darien. She had heard Ben tell of rafthands who would ride a single log, sometimes for an entire day, through the mazes of streams which fed into the Ocmulgee River, hoping to add it to ones which they had waiting to be constructed into a raft at a boom on the river.

The conductor came through the coach, announcing that the train was stopping at the flag station, Old Number One, the first stop out of Brunswick, if anyone needed to debark. Seeing Micah, he came over and talked for a few minutes, asking him if he still liked the watch. Micah patted his chest pocket and told him he used it every day. The train was slowing to a whistling, bell-ringing stop, even as the conductor spoke and left their car.

Katharine looked out of the window and was surprised to see the Ocmulgee rafthands, Shep, Luke, and Hoke, waiting for the train. They looked even more filthy and disheveled than she remembered them on the raft, for now they were very intoxicated, carrying their whiskey bottles and crocks with them into the colored-only train coach.

"I thought they said they were going to stay in Darien a day or two," Katharine said. Micah, too, was looking at the three Ocmulgee rafthands.

"Guess they took my advice," he commented with a laugh, "and decided not to spend all their money before headin' home." He hesitated a minute before adding ruefully, "However, from the way they look, they spent a good bit of it on whiskey. They'll start their card games now and probably start some trouble, too, especially when they see the Oconee rafthands. There's bad blood between the different gangs on the rivers."

"Oh, I didn't know that," Katharine said with some alarm in her voice.

"The train conductors deal with it all the time, but maybe there won't be any trouble tonight. If they're like me, they'll be asleep in a few minutes. Then, maybe we won't hear anything out of 'em."

The train doors clanged shut and the locomotive once again rolled on its steel tracks through the dark night. Katharine tucked her feet under her and leaned back on the hard coach seat, attempting to be comfortable for the long ride ahead. The slow rocking of the train soon lulled her to sleep.

Chapter Twenty-three

Katharine awoke with a start, thinking she was dreaming, at first not knowing where she was. Then, she realized that their train coach had turned into a war zone where cursing, yelling black rafthands were fighting one another in the middle of the train aisle.

Micah, too, had just awakened and he jumped to his feet, yelling to the drunken men to stop fighting and to go back to their coach. Other passengers in the coach began screaming in fear, husbands standing in front of their wives to protect them. The parents with the three children, now squalling in terror, sought to calm them. The mother held one and put her arms around the other two, as the father positioned himself between his family and the aisle where the rafthands fought.

Katharine sat frozen in her seat, too terrified to make a sound or to move. Panic-stricken, she saw the large Oconee rafthand, Blue, produce a large switchblade knife which he held before the drunken Ocmulgee raftsmen.

"Let me hear dem words agin, raf'hand," Blue said.

"We ain' meanin' no harm, honest t'Gawd," Luke said.

"What's the trouble, Blue?" Micah said, coming behind the large Negro. "What's the problem?"

By this time, the conductor was in the coach, shouting at the rafthands that they had alarmed the whole trainload of passengers, and he was going to put them off the train. The Negro, Blue, flashed his knife at the conductor and shouted that he wasn't "gittin' off no train."

"Blue?" Micah said calmly, "Put up your knife. You don't want to go to jail or worse. Now, what's the problem?"

"Dese Ocmulgee raf'hands, dey say dey de bes' on de ribbers. Ah say us Oconee raf'hands de bes'," the Negro said in a threatening voice.

Fighting words came from the three white Ohoopee raftsmen who had been quiet in their seats near the door of the coach.

"You ain't neithuh one the best. The Ohoopee rafthands can outraft any of you," one of them called out in a menacing tone of voice. At this, two of the Oconee rafthands jerked the Ohoopee raftsmen from their seats and the fighting began anew, midst piercing screams from the women passengers and loud wailing from the children who were huddled up to their parents.

A gunshot sounded, which brought the raftsmen to their senses, if only momentarily. Shep had fired his rifle out of the open window and was set to fire again when Micah calmly lifted the gun from his hands. The conductor was red-faced and angry.

"I want all of you to give me your weapons, and I'm going to place them here by the door. When you reach your station, you can retrieve your guns." The conductor looked around the group of ragged rafthands and held out his hands for their weapons.

The raftsmen refused to acknowledge the conductor's outstretched hands. Rather, each one turned to Micah MacRae and handed over his rifle. Micah placed all of the rifles near the door, then turned to the Negro, Blue, and asked for the knife which he had in his possession.

At first, backing away from Micah, the large Negro refused to give up the knife. His bottom lip quivering and his large thick arms spread, he crouched in the middle of the train, daring anyone to challenge him. His dark eyes shifted to any person or noise which he considered a threat. For a few minutes, only the clacking of the train wheels sounded in the otherwise silent coach. Then the sounds of weeping women and squalling children returned, agitating the colored rafthand further.

Micah MacRae called out to him. "Blue, if you don't give me that knife, I'm goin' to agree with the conductor that we need to put you off the train. Now, give me the knife before somebody gets hurt and you go to jail...or get hanged."

The defiant rafthand flinched noticeably at the thought of the real possibility of being hanged. Men had been hanged for less cause and he knew it. Micah quickly moved toward him and held out his hand for the knife. His huge shoulders slumping, the Negro closed the knife and gave it to the backwoodsman.

As the passengers resumed their seats on the jolting train, midst audible sighs of relief, the conductor joined Micah and the Oconee rafthand in the aisle, berating the latter for the trouble he had caused on his train.

"I ought to put you in handcuffs and turn you over to the sheriff. And what are you colored people doing out of your own coach?"

The Negro looked past the conductor, not answering. The passengers, cowering in their seats, cast furtive glances his way, wondering with renewed uneasiness whether trouble might be brewing again.

Noting the Negro's sullen demeanor, the conductor said, "Well, Micah, when we've had trouble before with the different river gangs, you suggested we separate them and it worked out very well. I think we'll do that now." He added, "I'll leave the weapons there by the door and they can get them when they leave."

Micah suggested that the Ocmulgee rafthands, Shep, Luke, and Hoke, take seats in the coach with him, so that he could keep an eye on them. When the conductor agreed to this, Micah told the three colored rafthands to sit on the opposite end of the train coach from the Ohoopee raftsmen, as he needed to keep the two river groups separated. The Ocmulgee raftsmen hastened to their seats, looking away from the large Negro in the aisle, as they brushed past him to reach their seats.

The other Oconee rafthands had already left the coach and the conductor suggested that Blue join his friends in their own carriage car. The large, colored rafthand looked at Micah MacRae, as if seeking direction for what he should do.

"I've got your gun and your knife, Blue, and we'll leave 'em here until we get to Helena, where I guess you folks will get off and catch the S.A.M. train home. Is that what you're goin' to do?"

"Yassuh," the Negro said, with his head up, undaunted, but with his lower lip protruded.

"Well, we've got another two hours before we get to Helena, and it's the middle of the night. Why don't you all put up your cards and your whiskey and..." Before Micah could continue with his lecture, the conductor intervened.

"I'm seeing to that myself. You rascals aren't going to disrupt this train again. No drinking is allowed, either. You all know that. I'm going to see to it myself that your whiskey is poured out." He waited for a moment for the Negro to precede him out of the coach. As the conductor followed the large, silent rafthand, he turned back to Micah, gripping him on the shoulder.

"Micah, my friend, we're always glad to see you on our train. You help us keep down any trouble."

"Well, Conductor, as we've talked about it before, these men have families up the river, and they work hard and look after their families. When they get to Darien and Brunswick and have a little money to spend, well, you know the rest of it. They fill up on whiskey and, for the most part, don't even know what they're a-doin'. I think you're right to pour out the whiskey." As the backwoodsman resumed his seat by Katharine, he told the departing conductor to call on him if he needed him again.

Katharine found herself still shaking after the episode. No one had told her how dangerous the trains could be with the drunken rafthands onboard. Also, she didn't realize that the backwoodsman was so well known as a mediator, whether on the steamboat or the train. She had just never realized how rowdy and downright mean the raftsmen could be. She had heard rafthands described as "wild as the river, itself," and now she knew for a fact that they were, indeed. Actually, she admitted to herself, she had seen the reckless and steel-hard side of Micah MacRae that day in his sugar field, when he was furious about the way Maude and Pete Ivey had been treated by Norman Dodge. She turned sideways to look at him as he spoke to her.

"Ma'm, are you all right? You're still shakin'," he said, covering her hands clasped in her lap with one of his own.

"I'm all right now. I was afraid someone was going to get killed."

"For a minute there, I was wonderin' myself. It's gotten to the place that rafthands from the different rivers are lookin' for fights with one another. It's gotten worse lately. And I know it's hard to believe, but these same men, for the most part, are hard-workin' farmers who don't drink much, except when they come to Darien and Brunswick."

Micah moved his hand and Katharine thought how reassuring his touch had been. She had felt his great strength, and she knew that it was something she desperately needed.

The passengers in the coach were settling back in their seats. Some were already asleep. The children had dropped off to sleep almost immediately after the frightening bout with the Negro had ended. They all sat together on one seat with their small bodies relaxed against one another, their eyes closed and their little mouths open.

"Put your head on my shoulder, if you need to, Ma'm," Micah said.

"Oh, no...I don't need to," Katharine said, though she longed to do just that. She rested her head on the back of the seat and was soon asleep.

***

Through her dreams, she could only faintly hear the conductor's voice as he came through the coach, holding on to the seat backs to maintain his balance on the shifting train. Still half asleep, Katharine tried to concentrate on what he was saying.

"We'll be at Longview in five minutes. Micah, I'm stoppin' the train for you."

"No, I'll just jump off. No need to stop the train just for me. I'm usually the only one gettin' off."

"Well, it's a regular stop, and we're runnin' right on time. Our schedule shows Longview at 2:53, and my watch says 2:50. We'll be ahead of schedule if we don't stop, but you never want us to stop."

"No, it takes longer for the train to come to a stop, and I can be off it and gone before it can stop. Just saves us both a little time and trouble."

"All right, Micah. Until next time, take care of yourself. And again, thank you for coming to our assistance. I see that all the weapons are gone, so I guess the rascals picked them up when they got off in Helena."

"They did, and they had calmed down quite a bit. They didn't have any more whiskey to drink, so they had sobered up and were actually decent when they came to get their weapons. They didn't know where they had a-left their guns, so somebody told 'em where they were. One or two even apologized for the trouble they had caused." The conductor shook his head, finding it difficult to smile and dismiss the antics of the rafthands aboard his train. The two friends shook hands as the conductor continued his passage through the coach and on out the door.

Katharine was wide awake now, realizing with a sinking feeling in the pit of her stomach that her relationship with the backwoodsman was nearing its end, in fact minutes away. He was standing, gathering his few possessions, most of which were in the large croker sack which he slung over his shoulder, along with his rifle.

He had a lightwood knot and some matches in his other hand. She supposed this would be his source of light for the long, walking trip through the dark pine forest to his home on Bear Creek. Morning was nearly four hours away, and she wondered whether one lightwood knot would suffice for the lengthy trek. She knew that he had another one stashed away in the croker sack, or perhaps several more, if the need should arise. Without a doubt, he was the most self-sufficient person she had ever known.

He was standing, holding out his free hand to her. She rose, also, quickly observing that the other passengers in the coach had gone back to sleep, following their arousal by the conductor only a few minutes before.

Wordlessly, she stood on tiptoe and kissed his rough-bearded cheek. He put his arm around her and kissed her lightly on the mouth.

"Goodbye, Micah," she said, as he started toward the coach door.

"Here," he said, handing her the derringer. "I removed the bullets and I have a sack for you to use for the gun and the bullets, 'til you get home."

Katharine accepted the sack, wordlessly thanking him with another kiss, this time on his lips.

"Goodbye, Katharine," he said in a low voice, adding, "I'll be seein' about your other trees." He gave her a brief hug.

"I know you will," she said, not really knowing what else to say, as she followed him to the coach door.

Once on the platform outside, he turned briefly to her before leaping off the rolling train into the dark night. She hurried back to her seat, holding on to the seat backs to keep from falling. She peered out the window into the night, trying to see the backwoodsman, and was rewarded when she saw a light bobbing through the trees, though she could only dimly see his form illuminated. She was glad to know he had the burning lightwood knot. Maybe it would ward off bears and catamounts, though she knew he never worried about such.

The last few miles of the train journey were the longest to Katharine, because she traveled them alone without the reassuring presence of the large backwoodsman. The aching void in her heart, now that he was gone, seemed to grow as the train rolled on its clacking iron wheels through the night.

She thought of him, walking the tenebrous forest paths toward Bear Creek. She brooded about the real possibility that she might never see him again, after she moved back to New York.

The kerosene lights of the Godwinsville station, Number 12½, shone through the trees, as the train slowed to a jolting stop. Katharine looked out the window and saw her carriage with Big Hill sitting in it, studying the train windows, obviously looking for her. The two carriage lamps glowed on either side of the driver's seat, illuminating his face.

She hurried to the coach door and down the train steps, with the conductor holding a lantern for her to see. He looked at her curiously, and Katharine knew that he was wondering who she was, since she had sat on the train with his friend, Micah MacRae. She was thankful that she wouldn't have to put up with the deception any longer, now that home was only a short distance away. Smiling and waving, she quickly walked toward the carriage. The two grays bobbed their large heads up and down and sideways in excited recognition and she threw her arms around their thickly-maned necks, so great was her relief in finding her horses and carriage and Big Hill to meet her during the late night hour.

Big Hill climbed down from the Brougham, his black, weathered face beaming his nearly toothless smile. He made no mention of the fact that she was wearing the same clothing as when she left eight days before. When he looked for her bags to place them in the carriage, she said, simply, that she didn't bring any luggage back with her. He asked no questions, and for that she was grateful, but something about his appearance made her stop before stepping into the carriage. He was wanting to tell her something.

"It sho is good to have you back home agin, Miz Kat'rin, and Ah knows you is glad to be back home, too."

"Yes, Hill, it's been a long eight days."

"Ah come here yesterd'y evenin' and this evenin' too."

"Yes, well, I wasn't sure just when I'd be back, but thank you for being here, Hill." She looked closely at him. What was he about to say? His face shone with suppressed delight as he stood facing her.

"You got a big su'prise at yo' house, Miz Kat'rin."

"What? What do you mean, Hill? I can't stand surprises. You must tell me."

"No'm, dey wants you to be su'prised, and Ah ain't s'posed to let on nuthin'." Hill, looking mysterious, continued to smile in a conspiratorial sort of way. Katharine stamped her foot, annoyed by his maddening attempt to keep something secret from her. She was tired and she didn't want any surprises or secrets, either. She stared at Hill, until he relented and revealed the surprise and the secret, both being the same, which awaited her at home.

"It's yo' parents, Miz Kat'rin. They come day before yesterd'y."

"What? My parents?" Katharine froze, not wanting Hill to know the dismay that she felt. Involuntarily, she looked down at her dirty, wrinkled clothes. What would her parents think? She wanted to run somewhere and hide and wait for someone to bring her some clean, presentable clothes which she might put on before greeting her parents. But there was nowhere to run and no place to hide. Katharine felt the old Negro's smile fading into a curious stare and she summoned a proper response that would allay any puzzlement he might be feeling.

"Oh, Hill, I really am surprised...and pleased, too," she hastily added. "I'm just sorry I wasn't there to greet them. You say they came day before yesterday?"

"Yas'm," Hill said, helping her up to the carriage seat, now that her initial shock was over.

"Yas'm, dey say dey been worried 'bout you, and dey wuz goin' to come dahn and see 'bout you."

Katharine smiled weakly, trying to convey a pleasure she could not feel under the circumstances. If only they had let her know that they were coming, she thought, as Big Hill guided the carriage from the depot on to the dirt road which led directly to her house.

How she had looked forward to a lingering tub bath when she arrived home. What a strange turn of events! She thrashed about in her mind, trying to decide just what to tell her parents about her lengthy absence, her disheveled clothes which were her dead husband's, and her arrival back home in the middle of the night at the train station.

As the horses briskly pulled the carriage through the inky night, its lamps doing little to light the tree-topped path ahead, her thoughts began to settle, and the dismay which she had first felt when she heard of her parents' arrival was rapidly changing into the anticipation of seeing them. As for what to tell them, why, she would tell them the truth! She had long wanted and needed to confide in someone about all that was happening in the piney woods. She had kept everything to herself for so long, and now she had the opportunity to lay the facts before her parents and see how they reacted. After all, Katharine thought, I'm a grown woman, and I have a right to my own opinion, just as they have a right to theirs.

Finally, the team pulled the carriage onto the brick circular drive of her home, its facade barely recognizable in the dark night. Katharine insisted that Big Hill not help her from the carriage and she easily climbed from it unassisted. However, he held a lantern for her and waited until she entered the house before guiding the carriage on to the stables.

Katharine quickly lit a lamp and started toward her room, when she saw a moving glow from another lamp coming around the corner of the hallway. It was her parents, coming to greet her.

"Katharine, honey, is that you?"

"Yes, Father, I'm home."

"We've been here two days," her mother said, as Katharine ran to embrace them in the hallway. Katharine hugged her parents quickly, then stood away from them.

"I'm terribly dirty, I'm afraid. You'll never guess where I've been."

Her parents stared at her, taking in the man's attire she was wearing and the droopy hat which she held in her hand.

"Katharine, wherever have you been? You don't look like yourself. And whose clothes are you wearing?"

"Whoa-a-a..., wait," Katharine said, laughing. "One question at a time. Come on in the parlor, so we can talk. I'm so dirty, I'm going to sit on the floor," she said, as she led her parents into the parlor. They set their lamps on tables in the room, and Katharine lit candles to provide more light. Her parents continued to gaze at her as if they were looking at an apparition.

Katharine felt giddy, so intense was her need to tell them all that she knew about the Dodge family and the land war. She hardly knew where to begin, but begin she must, before her parents decided that she had become deranged during her residence in the remote piney woods of the South.

"Mother and Father, first of all, I'm wearing Frank's clothes, and I've had them on for eight days. I know you could smell me when you hugged me while ago." Her parents protested, no, that they didn't smell her, but their eyes remained glued to Katharine, awaiting an explanation about her appearance and her whereabouts. Katharine blurted out, to her parents' amazement, "I rode my raft to Darien and that's where I've been all week."

"You what?" Her parents said simultaneously, in horrified voices.

"Yes, I wanted to be assured of a good price for my timber. Also, I wanted to see Darien so I rode my raft."

Her mother and father looked at each other in astonishment, then back at Katharine. Neither said anything, waiting for their daughter to continue.

"Mother and Father, I'll come back to the raft trip in a few minutes. It was the experience of my life, but I'm glad it's over. If it were not for Micah MacRae, I would not be sitting here now. He saved my life on three different occasions."

"Oh, Katharine, darling," her mother said in an anguished voice, "whatever are you trying to tell us?"

"Yes, and who is this Micah MacRae?" her father asked.

"Micah MacRae is the pilot oarsman who cut my timber and rafted it to Darien. As I said, he saved my life three times, once from a catamount, once from a rattlesnake, and once from a Klansman who tried to attack me."

"A Klansman? You mean somebody in the Ku Klux Klan?" Ann Stuart's eyes were enormous and her mouth open, as she stared at her daughter. She had heard of the Klan but hadn't realized that it was active again in the South. Katharine forebore telling her parents about the Klan raids on her property. That would come later. She didn't want to frighten them about staying there at her home.

Her parents' rapid-fire questions elicited from Katharine much of what had happened in her life during the two years since her husband had died. She told them about the questionable deeds to over 300,000 acres of land in the surrounding counties which the Dodge family claimed. She told how the local people were fighting back by tearing up the railroad tracks and tram roads and by sabotaging the sawmill at Normandale, but the Dodges continued to win the cases in court.

"A lot of people, including Frank and John Forsyth, have died, so far," Katharine said. "I know William E. Dodge was your friend, Father," she continued, "but what he did here was inexcusable, and now his sons are continuing the seizure of lands, using questionable deeds. People are being thrown off their land at gunpoint and they don't have anywhere to go. I saw one family myself, living in a pole shanty. It was heartbreaking."

Katharine looked at her parents with tears in her eyes, then continued, "I suppose I'm a part of it, too. Frank bought our land from William E. Dodge and I don't know whose it was before Mr. Dodge came into possession of it. For all I know, someone is living in a pole shanty because Mr. Dodge seized their land, then sold it to Frank and me." Tears began to roll down her cheeks.

Her parents, though traumatized by all they were hearing, became upset when they saw their daughter crying.

Katharine, honey, you're carrying this thing too far," her father said gently. "This land belongs to you and Frank, and rightfully so. That's why we have courts of law. You say the Dodges are winning their court cases. Well, then, justice has been done. It's not for you to worry about, honey."

"But, Father, the cases are being tried in the federal courts, rather than the state courts, and the local people have no way of winning."

"Ejectment suits would normally be tried by the superior court, right here in the county where the ejectments take place."

"That's what I'm trying to tell you, Father. They are being tried in the federal courts. Dodge and his lawyers are using a conspiracy charge, something like a conspiracy to deprive Dodge of his lands through forged deeds and perjured testimony. They used the same conspiracy argument two years ago to move the Forsyth murder case to the federal court in Macon, rather than the superior court here."

Katharine's father seemed intrigued but nonplused by what she was saying.

"Katharine, honey, I don't know all of the particulars of the cases you're talking about, but it is highly unusual that the jurisdiction was changed to the federal courts. Obviously, the Dodge sons had the best lawyers money could obtain and they were able to change the jurisdiction to their advantage." Mather Stuart produced a handkerchief from his vest pocket and handed it to Katharine to wipe her tears.

She dabbed at her eyes, feeling that she hadn't even scratched the surface of all that had happened and the ambivalence of her own feelings.

"I know you and Mother are sleepy, Father. We can talk again tomorrow, if you want to, after we all are rested."

"Katharine, darling," Ann Stuart interposed, "You are the one who is so tired. Look at you!"

Katharine looked down at her soiled, too-big clothes. She felt she owed her parents an extended explanation for her appearance, yet she felt that nothing she could say would really be a plausible reason for looking the way she did. She dreaded the questions, which she knew would be forthcoming, about who was on the raft with her. She decided to bide for time.

"Yes, it is late and I am tired. However, I'm still going to wash in my tub. Father, will you help me bring in some hot water? I'm sure Big Hill and Ollie are asleep."

"Sure thing, honey."

"I'll help, too," Ann Stuart said.

They went to the back porch and found the buckets, then proceeded to the kitchen where they emptied the wood stove reservoir of hot water into the pails.

Tears misted Katharine's eyes as her parents helped to fill her tub with the hot water. They had always been so good to her, so protective, so loving. And she loved them dearly. However, she felt that she had stepped out of their world since Frank's death and especially since the raft trip.

Katharine knew that, for some strange reason, she had changed forever, since making the river trip to Darien. The staid, comfortable, conforming world which she had known all of her life seemed to have crumbled, and in its place was...what? She didn't yet know the answer to that question.

"Think that's enough hot water now?" her father asked.

"Yes, thanks so much. Now, you two go on back to sleep and I'll see you both in the morning. Ollie will have breakfast ready. Goodnight."

"'Night, dear," her mother said, followed by, "'Night, honey," from her father, as they left the room and closed the door behind them.

Katharine peeled off the old clothes, vowing to herself to bury them at the first opportunity, and added a little cold water to the hot water in the tub. Turning off the tap, she climbed in the water and sat down in it, resting her head on the back of the tub. This was what she had looked forward to for a week!

She luxuriated in the water, soaping herself, then washing her long hair. The grime of the past week washed away and she let the water out of the tub. Reaching for a towel, she climbed out of the tub and rubbed herself dry. For the first time, she noticed the insect bites on her body. In spite of the long, protective clothing, mosquitoes had found their way under it and had left their red, itching marks. Noting the ugly bites, she could only be thankful that they were left by mosquitoes and not rattlesnakes or alligators. Slipping into her soft gown, she towel-dried her hair and brushed it free of tangles.

Her feather-soft bed, with its down-filled mattress, looked almost unreal to her and as she crawled into it, she remembered how she had slept the past week, with only a blanket between herself and the logs in her raft, or the hard ground on the riverbank. She sighed as she stretched her full length on the white linen sheets, feeling herself slowly sinking into the mattress which cupped around her body.

She thought of Micah and guessed he was still walking the lonely, dark, dirt roads to his house near Bear Creek. She resolved to pay one final visit to his place, to tell his mother and children goodbye. She could not bring herself to tell Micah goodbye. Their parting words on the train would have to suffice. Anyway, he would not likely be at home, as it was laying-by time for the farmers and Micah would be in his fields.

Katharine found herself tossing and turning in the large feather bed. Strange, she thought, that sleep came more easily on the raft than in her own bed. She sighed again, thinking of the backwoodsman trudging homeward. She wondered whether the Dodge logchoppers had already begun their dastardly cutting of the centuries-old pines which surrounded his place. God in heaven, she prayed, hands clutched upward, please protect Micah and his family!

Sleep finally came, but with it came dreams that she was once again on the drifting raft. The gentle rocking of the raft jarred fresh memories of the past week, and in each cameo-like remembrance was the backwoodsman, ever laughing, teasing, protecting, or just piloting the long raft, his brown eyes flecked with gold in the sunlight.

When she finally opened her eyes, she almost expected to hear the lusty river hollers, so real was her dreaming. Instead, she heard nothing but the rhythmic ticking of the mantel clock and the muffled voices of her parents in the guest chamber down the hallway.

She was out of bed in a hurry and quickly dressed for the day. She braced herself for more questions from her parents. She knew she had presented a shocking appearance to them the night before. She smoothed her hair which she had braided into a chignon at the nape of her neck and stepped into the hallway.

"Mother, Father, are you ready for breakfast or have you already eaten?"

"No, Katharine, dear, we've been waiting for you. Did you sleep well?" her mother asked.

"Yes, somewhat," she said, trying not to stretch the truth. "I'm just a little hungry. Let's go to the dining room. Maybe Ollie has our breakfast ready."

The three walked, arm in arm, to the large dining room where Ollie stood in her neat white uniform, one of several which Katharine had bought for her. The stout colored woman looked pleased as Katharine gave her a quick hug and hello.

"It sho is good to have you back, Miz Kat'rin. Ah's goin' on back to de kitchen. Ah knows you and yo' mama and papa wants to talk."

"Thank you, Ollie. I appreciate your preparing meals for Mother and Father while I was gone. They pleasantly surprised me. I didn't know they were coming."

"Yas'm, well, you had 'nuff veg'tabules what Miz Tilda put up, and 'nuff meats in de smokehouse, so's dat's what Ah's been cookin'." Ollie smiled as she left for the kitchen, telling Katharine to let her know if they needed anything.

Katharine rejoiced in the cream for her coffee and the eggs and baked bread. Her father and mother steeped their tea in her porcelain cups.

Katharine looked at her parents almost as though a chasm stretched between her and them. She felt that all she had told them about the land war and the legal troubles had simply not registered with them. They were smiling and talking about people and places in New York, and Katharine found herself not really hearing what they were saying. Her mother was relating the news of Katharine's friends in New York, who had continued with their lives following her own exodus to the South some six years prior. For several years, Katharine had exchanged letters with these friends and visited them when she made her rare trips back to New York. However, since even before Frank's death, she had had no communication with them.

But, life goes on, she thought, as her mother told her about Clara's three children and one on the way, Joan's divorce from her husband, and Susan's husband who had arrived back in New York recently, only to have his steamship quarantined because of the cholera scare and lying at anchor off the wooded heights of Staten Island.

Katharine concentrated on hearing about her friends' lives, feeling an odd detachment, as though so much time had passed and so many events had occurred, that it was difficult to feel a part of the place she had always called home. Also, she kept waiting for her parents to return to the matters at hand in the piney woods of Georgia - the land war, the Dodges' court cases involving the local people, and her own timber harvests and sales.

However, for reasons she would never know, her parents steered clear of the previous night's conversation. In fact, to Katharine, it seemed that they purposely avoided everything that she had talked about.

"Katharine, honey," her father said, "we're going on back to New York tomorrow. You'll be moving back home, anyway, in the next few weeks. I've got business to tend to just as soon as I get back."

"But you haven't been here long. Can't you stay awhile longer?" Katharine could not bear for them to leave so soon. She had much more to tell them but obviously they were not interested in hearing it.

Looking from one of her parents to the other, she finally acknowledged to herself that they did not want to hear any unpleasantries about their old friend, William E. Dodge, now deceased, nor his sons who were now heavily involved in numerous land ejectment cases. The cases had been tried in court, hadn't they? And the Dodges had won, fair and square.

Also, her parents, whether intentionally or not, conveyed the impression that their daughter's early widowhood had left her overly sensitive and perhaps too rash in her judgments. Their feeling appeared to be that once their daughter returned to New York, she would leave the piney woods and its land troubles behind forever, and she would be restored to the Katharine she used to be.

"Have you got someone you can trust to look after cutting your timber and shipping it to Darien?" her father asked.

"Oh, yes, Micah MacRae is to raft it for me. However, he may want to send some of it by rail to Brunswick. He's busy in his fields now."

Her parents did not ask any questions about Micah MacRae, and for this Katharine was thankful. She was afraid her face would betray her if she even mentioned his name once more.

After finishing breakfast, the three of them walked around the grounds of Sighing Pines, visiting the stables where Big Hill was shoeing the geldings. Mather Stuart commented that he'd like to go horseback riding in the afternoon, but Ann Stuart said with a laugh that she certainly did not want to accompany him. She only rode horseback when she had to. Katharine told her father she would ride with him, though she was somewhat miffed by her parents' detachment from the subjects she had broached to them, upon her arrival home the preceding night.

However, realizing that her parents would be leaving in the morning, when she would again be alone, Katharine locked away for the time being the hurt she felt because they didn't share her assessment of the land troubles in the Georgia piney woods. The isolation which she had hoped to shatter by her parents' comforting agreement with her was now sealed by their strange refusal to be drawn into anything unpleasant in regard to their longtime friend, William E. Dodge. She almost wished that she had never confided in them, for she was unnerved by their denial of anything blatantly wrong being attributed to the man nor to his sons.

After the hasty midday meal, Big Hill brought the newly shod and saddled geldings to the front driveway for Katharine and her father to mount for their afternoon ride. They rode over her own acreage first, then headed down the sandy road toward the Normandale sawmill. Passing many acres of cut-over lands with large stumps left behind, Katharine knew her father had to notice the butchering of the once lofty trees, but he said nothing.

In fact, father and daughter rode mostly in silence. From time to time, Mather Stuart would praise the horse he rode or speak of the nice September weather and Katharine would smile in agreement. But the things she longed to talk about went unsaid, because she had opened her heart before and had been rebuffed with silence and denial.

As she rode along by her father, she thought about moving back to New York. She would be going back home...to New York. But what then...? She would live with her parents, at first, anyway. And what about all of her feelings about what was going on down here in the Georgia piney woods? Why, she'd have to bury these feelings. She'd have to find a new life in New York. Isn't that what she had wanted, had been looking forward to?

For some unexplainable reason, tears started in her eyes and she quickly brushed them away. She, too, engaged in small talk in an attempt to keep her feelings from showing. She was relieved when the ride was over and the horses turned into her circular front driveway.

The rest of the day was spent pleasantly enough, with Katharine and her mother playing duets on the grand piano, following an early supper. Mather Stuart, comfortably attired in his wine linen smoking jacket, puffed on his pipe as he listened to the music and thumbed through Katharine's books in her library.

Afterward, Katharine helped her parents pack for their trip the following morning to Normandale where they would board the train for the first leg of their journey back to New York. Her father wanted to board the train at Normandale, rather than Godwinsville which was nearer, as he wanted to look at the Dodges' tremendous sawmill at Normandale. Her parents offered to carry back with them anything which she might want to send ahead but Katharine demurred, saying she hadn't really packed anything yet for her final trip home to New York.

The following morning, Katharine had Big Hill hitch the Percherons to the Brougham and saddle General Lee for herself to ride. She planned to ride alongside the carriage to the train depot at Normandale. Once they were on their way, she planned to ride on over to Micah MacRae's place to say goodbye to his family. After thinking about it, she had decided that she did want to say goodbye, after all, to the backwoodsman. She did not want him to remember her as he had last seen her - dusty and rumpled in her husband's old clothes. She wanted to wear a pretty dress and a fetching ribbon in her hair. She wanted his last memory of her to be what he had several times said she was ... a beautiful woman, ...and she strove to accomplish this.

She brushed her hair until it shone, then gathered it with a wide ribbon, letting it fall down her back in long soft curls. She chose a sky blue cambric dress with a sweetheart neckline and full puffed sleeves, stopping just above her elbows. Its full skirt over a light crinoline fell from her slim, corseted waist. A slight, gathered bustle, an integument of the dress, rested on her hips. She pirouetted in front of her bedroom mirror, appreciating the opportunity to wear a lovely dress again. It would be somewhat uncomfortable apparel for the lengthy ride to the MacRae place, but she had told Big Hill to strap her sidesaddle onto General Lee, as it would better accommodate the dress.

As a last minute thought, she found the derringer and extra bullets, which she dropped into the large pockets of her dress. She would put these in the saddlebag later.

She joined her parents on the front porch. Hill had already carried the Stuarts' luggage in the break to the depot and had returned a short while before. He first helped Katharine into the sidesaddle on General Lee, then assisted her parents in stepping up into the carriage. Replete in his coachman's uniform which he seldom wore because Katharine didn't always require it, he was the epitome of dignity as he took his place on the driver's seat and brandished the reins over the horses' backs, clucking a signal for the trip to begin. He obviously felt that the occasion of driving her parents to the depot merited his change from mere driver to liveried coachman.

Katharine quickly and surreptitiously placed the loaded derringer and extra bullets into the saddlebag which draped over the horse's withers. She knew that danger always lurked in the piney woods, whether in the form of wild animals or mean convicts, and she planned to be prepared, whatever the eventuality.

General Lee was almost rearing at the bit, his pent-up energy ready for a long gallop but Katharine held the horse to the pace of the carriage, mentally promising the animal that the long stretch toward Bear Creek would provide an outlet for his running, once her parents were safely aboard the train.

The southbound train was slowly chugging into the Station Number 11½, as Katharine and the others arrived. After coming to a clanging, steam-gushing stop with smoke erupting from its smokestack, the train waited for its few passengers to climb onboard for the trip to Savannah. Actually, her parents would have to change to the Savannah, Florida and Western train in Jesup for the trip on into Savannah. Once in Savannah, they would board the fast train known as *No. 27*, which would whisk them home to New York in a record twenty-nine hours.

"We can't wait for you to come home, Katharine, honey, and leave all this mess behind," Mather Stuart said, as he and Ann Stuart embraced their daughter and kissed her goodbye.

"Oh, Katharine, we're planning a big coming-home party for you," her mother said. She added, "You'll forget about the petty land squabbles here. It's a shame that they've gotten you so upset."

"Just remember, honey," her father said, " the courts have made the final judgments. After all, this area of the country is still living in the dark ages. You'll be coming back to civilization when you come home in a few days. Then, you'll have a different perspective about everything." Mather Stuart kissed his daughter on the cheek, then continued in a sober voice, "Actually, I don't understand how you could defend the squatters when they killed your husband, Katharine."

Feeling as though a final blow had struck her, Katharine quietly replied, "Father, we still don't know who killed Frank. He was found dead, as you know, by a woods rider on some of the Dodge property near Camp Six. Everyone assumed that he was killed by a disgruntled person who was losing his land, but no one knows for sure just what happened or who was responsible."

"Mather, let's don't upset Katharine here at the train station, as we're about to leave," Ann Stuart said, putting her arm around Katharine's shoulders.

"See, you have her all upset," she continued, pulling a tiny lace handkerchief from her dress pocket for Katharine to wipe the tears from her eyes.

"Sorry, honey, guess I let my lawyer's take on matters supersede any personal feelings I might have. I will say this, however, in defense of your feelings..." He looked intently at his daughter and she braced for whatever he was about to say.

"I have to grant you this: the fact that these cases are being tried in federal court, rather than state court is strange to me. I just don't see how the jurisdiction could have been changed. I don't do much trial work, and I haven't kept up with the revised laws since the war." He paused for a moment. "However," he continued, "the courts have decided, and we are a nation of law and order. We must abide by the courts' decisions. Just don't worry your pretty head about it, honey. I wish you were going back home with us today. We miss you. Come home soon," he said, giving her a final hug and kiss before abruptly turning and following his wife to the train steps. They boarded the train, and Katharine could see them moving through the coach, finally spotting their luggage which the porter had placed onboard. Taking their seats by the window, they gave her a final wave as the train boisterously started up, then chugged with gathering momentum on out of sight.

Katharine, still holding her mother's delicate handkerchief, dabbed at the fresh tears which wet her face, then climbed into the saddle and turned the horse toward her carriage where Big Hill patiently waited, the reins held loosely in his hands.

"I should be back late this evening, Hill. I need to start packing for the move back to New York. We'll begin tomorrow."

"Yes, Miz Kat'rin," the old Negro said humbly, then clucked to the horses to commence the trip back to her house.

Katharine quickly turned General Lee toward the Eastman dirt road which was reached in only a few minutes by the swift horse. After crossing the road, she guided the gelding along the familiar path by the timber railroad which ran through the towering, wind-swaying pines. With their tallest limbs almost meeting over the tracks, a sliver of light followed the railroad through the shade of the green-needled woods.

As breezes rustled the large pines, Katharine listened, looking at the mammoth trees, some of which had survived untouched for hundreds of years. Though she didn't see or hear logchoppers, she wondered whether they were at work on Micah MacRae's trees. She would soon find out.

The trip to the MacRae homestead was longer than she remembered. She prayed that no wild dogs or other menacing animals would appear, as she guided the horse across the old wooden bridge over Sugar Creek. After another hour's ride, she turned left and followed the sandy path which ultimately led toward Bear Creek. The short, rickety bridge over the shallow creek meant that the MacRae house was only minutes away, as the horse cautiously picked his way over its clattering boards.

Katharine was torn between feelings of wanting to see the backwoodsman and his family, but dreading the final farewell and separation from the people who had brought so much light and friendship to her in the midst of the storm of land troubles and disputes and killings. She would never, ever forget them!

As she neared the MacRae home, her heart fluttered with the hope that she would see the man who, only a few days before, had bade her goodbye before jumping off the train near Longview. She had to see him this one last time.

Slowing the horse to a walk before entering the dirt path to the house, she had a strange sense of foreboding. She heard the sound of heavy hooves hitting the dirt and a child's excited, high-pitched voice.

She dug her heel into the horse's flank to quicken the pace and hurriedly guided the animal to the pathway on the left side of the house. At first glance, she realized that something was horribly wrong. The huge black bull in the wood fence enclosure to the left of the house was alternately snorting and pawing the earth. As Katharine watched, hypnotized, it began a quick lope around the fence, pausing from time to time to thrust its horns at the wood rails which, lashed together, formed the circular cage.

As Katharine reined in the horse to get her bearings, she again heard a child's clear, sweet voice.

"Cow...cow..."

She could see the movement of someone on the inside of the rail fence...a child. Then, she realized with a heart turned to stone that it was Little Roy! He had crawled through the rail fence and was inside with the menacing bull!

As Katharine frantically glanced toward the house, wondering where Mrs. Abby and the girls were, the child moved away from the fence and began toddling toward the brute animal which lowered its head, swinging it from side to side. Thick slobber hung in long strings from its mouth. The large black beast, now still, eyed the progress of the little boy who fell several times to the ground which stretched between them.

Katharine didn't realize that she was screaming until her anguished cry rent the air, causing the nervous bull to look her way momentarily. She screamed again as her fingers clawed the saddlebag, searching for the derringer. Her hand closing around the gun, she grabbed extra bullets and dropped them into her large dress pocket, simultaneously sliding from the horse and running toward the rail fence.

The front door opened and Abby MacRae hurried onto the porch, apparently not seeing Katharine but noticing Little Roy in the pen with the dangerous bull. Shouting and screaming , she ran out of the picket fence gate and headed toward the rail fence. At the fence, she yelled to Little Roy to come to her, but the child only laughed with delight and called again to the black "cow," which took several threatening paces toward him.

Without further ado, Abby MacRae feebly climbed the fence and was on her way to retrieve her grandson, calling his name with every labored breath. Her movements enraged the bull, for it pawed the ground, snorting and blowing from its large quivering nostrils before charging toward the old, gnarled woman, its loose dewlap flapping with each hoofbeat. Katharine, screaming and sobbing, quickly climbed the wood fence rails, snagging her dress on the rough wood, which she frantically pulled loose before dropping to the ground inside.

The enraged bull hit Abby with its head down, goring her repeatedly with its deadly horns. Then, it turned its furious attention to the child who was screaming and crying because his grandmother lay dying on the hard ground. No longer was the bull a friendly cow. It was now a mortal enemy and the child tried to escape it, running toward the fence as fast as his chubby little legs would take him, the maddened bull following closely behind him.

Running toward the animal, Katharine pulled the hammer of the derringer back and shot at it, grazing the bull on its thickset shoulder. The beast, trailing blood from its wound, caught the child and lifted him with its horns, throwing him, squalling, into the air, then stomping the little body with its deadly hooves when it plummeted to the ground.

Katharine, shrieking and crying, shot the bull again, this time clipping its ear and bringing it thundering toward her. She reached in her pocket for two extra bullets, her hands shaking as she dropped them in the open chamber.

The bull came on, ripsnorting and raking the air with its horns. Katharine raised the derringer with two hands and shot dead-center at its head, but the animal didn't even flinch. It kept coming and her heart beat wildly within her. As she took aim again, a bullet tore past her, hitting the animal in the head. The bull made one final lunge toward her and dropped dead at her feet. Blood oozed from the bullet entry, wetting the straw and dirt near its massive head.

Screaming and sobbing, Katharine turned and saw the backwoodsman, rifle in hand, running from the fields. At first, he didn't realize that his mother and child lay battered and dead within the fence.

Shrieking hysterically, Katharine raced to the fence and climbed over it, somehow hoping to ease the pain which she knew was to come. Sobbing, she ran to the backwoodsman, wiping her eyes with the sleeve of her dress, still holding the cocked derringer in her other hand.

"Whoa, wait a minute, Ma'm. You're a-gonna get yourself killed, a-runnin' with a gun cocked like that." He gently took the gun from Katharine, her face contorted with horror and tears, and eased the hammer down, then placed it inside the saddlebag, draped over her horse.

"Now, what's happened? What were you a-doin' inside the bull pen? You could get hurt in there. A man was supposed to come last week..."

"Micah, your...son, Little Roy," Katharine sobbed out the words, "and your mother," she said, gesturing toward the fence.

"What?" The backwoodsman ran to the rail fence and looked at the carnage from hell which lay inside. He was over the fence in one large leap, followed by Katharine, ripping her dress again as she climbed, tears streaming, back over the rail fence.

"Lord," she whispered with a sob, "please help us." As she struggled to go to the backwoodsman, on his knees, cradling his dead child, she felt the churning in her breast and throat and fell to the ground, heaving and vomiting. Slowly, she retrieved the small handkerchief of her mother's, damp with her tears, and wiped her mouth.

Holding on to one of the fence rails, she weakly pulled herself up and again strove to reach the backwoodsman who had laid his child back on the ground and now was standing over his mother's inert and bleeding form. Katharine knelt beside the body, placing her hand over the tired heart which no longer beat.

The inhuman sound of grief that he uttered wrenched Katharine's soul and she stumbled over to him, brushing tears from her eyes with her dress sleeves. She stole to him, grasping him around his waist, feeling his hard, thick belt and the coarseness of his work denims and smelling the dried melon juice which clung to his hands and clothes.

He stood with arms by his side, shaking in his anguish and weeping without tears, the sobs in his chest intensifying. Katharine clung to him, wordless, her tears wetting his rough shirt, but still he stood as a standing dead man, the only show of life being the upheaval in his chest, the inward tears which would not cease.

Katharine stood with him, arms locked around his waist, for what felt like an eternity, waiting for the sobs to subside and for some answers as to what must be done.

It was then that she noticed the dog, lying on its side, not moving, near the far end of the rail fence. Obviously, she thought, the child had followed the dog through the fence, not knowing that the dangerous bull was not playing games with them.

She heard men's voices coming from the fields and then she saw the men, hurrying toward them. One of the men was Pete Ivey and the other was a one-legged man who lagged behind, unable to walk as fast with his peg leg.

The men, dusty and sweaty from the harvesting of the melons, were angels of mercy to Katharine. Tears streaming, she quickly ran to the fence, wanting to prepare them for what they were about to witness, but they were already climbing the rails, their faces reflecting the horror of all that lay before them.

"What the...?" the peg-legged man began. Pete Ivey nodded to Katharine, then hurried over to Micah, mutely observing the backwoodsman's anguish and grief.

"I don't know exactly how it all happened," Katharine began in a trembling voice. "When I came a few minutes ago..." She stopped. Had it only been a few minutes? It seemed like hours or even days. She began again, tears starting afresh.

"When I arrived, Little Roy was inside the fence. Then, Mrs. Abby came running from the house and climbed over the fence, trying to get Little Roy out. I had a gun in my saddlebag and I kept shooting at the bull, but it attacked Mrs. Abby first, then Little Roy. It turned on me then, but Micah shot it before it reached me. I guess he heard the shots and came to see what was going on." She wiped her eyes on her damp dress sleeve.

The peg-legged man spoke up, his voice etched with the pain and horror of the scene before him.

"Yes, Ma'm, Micah told us to go on workin', that he was a-gonna see what was goin' on, said he'd be back in a few minutes. Well, when he weren't back and we heard more shots, we figgered we better come see 'bout 'im." The crippled man, sweat popping out on his forehead, gulped, then tried to talk evenly.

"I'm Joe Little, Ma'm. I'm the nearest neighbor to the MacRae fam'ly, 'ceptin' Pete here. He lives here on Micah's place. My place is about three miles down the road." He pointed in the direction of his farm, then continued,

"I seen some bad things in the war, terrible bad," he said, "but I ain't seen nuthin' like this - guess it's 'cause it's my best friend..." His voice broke, then trailed off as he stood, cap in hand, trying to comprehend just what had happened.

Katharine shook her head, as if to shake off the gradual numbing of her senses.

"I'm Katharine Fremont. Mr. MacRae has done some lumber work for me, and I had come over to speak to his mother and children, actually to tell them goodbye, as I'm planning to move back to my home in New York within the next week or so. I taught his daughters music. By the way, where are Carrie and Mary Sue?" Katharine, tears starting again, looked expectantly toward the house, thinking perhaps the girls were too frightened to come outside.

"They're a-spendin' a few days with Ida, my wife," Joe Little said in a hushed whisper. My wife's been a-doin' all the cookin' while we all been a-helpin' Micah with his crops. The two girls have been good help to 'er." Joe Little wiped his eyes and blew his nose on an old, rumpled handkerchief which he withdrew from his dusty overalls pocket.

Everyone looked at Micah, still bent over his dead mother, his shoulders heaving but no sound coming from him. Slowly, the backwoodsman rose and took a few steps toward his child, raising a large forearm and rubbing it across his eyes. He stopped a few feet from his son's lifeless body, despair written in the slump of his shoulders and the droop of his head.

Pete Ivey, cap in his hands over his heart, stood with tears flowing unchecked near his friend and benefactor. He finally reached out and touched Micah on the shoulder in an awkward attempt at sympathy, but the backwoodsman appeared to be cast in stone, his countenance rigid and unresponsive.

Joe Little was the first to make a suggestion about any action to be taken, though he still intermittently reached for the used handkerchief in his overalls pocket.

"Miz Katharine, Ma'm, maybe if Pete and myself can get Micah to the house, then you can stay with 'im while we see about ever'thin' here. Guess we'll be havin' two funerals here at the same time. I'll have to make some coffins for 'is mama and little boy. 'Course, Pete can't hold out to do much, but I got two boys can help."

Katharine nodded mutely as Joe Little limped over to Micah.

"Micah, my friend, you got Pete and me here. We're a-gonna see about ever'thin'. And Miz Kath'ryn over there...she's gonna see about you. Let's go to the house. You need to rest some, son."

For the first time, the backwoodsman's grief-stricken brown eyes looked at Katharine, and she wanted to run to him and again throw her arms around him, but she maintained decorum in front of the other two men. She walked over to him, tears streaming from her eyes. Oh, how she did want to be strong...for him. Resolutely, she wiped her eyes with her dress sleeve, then willed herself to be strong for the man who had been like a refuge for her, since the day she first met him.

"Come, Micah, let's go inside. Mr. Little and Pete will do what needs to be done." She grasped his hand and felt his pain anew, for his large hands, usually steady and warm, were trembling and cold.

She led him through the split-rail gate and on through the picket gate, then up the steps and into his house. They sat in silence in the front room, the same room where she had taught his daughters music and where his dead wife's photograph still rested on the little round table near the piano.

"Katharine?" The backwoodsman's voice startled her. She looked at him.

"Yes?"

"Did I ever tell you that I love you?"

"What?" She felt as though the breath had been knocked out of her.

"What?" she said again, her lips parted.

"I said that I love you," he said simply.

"Micah, darling, you are upset. You don't know what you're saying." She had heard of people enduring traumatic experiences and afterward suffering from delusions, and she feared this was happening to Micah. The fact that she had just referred to him as "darling" still hadn't registered in her mind.

"You'll feel differently tomorrow, when you've had some rest. Come, lie down on the settee. You need to rest."

Micah allowed her to lead him to the old settee where he stretched out, his long legs dangling over the arm rests. He sat up abruptly.

"Think I'll lay down on my bed."

"Come, darling." This time she was aware of calling him the intimate name but it didn't matter. Hadn't he just lost his mother and his little boy? Anything she could say to comfort him, she would say.

She led him to his room and he fell across his bed, opening his arms for her to go into them. She hesitated, then lay down with him, feeling his hard body, steel-muscled from handling the plow and the axe and the pilot oar. The lingering smell of ripe melon wafted from his clothes and his breath.

Someone was walking down the dogtrot, and from the thumping sounds on the wood floor, Katharine knew it must be the stump-legged Joe Little. She was correct, for he called out to her, as he stopped midway the length of the dog run.

"Coming, Mr. Little." Katharine removed Micah's arms and rose from the bed, straightening her dress and patting her hair. Heretofore, she would not have been found with a man, not her own husband, in his bedchamber, but the circumstances were such that she didn't care what Joe Little thought, as she emerged from Micah's room.

To his credit, however, she detected no curiosity nor judgment in the man's manner as he addressed her, only the aching pain he felt for his friend and neighbor.

"Miz Fremont, we put the corpses on the wagon and I'm a-takin' 'em to my place. Pete's stayin' here, and my grandsons and me are a-gonna make the coffins. We'll have to dig the graves, too. Guess Micah'll bury 'em where his grandparents and 'is wife are buried, on back behind the cotton fields. It's higher ground back there, where they got the family cemetery." Joe Little wiped his eyes, then asked Katharine if she could find proper burial clothes for Mrs. Abby and Little Roy.

"Of course. I'll look for them while you talk to Micah. He's just lying down, resting. Go on in." Katharine opened the door and Joe Little went in, hat in hand.

Katharine stirred herself to the task of finding suitable clothes for the two bodies. She entered Abby MacRae's room and hastened over to the old chifforobe. She found the brown dress which Abby had worn to the church meeting that she had attended with her and her grandchildren. It was the only suitable dress she could find. Since Little Roy slept in a little bed in his grandmother's room, she looked for his clothes in the old dresser and found a clean white, homespun shirt and pants. She folded the clothes and placed them on the bench just outside the door.

Katharine walked up and down the dogtrot, trying to sort out her thoughts. She dared not look out at the wagon. She could not bear to see the lifeless bodies of Abby MacRae who had been a second mother to her here in the piney woods, whom she had loved as much as her own mother, and Little Roy, only alive for three short years on the face of the earth.

She paced the dogtrot and jerked around nervously when the door opened and Joe Little emerged from Micah's room, closing the door quietly behind him.

"He pretty much wants ever'thin' done the way I figgered, Ma'm. I done told 'im, too, me and Pete done buried 'is dog. Micah says he's puzzled by the dog. It never did go in that pen and mess with any of the bulls he pent up. We can't figger just what happened or how the baby got away from Miz Abby." The man shook his head slowly, then said, "Weren't no finer woman anywhere than Miz Abby. She had a hard life, but it was a good life. Well..." the man paused again, "me and Pete's got to go and tell ever'body in the fields what all has happened, and it ain't somethin' I'm a-lookin' forward to doin'..." Almost as an afterthought, he said as he placed his cap back on his head, "We gonna get some help from the rest of 'em in the field to cut up the meat. Maude and Pete'll want some. Micah don't want none of it, but I won't turn it down. Times are too hard, what with the company about to come on my land."

He abruptly hushed talking, as though he remembered that Katharine was closely associated with the despised company. She spoke quickly, to let him know that she didn't approve of everything the company did.

"Don't tell me that they're about to start cutting on your land, too, Mr. Little!" Katharine exclaimed. "I have heard Micah say that they were coming soon to his land. Let me tell you...I don't think it's right. I realize that some people do illegally settle on other people's lands, but the MacRaes have been living on this land for generations, and paying taxes. I honestly don't know why the courts are ruling against the local people."

"Excuse me, Miz Fremont, but I know why they're a-rulin' that way - it's because it's the Yankee courts. When our land cases were a-bein' heard in the state courts, we won just about ever'time, but when they changed the jurs'dicshun, why, that's why Dodge is a-winnin' ever' time. He's a damn Yankee, ain't he?" Joe Little's dander was up and fire had come to his voice. Then, he thought about the fact that he had cursed in front of a lady, albeit a Northern lady, and he was apologetic.

"Miz Fremont, forgive me. You are a nice lady, and I didn't mean to be so plainspoken to you. You ain't like the other thievin' North'ners - excuse me agin, Ma'm - I ain't a-meanin' to hurt your feelin's."

"You are forgiven, Mr. Little," Katharine said quietly, then changed the tragically sensitive subject to Micah's young daughters.

"Who will tell Mary Sue and Carrie about their grandmother and Little Roy?"

"I'll tell 'em, Miz Fremont. 'Course, they'll see the corpses. Gotta put 'em on coolin' boards first. We'll put 'em in the front room after we get the coffins made. I got a ol' shed on my place - never use it no more. Oughta be 'nuff wood to make the coffins, specially with one a-bein' sech a small one."

Katharine's tears almost started again, at his mention of the small coffin, but she steeled herself to be strong for the man who, only minutes before, had told her he loved her.

"Here are the burial clothes, Mr. Little. They were the only ones I could find."

"My wife'll put 'em on the bodies, after she washes 'em and they cool a bit," he said, draping the clothes over an arm.

After Joe Little left to tend to the sad duties that awaited him, Katharine silently opened Micah's door, only to find the bereaved backwoodsman with his eyes closed, one arm hanging over the side of the bed, his chest still shuddering from time to time with pent-up grief. Katharine gently placed his arm back on the bed, the movement causing him to turn restlessly onto his side, his eyes still closed. She quietly tiptoed out of the room, closing the door noiselessly behind her.

Grasping her elbows in front of her, she walked to the front of the house and braved a look toward the bullpen. Maude Ivey and her husband, Pete, were busy butchering the animal which had wrought such havoc and brought such pain.

Joe Little had hitched his own mule to Micah's wagon which held the battered bodies of Abby MacRae and her little grandson. Katharine watched as the one-legged man nimbly climbed up to the seat of the wagon and grabbed the reins. Clucking and flipping the loose reins, he guided the mule along the dirt pathway which led from the house to the road, turning left onto the sandy road which led to his neighboring farm.

Katharine sighed, not knowing what to do with herself. She walked the length of the dogtrot, back and forth, taking care not to step on any creaking boards which might rouse the backwoodsman.

Shadows lengthened as the day wore on, and still she walked, keeping within hearing distance of Micah MacRae, in the event he should need her. She had early on decided to stay the night, as he needed someone with him. She assumed that Joe Little would bring the girls back home, when he came back to dig the graves. They, too, would need someone.

Hearing hooves on the sandy road, along with the squeaking of the old wagon, she looked out and saw Joe Little returning with Micah's young daughters and his two large grandsons. Katharine met the girls at the picket gate, their youthful faces pinched and wet with their grief. Soundlessly, she hugged them as Joe Little looked down at them.

"We're a-goin' to dig the graves now, Miz Kat'rin. Pete's a-gonna meet us there at the ol' graves."

"All right, Joe," Katharine said, calling him by his first name, rather than "Mr. Little," for she felt that she had known him a lifetime.

"Micah wants to have the funerals in the mornin'. Then, we got to get back to work in the fields after'ards."

Katharine silently nodded to him, as he guided the mule toward the graves' site on past the cotton fields. She looked down at her young charges, still holding on to her. Their slender shoulders shook with the weight of their sorrow and she heard them sobbing as they pressed their golden heads to her bosom. The three of them stood as though welded together at the picket gate.

Mary Sue was the first to speak and her words were heartrending.

"We won't never see 'em agin, will we, Miz Katharine?" Katharine hesitated before answering.

"Not in this life, dearest."

"Why did it have to happen?" This was Carrie's question, and Katharine was at a loss for words. She, too, had wondered the same thing. Why?...Why?...Why? There were so many "whys" that remained unanswered.

"I really don't know why, Carrie, dearest. We are still trying to piece together just what happened, but there are things in life that we just don't understand...and will never understand. We just have to accept what life throws us and try to make the best of it." Katharine looked at the two young girls who had lost their mother only two years prior and now had lost their beloved grandmother and little brother. They knew, better than she, how difficult life could be.

"Well, it's getting late, dear ones, and I think you should eat something before going to bed."

"Where is Papa?" Carrie asked.

"I'm here, Carrie."

Katharine spun around at hearing his voice and the girls ran to his outstretched arms. He easily picked up both of them, holding one with each strong arm, their heads resting on his shoulders. As their young tears started again, he sat on the top porch step with them and wiped their wet faces with a handkerchief which he pulled from his back pocket.

"We saw 'em, Papa," Mary Sue sobbed, "they're in the coffins that Mr. Little made and they're there in their front room."

"Mama's gone and now Gramma's gone, Papa," Carrie said in a low voice between sobs.

"That's true," the backwoodsman said, his voice almost breaking. "However, I'm here and Miz Katharine is here."

"I surely am," Katharine said, struggling to speak in a calm voice, "and I'm going to the kitchen to prepare something for you to eat."

"Thanks, but nothin' for me," Micah said. "Fix somethin' for yourself and the girls, if you want to, but I ain't hungry."

"I'm not, either," Katharine said, and the girls, looking at her with tear-streaked cheeks, said that they couldn't eat anything.

The long day was finally coming to an end. Before darkness set in, Micah drew water from the well and brought it to the house. He then retired to the front room, while Katharine helped the girls prepare for bed.

Looking at them as they lay in their bed on the cornshuck mattress, their eyes swollen from crying, Katharine realized how much she would miss them. It was almost as if they were her own, especially now that their grandmother was gone. She bent down to kiss them and was moved to tears when each child gave her a hug and kiss.

"Try to get some rest. I'll be sleeping in your grandmother's room, if you need me during the night."

Katharine quickly left the room, carrying a burning candle with her to the front room. Micah sat still in one of the chairs with the thin cushions. He appeared to be brooding. Katharine slipped in and sat in the other rocking chair. She could sense that he needed to talk.

"A man was s'posed to come last week to get the bull. I wish now that I'd a-gone on and turned the bull out of the pen, but I kept thinkin' the man was a-comin'. Once you turn 'em back out in the woods, it's near about impossible to round 'em up again. I had my crops to lay by, too."

"Don't blame yourself, Micah."

"Come here, Katharine."

"W..what?"

"I said, come here. I want to hold you."

Katharine went to him, and he pulled her to his lap, holding her with both arms and bending his head over her face.

"I need you, Katharine," he said, his voice hoarse.

"I'm here, Micah," she said, lifting her face and kissing him on the forehead.

"I don't want you to go," he said.

"I'm not about to go anywhere. I'll stay here several days, if need be."

"No, I mean I don't want you to leave me...ever."

"What are you saying, Micah?"

"When I saw you in the pen with the bull and I thought you were about to be killed, or bad hurt, it seemed like the life was goin' out of me. You looked so beautiful. You stood there and faced what many a man would of run from." His voice broke as his strong arms pulled her closer to him.

"And then," he continued, "when I saw why you were a-standin' your ground and firin' that dang derringer that'd only hold two bullets at the time...when I saw my little boy and my mama, I knew then what kind of woman you are."

He kissed her on the mouth, and Katharine wept as she returned his kiss with the fervor and love which she had kept locked inside her and which had ripened and grown since she first laid eyes on him, only a little over a year prior.

"I loved your mother...and your son, too," Katharine said in a voice so low that Micah bent further toward her to hear.

"Do you love me?"

Katharine didn't know what to say. Things were moving too fast. Her whole life was being turned upside down. She looked into his brown eyes, startled by the naked love which she saw in them.

The sound of hoofbeats on the soft dirt in the front yard drew their attention. Then, a man's voice calling loudly caused them to look at each other questioningly. Who would be riding in the darkness, and what message did he bring? They quickly rose from the comfort of each other's arms. Micah grabbed the burning oil lamp and they walked out onto the dogtrot. By the moon's light and the flickering lamp, they could barely see a man, still astride his shifting horse at the gate. The man yelled excitedly.

"It's burnin', Micah! You can see it from here!"

"Norris Burch!" Micah said, holding the lamp before him toward the mounted man. "I just realized it was you. What's a-burnin'?"

"It's the mill, the Yellow Pines Lumber Mill at Normandale! It's on fire!" A laugh of vengeful glee issued from the man as he quickly spurred his horse to the road, calling back over his shoulder that he had others to tell about the fire.

Katharine hastened down the steps, picking up her long dress with one hand as Micah followed. Drawing her to him, Micah held her, and they both watched the burning of the Normandale lumber mill, some several miles from Bear Creek, gasping at the fiery display against the night sky.

Orange, jagged flames shot upward over the treetops, accompanied by billowing gray smoke. Red sparks darted to the sky, as if fired from a cannon below. Gunpowder sounds - Boom! Boom! Boom! - burst through the dark night, and Micah commented to Katharine that the barrels of turpentine and kerosene must be exploding.

Both stood in silent awe, contemplating the outcome of what they were witnessing. It was unbelievable that all of the wealth and brains and power of the Dodge industry could not have prevented what was now happening.

"I wonder how it started," Katharine mused aloud with some alarm in her voice. She glanced at Micah, noticing the strange look on his face. His eyes in the lamp's dim glow had a faraway look. Her mind racing, she looked back at the flames which licked at the stars. Had the fire been intentionally set? Did the local people have anything to do with it? Thank God that Micah was at home when the fire began!

Hearing the squeak of the returning wagon, they walked to the edge of the house and peered through the darkness. Joe Little, holding a burning lantern in one hand and the reins in his other hand, was guiding his mule toward them. He alternately clucked and spoke to the animal, trying to hasten the progress of the old wagon.

"Got 'em dug, Micah," he called out as he neared the picket fence. "Had to dig most of it by lamplight. 'Course, the moon helped some. Don't look like no rain for tomorrow." He paused, looking toward the burning sky in the distance over the treetops. "Wonder what's a-goin' on," he said.

"It's the mill burnin', Joe. Norris Burch came by a few minutes ago and told us."

Katharine noticed that a strange look also appeared on Joe Little's face. He glanced quickly at Micah, then at Katharine, obviously wanting to say something to Micah but not in Katharine's presence. Katharine, realizing that the two men needed to talk, told Micah that she was going to bed. It had been a long day and she was tired. Micah handed her the lantern and she hurried up the steps. Her dress caught under her foot as she entered the dog run, and she set down the lantern to see whether it might be torn.

The men's voices drifted over to her as she inspected the dress which appeared not to have suffered any more damage, since tearing it on the fence rails. Though feeling a little ashamed to be listening, she felt compelled to hear what they were saying. Also, she wasn't terribly surprised at herself for her lack of concern in regard to the burning of the Yellow Pines Lumber Mill. In fact, she felt a cool detachment, her only concern in the matter being the absolving of Micah MacRae in the cause of the fire.

"Who done it?" Joe Little's voice posed the blatant question. "We ain't had our meetin' yet."

"No, I was waitin' 'til my crops was laid by. Actually, Joe, I'd been thinkin', and this was what I was a-goin' to tell our people. Ain't no use tryin' to fight the Dodge people. Court'll rule with 'em ever' time. We're a-fightin' somethin' we can't win."

"You're right, Micah, but what are we supposed to do?"

"I guess it's not what we do, but what they do to us, to begin with. Seems we lose our land, one by one, and we better hope we have the money to buy it back, once the Dodge people cut and sell all the trees on it."

"Yep, but they ain't gonna have no sawmill left at Normandale." Joe Little looked at the distant but still raging fire. "Leastways, that's the way it looks from here," he added.

"They've still got the railroad and they got the sawmill at Willcox Lake. They can send the logs by train or raft 'em from Willcox Lake at Temperance."

"You're right, neighbor. It might slow 'em down some, but it ain't a-gonna stop 'em."

Katharine picked up the lantern and crept quietly down the dogtrot to Abby MacRae's bedchamber. Obviously, she thought, from hearing their conversation, the local people had considered burning the lumber mill, but they were to meet again to finalize their plans. Again, she was thankful that Micah had been home when the fire began. "The Lord works in mysterious ways," she thought.

Entering the room, she gently closed the door behind her and set the lantern on the dresser by the bowl of water which Micah had earlier placed there. She fumbled with her dress buttons and the tight laces of her corset, finally stepping out of her dress and pulling the corset over her head. She draped her clothes over the sole chair in the room, then washed her face and hands. Clad only in her sheer chemise, she lay down on top of the bedcovers, refusing to crawl between them and disturb the tidiness of Abby MacRae's room. She pulled up the old, knitted afghan at the foot of the bed which she was certain had been hand-purled by the caring, burred hands of Abby MacRae. She closed her eyes but sleep would not come.

Footsteps at her door told her that Micah MacRae stood just outside. She heard his hand grasp the handle and open the door, holding his lamp out into the room, so as to see her. She lay with eyes closed, knowing that if he chose to lie with her, she would not refuse him.

Men were different, she thought, and yet maybe not so different. Death and life often traveled together, hand in hand, and sometimes the presence of life made death more bearable, less painful.

As she lay under his scrutiny, however, she prayed that he wouldn't take this "life" from her that he wanted, needed, as she knew it was not the right thing to do, aside from the fact that they were not married. She was quite aware, as she lay there under his burning gaze, that he had not even mentioned marriage.

Her propriety made a swift return at this sober realization, and she was able to pull the afghan completely over her bosom and to turn over, away from him, in a final gesture of denial, and though her heart beat like a thundering storm, she thanked God for the strength to do this. She heard him silently leave the threshold and close the door behind him.

After finally sinking into a fitful sleep, she once again heard the unmistakable, shrill groaning of the wagon as the mule pulled it to the picket gate. Then, she heard mingled voices discussing the transport of the dead, and she knew that the bodies of Abby and Little Roy MacRae had been brought back home for their final rest.

Something told her that she didn't need to be sleeping during this time. She really didn't know what, if anything, was expected of her. She knew that backwoodsmen, especially Primitive Baptist backwoodsmen, would keep a vigil or wake over a corpse during the night. Perhaps this was what was beginning.

As she hurriedly redressed, she could hear more and more people walking along the dogtrot, whispering and weeping. She dreaded facing the sorrow and anguish, so recently multiplied, as others became informed of the terrible fate of Micah MacRae's mother and little boy.

Opening the door, she heard women's voices from the back porch and as she stepped onto the dogtrot, she heard three women, their backs to her, singing old-time hymns of the backwoods. They sang without any accompaniment, a cappella, the Sacred Harp music of their faith, and its haunting beauty stirred her soul.

People were coming up the porch steps, then entering the front room where the corpses lay, as others departed. Katharine felt a peculiar estrangement from these people, though for some odd reason she yearned to be a part of them - to grieve with them. Though she had never felt timorous in her life, she suddenly felt isolated as she stood alone on the dogtrot, knowing that she should go into the front room where the bodies lay, but dreading the viewing of them.

She looked toward the kitchen, across the back yard where women worked by the light of many burning oil lamps. More women were arriving with food.

With a start, she saw Micah MacRae coming down the kitchen steps as several young women arrived, some bearing more food. Katharine stood and watched as three of the women took advantage of the opportunity to fling themselves into his arms. One even attempted to kiss him on the mouth, but was disappointed when he turned his head and the kiss landed on his cheek, instead. Katharine recognized the brazen woman as the one who had sat behind the backwoodsman during the church service in Eastman the past winter. It was clear that she was wanting to be the next Mrs. Micah MacRae.

In an attempt to quell the jealousy that she felt rising in her breast, Katharine turned away and followed several more people who were entering the front room to pay their final respects to Abby MacRae and her little grandson, before their coffins were nailed shut forever. Katharine stood just inside the door, waiting for the farmer in his clean overalls and his tearful wife to leave the room. As they walked out, the man wiped tears from his own eyes.

Katharine forced herself to walk over to the coffins, covered with black cloth - one adult size and one very small. Joe Little had done a remarkable job, fashioning them from the heart pine wood of his old barn. He, or perhaps his wife, had also lined them with fluffy cotton batting, the cotton which Abby MacRae had planted and plowed herself, behind a mule, during many summers. Now, it cradled her and the child whom she had loved as her own.

Katharine didn't know why the faces of the bodies were covered with wet cloths. As she contemplated the reason for this, she was aware that someone had come into the room and was standing behind her. She turned around quickly and almost bumped into a plump, past middle-age, woman whose hair was pulled straight back into a wiry, gray bun on the back of her head.

"I'm Ida Little, Joe's wife. You must be Miz Katharine."

"Oh, Mrs. Little. I'm glad to meet you. Yes, I'm Katharine Fremont. I think your husband did a beautiful job making the coffins."

"Thank you, Ma'm. He usually has better wood on hand, but they turned out all right. I had some black cloth, set by for my own or Joe's coffin, but I give it to Joe to cover the coffins. I'll get some more, next time I go in to McRae."

Ida Little paused, then confided, "I been a-keepin' the handkerchiefs on their faces rinched in soda water. Keeps the blood from a-settlin' on the bottom of the corpses, and the faces from a-turnin' so brown. Here, let me move 'em, so you can see their faces. I need to wet the handkerchiefs again, anyhow."

Ida Little adeptly removed the face cloths and Katharine took a last look at the expressionless faces. Nickel coins kept Abby's eyes shut, while silver dimes served the same purpose on the eyes of Little Roy. As Katharine silently looked at the remains of the two people she had loved, Ida Little dabbed the handkerchiefs in a bowl of soda water and wrung them out. Seeing that Katharine had turned away from viewing the bodies, she replaced the wet cloths, commenting that she only used nickel and silver coins for the eyes, since copper pennies left a green color on the skin of corpses.

Katharine sat in one of the rocking chairs in the room. She supposed that the wake would go on all night, until the time of the funerals. Then, after the interments, the men would return to the fields. How they would feel like working without any rest, she didn't know, but this was their way of life.

She sat still in the chair, aware of a slight odor emanating from the nearby corpses. She knew that Primitive Baptists did not believe in embalming, as it was unscriptural, and she knew that the smell would become stronger as the night faded into day. It was for this reason that they never waited longer than necessary to conduct the funeral and bury the body.

Being through for the time being with her funereal preparations, the kindly Mrs. Little advised Katharine that she was going to eat something in the kitchen and wouldn't Katharine like to accompany her. Since the very thought of food made Katharine feel nauseous, she thanked her but replied, no, that she would just sit where she was for awhile. She really didn't think she could eat anything.

She sat with her head resting on the top chair slat, her eyes closed, thinking of the women who had made it plain to Micah MacRae that they were interested in him, particularly the woman who sought to kiss him on the mouth. It was obvious to Katharine that he wasn't interested in that young woman, or any of them, for he had not remarried during the two years of his widowerhood. She wondered about this. He had said that he loved her but did he really love her, or was he trying to exact some revenge on the hated lumber company by lying with her, then casting her aside? And what were her feelings for him?

Did she love him, as he had asked her earlier? Of course, she did, but she was old enough to be practical. She was no fawning, virginal, sixteen-year-old, though if the truth were known, she probably felt the same as one in his presence.

Could she live without him? Just the thought made her heart ache, for she had never even considered answering the question. Heretofore, when it would arise, she would summarily banish it to the secret recesses of her mind. But now, it would not be put away. It lingered for her to mull over and to thrash about in her thoughts.

The sound of uncontrolled sobbing signaled that someone was standing over Abby MacRae's coffin, openly grieving. Katharine decided to tiptoe quietly from the room, so as not to witness the woman's very private pain. However, as the mourner turned her head, Katharine realized she was Maude Ivey with tears streaming unwiped down her brown, splotched face.

Katharine reached out to her and the two embraced as partners in life against their common enemy...death. Maude's thin shoulders shook as she wept and Katharine found it difficult to restrain her own tears.

"She wuz so good to me and Pete and our young'uns. I wuz a-hopin' one day to pay 'er back for all she done for us. I loved Miz Abby. We all loved 'er." With this, a wail of sheer sorrow, that raised goosebumps on Katharine's arms, came from the stricken woman's lips.

Shaken, Katharine heard the door open and was relieved when Pete Ivey, followed by Ida Little, entered the room. Pete, his hunched shoulders more stooped than ever, gently retrieved his grieving wife from the open casket which held the earthly remains of their friend, neighbor, and benefactor, and shepherded her out of the room.

Watching them leave, Katharine thought dimly that somehow their roles now were reversed. When she first met them at the pole shanty, Maude had been the stronger of the two. Now, Pete appeared to be holding up better than Maude.

Ida Little reported to Katharine that the preacher had arrived, and the funerals were to take place as soon as the bodies could be carried to the graves' site. Katharine sensed that the bustling, plump woman was only affecting an air of serenity in the throes of sorrow, for she knew of the attachment of the two friends who had known each other all of their lives, whose husbands had marched away together to fight in the war.

Though the war had claimed her husband's leg, it had taken the life of Royston MacRae, leaving her neighbor to fend for herself and her young son in a harsh, cruel world. Ida briskly wiped away the tears that came, anyway, in spite of her stolid appearance.

Chapter Twenty-four

They came from miles around to the funerals of the MacRae family, for the deceased were ones of their own. The nailed-shut, black cloth-covered coffins, laden with the bodies of Abby MacRae and her grandson, were borne by a mule-pulled wagon, driven by Joe Little, to their eternal earthly abodes. Horse, mule, and ox-drawn wagons, buggies, buckboards, and simple carriages arrived at the MacRae homeplace, their passengers wearing the usual drab attire of backwoods people, with more than usual black cotton dresses and ill-fitting suits interspersed among the mourners. Those who didn't own conveyances either rode their animals or walked. Following the slow-moving wagon on the winding cow path to the grave sites on the far side of Micah MacRae's cotton fields, the solemn procession moved onward in the approaching warmth of the early morning sun.

Many cast their eyes toward the empty bullpen where the good woman Abigail MacRae and her little grandson had almost simultaneously met their Maker only the day before. Women and men alike blew their noses and wiped their eyes.

The heady aroma of beef smoking and the curling wisps of smoke from the smokehouse were reminders that some good would be found in the deadly bull, after all, that it would not be disposed of in the iniquity of its heinous slaughters but, rather, its remains would renew the lives of those who consumed it.

All resolved to be more careful in handling the farm animals which roamed freely in the woods surrounding their homes, often venturing into their yards, sometimes jumping over their protective picket fences. After all, they thought, look what happened to Abby MacRae who had plowed behind mules and oxen, who had milked cows and butchered hogs and cows.

Yes, life could be most difficult in the piney woods, especially for a woman, and though Micah had eased his mother's lot as best he could, she still had met with a terrible death that he could not prevent. Women leaned on their husbands who put protective arms around them, as they walked the last steps to the open graves awaiting the simple, pine coffins.

The old family cemetery was in the midst of a pine-clad knoll, encircled by a small stand of scrub oaks, several cedar trees, and patches of evergreen, cherry laurel bushes. On every side the verdant forest with its thick carpet of wiregrass provided a shady canopy.

Standing near the freshly dug graves, Katharine noticed the nearby graves of Micah's wife, his grandparents, and great-grandparents. The lightwood boards which served as headstones for the graves were simply carved, depicting the names and dates of births and deaths of the ones who were buried there. Jenny's marker read: "Virginia Sue Cameron MacRae, April 26, 1863 - July 15, 1889, Loving Wife and Mother."

The marking boards at the grandparents' graves bore birth dates in the 1840s, and the still legible wood markers at the great-grandparents' graves testified to the fact that both were born in the early 1820s. This should be proof enough to any court, Katharine thought, that the MacRae land ownership began much earlier than any pretended Dodge possession, and yet she knew now without doubt that it wasn't proof that was lacking. It was, as she had heard Micah and Joe Little say, the fact that the cases were being tried in federal court, rather than state court, and the local Southerners were being ruled against by vengeful judges with Northern sympathies. It was a pitiful continuation of the war which was supposed to have ended in 1865, but had been ongoing in the federal courtrooms of South Georgia for several more decades.

Katharine was as certain of this as she was of her own name. She wished that her parents could see the grave markers and the dates. She recalled her father saying that America was a nation of law and order and that all should abide by the courts' decisions, but what if the courts were flagrantly wrong, what then? What if you were about to lose your land and your home and your way of making a living? It was too terrible to contemplate. She could not imagine what it would be like to be in the same position and to know that everything was about to be taken away from her.

Her thoughts returned to the war fought over the veiled concept of state's rights, specifically over the emancipation of slaves. These people didn't even own any slaves, yet they volunteered or were conscripted to fight for the right of those who did, leaving behind them for four long years wives and children who had to learn to fend for themselves. Now, all they wanted was to live their disrupted lives in peace which still eluded them nearly thirty years after the war's end.

Katharine stood near the yawning graves with her arms around Carrie and Mary Sue. She wore the same dress which she had worn the day before, since she had no other to wear.

Across each grave, two flat fence rails were laid to support the coffins. Cotton lines from the animal harnesses were slipped under the coffins, to ease their lowering into the wood vaults which had been constructed in the three-feet by seven-feet, shoveled enclosure for the adult body and the smaller excavation for the child's body.

The girls wore Sunday-best dresses of dark gray cotton, which Katharine had laid out for them. The dresses were old and frayed, but clean. Katharine had brushed their hair, catching it with clasps over their ears and letting it hang down their shoulders in curls.

Micah stood by them, his head bowed. To Katharine's amazement, the young woman who had tried to kiss him earlier now inched her way to him, managing to stand only a few feet from him as the simple service began. The backwoodsman appeared totally unaware of her.

The preacher, noticeably weary from his four-hour horseback ride which began in the dark of the early morning hours, spoke of the Christian life of the gentle lady, Abigail MacRae, and the full innocence of the young child who looked to her as the only mother he had ever known. The soulful preacher also made mention of the fact that the dead child was named for Mrs. Abby's husband who had been killed in the war, some thirty years before. Micah had done this for his mother, knowing it would please her, though Micah himself never knew the father who died when he was only a few years old. Opening his old, worn Bible, the preacher read a few words from the Old and New Testaments, ending with "ashes to ashes; dust to dust."

As the mourners sang a closing hymn, without instruments or books, the men who stood at either end of the vault ledge first settled Abby MacRae's coffin into place, then screwed down the lid on the box. They placed short boards to cover the vault, so that the earth might not touch the coffin.

After following the same procedure with the coffin which held the child's remains, the men who had dug the graves, Joe Little and his grandsons, took up hoes and shovels and replaced the dirt on top of the graves. At the head and foot of each grave, they set lightwood boards, still smooth, awaiting the carved names and dates and epitaphs of those who lay beneath.

The funerals were over. The dead had been buried. Now, the living had to resume the task of living.

The bold, shameless young woman who so coveted the attention of Micah MacRae now stood before him. As he turned to begin the long walk back to the house, she fell in step with him, brushing against him and, at the rough places on the path, holding on to his arm.

Katharine, following behind with his two young daughters, could hear only fragments of the fairly one-sided conversation, but she heard enough and saw enough to know that the girl loved Micah MacRae and was letting him know how she felt in a roundabout, yet obvious, way. Katharine could not see the backwoodsman's face, but she knew that any man would feel flattered by the tenor of the conversation from an attractive young woman such as she.

Katharine also knew that Micah needed someone, now more than ever, since his mother was gone. He had two young daughters who needed a mother. He himself had need of a wife. She knew he could not, and would not, wait much longer to marry.

She assessed the situation in a cool, objective way, priding herself on her ability to remain aloof and to reason with herself in a mature manner. She swallowed hard and it was then that she realized that she was trembling.

Something larger than she had her in the palm of its hand, tossing her about at its every whim and caprice. She was in the midst of a tempest, a storm raging in her heart.

She was unaware that the two sweet little girls who clung to her on either side often looked up, searching her face, as she stared straight ahead, trying not to be consumed by jealousy of the pretty young woman who tripped along by Micah MacRae, holding onto him and looking up at him with her heart in her face.

After all, Katharine thought, trying to think through thoughts and feelings that had infused her mind and heart and soul since she first met Micah MacRae, after all, the backwoods girl who walked ahead of her was from the same background as he. Perhaps he was reconsidering. He might not even remember telling her, Katharine, that he loved her.

Regardless, Katharine thought, feeling herself still trembling, regardless of how they felt about each other, she knew that she had never even considered marrying him, because she would never want to live in the South. Hadn't she been counting the days before she would be moving back home? Again, she swallowed hard. For some reason, her former home now was remote and unappealing, and she couldn't bear to think about returning there, though her parents were expecting her within the next few days.

Several children in the procession of mourners whispered and motioned to Carrie and Mary Sue. Seeing them, Micah MacRae turned around and told his daughters that their friends were leaving and were wanting to tell them goodbye. As the girls hurried along the cow trail ahead of them, Micah turned to Katharine, putting his arm around her waist, appearing not to notice the young woman who had walked beside him.

Katharine was as surprised by this gesture as the other woman, who for the first time looked directly at Katharine, trying to decide who she was. Micah introduced them.

"Katharine Fremont...Nancy Perry."

The younger woman appeared to be stunned yet still uncomprehending. Katharine couldn't help but feel compassion for her, as the expression on her face was a mixture of disbelief, anger, and hurt.

Though the other woman said nothing, Katharine smiled and told her she was glad to meet her. Nancy Perry looked confused and relieved when someone called to her up ahead. She gave Micah and Katharine a long searching look, then hurried away from them.

Micah slowed their pace, pulling back from the rest of the procession until they were alone with nothing but tall timber between them and the others. Katharine felt herself trembling again. She looked at Micah and for the first time, suddenly, everything became as clear as the sun breaking through the clouds.

How, she thought, could she love this man and not love the South, for he was the South?

She faced him and stood directly in front of him. Slowly, she twined her arms around his neck, looking into his brown eyes. His arms pulled her to him, and all she could think was, God in Heaven, I'm home at last, for home is where Micah is.

She stood on tiptoe, feeling the full length and strength of the man she loved. Yes, Micah was this special part of the South with its wiregrass and piney woods. His eyes were the color of pine bark, his hair burnished with gold from the southern sun. He was strong and enduring like the stalwart pines which swayed above them and around them.

Micah's mouth found hers and she kissed him without restraint, feeling his arms around her.

"Do you love me, Katharine?"

"Yes."

He held her away from him, searching her blue eyes.

"Are you sure?"

"Oh, yes, darling."

"Will you marry me?"

"Yes," she said in a small voice.

"And what about goin' home to New York?" he teased, still holding her at arms' length.

"Home is where you are, Micah," she said, as he pulled her back into his arms.

"As you more'n apt know, this place won't be home to me much longer."

"I know that, Micah, but I've still got my place. We can live there."

"Katharine, my love, you're not marryin' a man without any plans. I made some money with my raftin', and I'm about to start my own businesses there in Eastman and McRae."

"You are? What kinds of businesses?"

"Prob'ly a cannery and ice house first. Then...who knows, I may add fertilizer and I just might go into the electric lights business. Won't be long before Eastman and McRae have electric lights. I've already got my buildin's up in Eastman and McRae."

"Is your building in Eastman near the post office?"

"It sure is."

"Why, Micah, I saw the building several months ago when I was in Eastman and I remember asking the postmaster whose it was. He said it belonged to a man in McRae but I never dreamed it was yours."

"I don't think we'll starve, Ma'm," he said, teasingly.

"And don't forget you've got all my timber to see about," she said.

"Well, seein' as how I'm gonna be a married man, I may just see about sendin' that timber by train, rather than raftin' it. Don't think I want to be gone for a week at the time, leavin' my beautiful wife."

"Micah?"

"Yes, Katharine?"

Katharine didn't know exactly how to question him about the lumber mill burning, but if they were to be married, she would like to have some answers.

"Micah," she began again, "I overheard you and Joe Little talking about the fire at the lumber mill, and I understood that the local people had been planning to burn the mill."

"You heard right," he said, harshly. "We had a meetin' a few months ago, and we talked about it. I was a-gonna call another meetin' after my crops were laid by. Then, the mill burned. Actually, though, the situation has changed since our last meetin'. It's no use tryin' to fight the ejectment cases, because they're bein' tried in federal court - Yankee court - now. We're gonna lose ever'thin', anyway. Might as well swallow it the best we can and get on with our lives."

He hesitated, then said, "But the main reason I couldn't have no part in the mill burnin' is you, Katharine."

"Me?" Katharine was humbled by the goodness and the love in his eyes as he looked down at her.

"Yes, you, Katharine. I don't know how much you have invested in it, but I couldn't hurt nothin' of yours." He drew her to him, and again she thought how wonderful it was, at last, to be home.

The wind stirred through the lofty boughs of the virgin longleaf yellow pines which had been standing in their shaded places for centuries. As she kissed the man she loved, she could feel the breeze, lifting her dress and filtering through her hair.

She nestled her head against Micah's chest and listened to the wind rustling through the woods. For the first time, she could detect what Abby MacRae had tried to explain to her. The tall yellow pines no longer sighed in an ominous way.

"Micah," she said, holding her head back and looking into his eyes, her own blue eyes shining with discovery, "I hear the pines soughing."

"They're soughin' for us," he said, pulling her to him and kissing her again.

Chapter Twenty-five

EARLY SPRING, 1895

Katharine sat at the rosewood desk in her bedroom, opening her mail. She had saved the letter from her parents until last, prolonging her anticipation of reading it. She wondered how Carrie and Mary Sue were enjoying New York. This was their first trip to the big city...actually, their first train trip out of the backwoods of Telfair County, Georgia, and she could hardly wait to read her parents' account of the girls' visit.

She looked at her mother's round, letter-perfect script on the envelope before breaking the wax seal and spreading the ivory, monogrammed stationery on her desk. Hearing a door close, she realized that Micah had just returned home from his trip to Eastman.

She rose from the desk, thinking the letter could wait, for she wanted to see her husband. Though they had been married over two years, she still felt like a newlywed. She yet felt the need to touch him, to be held by him, and she could hardly wait for him to put his arms around her and draw her close to him. She waited, almost breathless, as he walked through the house.

"Katharine?" he called.

"I'm in our bedchamber, Micah," she said.

As he entered the room, she felt the familiar warmth course through her body, just from the nearness of him. She walked toward him and he met her, enfolding her with his arms and kissing her.

She stepped back, eyeing the grège linen sack suit, the fine-threaded broadcloth shirt, and the four-in-hand tie which he was rapidly in the process of removing. Her eyes moved on to his dress oxfords.

"Do I pass inspection, Ma'm?" he asked, teasingly, tossing the tie on a nearby chair and unbuttoning his shirt collar.

"You do, sir," she said with mock gravity. "You are very handsome in your town clothes."

"And you are very beautiful," he said, brushing her mouth

with his lips. "Well," he continued, "I have some news ..., news which I think will interest you." His voice had suddenly changed from teasing to serious. Katharine was taken aback. She really didn't know what business he had been involved with in Eastman. He had mentioned joining the Alliance cooperative, but that was a year ago. As she understood it, the Alliance was a group of farmers who joined together to stockpile their needs in a common warehouse. They were also politically active. She moved back to her desk chair, eager to hear what he was about to tell her.

"I met with some of the Alliance men, but it's not much more organized since the last meetin'. We met in my buildin', which they want to use as a storage house," he continued, "the same as my new buildin' in Telfair County. In fact, they're wantin' storage houses for the farmers in Dodge, Laurens, Montgomery and Telfair. They'll prob'ly be the largest in the South."

"So you have joined the Farmers Alliance?" Katharine asked, wondering why this would have brought the ring to his voice and the elation shining in his eyes.

"Yes," he said, mysteriously, "but that is not all, Mrs. MacRae."

"What?" she said, smiling, then furrowing her brow, "You know I don't like secrets, Micah. What are you keeping from me?"

"Mrs. MacRae," he said solemnly, "you're lookin' at the newest member of the Eastman Stock and Investment Company."

"Oh, why that's wonderful, Micah," Katharine said, wondering just what the Eastman Stock and Investment Company might be. She vaguely remembered hearing Julia and Ben Winslow talking about such a company several years prior. As if reading her mind, Micah leaned against the bedpost, arms folded across his chest, and related that her friend, Ben Winslow, was one of the forty members of the company which was formed in 1890.

In fact, Micah informed her, Ben was the one who had come to his place of business, after the Alliance meeting, and invited him to meet with his company at the bank. At the bank meeting, Micah said, he was surprised that everyone was aware that he was making money in the fertilizer business. They also knew about his lucrative diversified farming. At any rate, they needed more capital, so he was asked to join their company. Before Katharine could question him, Micah recounted the purposes of the company for her, describing it in such a way that she could see its money-making potential.

It was to be a general manufacturing business, chartered for a period of twenty years. It was to establish and operate factories for the manufacture of ice, guano, cotton-seed oil, as well as an artesian waterworks and an electric lights plant in Eastman or elsewhere in the county.

"In other words, Katharine," Micah said, noticing the dawning glow of appreciation on his wife's face, "rather than me strugglin' to run my business alone, a-dealin' in one aspect of farmin', I'd be workin' with a company engaged in meetin' the needs of a growin' town. Electric lights will be here in a few years." Katharine was feeling his excitement.

"Oh, Micah, it all sounds absolutely thrilling. I've always known you have a head for business!"

"This will mean that we can build the house we talked about, wired for the new electric lights and with indoor plumbin'. It also means we can easily send Carrie and Mary Sue and our other young'uns to college and do anything else we want to. Oh, and by the way...," Micah said, surprising her again, "you might not want that new house when I tell you about another possibility. Somethin' else Ben told me this mornin' is that he and Julia are a-plannin' to move back to New York in another year or so, after most of the timber is cut. They're wantin' to sell their home, and they are hopin' we'll be interested in buyin' it."

"Winslow Hall?" Katharine knew that Ben and Julia had talked about their move back to New York for several years, but now that the time was close at hand, it almost seemed unreal. And to think that she and Micah now had the opportunity to own Winslow Hall! She had never even thought about owning the place! She knew that few people could afford to buy the splendid estate, and she marveled that Micah was now one of the few who could.

Micah was studying her, trying to fathom her thoughts. He himself was not interested in the Winslow home but he had thought that Katharine would be. Now, it puzzled him to see some hesitation on her part.

"I don't know, Micah. I have always loved it. I don't deny it. But visiting there and living in it are two different things. It's so big, it would take a fortune to maintain it. And it would take servants. I'm afraid Big Hill and Ollie and Tillie wouldn't be enough for Winslow Hall!"

"Well, be thinkin' about it. They don't need to know right away. Julia says their servants would likely stay on with whoever buys the place."

"Micah, I know you've always wanted to go back to your homeplace on Bear Creek."

"Not really, Katharine. It won't ever be the same with all the trees gone."

"But can't they be replanted?"

"Maybe, someday, there'll be a way, but to my knowledge, it can't be done. No, I'm afraid the land in this section of the state will never look as it did when the Dodges first laid eyes on it, after the war."

He continued, "But, even if the pines could be replanted, how long does it take a longleaf pine to grow?" He paused a few moments, before answering his own question: "Prob'ly fifty or sixty years to be of any value. The trees the Dodges started cuttin' took maybe several hundred years to grow. And, as I've said before, they aren't leavin' the small saplin's to replenish the stands. They're clear-cuttin', which should be illegal."

Katharine shuddered at his question, "How long does it take a longleaf pine to grow?", for she remembered asking the question herself at a timber company meeting several years before. The devastation that had been wrought in the piney woods of Georgia by outside forces was inexcusable, and the fact that it was continuing made it even more horrendous and unbelievable. She still felt guilty for her own part in the senseless deforestation of the piney woods. If only there were a way to replant the pines! And there were large stumps and treetops everywhere one looked! Not only were they unsightly but they also took up valuable space that could be used for crops. Katharine realized that Micah was looking at her in a questioning way, and she remembered that he had mentioned college for Carrie and Mary Sue and their own unborn children.

"Oh, Micah," she exclaimed again, thinking about all of the possibilities, "we have a wonderful new college right there in McRae, and from all I hear, the music department is the best!"

Her eyes shining, she rose quickly and hurried to his outstretched arms. Holding her against him, he kissed her neck and throat, then turned her around and encircled her slim waist with his arms, cradling her rounded stomach with his hands.

"He's kickin' today. Sure feels like a boy," he said, smiling, turning her back around and pulling her to him.

"He is, Micah. I don't want you to be disappointed."

"If the baby's a girl, I won't be disappointed...just want her to be healthy," he said, kissing her upturned mouth.

Katharine slid her arms around his neck and looked into the brown eyes that still set her heart aflutter.

"I know you want a boy, Micah," she said simply, "and we need to go ahead and be thinking of his name. However," she continued, moving away, "first things first." She retrieved the letter from the desk.

"It's a letter from Mother and Father. I was about to read it."

With one fell swoop Micah lifted her, startled but laughing, to the large bed where he lay down beside her, his hands under his head on the pillow. Katharine sat bolt upright, still laughing. Crossing her legs under her long, full dress, she smoothed the crinkled folds from the pages and began reading the letter, dated March 3, 1895:

Dearest Katharine and Micah,

The train trip home was delightful, for we experienced it through the eyes and feelings and questions of Carrie and Mary Sue. They enjoyed looking out the windows at the scenery in all the different states we traveled through, but they were especially intrigued by the Pullman berth where they slept soundly during the night. They also enjoyed the meals in the dining car. It hardly seems that they have been here a month already, for we have stayed busy, introducing them to New York City. They are lovely young girls with beautiful manners and natural grace. We have become very attached to them (as I really believe they are to us!). In fact, we look upon them as our grandchildren.

Upon reading this, Katharine wiped tears from her eyes. She had not told her parents that she was expecting a baby, afraid that her past problems with pregnancy might surface again and disappoint them another time. She would wait awhile yet to inform them. She glanced at Micah, glad that his eyes were closed and that he didn't see her tears. Quickly, she resumed reading the letter.

We took them to see the statue of *Liberty Enlightening the World* on Bedloe's Island in the harbor. I wish you could have seen their faces. They especially liked the torch which is lighted by the new electricity.

The girls enjoyed going to the Metropolitan Museum of Art and also the Lenox Library's Picture-Gallery. The statuary in the West Entrance Hall and the pictures by the Old Masters in the East Gallery of the Museum just entranced them. However, we believe their favorite painting was one in the Lenox collection, titled *Blind Milton Dictating Paradise Lost to His Daughters* by Munkacsy. I suppose Carrie and Mary Sue could see themselves as the 'daughters' in the picture.

Of course, every day we are a part of the carriage parade on the East Drive of Central Park. The girls have delighted in the zoo, Carousel, boats, swings, and pony and goat rides.

Needless to say, we're all having a wonderful time. We miss you, but we stay so busy that the girls haven't yet seemed terribly homesick. Carrie and Mary Sue send their love and kisses, along with ours.

> Our love,
> Mother and Father

After reading the letter, Katharine refolded it thoughtfully.

"They love the girls as I knew they would," she said, almost absently.

"Seems that the girls love them, too. Your parents are good people."

"You're right, Micah, they are, but they still refuse to discuss all that's happened here in the piney woods since the war. They still think the Dodges are fine upstanding people. Even though they legally might claim over 300,000 acres of land, I don't see how they could morally or ethically own it, because their deeds are certainly questionable, to say the least. Also, I think the Dodges have had friends in high places who have favored them in the court cases."

Micah reached for her hand and held it to his cheek. Katharine looked at him quickly, realizing that he had further news to tell her.

"I heard somethin' else while I was in Eastman today."

"What, Micah?" He had turned dead serious, and Katharine knew that whatever he was about to relate to her involved the ongoing land war. She braced herself, always fearful that he might return to the fray and be imprisoned or killed.

"As you know, back last summer, Dodge named 381 people as trespassers on 'is lands and filed a bill of peace against 'em. One of 'em was Joe Little."

"Yes, but Micah, Mr. Joe's known this for several years."

"He's changed, though, Katharine. When he saw how the Dodges left my land after cuttin' all the trees and leavin' the big stumps behind, he swore they'd have to kill 'im before he'd give up 'is land."

"He doesn't sound like the man I remember," Katharine said. Memories of Joe Little, after the deaths of Abby MacRae and Little Roy, flooded her mind. He had made the coffins and dug the graves for the two victims. Katharine hadn't seen him or his wife, Ida, much during the past two years. Micah had been so busy with his new business ventures and, from all she had heard, Joe Little had been busy cutting the timber on his land...or what was once his land, trying to stay ahead of the Dodge logchoppers.

Micah continued, talking softly about his long-time friend. "You may not know it, but Joe killed a man not long ago."

Katharine was stunned. "What?" she exclaimed. "No, I didn't know!" The timber war had undoubtedly claimed another victim.

"He killed a colored fella, one of Dodge's logchoppers. Seems they came on Joe's land to lay tracks for a railroad through 'is land. Some of 'em were a-sawin' on 'is trees when Joe came up on 'em in the woods, a-carryin' a Winchester rifle. Joe claimed the company didn't have the right to use 'is lands in any way, while the titles are in dispute and the right of possession pendin' in the courts."

"I have to agree with him," Katharine said, incredulous that anyone would believe otherwise.

"I'm afraid Joe's in a lot of trouble now. Before, he was only charged with contempt of court and was served with somethin' called a "rule nisi," which he ignored. Also, he's been fined $2,000 and has sustained an execution on 'is property in order for him to pay the fine. Now, he's charged with murder!"

Katharine's face was unbelieving, her dark blue eyes transfixed on her husband's face. Joe Little a murderer? Were military men murderers when they killed the enemy? Wasn't this a war? Could a man in America actually be tried for murder when he was protecting what he truly believed was his own land and timber? Again, she had no answers but she feared for Joe Little and his family. Also, she feared what Micah might do, for Joe Little was the father whom Micah never knew.

Micah said, "Somebody gave me this article by our own Judge Roberts in the *Atlanta Constitution*. You might want to read it later. It pretty much disputes the Dodges' claims to all the lands here." Micah threw the paper on the desk, realizing that Katharine still had her mind on Joe Little and hadn't really heard what he had said.

Dazed by the revived intensity of the land war, her thoughts jumbled in trying to assimilate the latest news involving Joe Little, she was disconcerted by a loud continuous rapping on the front door and a woman's high-pitched voice, calling out Micah's name. Katharine followed Micah to the door which he opened to Ida Little, her face tear-streaked and her gray hair wisping away from the severe bun on the back of her head to frame her face. Her two grandsons remained seated on the wagon in the driveway. They nodded and spoke, but refused Micah's invitation to come inside. Rather, they said, looking frightened and edgy, they would wait outside for their grandmother.

Ida Little needed little persuasion to come inside. She nearly fell into the welcoming arms of her two young friends who guided her to a seat in the parlor. Repeatedly, she dabbed at her eyes with a wrinkled handkerchief while informing them of her husband's dire situation.

"The federal marshals are after Joe," she said, her voice breaking and tears streaming.

"I know, Miz Ida," Micah said. "I heard it this mornin' in Eastman."

"He's wanted for murder. He killed a black fella, one of Dodge's logchoppers. He weren't tryin' to kill nobody, just wanted 'em to leave our land and timber alone. I can't believe it - my Joe wanted for murder!" Again, the tears flowed freely and Ida Little looked at Micah beseechingly, as though he could right her upside-down world again and somehow make the pain and heartache go away.

"Where is Joe, Miz Ida?" Micah asked, gently.

Ida Little faltered, looking around the room for unseen ears which might be listening, then lowered her voice to a whisper.

"He's a-hidin' out in the river swamp," she said.

"The talk around Eastman this mornin' was that he was arrested once but managed to get away," Micah said.

"That's right," Ida Little said, tears shimmering again in her eyes, "they came to the house and had our boys, Billy Bob and Junior, in the buggies with 'em. Our boys were with Joe when the colored man was killed. They were arrested on attempted murder. Anyway, the marshal and 'is deputies came down on the train from Macon and rented the two buggies in Helena. They put handcuffs on all three of 'em and were carryin' 'em back to Helena to put 'em on the train to Macon.

"Well," she continued, "they hadn't left the house for long when some of our neighbors waylaid 'em on the road near Longview. They all, 'bout thirty men, came out of the woods and stopped the horses. All of 'em pointed their rifles at the marshal and 'is deputies.

"They freed Joe and the boys and made the deputies take off their handcuffs, then sent the marshal and 'is deputies on their way back to the train station in Helena. Now, Joe and the boys are in worse trouble for resistin' arrest!"

"You know, Miz Ida, I talked to Joe many times, tryin' to make him see that he was a-fightin' a lost cause. I told 'im I'd hire 'im to work as manager of my McRae store but he wouldn't hear of it."

"I know you did, Micah, son," Ida said, "and I told 'im that was the thing to do. I don't like it no more'n he does that the Dodges are a-takin' our land but when the courts gave 'em the right to do it, well, as you just said, Micah, he's a-fightin' a lost cause."

"Whereabouts in the river swamp is he hidin' out, Miz Ida?" Micah asked.

Again, Ida Little looked around the room, as if fearful that someone might be lurking in its shadows, then whispered.

"They're a-campin' out in the woods near the mouth of Big Horse Creek, a place called 'Possum Creek, on farther towards Lumber City. My grandsons been a-gettin' rations to 'em, but that's stopped now, Micah. That's why I came to see you. See, they watch ever'thin' we do now, but they don't know that we know it.

"When we came to your house," she continued, "we lit out through the woods, knowin' they wouldn't know how to follow us. They came after us on the main roads, thinkin' they'd see us a-comin' out on the other side of the woods on the Eastman road, but we kept to the woods, and I guess they're still a-lookin' for us a few miles from here. We didn't want to involve you and Miz Katharine in any way, Micah, but I'm too desperate to do anythin' else." Ida Little placed her hands over her face and rocked back and forth in the still chair.

Katharine was appalled at the change in Ida Little from a plump, aging, serene woman to the thin, hysterical creature who now wept uncontrollably behind clinched fingers, hiding her downcast face. Katharine wanted to comfort her, to reassure her that everything was going to be all right, but she knew that everything was not going to be all right, that her husband and sons were in deep trouble. She knelt down in front of Ida Little and put her arms around her.

"Mrs. Ida, let me make you a cup of hot tea or coffee. Which would you prefer? And how about something to eat with it? I have some blueberry cobbler."

"Oh, no, chile," Ida said, her eyes again brimming with tears, "I couldn't eat or drink nothin'. Thank you though, Katharine.

462

You were always so sweet. I remember how Abby loved you." This brought tears to Katharine's eyes and she quickly brushed them away.

Micah was at the window, looking out at Ida's grandsons who were standing by the wagon, waiting on their grandmother. They appeared to be chilled in the blustery, early spring weather, hopping from one foot to the other with their hands jammed into the pockets of their wool jackets. The evening was turning colder.

"Billy and Joey are cold, Miz Ida. They need to come on inside."

"No, Micah, they're a-lookin' out for the deputies. We all gotta go and get away from your place. As I said while ago, I wouldn't a-come here, but I was desperate!"

"What can I do to help you, Miz Ida?" Micah asked.

"I got to get food to Joe and my boys some way, Micah, and I got to talk 'im into givin' himself up, him and our boys, too. The deputies will follow me or my grandsons, and I don't know what would happen. I'm wantin' you, Micah, to try to talk some sense into 'im. You're the only one can do it. I'm hopin' you can get Joe and Billy Bob and Junior to come on home, whatever happens. They can't stay in the river swamp forever, and in a few months, the heat and 'skeeters'll be so bad, they'll be a-comin' out, anyway."

"The company's cut the timber along Horse Creek," Micah said, knowing that she would grasp the significance of his terse words, since there would be no protective cover for anyone who dared to carry anything to the escaped prisoners in the swamp.

"That's right, Micah, it'd be a-takin' a chance a-followin' the creek with all the timber gone, but that's the only way to go to make any time."

"When do you want me to carry rations to 'em, Miz Ida?" Micah asked.

"They need 'em now, son. It's been awhile since any of us could get food to 'em. The deputies are watchin' our neighbors, too, so I don't have nobody to call on but you, Micah, and I hate havin' to do it." The relentless tears were rolling down her lined cheeks, and she swiped at them with the handkerchief which she kept knotted in her fist. However, for the first time she appeared to be calming down. Her voice was stronger, surer, more like herself when she spoke again.

"I knew you'd do it, Micah, so I put food and dry matches, and anythin' else I could think of, in the wagon. I knew you'd have to ride your horse rather than take a wagon down there in the river swamp, so I didn't pack much."

Micah began slowly pacing the room, obviously in deep thought. Katharine knew that he was studying every aspect of the situation, trying to decide on the best course of action. He stopped from time to time at the window, his hands on his hips, and stared outside for a few minutes before walking to the fireplace and stoking the low fire which burned within it. He knew of the terrible risks involved and that anything he did might be construed as aiding escaped prisoners, though he would try to talk them into giving up and turning themselves in to the deputies. Resting his arm on the mantel, he turned around and faced Katharine and Ida Little who had both sat wordlessly, watching him.

"Miz Ida, I'll go on tonight, as dark sets in, but I'm a-wantin' you to stay here with Katharine. I don't want to leave her alone. Will you do that?"

"Oh, yes, Micah, you know I will! Oh, and let me tell you, son, Joe said to tell you that they tied some gourds together, 'bout a quarter mile from the river. They hacked out a path through the swamp to their camp. They don't put out the gourds, lessen they know somebody's a-comin with rations. Joe said you should be a-gettin' near their hideout about midnight, whether you go tonight or tomorrow night, so he plans to shoot 'is Winchester in the air ever' fifteen minutes. They also have a fire goin' that you might see, maybe the smoke from it, anyways."

"I'll be a-listenin' for the gunshots, Miz Ida, and maybe I'll see their fire. I'll find 'em. Don't worry. I'll get the rations from the wagon and let Billy and Joey take the woods paths back home, not travel the main roads, so maybe they won't be spotted by the deputies. When I come back, we'll carry you home, Miz Ida. I might have to stay a day or so in the swamp, tryin' to talk Joe into comin' back with me."

"I hope you can talk some sense into 'im, Micah, and the boys, too. They're gonna do just what their Pa does, and I used to be happy 'bout that, 'cause Joe always tried to do the right thing. Now, I don't know what to think. He says he ain't a-gonna be taken alive!"

Ida Little reached in her pocket for the wrinkled handkerchief and wiped her eyes. She looked ten years older, Katharine thought, for the fretting and worrying had taken their toll. Feebly, with Katharine's help, she rose from her chair, and the two of them followed Micah outside, onto the wide front porch.

Micah was at the wagon, explaining to the young cousins what the plan was, in regard to their fathers and grandfather. After they quickly unloaded the rations, Micah insisted that they hurry and keep to the woods paths and back roads to avoid detection by the deputies. The young boys jumped quickly to the wagon seat and clucked to the rested horse, hastily shaking the reins over his back. In a few moments, the wagon rumbled to the main dirt road, then out of sight. Katharine knew the boys would head through the piney woods farther on down the road where myriad buggy and wagon trails crisscrossed the wiregrass and where no outsider would dare follow.

As Katharine and Ida Little went inside, Micah disappeared around the corner of the house, on his way to the stables. Though Big Hill and Ollie still helped them, Micah had always told Katharine that he preferred saddling his own horse. He was unused to someone else doing it for him.

He had purchased his large horse only within the past year, after he was convinced that his fertilizer business was on solid ground. Katharine had urged him to ride Harry, the gelding, but he always declined, and Katharine knew it was because the horse had belonged to her first husband. They drove both of the geldings with their carriages, but Micah wanted his own animal to ride.

Katharine set about lighting lamps in the house, for darkness had crept up on them. She knew Micah would have four or five hours of hard riding to reach the remote area in the Ocmulgee swamp where the Littles were encamped. She looked out the window at the full moon in the evening sky, which would be his only source of light during the cold night ride. She remembered her own frightening midnight ride with the young colored girl several years before, and the memory brought cold shivers.

Katharine accompanied Ida Little to one of the guest rooms, knowing that the distraught woman needed to lie down and rest before their evening meal. As she started a fire in the marble-encased fireplace, she heard Micah enter their bedroom down the hall to change clothes for the lengthy horseback ride.

Katharine turned around to speak to Ida Little, but silenced herself when she saw her guest already in deep sleep on the large, four-poster bed. She hadn't even pulled down the bedcovers, so great was her exhaustion. Katharine picked up the large, silk-threaded afghan at the foot of the bed and spread it over her, feeling great sorrow for the personal battles which her friend was having to endure. She closed the guest room door and tiptoed down the hallway.

Micah was standing in their bedchamber, dressed in his leather pants and jacket and homespun shirt, looking almost the way he did the first time she ever saw him at the Yellow Pines Lumber Mill. Katharine gasped at the memory. Micah looked up after tying his leather boots and held out his arms for her.

As she felt his strong arms close about her, she knew that his love was as necessary as the air she breathed. She basked in it, holding him around his neck and laying her head on his chest. She closed her eyes and felt his lips on her hair and cheeks and forehead before finding her mouth. She clung to him, not wanting him to go, yet knowing that he must.

"Be careful, Micah" she said.

"I will," he said, adding, "I think you know, Katharine, that I wouldn't do this, except I feel like I have to. Joe Little was like a daddy to me all my life."

"I know," she said, as they walked arm in arm to the front porch. Micah's magnificent roan stallion was tethered to the hitching post at the driveway, his large bulk glistening in the moonlight. The ponderous saddlebag, bulging with food and provisions for the prisoners in hiding, was draped over the horse's withers. Two large sacks filled with oats for the horse were tied together, then attached to the back of the saddle, along with a tightly rolled bundle of blankets.

Without further delay, Micah spun Katharine around and cupped her face in his hands. With his thumbs, he traced the curve of her cheeks and the moist crevices of her mouth. He kissed her, his strong body shaking.

"I love you," he said.

"I love you, Micah," Katharine said. "Please be careful because I can't live without you." Her voice broke when she said this and, once again, he held her.

"Go ahead, Micah. I'll be all right," she said, resolutely wrenching away from him. "I know this is something you have to do. Just be careful."

Micah leaned down and kissed her one last time before picking up his rifle and slinging it over his shoulder and chest. Leaving the porch in one jump, he was quickly in the saddle. A moment later, he had reached the dirt road, and Katharine could hear the horse's hooves, beating a crescendo at first, then gradually diminishing into the other sounds of the moonlit night.

Katharine went back into the house and blew out the lamps which she had lit earlier. In their bedchamber, she added more lightwood to the fire, stoking it until the flames blazed upward. She quickly put on a warm gown and climbed into bed. Lying back on her pillow, she stretched her hand to Micah's side of the bad, pretending he was lying beside her.

As she lay there, gazing into the fireplace which lit up the room with its burning, hissing fire, she felt the twitchings in her womb, and she cupped her hands over it, already loving the tiny life which flickered inside.

Chapter Twenty-five

The backwoodsman rode the large stallion hard for the first few miles, letting the animal expend the enormous power and energy which had accumulated during several days of restless inactivity. Micah had thought about building a larger fenced-in pasture for their horses, as he felt they were not being exercised enough, especially now that Katharine didn't ride as often as she had in the past. He resolved to begin the fencing, once he returned from the trip to the swamp. Big Hill had always exercised the two geldings, but he refused to ride the new horse, claiming he was too old to ride a young stallion.

Just thinking about his horse's name brought a smile to the lips of the backwoodsman. Katharine had suggested the name, "Pegasus," a winged horse of Greek tragedy, she had said, but when he had suggested "Ulysses," she first thought he had taken the name from other Greek mythology. No, he had countered, he knew little about Greek mythology. He was merely following her lead in naming the geldings after Southern military leaders. His horse would be named after a Northern general. After all, the North had won the war! Katharine had laughed at this, but the name seemed to fit the froward stallion. Katharine was further amused when Big Hill was informed that the horse was named for General Ulysses Grant. The old colored attendant solemnly referred to the horse, from that time forward, as Gen'l Grant. Katharine and Micah always chuckled when they heard him. It never dawned on either of them that their faithful servant could not pronounce the name, "Ulysses."

The horse was still galloping when they reached the small settlement of Normandale, almost completely vacated since the fire which had destroyed the Yellow Pines Lumber Mill over two years prior. The town's populace of six hundred persons had left as quickly as they had arrived. The rumor was being circulated that some German colonists were planning to settle in the area, though they hadn't yet arrived. Also, the town's name was to be changed to "Missler," he had heard.

Micah decided to follow the timber railroad from Normandale to Horse Creek, then follow the path of the former timber railroad along Horse Creek. Since the timber had been cut in large swaths in these areas, the uninhibited moonlight made his course more visible.

He wondered where the deputies were, but doubted they would be traveling even the relatively well-lit timber railroad routes at night. He knew he would raise their suspicions if he should meet up with them. However, they probably did not know of his close ties with the escaped prisoners. They would have no reason to detain him. Still, he ruminated about the possibility that he might be stopped for questioning in regard to the disappearance of Ida Little and her grandsons.

The night stretched on, along with the miles the horse had traveled. The Horse Creek trail which followed the former timber railroad ran parallel with the road which led past Joe Little's home and farm. Micah felt that this was the most dangerous part of his journey, for it was within only a few miles of the Littles' homeplace. However, he strongly doubted that the deputies would even know of the existence of the former timber railroad which ran close by Horse Creek.

The thought occurred to him that he should ride in the creek, so the horse's hooves wouldn't leave their imprints on the soft dirt on the banks. This he did, guiding the large stallion into the low creek water and sloshing along for several miles.

Sensing that the danger of detection had been greatly lessened, now that he was substantially farther away from the Littles' farm, he guided the horse back to the former timber train path and let the animal run at top speed for several miles, attempting to make up for time lost in following the creek.

He was traveling farther toward the river, and he figured he should be at his destination within an hour. In fact, he'd be at the river itself within an hour, he guessed. The road, almost overgrown since the removal of the timber railroad tracks some years before, led in a westerly direction, for it followed Big Horse Creek which emptied into the Ocmulgee River, now only a few miles distant.

The backwoodsman relaxed in his saddle, aware that the worst part of the trip was behind him, and if he could convince Joe and his boys to come out of hiding and to give themselves up, then maybe everything wouldn't be as bad as everyone thought. Maybe there would be some leniency because of Joe Little's age and the fact that he was so troubled over losing his land and timber. Maybe...maybe.

A gunshot sounded to his left, and Micah figured this was Joe Little's signal from his encampment. Micah turned the horse to the left, toward what he guessed was the Opossum Creek area of the swamp. He could smell lightwood burning, though he couldn't yet see the campfire.

He looked for the gourds which Ida Little had described and, within only a few minutes, found them suspended from the low limb of a pine tree. Behind the tree, a crude path led into the Ocmulgee River swamp. The swamp was a tangle of tall slash pines and vines, and he was having trouble seeing anything at all, now that the moon's light was eclipsed. He had to rely on the horse to pick his way through the dense undergrowth.

Another gunshot sounded toward the river and the stallion shied, for it was closer and louder in the swamp, and then Micah saw the glow of a campfire through the trees. He almost dreaded facing his lifelong friends, for he knew that he would become a part of the life and death struggle which had the Littles in its iron grip.

He hallooed through the woods and he could see the three men moving to their weapons, in the event he were the enemy. He hallooed again and called them by name, reassuring them that he was their longtime friend and former neighbor. They peered through the woods, hearing him but not yet seeing him. The big stallion finally entered the circle of light from the lightwood fire and Micah dismounted, tying the reins over a low tree branch.

The short, stocky Joe Little limped over to Micah and embraced him in a bear hug, his tears rolling unashamedly down his bearded face. His two sons took turns embracing the friend they had known since childhood. Though their bearded faces were strained with the urgency of their plight, they manfully held back the tears which their father, in his older years, could unreprovingly shed.

No one spoke at first, the gravity of the circumstances of the three men weighing what needed to be said. Finally, Joe Little spoke in a voice hoarse with pent-up grief - grief for the slow death of his way of life at the hands of the Northern timber barons, though his words were only simple words of greeting.

"Micah, it's good to see you! I knew you'd come. That's a fine horse there. Did you get shed of your mule?"

"No, but Ol' Doll died about a year ago. I think she missed my mama. Ol' Doll was nearly as old as me. She was probably thirty years old but I think she just gave up and gave out when my mama died." In the somewhat awkward silence which followed, Micah looked around the encampment, then returned to the business at hand.

"I got rations for you in the saddlebag. Miz Ida sent some meat from the smokehouse and some of her biscuits and cane syrup. You folks hungry?"

"We been without food now goin' on the second day, son, and before that, it was hardtack ever' day for close to a week. It'll be good to eat Ida's biscuits. Ain't had one of her biscuits in awhile."

Billy Bob and Junior Little both expressed their appreciation to Micah for his willingness to bring them provisions, realizing that he was putting himself in jeopardy. Micah countered that he had to help them, for their papa had always been like a father to him, and he reckoned that they were the brothers he had never had.

Micah lifted the heavy saddle and stuffed saddlebag from the horse and set them on the ground, urging the men to eat the food he had brought, while he tended to his horse's needs. Since the river was only a few hundred yards away, he led the horse to the water to drink. The horse took long drafts of the flowing water. After returning to the campfire, Micah rubbed down the horse with the old blanket which he had placed under the saddle for the trip. This accomplished, he removed one of the sacks from the saddle and placed the sack under the horse's mouth as a manger of sorts. Munching the oats, the horse whickered his contentment.

The Littles were busy eating, also, cutting into the ham which Joe Little had hung in his smokehouse back in the fall. Ida Little's biscuits were eaten, one by one, and the men didn't even bother to heat them on the fire. Rather, they ate them cold, pouring the thick cane syrup over them. Micah joined them, eating sparingly, for the food might be needed for awhile, if the men should refuse to return home.

The men talked little as they ate, for each had his own troubled thoughts. They did, however, ask about their family, about "Miz Katharine," and also inquired about the deputies. Micah knew nothing to tell them about the deputies, other than the fact that Billy and Joey had outrun them by taking the paths through the piney woods to his and Katharine's home.

"We don't want you and Miz Katharine to be drawn into our troubles, son," Joe Little said, adding, "You say Miz Katharine is a-doin' all right?"

"She's fine, Joe. Ida's stayin' with her till I get back. Katharine's about five months along, as you know, and I need to get back to her as soon as I can."

"I understand that, Micah, son, but you need to rest and go back tomorrow."

"That's what I'm plannin' to do, Joe, but I'm a-wantin' you all to come back with me. Ain't no use in fightin' somethin' you can't win."

"They'll kill me if I go back, Micah," he said, coughing and clearing his throat.

"You'll have a trial, Joe, and there's a chance you could get acquitted."

"Not a chance, Micah. I killed a colored fella. Didn't mean to. I was tryin' to scare 'em off my land but one of my bullets killed one of 'em."

"I know that, Joe, but you didn't mean to do it. You just said so. That'll count for somethin' in a court of law."

"We ain't got no 'court of law' now, son. It's the Yankee court now and the law don't seem to count for nothin' no more."

"I agree with you. I think you're right, and I don't like the Yankee court anymore than you do. Only difference is I ain't a-gonna fight somethin' I know, from the outset, that I can't win. You got Miz Ida and your young'uns and grandyoung'uns to think about. Miz Ida was all upset today when she and Billy and Joey came to my house. They're worried about all of you."

"Ida was upset, you say?" Joe Little asked, mounting concern evident in his voice, followed by a fit of coughing.

"Of course, she's upset. She and the rest of your family are like prisoners in their own homes. The deputies want to know just about everthin' they do. As you know, they can't bring you rations no more, because the deputies would follow 'em here. By the way," Micah said, "how long have you three been a-hidin' out in the swamp?"

"I 'bout lost track of time, son, but we prob'ly been here two months, maybe longer." The weariness in Joe Little's voice was painful to hear.

He continued, "We catch all the fish we can, but we need grease and meal to cook 'em. I'm glad Ida sent some meal and sowbelly, too."

"The thing is, Joe, that I don't know how long Miz Ida can send food to you. As I said, they watch everthin' she does, along with the rest of your family. Won't be long before the marshal and 'is deputies figure out how to follow 'em through the woods. It's just a matter of time before they find you."

Joe Little's sons had remained silent during their father's exchange with Micah MacRae. They, too, were tired and they missed their homes and families. Though they remained loyal to their father, they were aware of their own violations of the law. They had fired at the Dodge logchoppers and had been arrested for attempted murder, though they never intended to harm anyone. After their arrest, their neighbors had helped them and their father escape, so all three of them were considered escaped prisoners. The marshal had interrogated their neighbors, trying without success to ascertain who had taken part in the escape. The term, "escaped prisoners," applied to themselves, was difficult enough to bear, but their father's being wanted on murder charges was unbelievable, for the three of them had shot up into the air, over the heads of the logchoppers, and it was just about impossible that one of their high-ranging shots could have killed one of the Dodges' men. The fatal bullet had, however, come from their father's Winchester rifle, as the brothers had both fired shotguns.

As Micah talked on, now pleading with Joe Little to give himself up and face the mounting charges against him, his sons mutely prayed that their father would heed the advice, even if it meant court trials and possible incarceration, or worse, for their father. They knew the inevitability of their situation and they were beginning to doubt the judgment, and even the sanity, of their father.

They knew that Micah was offering them a way out, even at his own peril, and they perceived that now was the time to act. The brothers looked at each other, briefly but meaningfully, establishing that their thoughts were the same. Junior Little, the elder son, spoke first.

"Pa, Micah's right. We don't like the Dodge people anymore than you do, but our hands are tied. We can't fight the Yankee courts. It's time to quit and go home. We got wives and young'uns to think about."

"That's right, Pa," Billy Bob hastened to agree, "you already got a cold from a-bein' out here in the swamp. It could go into somethin' worse. You're too old, Pa, to be a-campin' out here in the cold in the swamp."

A paroxysm of coughing left the older man gasping and blowing his nose. The look of defeat on his white-bearded face brought expressions of despair to the faces of his sons who stood looking downward, as though searching for answers on the ground below them.

In the hours which followed, while Joe Little and his sons wrestled with what to do, talking among themselves from time to time during longer periods of silence, Micah carried the kerosene lantern into the woods to find fat lightwood to add to the fire, for the night was growing colder.

As the fire blazed higher and the swamp sounds chirped and croaked around them, the four men unrolled their quilts and blankets and lay down for a restless night of wakefulness, interspersed with only a few hours of sleep. Micah, too, found it difficult to relax, always on guard for the possibility that the deputies might find the secluded hideout. Though the fire was a necessity in the now bitter-cold night, the smell of lightwood and the smoke rising above the treetops were dead giveaways.

The gray dawn found the men huddled in their spare bedding around a dwindling fire. Lusty hollers from a raft on the nearby river reminded them that if their pursuers chose to scour the river in the Horse Creek area, they would be only a few hundred yards from their camp.

Joe Little's cough had worsened during the night, contributing to the younger men's lack of sleep. The two sons, haggard from worry and sleeplessness, tumbled from their blankets and set about finding more wood for the fire, while their father sat up, coughing and gagging and trying to clear his throat.

Micah rolled his quilt and blanket tightly together. He had decided to leave as soon as possible. The longer he stayed, the more precarious his own situation became.

As his friends began their meager breakfast preparations in the gelid morning air, still undecided about what to do, Micah quietly untethered his horse and led him to drink in the river. Upon returning to the camp, he opened the last sack of oats for the animal before settling down near the roaring fire to eat a biscuit with syrup and some of the fried fatback, along with a tin cup of strong coffee.

Feeling revived, he saddled Ulysses and threw the empty saddlebag over the horse's neck. He would travel lighter going back, with the saddlebag and the sacks now empty. He only had his bedroll, tied to the saddle, and his rifle slung over his shoulder. He was ready to go.

The three wanted men had watched Micah's preparations for his return trip with troubled hearts, each sipping the last coffee dregs from their tin cups, savoring the heat in the cold air. The two brothers rose from their places around the fire, glancing at each other, then eyeing their father whose hacking cough racked his body.

Joe Little held up an arm for assistance and his son, Junior, helped his father to his feet. Coughing and gagging, the man accused of murder limped over to Micah, still supported by his son.

"I been a-thinkin' 'bout all you said, Micah, and I know you're right. I'm an old man, and I'm a sick man. I know I won't last much longer here in the swamp. More'n all that, though," he said, his eyes filling with tears, "I want to see Ida." He repeated, "I want to see my Ida," then added softly, "before I die."

He turned to his sons and said, "Let's get our things together and a-go home, boys." Relief, intermingled with hope, shone in his sons' eyes as they grasped Micah's hand and wished him a safe journey home.

"Mr. Joe," Micah said in a rare deference to his friend's age and illness by the formal title of regard, "you ain't able to walk back home..." Before Micah could conjecture about a way for the escaped prisoner to return home, Junior Little quickly intervened.

"We done thought of that, Micah. I'm gonna go home and get my horse and wagon. Pa can lay down in the wagon. I'll just follow along the old timber railroad - same way you came in."

"Mr. Joe," Micah said, again addressing his friend with loving respect, "I got warehouses in McRae and Eastman, and I need men to work in both places. You and Junior and Billy Bob can work for me. Then, when Dodge is through a-cuttin' your trees, you can buy your land back.

"It ain't right," Micah continued, looking at each of the forlorn, beaten men, "God knows it ain't right, but as I see it, it's the only way. It's what I had to do."

The three Littles each unashamedly threw their arms around Micah's neck, thanking him repeatedly for coming to them and for remaining their friend during their tribulations. They appreciated his job offers, and if they could work out their troubles with the law, they would be seeing him. Finally, they said, he had made them realize that they had to cut the ties with their land, for the land was no longer theirs.

Micah mounted his horse and saluted his friends. This simple gesture brought about a change in the bearings of the three men who stood below him, for they straightened their shoulders and set their chins.

Captain Joe Little stepped forward, without assistance, in front of his sons, and for a fleeting moment he was the Confederate officer who had defended his beloved Southland and who had paid dearly with the loss of his right leg. Never again would his face register the pride and honor which briefly appeared and as quickly disappeared.

"We love you, son," the old man said. "Be careful and have a safe trip home." He slowly turned away, slumping and coughing, as his sons led him back to the warmth of the campfire.

Micah guided the large stallion through the dense swamp toward the path which followed Horse Creek. The sun was coming up, warming the day a bit.

Chapter Twenty-six

On the second day after Micah's return from the swamp, he and Katharine prepared to take Ida Little back home. After hearing that her husband was likely to be home when she arrived, that lady had regained her composure and her grit, and her eyes fairly snapped at the prospect of having her "dear husband" home again with her once more. For the time being, she refused to grapple with the fact that he was wanted on murder and escaping arrest charges.

Big Hill brought the large curtain rockaway, which Micah had purchased shortly after he and Katharine married, to the front driveway. The two geldings were hitched to it. The colored servant held the reins while Micah assisted the ladies in stepping up to the carriage, before vaulting aboard himself. Katharine sat on the driver's seat with Micah, as she thought Ida Little would probably want to sleep on the return trip to her home, and the extra room inside the carriage would make her friend more comfortable. Since the day was warming up, Big Hill had rolled up the carriage curtains.

Handing up the loose reins to Micah, Big Hill inquired whether he should start putting up the rail fencing for the horse pasture which they had talked about. The fact that the old Negro was always aware of what needed to be done, and was willing to be of service in any way, was ever pleasing to Micah, and he could understand why Katharine had always treated Big Hill and his wife, Ollie, who more than earned her keep, also, with such affection. They were like members of their extended family, he thought, looking into the earnest brown eyes which peered from the wrinkled, dark face.

"Yes, you can get started, Hill. You remember, I showed you yesterday how part of the pasture will be in the trees near the house and part near the creek where the trees have been cut. We'll get up the stumps later."

"Yassuh, Ah knows, Mistuh Micah. Ah be done stahted when you and Miz Kat'rin gits back. Yo' Gen'l Grant, he too big to keep shet up in de stables." Micah and Katharine smiled at this.

"We'll be comin' back this evenin', Hill. It'll prob'ly be too late to do much after I get back but we can get started early in the mornin'."

"Sho nuff, Mistuh Micah. I gonna get stahted now. You all be careful now, heah?"

The carriage was soon on the dirt road, the geldings pulling it toward the ghost town of Normandale. The three travelers rode mostly in silence, though Ida Little from time to time questioned Micah about his trip to the swamp to see her husband and sons.

Micah debated whether or not to tell her about Joe Little's sickness. He really felt that his friend needed a doctor, though he knew that Ida Little had her own home remedies and would probably use them before sending for a doctor. Oftentimes, the elixirs and poultices of the backwoods people were as healing as the latest methods of treatment which physicians employed. He decided to let Ida Little make her own judgment about her husband's illness.

Katharine felt an uneasiness and a weariness as she rode along in the carriage. She really had not felt like making the trip, but she could not bear to be away from Micah anymore, so here she was, rocking along beside him.

She reminisced about their marriage and the fact that she had prevailed upon him to live at her home, since his land and timber were involved in one of the Dodge ejectment suits. She knew he didn't want to live in Frank Fremont's home but it was the most sensible option at the time. He had refused at first, but when he found out that she owed money on the house, he had stepped in and paid the balance of what was owed, which was more than half the cost of the house. She knew that it was money he had saved to reinvest in his fledgling businesses which hadn't yet had time to prosper, and she feared that they might suffer, but only then had he agreed to live there, and it was none too soon, for the Dodge loggers had already begun cutting his trees. His business ventures continued to thrive, however, causing her to acknowledge once again his unusual business acumen.

After the timber was cut, Micah swallowed his wrath and his anguish over the desecration of his homeplace and bought back his land which was left treeless with large stumps. This year was the second time he had planted, since buying the land back from the Dodges. He had planted cotton, corn, sugar cane, peanuts, sweet potatoes, peas, oats, rice, and barley.

Her thoughts shifted to the U.S. Marshal and his deputies. She wondered about the possibility that they had been lying in wait for Joe Little and his sons when they returned from their swamp hideout. What if they had already been arrested and were in the Macon or Savannah jail? Katharine quickly glanced back at Ida Little who was already sound asleep. Katharine hoped that the three families involved would have some time together - a week or even a day - before the deputies arrived with arrest warrants.

She stole a look at Micah, dressed in his usual leather and homespun clothing for the trip into the backwoods of Telfair County. She knew he was more comfortable in such attire as he had worn it all of his life, though it had seemed so foreign to her when she first had seen the backwoodsmen of the Georgia piney woods. And to think that she had married one! She smiled at this, happy in her thoughts.

She studied his profile, the clean-shaven face, the set of his chin. She looked at his large, capable hands, loosely holding the reins and his strong legs, straining against the snug leather pants.

Micah suddenly turned the horses onto the road which followed the timber railroad at Normandale. Katharine looked away from her husband to the landscape on both sides of the railroad for perhaps a quarter of a mile and ahead of the tracks as far as the eye could see. It was a wasteland of large stumps where once there had been a pine forest rising out of an ocean of wiregrass. She remembered the huge trees with spreading crowns which nearly touched above the railroad tracks only a few years before.

She remembered the songbirds and the deer and the mellifluous tones of the forest which was home to so many creatures, including man. She remembered how the sounds of the rustling pine trees were at first ominous to her, as if the pines themselves knew of their imminent demise. Then, she remembered Abby

MacRae's enlightening her about the Southern meaning of the whishing sounds which the pine branches made when the wind brushed them together.

Katharine, too, had heard this "soughing" of the pines, sounds of contentment which the local people had lived under for many lifetimes. Now, the "soughing" was being hushed not only in Dodge and Telfair Counties but also in the adjoining counties of Pulaski, Laurens, and Montgomery - a five hundred square mile expanse of virgin timber which was possibly two hundred years old. When it would end was anyone's guess, for the logchoppers had been cutting for twenty years in the area, and someone had said there was enough timber to last another ten to twenty years.

She remembered Mary Sue's childish words, "Prob'ly for miles and miles and miles - nuthin' but big ole tree stumps!" "Out of the mouth of babes...," Katharine thought, for the child's words had been prophetic. In a few more years, they would sadly ring true.

She sighed, thinking about the wanton ravaging of the piney woods. Without looking at him, she felt Micah's eyes on her.

"You're awfully quiet, Katharine," he said.

"Aren't we all!" she replied, smiling at him, then at Ida Little who was still asleep.

Not having received any explanation for Katharine's silence, Micah returned to the business of guiding the horses onto the path which followed Bear Creek. Though some of this timber had also been cut, they were soon riding under thick-trunked yellow pines which hadn't yet felt the axe of the logchoppers.

Shy swamp birds trilled their plaintive songs, and Katharine imagined that they were warning the other forest creatures and the trees, also, what was to come, when the world they had known would soon come crashing down around them. An air of expectancy hovered in the air, though she couldn't decide whether it related to the imminent destruction of the remaining forest land or to the fate of Ida Little's husband and sons.

The carriage was now crossing the short, rumbling bridge over Bear Creek and Katharine tried to shake off her troubling thoughts. However, when they passed by Micah's homeplace, her melancholy returned, for though his land near the road was planted with cotton, the large stumps left by the logchoppers protruded every few feet above the square-budded plants. These would soon produce white blooms, followed by the white-tufted bolls. Micah had removed some of the stumps, but it was a time-consuming process that would probably take years to complete. Though she didn't voice her thoughts, she could certainly understand why Joe Little had fought to keep his land, but she agreed with Micah that it was a losing battle.

She was glad to know, however, that the MacRae home was now occupied by the Ivey family, although no one was visible on the premises. The well-swept yards and tended flowers were testaments of the Iveys' love for the family who once called the place home.

The Iveys were now in charge of Micah's farming operations and Katharine was certain they were in one of the fields, looking after his crops. Pete's health had improved, and he and Maude and their five children rather easily handled the daily farm work. They also used the services of a colored family who lived not far from the homeplace. One of the sons was the young boy who had brought word, several years past, that Katharine was to stop teaching music to Micah's daughters. She remembered the hurt she had felt, when the boy had leaned down from his mule and handed her the envelope with money which Micah had sent for the music lessons.

They were arriving now at the Littles' homestead and the horses pulled the carriage on up to the front porch which ran the length of the house. A man was asleep in a swing on the porch, but he sat up when the carriage arrived near his front steps.

It was Joe Little! Ida uttered a sob as she took Micah's outstretched hand and half-fell from the carriage seat to the ground. As the older couple moved to meet each other, Micah lifted Katharine from the carriage and they stood, watching the tearful reunion of their friends and former neighbors.

Joe and Ida Little embraced and wept, holding on to each other, though he turned aside from time to time to cough and gag.

"Joe, honey," Ida Little said lovingly, "you done got yourself sick down there in the swamp. Sounds like you got pneumonie again, but I got a remedy for it. You got fever, too," she said, feeling his forehead with tender, caring hands.

Though she looked worried, Ida Little, however, pulled away from her husband and faced Micah and Katharine who were now standing by them. As if with one accord, she and Joe Little threw their arms around Katharine and Micah, expressing their love and appreciation for all that had been done on their behalf. Overcome by coughing and gasping for air, Joe Little turned away and started up the porch steps.

"Just go inside and lay down, Joe. I'll fix you a poultice that'll get rid of that cough," Ida said, turning back to her young friends.

"Katharine, honey, you take care of yourself. Seems like you're a-gettin' along real good and you never looked any prettier'n you do now."

"Thank you, Mrs. Ida," Katharine said, adding, "I really believe everything's going to be all right this time."

"When I was a good bit younger, I used to be a midwife in this part of the county. I could always tell whether it was gonna be a boy or a girl. Never was wrong, not even one time."

"Well, tell us what we're havin', Miz Ida," Micah said, smiling.

"You're havin' a boy, I'd say," Ida Little said, eyeing Katharine's slim figure which rounded slightly below her waist. "However, I'd really have to see you closer to time to say for sure," she said with a smile, as Micah helped Katharine to the carriage seat.

"Goodbye, Mrs. Ida. Take care of yourself and Mr. Joe," Katharine said, pulling her skirt aside for Micah to sit beside her.

"Goodbye, dear ones," Ida Little said, blowing a kiss to them as Micah turned the horses toward home. The horses quickly pulled the carriage to the road, and Micah and Katharine both turned around and waved until they could see her no more.

"I'm glad Mr. Joe was home when we got there," Katharine said, reaching for Micah's free hand, "but he seems very ill. Do you think he'll be all right?"

"Yes, I do, my dearest," Micah said, cradling Katharine's small, soft hand in his large, rough one. "I think Miz Ida is at work right now with her tea of butterfly weed and whiskey and maybe her poultice of quinine and hog lard."

Katharine looked sideways at him unbelievingly, but he stirred her further by stating that skunk oil was also used for pneumonia. Though he had never been administered skunk oil himself, he said, he knew others who had, and it was known to help cure a person who suffered from pneumonia.

Though he talked in a lighthearted manner, enjoying her raised-eyebrow puzzlement, she knew that he probably spoke the truth, for the backwoods people were known for their curative potions and poultices. Whatever treatment he received, she silently prayed that Joe Little would recover quickly and that somehow he could rid himself of the murder charge which threatened to separate him, for the rest of his life, from his beloved family and friends.

The trip home was uneventful. Katharine found herself dozing against Micah's shoulder. The rhythmic rocking of the carriage and the horses' hooves hitting the dirt in pummeling cadence finally lulled her into deep sleep, broken only by their arrival home, when the geldings' hooves struck the resounding brick driveway and awakened her. Only then did she realize that Micah had held her for hours, with an arm around her, to keep her from falling in her sleep.

Still half asleep, she leaned over and kissed him on the mouth. He pulled the horses to a halt, then lifted her into his lap. He pulled her against him, until her full breasts felt the buttons on his shirt. His hands moved with familiar exploration over her body and she mutely wondered whether she was attractive to him any more, now that her pregnancy was showing.

His hand found a breast under her bodice, cupping it toward his mouth. His beard grazed her bosom as his mouth covered it with kisses. Not realizing it, he had answered her silent question. He could still make her feel beautiful and desirable. She kissed him, parting her lips for the hotness of his mouth which sent warm shivers through her body.

"Let's go to bed," he said abruptly, hoarsely, lifting her from the carriage. "I'll see to the horses."

"All right, Darling. I'll be waiting for you," she said, as he opened the door and lit a candle for her.

***

Katharine awoke while it was yet dark and lay in bed, undecided whether to add more lightwood to the smoldering fire in the fireplace in their bedroom or whether to turn over and sleep some more. Micah's regular, heavy breathing indicated he would sleep awhile longer, so she decided not to replenish the fire just yet but snuggled against him for warmth. He acknowledged her near presence by pulling her even closer to him, so that she nestled in the inward crook of his body with his arm around her. She remembered the nights on the raft when she had longed to lie within his arms as she did now. She thought about their lovemaking the night before and her body arched involuntarily from her memory of it. She breathed deeply, feeling that she was experiencing the beauty of life at its richest, for she had the love which God had created for man and woman to enjoy. She knew without doubt that this was one of the meanings of life and she thanked God for bringing her to the once-hated piney woods of South Georgia and to the man who now held her in his arms.

She lay quietly, drifting in and out of slumber until the dawn brought subdued light into the room. Then she carefully removed Micah's arms, trying not to awaken him, and crawled out of bed. She knew that he wanted to start early, putting up the pasture fence for the horses, and he had said he wanted to begin at daybreak, but she also knew he had experienced two grueling trips in the last two days, so he needed to rest. She crept about, dressing for the day and brushing her hair over her ears, where she caught it with a pretty green-gold ribbon, the same color as her dress.

She moved quietly about the house, picking up the newspaper which Micah had left on the desk in their bedchamber and finally entering the front parlor. After adding lightwood knots to the wood in the fireplace, she struck a match, lighting the fire, then settled in a nearby chair to read the long *Atlanta Constitution* newspaper article which was written by the judge of the Dodge County court, Judge David M. Roberts. It was titled "The Other Side." Katharine read the article quickly, surprised that the judge was publicly taking the side of the embattled "squatters."

In the article, he stated that the attorney, Luther Hall, and the others presently serving prison time in the Ohio State Penitentiary were not guilty of the murder of the Dodges' superintendent, John C. Forsyth, in 1890. In fact, she read, her heart beating faster, that the person who turned state's evidence against the others and who pretended to suffer from hemorrhage and pneumonia, appearing to be on his death bed during the notorious murder trial held in Macon, was in fact seen fox hunting in the Sugar Creek area of Telfair County three days after his return from Macon, following his pusillanimous betrayal of his fellow defendants.

Katharine read rapidly, knowing that the judge's words would vindicate the way she had felt about the land war during the past four years. She almost laughed out loud when she read:

> Mr. Dodge seems to be, from the tone of his defender's article, a gentleman who is utterly incapable of anything like wrong, and while we are not prepared to deny the assumption that this king can do no wrong, and the killing of his house cat would be high treason against the government, to suppress which all the United States marshals would be ordered out. Yet I feel constrained to refer to two little circumstances of history connected with this land matter that smack very strongly of something diametrically opposed to honesty and fairness. About 1879 or 1880 the Georgia legislature passed an act prohibiting any foreign corporation owning more than 5,000 acres of land in this state unless it should by a certain time mentioned in said act be incorporated under the laws of the state of Georgia. The Dodges then claimed, under the corporate name of the Georgia Land and Lumber Company, all the land to which Mr. Norman W. Dodge now holds titles, but the law was evaded by the corporation transferring the property to George E. Dodge. The effect of this act would have been to require the Dodges to try all these land cases in the state courts in the several counties where the lands are situated.

Katharine read on, still silently laughing about the reference to the killing of Dodge's house cat being "high treason against the government." Also, she remembered Micah's talking about the cases tried in the state courts being often decided in favor of the local people, whereas the ones which were tried in the federal courts were usually decided in favor of the Dodges. No wonder the Dodges had the cases moved into the federal courts, using the flimsy excuse of a "conspiracy" being promulgated against them. She continued reading:

> There is another fraud I desire to call attention to which is being perpetrated by Mr. Dodge, and is no doubt an imposition upon the federal court. Mr. Dodge is using these bills of peace not only to recover the land embraced in Judge Speer's decree, but he embraces in the same batches of lots lands that are not covered by the decree; notably lands sold under wild land tax executions that had been transferred and the title of which has been pronounced to be void by at least two adjudications of the Supreme Court of Georgia.
>
> In conclusion, I would say that there is not a man in Georgia who deprecates forgery more that I do. I abhor and detest it and utterly condemn it whether it is the forgery of a land title, a bank check, or anything else.
>
> Judge Roberts further stated... that he was "with the people in this matter."

Katharine folded the paper, thinking that she would mail it to her parents. Maybe then they would understand what she had tried to explain to them that night, after she first returned home from the rafting trip. She had never, ever, brought up the subject again but it had remained an invisible wall in their relationship. The article only cemented what she had observed for herself, since her first husband's death, that the confiscation of over 300,000 acres of the finest longleaf yellow pine in the world by the Dodge family had been done with questionable deeds, strong-arm tactics, and spurious legal finaglings. However, though she felt justified in her convictions about the land war, she wondered whether anything could be done to assuage the effects of years of pillage and depletion of the longleaf yellow pine. She doubted it. She felt the yoke of despoilment as surely as Micah and the other local, displaced people felt it.

She sighed, laying down the paper, and picked up the tiny baby sacque which she had been embroidering for several weeks. As her fingers worked the long embroidery needle, she felt the baby stir within her, and a sense of contentment swept over her, replacing the turmoil she had felt after reading the article.

Her life was so full now, so meaningful. She had ten regular piano students, and more were wanting to take lessons. She also taught school to Carrie and Mary Sue and some of their friends. Micah had built a school room there at Sighing Pines, which would accommodate ten children around the ages of Carrie and Mary Sue. He had also bought a piano for the schoolroom, and this was where she instructed the children in the study of music.

Both Micah and she were active in community affairs, and all four of the family had joined the Methodist Church in Eastman. In spite of the smouldering land war which alternately flared up, then simmered down, they managed the semblance of a secure, sheltered life. Though there were still grievances in regard to the continued Dodge presence in the area, the consensus among the local people was that it was foolhardy to mount any real opposition to the wealthy Northern family, for all efforts to do so were ultimately futile.

She worked on the tiny linen sacque, scarcely as large as her two hands, embellishing it with the soft pastel threads which she pulled through the cloth in varying patterns of chains and knots. She was looking forward to dressing their baby in the little sacque.

Thinking she heard horses' hooves on the driveway, she laid down the embroidery, then hurried to the foyer and looked out the side panels of glass. A man was leaping from his horse which he didn't even bother to tether. Katharine thought he looked familiar as he rushed up the front steps and held out a fist to pound on the door.

She quickly opened the door and recognized Norris Burch, obviously winded from a lengthy horseback ride.

"Miz Katharine, wh...where's Micah?" he said, swallowing hard and gasping as the words spilled out.

Before Katharine could answer, Micah was beside her, fully dressed, and grimly eyeing their visitor.

"What is it, Norris? No, don't tell me. I think I know. They arrested Joe, right?"

"Micah, my fr...friend," Norris Burch said, still huffing and stammering, "I wish that was all. God knows..." His voice trailed off. He held his deerskin hat in his hands, and his eyes filled with tears as he looked down at the porch floor.

"What's happened? Tell me, man!" Micah demanded, shaking the tearful messenger with both hands.

"They killed Joe!" the man screamed, sobbing, tears streaming down the creases of his face.

Katharine felt a jolt around her heart and she held on to the porch column nearest her. She glanced at Micah, and the stony expression on his face was reminiscent of the time in the bull pen, when he first realized his mother and son were dead. She longed to comfort him, to hold him, but she could only support herself and then she could not even do that. She had no strength at all. Her hands slipped down the smooth white column and she slumped on the cold wood porch.

She awoke on the bed with Micah leaning anxiously over her. At first, she wondered why she was lying in bed, fully dressed, but then she remembered the pain that Norris Burch had brought and she felt it settle around her heart, the cold reality that Joe Little was dead! Another statistic in the never-ending land war, she thought. Then she remembered something else that Norris Burch had said just before she had fainted.

"Micah?" she asked, her voice trembling.

"Yes, Katharine?" he said, holding her hand. "Are you all right? You gave me quite a scare!"

"Yes, I'm all right, but Micah, didn't I hear Norris Burch say that eighty-one bullets were fired into their home?"

"Yes, Katharine, but you need to get your mind off Joe Little. I hate it worse'n just about anythin', specially since I talked him into leavin' the swamp and goin' on back home. But, then, I'm thinkin' Joe was spared havin' to put himself and 'is family through 'is murder trial, which very well could have ended in life behind prison bars. Maybe he was spared all of that."

"How is Mrs. Ida?" Katharine asked, her eyes brimming with tears.

"Norris Burch said she was all right, just scared to death. She said that Joe was asleep on the front porch of his house, when they heard the first bullets. Billy Bob and his boys were in the fields, but Joe told Ida to run to the back porch and wait for him there, 'til the shootin' was over. I think, deep down, she felt like Joe had already been taken from her, and the murder trial would've just prolonged the fact. So, in a terrible sort of way, his quick death was like gettin' it all over with, rather than draggin' ever'thin' out. The thing she's askin', and what we're all a-wonderin, and what you just asked... is why it took eighty-one bullets to kill the man. The Telfair sheriff has gone to Macon to bring charges against the federal deputies who fired all of those shots."

Micah looked at Katharine with eyes that were red-rimmed but tearless. He walked over to the window and looked outside at the cold, windy day. She knew that he was putting up a brave front for her sake. He was attempting to spare her his own private anguish, though she felt it almost as keenly as he.

Micah continued in a tired, flat voice, "Norris said they're havin' the funeral this mornin', probably long about now."

"But we won't be there!" Katharine exclaimed, tears streaming down her face.

"No, they don't expect us to. We'll see Miz Ida later. They know your condition, Katharine. Norris won't be there, either, but they wanted us to know what happened. He's been a-ridin' hard since early this mornin'. Said he had others to tell about it before headin' on back home. He was worried about you...said he shouldn't have gotten so upset in front of you. He didn't know about your condition. He's down at the stables now, feedin' and waterin' and restin' his horse. I offered one of our horses but he wouldn't hear of it - said his would be all right after some water and oats."

"Where will Joe be buried?"

"Norris said they're a-gonna bury him there on their homeplace in the family cemetery, even though the Dodge logchoppers are already at work. Joe's sons plan to buy back the land from Dodge, once the timber is cut, the way I did."

"Where will they get the money, if Dodge is taking their land?"

"They're both a-gonna work in my warehouses. I need a good manager for each of my warehouses in Eastman and McRae. Won't take 'em long to make enough money to buy back the cut-over land. Of course, they'll have to settle their legal problems first, but I think they'll be cleared of everything."

With a certain sadness, she realized that she was no closer to understanding the lingering conflict in the Georgia piney woods than she had been when she first moved south, a decade ago. She honestly felt that she herself now harbored more rancor toward the Northern timber people than the Southerners did.

There was no reasonable explanation for pumping eighty-one bullets into a man's house. She had the feeling that this ruthless overkill and desecration of a Southern "squatter" and his home would forever quell any further resistance on the part of any of the other 380 defendants in the Dodges' present mass ejection suit in the federal court in Macon, which originally named Joe Little as a defendant. A bitter rage welled in her heart and she longed to lash out at those who had brought such suffering and destruction and desecration to the people she loved and to their lands which grew the fabulous longleaf yellow pine.

When Micah turned to face her, she expected to see the anger and despair, which she herself felt, reflected in his face. Instead, however, his expression was one of preoccupation which effectively pushed his grief aside. The glint in his eyes she later would construe to be hope itself. He had worked through his anger and his desire for avengement. Strangely, she had not.

"I've got to work on my plow. Still not workin' the soil the way it should," he said, walking down the hallway with her following behind.

"Micah?" she said, not really knowing why she called his name. He stopped and put his arm around her as they continued on to the front door. He opened the door and they stepped onto the porch where they hesitated before walking down the steps and out into the front yard.

Wind was blowing through the large pines, its rustling sounds bringing a comforting balm. She looked into the eyes of the man beside her, once filled with hatred for the Northern people who had dispossessed him and his family not only of their land and home, but now of the only father he had ever known.

As always, she felt his strength, and now for the first time she also sensed his peace. They stood with arms around each other, facing the morning sun as it rose like a golden crown over the swishing, soughing pines. Almost as though he could read her thoughts, Micah stated that a new day was dawning in the piney woods. The timber era would be over in a few years, and the plow was coming into its own again.

Katharine thought back to the church service she had attended in Eastman several years before, when the Methodist preacher had preached from the little book of *Micah*. She now remembered his text: "They shall beat their swords into plowshares and their spears into pruning hooks: nation shall not lift up a sword against nation, neither shall they learn war any more."

The words were like soothing prophecy which would one day be fulfilled. A sense of peace flooded over her. In a few years, a new century would begin and the large pines would be gone. What then? Cotton, the "great staple" which had been removed from taxation, largely and ironically by the efforts of William E. Dodge, was reclaiming its kingdom. Long a mainstay of the Southern economy, it was a steady, lucrative crop that could be harvested each year, unlike the tall pines which required a fifty-year growing period.

Maybe, someday, someone would find a way to replant the longleaf yellow pine. At the present, neither knowledge nor tools were available to make this possible.

But life goes on, Katharine thought, listening to the soughing of the great yellow pines, some of the very few that remained in the Georgia piney woods, for at that moment she felt again the flutter of new life within her. Someday, she would try to explain away the massive stumps that scarred the landscape and thwarted the plow and uprooted the lives of people and animals.

"This is not the way it once looked," she would tell her children and grandchildren, and anyone else who would listen, "for if one could have taken flight, like the crow or the eagle, one could have looked down and have seen hundreds and hundreds of miles of thick-trunked, soughing, longleaf yellow pines...."